THE GLASS BOOKS of the DREAM EATERS

THE GLASS BOOK

the DREAM EATERS

Gordon Dahlquist

BANTAM BOOKS

THE GLASS BOOKS OF THE DREAM EATERS
A Bantam Book / September 2006

Published by
Bantam Dell
A Division of Random House, Inc.
New York, New York

BOOK DESIGN BY GLEN M. EDELSTEIN

Library of Congress Cataloging in Publication Data
Dahlquist, Gordon.
The glass books of the dream eaters / Gordon Dahlquist.
p. cm.
ISBN-10: 0-385-34035-4
ISBN-13: 978-0-385-34035-9
I. Title.

PS3604.A345 G58 2006 2006040740
813/.6 22

Printed in the United States of America

Published simultaneously in Canada

www.bantamdell.com

10 9 8 7 6 5 4 3 2 1

BVG

Time spent in an imaginary city calls forth a startling array of generosity and patience. To these people, places, and events this book is indebted, and to each I offer my thanks, grateful for the opportunity to do so.

Liz Duffy Adams, Danny Baror, Karen Bornarth, Venetia Butterfield, CiNE, Shannon Dailey, the Dailey family, Bart DeLorenzo, Mindy Elliott, Evidence Room, *Exquisite Realms,* Laura Flanagan, Joseph Goodrich, Allen Hahn, Karen Hartman, David Levine, Beth Lincks, Todd London, the Lower East Oval, Honor Molloy, Bill Massey, John McAdams, E. J. McCarthy, Patricia McLaughlin, *Messalina,* David Millman, Emily Morse, New Dramatists, Octocorp@30th & 9th [RIP], Suki O'Kane, Tim Paulson, Molly Powell, Jim and Jill Pratzon, Kate Wittenberg, Mark Worthington, Margaret Young.

My father, my sister, my cousin Michael.

THE GLASS BOOKS of the DREAM EATERS

ONE

Temple

From her arrival at the docks to the appearance of Roger's letter, written on crisp Ministry paper and signed with his full name, on her maid's silver tray at breakfast, three months had passed. On that morning, her poached eggs steaming their silver bowl (gelatinous, gleaming), Miss Temple had not seen Roger Bascombe for seven days. He had been called to Brussels. Then to the country house of his infirm uncle, Lord Tarr. Then he had been required at all hours by the Minister, and then by the Deputy Minister, and finally by a pressing request from a cousin desperate for discreet advice about matters of property and law. But then she found herself in the same tea shop as that same cousin—the over-fed, over-wigged Pamela—exactly when Roger was said to be soothing her distress. It was quite clear that Pamela's only source of disquiet was a less than ready supply of buns. Miss Temple began to feel tremulous. A day went by with no word at all. On the eighth day, at breakfast, she received the letter from Roger regretfully severing their engagement, closing with the politely expressed desire that she take pains to never contact nor see him in any way for the complete remainder of her days. It contained no other explanation.

Such rejection had quite simply never occurred to her. The manner of dismissal she barely noticed—indeed, it was just how she would have done such a thing (as in fact, she had, on multiple galling occasions)—but the fact of it was stinging. She had attempted to re-read the letter, but found her vision blurred—after a moment she realized she was in tears. She dismissed the maid and unsuccessfully attempted to butter a slice of toast. She placed the toast and her knife carefully on the table, stood, and then walked rather hurriedly to her bed, where she curled into a tight ball, the entirety of her small frame shaking with silent sobs.

For an entire day she remained indoors refusing all but the most bitter Lapsang Soochong, and even that watered down (without milk *or* lemon) into a thin, rusty beverage that managed to be both feeble and unpleasant. In the night she wept again, alone in the dark, hollow and unmoored, until her pillow was too damp to be borne. But by the next afternoon, her clear grey eyes ringed red and her sausage curls lank, waking in pallid winter light (a season quite new to the warm-blooded Miss Temple, who judged it objectively horrid), the bedding tangled about her, she was once more determined to be about her business, and brisk.

Her world had been changed—as she was willing to admit (she had a young lady's classical education) did happen in life—but it hardly meant she was obliged to be docile, for Miss Temple was only docile on the most extraordinary occasions. Indeed, she was considered by some a provincial savage if not an outright little monster, for she was not large, and was by inclination merciless. She had grown up on an island, bright and hot, in the shadow of slaves, and as she was a sensitive girl, it had marked her like a whip—though part of that marking was how very immune from whips she was, and would, she trusted, remain.

Miss Temple was twenty-five, old to be unmarried, but as she had spent some time disappointing available suitors on her island before being sent across the sea to sophisticated society, this was not necessarily held against her. She was as wealthy as plantations could make her, and sharp-witted enough to know that it was natural for people to care more for her money than for her person, and she did not take this point of materialist interest to heart. Indeed, she took very little to heart at all. The exception—though she found herself now hard-pressed to explain it, and though lacking explanations of any kind vexed her—was Roger.

Miss Temple had rooms at the Hotel Boniface, fashionable but not ridiculous, consisting of an outer parlor, an inner parlor, a dining room, a dressing room, a sleeping room, a room for her two maids, and a second dressing and sleeping room for her aged Aunt Agathe, who lived on a small plantation-derived stipend, and who generally alternated between meals and slumber but was enough respected to be a suitable chaperone, despite her lack of attention. Agathe, whom Miss Temple had only first met upon her disembarkation, was acquainted with the Bascombe family. Quite simply, Roger was the first man of reasonable status and beauty to whom Miss Temple had been introduced, and being a young woman of clarity and loyalty, she found no further reason to search. For his part, Roger gave every impression of finding her both pretty and delightful, and so they were engaged.

To all accounts it was a good match. Roger's expressed opinion aside, even those who found Miss Temple's directness difficult would admit to her adequate beauty. They would also happily admit to her wealth. Roger Bascombe was a rising figure in the Foreign Ministry, cresting the verge of palpable authority. He was a man who looked fine when well-dressed, displayed no flagrant vice, and who possessed more chin and less stomach than any the Bascombes had produced in two generations. Their time together had been brief but, to Miss Temple's experience, intense. They had shared a dizzying variety of meals, strolled through parks and galleries, gazed deeply into each other's eyes, exchanged tender kisses. All of this had been new to her, from the restaurants and the paintings (the scale and strangeness of which prompted Miss Temple to sit for several minutes with a hand pressed tightly over each eye), the variety of people, of smells, the music, the noise, the manners and all the new words, and further to the particular strength of Roger's fingers, his arm around her waist, his kindly chuckle—which even when she felt it came at her expense she strangely did not mind—and his own smells, of his soap, his hair oil, his tobacco, his days in meeting rooms amidst piles of thick documents and ink and wax and wood varnish and felt-topped tables, and finally the, to her mind, devastating mixture of sensations she derived from his delicate lips, his bristling side whiskers, and his warm searching tongue.

But by Miss Temple's next breakfast, though her face was blotched and swollen about the eyes, she met her eggs and toast with customary ferocity, and met the maid's timorous gaze just once with a narrow peremptory glance that served as a knife drawn across the throat of any speech, much less consolation. Agathe was still asleep. Miss Temple had been aware (from the husky, insistent, violet-scented breathing) that her aunt had lingered on the opposite side of her door through the day of her (as she now thought of it) Dark Retreat, but she wanted no part of that conversation either.

She launched herself out of the Boniface, wearing a simple but frankly quite flattering green and gold flowered dress, with green leather ankle boots and a green bag, walking crisply toward the district of expensive shops that filled the streets on the near bank of the river. She was not interested in actively buying anything, but had the idea that looking at the assembled goods of the city—of the world—making their way from so many different lands to this collection of shops might serve as a spur to new thinking about her own new state of affairs. With this in mind, she found herself eager, even restless, moving from stall to stall, her eyes roving without lingering over fabrics, carved boxes, glassware, hats, trinkets, gloves, silks, perfumes, papers, soaps, opera glasses, hairpins, feathers, beads, and lacquered items of all kinds. At no point did she actually stop, and sooner than she had imagined possible Miss Temple found herself on the district's other side, standing at the edge of St. Isobel's Square.

The day above her was a cloudy grey. She turned and retraced her steps, gazing still more intently into each exotic display, but never—if she herself were a fish—finding the item that would hook her attention into place. On the Boniface side again, she wondered exactly what she thought she was doing. How, if she was with clarity embracing her new sense of loss and redefinition, did nothing—not even an especially cunning lacquered duck—generate interest? Instead, at each object, she felt herself driven onward, prey to some nagging urge she could not name, toward some unknown prize. That she had no conscious idea what this prize might be irked her, but she took comfort from the implication that it did exist, and would be potent enough to alert her when it came into view.

So, with a resolute sigh, she crossed back through the shops for a third time, her attention entirely elsewhere, confident, as she crossed the square toward the nest of monumental white stone buildings that made up the government Ministries, that her interest was—in a word—disinterested. The matter lay not so much with the perceived faults of her own person, if any, nor the perceived superiority, if any, of a rival (whose identity she was, out of idle curiosity alone, in the back of her mind trying to guess), but merely that her own case was the best example at hand. Or was it the only example? Still, it did not mean she was *troubled* by it, or that she'd no perspective, or that for any future affections of the now-beyond-her Roger Bascombe she would give two pins.

Despite these absolutely rational thoughts, Miss Temple paused upon reaching the center of the square, and instead of continuing on to the buildings where Roger was undoubtedly even now at work, she sat on a wrought-metal bench and looked up at the enormous statue of St. Isobel at the square's center. Knowing nothing of the sainted martyr and in no way devout, Miss Temple was merely disquieted by its vulgar extravagance: a woman clinging to a barrel in surging surf, clothes torn, hair wild, ringed by the flotsam of shipwreck, with the water about her churned to froth by a roiling tangle of serpents that wrapped around her flailing limbs, coiled under her garments and wound across her throat even as she opened her mouth to cry to heaven—a cry one saw to be heard by a pair of angels, winged, robed, and impassively gazing down from above Isobel's head. Miss Temple appreciated enough the size of the thing and the technical achievements involved, but it nevertheless struck her as coarse and unlikely. Shipwreck, as an island girl, she could accept, as she could martyrdom by snakes, but the angels seemed fatiguingly presumptuous.

Of course, as she looked into the unseeing stone eyes of the forever serpent-beset Isobel, she knew she could have scarcely cared less. Her gaze finally followed her true interest, toward the nest of white buildings, and so, quickly, she formed a plan, and with each step of that plan, a perfectly sound justification. She accepted that she was forever divided from Roger—persuasion and reunion were no part of her aims. What she sought, what she in fact required, was information. Was it strict rejection alone—that Roger would rather be alone than be burdened with her? Was it a matter of personal ambition—that she must be shunted aside in favor of promotion and responsibility? Was there simply another woman who had supplanted her in his affections? Or was there something else that she could not presently imagine? They were all equal in her mind, of neutral *emotional* value, but crucial as far as Miss Temple's ability to situate herself in her new loss-inflected existence.

It would be simple enough to follow him. Roger was a man of habits, and even when his hours of work were irregular he would still take his mid-day meal, whenever he did take it, at the same restaurant. Miss

Temple found an antiquarian book shop across the street where, as she was obliged to purchase something for standing so long watching through its window, she on impulse selected a complete four-volume *Illustrated Lives of Sea Martyrs.* The books were detailed enough to warrant her spending the time in the window, apparently examining the colored plates, while actually watching Roger first enter and then, after an hour, re-emerge, alone, from the heavy doors across the street. He walked straight back into the Ministry courtyard. Miss Temple arranged for her purchase to be delivered to the Boniface, and walked back into the street, feeling like a fool.

She had re-crossed the square before her reason convinced her that she was not so much a fool as an inexperienced observer. It was pointless to watch from *outside* the restaurant. It was only from inside that she could have determined whether or not Roger dined alone, or with others, or with which particular others, with any of whom he might have shared significant words—all crucial information. Further, unless he had merely thrown her over for his work—which she doubted, scoffing—she was like to learn nothing from observing his working day. It was after work, obviously, that any real intelligence would be gathered. Abruptly, for by this time she was across the square and in the midst of the shops, she entered a store whose windows were thick with all shapes of luggage, hampers, oilskins, gaiters, pith helmets, lanterns, telescopes, and a ferocious array of walking sticks. She emerged some time later, after exacting negotiations, wearing a ladies' black traveling cloak, with a deep hood and several especially cunning pockets. A visit to another shop filled one pocket with opera glasses, and a visit to a third weighed down a second pocket with a leatherbound notebook and an all-weather pencil. Miss Temple then took her tea.

Between cups of Darjeeling and two scones slathered with cream she made opening entries in the notebook, prefacing her entire endeavor and then detailing the day's work so far. That she now had a kind of uniform and a set of tools made everything that much easier and much less about her particular feelings, for tasks requiring clothes and accoutrements were by definition objective, even scientific, in nature. In keeping with this, she made a point to write her entries in a kind of cipher, replacing proper names and places with synonyms or word-play that hopefully would be impenetrable to all but herself (all references to the Ministry were to "Minsk" or even just "Russia", and Roger himself—in a complex train of thought that started with him as a snake that had shed his skin, to a snake being charmed by the attractions of others, to India, and finally, because of his still-remarkable personal presence—became "the Rajah"). Against the possibility that she might be making her observations for some time and in some discomfort, she ordered a sausage roll for later. It was placed on her table, wrapped in thick waxed paper, and presently bundled into another pocket of her cloak.

Though the winter was verging into spring, the city was still damp around the edges, and the evenings colder than the lengthening days seemed to promise. Miss Temple left the tea shop at four o'clock, knowing Roger to leave usually at five, and hired a carriage. She instructed her driver in a low, direct tone of voice, after assuring him he would be well paid for his time, that they would be following a gentleman, most likely in another carriage, and that she would rap on the roof of the coach to indicate the man when he appeared. The driver nodded, but said nothing else. She took his silence to mean that this was a usual enough thing, and felt all the more sure of herself, settling in the back of the coach, readying her glasses and her notebook, waiting for Roger to appear. When he did, some forty minutes later, she nearly missed him, amusing herself for the moment by peering through the opera glasses into nearby open windows, but some tingling intuition caused her to glance back at the courtyard gates just in time to see Roger (standing in the road with an air of confidence and purpose that made her breath catch) flag down a coach of his own. Miss Temple rapped sharply on the roof of the coach, and they were off.

The thrill of the chase—complicated by the thrill of seeing Roger (which she was nearly certain was the result of the task at hand and not any residual affection)—was quickly tempered when, after the first few turns, it became evident that Roger's destination was nowhere more provocative than his own home. Again, Miss Temple was forced to admit the possibility that her rejection might have been in favor of no rival, but, as it were, immaculate. It was possible. It might even have been preferable. Indeed, as her coach trailed along the route to the Bascombe house—a path she knew so well as to once have considered it nearly her own—she reflected on the likelihood that another woman had taken her place in Roger's heart. To her frank mind, it was not likely at all. Looking at the facts of Roger's day—a Spartan path of work to meal to work to home where undoubtedly he would, after a meal, immerse himself in still more work—it was more reasonable to conclude that he had placed her second to his vaulting ambition. It seemed a stupid choice, as she felt she could have assisted him in any number of sharp and subtle ways, but she could at least follow the (faulty, childish) logic. She was imagining Roger's eventual realization of what he had (callously, foolishly, blindly) thrown aside, and then her own strange urge to comfort him in this sure-to-be-imminent distress when she saw that they had arrived. Roger's coach had stopped before his front entrance, and her own a discreet distance behind.

Roger did not get out of the coach. Instead, after a delay of some minutes, the front door opened and his manservant Phillips came toward the coach bearing a bulky black-wrapped bundle. He handed this to Roger through the open coach door, and then in turn received Roger's black satchel and two thickly bound portfolios of paper. Phillips carried these items of Roger Bascombe's work day back into the house, and closed the door behind him. A moment later, Roger's coach jerked forward, returning at some pace into the thick of the city. Miss Temple rapped on her coach's ceiling and was thrown back into her seat as the horses leapt ahead, resuming their trailing surveillance.

By this time it was fully dark, and Miss Temple was more and more forced to rely on her driver that they were on the right path. Even when she leaned her head out of the window—now wearing the hood for secrecy—she could only glimpse the coaches ahead of them, with no longer a clear confidence about which might be Roger's at all. This feeling of uncertainty took deeper hold the longer they drove along, as now the first tendrils of evening fog began to reach them, creeping up from the river. By the time they stopped again, she could barely see her own horses. The driver leaned down and pointed to a high, shadowed archway over a great staircase that led down into a cavernous gas-lit tunnel. She stared at it and realized that the shifting ground at its base, which she first took to be rats streaming into a sewer, was actually a crowd of dark-garbed people flowing through and down into the depths below. It looked absolutely infernal, a sickly yellow portal surrounded by murk, offering passage to hideous depths.

"Stropping, Miss," the driver called down and then, in response to Miss Temple's lack of movement, "train station." She felt as if she'd been slapped—or at least the hot shame she imagined being actually slapped must feel like. Of course it was the train station. A sudden spike of excitement drove her leaping from the cab to the cobblestones. She quickly thrust money into the driver's hand and launched herself toward the glowing arch. Stropping Station. This was exactly what she had been looking for—Roger was doing something *else.*

It took her a few desperate moments to find him, having wasted valuable seconds gaping in the coach. The tunnel opened into a larger staircase that led down into the main lobby and past that to the tracks themselves, all under an intricate and vast canopy of ironwork and soot-covered brick. "Like Vulcan's cathedral." Miss Temple smiled, the vista spreading out beneath her, rather proud of so acutely retaining her wits. Beyond coining similes, she had the further presence of mind to step to the side of the stairs, use a lamp post to perch herself briefly on a railing, and with that vantage use the opera glasses to look over the whole of the crowd—which her height alone would never have afforded. It was only a matter of moments before she found Roger. Again, instead of immediately rushing, she followed his progress across the lobby to a particular train. When she was sure she had seen him enter the train, she climbed off of the railing and set off first to find out where it was going, and then to buy a ticket.

She had never been in a station of such size—Stropping carried all traffic to the north and west—much less at the crowded close of a working day, and to Miss Temple it was like being thrust into an ant-hill. It was usual in her life for her small size and delicate strength to pass unnoticed, taken for granted but rarely relevant, like an unwillingness to eat eels. In Stropping Station, however, despite knowing where she was going (to the large blackboard detailing platforms and destinations), Miss Temple found herself shoved along pell-mell, quite apart from her own intentions, the view from within her hood blocked by a swarm of elbows and waistcoats. Her nearest comparison was swimming in the sea against a mighty mindless tide. She looked up and found landmarks in the ceiling, constellations of ironwork, to judge her progress and direction, and in this way located an advertising kiosk she had seen from the stairs. She worked her way around it and launched herself out again at another angle, figuring the rate of drift to reach another lamp post that would allow her to step high enough to see the board.

The lamp post reached, Miss Temple began to fret about the time. Around her—for there were many, many platforms—whistles fervently signaled arrivals and departures, and she had no idea, in her subterranean shuffling, whether Roger's train had already left. Looking up at the board, she was pleased to see that it was sensibly laid out in columns indicating train number, destination, time, and platform. Roger's train—at platform 12—left at 6:23, for the Orange Canal. She craned her head to see the station clock—another hideous affair involving angels, bracketing each side of the great face (as if keeping it up with their wings), impassively gazing down, one holding a pair of scales, the other a bared sword. Between these two black metal specters of judgment, Miss Temple saw with shock that it was 6:17. She threw herself off the lamp post toward the ticket counter, burrowing vigorously through a sea of coats. She emerged, two minutes later, at the end of an actual ticket line, and within another minute reached the counter itself. She called out her destination—the end of the line, round-trip—and dropped a handful of heavy coins onto the marble, pushing them peremptorily at the ticket agent, who looked beakily at her from the other side of a wire cage window. His pale fingers flicked out from under the cage to take her money and shoved back a perforated ticket. Miss Temple snatched it and bolted for the train.

A conductor stood with a lantern, one foot up on the stairs into the last car, ready to swing himself aboard. It was 6:22. She smiled at him as sweetly as her heaving breath would allow, and pushed past into the car. She had only just stopped at the top of the steps to gather her wits when the train pulled forward, nearly knocking her off her feet. She flung her arms out against the wall to keep her balance and heard a chuckle behind her. The conductor stood with a smile at the base of the steps in the open doorway, the platform moving past behind him. Miss Temple was not used to being laughed at in any circumstance, but between her mission, her disguise, and her lack of breath, she could find no immediate retort and instead of gaping like a fish merely turned down the corridor to find a compartment. The first was empty and so she opened the glass door and sat in the middle seat facing the front of the train. To her right was a large window. As she restored her composure, the last rushing view of Stropping Station—the platform, the trains lined up, the vaulted brick cavern—vanished, swallowed by the blackness of a tunnel.

The compartment was all dark wood, with a rather luxurious red velvet upholstery for the bank of three seats on either side. A small milk-white globe gave off a meager gleam, pallid and dim, but enough to throw her reflection against the dark window. Her first instinct had been to pull off the cloak and breathe easily, but though Miss Temple was hot, scattered, and with no sense of where she was exactly going, she knew enough to sit still until she was thinking clearly. Orange Canal was some distance outside the city, nearly to the coast, with who knew how many other stops in between, any one of which might be Roger's actual destination. She had no idea who else might be on the train, and if they might know her, or might know Roger, or might in fact be the reason for the journey itself. What if there were no destination at all, merely some rail-bound assignation? In any case, it was clear that she had to find Roger's location on the train or she would never know if he disembarked or if he met someone. As soon as the conductor came to take her ticket, she would begin to search.

He did not come. It had already been some minutes, and he had only been a few yards away. She didn't remember seeing him go past—perhaps when she entered?—and began to get annoyed, his malingering on top of the chuckle making her loathe the man. She stepped into the corridor. He was not there. She narrowed her eyes and began to walk forward, carefully, for the last thing she wanted—even with the cloak—was to stumble into Roger unawares. She crept to the next compartment, craned her head around so she could peer into it. No one. There were eight compartments in the car, and they were all empty.

The train rattled along, still in darkness. Miss Temple stood at the door to the next car and peered through the glass. It looked exactly like the car she was in. She opened the door and stepped through—another eight compartments without a single occupant. She entered the next car, and found the exact same situation. The rear three cars of this train were completely unoccupied. This might explain the absence of the conductor—though he still must have known her to be in the rear car and if he had been polite could have taken her ticket. Perhaps he merely expected her to do what she was doing, moving ahead to where she should have been in the first place, if she hadn't been so late to reach the train. Perhaps there was something she didn't know about the rear cars, or the etiquette on this particular trip—would that explain the chuckle?—or about the other passengers themselves. Perhaps they were in a group? Perhaps it was less a journey and more of an excursion? Now she despised the conductor for his presumption as well as his rudeness, and she moved forward in the train to find him. This car as well was empty—four cars!—and Miss Temple paused at the doorway into the fifth, trying to recall just how many cars there were to begin with (she had no idea) or how many might be normal (she had no idea) or what exactly she could say to the conductor, upon finding him, that would not reveal her complete ignorance (she had no immediate idea). As she stood thinking, the train stopped.

She rushed into the nearest compartment and threw open the window. The platform was empty—no one boarding, and no one leaving the train. The station itself—the sign said Crampton Place—was closed and dark. The whistle blew and the train—throwing Miss Temple back into the seats—lurched into life. A chill wind poured through the open window as they gathered speed and she pulled the window closed. She had never heard of Crampton Place, and was happy enough not to be going there now—it struck her as desolate as a Siberian steppe. She wished she had a map of this particular line, a list of stops. Perhaps this was something she might get from the conductor, or at least a list she could write down in her book. Thinking of the book, she took it out and, licking the tip of the pencil, wrote "Crampton Place" in her deliberate, looping script. With nothing else to add, she put the book away and returned to the corridor and then, with a sigh of resolve, stepped into the fifth car.

She knew it was different from the perfume. Where the other corridors were imbued with a vague industrial mixture of smoke and grease and lye and dirty mop-water, the corridor of the fifth car smelled—startling because she knew them from her own home—of frangipani flowers. With a surge of excitement, Miss Temple crept to the nearest compartment and slowly leaned forward to peer into it. The far seats were all occupied: two men in black topcoats and between them a woman in a yellow dress, laughing. The men smoked cigars, and both had trimmed and pointed beards, with hearty red faces, as if they were two examples of the same species of thick, vigorous dog. The woman wore a half-mask made of peacock feathers that spread out over the top of her head, leaving only her eyes to pierce through like gleaming stones. Her lips were painted red, and opened wide when she laughed. All three were gazing at someone in the opposite row of seats, and had not noticed Miss Temple. She retreated from view, and then, feeling childish but knowing nothing else for it, dropped to her hands and knees and crawled past, keeping her body below the level of the glass in the door. On the other side, she carefully rose and peered back at the opposite row of seats and froze. She was looking directly at Roger Bascombe.

He was not looking at her. He wore a black cloak, closed about his throat, and smoked a thin, wrapped cheroot, his oak-colored hair flattened back over his skull with pomade. His right hand was in a black leather glove, his left, holding the cheroot, was bare. At a second glance Miss Temple saw that the right gloved hand was holding the left glove. She also saw that Roger was not laughing, that his face was deliberately blank, an expression she had seen him adopt in the presence of the Minister or Deputy Minister, or his mother, or his uncle Tarr—that is, those to whom he owed deference. Sitting against the window, the seat between them unoccupied, was another woman, in a red dress that flashed like fire from beneath a dark fur-collared cloak. Miss Temple saw the woman's pale ankles and her delicate throat, like white coals beneath the flaming dress, flickering in and out of view as she shifted in her seat. Her darkly red mouth wore an openly provocative wry smile and she puffed at a cigarette through a long black lacquered holder. She also wore a mask, of red leather, dotted with glittering studs where the eyebrows would be, and then—Miss Temple noted with some discomfort—forming a gleaming tear, just ready to drop from the outer corner of each eye. She had obviously said whatever the others were laughing at. The woman exhaled, a deliberate stream of smoke sent to the other row of seats. As if this gesture were the conclusion of her witticism, the others laughed again, even as they waved the smoke from their faces.

Miss Temple stepped clear of the window, her back flat against the wall. She had no idea what she ought to do. To her right was another compartment. She risked a peek, and saw the far seats occupied with three women, each with a traveling cloak wrapped around what seemed to be, judging from their shoes, elegant evening wear. Two wore half-masks decorated with yellow ostrich feathers while the third, her face uncovered, held her mask on her lap, fussing with an uncooperative strap. Miss Temple pulled her own hood lower and craned to see that the other seat held two men, one in a tailcoat and one in a heavy fur that made him seem like a bear. Both of these men wore masks as well, simple black affairs, and the man in the tailcoat occupied himself with sips from a silver flask, while the man in the fur tapped his fingers on the pearl inlaid tip of an ebony walking stick. Miss Temple darted back. The man in the fur had glanced toward the corridor. In a rush she scampered past Roger's compartment, in open view, and through the connecting door to the previous car.

She shut the door behind her and crouched on her hands and knees. Interminable seconds passed. No one came to the door. No one entered in pursuit, or even curiosity. She relaxed, took a breath, and brought herself sharply to task. She felt out of her depth, beyond her experience—and yet, frankly, Miss Temple had no confirmation why this must be true. Despite being assailed with sinister thoughts, all she had definitely learned was that Roger was attending—without obvious pleasure, nor anything more evident than obligation—an exclusive party of some kind, where the guests were masked. Was this so unusual? Even if to Miss Temple it was, she knew this did not figure, so much was strange to her sheltered life that she was no objective judge—had she been in society for an entire season, this kind of entertainment might seem, if not so routine as to be dull, at least a known quantity. Further, she reconsidered the fact that Roger was not sitting *next* to the woman in red, but apart from her—in fact, apart from everyone. She wondered if this was his first time in their company. She wondered who this woman was. The other, in yellow with the peacock feathers, interested her much less, simply for having been so vulgarly receptive to the more elegant woman's wit.

Clearly the men were unconcerned about hiding their identities—they must all know each other and be traveling as a group. In the other compartment, all being masked, perhaps they didn't. Or perhaps they did know each other but were unaware of it *because* of the masks—the whole pleasure of the evening would lie in guessing, she realized, and in remaining hidden. It struck Miss Temple as perhaps a great deal of fun, though she knew that her own dress, if fine for the day, was nothing to wear to such an evening, and that her cloak and hood, though they protected her identity for the moment, were nothing like the proper party mask everyone else would have.

Her thoughts were interrupted by a clicking sound from the other corridor. She risked a look and saw the man in the fur—quite imposing when not seated, nearly filling the corridor with his wide frame—stepping out of Roger's compartment and closing the door behind him. Without a glance toward her, he returned to his own. She sighed, releasing a tension she had been unable to fully acknowledge; he had not seen her, he was merely visiting the other compartment. He must know the woman, she decided, even though he could have stepped into the compartment to speak to any person in it, including Roger. Roger saw so many people in his day—from government, from business, from other countries—and she realized with a pang how small her own circle of acquaintance actually was. She knew so little of the world, so little of life, and here she was cowering in an empty train car, small and ridiculous. While Miss Temple was biting her lip, the train stopped again.

Once more she dashed into a compartment and opened the window, and once more the platform was empty, the station shuttered and dark. This sign read Packington—another place she had never heard of—but she took a moment to enter it into her notebook just the same. When the train began to move again she closed the window. As she turned back to the compartment door she saw that it was open, and in it stood the conductor. He smiled.

"Ticket, Miss?"

She fished her ticket from her cloak and handed it to him. He took it from her, tilting his head to study the printed destination, still smiling. In his other hand he held an odd metal clamping device. He looked up.

"All the way to Orange Canal, then?"

"Yes. How many more stops will that be?"

"Quite a few."

She smiled back at him, thinly. "Exactly how many, please?"

"Seven stops. Be the better part of two hours."

"Thank you."

The clamping device punched a hole in the ticket with a loud snapping sound, like the bite of a metal insect, and he returned it to her. He did not move from the door. In response, Miss Temple flounced her cloak into position as she met his gaze, claiming the compartment for herself. The conductor watched her, glanced once toward the front of the train and licked his lips. In that moment she noticed the porcine quality of his heavy neck, particularly how it was stuffed into the tight collar of his blue coat. He looked back at her and twitched his fingers, puffy and pale like a parcel of uncooked sausages. Confronted with this spectacle of ungainliness, her contempt abated in favor of mere disinterest—she no longer wanted to cause him harm, only that he should leave. But he wasn't going to leave. Instead, he leaned closer, with a feeble kind of leer.

"Not riding up with the others, then, are you?"

"As you can see, no."

"It's not always safe, a young lady alone..." He trailed off, smiling. The conductor persisted in smiling at all times. He fingered the clamping device, his gaze drifting toward her well-shaped calves. She sighed.

"Safe from what?"

He did not answer.

Before he could, before he could do anything that would cause her to either scream or feel still more galling pitiful disdain, she raised her open palm to him, a signal that he need not answer, need not say anything, and asked him another question.

"Are you *aware* where they—where *we*—are all going?"

The conductor stepped back as if he had been bitten, as if she had threatened his life. He retreated to the corridor, touched his cap, and turned abruptly, rushing into the forward car. Miss Temple remained in her seat. What had just happened? What she'd meant as a question the man had taken as a threat. He must *know,* she reasoned, and it must be a place of wealth and influence—at least enough that the word of a guest might serve to cost him his position. She smiled (it had been a satisfying little exchange, after all) at what she had learned—not that it was a surprise. That Roger was attending in a subordinate position only reinforced the possibility that representatives from the upper levels of government might well be present.

With a vague gnawing restlessness, Miss Temple was reminded that she was actually getting hungry. She dug out the sausage roll.

Over the next hour there were five more stops—Gorsemont, De Conque, Raaxfall, St. Triste, and St. Porte—every name going into her notebook, along with fanciful descriptions of her fellow travelers. Each time, looking out the window, she saw an empty platform and closed station house, with no one entering or leaving the train. Each time also she felt the air getting progressively cooler, until at St. Porte it struck her as positively chill and laced with the barest whiff of the sea, or perhaps the great salt marshes she knew to exist in this part of the country. The fog had cleared, but revealed merely a sliver of moon and the night remained quite dark. When the train started up again, Miss Temple had at each station crept into the corridor and carefully peered into the fifth car, just to see if there was any activity. Once she had a glimpse of someone entering one of the forward compartments (she had no idea who—black cloaks all looked the same), but nothing since. Boredom began to gnaw at her, to the point that she wanted to go forward again and get another look into Roger's compartment. She knew this to be a stupid idea that only preyed upon her because of restlessness, and that further it was times like these when one made the most egregious mistakes. All she had to do was remain patient for another few minutes, when all would be clear, when she could get to the very root of the whole affair. Nevertheless, her hand was in the act of turning the handle to enter the fifth car when the train next stopped.

She let go of it at once, shocked to see that all down the corridor the compartment doors were opening. Miss Temple ducked back into her compartment and threw open the window. The platform was crowded with waiting coaches, and the station windows were aglow. As she read the station sign—Orange Locks—she saw people spilling from the train and walking very near to her. Without closing the window she darted back to the connecting door: people were exiting from a door at the far end, and the last person—a man in a blue uniform—had nearly reached it. With a nervous swallow and a flutter in her stomach, Miss Temple stepped silently through the door and rapidly, carefully, padded down the corridor, glancing into each compartment as she passed. All were empty. Roger's party had gone ahead, as had the fur-coated man.

The man in the blue uniform was also gone from view. Miss Temple picked up her pace and reached the far end, where an open door and a set of steps led off the train. The last people seemed to be some yards ahead of her, walking toward the coaches. She swallowed again. If she stayed on the train, she could just ride to the end and take the return trip easily. If she got off, she had no idea what the schedule was—what if the Orange Locks station were to close up like the previous five? At the same time, her adventure *was* continuing in the exact manner she had hoped. As if to make up her mind, the train lurched ahead. Without thinking Miss Temple leapt off, landing with a squawk and a stumble on the platform. By the time she gathered herself to look back, the train was racing by. In the doorway of the final car stood the conductor. His gaze was cold, and he held his lantern toward her the way one holds a cross before a vampire.

The train was gone and the roar of its passage faded into the low buzz of conversation and the clops and jingles and slams of the travelers climbing into their waiting coaches. Already full coaches were moving away, and Miss Temple knew she must decide immediately what to do. She saw Roger nowhere, nor any of the others from his car. Those remaining were in heavy coats or cloaks or furs, a seemingly equal number of men and women, perhaps twenty all told. A group of men climbed into one coach and a mixture of men and women piled into two more. With a start she realized that there was only one other coach remaining. Walking in its direction were three women in cloaks and masks. Throwing her shoulders back and the hood farther over her face, Miss Temple crossed quickly to join them.

She was able to reach the coach before they had all entered, and when the third woman climbed up and turned, thinking to shut the door behind her, she saw Miss Temple—or the dark, hooded figure that Miss Temple now made—and apologized, situating herself farther along on the coach seat. Miss Temple merely nodded in answer and climbed aboard in turn, shutting the door tightly behind her. At the sound, after a moment to allow this last person to sit, the driver cracked his whip and the coach lurched into motion. With her hood pulled down, Miss Temple could barely see the faces of the other passengers, much less anything out the window—not that she could have made sense of what she might have seen anyway.

The other women were at first quiet, she assumed due to her own presence. The two across from her both wore feathered masks and dark velvet cloaks, the cloak of the woman to the left boasting a luxurious collar of black feathers. As they settled themselves in the coach, the one to the right opened her cloak and fanned herself, as if she were over-hot from exertion, revealing a dress of shimmering, clinging blue silk that seemed more than anything else like the skin of a reptile. As this woman's fan fluttered in the darkness like a night bird on a leash, the coach filled with perfume—sweet jasmine. The woman sitting next to Miss Temple, who had preceded her into the coach, wore a kind of tricorn hat rakishly pinned to her hair, and a thin band of cloth tied over her eyes, quite like a pirate. Her wrap was simple but probably quite warm, made of black wool. As this was not as sumptuous, Miss Temple allowed herself to hope she might not be so out of place, as long as she kept herself well concealed. She felt confident her boots—cunningly green—if glimpsed, would not make her look out of place.

They rode for a time in silence, but Miss Temple was soon aware that the other women shared her own sense of excitement and anticipation, if not her feeling of terrible suspense. Bit by bit they began making small exploratory comments to one another—first about the train, then about the coach or about each other's clothing, and finally, hintingly, at their destination. They did not at first address Miss Temple, or indeed anyone in particular, merely offering comments in general and responding the same way. It was as if they were not supposed to be talking about their evening at all, and could only proceed to do so by degrees, each of them making it tacitly plain that they would not be averse to bending the rule. Of course Miss Temple was not averse in the slightest, she just had nothing to say. She listened to the pirate and the woman in silk compliment each other on their attire, and then to both of them approve of the third woman's mask. Then they turned to her. So far she had said nothing, merely nodding her head once or twice in agreement, but now she knew they were all examining her quite closely. So she spoke.

"I do hope I have worn the right shoes for this cold an evening."

She shifted her legs in the tight room between seats and raised her cloak, exhibiting her green leather boots, with their intricate lacing. The other three leaned to study them, and the pirate next to her confided, "They are most sensible—for it will be cold, I am sure."

"And your dress is green as well . . . with flowers," noted the woman with the feathered collar, whose gaze had moved from the shoes to the strip of dress revealed above them.

The woman in silk chuckled. "You come as a Suburban Rustick!" The others chuckled too and, so bolstered, she went on.

"One of those ladies who live among novels and flowered sachets—instead of life itself, and life's gardens. The Rustick, and the Piratical, the Silken, and the Feathered—we are all richly disguised!"

Miss Temple thought this was a bit thick. She did not appreciate being termed either "suburban" or "rustick" and further was quite convinced that the person who condemns a thing—in this case novels—is the same person who's wasted most of her life reading them. In the moment, as she was being insulted, it was all she could do not to reach across the coach (for it was an easy reach) and take sharp hold of the harpy's delicate ear. But she forced herself to smile, and in doing so knew that she must place her immediate pride in the service of her adventure, and accept the more important fact that this woman's disdain had given her a costume, and a role to play. She cleared her throat and spoke again.

"Amongst so many ladies, all striving to be most elegant, I wondered if such a *costume* might be noticed all the more."

The pirate next to her chuckled. The silken woman's smile was a little more fixed and her voice a bit more brittle. She peered more sharply at Miss Temple's face, hidden in the shadow of her hood.

"And what is your mask? I cannot see it . . ."

"You can't?"

"No. Is it also green? It cannot be elaborate, to fit under that hood."

"Indeed, it is quite plain."

"But we cannot see it."

"No?"

"But we should like to."

"My thinking was to make it that much more mysterious—it being in itself, as I say, plain."

In reply the silken woman leaned forward, as if to put her face right into the hood with Miss Temple, and Miss Temple instinctively shrank back as far as the coach would allow. The moment had become awkward, but in her ignorance Miss Temple was unsure where the burden of *gaucherie* actually lay—with her refusal or the silken woman's gross insistence. The other two were silent, watching, their masks hiding any particular expression. Any second the woman would be close enough to see, or close enough to pull back the hood altogether—Miss Temple had to stop her in that very instant. She was helped, in this moment, by the sudden knowledge that these women were not likely to have lived in a house where savage punishment was a daily affair. Miss Temple merely extended two fingers of her right hand and poked them through the feathered mask-holes, straight into the woman's eyes.

The silken woman shot back in her seat, sputtering like an over-full kettle coming to boil. She heaved one or two particularly whingeing breaths and pulled down her mask, placing a hand over each eye, feeling in the dark, rubbing away the pain. It was a very light touch and Miss Temple knew no real damage had been done—it was not as if she had used her nails. The silken woman looked up at her, eyes red and streaming, her mouth a gash of outrage, ready to lash out. The other two women watched, immobile with shock. Again, all was hanging in the balance and Miss Temple knew she needed to maintain the upper hand. So she laughed.

And then a moment after laughing pulled out a scented handkerchief and offered it to the silken woman, saying in her sweetest voice, "O my dear . . . I *am* sorry . . . ," as if she were consoling a kitten. "You must forgive me for preserving the . . . *chastity* of my disguise." When the woman did not immediately take the handkerchief Miss Temple herself leaned forward and as delicately as she could dabbed the tears from around the woman's eyes, patiently, taking her time, and then pressed the handkerchief into her hands. She sat back. After a moment, the woman raised the handkerchief and dabbed her face again, then her mouth and nose, and then, with a quick shy glance at the others, restored her mask. They were silent.

The sounds of the hoofbeats had changed, and Miss Temple looked out of the coach. They were passing along some kind of stone-paved track. The country beyond was featureless and flat—perhaps a meadow, perhaps a fen. She did not see trees, though in the darkness she doubted she could have had they been there—but it did not *seem* like there would be trees, or if there had been once, that they had been cut down to feed some long-forgotten fire. She turned back to her companions, each seemingly occupied with her own thoughts. She was sorry to have ruined the conversation, but did not see any way around it. Still, she felt obliged to try and make amends, and attempted to put a bright note in her voice.

"I'm sure we shall be arriving soon."

The other women nodded, the pirate going so far as to smile, but none spoke in reply. Miss Temple was resilient.

"We have reached the paved road."

Exactly as before, all three women nodded and the pirate smiled, but they did not speak. The moment of silence lengthened and then took hold in the coach, each of them sinking deeper, as the air of solitude intruded, into her own thoughts, the earlier excitement about the evening now somehow supplanted by an air of brooding disquiet, the exact sort of gnawing, unsparing unrest that leads to midnight cruelty. Miss Temple was not immune, especially since she had a great deal to brood about if she were to shift her mind that way. She was keenly reminded that she had no idea what she was doing, where she was going, or how she would possibly return—and indeed, more than any of these, what she would return *to.* The stable touchstone of her thoughts had disappeared. Even her moments of satisfaction—frightening the conductor and besting the silken woman—now struck her as distant and even vain. She had just formed the further, frankly depressing, question "was such satisfaction always at odds with desire?" when she realized that the woman in the feathered cloak was speaking, slowly, quietly, as if she were answering a question only she had heard being asked.

"I have been here before. In the summer. It was light in the coach... it was light well into the evening. There were wildflowers. It was still cold—the wind is always cold here, because it is close to the sea, because the land is so flat. That is what they told me... because I was cold... even in summer. I remember when we reached the paved road—I remember because the movement of the coach changed, the bouncing, the rhythm. I was in a coach with two men... and I had allowed them to unbutton my dress. I had been told what to expect... I had been promised this and more... and yet, when it happened, when their promises began to be revealed . . . in such a desolate locale . . . I had goosebumps everywhere." She was silent, then glanced up, meeting the eyes of the others. She wrapped her cloak around her and looked out the window, smiling shyly. "And I am back again . . . you see, it gave me quite a thrill."

No one said a word. The clattering hoofbeats changed once more, drawing the coach onto uneven cobblestones. Miss Temple—her mind more than a little astir—glanced out the window to see that they had entered a courtyard, past a large, tall iron gate. The coach slowed. She could see others already stopped around them, passengers piling out (adjusting cloaks, putting on hats, tapping their walking sticks with impatience), and then a first glimpse of the house itself: splendid, heavy stone, some three tall stories high and without excessive ornament save for its broad windows, now streaming out welcoming golden light. The entire effect was of a simplicity that, when employed on such massive scale, bespoke a hard certainty of purpose—in the same way as a prison or an armory or a pagan temple. She knew it must be the great house of some Lord.

Their coach came to a halt, and as the last person in Miss Temple took it upon herself to be the first person out, opening the door herself and taking the coachman's large hand to aid her descent. She looked up to see, at the end of the courtyard, the entrance to the house, double doors flung open, servants to either side, and a stream of guests disappearing within. The massive splendor of the place amazed her, and she was again assailed by doubt, for surely once inside she would have to remove her hood and cloak and be revealed. Her mind groped for a solution as her eyes, brought back to their task, scanned the milling crowd for a glimpse of Roger. He must already be in the house. Her three companions were all out of the coach and had begun walking toward the doors. The pirate paused for a moment, looking back, to see if she was with them, and in another sudden decision Miss Temple merely gave in answer a small curtsey, as if to send them on their way. The pirate cocked her head, but then nodded and turned to catch up with the other two. Miss Temple stood alone.

She looked about the courtyard—was there perhaps some other way inside?—but knew that her only hope, if she wanted to truly discover what Roger was doing and why, in service to this, he had so peremptorily thrown her over, was to present herself at the grand entryway. She fought the urge to run and hide in a coach, and then the urge to just put things off long enough to record her most recent experiences in the notebook. If she must go in, it was better to go in at the proper time, and so she forced her legs to take her with a sureness of step that her racing heart did not share. As she got closer she moved among the other coaches, whose drivers were being directed by grooms toward the other side of the courtyard, more than once causing her to dodge rather sharply. When her path was finally open, the last of the other guests—perhaps her three companions?—had just cleared the entryway and vanished from her view. Miss Temple lowered her head, throwing more shadow over her face, and climbed the stairs past footmen on either side, noting their black livery included high boots, as if they were a squadron of dismounted cavalry. She walked carefully, raising her cloak and her dress high enough to climb the stairs without falling, but without being so vulgar as to expose her ankles. She reached the top of the stairs and stood alone on a pale marble floor, with long, mirrored, gas-lit hallways extending before her and to either side.

"I think perhaps you're meant to come with me."

Miss Temple turned to see the woman in red, from Roger's car. She no longer wore her fur-collared cloak, but she still had the lacquered cigarette holder in her hand, and her bright eyes, gazing fixedly at Miss Temple through the red leather mask, quite belied their jeweled tears. Miss Temple turned, but could not speak. The woman was astonishingly lovely—tall, strong, shapely, her powdered skin gleaming above the meager confines of the scarlet dress. Her hair was black and arranged in curls that cascaded across her bare pale shoulders. Miss Temple inhaled and nearly swooned from the sweet smell of frangipani flowers. She closed her mouth, swallowed, and saw the woman smile. It was very much how she imagined she had so recently smiled at the woman in blue silk. Without another word, the woman turned and led the way down one of the mirrored halls. Without a word Miss Temple followed.

Behind, she heard a distant buzz, of movement, of conversation, of the party itself—but this was fading before the sharp report of the woman's footfalls on the marble. They must have gone fifty yards—which was but half the length of the hall—when her guide stopped and turned, indicating with her outstretched hand an open door to Miss Temple's left. They were quite alone. Not knowing at this point that she could do anything else, Miss Temple went into the room. The woman in red followed, and shut the heavy door behind them. Now there was silence.

The room was spread with thick red and black carpets which absorbed the sound of their passage. The walls were fitted with closed cabinets, and between them racks of hooks, as if for clothing, and a full-length mirror. A long, heavy wooden work table was shoved against one wall, but Miss Temple could see no other furniture. It looked like some kind of attiring room, for a theatre, or perhaps sport, for horseback riding, or a gymnasium. She imagined a house of this size might well have its own anything it wanted, if the owner was so inclined. On the far wall was another door, not so fancy, set into the wall to look at first glance like one of the cabinets. Perhaps that led to the gymnasium proper.

The woman behind her said nothing, so she turned to face her, head inclined so as to shadow her face. The woman in red wasn't looking at Miss Temple at all, but was fitting another cigarette into her holder. She'd dropped the previous one on the carpet and ground it in with her shoe. She looked up at Miss Temple with a quick ghost of a smile, and strode over to the wall, where she jammed the new cigarette into one of the gas lamps and puffed on the holder until it caught. She exhaled, crossed to the table and leaned back against it, inhaled, and exhaled again, gazing at Miss Temple quite seriously.

"Keep the shoes," the woman said.

"Beg pardon?"

"They're quaint. Leave the rest in one of the lockers."

She gestured with the cigarette holder to one of the tall cabinets. Miss Temple turned to the cabinet and opened it; inside, hanging from hooks, were various pieces of clothing. On the hook right in front of her face—as if in answer to her fears—was a small white mask, covered in closely laid small white feathers, as if from a dove or a goose or a swan. Keeping her back to the woman in red, she threw off her hood and tied the white mask into place, weaving the strap beneath her curls, pulling it tight across her eyes. Miss Temple then shucked off her cape—glancing back once to the woman, who seemed to be smiling with wry approval of her progress—and hung it on a hook. She selected what seemed to be a dress from another hook—it was white, and silken—and held it out in front of her. It wasn't a dress at all. It was a robe, a very short robe, without any kind of buttons or sash, and quite thin.

"Did Waxing Street send you?" the woman asked, in a disinterested, time-passing tone.

Miss Temple turned to her, made a quick decision, and spoke deliberately.

"I do not know any Waxing Street."

"Ah."

The woman took a puff of her cigarette. Miss Temple had no idea whether her answer had been wrong—whether there had been a right or wrong answer—but she felt it was better to tell the truth than to guess foolishly. The woman exhaled, a long thin stream of smoke sent toward the ceiling.

"It must have been the hotel, then."

Miss Temple said nothing, then nodded, slowly. Her mind raced—what hotel? There were hundreds of hotels. *Her* hotel? Did they know who she was? Did her own hotel supply young women as guests to luxurious parties? Did any hotel do such a thing? Obviously so—the mere question told her that—yet Miss Temple had no idea what this meant as far as her own disguise, what she ought to say or how she was expected to behave or what this exactly implied about the party, though she was beginning to have suspicions. She looked again at the wholly inadequate robe.

She turned to the woman. "When you say *hotel*—"

Her words were cut off brusquely. The woman was grinding out her second cigarette on the carpet, and her voice was suddenly annoyed.

"Everything is waiting—it's quite late. *You* were late. I have no intention of serving as a nursemaid. Get changed—be quick about it—and when you're presentable, you can come find me." She walked directly toward Miss Temple, reached out to take hold of her shoulder—her fingers surprisingly hard—and spun her so her face was half-way into the cabinet. "This will help you get started—given the fabric, think of it as an act of mercy."

Miss Temple squawked. Something sharp touched the small of her back, and then shifted its angle, driving upward. With a sudden ripping sound, and a simultaneous collapse of her garment, Miss Temple realized that the woman had just sheared through the lacings of her dress. She whirled around, her hands holding it to her bosom as it peeled away from her back and off of her shoulders. The woman was tucking something small and bright back into her bag, crossing to the small inner door, and jamming a third cigarette into her holder as she spoke.

"You can come in through here."

Without a further glance at Miss Temple the woman in red opened the door with impatience, paused to get a light from the nearest wall sconce, and strode from view, pulling the door behind her so it slammed.

Miss Temple stood, at a loss. Her dress was ruined, or at least ruined without immediate access to new lacing and a maid to tie it up. She pulled it off of her upper body and did her best to shift the back section around so she could see it—fragments of green lacework were even now tumbling to the floor. She looked at the door to the hallway. She could hardly leave like this. On the other hand, she could hardly leave in her corset, or in the pitifully gossamer silk robe. She remembered with relief that she did still have her cloak, and could surely cover any less than decorous attire with that. This made her feel a little better and, after a moment of steady breathing, she was in less of a hurry to escape, and began to wonder once more about the woman, the party, and of course, never far from her thoughts, Roger. If she could return to fetch her cloak at any time and simply put it over her corset or ruined dress, then what was the harm in perhaps investigating further? On top of this, she was now intrigued by the reference to the hotel—she was determined to find out if such things happened at the Boniface, and how other than by continuing could she pursue her brave plan? She turned back to the cabinet. Perhaps there were other things than the robe.

There were, but she wasn't sure if she was any more comfortable at the thought of putting them on. Several items could only be described as undergarments, and probably from a warmer climate than this—Spain? Venice? Tangier?—a pale silken bodice, several sheer petticoats, and a pair of darling little silk pants with an open seam between the legs. There was also another robe, similar to the first, only longer and without any sleeves.

The ensemble was all white, save for the second robe, which had a small green circle embroidered repeatedly as a border around the collar and the bottom hem. Miss Temple assumed this was why she was allowed to keep her shoes. She looked at her own undergarments—shift, petticoats, cotton breeches, and her corset. Except for the corset, she didn't see too much of a difference between what was in the cabinet and the items on her body—save for the former being made of silk. Miss Temple was not in the habit of wearing silk—and it was only rarely that she was provoked into a choice outside her habits. The problem was getting out of her corset and then back into it, without assistance. She felt the silken pants between her fingers and resolved to try.

Her fingers tore behind her at the knotwork of the corset, for now she was concerned about taking too long, and did not want anyone coming in to collect her when she was half-naked, and once she was free of it—and taking deeper breaths than she was used to—she pulled the corset and her shift over her head. She pulled on the silk bodice, sleeveless, with tiny straps to keep it up, and tugged it into place over her bosom. She had to admit that it felt delicious. She pushed her petticoats and breeches down to the floor and, balancing on one foot and then the other, kicked her shoes free of them. She reached for the little pants, feeling a strange thrill at standing in such a large room wearing nothing but the bodice, which did not stretch below her ribs, and her green ankle boots. Stranger still, pulling on the pants, was how she felt somehow even more naked, with the open seam along her delicate curls. She ran her fingers through them once, finding the exposure both exquisite and a little frightening. She removed her fingers, sniffed them by habit, and reached for the silken petticoats, holding them open and stepping through the circle one foot at a time. She pulled them up, tied them off, and then reached again for her corset.

Before she put it on, Miss Temple stepped in front of the large mirror. The woman who stared back was unknown to her. It was partially the mask—the experience of looking at herself in a mask was extremely curious, and not unlike running her fingers along her open pants. She felt a tingle crawl down her spine and settle itself right among her hips, a ticking restless hunger. She licked her lips, and watched the woman in the mask of white feathers lick hers as well—but this woman (her pale arms bare, her legs muscular, throat exposed, roseate nipples at plain view through the bodice) licked them in quite a different way than seemed normal to Miss Temple—though once she saw that image, its sensation was, as it were, taken into her, and she licked them again as if some transformation had indeed been made. Her eyes glittered.

She dropped the corset back into the cabinet and put on the robes, first the shorter one with sleeves, and then over it the larger, almost like a tunic, with the borders of green embroidery, which did in fact have several hooks to keep it closed. She looked at herself again in the mirror, and was happy to see that together the two layers of robe provided enough of a barrier for decency. Her arms and lower legs were still semi-visible through their single layers, but the rest of her body, though suggested, could not in any detail be seen. As a final precaution, because she had not fully lost her sense of place or perspective, Miss Temple fished in the pocket of her cloak for both her money and her all-weather pencil, which was still rather sharp. Then she knelt on alternating knees, stuffing the money into one boot and wedging the pencil into the other. She stood, took a couple of steps to test comfort, closed the cabinet, and then walked through the inner door.

She was in a narrow unfinished hallway. She walked a few paces in gradually growing light and reached a turn where the floor slanted up toward the bright light's source. She stepped into glaring light and raised a hand to block it, looking around her. It was a kind of sunken stage—above and around it rose a seating gallery pitched at a very steep angle, covering three sides of the room. The stage itself, what she took for playing space, was taken up with a large table, at the present moment flat but with a heavy apparatus underneath, which, she assumed from the large, notched curve of steel running the length of the table, could tilt the table to any number of angles, for better viewing from the gallery. Behind the table, on the one wall without seating, was a common, if enormously large, blackboard.

It was an operating theatre. She looked to either side of the table and saw holes that dangled leather belts, to restrain limbs. She saw a metal drain on the floor. She smelled vinegar and lye, but beneath them some other odor that prickled the back of her throat. She looked up at the blackboard. This was for teaching, for study, but no mere man of science could afford such a home. Perhaps this Lord was their patient—but what patient would want an audience for his treatment? Or patron to some medical prodigy—or himself a practicing amateur—or an interested spectator? Her flesh was chilled. She swallowed, and noticed something written on the board—she hadn't seen it from the entrance because of the light. The surrounding text had been erased—indeed, half of this word had been erased—but it was easy to see what it had been: sharp block printing, in chalk, the word "ORANGE."

Miss Temple was startled—indeed, she may have squeaked in surprise—by a throat being cleared on the far side of the stage, from shadow. There was an opposite rampway rising up from the floor she hadn't seen, hidden by the table. A man stepped into view, wearing a black tailcoat, a black mask, and smoking a cigar. His beard was elegantly trimmed, and his face familiarly ruddy. It was one of her two dogs from the train, who had been sitting across from Roger. He looked at her body quite directly, and cleared his throat again.

"Yes?" she asked.

"I have been sent to collect you."

"I see."

"Yes." He took a puff on the cigar but otherwise did not move.

"I'm sure I'm sorry to make anyone wait."

"I didn't mind. I like to look around." He looked again, frankly examining her, and stepped fully up from the ramp into the theatre, raising his cigar hand above his eyes to block the light. He glanced over the gallery, to the table, and then to her again. "Quite a place."

Miss Temple adopted, without difficulty, a knowing condescension. "Why, have you never been here?"

He studied her before answering, then decided not to answer, and stuck the cigar into his mouth. With his hand free, he pulled a pocket watch from his black waistcoat and looked at the time. He replaced the watch, inhaled, then removed the cigar, blowing smoke.

Miss Temple spoke again, affecting as casual an air as possible.

"I have always found it to be an elegant house. But quite . . . particular."

He smiled. "It is that."

They looked at each other. She very much wanted to ask him about Roger, but knew it wasn't the time. If Roger was, as she suspected, peripheral, then asking for him by name—especially a guest in her strange position (as much as she did not fully understand what that was)—would only arouse suspicion. She must wait until she and Roger were in the same room and—while both were masked—try to engage someone in conversation and point him out.

But being alone with anyone was still an opportunity, and despite her terrible sense of disquiet and unease, in order to try and provoke this canine fellow further, she let her eyes wander to the blackboard, looking fixedly at the half-erased word, and then back to him, as if pointing out that someone had not fully done their job. The man saw the word. His face twitched in a quick grimace and he stepped to the board, wiping the word away with his black sleeve, and then beating ineffectually on the sleeve to get rid of the chalk smear. He stuck the cigar in his mouth and offered her his arm.

"They *are* waiting."

She walked past the table and took it, bobbing her head as she did. His arm was actually quite strong and he held hers tightly, even awkwardly, as he was so much taller. As they walked down the ramp into darkness, he spoke, nodding his head back to the theatre. "I don't know why they had you go through there—I suppose it's the shortest way. Still, it's quite a sight—not what you'd expect."

"That depends," Miss Temple answered. "What do *you* expect?"

In response, the man only chuckled, and squeezed her arm all the harder. Their ramp made a turn just like the other had, and they walked on level ground to another door. The man pushed it open and thrust her deliberately into the room. When she had stumbled several steps forward he came in behind and closed the door. Only then did he let go of Miss Temple's arm. She looked around her. They were not alone.

The room was in its way the opposite of where she had changed clothes, for just as it was on the opposite side of the theatre so it must be used for an opposite kind of preparation—an entirely different kind of participant. It felt like a kitchen, with a flagged stone floor and white tiled walls. There were several heavy wooden tables, also fitted with restraints, and on the walls various bolts and collars, clearly meant for securing the struggling or insensible. However, and strangely, one of the wooden tables was covered with an array of white feather pillows, and on the pillows sat three women, all wearing masks of white feathers and white robes, and each of them dangling their naked calves off of the table, the robes reaching just below their knees. All of their feet were bare. There was no sign of the woman in red.

No one was speaking—perhaps they'd gone silent at her arrival—and no one spoke as her escort left her where she was and crossed to one of the other tables, where his companion, the other dog-fellow, stood drinking from a flask. Her escort accepted the flask from him, swallowed manfully, and returned it, wiping his mouth. He took another puff from his cigar and tapped it against the edge of the table, knocking a stub of ash to the floor. Both men leaned back and studied their charges with evident pleasure. The moment became increasingly awkward. Miss Temple did not move to the table of women—there wasn't really room, and none of the others had shifted to make any. Instead, she smiled, and pushed her discomfort aside to make conversation.

"We have just seen the theatre. I must say it is impressive. I'm sure I don't know how many it will seat compared to other such theatres in the city, but I am confident it must seat plenty—perhaps up to one hundred. The notion of so many attendees in such a relatively distant place is quite a testament to the work at hand, in my own opinion. I should find it satisfying to be a part of that endeavor, however much as a tangent, even as a distraction, even for only this evening alone—for surely the fineness of the facility must parallel the work done in it. Do you not agree?"

There was no reply. She continued—for this was often her experience in public conversation and she was perfectly able to press on, adopting the pose of the knowing veteran.

"I am also, of course, happy for any excuse to be wearing so much silk—"

She was interrupted when the man with the flask stood and crossed to the far door. He took another nip and stuffed the flask into his tailcoat as he walked, then opened the door and closed it behind him. Miss Temple looked at the remaining man, whose face in the interval had gone even redder, if that were possible. She wondered if he were in the midst of some kind of attack, but he smiled passively enough and continued to smoke. The door opened again and the man with the flask poked his head through, nodded to the man with the cigar, and disappeared from view. The man with the cigar stood and, smiling once more at them all—the gaze of each woman following him closely—crossed to the open doorway. "Any time you're ready," he said and walked out, closing the door behind him. A moment later Miss Temple heard the distinct sharp click of that door being locked. Their only path led back to the theatre.

"You've kept your shoes," said one of the women, on the right.

"I have," said Miss Temple. It was not what she wanted to talk about. "Have any of you been *in* the theatre?" They shook their heads no, but said nothing more. Miss Temple indicated the restraints, the bolts, the collars. "Have you looked at this room?" They blandly nodded that they had. She became almost completely annoyed. "He has locked the door!"

"It will be fine," said the woman who had spoken before. Miss Temple was suddenly caught up—did this voice seem familiar?

"It is merely a room," said the woman in the middle, kicking at one of the leather restraints hanging near to her leg. "It's not what it is used for *now.*"

The others nodded blankly, as if no more needed saying.

"And what exactly would *that* be?" demanded Miss Temple.

The woman giggled. It was a giggle she'd heard before too. It was from the coach. This was the woman who'd let the men unbutton her dress. Miss Temple looked at the other two—seeing them in such different apparel, such different light—were they the pirate and silken woman whose eyes she had poked? She had no idea. She saw that they were smiling at her too, as if her question had indeed been very foolish. Were they drunk? Miss Temple stepped forward and grasped the woman's chin, tilting her face upwards—which she passively, strangely, allowed—and then lowered her own face to the woman's mouth and sniffed. She well knew what alcohol—particularly rum—smelled like, and its squalid influence. The woman wore perfume—sandalwood?—but there was another odor that Miss Temple did not recognize. It was not alcohol, or indeed anything she had smelled before—nor, further, did the odor emanate from around the woman's mouth (again occupied with giggling), but higher on her face. The odor was vaguely mechanical, almost industrial, but it wasn't coal, nor rubber, nor lamp oil, nor ether, nor even burnt hair, though it seemed adjacent to all of these unpleasant smells joined together. She could not place it—not in her mind, nor on the woman's body—was it around her eyes?—behind the mask? Miss Temple released her and stepped away. As if this were a signal to all three of them, they hopped off the table as one.

"Where are you going?" Miss Temple asked.

"We are going in," said the one in the middle.

"But what have they told you? What will happen?"

"Nothing will happen," said the woman on the right, "save everything we desire."

"They are expecting us," said the woman on the left, who had not yet spoken. Miss Temple was certain it was the woman who had arrived wearing the blue silk dress.

They pushed past her to the door—but there was so much more to ask them, so much more they could say! Were they invited guests? Did they know of any hotel? Miss Temple sputtered, dropping for the moment her condescending pose, crying to them all, "Wait! Wait! Where are your clothes? Where is the lady in red?"

All three erupted into stifled laughter. The one in front opened the door, and the one in the rear dismissed Miss Temple with a derisive flip of her hand. They walked out, the last closing the door behind them. There was silence.

Miss Temple looked around her at the cold, menacing room, her early confidence and pluck having quite ebbed away. Obviously, if she were bold, the path to full investigation lay up the dark ramp and into the theatre. Why else had she met the challenge of changing clothes, of formulating questions, of coming *all this way*? At the same time, she was not a fool, and knew enough that this room and the theatre, this party—all legitimately disquieting—could well pose a keen danger to both her virtue and her person. The outside door was locked, and the men outside that locked door horrid. The room held no cabinets or alcoves in which to crouch concealed. She pointed out to herself that the other women—who must know more than she—were unconcerned. The other women might equally be whores.

She took a breath, and chided herself for so brusque a judgment—after all the women had been finely dressed. They might be unchaste, even slatternly, they might indeed be here by way of some hotel—who knew the complications of another's life? The true question was whether this must lead perforce to a situation beyond her skills to manage. There were great gaps in Miss Temple's experience—which she would freely acknowledge, when pressed—that were only generally filled in with equally great swathes of inference and surmise. About many of these things she nevertheless felt she had a good idea. About others, she preferred to find pleasure in mystery. In the matter of the strange theatre, however, she was determined that no gaps, so to speak, should be filled at all.

She could at least listen at the door. With care she turned the knob and opened the door perhaps an inch. She heard nothing. She opened it a bit wider, enough to insert her head through the gap. The light looked the same as before. The other women had only just gone out—she could only have dithered for the space of a minute. Could it be that the crowd was so soon in hushed concentration? Was there already some ghastly tableau on display? She listened, but heard nothing. Peering around the corner, however, just gave her the glaring light in her eyes. She crept forward. She still heard nothing. She lowered herself to a crouch, then to her hands and knees, all the while gazing up the ramp at an uncomfortable angle. She saw and heard nothing. She stopped. She was at the point where any further movement would reveal her to the gallery—she was already fully visible from the stage, had anyone been there to see her. She shifted her gaze to the table. There was no one upon it. There was no one at all.

Miss Temple was extremely annoyed, if also relieved, and further, more than a little curious as to what had actually happened to the three women. Had they merely gone out the other side? She resolved to follow them, but happened in crossing the stage to glance up again at the blackboard, the glaring light now out of her eyes. In the same block letters, someone had inscribed, "SO THEY SHALL BE CONSUMED". Miss Temple visibly started, as if someone had blown in her ear. The words had definitely not been there before.

She whirled around to the gallery seats again, looking for anyone hiding on their hands and knees. There was no one. Without delay she continued across to the first ramp and down it, rounding the corner to the door. It was closed. She put her head to the door and listened. She heard nothing—but this meant nothing, the doors were thick. Tired as she was of unnecessary stealth, she again turned the knob with excruciating patience and opened it just enough to peek through. She widened the opening, listened, heard nothing, and widened it again. Still nothing. Annoyance getting the best of her, Miss Temple opened the door completely, and gasped with shock.

Strewn across the floor were the tattered, savaged remains of her hooded cloak, her dress, her corset, and her undergarments—all slashed beyond repair, nearly beyond recognition. Even her new notebook had been destroyed—pages torn out and scattered like leaves, the binding snapped, the leather cover pitted and gashed. Miss Temple found herself shaking with outrage, and with fear. Obviously she had been discovered. She was in danger. She must escape. She would follow Roger another time, or she would engage professional operatives, men who knew their business—stout fellows who would not be so easily tricked. Her efforts had been ridiculous. They might well be her undoing.

She crossed to the wall of cabinets. Her own clothing was destroyed, but perhaps one of the others held something she could use to cover herself. They were all locked. She pulled with all her strength, to no avail. She looked around for anything to force the cabinet doors, to pry them open, but the room was bare. Miss Temple released a cry of guttural frustration, an unexpectedly plangent whine—which when she heard it herself, with a certain shock, made clear the true extent of her desperate position. What if she were discovered and her name made known? How could she distinguish herself from any of these other similarly clad women? How could she face Roger? She caught herself. Roger! It was exactly the thing to restore her resolve. The last thing she wanted was to be in any way subject to his scrutiny—the very thought of it filled her with rage. *He* filled her with rage. In that moment she despised Roger Bascombe and was newly determined to get free of this horrid predicament and then, at her leisure, dedicate herself to ruining him utterly. And yet, even in the act of imagining that ruin, and herself sneering in triumph above him, Miss Temple felt a stab of pity, of proprietary concern for what the foolish man had managed to become involved in—what depravity, what danger, what career-destroying scandal was he here so blithely courting? Was it possible he did not understand? If she were to somehow speak to him, could she apprise him of his peril? Could she at least divine his mind?

Miss Temple walked to the hallway door and opened it. The hallway seemed empty, but she craned her head out as far as she could, listening closely. One way took her back to the front, to the thick of the party and directly past—she assumed—other guests, servants, *everyone.* It would also take her to the coaches, if in her present costume she were able to get out of the house without being discovered, exposed, ridiculed, or worse. The *other* way took her deeper into the house, and deeper into danger but also deeper into intrigue. Here she might legitimately hope to find a change of clothing. She might find an alternative route to the coaches. She might even find more information—about Roger, about the woman in red, about the Lord in residence. Or she could find her own destruction. While Miss Temple posed the question to herself as one of "running away" versus "bravely pushing on" it was also true that going deeper into the house, though more frightful as a whole, served to postpone any immediate confrontation. If she were to go back to the entrance she was certain to run into servants at least. If she went forward anything at all might happen—including an easy escape. She took one more look toward the great entrance, saw no one, and darted in the opposite direction, moving quickly and close to the wall.

She came to three successive doors on her side and one across the mirrored hall, all of which were locked. She kept walking. Her shoes seemed impossibly loud on the tiled floor. She looked ahead of her to the end of the hallway—there were only two more doors before she'd have to turn around. Another door across the hall—she glanced backwards again and, seeing no one, dashed across to it. The handle did not budge. Another look—still no one—and she trotted back to the other side, and up to the last door. Beyond it, the hallway ended in an enormous mirror that was inset with panes and posts to look like one of the great windows that faced out from elsewhere in the house—only the view here was ostentatiously and pointedly turned inward, as if to confide that (frankly, behind doors) such an interior view was truly the more important. To Miss Temple it was chastening, for she saw herself reflected, a pale figure skulking on the border of opulence. The earlier pleasure she'd felt upon seeing herself so masked was not wholly absent, but tempered with a better understanding of a risk that seemed to be its twin.

At the final door her luck changed. As she neared it, she heard a muffled voice and sounds of movement. She tried the knob. It was locked. There was nothing else for it. Miss Temple squared her shoulders and took a deep breath. She knocked.

The voice went silent. She braced herself, but heard nothing—no steps to the door, no rattle of the lock. She knocked again, louder, so that it hurt her hand. She stepped back, shaking her fingers, waiting. Then she heard quick steps, a bolt being drawn, and the door snapped open a bare inch. A wary green eye stared down at her.

"What is it?" demanded a querulous male voice, openly peeved.

"Hello," said Miss Temple, smiling.

"What the devil do you want?"

"I'd like to come in."

"Who the devil are you?"

"Isobel."

Miss Temple had seized the saint's name on instinct, from nerves—but what if it gave her away, if there were another Isobel who was known to be somewhere else, or didn't look anything like her, some fat blotchy girl who was always in a sweat? She looked up at the eye—the door had not opened a jot farther—and desperately tried to gauge the man's reaction. The eye merely blinked, then quickly ran up and down her body. It narrowed with suspicion.

"That doesn't say what you want."

"I was directed here."

"By whom? By *whom*?"

"Whom do you think?"

"For what purpose?"

Though Miss Temple was willing enough to continue, this was going *on,* and she was acutely aware of being so long visible in the hallway. She leaned forward, looked up to the eye, and whispered, "To change my *clothing.*" The eye did not move. She glanced around her, and back to the man, whispering again. "I can hardly do so in the *open air*..."

The man opened the door, and stepped away, allowing her to enter. She took care to scamper well past his possible grasp, but saw that he had merely closed the door and indeed stepped farther away. He was a strange creature—a servant, she assumed, though he did not wear the black livery. Instead, she noted that his shoes, though they had once been fine, were scuffed and clotted with grime. He wore a white work smock over what looked to be a thoroughly simple and equally worn brown shirt and pants. His hair was greasy, smeared back behind his ears. His skin was pale, his eyes sharp and searching, and his hands black as if they had been stained with India ink. Was he some kind of printer? She smiled at him and said thank you. His reaction was to audibly swallow, his hands worrying the frayed hem of his smock, and then study her while breathing through his open mouth like a fish.

The room was littered with wooden boxes, not as long or deep as a coffin, but lined with cushioning felt. The boxes were open, the tops haphazardly propped up against the wall, but their contents were not apparent. In fact, they all seemed empty. Miss Temple took it upon herself to glance into one of them when the man snapped at her, traces of spittle lancing into the air with his vehemence.

"Stop that!"

She turned to see him pointing at the boxes and then, his thoughts shifting, to her, her mask, her clothing.

"Why did he send you here? Everyone's supposed to be in the other rooms! I have work to do! I can't—I won't be the butt of his jokes! Hasn't he done enough to me already? Hasn't his lap-dog Lorenz? Do this, Crooner! Do that, Crooner! I have followed every instruction! I am just as responsible for . . . my own designs—one momentary, regrettable lapse—I have agreed to every condition—submitted utterly, and yet—" He gestured helplessly, sputtering at Miss Temple. "This *torment*!"

She waited for him to stop speaking and, once he did, to stop huffing like an ill-fed terrier. On the far side of the room was another door. With a serious nod and a respectful dip of her knee, Miss Temple indicated this door and whispered, "I will trouble you no further. If you-know-who *does* happen to question me, I will make plain that you were solely focused on your task." She nodded again and walked to the door, very much hoping it was not a closet. She opened it and stepped into a narrow hallway. Shutting the door behind her, Miss Temple sagged with relief against the wall.

She knew there was no time to rest and forced herself on. The hallway was an unadorned servants' corridor, allowing swift, undisturbing passage between vital parts of the house. With a surge of hope, Miss Temple wondered if it might lead her to the laundry. She padded as softly as her boots would allow to the door at the far end. Before turning the knob, she noticed a metal disk the size of a coin fixed to the door with a tiny bolt. She swiveled it to the side and revealed, set into the wood, a spy hole. Obviously this was so a careful servant could be sure not to interrupt his master with an untimely entrance. Miss Temple fully approved of this engine of discretion and tact. She stood on her toes and peeked in.

It was a private closet, luxurious in size, dominated by a large copper bath. On a table sat an array of bathing implements—sponges, brushes, bottles, soaps, and stacks of folded white towels. She saw no person. She opened the door and crept in. Immediately, she lost her footing—her heel skidding on the wet tile floor—and sat down hard on the floor in an awkward, spraggling split. A sharp ripping sound told her the outer robe had torn. She froze in place, listening. Had anyone heard? Had she actually yelped? There was no answering sound from beyond the open closet door. Miss Temple gingerly stood. The floor had been liberally splashed with water, a number of used towels dropped without care on the floor, crumpled and soaked. She carefully leaned over and dipped her fingers into the bath. It was tepid. No one had been in the tub for at least thirty minutes. She dabbed her fingers on one of the towels—no servant had been in the room either, or all would have been cleared and swabbed. This meant that either the occupant was still there, or that the servants had been warned away.

It was then that Miss Temple noticed the smell, drifting in from the room beyond. She probably hadn't detected it immediately because of the residue of flowered soaps and oils, but as soon as she had taken a step toward the door her senses were assailed with the same strange unnatural odor she had found on the masked woman's face, only now much stronger. She put a hand over her nose and mouth. It seemed a mixture of ash and burnt cork perhaps, or smoldering rubber—she wondered suddenly what burning glass smelled like—yet what were any of those smells doing in the private quarters of a country mansion? She poked her head out of the bathing closet and into a small sitting room. A quick glance took in chairs, a small table, a lamp, a painting, but no source of new clothing. She stepped across to the far doorway leading out, which was when she heard the noise.

Heavy footsteps, approaching nearer and nearer. When they had practically reached her—when she was just about to bolt back to the closet—the footsteps stumbled and Miss Temple heard the distinct screech and crash of something heavy being knocked into something else, which in turn toppled to the floor and shattered. She flinched to see a spray of China blue glass jet through the open doorway past her feet. A pause. The footsteps resumed, again lurching, and faded away. Miss Temple risked a peek around the corner. At her feet were the scattered remains of an enormous vase, the lilies that had been inside, the broken marble pedestal it had rested upon, and an end table knocked askew. The room held a large canopied bed with all its linen stripped away. Instead, the bed held three wooden boxes, identical to those the strange servant had opened in the room off the hall. These too were open and lined with felt—orange felt, as she now fully took in, recalling the word on the blackboard. The boxes were all empty, but she picked up one of the discarded lids and saw that letters—also in orange—had been stenciled on the wood: "OR-13". She looked at the other two lids and saw that they had in turn been stenciled "OR-14" and "OR-15". She snapped her head up to the archway. The footsteps had returned, careening even more recklessly. Before Miss Temple could do a thing to hide there was a thicker, meaty crash, and then another silence.

She waited, heard nothing, and crept to the archway. The smell was even stronger. She gagged, holding part of her sleeve across her nose and mouth. This was another sitting room, more fully furnished, but with every item covered by a white cloth, as if this part of the house were closed. On the floor, poking from behind a white-shrouded sideboard, were a pair of legs: bright red trousers with a yellow cord on the outside seam, stuffed into black boots. A soldier's uniform. The soldier did not move. Miss Temple dared to step into the room and look at him fully. His coat was also red, draped with golden epaulettes and frogging and he had a thick black moustache and whiskers. The rest of his face was covered by a tight red leather mask. His eyes were closed. She did not see any blood—there was no immediate indication that he had hit his head. Perhaps he was drunk. Or overwhelmed by the smell. She poked the man with her foot. He did not stir, though she saw from his gently moving chest that he lived.

Wadded up in his hands—and perhaps tripping on this had been his difficulty—was a black cloak. Miss Temple smiled with satisfaction. She knelt and gently prized it free, and then stood, holding it open before her. There was no hood, but it would cover the rest of her very well. She smiled again with cunning and knelt at the man's head, carefully unfastening his mask and then peeling it away from his face. She let out a gasp. Around his eyes the man bore what looked like a strange brand, an impression on the skin, as if a large pair of metal glasses had been pressed into his face and temples. The flesh was not burned, but discolored a visceral shade of plum, as if a layer of skin had been rubbed away. Miss Temple examined the other side of his mask with distaste. It did not seem fouled or bloody. She wiped it on one of the white chair covers. It left no stain. Still, it was with distrust that she pulled off her own white mask and exchanged it for the red. She then pulled off her white robes and wrapped herself in the black cloak. There was no mirror, but she still felt as if she had regained some of her footing. She stuffed the discarded things into the sideboard and made her way to the next doorway.

This was quite large, clearly the main entrance to this suite of rooms, and it opened directly onto a crowd of finely dressed guests moving purposefully past her down a large, well-lit corridor. A man noted Miss Temple's appearance in the doorway and nodded, but did not pause. No one paused—in fact there seemed to be some hurry. Happy not to be causing alarm, Miss Temple stepped into the moving mass and allowed herself to be swept along. She was mindful to hold her cloak closed, but otherwise had leisure to study the people around her. They all wore masks and elegant evening wear, but seemed a variety of types and ages. As she shuffled along several others nodded or smiled to her, but no one spoke—in fact, no one was speaking at all, though she did sense an occasional smile of anticipation. She was convinced that they were all going toward something that promised to be wonderful, but that very few, if any, of them actually knew what it was. As she looked ahead and behind, she saw it was really no great group in the corridor—perhaps forty or fifty. Judging from the number of coaches at the front of the house, this was but a fraction of those attending the party. She wondered where everyone else was, and how they had explained the absence of this group. Further, where were they going? And how long was the corridor? Miss Temple decided that whoever laid out the house was unhealthily fixated with *length*. She stumbled abruptly into the person ahead of her—at this point a short woman (which was to say, of her own height) in a pale green dress (a color similar to Miss Temple's own, she noted with a pang) and an especially ingenious mask made from strings of hanging beads.

"Oh, I am so sorry," Miss Temple whispered.

"Not at all," the woman replied, and nodded at a gentleman in front of her, "I trod on *his* heel." They were stopped in the hall.

"We are stopped," observed Miss Temple, trying to keep up the conversation.

"I was told the stair is quite narrow, and to be careful with my shoes. They never build for ladies."

"It is a terrible truth," agreed Miss Temple, but her gaze had shifted over their heads, where indeed she saw a line of figures winding their way up a spiral staircase, fashioned of bright metal.

Her heart leapt in her throat. Roger Bascombe—for it could be no one else, despite the plain black mask across his eyes—was even as she watched moving around the upper spiral, and for the moment facing her directly. Once more, his expression was guarded, his hand tapping impatiently on the rail as he climbed, one step at a time, other guests immediately above and below him. He so disliked the crush of a crowd—she knew he must be miserable. Where was he going? Where did he *think* he was going? Then all too brusquely Roger had reached the top, a narrow balcony, and disappeared from sight.

Miss Temple turned her gaze to the people around her—she had shuffled another few steps forward, her thoughts fully awhirl—and realized the woman in green had been whispering. "I'm sorry," Miss Temple whispered back, "I was suddenly distracted with excitement."

"It is very exciting, isn't it?" confided the woman.

"I should say it is."

"I am feeling quite girlish!"

"I am sure you speak for everyone," Miss Temple assured her, and then blithely wondered, "I did not expect so many people."

"Of course not," answered the woman, "for they've been very careful—the hiding of this group within the larger function, the subtlety of our invitations, the concealment of identity."

"Indeed." Miss Temple nodded. "And what a cunning mask you have."

"It *is* very cunning, is it not?" The woman smiled. By this time she had taken a half-step back so she could walk next to Miss Temple and they could speak lower without attracting the attention of others. "But I myself have been intending to compliment your cloak."

"Ah, well, that is kind of you to say."

"Rather *dramatic,*" the woman muttered, reaching to touch a border of black ribbon edging the collar that Miss Temple had not noticed. "It looks almost like a soldier's."

"Is that not the fashion?" Miss Temple smiled.

"Indeed"—here the woman's voice went lower still—"for are *we* not soldiers now, in our own way?"

Miss Temple nodded, and spoke in quiet solidarity. "My feeling is the same."

The woman met her gaze significantly, and then ran her eyes quite happily over the cloak. "And it is quite long—it covers you completely."

Miss Temple leaned closer. "So no one will know what I am wearing."

The woman smiled wickedly and leaned in closer still. "Or if you are wearing anything at all . . ."

Before Miss Temple could respond they were at the foot of the staircase. She gestured for the woman to go first—the last thing she wanted was for these impulsive words to prompt her companion to look under her cloak from below. As they rose, she looked down—there were only a scattered dozen people still in the corridor. Then she swallowed—for behind them all, advancing slowly, almost as if to herd them like sheep, was the woman in red. Her gaze fell across Miss Temple, who could not suppress a flinch, and then slid past her toward the balcony. Miss Temple kept climbing and was soon around the other side of the spiral, out of sight. When she once more rotated out into the open she steeled herself to merely face upward into the green woman's back. The nape of her neck prickled. It was all she could do not to look, but she held to her will, resisting the destructive urge—sure she'd been discovered. Then the green woman stopped—there was a delay above them. Miss Temple felt fully exposed, as if she wore no cloak and no mask, as if she and the woman in red were alone. Again, she sensed that gaze boring into her and distinctly heard those footfalls she remembered from the mirrored hall. The woman was coming closer . . . closer . . . she had stopped directly below. Miss Temple looked down—and for a terrible flashing moment met that pair of glittering eyes. Then, an infinitesimal shift, and the woman was looking—or trying to look, partially blocked by the step she was standing on—up her cloak. Miss Temple held her breath.

The woman above her climbed on, and Miss Temple followed, aware that as she moved her cloak by necessity opened around her feet, but she was unable to look down again to confirm if the woman had recognized her, or had merely examined her along with all the others. Three more steps and she was on the balcony, walking across it and through a small, dark door. Here the woman in green paused, as if to suggest they continue together, but Miss Temple was now too frightened of exposure and wanted to hide alone. She nodded to the woman, smiling, and then walked deliberately in the opposite direction. It was only then she actually perceived where she was.

She stood in an aisle that ran along the top of the steeply raked gallery, looking down at the operating theatre. The gallery itself was largely full, and she forced herself to search for an empty seat. On the stage she saw the man from the train, the very large man in the fur coat—no longer wearing the coat, but still fingering his silver walking stick. He glared up at the gallery, impatiently waiting for people to situate themselves. She knew how bright the light in his eyes actually was, that he could not see, but nevertheless felt his gaze restlessly pass over her, hard as a rake across gravel, as she stepped to the far aisle. She dared not stray from the upmost row—the lower one sat, the more visible one was from the stage—and was relieved to find an empty seat three places in, between a man in a black tailcoat and a white-haired fellow in a blue uniform with a sash. As each was some inches taller than she, Miss Temple assured herself that she was less visible between them—though what she felt was fully trapped. Behind her, she knew the woman in red must have entered. She forced her gaze to the stage, but what she saw didn't help her fears in the slightest.

The powerful man extended his hand into the shadow of a rampway and pulled it back, now gripping the pale shoulder of a masked woman in white silk robes. The woman walked carefully, blinded by the light, allowing the man to guide her. He then—with no ceremony at all—hoisted her with both hands into a sitting position on the table, legs dangling. He scooped up her legs and pulled them around to the table front, rotating her. He was obviously speaking to her, too low for anyone else to hear, for with a shy smile she lay back on the table, and shifted her body to be properly in the center. As she did this, the man matter-of-factly positioned each of her ankles to opposite corners of the table and threaded a leather belt around them. He tightened the belts with a sharp tug and let the slack drop. He moved up to her arms. The woman said nothing. Miss Temple was unsure which of the three women was on the table—perhaps the pirate?—and while she was trying to guess, the man bound the woman's arms. Then, carefully, he cleared away her elegantly curled hair and threaded another belt across her pale, delicate throat. This was also tightened, in a firm but not so muscular manner, leaving the woman completely secured. The man then stepped behind her and took hold of a metal handle, like that of a pump. He pulled it. The machinery answered with a percussive snap, loud as a gunshot, and the top of the table lurched upwards, rotating toward the gallery. Three more snaps and the woman was perhaps half-way to being vertical. He released the handle and walked off the stage into shadow.

The woman had no particular expression, aside from a bland smile, but this could not disguise the fact that her legs were shaking. Miss Temple risked a glance over the shoulder of her neighbor, back toward the door, and quickly turned her eyes back to the stage. The woman in red stood directly in the doorway, as if on guard, glancing idly across the crowd as she worked a new cigarette into her holder. Miss Temple's only other escape would be to vault onto the stage and rush down a rampway, which was hardly possible. Restlessly, she looked across the crowd herself, trying to find some idea, some new avenue. Instead, she found Roger, directly in the center of the gallery, sitting between a woman in yellow—she must be the laughing woman from his train compartment—and, of all things, an empty seat. It must be the only empty seat in the theatre. Somewhere behind her, Miss Temple smelled burning tobacco. She was certain that seat belonged to her scarlet nemesis—but what could explain the connection of that woman and Roger Bascombe? Was she some diplomatic figure—or a mysterious courtesan, or decadent heiress? Simply by collecting Miss Temple at the door, she proved herself part of whatever the crowd had here gathered to watch. Roger had been with her on the train—but did that mean he knew what they'd see as well? But then, with a sudden stab of doubt, Miss Temple wondered instead if the seat *she* occupied had been the woman's—but what could she possibly do now?

The powerful man returned to the light, now bearing in his arms another of the white-robed women. This was certainly the one in blue silk, for her long hair was undone and trailed down toward the floor. He walked to the center of the stage, in front of the table, and cleared his throat.

"I believe we are ready," he began.

Miss Temple was surprised at his voice, which far from being harsh or commanding, was faint, almost a rasp, if still in a bass register. It emerged from his throat like something scarred, no longer whole. He did not raise his voice either, but relied on others to pay attention—and his bearing was such that his audience did so completely. He cleared his throat again and lifted the woman in his arms, as if she were a text he would expound.

"As you can see, this lady has become fully subject. You will understand that no opiates nor other coercive medicines have been employed. Further, while she seems quite helpless, this is merely what has become her preferred state. It is hardly a necessity. On the contrary, a high level of responsiveness is perfectly within her grasp."

He swung the woman's body in such a way as to lift the upper half and sweep her legs into position beneath it, dropping her feet to the floor. He then stepped away, releasing his grip. The woman tottered, her eyes still glassy, but she did not fall. Without warning he slapped her sharply across the face. A gasp rippled across the gallery. The woman reeled, but she did not go down—on the contrary, one of her own arms shot out toward the man's own face, ready to strike. He caught her hand easily—he had clearly expected her blow—and then slowly lowered her arm to her side and released it. She did not move to swing again, and in fact her staid manner was as if the slap had never occurred. The man looked up into the gallery as if to acknowledge this, and then reached again toward the woman, this time putting his powerful hand around her throat. He squeezed. The woman reacted violently, clawing at his fingers, slapping at his arm, then kicking at his legs. The man held her at arm's length and did not waver. She could not reach him. The woman's face was red, her breath labored, her struggles more desperate. He was killing her. Miss Temple heard a murmur of shock from the uniformed man next to her—a murmur echoed elsewhere in the crowd—and felt him shift in his seat, as if he was going to stand. Anticipating this exact moment of protest, the man on stage released his grip. The woman staggered, her breath a series of ragged whoops—but her struggles soon abated. At no time did she refer to the man. After a minute or so regaining her strength, she stood once more with a placid stance and blank expression, exactly as if he were not there at all.

Again, the man looked up at the gallery, registering his point, and then stepped behind his subject. In a swift movement he flipped up the back of her robes and plunged his hand beneath them, deliberately digging. The woman stiffened, wriggled, and then bit her lip—the rest of her facial features consistently blank. The man remained behind her, his unseen fingers working. His expression remained impassive—he might have been repairing a clock—as before him the woman's breathing deepened, and her posture subtly shifted, leaning forward and placing that much more of her weight on her toes. Miss Temple watched, rapt—she knew what access the woman's silken pants would provide and exactly where he was occupied—as the slow arc of accelerating pleasure took hold on the woman's face—an audible gasp, a blush spreading over her throat, her clutching fingers. Again, abruptly, the man removed his hand and stepped away, taking a moment to wipe his fingers on the back of her robes. For her part, once he was clear, she immediately relaxed into her passive stance and expression. The man snapped his fingers. Another man stepped from the shadows—Miss Temple saw he was her own canine escort from earlier—and took the woman's hand. He led her down the rampway and out of sight.

"As you see," the man on stage continued, "the subject is both highly responsive and content to remain within her self. Such are the *immediate* effects, along with varying degrees of dizziness, nausea, and narcolepsy. It is why, during these early stages, supervision—protection—is of vital concern." He snapped his fingers again and from the opposite rampway emerged the second canine escort, guiding the last of the three women in white. She was led to the powerful man, walking perfectly normally, where she curtsied. He took her hand from the escort (who departed the stage) as she straightened, and turned her to face the gallery. She curtsied again.

"This lady," the man went on, "has been our subject for three days. As you see, she remains in complete control of her faculties. More than this, she has been *liberated* from strictures of thought. She has in these past three days embraced a *new method of life.*"

He paused for his dramatic words to register fully, and then continued, a note of dry disdain audibly rising in his voice.

"Three days ago, this woman—like so many others, like so many others here this evening, I presume—believed herself to be in *love.* She is now positioning herself, with our assistance, to be in *power.*" He paused and nodded to the woman.

As she spoke, Miss Temple recognized the low voice of the woman in the feathered cloak. Her tone was the same as when she told the story of being with the two men in the coach, but the cold dreamy distance with which she spoke of herself gave Miss Temple chills.

"I cannot say how I was, for that would be to say how I was a child. So much has changed—so much has become clear—that I can only speak of what I have become. It's true I thought myself to be in love. In love because I could not see past the ways in which I was subject, for I believed, in my servitude, that this love would release me. What view of the world had I convinced myself I understood so well? It was the useless attachment to another, to *rescue,* which existed in place of my own action. What I believed were solely consequences of that attachment—money, stature, respectability, pleasure—I now see merely as elements of my own unlimited capacity. In these three days I have acquired three new suitors, funds for a new life in Geneva, and gratifying employment I am not permitted"—here she shyly smiled—"to describe. In the process I have happily managed to acquire and to spend more money than I have hitherto in my entire life possessed."

She had finished speaking. She nodded to the gallery, and took a step backwards. Once more the escort appeared, took her hand, and walked her into darkness. The powerful man watched her exit, and turned back to his audience.

"I cannot give you details—any more than I would provide details about any of you. I do not seek to *convince,* but to offer *opportunity.* You see before you examples of different stages of our Process. These two women—one transformed three days since, the other just this night—have accepted our invitation and will benefit accordingly. This third... you will watch her transformation yourselves, and make your own decisions. You will bear in mind that the severity of the procedure matches the profundity of this *transformation.* Your attention—along with your silence—is quite the limit of what I ask."

With this, he knelt and picked up one of the wooden boxes. As he crossed with it to the table, he casually pried the top back with his fingers and tossed it aside with a flat clatter. He glanced at the woman, who swallowed with nervousness, and placed the box onto the table, next to her leg. He pulled out a thick layer of orange felt, dropped it onto the floor, and then frowned, reaching into the box with both hands, performing some adjustment or assembly. Satisfied, he removed what looked to Miss Temple like an overly large pair of glasses, the lenses impossibly thick, the frames sheathed in black rubber, trailing hanks of copper wire. The man leaned across the woman's front, blocking her from view, and tossed her white mask to the side. Before they might know her identity, he lowered the strange piece of machinery onto her open face, tightening it with short powerful movements of his hands that caused the woman's legs to twitch. He stepped back to the box. The woman was breathing hard, her cheeks were wet, the sleeves of her robe balled up in her fists. The man removed a wickedly toothed metal clamp, attached one end to the copper wire, and secured the other inside the box to something Miss Temple could not see. Upon his doing this, however, the thing inside the box began to glow with a pallid blue light. The woman caught her breath and grunted with pain.

In that exact moment, Miss Temple did the same, for a sharp stabbing sensation pricked her spine directly between the shoulders. And as she turned her head to see the woman in red was no longer in the doorway, she felt from her other side that woman's breath in her ear.

"I'm afraid you must come with me."

Throughout their passage from the darkened gallery, across the balcony, and down the stairs themselves, the woman had maintained the pressure of her pinpoint blade, convincing Miss Temple not to call out, pretend a faint, or even to trip her adversary so she might fly over the railing. Once they had reached the long marble corridor, the woman stepped away and tucked her hand back into a pocket—but not before Miss Temple could note the bright metal band across her fingers. The woman glanced up to the balcony, to make sure no one had followed, and then indicated that Miss Temple should lead the way back down the corridor toward the rest of the house. Miss Temple did so, desperately hoping for an open door she could dash through, or the intervention of some passer-by. She already knew that there were other guests—that the events in the operating theatre were hidden from outside eyes within the larger gathering taking place in the whole of the house. If she could only reach *that* collection of people, she was certain she would find aid. They passed several closed doors, but Miss Temple's journey to the staircase had been so focused on the people around her that she had little memory of anything else—she'd no idea where these might go, or even if one of these doors might be where she had entered. The woman drove her ahead with sharp shoves past any landmark where she thought to linger. At the first of these offensive gestures, Miss Temple felt her sense of propriety to be fully overwhelmed by her fear. She was frankly terrified what was going to happen to her—that she could be so subject to abuse was just another sign of how low she had fallen, how desperate her straits. At the second shove, a rising level of annoyance was still nevertheless overborne by her own physical frailty, the woman's weapon and obvious malice, and the knowledge that, as she could certainly be accused with trespassing and theft, she had no legal ground to stand on whatsoever. At the third such shove, however, Miss Temple's natural outrage flared and without thinking she whipped round and swung her open hand at the woman's face with all the strength in her arm. The woman pulled her head back and the blow went wide, causing Miss Temple to stumble. At this the woman in red chuckled, insufferably, and once more revealed the device in her hand—a short vicious blade fixed to a band of steel that wrapped across her knuckles. With her other hand she indicated a nearby doorway—by all appearances identical to every other in the corridor.

"We can speak in there," she said. Glaring her defiance quite openly, Miss Temple went in.

It was yet another suite of rooms, the furniture covered with white cloths. The woman in red closed the door behind them, and shoved Miss Temple toward a covered divan. When Miss Temple turned to her, eyes quite blazing, the woman's voice was dismissive and cold.

"Sit down." At this, the woman herself stepped over to a bulky armchair and sat, digging out her cigarette holder and a metal case of cigarettes. She looked up at Miss Temple, who had not moved, and snapped, "Sit down or I'll find you something *else* to sit on—*repeatedly.*"

Miss Temple sat. The woman finished inserting the cigarette, stood, walked to a wall sconce and lit it, puffing, and then returned to her seat. They stared at each other.

"You are holding me against my will," Miss Temple said, out of the hope that standing up for herself had prompted this conversation.

"Don't be ridiculous." The woman inhaled, blew smoke away from them and then tapped her ash to the carpet. She studied Miss Temple, who did not move. The woman did not move either. She took another puff, and when she opened her mouth to speak, smoke came out along with her words.

"I will ask you questions. You will answer them. Do not be a fool. You are alone." She looked pointedly at Miss Temple and then, shifting her voice to a slightly more dry tone of accusatory recitation, began in earnest. "You arrived in a coach with the others."

"Yes. You see, I am from the hotel," Miss Temple offered.

"You are not. It will not aid you to lie." The woman paused for a moment, as if trying to decide her best course of questioning. Miss Temple asserted herself.

"I am not afraid of you."

"It will not aid you to be stupid either. You came on the train. How did you know what train to take? And what station? Some person told you."

"No one told me."

"Of course someone told you. Who are your confederates?"

"I am quite alone."

The woman laughed, a sharp scoffing bark. "If I believed that, you'd be headfirst in a bog and I'd be done with you." She settled back into her chair. "I will require names."

Miss Temple had no idea what to say. If she simply made up names, or gave names that had nothing to do with the matter, she would only prove her ignorance. If she did not, the risk was even greater. Her knee was trembling. As calmly as she could, she put a hand on it.

"What would such a betrayal purchase me?" she asked.

"Your life," answered the woman. "If I am kind."

"I see."

"So. Speak. Names. Start with your own."

"May I ask you a question first?"

"You may not."

Miss Temple ignored her. "If something were to happen to me, would this not be the most singular signal to my confederates about the character of your activities?"

The woman barked again with laughter. She regained control over her features. "I'm sorry, that was so very nearly amusing. Please—you were saying? Or did you want to die?"

Miss Temple took a breath and began to lie for all she was worth.

"Isobel. Isobel Hastings."

The woman smirked. "Your accent is . . . odd . . . perhaps even fabricated."

As she was speaking in her normal voice, Miss Temple found this extremely annoying.

"I am from the country."

"What country?"

"This one, naturally. From the north."

"I see . . ." The woman smirked again. "Whom do you serve?"

"I do not know names. I was given instructions by letter."

"What instructions?"

"Stropping Station, platform 12, 6:23 train, Orange Locks. I was to find the true purpose of the evening and report back all I had witnessed."

"To whom?"

"I do not know. I was to be contacted upon returning to Stropping."

"By whom?"

"They would reveal themselves to me. I know nothing, so I can give nothing away."

The woman sighed with annoyance, stubbed out her cigarette on the carpet, and rummaged for another in her bag. "You've some education. You're not a common whore."

"I am not."

"So you're an *un*-common one."

"I am not one at all."

"I see," the woman sneered. "Your expenses are paid by the work you do in a *shop*." Miss Temple was silent. "So tell me, because I do not understand, just who are you to be doing this kind of... 'investigation'?"

"No one at all. That is how I can do it."

"Ah."

"It is the truth."

"And how were you first... recruited?"

"I met a man in a hotel."

"A *man*." The woman sneered again. Miss Temple found herself studying the woman's face, noting how its almost glacially inarguable beauty was so routinely broken by these flashes of sarcastic disapproval, as if the world itself were so insistently squalid that even this daunting perfection could not stand up against the onslaught. "What *man*?"

"I do not know him, if that is what you mean."

"Perhaps you can say what he looked like."

Miss Temple groped for an answer and found, looming out of her unsettled thoughts, Roger's supervisor, the Deputy Foreign Minister, Mr. Harald Crabbé.

"Ah—let me see—a shortish man, quite neat, fussy actually, grey hair, moustache, polished shoes, peremptory manner, condescending, mean little eyes, fat wife—not that I saw the wife, but sometimes, you will agree, one just *knows*—"

The woman in red cut her off.

"What hotel?"

"The Boniface, I believe."

The woman curled her lip with disdain. "How *respectable* of you..."

Miss Temple continued. "We had tea. He proposed that I might do such a kind of task. I agreed."

"For how much money?"

"I told you. I am not doing this for money."

For the first time, Miss Temple felt the woman in red was surprised. It was extremely pleasant. The woman rose and crossed again to the sconce, lighting a second cigarette. She returned to her seat in a more leisurely manner, as if musing aloud. "I see... you prefer... leverage?"

"I want something other than money."

"And what is that?"

"It is my business, Madam, and unconnected to this talk."

The woman started, as if she had been slapped. She had been just about to sit again in the armchair. Very slowly, she straightened, standing tall as a judge over the seated Miss Temple. When she spoke, her voice was clipped and sure, as if her decision had already been made, and her questions now merely necessary procedure.

"You have no name for who sent you?"

"No."

"You have no idea who will meet you?"

"No."

"Nor what they wanted you to find?"

"No."

"And what *have* you found?"

"Some kind of new medicine—most likely a patent elixir—used on unsuspecting women to convert them to a lifetime spent in the service of corrupted appetites."

"I see."

"Yes. And I believe *you* are the most corrupted of them all."

"I'm sure you are correct in every degree, my dear—you have much to be proud of. Farquhar!"

This last was shouted—in a surprisingly compelling voice of command—toward a corner of the room blocked from view by a draped changing screen. Behind it Miss Temple heard the sound of a door, and a moment later saw her escort from before emerge, his complexion even redder, wiping his mouth with the back of a hand. "Mmn?" he asked; then, making the effort to swallow, did so, and cleared his throat. "Madam?"

"She goes outside."

"Yes, Madam."

"Discreetly."

"As ever."

The woman looked down at Miss Temple and smiled. "Be careful.

This one has *secrets.*" She walked to the main door without another word and left the room. The man, Farquhar, turned to Miss Temple.

"I don't like this room," he said. "Let's go somewhere else."

The door behind the screen led them into an uncarpeted serving room with several long tables and a tub of ice. One of the tables held a platter with a ravaged ham on it, and the other an array of open bottles of different shapes. The room smelled of alcohol. Farquhar indicated that Miss Temple should sit in the only visible chair, a simple wooden seat with no padding, a high back, and no arms. As she did, he wandered over to the ham and sawed away a chunk of pink meat with a nearby knife, then skewered the chunk on the knife and stuck it into his mouth. He leaned against the table and looked at her, chewing. After a moment he walked to the other table and leaned against it, tipping a brown bottle up to his teeth. He exhaled and wiped his mouth. After this moment of rest, he continued drinking, three deep swallows in succession. He put the bottle on the table and coughed.

The door on the far side of the room opened and the other escort, with the flask, stepped in. He spoke from the doorway. "See anything?"

"Of what?" Farquhar grunted in reply.

"Fellow in red. Nosing about."

"Where?"

"Garden?"

Farquhar frowned, and took another pull from the brown bottle.

"They saw him out front," continued the other man.

"Who is he?"

"They didn't know."

"Could be anybody."

"Seems like it."

Farquhar took another drink and set the bottle down. He nodded at Miss Temple.

"We're to take her out."

"Out?"

"Discreetly."

"Now?"

"I expect so. Are they still occupied?"

"I expect so. How long does it take?"

"I've no idea. I was eating."

The man in the door wrinkled his nose, peering at the table. "What is that?"

"Ham."

"The drink—what's the drink?"

"It's . . . it's . . ." Farquhar rummaged for the bottle, sniffed it. "Spiced. Tastes like, what's it . . . cloves? Tastes like cloves. And pepper."

"Cloves make me vomit," the man in the doorway muttered. He glanced behind him, then back into the room. "All right, it's clear."

Farquhar snapped his fingers at Miss Temple, which she understood to mean that she should stand and walk to the open door, which she did, Farquhar following after. The other man took her hand and smiled. His teeth were yellow as cheese. "My name is Spragg," he said. "We're going to walk quietly." She nodded her agreement, eyes focused on the white front of his dress shirt, stained with a thin spatter of bright red blood. Could he have been just shaving? She pulled her eyes away and flinched as Farquhar took her other hand in his. The two men glanced at each other over the top of her head and began to walk, holding her firmly between them.

They made directly for a pair of glass double doors, covered with a pale curtain. Spragg opened the doors and they stepped out into a courtyard, footfalls rustling onto gravel. It had become cold. There were no stars, nor any longer palpable moonlight, but the courtyard was ringed with windows that threw out a general glow, so it was easy enough to see their path, winding among shrubbery and statues and great stone urns. Across, in what must be another wing of the house, Miss Temple fancied she could see the movements of many people—dancing perhaps—and hear the faint strains of an orchestra. This must be the rest of the party, the main party. If only she could break free and run across to it—but she knew that while she might stamp on the foot of one of her escorts, she could not do it to both of them. As if they knew her thoughts, both men tightened their grip on Miss Temple's hands.

They guided her toward a small darkened archway, a passage running between wings of the house, for gardeners or others having no acceptable business indoors. It allowed the three of them to skirt the main party completely, as well as the main entrance to the great house, for when they had emerged on the other side, Miss Temple found herself at the large cobblestone courtyard where the coaches were waiting, and where she had so long ago—so it seemed—arrived.

She turned to Farquhar. "Well, thank you, and I am sorry for the inconvenience—" but her attempts to extricate her hand were of no avail. Instead, Spragg gave her right hand to Farquhar to hold as well, and stalked off to where a small knot of drivers huddled over a hot brazier. "I will go," insisted Miss Temple. "I will hire a coach and leave, I promise you!" Farquhar said nothing, watching Spragg. After a moment of negotiation, Spragg turned and pointed to an elegant black coach, and began walking to it. Farquhar pulled Miss Temple to join him.

Farquhar looked at the empty driver's seat. "Who's up?" he asked.

"Your turn," answered Spragg.

"It isn't."

"I drove to Packington."

Farquhar was silent. Then, with a huff, he nodded at the coach door. "Get in then."

Spragg chuckled. He opened the door and climbed in, reaching out with both of his meaty hands to collect Miss Temple. Farquhar huffed again and hoisted her up, as if her weight meant very little. As Spragg's hard fingers grabbed her arms and then her shoulders, Miss Temple saw her cloak fall quite away from the rest of her body, giving both men lurid views of her silken underthings. Spragg pushed her roughly onto the seat across from him, her legs awkwardly splayed and her hands groping for balance. They continued to stare as she collected the cloak tightly around herself. The men looked at each other. "We'll get there soon enough," Farquhar intoned to Spragg. Spragg merely shrugged, his face an unconvincing mask of disinterest. Farquhar closed the door of the coach. Spragg and Miss Temple gazed at each other in silence. After a moment, the coach swayed with the weight of Farquhar climbing up into the seat, and after another moment, leapt forward into life.

"I heard you mention Packington," Miss Temple said. "If it is convenient, you may leave me off there, where I can meet the train with little trouble."

"My goodness." Spragg smiled. "She's a *listener.*"

"You were not exactly whispering," replied Miss Temple, not liking his tone—in fact, not liking Spragg at all. She was annoyed with herself for not managing her cloak when she entered the coach. Spragg's gaze was positively crawling across her without shame. "Stop looking at me," she finally snapped.

"Oh, what's the harm?" He chuckled. "I saw you earlier, you know."

"Yes, I saw you earlier as well."

"Earlier than that, I mean."

"When?"

Spragg picked a bit of grime from under his thumbnail. "Did you know," he asked, "that in Holland they've invented glass that works like a mirror on one side, and a clear picture window on the other?"

"Really. Well, how do you beat that for cleverness?"

"I don't think you do." Spragg's smile widened further into satisfaction, if not outright malice. Miss Temple blanched. The mirror where she'd changed her clothes, where she put on the feathered mask and licked her lips like an animal. They had watched her through all of it, watched her together, as if she were an Egyptian vaudeville.

"My Lord it's hot in here." Spragg chuckled, tugging at his collar.

"I find it quite cold, actually."

"Perhaps you'd like a drink to warm you up?"

"No thank you. But may I ask you a question?"

Spragg nodded absently, digging in his coat for the flask. As he sat back and unscrewed the cap, Miss Temple felt the coach shift. They had left the cobblestones for the paved road that must lead to the border of the estate. Spragg drank, exhaling loudly and wiping his mouth between pulls. Miss Temple pressed on. "I was wondering... if you knew—if you could tell me—about the other three women."

He laughed harshly. "Do you want to know what *I* was wondering?"

She did not answer. He laughed again and leaned across to her. "*I* was wondering..." he began, and placed his hand on her knee. She swatted it away. Spragg whistled and shook his hand, as if it were stinging. He sat back and took another pull on the flask, and then tucked it away in his coat. He cracked his knuckles. Outside the coach was darkness. Miss Temple knew she was in a dangerous spot. She must act carefully.

"Mr. Spragg," she said, "I am not convinced we understand one another. We share a coach, but what do we really know about the other person? About what advantage that person can offer—advantage, I must point out, that may remain secret from other interested parties. I am speaking of money, Mr. Spragg, and of information, and, yes, even of *advancement.* You think I am a wayward girl without allies. I assure you it is not the case, and that it is indeed you who is more in need of *my* assistance."

He looked back at her, impassive as a fish on a plate. In a sudden movement, Spragg leapt across the coach and fully onto her body. He caught up both her hands in his and blocked her kicking legs with the bulk of his middle, crushing them to her so she could not swing with any force. She grunted with the impact and pushed against him. He was quite strong, and very heavy. With a quick jerk he adjusted his grip so that one of his large hands held both of hers, and with his free hand ripped at the ties of her cloak, tearing it away from her. Then the hand was pawing her body as it had never been touched before, with a crude insistent hunger—her breasts, her neck, her stomach—his mauling touch so rapidly invasive that her understanding lagged behind the spasms of pain. She pushed against him with all of her strength, with such a desperate exertion that she was gasping, her breath now coming in sobs. She had never in her life known that she could struggle so, but still she could not move him. His mouth lurched closer and she turned her head to the side, his beard scratching her cheek, the smell of whisky suddenly overwhelming. Spragg shifted again, wedging his bulk between her legs. His free hand took hold of an ankle and roughly pushed it up, forcing her knee toward her chin. He let go, doing his best to pin it in place with his shoulder, and dropped his hand between her thighs, pulling apart her petticoats. Miss Temple whined with fury, thrashing. His fingers tore the silk pants, blindly stabbing her delicate flesh, digging deeper, catching her with his ragged nails. She gasped with pain. He chuckled and drew his wet tongue across her neck.

She felt his hand leave her, but sensed through the movements of his arm that it was occupied elsewhere—with loosening his own clothing. She arched her back to throw him off. He laughed—he *laughed*—and shifted his grip from her wrists to around her throat. Her hands fell free.

He was choking her. His other hand was back between her legs, pushing them apart. He pressed his body nearer. In a moment of clarity, Miss Temple recalled that the leg bent awkwardly against her chest wore the shoe which held her sharpened all-weather pencil. It was within her reach. She desperately groped for it. Spragg leaned away from her, allowing himself the pleasure of looking down between them—at the spectacle of their bodies—one hand choking her, the other wedging her thighs apart. He was about to thrust himself forward. She drove the pencil deep into the side of his neck.

Spragg's mouth opened with surprise, the hinges of his jaw twitching. His face went crimson. Her fingers were still gripping the pencil and she wrenched it free, ready for another blow. Instead, this released a thick pulsing jet of blood that sprayed like a fountain across her body and onto the walls of the coach. Spragg gasped, groaned, rattled, jerking like a puppet above her. She kicked her way free—she was screaming, she realized—everything wet and sticky, blood in her eyes. Spragg dropped with a thud between the seats. He thrashed for another few moments and became still. Miss Temple held the pencil, breathing hard, blinking, covered in gore.

She looked up. The coach had stopped. She groaned aloud with dismay. She heard the distinct crunch of Farquhar jumping down from the driver's seat. With a sudden thought she threw herself on top of Spragg's leaden body and pawed at his coat, trying to locate the pockets in the dark, hoping he had a knife, a pistol, any kind of weapon. The latch turned behind her. Miss Temple wheeled and, bracing her legs, threw herself forward just as Farquhar pulled open the door. She cannoned into his chest, flailing with the pencil, screaming. His hands came up instinctively to catch her, and she stabbed over them at his face. The tip of the pencil ripped deeply into Farquhar's cheek, dragging an ugly gash, and then snapped. He howled and flung her away. She landed heavily and rolled, the breath knocked from her body, her knees and forearms stinging from the gravel. Behind her, Farquhar was still howling, mixed with inarticulate curses. She crawled to her hands and knees. She looked at the broken stub in her hand and let go of it with an effort. Her fingers felt tight and strange. She wasn't moving quickly enough. She needed to be running. She looked back at Farquhar. One side of his face seemed split in two: the lower half dark and wet, above it almost obscenely pale. He was silent. Farquhar had looked into the coach.

He reached into his coat and removed a black revolver. With his other hand he fished out a handkerchief, flapped it in the air to open it, and then pressed it against his face, wincing at the contact. When he spoke, his voice was run through with pain.

"God damn . . . God damn you to hell."

"He attacked me," Miss Temple said, hoarsely. They stared at each other.

She very carefully shifted her weight so she could straighten up, sitting on her heels. Her face was wet and she kept having to blink. She wiped her eyes. Farquhar didn't move. She stood, which took a bit of an effort. She was sore. She glanced down at herself. Her underthings were ripped apart and soaked with wide scarlet stripes, clinging and torn—she may as well have been naked. Farquhar kept staring at her.

"Are you going to shoot me?" she asked. "Or shall I kill you as well?"

She looked around her. Near her on the ground she saw a jagged stone, perhaps twice the size of her fist. She bent over and picked it up.

"Put that down!" Farquhar hissed, raising the pistol.

"Shoot me," Miss Temple replied.

She threw the stone at his head. He squawked with surprise and fired the pistol. She felt a scorch along the side of her face. The stone sailed past Farquhar and slammed into the coach. This impact, occurring in nearly the same moment as the shot, caused the horses to leap forward. The open coach door smacked into the back of Farquhar's head and spun him off balance toward the advancing rear wheel. Before Miss Temple could quite understand what she was watching, the wheel clipped the man's legs, and with a shocked cry he toppled beneath. The wheel went over Farquhar's body with a hideous snapping sound and he rolled to an awkward stillness. The coach continued away, out of her sight and hearing.

Miss Temple fell onto her back. She stared up into the depthless black sky, growing cold. Her head swam. She could not tell what time had passed. She forced herself to move, to roll over. She vomited onto the ground.

After another set of trackless minutes, she was on her hands and knees. She was shivering, a mass of aches and dizziness. She touched the side of her head, and was surprised to realize she was no longer wearing the mask. It must have come off in the coach. Her fingers traced a raw line above her ear, scored by Farquhar's bullet. Her throat heaved again as she touched it. It was sticky. She smelled blood. She had never known so much blood at a time, to know that it had a smell at all. She could not now imagine ever forgetting it. She wiped her mouth and spat.

Farquhar remained in place on the ground. She crawled to him. His body was twisted and his mouth was blue. With great effort, Miss Temple pulled off his coat—it was long enough to cover her. She found the revolver and shoved it into one of the pockets. She began to walk down the road.

It was an hour before she reached the Orange Locks station. Twice she'd staggered from the road to avoid a coach on its way from the great house, crouching on her knees in a field as it passed. She had no idea who might be in them, and no desire to find out. The platform itself was empty, which gave her hope that the train was still running—as the occupants of the coaches she had seen were gone. Her first instinct was to hide while she waited, and she had curled herself into a shadowed corner behind the station. But she kept catching herself nodding into sleep. Terrified of missing the train if it should come, or of being discovered in so vulnerable a state by her enemies, she forced herself to wait on her feet, until she was weaving.

Another hour passed, and no other coaches had arrived. She heard the whistle of the train before she saw its light, and hurried to the edge of the platform, waving her arms. It was a different conductor who lowered the steps, openly staring as she climbed past him into the car. She lurched into the corridor and bent down for the money in her other shoe. She turned to the conductor—she had lost her ticket with her cloak and her dress—and stuffed a note worth twice the fare into his hand. He continued to stare. Without another word she made her way down toward the rear of the train.

The compartments were all empty, save for one. Miss Temple glanced into it and stopped, looking at a tall, unshaven man with greasy black hair and round spectacles of dark glass, as if he were blind. His equally unkempt topcoat was red, as were his trousers and his gloves, which he held in one hand, a thin book in the other. On the seat beside him was an open razor, lying on a handkerchief. He looked up from his book. She nodded to him, and just perceptibly dipped her knee. He nodded in return. She knew that her face was bloody, that she was dressed in rags, and that yet somehow he understood that she was more—or other—than this appearance. Or was it that in this appearance she was revealing her true nature? He smiled faintly. She wondered if she had fallen asleep on her feet, and was actually dreaming. She nodded again and made her way to another compartment.

Miss Temple dozed with one hand on the revolver until the train reached Stropping, early in the morning, the sky still thick with shadow. She saw nothing more of the man in red, nor of anyone she recognized, and was forced to pay three times the usual fare to get a coach to the Boniface, and then to bang on the glass front of the hotel with the revolver to be let in. Once the staff was convinced who she was and allowed her to enter—faces white, eyes wide, jaws gaping—she refused to say another word and, clutching the coat around her body, went directly to her rooms. Inside was warm and still and dark. Miss Temple staggered past the closed doors of her sleeping maids and her sleeping aunt to her own chamber. With the last of her strength she dropped the coat behind her to the floor, tore away the bloody rags and crawled naked but for her green boots into the bed. She slept like a stone for sixteen hours.

TWO

Cardinal

He was called Cardinal from his habit of wearing a red leather topcoat that he'd stolen from the costume rack of a traveling theatre. It had been winter, and he'd taken it because the ensemble included boots and gloves as well as the coat, and at the time he was lacking all three. The boots and gloves had since been replaced, but he had preserved the coat, despite wearing it through all weathers. Though few men in his line of work sought to identify themselves in any way at all, he found that, in truth, those who sought him out—for employment or punishment—would find him even if he wore the drabbest grey wool. As for the name, however ironic or mocking, it did bestow a certain veneer of mission—given his life was a persistent and persistently vicious struggle—onto his itinerant church of one, and though he knew in his heart that he (like everyone) must lose at the finish, the vain title made him feel less through the course of his days like an animal fattened in a pen.

He was called Chang for more immediate reasons, if equally ironic and mocking. As a young man he'd been deeply slashed by a riding crop over the bridge of his nose and both eyes. He'd been blinded for three weeks, and when his vision finally cleared—as much as it was ever going to clear—he was greeted with the blunt scars that crossed and then protruded out from the corners of each eyelid, as if a child's caricature of a slant-eyed menacing Chinaman had been scrawled with a knife over his features. His eyes were thereafter sensitive to light, and tired easily—reading anything longer than a page of newspaper gave him a headache that, as he had learned many times over, only the deep sleep of opiates or, if such were unavailable, alcohol, might assuage. He wore spectacles with round lenses of dark smoked glass in all circumstances.

It was a gradual process by which he accepted these names, first from others, and then finally used them himself. The first time he replied "Chang" when asked his name, he could too easily recall the taunting comments as he waited day after day in the sickroom for his sight to return (it was a name to be always accompanied by a bitter smile), but even those associations seemed more real—more important to carry forward—than an earlier identity marked with failure and loss. More, the names were now a part of his working life—the rest were distant landmarks on a sea voyage, faded from sight and usage.

The riding crop had also damaged the inside of his nose, and he had little sense of smell. He knew abstractly that his rooming house was more objectionable than his own experience told him—he could see the nearby sewers, and knew by logic that the walls and floors had fully absorbed the fetid airs of their surroundings. But he was not uncomfortable. The garret room was cheap, isolated, with rooftop access and, most importantly, in the shadow of the great Library. For the smell of his own person, he contented himself with weekly visits to the Slavic baths near the Seventh Bridge, where the steam soothed his ever red-rimmed eyes.

At the Library, Cardinal Chang was a common sight. It was knowledge that put him ahead of his competitors, he felt—anyone could be ruthless—but his eyes prevented long hours spent in research. Instead, Chang made the acquaintance of librarians, engaging them in long interrogative conversations about their given responsibilities—specific collections, organizational theories, plans for acquisition. He pursued these topics in calm but relentless inquiry, so that eventually—through memory and rigorous mental association—it had become possible for him to isolate at least three-quarters of what he needed without actually reading a word. As a result, though he haunted its marbled halls nearly every day, Cardinal Chang was most often found pacing a Library corridor in thought, wandering through the darkened stacks by memory, or exchanging keen words with a blanching though professionally tolerant archivist as to the exact provenance of a new genealogical volume he might need to consult later in the day.

Before the incident with the riding crop and the young aristocrat who wielded it, Chang had been a long-time student—which meant that poverty did not trouble him, and that his wants, then from necessity and now by habit, were few. Though he had abandoned that life completely, its day to day patterns had marked him, and his working week was divided into a reliably Spartan routine: the Library, the coffeehouse, clients, excursions on behalf of those clients, the baths, the opium den, the brothel, and bill collecting, which often involved revisiting past clients in a different (to them) capacity. It was an existence marked by keen activity and open tracts of ostensibly lost time, occupied with wandering thought, thick sleep, narcotic dreams, with willful nothingness.

When not so pacified, however, his mind was restless. One source of regular consolation was poetry—the more modern the better, as it usually meant a thinner text. He found that by carefully rationing out how many lines he read at a time, and closing his eyes to consider them, he could maintain a delicately steady, if perhaps finally grinding, pace through the whole of a slim volume. He had been occupying himself in such a manner, with Lynch's new translation of the *Persephone* fragments (found in some previously unplundered Thessalonikan ruin), when he looked up and saw the woman on the train. He smiled to think of it, as he lay just awake on his pallet, for the lines he'd been reading at the time—"battered princess / that infernal bride"—had seemed to exactly illustrate the creature before him. The filthy coat, the blood-smeared face, her curls crusted and stiff, her piercing grey eyes—a meeting of such beauty and such spoilage—he found it all perfectly impressive, even striking. He had decided at the time not to follow, to allow the incident its own distinction, but now he wondered about finding her, remembering (with a stirring of lust) the lines fallen tears had traced down her cheeks. After consideration, Chang decided he would ask at the brothel—any new whore so covered in blood would certainly have *someone* talking about her.

The grey light from his window told him that he had slept later than usual. He rose and washed his face in the basin. He dried himself vigorously on an old towel and decided he could go another day without shaving. After a moment of indecision, he decided to swirl a mouthful of salt water around his teeth, spat into his chamber pot, pissed in the pot, and then ran his fingers through his hair in lieu of a comb. His clothes from the previous day were still clean enough. He put them on, re-knotted a black cravat, tucked his razor into one coat pocket and the slim volume of *Persephone* into another. He put on his glasses, relaxed as even this day's pallid light was dimmed, grabbed a heavy, metal-knobbed walking stick, and locked his door behind him.

It was just after noon, but the narrow streets were empty. Chang was not surprised. Years ago the neighborhood had been fashionable, rows and rows of six-story mansions crowded near the river, but the growing stench of the river itself, the fog and the crime it covered, along with the city's expansion elsewhere into broad landscaped parks had caused the mansions to be sold, each of them cut up into a myriad of smaller rooms, rough unpainted walls thrust between the once elaborate stucco moldings, catering to a vastly different caste of occupants—disreputable occupants such as himself. Chang walked some distance out of his way, north, to find a morning newspaper, and tucked it under his arm unread as he turned back toward the river. The Raton Marine was historically a tavern—and still functioned as such—but during the daylight had taken to serving coffee, tea, and bitter chocolate. In this way it had expanded its role as a place of itinerant business, where men might linger to seek and to be found, in rooms both public and unseen.

The Cardinal took a table inside the main room, away from the glare of the open walkway, and called for a cup of the most dark and acrid South American chocolate. This morning he didn't want to speak to anyone, or at least not yet. He wanted to read the newspaper, and that was going to take time. He spread the front page over his table and squinted so that he could really only make out the largest size of type, sparing his eyes as much unwanted text as possible. In this way he skimmed through the headlines, moving quickly past international tragedies and domestic scandals, the perfidies of weather and disease, the problems of finance. He rubbed his eyes and took a hot mouthful of chocolate. His throat clenched against the bitter taste, but he felt his senses sharpened all the same. He returned to the paper, moving into the inner pages, bracing himself for smaller type, and found what he was after. Chang took another fortifying swallow of his drink, and plunged into the dense column of text.

REGIMENTAL HERO MISSING

Col. Arthur Trapping, commander of the 4th Dragoons, decorated hero of Franck's Redoubt and Rockraal Falls, was reported missing today from both his regimental quarters and his own dwelling on Hadrian Square. Col. Trapping's absence was noted during the formal investiture of the 4th Dragoons as the "Prince's Own", with newly designated responsibilities as a Household Regiment for Palace defense, Ministry escort, and ceremonial duties. Acting for Col. Trapping in the ceremony was the regiment's Adjutant-Colonel, Noland Aspiche, who received the formal charge of duty from the Duke of Stäelmaere, attended by Palace representatives. Despite concerns expressed from the highest levels of government, the authorities have been unable to locate the missing officer. . . .

Chang stopped reading and rubbed his eyes. It told him all he needed to know—or all he was going to learn for the moment. Either the truth was being suppressed, or indeed the facts had somehow remained unknown. He could not believe that Trapping's movements were so much a secret—he'd followed the man easily enough, after all—but any number of things could have happened between then and now to alter what appeared to be the facts. He sighed. Though his involvement ought to have been finished, it was more likely to be merely beginning. It would depend on the client.

He was about to turn the page when another headline caught his eye. A country aristocrat—Lord Tarr, whom he'd never heard of—had been murdered. Chang peered at the text, and learned that the ailing Tarr had been found in his garden, in his nightshirt, with his throat torn out. While there was a chance that he'd been attacked by an animal, it was now suspected that the wound had been brutally enlarged to disguise the deep cross-cut of a blade. Inquiries were pending. Inquiries were *always* pending, Chang thought to himself, reaching for his cup—that was why he had regular work. No one liked to wait.

As if on cue, someone near him coughed discreetly. Chang looked up to see a uniformed trooper—red coat and trousers, black boots, a brass helmet with a horse-tail crest in one hand, the other resting on the hilt of a long saber—standing at the doorway, as if actually entering the Raton Marine would foul his military crispness. Upon getting Chang's attention, the trooper nodded and clicked his heels. "If you'll accompany me,

Sir," he deferentially called over to Chang. None of the other customers acted as if they'd heard a word. Chang nodded to the trooper and stood. This was happening more quickly than he'd expected. He collected his walking stick and left the paper for someone else to read.

They did not speak as Chang was led to the river. The bright uniform of his guide seemed to vibrate against their monochrome surroundings of stone paving, grey mottled plasterwork, and black pools of standing fetid water. Chang knew that his own coat had a similar effect, and smiled at the thought that the two of them might be seen as a strange kind of pair—and how much the trooper would loathe such an idea. They rounded a corner and walked onto a stone balcony that overhung the river itself. The wide black water slipped past beneath them, the far bank just visible through the tracings of fog that had either not fully abated from the night or were already beginning to gather. The balcony had been a wharf for pleasure craft and boats for hire when the district was thriving. It had since been left to rot, despite being regularly used for nefarious transactions after nightfall.

As he expected, Adjutant-Colonel Noland Aspiche stood waiting for him, with an aide and three other troopers standing behind, and two more waiting in the trim launch tied up to the stairwell. Chang stopped, allowing his escort to continue on to his commander, click his heels and report, gesturing back to Chang. Aspiche nodded, and then after a moment walked over to Chang, out of earshot from the others.

"Where is he?" he snapped, speaking quietly. Aspiche was a hard, lean man, with receding hair cut close to his skull. He dug a thin black cheroot from his red jacket, bit the tip off, spat, and pulled out a small box of safety matches. He turned away from the wind and lit one, puffing until the flame took. He exhaled a blue plume of smoke and returned his sharp gaze to Chang, who had not answered. "Well? What have you got to say?"

Chang despised authority on principle, for even when veiled by the rubric of practical necessity or the weight of tradition he could not see institutional power as anything but an expression of arbitrary personal will, and it galled him profoundly. Church, military, government, nobility, business—his skin crawled at every interaction, and so though he granted Aspiche his probable competence there was an urge in Chang, rising at the very manner in which the officer bit off the tip of his cheroot and spat, to savage the man with his razor then and there, no matter the consequences. Instead he was still, and answered Adjutant-Colonel Aspiche as calmly as possible.

"He's dead."

"Are you sure? What did you do with the body?" Aspiche spoke moving only his mouth, keeping the rest of his body still—from the back, as his men saw him, he was merely listening to Chang.

"I didn't do anything with the body. I didn't kill him."

"But—we—you were instructed—"

"He was *already* dead."

Aspiche was silent.

"I followed him from Hadrian Square to the country, to the Orange Canal. He met a group of men, and together *they* met a small launch sailing up the canal. From the launch they unloaded a cargo onto two carts, and drove the carts to a nearby house. A great house. Do you know what house that was, near the Orange Canal?"

Aspiche spat again. "I can guess."

"Evidently it was quite an occasion—I believe the given excuse was the engagement of the Lord's daughter."

Aspiche nodded. "To the German."

"I was able to enter the house. I was able to find Colonel Trapping, and with a fair amount of difficulty, I was able to introduce a substance to his wine—"

"Wait, wait," interrupted Aspiche, "who else was there? Who else was with him at the canal? What happened to the carts? If someone else killed him—"

"I am telling you," hissed Chang, "what I am going to tell you. Are you going to listen?"

"I'm contemplating having you horsewhipped."

"Are you *really*?"

Aspiche sighed and glanced behind him at his men. "No, of course not. This has been very difficult—and not hearing from you—"

"I was awake into the early morning. I explained that this was likely to happen. And instead of paying attention you first sent a uniformed man to collect me, and then appeared yourself in a part of the city you can have no decent social or professional business in whatsoever. You might as well have set off fireworks. If anyone has suspicions—"

"No one has suspicions."

"That you know of. I will have to go back to the coffeehouse and give ready money to the five men who saw me so *collected*—to protect the both of us. Are you this careless with the lives of your men in action? Are you this careless with yourself?"

Aspiche was not accustomed to such a tone, but his silence itself was admission of his error. He turned away, gazing back into the fog. "All right. Get on with it."

Chang narrowed his eyes. So far it had been simple enough, but here he was in the dark as much as Aspiche was at least pretending to be. "There were hundreds of people in the house. It was *indeed* an engagement party. Perhaps that is not all it was, but it was certainly that, which created both confusion for me to blend into, and confusion that got in my way. Before the substance could take effect, Colonel Trapping eluded me, leaving the main gathering by way of a back staircase. I was unable to follow directly, and was forced to seek him through the house. When I finally did find him, he was dead. I could not see why. The substance I gave him was not in a quantity to kill, yet he had no marks of mortal violence about his body."

"You're sure he was dead."

"Of course I am."

"You must have miscalculated your poison."

"I did not."

"Well, what do you *think* happened? And you still haven't explained what happened to the body!"

"I suggest that you calm yourself and listen."

"I suggest that you get damned on with your explanation."

Chang let that pass, retaining his even tone. "There were marks on Trapping's face, like burns, around the eyes, but of a regular, precise nature, as if from a brand—"

"A *brand*?"

"Indeed."

"On his *face*?"

"As I said. Further, the room—there was a strange odor—"

"What was it?"

"I cannot say. I have no ability with odors."

"A poison?"

"It is possible. I do not know."

Aspiche frowned, thrown into thought. "All this—it makes no sense," he snapped. "What about these burns?"

"That is my question to you."

"What does that mean?" said Aspiche, taken aback. "I don't have a clue."

They stood in silence for a moment. The Adjutant-Colonel seemed genuinely perplexed.

"My examination was interrupted," continued Chang. "I was again forced to make my way through the house, this time away from pursuit. I managed to lose my pursuers on my way back to the canal."

"All right, all right. What was in those carts?"

"Boxes. Of what I don't know."

"And his confederates?"

"No idea. It *was* a masked ball."

"And this—this *substance*—you don't think you killed him?"

"I know I did not."

Aspiche nodded. "It's good of you to say. Still, I'll pay you as if you had. If he turns up alive—"

"He won't."

Aspiche smiled tightly. "Then you'll merely owe me the job."

He pulled a thin leather wallet from his jacket and handed it to Chang, who tucked it into his coat.

"What happens next?" asked Chang.

"Nothing. My hope is that it's over."

"But you know it isn't," Chang snarled. Aspiche did not reply. Chang pressed him. "Why has there been no further word? Who else is involved? Vandaariff? The Germans? Any one of three hundred guests? You know the answers or you don't, Colonel. You'll tell me what you want to. But someone's hidden your body, and you're going to have to know why. You've come this far—it'll have to be finished."

Aspiche did not move.

As Chang gazed at the man—stubborn and dangerously proud—one of the *Persephone* fragments rose to his mind:

His willful suit, imperious and cold
Pay'd court perfum'd by graves and fetid mold

"You know how to find me... discreetly," Chang muttered. He turned and stalked back to the Raton Marine.

Chang had spent the previous three days planning the murder of Arthur Trapping for a fee. It had seemed simple enough. Trapping was the ambitious brother-in-law of Henry Xonck, a wealthy arms manufacturer. To find a position fitting to his newly married status, he had with his wife's money purchased a prestigious commission as commander of the 4th Dragoons, but he was no soldier and his decorations resulted from his mere presence at two provincial engagements. Trapping's actual exploits were limited to consuming heroic quantities of port and a lingering patch of local dysentery. When his regiment was rewarded with a significant change of duties, Trapping's executive officer, the long-suffering Adjutant-Colonel—a professional soldier who, if he were to be believed, didn't desire the command so much for himself, but only to clear the place for any genuinely worthy figure—had taken the quite remarkable step of engaging Cardinal Chang.

Outright assassination was not Chang's usual line, but he'd done murder before. More often, as he preferred to see it, he was engaged to influence behavior, through violence, or information, or both, as necessary. In recent months, however, he'd felt a growing disquiet, as if there were behind his every step the barely audible ticking of a clock, that his life wound toward some profound *accounting*. Perhaps it was a malady of his eyes, a general gnawing anxiety that grew from seeing as much as possible in shadow. He did not allow this lurking dread to influence his movements, but when Aspiche had offered a high fee, Chang saw it as an opportunity to withdraw from view, to travel, to disappear into the opium den—anything until the cloud of foreboding had passed by.

Not that he trusted what Aspiche had told him of the job. There was always more to it—clients always lied, withheld. Chang had spent the first day doing research, digging through social registers, old newspapers, genealogies, and as ever, the connections were there for the finding. Trapping was married to Charlotte Xonck, the middle child of three, between Henry, the oldest, and Francis, as yet unmarried and just returned from a lengthy tour abroad. Though poor Adjutant-Colonel Aspiche might assume that the regiment's rise in stature had been earned by its colonial triumphs, Chang had found that the order to invest the 4th Dragoons as the Prince's Own (or Drunken Wastrel Whoremongering Sodomite's Own, as Chang preferred to think of it) was issued one day after the Xonck Armory agreed to lower terms for an exclusive contract to re-fit the cannons of the entire navy and coastal defenses. The mystery was not why the regiment had been promoted, but why Henry Xonck thought it worth such a costly bargain. Love for his only sister? Chang had sneered and sought out another archivist to badger.

The precise nature of the regiment's new duties was not part of any official document he could find, every account merely parroting what he'd read in the newspaper—"Palace defense, Ministry escort, and ceremonial duties"—which was gallingly vague. It was only after pacing back and forth that it occurred to him to confirm where the announcement had actually been issued. He again dragged the archivist away from his other duties to retrieve the folio of collected announcements, and then saw it on the cover of the folio itself—it was from a Ministry office, but not the War Ministry. He peered at the paper, and the seal at the top. The Foreign Ministry. What business had the Foreign Ministry with announcing—and thus, by inference, arranging—the installation of a new regiment of "Palace defense, Ministry escort, and ceremonial duties"? He snapped at the archivist, who merely stammered, "Well, it *does* say Ministry escort—and the F-Foreign Ministry is indeed one of the, ah, M-M-Ministry offices—" Chang cut him off with a brusque request for a list of senior Foreign Ministry staff.

He'd spent a good hour wandering through the darkened stacks—the staff had conceded access to Chang, reasoning it was less bother to have him out of their sight than in their faces—pushing these rudimentary pieces around in his mind. No matter what else it did, the most important work of the regiment would be under the aegis of the Foreign Ministry. This could only refer to diplomatic intrigues of one kind or another, or internal government intrigues—that somehow in exchange for Xonck's lowered fee, the War Ministry had agreed to put the regiment at the Foreign Ministry's disposal. For Xonck, Trapping would obviously function as his spy, alerting him to any number of international situations that might influence his business, and the rise and fall of the business of others. Perhaps this was reward enough (Chang was unconvinced), but it did not explain why one Ministry would be doing such an outlandish service for another—or why the Foreign Ministry might require its own troops in the first place.

Nevertheless, this much information allowed Chang, after making himself familiar with Trapping's person, the location of his house, his coach, and the regimental barracks, to position himself outside the Foreign Ministry itself, convinced that this was the crucial point of revelation. Such was Chang's way, and while he performed such investigation to better understand what he was engaged with, it's also true that he did it to occupy his mind. If he was but a brute murderer, he could have cut Arthur Trapping down at any number of places, simply by following him until he was isolated in the street. The fact that Chang might well end up doing that very thing in the end didn't alter his desire to understand the reasoning behind his actions. He was not squeamish about his work, but he was well aware that the risk was his, and that a client might always wonder about furthering their own security by arranging things so that Chang too might fall victim to unpleasant circumstance. The more he knew—about the clients and their objects—the safer he was going to feel. In this case, he was keenly aware that the forces involved were far more powerful and vast than Trapping and his bitter Adjutant-Colonel, and he would need to be careful not to provoke their interest. If 'twere done, 'twere best done as invisibly as possible.

On the afternoon of that first day and again on the second, Trapping's coach had taken him from the regimental barracks to the Foreign Ministry, where he had spent several hours. At each evening the coach had taken him to his house on Hadrian Square, where the Colonel remained at home, without any notable visitors. On the second night, as he watched Trapping's windows from the shadow of decorative shrubbery, Chang was startled to see a coach move past, the doors painted with the Foreign Ministry crest. The coach did not stop at Trapping's door, however, but continued on to a house on the other side of the square. Chang quickly loped after it, in time to see a trim man in a dark coat exit the coach and enter the door of number 14, weighed down with several thick satchels. The coach drove away. Chang returned to his surveillance. The next morning at the Library he again consulted the list of Foreign

Ministry staff. The Deputy Minister, Harald Crabbé, made his residence at 14 Hadrian Square.

On the third day he'd once again gone to the Ministry, passing his time on the edge of St. Isobel's Square, at a point where he could observe both the coach traffic in front of the building and the intersection where any coach by way of the rear alley would have to exit. By now he'd become familiar with at least some of the Ministry staff, and studied them as they went in and out, waiting for Trapping to arrive. Despite all the suggestions of intrigue around the Colonel, Chang judged the man himself to be a reasonably simple target. If he repeated his pattern of the previous two nights, it would be easy enough to enter through a second-story window (accessible from a drain pipe whose strength Chang had tested the night before) and creep down to Trapping's chamber (whose location he had established from watching the appearance of light in the windows as Trapping climbed to the third floor to sleep). The precise method wasn't settled in his mind, and would depend on the exact circumstances in the room. He would have his razor, but also come equipped with a poison that would, to a careless eye, suggest an apoplexy not unheard-of for a man of Trapping's age. Whether anyone would consider it murder would be one more signifier of the intrigue, and the stakes of Trapping's elevation. Chang was not overly concerned about anyone else in the house. Mrs. Trapping slept apart from her husband, and the servants, if he chose his time correctly, would be far from the room.

He crossed the square at two o'clock and bought a meat pie, breaking it into pieces and consuming them one at a time while he walked back to his position. As he passed the sculpture of St. Isobel, he smiled, his mouth full. The truly hideous nature of the composition—garish sentiment, cloying pathos—never prevented him from finding lurid satisfaction in the image of the saint herself, the coiling serpents swarming across her slippery flesh. It amazed him that such a piece had been erected at public expense in such an open space, but he found the blithe veneration of something so obviously rank to be a comfort. Somehow it restored his faith that he indeed had a place in the world. He finished the meat pie and wiped his hands on his trousers.

At three o'clock, Trapping's regimental coach appeared, empty, at the alleyway exit, and turned left, heading back to the 4th Dragoons barracks. The Colonel was inside by way of the rear entrance, and intending to leave by other means. It was four-fifteen when Chang saw a Ministry coach at the same spot. On one side of the coach sat Harald Crabbé and in the seat opposite, a splash of red and gold through the window, sat Arthur Trapping. Chang dropped his gaze while they passed and watched them go. As soon as they rounded the corner he sprinted for a coach of his own.

As he expected, the Ministry coach was on its way to Hadrian Square, and easily followed. What he did not expect was that it would stop in front of number 14 and that both men would enter, nor that, when they reappeared some minutes later, their coach would take them on a direct path northwest of the city. The fog was growing, and he moved next to his driver to better see—though his distant vision was at its limit in the falling dusk—where his quarry took him. His driver grumbled—this was far beyond his normal reach—and Chang was forced to pay him far more than he would have liked. He thought of simply taking the coach for himself, but he trusted neither his own vision nor his driving skills, besides not wanting to spill any unnecessary blood. As it was, they were soon beyond the old city walls, and then beyond the sprawl of new building and into the country itself. They were on the road to the Orange Canal, which went as far as the ocean, and the coach ahead of them showed no sign of stopping.

They rode for nearly two hours. At first Chang had made his driver pull back, allowing the other coach to drift to the edge of sight, but as the darkness grew they were forced to close, being unable to see if the other coach should turn from the road. He had followed Trapping initially as merely a continuation of his plan, and then farther at the prospect of isolating him at some vacant place in the country where a murder might be more easily managed. But the farther he went in pursuit, the more wrong-headed it seemed. If he were merely trying to kill the man, he should turn around and try again the next night—simply repeating the plan until he was able to get Trapping alone in his room. The long coach journey with Deputy Minister Crabbé was a matter for intrigue, for

Xonck and the War Ministry, and while Chang was certainly curious, he had no idea what he was riding into, and that was always foolish. Aside from these doubting thoughts, he realized he was cold—a bitter wind from the sea had chilled him utterly. He was forming the very words to tell his driver to stop when the man grabbed his shoulder and pointed ahead at a distant knot of torchlight.

Chang ordered him to stop the coach, and instructed him to wait for fifteen minutes. If he had not returned, the man was free to leave him and return to the city. The driver did not argue—he was certainly as cold as Chang, and still bitter over the unexpected length of this particular fare. Chang climbed from the coach, wondering if the man would even wait that long. He gave himself five minutes to make a decision—the last thing he wanted was to be stranded in the darkness, all but blind. As it was, he had to move extremely cautiously. He pulled off his glasses, this being a case where any light was better than none, and tucked them into the inner pocket of his coat. Ahead of him he could see the Ministry coach, waiting among several others. He moved into the grass and toward the torchlight, some thirty yards away, where two figures were walking toward a larger group. Chang crept as close as he dared on the path, and then stepped away from it and crouched, his eyes just clear of the grass to see.

There was a low brisk conversation—it was clear Trapping and Crabbé were late—and what seemed like a perfunctory shaking of hands. As his eyesight grew accustomed to the torches, Chang saw that something was reflecting them—water—and what seemed to have been an abstract mass of shadow resolved itself into an open launch, tied up at the canal. Trapping and Crabbé followed the others along the canal and to what looked like carts (Chang could just make out the wheel tops above the grass). A canvas sheet was pulled back from one cart to show the late arrivals a number of wooden boxes, obviously loaded from the launch. Chang could not make out the faces of any other men, though he counted six of them. The canvas sheet was pulled down again and tied, and the men began to climb onto the carts. At a sharp whip crack, they drove off, away from the coaches, down a road that Chang from his place could not see.

Chang moved quickly after them, pausing to glance into the launch—which told him nothing—and down the road, which was little more than a country path worn through the grass. He thought again about what he was doing. Pursuing the carts meant losing his coach. He resolved himself to being abandoned—worse things had happened to him, after all, and this still might be a perfect opportunity to execute his task. The carts moved much faster than he, however, and soon enough he was walking on his own, alone in the dark. The wind was still cold, and it was at least thirty minutes before he came upon the carts tied up at the kitchen entrance of what looked like a formidable building—though whether it was a dour mansion or a splendid fortress, he could not say. The boxes were gone, as were the men . . .

Still annoyed from his interview with Aspiche, Chang walked back into the Raton Marine and was relieved to see that everyone who had been present at the trooper's arrival was still there. He stood in the doorway a moment, allowing each person to glance up at him, in order to return those glances with a meaningful nod. He then went around to each man—including Nicholas the barman—and placed a gold coin next to his glass. It was all he could do—and if one of them were to go behind his back, it would at least be seen by others as a broken agreement reflecting poorly on the Judas. He ordered another cup of bitter chocolate and drank it outside. For all practical purposes, he was waiting for Aspiche to do something, but Noland Aspiche was at best a fool who hoped to profit from someone else killing his Colonel, or at worst part of the larger intrigue, which meant he had been lying to Chang from the start. In either case, Aspiche was unlikely to act. Despite the wallet in his coat, Chang was regretting the entire affair. He took a swallow of chocolate and grimaced.

As soon as he'd seen the size of the house, he'd known where he was, for there was only one such dwelling on the coast near the Orange Canal, that of Robert Vandaariff, recently made Lord Vandaariff, the financier whose daughter was famously engaged to a German prince of some small state, Karl-Horst von Somesuch-or-other. Chang couldn't remember—it was in any number of headlines he'd skipped past—but he was quick to realize, as he pushed his gloved hand through the pane of a delicate glass doorway, that he was trespassing into a rather large social occasion, some kind of formal masked ball. He watched from the shadows until he found a drunken guest from whom he could safely wrestle a mask, and then so covered (though again it meant taking off his glasses) moved out in direct search of Trapping. As most of the men were in formal black topcoats, the red-uniformed Colonel was relatively easy to find. Chang himself attracted attention for the same reason—the willfully brazen figure he cut in his usual environment, where intimidation balanced concealment, hardly lent itself to a fancy-dress party in a lavish mansion. But he simply carried himself with the disdainful air of a man who belonged. It amazed him how many people immediately assumed that, because of an unpleasant arrogance, he possessed more rights than they.

Trapping was drinking heavily, in the midst of a rather large party, though it did not seem like he took an active part in the conversation. As he watched, he now realized that Trapping stood between two groups. One gathered around a heavy, balding man to whom all the others deferred—most prominently a young man with thick red hair and an exceedingly well-dressed woman (could this possibly be Trapping's wife, Charlotte Xonck, and the men her brothers Henry and Francis?). Behind this woman was another, whose gown was more demure and who, much like Chang, occupied herself with subtly studying the figures around her—and in this struck him as the figure in the party to most carefully avoid. The other group was made of men, in both formal attire and military uniforms. Chang could not tell if Crabbé was present or not—the masks made it difficult to be sure. As curious as he was to watch such parties gathered around as unimpressive a figure as the Colonel—and to discover *why*—Chang was aware he could not linger. Bracing himself, he strode quite near to them, avoiding eye contact and addressing the servant at the nearby table, calling for a glass of wine. The conversation faded around him as he waited, feeling the impatience of both groups for him to leave. The servant handed him a full glass, and Chang took a swallow, turning to the man next to him—who was, of course, Trapping—fixing him with his gaze. Trapping nodded, then could not help but stare. Chang's scarred eyelids, visible through the mask-holes, gave Trapping pause, for though he could not be certain what he was seeing, he knew something was not quite right. The length of the contact, though, allowed Chang to speak.

"A fine occasion."

"Indeed," answered Colonel Trapping. His gaze had dropped from Cardinal Chang's eyes to his coat, and then to the rest of his garments, which though striking were hardly appropriate for the occasion, or even quite reputable. Chang looked at his own clothes, caught Trapping's eye again and scoffed, chuckling.

"Had to come straight from the crossing. Been riding for days. Still, couldn't miss it, eh?"

"Of course not." Trapping nodded, vaguely mollified, but looking somewhat helplessly over Chang's shoulder, where the rest of his group was drifting distinctly in the other direction to resume their conversation.

"What are you drinking?" demanded Chang.

"I believe it is the same as what you are drinking."

"Is it? Do you like it?"

"It is indeed fine."

"I suppose it is. I suppose it would be, eh? Here's to the host."

Chang touched his glass to Trapping's and tossed off the contents, more or less forcing Trapping to do the same. Before he could move, Chang snatched the glass from him and held them both out toward the servant, barking for more wine. As the servant leaned forward to pour, and as Trapping groped for excuses behind him to leave, Chang deftly dusted a small amount of white powder onto his thumb, and—distracting the servant with a brusque question about a possibly spoiled cork—rubbed it along the rim of Trapping's glass as he picked it up. He handed the glass to the Colonel, and they drank again—Trapping's lips touching the rim of his glass where he'd placed the powder. Once this was done, just as abruptly as he'd arrived, Chang nodded to Trapping and walked out of the room. He'd watch from the margins until the drug took hold.

From there it had quickly gone wrong. The group of men—Crabbé's faction?—finally claimed Trapping from the group Chang guessed to be the Xoncks and walked with him to a rear corner of the room and through a doorway flanked by two men who stood, casually but unmistakably, as sentries. Chang watched his quarry disappear, and looked around for another way, just for one moment catching the eye of Charlotte Xonck's companion, who looked away—not quite quickly enough—in the same instant. He stalked from the main rooms before he attracted any more unwanted attention. It had taken him at least an hour—time spent dodging servants, guests, and what looked to be a growing number of openly suspicious faces—before he finally found himself in a long marbled corridor, lined with doors. It was an exact epitome of his ridiculous situation, and how his decision to risk first entry and then bold exposure to Trapping had utterly failed. By this time Trapping should have been dead, but instead he was most likely shaking off what he would explain to himself as a bit too much wine. Chang had given him only enough of the drug to guarantee his pliability—thinking to drag him into the garden—but now it was just another mistake. He stalked down the corridor, trying the doors as he went. Most were locked, and he was forced to move on to the next. He had perhaps reached the mid-point when he saw, ahead of him at the far end, a crowd begin to emerge from a balcony above, and make its way down a spiral staircase. He lunged for the nearest door. It was open. He dashed through and closed it behind him.

On the floor was Trapping, dead, his face branded—seared? scarred?—but with no immediately apparent cause. Chang detected no wound, nor any blood, any weapon, even another glass of wine that might have been drugged. Trapping was still warm. It couldn't have been long—no longer than thirty minutes, at most—since he had died. Chang stood above the body and sighed. Here was the result he wanted, but in a far more disturbing and complicated manner. It was then that he'd noticed the smell, vaguely medicinal or mechanical—but thoroughly out of place in that room. He had bent down again to go through Trapping's pockets when there was a knock at the door. At once, Chang stood and walked quietly to the next room of the suite and from there into the bath closet, looking for some place to hide. He found the servants' door just as the hallway door was opened, and someone called to Colonel Trapping by his Christian name. Chang was carefully, silently easing the latch behind him when the voice began calling harshly for help.

It was time to get out. The narrow dark corridor led to a strange man in a room—a crabbed, officious creature—surrounded by familiar-looking boxes. The man wheeled at his entry and opened his mouth to shout. Chang crossed the distance to him in two steps and clubbed him across the face with his forearm. The man fell onto a table, scattering a pile of wooden box pieces. Before he could rise, Chang struck him again, across the back of the head. The man smashed into the table and slumped to the floor, groping, gasping damply. Chang glanced quickly at the boxes, which all seemed to be empty, but knew that he had no time. He found the next door and stepped into an even larger corridor, lined with mirrors. He looked down the length and knew that it must lead to the main entrance, which would never do. He saw a door across the hall. When he found that it was locked, he kicked it until the wood around the lock buckled in, and shouldered his way through. This room had a window. He snatched up a side chair and hurled it through the glass with a crash. Behind him there were footsteps. Chang kicked the broken shards free from the panes and leapt through the opening. He landed with a grunt on a bed of gravel and ran.

The pursuit had been half-hearted—for he was near-blind in the night and by all rights any serious attempt should have taken him. When he was sure that they had stopped following, Chang eased into a walk. He had a general notion of where he was in relation to the sea and so turned away from it and eventually struck the rail tracks, walking along them until he reached a station. This turned out to be Orange Canal, and the end of this particular line. He boarded the waiting train—pleased that there *was* a waiting train—and sat brooding until it finally began to move, carrying him back to the city and, in the midst of that journey, his moment with the battered Persephone.

At the Raton Marine, he finished his drink and put another coin on the table. The more he worried over the events of the previous day and night, the more he berated himself for impulsive nonsense—all the more that now there was no announcement of Trapping's death. He felt like going back to sleep for as long as he could, perhaps for days in the opium den. What he forced himself to do instead was walk to the Library. The only new information he had was the possible association of Robert Vandaariff or his high-placed prospective son-in-law. If he could explore their connection to Xonck, or to Crabbé, or even to Trapping himself, he would then be able to obliterate his senses with a clear conscience.

He walked up the grand steps and through the vaulted lobby, nodding at the porter, and climbed to the main reading room on the second floor. As he entered, he saw the archivist he was looking for—Shearing, who kept all records relating to finance—in conversation with a woman. As he approached, the small gnarled man turned to him with a brittle smile and pointed. Chang stopped as the woman turned to face him, and dipped her knee. She was beautiful. She was walking toward him. Her hair was black, and gathered behind to hang in curls over her shoulders. She wore a tiny black wool jacket that did not reach her thin waist over a red silk dress, subtly embroidered in yellow thread with Chinese scenes. She held a small black bag in one hand, and a fan in the other. She stopped, a mere few feet away, and he forced himself to look at her eyes—past her pale throat and fiercely red lips—which were fixed upon him with a certain seriousness of manner.

"I'm told your name is Chang," she said.

"You may call me that." It was his customary answer.

"You may call me Rosamonde. I have been directed to you as a person who might provide me with the aid I require."

"I see." Chang shot a look back at Shearing, who was gawking at them like an idiot child. The man ignored the look entirely, beaming at the woman's splendid torso. "If you'll walk this way"—Chang smiled stiffly—"we may speak more discreetly."

He led her up to the third floor map room, which was rarely occupied, even by its curator, who spent most of his time drinking gin in the stacks. He pulled out a chair and offered it to her, and she sat with a smile. He chose not to sit, leaning back against a table, facing her.

"Do you always wear dark glasses indoors?" she asked.

"It is a habit," he answered.

"I confess to finding it disquieting. I hope you are not offended."

"Of course not. But I will continue to wear them. For medical reasons."

"Ah, I see." She smiled. She looked around the room. Light came in from a high bank of windows that ran along the main wall. Despite the grey of the day, the room still felt airy, as if it were much higher off the ground than its three stories raised it.

"Who directed you to me?" he asked.

"Beg pardon?"

"Who directed you to me? You will understand that a man in my position must have references."

"Of course. I wondered if you had many women for clients." She smiled again. There was a slight accent to her speech, but he could not place it. Nor had she answered his question.

"I have many clients of all kinds. But please, who gave you my name? It is quite the final time I will ask."

The woman positively beamed. Chang felt a small charge of warning on the nape of his neck. The situation was not what it appeared, nor was the woman. He knew this utterly, and strove to keep it in the fore of his mind, but in the same moment was transfixed by her body, and the exquisite sensations emanating from its view. Her chuckle was rich, like the flow of dark wine, and she bit her lip like a woman play-acting the schoolgirl, doing her level best to fix him with her riveting violet eyes, like an insect stuck on a pin. He was unsure she had not succeeded.

"Mr. Chang—or should I say *Cardinal*? Your name, it is so amusing to me, because I have known Cardinals, for I was a child in Ravenna—have you been to Ravenna?"

"No. I should of course like to. The mosaics."

"They are beautiful. A color of purple you have never seen, and the pearls—if you know of them you *must* go, for not seeing them will haunt you." She laughed again. "And once you have seen them they will haunt you all the more! But as I say, I have known Cardinals, in fact a cousin of mine—who I never liked—held such an office—and so it pleases me to see a figure such as yourself hailed with such a name. For as you know, I am suspicious of high authority."

"I did not know."

As the moments passed, Chang became painfully more aware of his rumpled shirt, his unpolished boots, his unshaven face, that his whole life was at odds with the splendid ease, if not outright grace, of this woman. "But you still, forgive my insistence, have not told me—"

"Of course not, no, and you are so patient. I was given your name, and a notion of where you might be found, by Mr. John Carver."

Carver was a lawyer who, through a number of unsavory intermediaries, had engaged Chang the previous summer to locate the man who had impregnated Carver's daughter. The daughter had survived the abortion her father—a harsh pragmatist—insisted upon, but had not been seen in society since—apparently the procedure had been difficult—and Carver was especially distraught. Chang had located the man in a seaside brothel and delivered him to Carver's country house—not without injury, for the man had struggled hard once he realized the situation. He left Carver with the wandering lover trussed on a carpet, and did not concern himself further with the outcome.

"I see," he said.

It was extremely unlikely that anyone would associate his name with Carver's unless the information came from Carver himself.

"Mr. Carver has drawn up several contracts for me, and has come to share my confidence."

"What if I were to make it quite clear to you that I have never met nor had any acquaintance with John Carver?"

She smiled. "It would be exactly as I feared, and I must turn for assistance elsewhere."

She waited for him to speak. It was his decision, right then, to accept her as a client or not. She clearly understood the need for discretion, she was obviously rich, and he would certainly welcome a distraction from the unsettled business of Arthur Trapping. He shifted his weight and hopped onto the table top, sitting. He bent his head toward hers.

"I am sorry, but seeing as I do not know Mr. Carver, I cannot in conscience accept you as a client. However, as a man of sympathy, and since you have come all this way, perhaps I can listen to your story and in return provide you with whatever *advice* I am able, if you are willing."

"I would be in your debt."

"Not at all." He permitted himself a small smile in return. At least this far, they understood one another.

"Before I begin," she said, "do you need to take notes?"

"Not as a rule."

She smiled. "It is after all a simple situation, and one that while *I* am unable to answer it doesn't strike me as particularly unanswerable for the man with the proper set of skills. Please interrupt me if I go too fast, or seem to leave anything out. Are you ready?"

Chang nodded.

"Last night there was a gathering at the country home of Lord

Vandaariff, celebrating the engagement of his only daughter to Prince Karl-Horst von Maasmärck—you surely have heard of these people, and appreciate the *degree* of the occasion. I was in attendance, as a school friend—acquaintance, really—of the daughter, Lydia. It was a masked ball. This is important, as you will see later. Have you ever been to a masked ball?"

Chang shook his head. The warning tingle on his neck had by now traveled the whole length of his spine.

"I enjoy them, but they are disquieting, for the masks provide license for behavior beyond the social norm, especially at a gathering this large, at a house this expansive. The anonymity can feel profound, and quite frankly anything can happen. I'm sure I do not need to explain further."

Chang shook his head again.

"My escort for the evening was, well, I suppose you would describe him as a family friend—somewhat older than I, an essentially good fellow whose weak resolve had led him to repeated degradations, through drink, gambling, and foolish, even unnatural, indulgence—and yet through all of this, for our family connection and his, I do believe, essential inner kindness, I was resolved to try and do my part to return him to the better graces of society. Well, there is no way of putting it cleanly. The house is large and there were many people—and in such a place, *even* in such a place, people enter who should not, without invitation, without regard, without any intention beyond, if I may say so, *profit.*"

Chang nodded in agreement, wondering exactly when he ought to run from the room, and how many confederates she might have on the staircase below.

"Because—" her voice broke. Tears formed at the corners of each eye. She dug for a handkerchief in her bag. Chang knew he ought to offer her one, but he also knew what his own handkerchief looked like. She found her own and dabbed at her eyes and nose. "I am sorry. It has all been so sudden. You must see people in distress quite often."

He nodded. Distress that he himself *caused,* but he needn't point that out.

"That must be terrible," she whispered.

"One becomes used to anything."

"Perhaps that is the worst thing of all." She folded the handkerchief back into her bag. "I am sorry, let me continue. As I say, it was a large affair, and one was required to speak to many people, aside from Lydia and Prince Karl-Horst, and so I was quite busy. As the evening went on, I realized that I had not seen my escort for some time. As I looked for him, he seemed to be nowhere. I was able to engage the assistance of mutual friends and, as discreetly as possible, we searched the adjoining rooms of the house, hoping that he had merely overindulged in drink and fallen asleep. What we found, Mr. Chang—Cardinal—was that he had been murdered. After conversation with other guests I am convinced that I know the identity of his killer. What I should like—what I should have liked, were you able to accept this task—is for this person to be found."

"And delivered to the authorities?"

"Delivered to me." She met his gaze quite evenly.

"I see. And this person?" He shifted in his seat, ready to leap at her. With the razor at her throat he could force his way past any phalanx of waiting men.

"A young woman. An inch or two above five feet but no more, chestnut hair in sausage curls, a fair complexion, pretty enough in a common style. She wore green boots and a black traveling cloak. Due to the manner in which my friend was killed, it is safe to say that she bore significant traces of blood. She gave her name as Isobel Hastings, but that is undoubtedly a lie."

He had asked other questions after this, but a part of his mind was elsewhere, attempting to make sense of the coincidence. Rosamonde could not say anything else about the woman—she was assumed to be a prostitute of some high stature, otherwise it was not known how she could have entered the house so easily, but Rosamonde had no idea how she had arrived nor how she had escaped. She asked him, as a point of reference, about his usual fee. He told her, and suggested that, again, if he had been able to accept her as a client, they would choose a place to meet or leave word. She looked around her and declared that the Library suited her fine for such a meeting, and that word could be left for her at the St. Royale Hotel. With that she rose and offered him her hand. He felt like a fool but found himself bending over to kiss it. He remained where he was, watching her leave, the stirring vision of her walking away quite matched by the seething disquiet in his mind.

Before anything else, he sent a message to John Carver, asking for confirmation, via the Raton Marine, that his name had been given to a young woman in need. Next, he required something to eat. It had been since the meat pie in St. Isobel's Square the day before, and Chang was famished. At the same time, as he walked down the marble steps outside the Library and into the open air, he was keenly suspicious of having been exposed. He made his way west, toward the Circus Garden and its shops, then stopped at a news kiosk, pretending to look at a racing pamphlet. No one seemed to have followed him from the Library, but this meant nothing—if they were skilled he might have men waiting for him at any particular haunt, as well as his rooming house. He put down the pamphlet and rubbed his eyes.

The food stalls gave him another meat pie—the Cardinal was not expansive in his diet—and a small pot of beer. He finished them quickly and continued to walk. It was nearing four o'clock, and already he could feel the day turning toward darkness, the wind acquiring its evening bite. As Chang saw it, he had three immediate choices: first, back to the Raton Marine to await contact from either Carver or Aspiche; second, stand watch at the St. Royale and find out everything he could about his new client, beginning with her true name; or third, start visiting brothels. He smiled—a rather simple choice, after all.

In truth, it made sense to see the brothels now, for there the business day would have just begun, and his chances were better to get information. The name Isobel Hastings was a place to start, for even if it was false, Chang knew that people grew attached to their disguises, and that a false name used once would most likely be used again—and if it were her true name, then all the easier. He walked back toward the river, farther along the strand, into the decayed heart of the old city. He wanted to visit the lowest of the houses first, before it became too thick with clientele. The house was known as the South Quays because it fronted the river, but also as a joke (for there were no south quays in the city) on the various points of moorage one might consider on the body of a whore. It catered to men of the sea and had a pitiless changeover among its available women, yet it was the best place to look for someone new. The South Quays was a drain that drew down into it all the loose and soiled flotsam of the city.

As he walked, he also regretted giving up the newspaper—he'd have to find another—now wanting to search for this new killing; even another vague reference to Rosamonde's companion as "missing" would at least provide him with a name. A second death on Robert Vandaariff's premises, on such an occasion, certainly added to the financier's reasons for keeping things quiet, though Chang wondered how long Trapping's death could remain so. Chang knew that even if Rosamonde had not actually lied to him, there was more to the story. His own memory of Persephone (which he preferred to Isobel) in the train told him that much. But pursuing Rosamonde's (whoever she actually was) investigation was a way to also pursue the intrigue around Trapping, and keep abreast of his own vulnerability in that regard—for it must mean learning more about the house, the guests, the party, the circumstances. But she had told him nothing about any of that, merely about the woman she wanted found. He clucked his tongue with annoyance as he walked, knowing that his best path to protect himself was also the path most likely to expose his involvement.

When he reached it, Dagging Lane was still empty. This was the rear of the house, whose front overhung the river itself and allowed for easy disposal of those contentious or unable to pay. A large man lounged outside a small wooden door, whose bright yellow paint stood out in a street of dirty brick and weather-stained wood. Chang walked up to him and nodded. The man recognized him and nodded in return. He knocked three times on the door with his meaty fist. The door opened and Chang stepped into a small entryway, cheaply carpeted, and lit with yellow lantern light instead of gas. Another large man demanded his walking stick, which Chang gave over, and then indicated with a practiced leer that he should proceed past a beaded curtain into a side parlor. Chang shook his head.

"I am here to speak to Mrs. Wells," he said. "I will pay for the time."

The man considered this, then walked through the curtain. After a brief interval, which Chang passed by looking at a cheap print framed on the wall (illustrating the intimate life of a Chinese contortionist), the man returned and ushered him through the parlor—past three sofas full of half-dressed, over-painted women, all appearing equally young and equally ravaged in the dim sickly light and who seemed to be generally yawning, scratching themselves, or in several cases, coughing thickly into napkins—and then to Mrs. Wells's own inner room, where the woman herself sat next to a crackling fire with an account book on her knees. She was grey, small, and thin, and in her work as routinely nurturing and dispassionately brutal as a farmer. She looked up at him.

"How long will this take?"

"Not long, I am sure."

"How much were you expecting to pay?"

"I was expecting this."

He reached into his pocket and removed a crumpled note. It was more than he ought to have offered, but the risk in this matter was closer to his person, so he didn't begrudge it. He dropped the banknote onto her ledger book and sat in the chair across from her. Mrs. Wells took the note and nodded at the large man, still standing in the doorway. Chang heard the man leave and close the door, but kept his gaze on the woman.

"I am not in the custom of providing information about my customers—" she began. Her teeth clicked when she spoke—some large percentage were made of white porcelain, which rather hideously showed the true color of those real teeth that remained. Chang had forgotten how much this annoyed him. He raised his hand to cut her off.

"I am not interested in your customers. I am looking for a woman, almost assuredly a whore, whom you may know of, even if you do not employ her directly."

Mrs. Wells nodded slowly. Chang didn't quite know what that meant, but as she did not then speak, he went on.

"Her name may be, or she may call herself, Isobel Hastings. Out of her shoes she is most likely five feet in height, with chestnut hair, in curls. The most salient fact is that she would have been seen early this morning wearing a black cloak and quite liberally—her face, her hair, her person—covered in dried blood. I expect that such a girl returning to your house, or any house, in such a manner—though it is not unheard-of—would have caused remark."

Mrs. Wells did not answer.

"Mrs. Wells?"

Still Mrs. Wells did not answer. Very quickly, and before she could slam the book, Chang darted forward and snatched the banknote away from her. She looked up at him in surprise.

"I am happy to pay for whatever you know, but not for abject silence."

She smiled as slowly and deliberately as a blade being unsheathed. "I am sorry, Cardinal, I was merely thinking. I do not know the girl you speak of. I do not know the name, and none of mine came home so bloodied. I would certainly have heard, and as certainly demanded reparations."

She stopped, smiling. There was more, he saw it in her eyes. He returned the banknote. She took it, placed it in the heavy ledger as a bookmark, and closed the book. Chang waited. Mrs. Wells chuckled, a particularly unpleasant noise.

"Mrs. Wells?"

"It is nothing," she replied. "Merely that you are the third to come asking for this same creature."

"Ah."

"Indeed."

"Might I ask who those others were?"

"You might." She smiled, but did not move, a silent request for more money. Chang was torn. On one hand, he had already paid her far more than he should. On the other, if he attacked her with his razor, he'd have to deal with the two men at the door.

"I believe I have been fair with you, Mrs. Wells . . . have I not?"

She chuckled again, setting his teeth on edge. "You have, Cardinal, and will be so in the future, I trust. These others were less . . . respectful. So I will tell you that the first was this morning, a young lady claiming to be this person's sister, and the second, just an hour ago, a man in uniform, a soldier."

"A red uniform?"

"No no, it was black. All black."

"And the woman"—he tried to think of Rosamonde—"she was tall? Black hair? Violet eyes? Beautiful?" Mrs. Wells shook her head.

"Not black hair. Light brown. And she was pretty enough—or would have been without the burns on her face." Mrs. Wells smiled. "Around the *eyes,* you know. Such a *dreadful* thing to have happen. Windows to the soul, don't you know."

Chang stalked back to the Raton Marine in a fury. It would have been one thing to learn that he was but one of several out to find this woman, but when he himself was so close to dire exposure in the same affair—whether he'd actually killed Trapping or not, he could just as easily hang for it—it was doubly maddening. His mind was spinning with suspicion. When he reached the Raton Marine it was nearly dark. No word had come from John Carver. Not quite ready to question his client directly, he began walking to the next likely house, near the law courts. This was known as the Second Bench, and was not too far and in a marginally safer location. He could thrash through his thoughts on the way.

As he forced himself to break the parts into discrete elements, he admitted that it was not strange that Mrs. Wells did not know his Persephone. When he had seen her on the train, there was the distinct sense that the image she then made was spectacular—that it was unusual to her, however telling or revelatory, or however large a story lay behind it. Her curls, though bloody and ruined, bespoke a certain care—perhaps the assistance of a servant. This would mean the Second Bench, or even the third house he had in mind, the Old Palace. These respectively offered an escalating class of whore, and served an escalating class of clientele. Each house was a window into a particular stratum of the city's traffic in flesh. Chang himself could patronize the Palace only when he possessed significant cash, and even then solely because of services rendered its manager. The unsavory nature of the South Quays only raised the question of how the other two searchers had found it, or thought to go there. The soldier he could understand, but the woman—her sister? There were, frankly, only so many ways a woman would know of such a place's existence, for the South Quays was nearly invisible to the greater population. That Rosamonde would know of it, for example, he would find more surprising than a personal letter from the Pope. But the others searching *did* know. Who were they, and whom did they serve? And who was this woman they all sought?

This did nothing to support his client's story of her poor murdered friend, who could be no disconnected innocent, but someone about whom other issues—inheritance? title? incrimination?—must be spinning, all of which she had withheld in their interview. Chang cast his mind back to the train, looking into those unreadable grey eyes. Was he looking at a killer, or a witness? And if she *had* killed... as an assassin, or in defense? Each possibility altered the motives of those searching for her. That none of them had gone to the police—even if it was at the specific, powerful request of Robert Vandaariff—did not reflect well on anyone's good intentions.

Not that good intentions were any normal part of Chang's life. The Second Bench was his usual choice in brothels, though this had more to do with a desire to balance his financial resources against the likelihood of disease than with any particular merits of the house. Still, he was acquainted with the staff and with the current manager, a fat greasy fellow with a shaved head named Jurgins who wore a number of large rings on his fingers—the very image of a modern court eunuch, it always seemed to Chang. Jurgins affected a jolly manner, though this was pushed aside like a curtain every time money came into the conversation, to be shot back into place once his insistent greed was no longer at the fore. As so many of the place's customers were drawn from business and the law, this mercenary manner was barely noticed, and certainly no cause for offense.

After a few quiet words with the men at the door, Chang was guided into Jurgins's private room, hung with tapestries and lit with crystal lamps whose shades dangled all kinds of delicate fringe, the air so thick with incense that even Chang found it oppressive. Jurgins sat at his desk, knowing Chang well enough to both see him alone and to also keep the door open with a bodyguard at close call. Chang sat in the chair opposite, and removed a banknote from his coat. He held it up for Jurgins to see. Jurgins could not help but tap his fingertips on the desk with anticipation.

"What may we do for you today, Cardinal?" He nodded at the banknote. "A formal request for something elaborate? Something... *exotical*?"

Chang forced a neutral smile. "My business is simple. I am looking for a young woman whose name may be Isobel Hastings, who would have arrived back here—or at another such establishment—early this morning, in a black cloak, and quite covered in blood."

Jurgins frowned thoughtfully, nodding.

"So, I am looking for her."

Jurgins nodded again. Chang met his gaze, and deliberately smiled. Out of a natural sycophantic impulse, Jurgins smiled as well.

"I am *also*"—Chang paused for companionable emphasis—"interested in the two people who have already wasted your time asking for her."

Jurgins smiled broadly. "I see. I see indeed. You're a clever man—I have always said it."

Chang smiled thinly at the compliment. "I would expect them to be a man in a black uniform and a woman, brown hair, well-dressed, with a... *burn* of strange design around her eyes. Would that be accurate?"

"It would!" Jurgins grinned. "He came first thing this morning—he woke me up—and she some time after luncheon."

"And what did you tell them?"

"What I will be forced to tell you, I'm afraid. The name means nothing. And I have heard no news about such a bloody girl, neither from here or any other house. I am sorry."

Chang leaned forward and dropped the banknote onto the desk. "No matter. I did not expect that you had. Tell me about the other two."

"It was just as you said. The man was an officer of some kind—I do not follow the military, you know—and perhaps your own age, quite the insistent brute, not understanding that I was not of his command, if you get me. The woman said the girl was her sister, quite lovely—as you say, except for the burn. Even then, we get people who fancy that kind of thing directly."

"And what were their names—or the names they gave you?"

"The officer called himself *Major Black*." Jurgins smirked at its obvious falseness. "The woman gave herself as a Mrs. Marchmoor." He chuckled with a lurid relish. "As I say, I would have been happy to offer her employment, if not for the delicacy of the occasion, her missing a relative and all."

The Second Bench and the Old Palace were on opposite sides of the north bank, and his path to the Palace took him close enough to the Raton Marine that he decided to stop by to see if Carver had left word.

He had not. It was unlike Carver, who fancied himself so important that he kept messengers and runners on hand at all hours—and certainly well into the evening. Perhaps Carver was in the country, which made it less likely that between last night and today Rosamonde could have received his recommendation. It was still possible, however, and he pushed the matter aside until he heard either way. He'd pressed Jurgins for more detail about the officer's uniform—silver facings and a strange regimental badge of a wolf swallowing the sun—and could just return to the Library before its doors shut for the day. Instead, he decided it was important to reach the Palace. In the unlikely case that he did find direct information, he wanted to get it as soon as possible—certainly the major and the sister were there now or had been already. He could easily find the regiment and identify the officer in the morning, if it was still of importance.

Outside the Raton Marine, he paused, and looked at his garments as objectively as possible. They wouldn't do, and he'd have to quickly visit his rooms to change. The Palace was particular about who it allowed in, and if he were to expect further to interrogate its manager then he would have to look close to his best. He cursed the delay and strode quickly along the darkened street—more peopled than before, some nodding to him as he passed, others simply pretending he didn't exist, which was the normal way of the district. Chang reached his door, fishing a key from his pocket, but found when he tried to insert it into the lock that the lock had been dislodged in its frame. He knelt and studied it. A sharp kick had snapped the wood around the bolt. He pushed the door with a gentle touch and it swung open with its habitual creak.

Chang looked up the empty, dimly lit staircase. The building was silent. He rapped on his landlady's door with his stick. Mrs. Schneider was a gin drinker, though this was a bit early for her to be insensible. He tried the knob, which was locked. He knocked again. He cursed the woman, not for the first time, and turned back to the stairs. He advanced quickly and quietly, holding his stick before him in readiness. His room was at the top, and he was used to the climb, striding across each landing with a glance to the doorways, all of which seemed to be closed, the occupants silent. Perhaps the lock had merely been kicked in by a tenant who'd misplaced his own key. It was possible, but Chang's natural suspicion would not rest until he reached the sixth-floor landing . . . where his own doorway gaped wide open.

With a swift tug Chang pulled the handle out of his stick, revealing a long, double-edged knife, and reversed his grip on the remaining portion in his other hand, allowing him to use the polished oak as a club or to parry. With both hands so armed, he crouched in the shadow and listened. What he heard were the sounds of the city, faint but clear. His windows were open, which meant that someone had gone onto the roof—perhaps to escape, perhaps to explore. He kept waiting, his eyes fixed on the door. Anyone inside would have heard him come up the stairs, and must be waiting for him to enter... and they must be getting as impatient as he. His knees were stiffening. He took in a breath and quietly sighed, willing them to relax, and then heard a distinct rustle from the darkened room. Then another. Then a fluttering of wings. It was a pigeon, undoubtedly entering by way of the open window. He stood with disgust and walked to the door.

As he entered, the combination of the darkened room and his glasses left Chang not altogether blind, but certainly in the realm of deep nightfall, and perhaps this deprivation had sharpened his other senses, for as his foot crossed the open doorway he sensed movement from his left side and by instinct—and by his embedded knowledge of the room—threw himself to the right, into a nook between a tall dressing cabinet and the wall, raising the length of his stick before him as he did. The bit of moonlight from the window caught the flashing scythe of a saber sweeping down at him from behind the door. He'd stepped clear of the main blow and stopped the rest of it on his stick. In the same instant Chang drove himself directly back into his assailant. As he did, he thrust the stick across the man's blade—which, in the close quarters, the man was awkwardly pulling back—and so prevented a second blow. Chang's right hand, holding the dagger, shot forward like a spike.

The man grunted with pain and Chang felt the thick, meaty impact—though in the darkness he could not tell where the blow had landed. The man struggled with his long blade, to get the edge or the point toward Chang's body, and Chang dropped his stick to grab the man's sword arm, grappling to keep it clear. With his right hand he pulled the dagger back and rapidly stabbed forward three times more, like a plunging needle, twisting it as he yanked it clear. By the final thrust he felt the strength ebbing from the man's wrist, and he released his grip, stepping away. The man collapsed to the floor with a sigh, and then a choking rattle. It would have been better to question him, but there was nothing for it.

When it came to violence, Chang was realistic. While experience and skill would increase his chances of survival, he knew that the margins for error were tiny and often subject not so much to luck as to a certain authority of intention, or will. In those minute spaces of variability a firm, even grim, determination was crucial, and hesitation of any kind a mortal flaw. Any man could be killed by any other, no matter what the circumstances, and there was always the blue moon chance that a fellow who has never carried a sword will do a thing with it no sane duelist would expect. Chang had in his life dealt out and received all sorts of punishment, and was under no illusion that his skills would protect him forever, or from everyone. In this particular instance, he was lucky that a desire for silence had led his opponent to choose—instead of a revolver—a weapon ridiculously unsuited for assassination in such close quarters. Once he'd missed with his first blow, Chang had stepped within his guard and stabbed home—but the window for action was very narrow. Had Chang paused, dodged farther into the room, or tried to dash back to the landing a second blow from the saber would have mown him down like fresh wheat.

Chang lit the lamp, located the pigeon and—feeling especially ridiculous stepping around the dead body—drove it out of the open window onto the rooftop. The room was not too much of a mess. It had been thoroughly searched, but without the intent to destroy anything and as his possessions were few it would be a brief matter to set things back to rights. He stepped to the still-open door and listened. There was no sound from the stairway, which meant either no one had heard, or that he was indeed alone in the building. He closed the door—the lock had been forced just like the front entrance—and braced the back of it with a chair. Only then did he kneel, wipe the dagger on the man's uniform, and slide it back into the body of his stick. He cast an eye along the length—he'd been fortunate enough to parry the saber on the flat of the blade, and hadn't cracked the wood. He set it against the wall, and looked down at his assailant.

He was a young man, blond hair cropped short, in a black uniform with silver facing, black boots, and a silver badge of a wolf devouring the sun. His right shoulder sported one silver epaulette—a lieutenant. Chang quickly went through the man's pockets, which aside from some small amount of money (which he took) and a handkerchief, were empty. He looked more closely at the body. The first dagger blow had landed just below the ribs from the side. The next three had driven up under the ribcage and into the lungs, judging by the bloody froth at the fellow's mouth.

Chang sighed and sat back on his heels. He didn't recognize the uniform at all. The boots suggested a horseman, but an officer might wear anything, and what young man foolish enough to *be* a military officer wasn't also going to want high black boots? He picked up the saber, feeling the balance of the weapon. It was an expensive piece, exquisitely weighted, and wickedly sharp. The length, the broad curve and flat width of the blade made it a weapon for horseback, for slashing. He'd be light cavalry—not a Hussar by his uniform, but perhaps a Dragoon or a Lancer. Troops for quick movement, reconnaissance, intelligence. Chang leaned over the body and unfastened the scabbard. He sheathed the blade and tossed it onto the pallet. The body he would get rid of, but the sword would certainly be worth something if he needed ready cash.

He stood up and exhaled, his nerves finally easing back to a more normal state of wariness. At the moment a corpse was the last thing he wanted to waste time with settling. He had no clear idea of the hour, and knew that the later he arrived at the Palace the harder it would be to speak to the manager, and the more of a lead his rivals would have upon him. He permitted himself a smile to think that at least one of these rivals would be thinking him dead, but then knew that this also meant that the Major would be expecting word—and undoubtedly soon—from this young agent. Chang could certainly expect another visit, this time in force, in the near future. His room was unsafe until the business was settled—which meant that he'd have to deal with the body now, for he really did not want to leave it unattended—possibly for days. His sense of smell was not *that* bad.

Quickly then, he made himself presentable for the Old Palace: a shave, a wash from his basin, and then a new change of clothes—a clean white shirt, black trousers, cravat and waistcoat—and a quick scrub and polish for his boots. He pocketed what money he had stashed about the room and three books of poetry (including the *Persephone*), and then combed his still-wet hair in the mirror. He balled up his old handkerchief and tossed it aside, then tucked a fresh one and his razor into the pocket of his coat. He opened the window to the roof, stepped out to see if any nearby windows were lighted or occupied. They were not. He returned to the room and took hold of the body under each arm, dragging it onto the rooftop, out to the far edge. He looked over, down at the alleyway behind the building, locating the trash heap piled around the habitually clogged sewer. He glanced around him once more, then hefted the body onto the edge and, checking his aim, pushed it over. The dead soldier landed on the soft pile. If Chang was lucky, it would not be immediately clear whether he had fallen or been murdered in the street.

He returned to his room, collected his stick and the saber, blew out the lamp, and crept back out the window, closing it behind him. It wouldn't lock, but given that the location was known to his enemies, it hardly mattered. He set off across the rooftops. The buildings of this block were directly connected, and his path was simple enough, with only a few slippery stretches of ornamental molding requiring caution. At the fifth building, which was abandoned, he pried open an attic hatchway and dropped down into darkness. He landed easily on the wooden floor, felt for a moment, and located a spot of loose planking. He pulled it back and shoved the saber inside, replacing the plank over it. He might never come back for it, but he had to assume his own room would be searched by more soldiers, and the less they found of their fallen comrade the better. He groped again and found the ladder to the landing below. In a matter of moments, Chang was on the street, still presentable and bound for the Palace, with yet another soul weighing upon his exiled conscience.

The house was named for its proximity to an actual royal residence given over—its fortified walls too out of fashion—some two hundred years ago, which had first been used as a home for various minor Royals, then as the War Ministry, then an armory, a military academy, to finally—and presently—as the home of the Royal Institute of Science and Exploration. While it would seem that such an organization would hardly encourage the nearby thriving of such an exclusive brothel, in fact the various endeavors of the Institute were almost all supported, in competitive fashion, by the wealthiest figures in the city, each striving against the others to finance an invention, a discovery, a new continent, or a newly located star to result in the immemorial attachment of their name to something permanent and useful. In turn, the Institute members strove against each other to attract patrons—the two communities of the privileged and the learned spawning between them an entire district whose economy derived from flattery, favoritism, and the excessive consumption that followed each. Thus, the Old Palace brothel—named, in another anatomical witticism, for perhaps the oldest palace of all.

The entry to the house was respectable and austere, the building itself crammed into a block-long row of identical stiff stackings of grey stone with domed rooftops, the doorway green and brightly lit, the walk from the street leading through an iron gate and past a well-occupied guard's hut. Chang stood so he was clearly seen, waited while the gate was unlocked, and made his way up to the door itself, where another guard allowed him into the house proper. Inside was warm and bright, with music and distant decorous laughter. A fetching young woman appeared for his coat. He declined, but gave her his stick and a coin for her trouble. He walked to the end of the foyer where a thin man in a white jacket hovered at a high rostrum, fitfully scribbling in a notebook. He looked at Chang with an expression that kept just barely to the prudent side of amusement.

"Ah," he said, as if to convey the multitude of comments regarding Chang's person he was, through compassion and kindness, withholding.

"Madame Kraft."

"I am not sure she is available—in fact, I am certain—"

"It is quite important," Chang said, meeting the man's eyes levelly. "I will pay for the lady's time—whatever fee she sees fit. The name is Chang."

The man narrowed his eyes, ran his gaze once more over Chang, and then nodded with a doubtful sniff. He scrawled a few lines on a small piece of green paper, stuffed the paper into a leather tube, and inserted the tube into a brass pipe fixed to the wall. With a gulping hiss, the tube was abruptly sucked from sight. The man turned back to his rostrum, making notes. Minutes passed. The man ignored him absolutely. With a sudden *chonk* the leather tube reappeared from another pipe, shooting into a brass pocket beneath. The man extracted the tube and dug a scrap of blue paper from it. He looked up with a blank expression that nevertheless exuded contempt.

"This way."

Chang was led through an elegant parlor and down a long hallway where the light was dim and the closely patterned wallpaper made the space seem narrower than it actually was. At its end was a metal-sheathed door where the man in white knocked, four times, deliberately. In answer, a narrow viewing slot slid back and then, the visitors having been seen, shot closed. They waited. The door opened. His guide gestured for Chang to enter a darkly paneled room with desks and blotters and ledgers and a large abacus screwed into prominent position on a side table. The door had been opened by a tall man in his shirtsleeves, a heavy revolver holstered under one arm, with black hair and skin the color of polished cherry wood, who nodded him toward another door on the far side of the office. Chang crossed to it, thought it would be polite to knock, and did so. After a moment, he heard a muted request to enter.

The room was another office, but with a single wide desk, across which was spread a large blackboard that had been painted with various columns and inset with strips of wood with holes bored into them, so that colored pegs could be inserted along the columns, cutting each into rows, the whole forming an enormous grid. The blackboard was already scrawled with names and with numbers and dotted with pegs. Chang had seen it before and knew it corresponded to the rooms in the house, the ladies (or boys) at work, and the segments of time in the evening, and that it was wiped and re-written fresh every night of the week. Behind the desk, a piece of chalk in one hand and a moist sponge in the other, stood Madelaine Kraft, the manager—and some said actual owner—of the Old Palace. A well-shaped woman of uncertain age, she wore a simple dress of blue Chinese silk, which set off her golden skin in a pleasant way. She was not beautiful so much as compelling. Chang had heard she was from Egypt, or perhaps India, and had worked her way from the front of the house to her present position through discretion, intelligence, and unscrupulous scheming. She was without a doubt a far more powerful person than he, with high-placed men from all over the land profoundly obligated to her silence and favor, and thus at her call. She looked up from her work and nodded to a chair. He sat. She dropped the chalk and sponge, wiped her fingers on her dress and took a drink of tea from a white china cup to the side of the board. She remained standing.

"You're here about Isobel Hastings."

"I am."

Madelaine Kraft did not reply, which he took as an invitation to continue.

"I was asked to find her—a . . . *lady* returning from an evening's work covered in blood."

"Returning from where?"

"I was not told—the understanding was that the quantity of blood was singular enough for her to be remembered."

"Returning from whom?"

"I was not told—the assumption being the blood was his."

She was silent for a moment, in thought. Chang realized that she was not thinking of what to say, but weighing instead whether or not to say what she was thinking.

"There is the missing man in the newspaper," she said, musing.

Chang nodded absently. "The Colonel of Dragoons."

"Could it be him?"

He answered as casually as he could, "It's entirely possible."

She took another sip of tea.

"You will understand," Chang went on, "that I am being honest."

This made her smile. "Why would I understand that?"

"Because I am paying you, and your bargains are fair."

Chang reached into his coat for the wallet and extracted three crisp banknotes. He leaned forward and set them down on the blackboard. Madelaine Kraft picked up the notes, glanced at the amount, and dropped them into an open wooden box next to her tea cup. She glanced at the clock.

"I'm afraid there is no great deal of time."

He nodded. "My understanding is that my client desires revenge."

"And you?" she asked.

"First, to know who else is searching for her. I know the agents—the officer, the 'sister'—but not who they represent."

"And after that?"

"That will depend. Obviously they have already been here asking questions—unless you are involved in this business yourself."

She cocked her head slightly and, after a moment of thought, sat down behind the desk. She reached over for another sip of tea, took it, and kept the cup, holding it between her breasts with both hands, watching him evenly across the desk top.

"Very well," she began. "To begin with, I do not know the name, and I do not know the woman. No person of my household—or of my household's acquaintance—appeared in the early hours of this morning displaying any quantity of blood. I have made it a point to *ask,* and I have received no such answer. Next, Major *Blach* was here this afternoon. I told him what I have just told you."

She pronounced the name unlike Jurgins or Wells, as if it was foreign... had he spoken with an accent? The others had not mentioned it.

"And the sister?"

She smiled conspiratorially. "*I* have seen no sister."

"A woman, scars on her face, a burn, claiming to be Isobel Hastings's sister, a 'Mrs. Marchmoor'—"

"I have not seen her. Perhaps she's still to come. Perhaps she does not know this house."

"That's impossible. She has been to two other houses before me, and she would know this one before all the rest of them."

"I am sure that's true."

Chang's mind raced, sorting quickly—Mrs. Marchmoor had known the other houses, she had bypassed this one—to a swift conclusion: she did not come because she would be *known.*

"May I ask if any women of your household have recently... graduated to other situations, perhaps without your consent? With light brown hair?"

"It is indeed the case."

"The type to be searching for a blood-soaked relative?"

"Hardly," she scoffed. "But you said burns across the face?"

"They could be recent."

"They would need to be. Margaret Hooke has been gone four days. The daughter of a ruined mill owner. She would not be known at any lower house."

"Does she have a sister?"

"She doesn't have a soul. Though it appears she's found something. If you can tell me what that is—or who—I'll be kindly disposed."

"You have a suspicion. That's why we're talking."

"We're talking because one of several regular customers of Margaret Hooke is presently in my house."

"I see."

"She saw many people. But anyone wanting to learn what might be learned... as I said, there's little time to talk."

Chang nodded and stood. As he turned to the door she called to him, her voice both quiet and more urgent at the same time. "Cardinal?" He looked back. "Your own part in this?"

"Madam, I am merely the agent of others."

She studied him. "Major Blach did ask for Miss Hastings. But he also sought any information about a man in red, a mercenary for hire, perhaps even this bloody girl's accomplice."

He felt a chill of warning. The man had obviously asked Mrs. Wells and Jurgins too, and they had said nothing, laughing at Chang's back. "How strange. Of course, I cannot explain his interest, unless he had been following my client, and perhaps observed us speaking."

"Ah."

He nodded to her. "I will let you know what I find." He stepped to the door, opened it, and then turned back. "Which lady of your house is entertaining Margaret Hooke's customer?"

Madelaine Kraft smiled, her thin amusement tinged with pity.

"Angelique."

He returned to the front of the house and collected his stick, then so armed—and untroubled by the staff who seemed to understand that it had been arranged—approached the man in white. Chang saw that he held another small piece of blue paper, and before he could speak the man leaned forward with a whisper. "Down the rear staircase. Wait under the stairs, and then you may follow." He smiled—Kraft's acceptance smoothing the way for his own. "It will provide the additional benefit of allowing you to leave unseen."

The man went back to his notebook. Chang walked quickly past him into the main part of the house, along wide welcoming archways that opened onto variously entrancing vistas of comfort and luxury, food and flesh, laughter and music—to a rear door, watched by another burly man. Chang looked up at him—he was tall himself and found the immediate density of so many taller, broader figures a little tiresome—waited for the man to open the door, and then stepped onto the landing of a slender wooden staircase leading down to a narrow, high passageway of some twenty yards. This basement passage was significantly cooler, moist-aired, and lined with brick. Directly beneath the staircase was a hutch with a door. Chang pulled it open and climbed inside, bending nearly double to fit, and sat on a round milking stool. He pulled the door closed and waited in the dark, feeling foolish.

The interview had raised more questions than it had answered. He knew his conversation with Rosamonde in the map room had been unobserved, so Black must know of him independently—either from some other informant, from seeing him at the Vandaariff mansion, or, he had to admit, from Rosamonde herself. If Mrs. Marchmoor was also Margaret Hooke, then Angelique was in danger of disappearing as well—though Madelaine Kraft's suspicion had not stopped her from accepting the regular client who might have been the cause. Perhaps this meant that the client was not as important as some other party, or some other power, yet hidden in the shadow—information she hoped Chang could provide. Chang rubbed his eyes. In the course of a day he had placed himself in the shadow of one murder, performed another, and set himself against at least three different mysterious parties—four if he counted Rosamonde—without any real knowledge of the larger stakes at hand. Further, none of this had brought him a step closer to finding Isobel Hastings, who grew more mysterious by the hour.

Despite his racing mind, it was only a minute before he heard the door open and the descending weight of footsteps on the stairs above his head. A man was speaking, but Chang couldn't make out the words over the noise—to his best guess there were at least three people in the party, perhaps more. Finally they were off the stairs and walking away from him down the passage. He cautiously opened the hutch door, and peeked out: the party could only walk single file in the narrow space, and all he could see was the back of the rear figure, an unremarkable-looking man in a formal black topcoat. He waited until they reached the far end of the passage before slowly pushing the door open and extricating himself. By the time he was once more standing at his full height, they had rounded a corner and disappeared. Walking as much as possible on his toes to reduce the sound of his footsteps, he followed at a trot to make up the distance.

At the corner he stopped, listening, and again heard the voice—low and strangely muttering—but not the words themselves, obscured by jingling keys and their fumbling at a lock. He silently dropped to a crouch and then risked edging one eye around the corner—knowing that anyone looking would be less likely to notice an eye at a less-than-normal eye height. The party was some ten yards away, standing in front of a locked, metal-bound door. The man in the rear still stood with his back to Chang, the closer view revealing him to be younger with thin, oak-colored hair plastered flat to his skull. Beyond him Chang could see parts of three other people: a small man in an ash-grey coat bent over the door, attempting to find the right key, a tall, broad-shouldered man in a thick fur, impatiently tapping a walking stick on the floor and leaning down—he was the one muttering—to the fourth person, tucked under his arm like a flower in a grenadier's bearskin: Angelique. Her dress was deep blue, and she did not react to whatever the man was saying, gazing without expression at the elegant grey man's hands as he sorted through keys. The lock turned—he'd found the right one at last—and he opened the door, looking back at the others with a trim twitch of a smile. It was Harald Crabbé.

At this the man in the fur snapped open a pocket watch and frowned. "Where in hell is he?" he said, his voice an iron rasp. He turned to the third man and hissed balefully, "Collect him."

Chang darted back around the corner, desperately looking around him for a place to hide. He was fortunate in that, being in a crouch, his eyes naturally looked upwards, and saw a pair of iron pipes, as wide as his arm, running the length of the passage just below the high ceiling. Behind him he heard another voice—Crabbé—interrupt the nearing footsteps of the third man, just at the corner, a step away from discovering Chang.

"*Bascombe.*"

"Sir?"

"Wait a moment." Crabbé's tone changed—clearly now he was addressing the man in the fur. "Another minute. I should rather not give him any insight into our growing displeasure, nor the satisfaction such knowledge would undoubtedly bring. Besides"—and here his voice changed again, to an awkward sugarish tone—"his *prize* is with us."

"I am no one's prize," replied Angelique, her voice quiet but firm.

"Of course you aren't," assured Crabbé, "but he needn't know that until we're ready."

Chang looked up in horror. At the far end of the passage, above the staircase, the door was opened. Someone was coming. He was caught between them. In a surge of strength he took three steps and jumped, bracing one foot against the wall and thrusting off, catching the other foot on the opposite side and thrusting again, higher, so that his outstretched arms could reach the pipes. A pair of legs were visible descending the stairs. The group around the corner would hear any second. He pulled himself up, wrapping his legs around the pipes, and then through sheer force rolled over above them, so he faced the floor, quickly tucking the ends of his coat so they didn't hang. He looked down with despair. His stick was still on the floor, close to the wall, where he'd set it when he'd peeked around the corner. There was nothing he could do. They were coming. How long had he taken? Had he been seen? Heard? A moment later—holding his breath despite his heaving chest—Chang saw the third man, Bascombe, step around the corner—standing bare inches from his stick. The footsteps neared from the other end—louder than he'd thought. It was more than one person.

"Mr. Bascombe!" one of them shouted, a kind of exuberant greeting made all the more hearty (or fatuous) by the fact that the men had most likely been apart for all of five minutes. But the tone served to announce that they were on an adventure together, an *evening*—and declare as well who was that evening's guide. Chang's skin prickled with loathing. He exhaled silently through his nose. He could not believe they had not seen him—and prepared to drop onto Bascombe, attack the newcomers, then run for the steps. The pair passed directly beneath. He froze, again holding his breath. One man, a sharp fellow in a crisp black tailcoat, bristling red side whiskers, and long, thick, curled red hair (obviously the man who had called out), supported the shambling steps of another taller, thinner man in a steel blue uniform, capped with a squat, blue-plumed shako, with medals across his chest and tall boots that unmercifully hampered his alcoholic gait. Once they were close enough, Bascombe stepped forward and took the uniformed man's other side, and the three of them vanished around the corner.

Chang stayed above the pipes until he heard the iron door close behind them, then swung himself down to hang by his arms and drop to the floor. He brushed himself off—the pipes were filthy—and picked up his stick. He exhaled, berating himself for being trapped so foolishly. He had only been saved by the uniformed man, he knew, whose stumbling drunken state had diverted attention away from anything else. He thought back to the conversation between the man in fur and Crabbé: which of the two men had they been waiting for—the drunken officer or the hearty fop? And though he resisted the thought—for it led to naught but slow disintegration of his peace—as he walked around the corner and stared at the iron door they'd closed behind them... which among them all had laid claim to Angelique?

She'd come from Macao as a child, orphaned when her father, a Portuguese sailor, had died in a knife fight his second day off the ship. Her mother had been Chinese, and her appearance had transfixed Chang from the moment he'd seen her in the main room of the South Quays—where she had found a kind of home after the cruelty of the public orphanage. Exotic beauty and a strangely compelling reserve had elevated her first from that squalid lair to the Second Bench and finally this last year, at the ripe age of seventeen, to the perfumed heights of the Old Palace, Madame Kraft having purchased her contract for an undisclosed amount. This had effectively placed her beyond Chang's reach. He had not spoken to her in five months. Of course he had barely spoken to her before that—he was not one for speaking in general, and still less to anyone for whom he might possess actual feelings. Though he told himself she was well aware of the special place she held within his—he could not say "heart", for what was that in a life like his (perhaps "panoramic painting" was a more accurate description of the rootless pageant of Chang's existence)—this had prompted no significant words on her part, for no matter her own feelings, she preferred silence as much as he. At first this might have been a question of language, but by now it had become an expression of professional manner, one with a bright smile, pliant body, and impossibly distant eyes. In the devastating moments they'd spent in what passed for intimacy, Angelique was never other than polite and practiced, but always allowed just a glimpse of a boundless inner landscape held firmly in reserve... a glimpse that went through Chang's very soul like a fishhook.

He tried the metal door, to no avail, and sighed with impatience. It was an old lock, intended more to delay determined pursuit than prevent it utterly. He groped in his coat for a ring of iron skeleton keys and flipped through them. The second key worked, and he swung the door open slowly—it was well-greased and did not creak—and stepped through into darkness. He pulled the door behind him, leaving it unlocked, and listened. His quarry's pace was slow, not surprising due to the combination of the drunken man and Angelique—her shoes and dress would not be suited to a darkened cobblestone tunnel. Chang followed quietly, stick before him, left hand feeling the wall. The tunnel was not long—judging by the distance just far enough to clear the alley and next block of houses. Quickly Chang tried to place the exact direction—the stairway down, then the passage, the corner, then the dark tunnel, which seemed to have a very gentle curve to the left... the block behind the brothel was the outlying wall of the Palace itself—additional buildings for the Institute. Undoubtedly the tunnel had been originally built as a secret bolt-hole from the Palace, perhaps to what was then the house of a mistress, perhaps as a way to escape a mob. Chang smiled to see the usage reversed, but retained his air of caution. He had never been within the walls of the Institute, and had no clear idea what he was going to find.

Ahead, they had stopped. Someone pounded on another iron door, a metallic rapping (the large man's stick?) that echoed sharply through the tunnel. In answer, Chang heard the working of a lock, the shrill ripple of chain pulled through an iron ring, and then the creak of heavy hinges. Orange light bled into the darkness. The party stood at the base of a short stone staircase, and above them an open hatch nearly flush with the ground, as to a cellar. Several men stood with lanterns, offering their hands one at a time as the party members climbed out. They did not close the door—perhaps because they would be bringing Angelique back?—so Chang took the opportunity to slip to the stone steps and crouch low, looking up. Above him, quite ghostly in the moonlight, were the leafless limbs of a tree.

He peeked over the edge and saw that it opened onto a large grassy courtyard between buildings of the Palace. The pool of lantern light moved farther away as the group was guided across the lawn, leaving him very much in shadow. Keeping low, Chang stole from the tunnel—it felt like leaving a crypt—and after them, drifting as he went toward the nearest tree, which gave a more substantial cover. The windows in the buildings around him were dark—he had no idea how much of the Palace the fellows of the Institute actually occupied, or in what manner, so could only hope to remain unobserved. He jogged along to another tree, now even closer to the walls, the thick turf swallowing the sound of his boots. It was easy to see where the party was headed—toward another man with a lantern, who stood marking the entrance to a strange structure at the courtyard's center, apart from and unconnected to any other building.

It was one low story, made of brick, without windows and, as near as Chang could tell, circular. As he watched, the group of six and their guides reached the doorway and entered. The man who had been at the door remained. Chang advanced to another tree, taking more care with any noise. He was perhaps twenty yards away. He waited, still, for several minutes. The guard did not move from the door. Chang studied the courtyard, wondering if he could creep around to the far side of the circular building, in case there might be another door, or a window, or access through the roof. Instead, he eased into a crouch and decided to wait, hoping that the guard would enter or some of the party would come out. The party itself he was still pondering. He did not recognize any of them save Crabbé and Angelique. The man Bascombe was a lackey for either the Deputy Minister or the man in the fur, it was unclear who—just as it was unclear who between those men was the superior power. The final two were a mystery—from his vantage point on the ceiling he could hardly see the face of either man, nor the details of the drunken officer's uniform. Obviously there was some relation to the gathering at Robert Vandaariff's house—Crabbé had been in both places. Had one of them courted Margaret Hooke in the same way as they were courting Angelique—Margaret Hooke who was looking for Isobel Hastings (who had also been at Vandaariff's) and who had the same scarring as the late Arthur Trapping? Her scarring had been recent, just as Trapping's had occurred in the few minutes between his leaving the main reception and Chang finding him on the floor—which at least told Chang that the scarring itself hadn't caused Trapping's death, as the woman had obviously survived. Most important was the disparate nature of the group, gathering for some shared purpose—a purpose that, perhaps only as a tangent, had killed Arthur Trapping and prompted a search for Isobel Hastings. Chang doubted this search was about revenge. His Persephone may indeed have killed Rosamonde's friend—the blood had come from somewhere—but she was being hunted for what she had seen.

The guard turned suddenly, away from Chang, and a moment later Chang himself heard footsteps from across the courtyard. Walking forward into the lantern's glow was a spare man in a long, dark, double-breasted greatcoat with silver buttons and bare epaulettes, his pale head bare, his hands joined behind his back. At the guard's request he stopped several yards away, nodding sharply and clicking his heels in salute. The man was clean-shaven and wore a monocle that reflected the light as he nodded his head, clearly requesting entry and then taking in the guard's refusal. The man exhaled with resignation. He looked behind him and gestured vaguely with his left hand—perhaps at a place where he might be allowed to wait. The guard turned his head to follow the hand. In one swift movement the man whipped his right arm forward, his thumb drawing the hammer of a gleaming black pistol, and aimed the barrel square at the guard's face. The guard did not move, but then very quickly, at the man's brisk, whispered instruction, dropped his weapon to the grass, put down the lantern, and then turned his face to the door. The man snatched up the lantern and placed the pistol against the guard's spine. The guard opened the door with a key and the two men disappeared inside.

They did not close the door either. Chang quickly loped across the lawn toward it and carefully craned his head so he could see in. The entrance led directly to a low staircase that descended several stories on a direct and very steep incline. The building was sunk deeply into the ground and Chang could just see the two figures leaving the stairwell, with only a flickering orange glow bleeding back from the disappearing lantern. Chang glanced around the courtyard, readied his stick, and crept down the stairs, moving slowly, silently, and keeping himself at all times ready to bolt back to the top. Once again he'd placed himself in a narrow corridor at the mercy of anyone appearing above or below him—but if he wanted information, he saw no other way. Just above the lower landing he stopped, listening. He could hear distant conversation, but the words were muddled by the strange acoustics. Chang looked above him. No one was there. He continued his descent.

The stairs opened onto a circular hallway curving away to either side, as if it formed a ring around a great central chamber. The voices were to Chang's left, so he went that way, pressing close against the inner wall to remain unseen. After some twenty yards, moving into a steadily brighter light, he stopped again, for suddenly—as if he had walked through a door—he could hear the voices perfectly.

"I do not care for the *inconvenience.*" The voice was angry but controlled. "He is insensible."

The accent sounded German, but perhaps something else—Danish? Norse? The words were met first with silence, and then the delicate speech of a practiced diplomat, Harald Crabbé.

"Doctor... of course... you must see to your duties—quite understandable, in fact, admirable. You will see, however... the delicacy, the *time* element—that there are requirements—*duties*—in competition. I believe we are all friends here—"

"Excellent. Then I will bid you a friendly good evening," replied the Doctor. In immediate answer came the ringing of steel—a sword being drawn—and the clicks of several guns being cocked. Chang could imagine the standoff. What he could not imagine were the stakes.

"Doctor . . . ," Crabbé continued, with a rising strain of urgency in his voice. "Such a confrontation suits no one—and your young master's wishes, if he were able to make them known—"

"Not my master, but my charge," cut in the Doctor. "His wishes in the matter count for very little. As I said, we will be leaving, unless you choose to kill me. If you do so choose, I promise that I will first blow out the brains of this idiot Prince—which I believe will quite spoil your plans, as well as leaving a powerful father . . . angry. Good evening."

Chang heard shuffling steps, and a moment later saw the Doctor, one hand holding up the tottering, insensible man in uniform, and the other occupied with the pistol. Chang retreated with him step for step, keeping out of view of the larger group which he had just glimpsed—Crabbé, Bascombe, the foppish red-haired man (who held the sword), and three guards (who held the pistols). There was no sign of the man in fur, nor of Angelique. As they retreated, no one spoke—as if the situation had progressed beyond words—and soon Chang found himself retreating past the staircase. He considered dashing up, but it would only expose him—they would have to hear his steps and he could not reach the top unseen. It might also be the exact distraction to get the Doctor killed, and right now Chang didn't know if that would be a good thing or not. He still hoped to learn more. The drunken, uniformed man, unless he was very wrong, must be Karl-Horst von Maasmärck. Once more, mysterious connections between Robert Vandaariff, Henry Xonck, and the Foreign Ministry seemed to be dancing just out of reach in his brain. Momentarily distracted with thought, Chang looked up. The Doctor had seen him.

He stood with the slumped von Maasmärck at the base of the stairwell, and had merely glanced down the other end of the corridor as a reflex and been shocked to see anyone, much less a strange figure in red. Chang knew he was beyond the curve of the wall and out of sight to the others, and slowly brought a finger to his lips, indicating silence. The Doctor stared. His skin was pale and the impression he gave nearly skeletal. His hair was ice-blond and shaved on the back and sides of his head in a nearly medieval fashion, long and plastered back in a part on top—though his struggles had broken it forward in lank, white clumps that hung over his eyes. It did not seem, for all his apparent confidence, that the Doctor was a man of action, or necessarily used to waving a pistol. Chang deliberately backed away from him, keeping eye contact, and made a gesture to indicate that the Doctor should exit—*now.* The Doctor darted his gaze back to the others and began to awkwardly mount the stairs, pulling up the near deadweight of the Prince along with him. Chang retreated farther from view, his thoughts once more askew upon seeing von Maasmärck's face: quite clearly livid with red circular burns around both of his eyes.

The group clustered around the lower door. "Doctor, I am sure we shall see you again," called Crabbé amiably, "and good night to your sweet prince." The Deputy Minister then muttered to the guards near him, "If he falls, take him. If he doesn't, one of you secure the door, and the other follow him. You"—he singled out the guard the Doctor had brought down at pistol point—"stay here." Two of the guards climbed rapidly from sight and one remained, his pistol in hand. Crabbé turned and, with Bascombe and the red-haired fop, disappeared down the hallway whence they'd come.

"It doesn't signify," he said to them cheerfully. "We shall find the Prince tomorrow—in some fashion—and the Doctor may be dealt with at leisure. There is no hurry. Besides"—and here he chuckled, speaking more intimately—"we have another engagement with *nobility*—yes, Roger?"

They passed out of hearing. Chang slowly retreated another ten yards, boxed in again. He would have to attack the guard to get out, or outlast them—assuming that when the party left they would take the guards along. He turned and continued down this half of the corridor, hoping the circle might join on the other side.

Chang advanced with his stick before him in both hands—one on the handle and one on the body—ready to pull it apart at a moment's notice. He had no real idea if he was the hunter or the hunted, but knew that if things went bad he could be fighting several men at once, which was almost always fatal. If the group of men kept their heads, one of them was always presented with an opening, and their lone opponent, no matter how vigorous or skilled, would fall. That man's only option was to attack at as many points as possible and through pure aggression separate the group into fragile individuals—who might then be prone to hesitation. Hesitation created tiny moments of single combat, winnowing the group, which in turn created more hesitation—ferocity pitted against presence of mind, fear trumping logic. In short, it meant attacking like a madman. But such a wanton strategy opened his defense with more holes than Mrs. Wells's natural smile—and any remaining presence of mind in his opponents—which was to say, if they were not inexperienced, stupid, easily rattled farmers—would leave him stuck like a pig. The better aim was to avoid it entirely. He took care to make no noise.

As the corridor curved, he detected a low humming from beyond the inner wall—from the central chamber, whatever that actually was. On the floor in front of him lay a profusion of long boxes, opened and emptied in a great tumbled pile, the same boxes he'd seen on the cart at the canal and in the house of Robert Vandaariff—though these were lined with blue felt rather than orange. The humming grew louder, then steadily louder still, until the very air seemed to vibrate. Chang put his hands over his ears. The discomfort bled horribly into pain. He stumbled forward. The corridor ended at a door, sheathed in metal. He picked his way across the boxes—the great throbbing noise covering the sound of his awkward steps—but he could not concentrate, tripping, knocking boxes aside. He tottered and shut his eyes. He sank to his knees.

It took Cardinal Chang several seconds of brutally reverberating echo in his ears to perceive that the sound had stopped. He sniffed, and felt his face. It was wet. He dug for his handkerchief—his nose was bleeding. He struggled to his feet amidst the littered boxes, shaking away a fog of dizziness, staring at the bright stains on the cloth as he doubled it over and dabbed again at his face. He collected himself, sniffed, stuffed the handkerchief into a side pocket, and stepped carefully to the door. He pressed his ear against it, listening, but it was too thick—which only made him wonder all the more at the true extremity of the throbbing hum, to have so touched him through the massive walls and this heavy door. What had happened to the people *within* the chamber? What was the cause of the noise? He stood for a moment, assessing just where he was in relation to his ostensible aims—to find the true killer of Arthur Trapping and the elusive Isobel Hastings. Chang knew he had pursued a dangerous tangent—perhaps trapped himself there. Then he thought of Angelique, perhaps on the other side of this door, involved he knew not how—but certainly without any protection he could trust. He turned the handle.

The heavy door swung open on silent well-oiled hinges, and Chang entered with all the noise of a ghost—and indeed, as he took in the spectacle before his eyes, the color drained from his face. He had entered a kind of ante-room, divided from a larger, vaulted chamber—whose high walls were lined with gleaming pipes, like a great organ, like a cathedral—which he saw through a large window of thick glass. The pipes ran together down to the floor and gathered under a stage-like platform upon which was a large table. On the table lay Angelique, quite naked, her head covered with an elaborate mask of metal and black rubber, her body a-swarm with black hoses and cables, an infernal, passive vision of St. Isobel's martyrdom. Standing on the platform next to her were several men, their heads covered with great helmets of brass and leather, with thick lenses for their eyes and odd inset boxes over the mouth and ears, all identifiable to Chang from their garments: a small man in grey, a crisp man in elegant black, a slender man who must be Bascombe, and a large man no longer in his fur, shirtsleeves rolled up, arms covered to his elbows by heavy leather gauntlets. They were all looking in his direction—not at him, but through the window at the delicate procedure taking place before Chang's eyes.

The ante-room was dominated by a wide stone trough of bubbling, steaming liquid, into which fed at least fifty of the slick black hoses, which were draped across nearly every inch of floor space. Suspended by chains above this hissing pool hung a dripping metal slab, obviously just retracted out of the trough. On the opposite side of the trough from Chang was a man in leather gloves, a heavy leather apron, and one of the strange helmets. He was awkwardly leaning forward and in his arms cradled a pulsing rectangular object, brilliantly opaque, the exact shape of a large book, only fabricated from dripping, steaming, gleaming, piercingly indigo blue glass. The glass book was perilously balanced on his open hands and forearms, as if it were too fragile or too dangerous to actually grip. With extreme concentration he had clearly just raised it from the roiling liquid and then taken it off the metal slab. Then the man looked up and saw Chang.

His concentration snapped. His balance shifted, and for an endless sickening moment Chang watched the glass book slide off the slick leather gauntlets. The man lurched, trying to correct the balance, but only sent it skidding uncontrolled in the other direction. He lurched again but it bobbled away from his grasp and dropped onto the edge of the stone trough, where it shattered in a cloud of sharp fragments. Chang saw the figures in the great chamber running toward the window. He saw the man reeling back, his clutching hands bristling with thin daggers of glowing glass. But mainly Chang was overwhelmed by the smell, the same smell he had known near the body of Arthur Trapping, now impossibly more intense. His eyes stung, his throat clenched, his knees sagged. Before him the man was screaming—the muffled shrieks echoed through the helmet. The others were quickly approaching the room. Chang could barely stand. He looked through the window at Angelique on the table, writhing as if the hoses were sucking out her life blood, and stumbled back, his hand over his mouth, his head swimming from the fumes, black spots floating up in front of his eyes. He ran for his life.

He clattered unheedingly through the litter of boxes, sucking in the cleaner air, shouts behind him, and tore his stick apart, readying each piece. He raced around the corridor, his legs pounding, his heart reeling from what he'd just seen, from abandoning Angelique—could he have freed her? Was she there willingly? What had he just *done*?—and charged straight at the guard, who had heard him coming and frantically dug for his pistol. The guard pulled the weapon free just as Chang reached him, swinging his stick at the barrel. The shot was knocked wide and then Chang's right hand was lancing forward. The man twisted desperately away and the blade caught on his right shoulder instead of his throat. The guard bellowed. Chang ripped the blade free and struck him across the face with the stick, knocking the man to his knees. He glanced behind—he could hear people charging through the boxes, and ran up the stairs. He was half-way up when a shot went off below—the guard trying with his left hand. The shot missed but would surely alert the man at the top, who would only have to slam the upper door to trap Chang completely. He pushed forward, his legs protesting—his head still dizzied from the fumes, his thoughts still on the table in the vaulted room, Angelique's thrashing masked face—gasping with effort. Another shot from below, another miss, and Chang had reached the top, charging into the courtyard, already swinging his arms in defense—but seeing no one. He stopped, stumbling, breathing hard, his eyes blind in the darkness.

He looked back to the door and located the guard... on the ground, face-down and still.

Before he could think—the Doctor?—two black shapes stepped from shadow, one of them slamming the door closed. Chang backed away onto the grass, and then wheeled at the sound of steps behind him. Two more shapes. He adjusted his angle of retreat away from both pairs, and then heard more steps—he was cut off again. He was surrounded in the dark by six men... all of whom seemed to be wearing black uniforms with silver facings. With a metallic ringing they each drew a saber. There was nothing he could do. Was Angelique dead? He didn't know—he didn't know anything. Chang abruptly sheathed his dagger into the body of his stick, and looked at the soldiers.

"Either you are going to kill me here or escort me to your Major." He pointed at the door. "But *they* will interrupt us any moment."

One of the soldiers stepped aside, making a gap in the circle, and gestured for him to walk that way—toward a large arch, the actual entrance to the courtyard. As Chang stepped forward the soldiers as a group extended their sabers toward him, and the one who had moved demanded, "Your weapon." Chang tossed his stick to him and walked on, half-expecting a blade in his back. Instead, they quickly marched him into the shadow of the archway and toward a black coach. The soldier with his stick sheathed his saber and drew a small pistol, which he held against Chang's neck. Once this was done, the others sheathed their blades as well, and set about their tasks—two climbed up to drive the coach, one opened the coach door and climbed in, turning to help Chang enter, two more ran to open the courtyard gates. The trooper with the pistol followed him in and closed the door behind. The three sat on the same side, Chang in the middle, the pistol tight against his ribs. Across and alone on the other side of the coach sat a hard man of middle age, his grey hair cropped short, his face without expression. He rapped his knuckled fist on the roof of the coach and they pulled forward.

"Major Black, how fortunate," said Chang. The Major ignored him, nodding to the man with the pistol, who handed across Chang's stick. The Major studied it, pulled it apart a few inches, sniffed disapprovingly and shot the pieces back together. He measured Chang with evident disdain, but did not speak. They rode in silence for several minutes, the hard muzzle of the pistol pressed unwaveringly against his side. Chang wondered what time it was—eight o'clock? Nine? Later? Usually he told time by his stomach, but his meals had lately been so arbitrary and sparse as to disrupt that normal sense. He had to assume that they were taking him to an isolated death. He made a point of yawning.

"That's an interesting badge," he said, nodding to the Major. "The wolf Skoll swallowing the sun—not exactly an uplifting image, a portent of Ragnarok—the final battle where the forces of order are doomed to fail, even the gods themselves. Unless you see yourself allied with chaos and evil, of course. Still, curious for a *regiment.* Almost whimsical—"

At a nod from the Major, the trooper on Chang's left drove his elbow deeply into Chang's kidney. Chang's breath caught in his throat, his entire body tensing with pain. He forced himself to smile, his voice choking with effort.

"And Miss Hastings—did you find her? Went to a shocking amount of trouble, didn't you—only to find out that all of your information about her was wrong. You don't have to tell *me,* I know just how you feel—*like a fool.*"

Another savage elbow. Chang could taste the bile in his throat. He'd have to be a little more direct if he wanted to avoid vomiting into his own lap. He forced another smile.

"Aren't you even the slightest bit curious about what I saw just now? Your men heard the shots—don't you want to know who was killed? I would expect it to change all sorts of things—balance of power, all that. Excuse me, may I? Handkerchief?"

The Major nodded, and Chang very slowly reached into his outside pocket. His hand was only just there when the man to his left slapped it away and reached into the pocket himself, pulled out the bloody handkerchief and passed it to Chang. Chang smiled his thanks and dabbed at his mouth. They had been traveling for some minutes. He had no idea in what direction. It was most probable that they would take him out to the country or down to the river, but that only meant they could be anywhere in between. He looked up. The Major was watching him closely.

"So," continued Chang. "Indeed. A struggle—shots—but the main point of interest being an *odor*—perhaps you have known it—strange, overpowering—and a noise, an excruciating buzzing noise, like a great mechanical hive, with the force of a steam engine. I'm sure you know all this. But what they were doing—what they had done, to that woman..." Chang's voice faltered for a moment, his momentum broken by the image of Angelique writhing beneath the mass of black hose, the men around her in leather masks—

"I do not care about the *whore,*" said Major Black in a thick Prussian accent, his voice as cold and hard as an iron spike. Chang looked up at him—already things had become easier—and coughed thickly into the handkerchief, wiping his mouth, muttering apologies, and as he spoke he casually stuffed the handkerchief into the *inside* pocket of his coat.

"So sorry—no, of course not, Major—you are concerned with the *Prince,* and with the *Minister,* the figures of *industry* and *finance*—all pieces in the great puzzle, yes? While, I beg your pardon, *I*—"

"You are no piece at all," the Major sneered.

"How kind of you to say," answered Chang, as he swept his hand from his pocket, flicking open the razor and laying it against the throat of the man with the pistol. In the moment of disorientation caused by the touch of cold steel, Chang closed the fingers of his other hand around the pistol and wrenched the aim away from him and toward the Major. The men in the coach froze. "If you move," Chang hissed, "this man dies, and the two of you must kill an angry man who holds a weapon that is very, *very* useful in tight spaces. Let *go* of the pistol."

The man desperately looked to Major Black, who nodded, his face furrowed by rage. Chang took the pistol, aimed it carefully at the Major's face, and pushed himself across the coach. He sat next to Black, placed the razor against his neck and then turned the pistol on the two troopers. No one moved. Chang nodded to the trooper nearest the door. "Open it." The trooper leaned forward and did so, the noise of the coach was abruptly louder, menacing, the dark street whipping past them. It was a paved road. They were still in the city—they must have been aiming for the river. Chang threw the pistol out of the coach and reached over for his stick. He knocked on the roof with the stick, and the coach began to slow. He glared at the two troopers and then turned to the Major. "I will tell you this. I have killed one of you already. I will kill all of you if I must. I do not appreciate your ways. Avoid me."

He launched himself through the door and tumbled into an awkward roll on the hard cobblestones. He pulled himself to his feet, stumbling ahead, and stuffed the razor into his coat. As he feared, the two troopers had leapt from the coach after him, along with one from the driver's seat. They had all drawn their sabers. He turned and ran, the bravado of a moment before vanished like any other hopeful bit of theatre.

Somehow, when he had fallen and rolled, his glasses had stayed on. The side pieces wrapped closely around his ears for that very reason, but he was still amazed that they were there. He was running on a block with gas lamps, so he could see *something,* but he had no idea where in the city he was, and so in that sense was running blind—and at top speed. He did not doubt that if they caught him they would cut him down—both that they would be able to do it, and that whatever plan they'd entertained of taking him away in the coach was quite fully abandoned. He rounded a corner and tripped on a broken stone, just managing to avoid sprawling on his face. Instead he careened full into a metal rail fence, grunted with the impact and drove himself forward, along the block. This was a residential street of row houses without coach traffic. He looked behind and saw the troopers gaining ground. He looked ahead and swore. The coach with Major Black had doubled back and was coming toward him on the street. He searched wildly about him and saw an alley looming to his left. He drove his legs to reach it before the coach, which was heading straight for him, the driver lashing his team for speed. Chang was close enough to see the horses rolling their white eyes when he darted into the dark passage, his foot slipping on the filthy brick, grateful that it was too narrow for the coach, which thundered past. For a moment he wondered about stopping, facing the troopers—perhaps one at a time. It was not narrow—or he yet stupidly desperate—enough for that. He ran on.

The alley separated two large houses, without any doors that he could see, or windows lower than the second story. With a sinking feeling he realized that if he were cut off at the other end, it would turn into another trap. His only immediate consolation came from knowing that the soldiers' boots were even less suited to this than his own, and even more prone to slipping on the slimy broken surface. He cleared the alley at a full run, saw no coach, and paused—his momentum carrying him well out into the street, lungs heaving—to grope for his bearings, for any sign or landmark he knew. He was in a part of the city where decent people *lived*—the last place he would know. Then, ahead of him, as sweetly welcome as a child's answered prayer, he saw that the next road began to slope down. The only downward slope in the city went toward the river, which at least told him where he was on the compass. He pushed himself after it—looking back to see the first trooper clearing the alley—for that almost certainly meant pushing himself into fog.

He raced down the street, careening a bit as the slope began to alter his balance. He could hear the troopers clattering after him, their determination positively Germanic. He wondered if Black and the Doctor were in league and if the soldiers were part of Karl-Horst von Maasmärck's retinue. Ragnarok was a Norse legend of destruction—it would have been adopted as a badge by only the harshest of regiments—and he could not immediately associate that with the intemperate insensible Prince. The Doctor he could understand—someone having personal charge of a Royal made a certain sense—but the Major? What interest of the Prince (or the Prince's father?) was served by killing Chang, or by hunting Isobel Hastings? Yet who else could he serve? How else could he be in a foreign country in such force? The first wisps of fog drifted over his feet as he ran. He inhaled the moist air in gulping lungfuls.

The road turned and Chang followed it. Ahead of him he saw a small plaza with a fountain and like a key turning open a lock he knew where he was—Worthing Circle. To the right was the river itself, to the left the Circus Garden, and straight ahead the merchants' district and beyond it the Ministries. There were people here—Worthing Circle was a place of some nefarious business after nightfall—and he veered to the right, for the river and the thicker fog. It was nearly his death. The coach was there in wait. With a whip crack the horses leapt forth, charging directly at him. Chang threw himself to the side, clawing his way clear. He was cut off from the river, and from the merchants—he scrambled to his knees as the coachman wrestled with the horses, trying to make them turn. Chang reached his feet and heard a shot whistle past his head. Black leaned out of the coach window with a smoking pistol. Chang cut across the plaza just ahead of the three troopers, once more right on his heels, and toward the Circus Garden into the heart of the city.

His legs were on fire—he had no idea how far he'd run, but he had to do something or he was going to die. He saw another alley and barreled into it. Once in he stopped and threw himself against the wall, pulling apart his stick. If he could take the first of them by surprise—but before he'd even finished the thought the first trooper charged around the corner, saw Chang, and raised his saber in defense. Chang slashed at his head with the stick, which the man parried, and then lunged with the dagger—but he was too slow and off target. The blade ripped along the man's front, cutting his uniform, but missing its mark. The trooper seized Chang's dagger arm around the wrist. The other troopers were right behind—a matter of seconds before someone ran him through. With a desperate snarl, Chang kicked at the man's knee and felt a horrible snap as it gave. The man shrieked and fell into the legs of the trooper behind. Chang wrenched his arm clear and stumbled back, his heart sinking as the third man hurtled past his struggling comrades, saber extended. Chang continued to retreat. The trooper lunged at him—Chang beat the weapon aside with the stick and stabbed with the dagger, his reach nowhere near the trooper. The trooper lunged again—again Chang beat it aside—and then followed with a sweeping cut at Chang's head. Chang raised the stick—it was all he could do—and saw it splintered to pieces. He dropped the broken fragment and ran.

As Chang careened away through the alley he told himself that in the loss of his stick he had divested himself of one trooper, but a dagger against a saber was no fight at all. Ahead of him he saw the alley's ending, and a knot of people in silhouette. He screamed at them, an inarticulate howl of menace, which had the desirable effect of making them turn and then scatter—but not quickly enough. Chang cannoned into the rearmost figure—a man who, as Chang actually took in the group of people, must have been in negotiation with one of the fleeing women—and seized the back of his collar. He twisted the man behind him and with a brutal thrust sent him directly into the nearest pursuing trooper. The soldier instinctively did his best not to run the fellow through, raising the saber out of the way and clubbing at him with his other arm, but Chang had turned as well, advancing behind his impromptu shield. The moment the bystander was knocked aside Chang's way was clear and he drove his dagger into the trooper's chest. Without looking back he pulled it free and wheeled, running again. He heard the women's screams behind him.

Was the third trooper still coming? Chang glanced over his shoulder. He was. Cursing all military discipline, Chang dodged across the road into another narrow alley—the last thing he wanted to see again was the coach.

He'd lost track of his exact location—nearer to the Circus, at least. This alley was cluttered with boxes and barrels, and as he ran he passed more than one doorway. The third trooper was lagging behind, if still determined. Momentarily out of his sight, Chang dashed up the next block in a low crouch until he found what he wanted, a sunken shop front whose entrance was below the street. Chang vaulted the handrail and went to his knees as he landed at the foot of a small set of stairs, dropping his head and doing his best to stifle his heaving breath. He waited. The street was dark and drifting with fog and generally empty—if he had been seen, it was still possible no one would point him out to the soldier. He was sheathed in sweat—he couldn't remember when he'd run as far, or last been in such an idiotic fix. Why had he thrown away the pistol? If it was going to come to murder, why hadn't he shot them all in the coach? He waited. Unable to bear it further, he inched up the steps and peeked into the road. The trooper stood in the street, his saber out, looking up and down the road. He too was unsteady on his feet—Chang could hear the man's ragged breathing and see it clouding in the cool night air—and clearly unaware which direction Chang had fled, taking a few steps one way, craning his head, and then walking back the other. Chang narrowed his eyes, his desperation simmering down closer to cold fury. He quietly transferred the dagger to his left hand, and fished out the razor with his right, flicking it open. The trooper still had his back to him, and stood perhaps fifteen yards away. If he could get up to the street in silence, he was sure that, at a dead run, he would cover half the distance before the man heard . . . another few yards while he turned . . . the final gap as the man raised his blade. The trooper would have one blow, and if Chang could avoid it, it would be over.

And if he didn't avoid it . . . well, it would be over either way—*"in each instant tenderness, and ash"*, to quote Blaine's *Jocasta*. He paused, balancing the outrage of being hunted like an animal through his own streets by a gang of foreign louts against patience and sanity . . . and then shifted his feet on the stairs, preparing to charge (he *had* promised to kill them). Suddenly he threw himself down into cover. A coach clattered near...and then stopped next to the trooper. Chang waited, listening. He heard the harsh interrogation from the Major, in German, then silence, and then a moment later the sweet metallic rush of the trooper sheathing his blade. Chang looked up in time to see the trooper hoisting himself onto the driver's bench, and the coach pulling away into the fog. He looked down at his hands and relaxed his grip on his weapons. His fingers ached. His legs ached, and his head was throbbing behind his eyes. He folded the razor into his pocket and tucked the dagger into his belt. He mopped his face with his bloody handkerchief—already the sweat on his neck and back was turning cold. He remembered dully that he had no place to sleep.

Chang crossed the road and entered the next alley, looking purposefully for the proper point of entry. He was between a pair of large buildings he didn't recognize in the dark, but knew this was a district of hotels and offices and shops. He located a first-story window near enough to a stack of barrels and climbed on top of them. The window was in reach. He wedged the dagger under the sill and twisted it, popping the window up, and then opened it the rest of the way with his hands. He stuck the dagger back into his belt and with an embarrassing amount of effort—his entire body wavering in the air as his arms nearly failed him—pulled himself through. He crawled gracelessly onto the floor of a dark room, and pulled the window closed. He groped around him. It was a supply room—shelves stacked with candles, towels, soaps, linen. He managed to find the door and open it.

As Chang walked down the carpeted hallway, paneled with polished wood and aglow with welcoming, warm gaslight, he found his mind chopping the figures of his day into factions. On one side there was Crabbé and the man in fur, who were responsible for the strange burns, so with them he placed Trapping, Mrs. Marchmoor, and Prince Karl-Horst. On the other was Major Black...perhaps with Karl-Horst's Doctor. Scattered between them were far too many others—Vandaariff, Xonck, Aspiche, Rosamonde...and of course, Isobel Hastings. The list always ended with her, the one person about whom he'd never seemed to learn a thing.

The hallway led him into the hushed silence of a lovely vaulted room, decorated with potted palms and walls of plate mirror, with a wide wooden reception desk and a man in a frogged coat behind it. He had broken into a hotel. Chang nodded briskly at the man and reached into his coat for the wallet. Over the day he'd managed to spend nearly everything Aspiche had given him, and this would take the rest of it. He didn't care. He could sleep, have a bath, a proper shave, a meal, and be fresh for the day to come. Tomorrow he could always fetch the saber in the attic and sell it for cash. This made him smile as he reached the desk, dropping the wallet onto the inlaid marble surface.

The desk clerk smiled. "Good evening, Sir."

"I hope it's not too late."

The clerk's eyes flicked to the wallet. "Of course not, Sir. Welcome to the Hotel Boniface."

"Thank you," answered Chang. "I should like a room."

THREE

Surgeon

Doctor Abelard Svenson stood at an open window overlooking the small courtyard of the Macklenburg diplomatic compound, gazing at the thickening fog and the few sickly gaseous lights of the city bright enough to penetrate its fell curtain. He sucked on a hard ginger candy, clacking it against his teeth, aware that a lengthy brood about his current situation was a luxury he could not indulge. With a shove from his tongue he pushed the candy between his left molars and smashed it to sharp pieces, smashed these pieces again, and then swallowed them. He turned from the window and reached for a porcelain cup of tepid black coffee, gulping it, finding a certain pleasure in the mix of sweet ginger syrup coating his mouth and the bitter beverage. Did they drink coffee with ginger in India, he wondered, or Siam? He finished the cup, set it down and dug for a cigarette. He looked over his shoulder at the bed, and the still figure upon it. He sighed, opened his cigarette case, stuck one of the dark, foul Russian cigarettes in his mouth, and took a match from the bureau near the lamp, striking it off of his thumbnail. He lit the cigarette, inhaled, felt the telltale catch in his lungs, shook out the match, and exhaled longingly. He couldn't put it off anymore. He would have to speak to Flaüss.

He crossed the room to the bolted door, skirting the bed, and—sticking the cigarette into his mouth to free both hands to pull the iron bolt clear—glanced back at the pale young man breathing moistly underneath the woolen blankets. Karl-Horst von Maasmärck was twenty-three, though pervasive indulgence and a weak constitution had added ten years to his appearance. His honey-colored curls receded from his forehead (the thinness especially visible with the hair so clumped together by sweat), his pallid skin sagged below his eyes and around his family's weak mouth and sunken jaw, and his teeth were already beginning to go. Svenson stepped over to the insensible man—overgrown boy, really—and felt the pulse at his jugular, antic despite the laudanum, and once more cursed his own failure. The strange looping pattern seared into the Prince's skin around the eyes and across his temples—not quite a burn, not exactly even raw, more of a deep discoloration and with luck temporary—mocked Doctor Svenson's every previous effort to control his willful charge.

As he looked down, he resisted the impulse to grind the cigarette into the Prince's skin and chided himself for his own mistaken tactics, his foolish trust, his ill-afforded deference. He'd focused on the Prince himself and paid far too little attention to those new figures around him—the woman's family, the diplomats, the soldiers, the high-placed hangers-on—never thinking he'd be tearing the Prince away from them at pistol-point. He barely even knew who they were—far less what part in their plans had been laid aside for the easily dazzled Karl-Horst. All that had been the business of Flaüss, the Envoy—which had either gone horribly wrong or . . . hadn't. Svenson needed to report to Flaüss on the Prince's health, but he knew that he must use the interview with the Envoy to determine whether he was truly without allies in the diplomatic compound. He noticed his overcoat slung across the bedpost and folded it over his arm—heavier than it ought to be from the pistol tucked into the pocket. He looked around the room—nothing particularly dangerous should the Prince wake up in his absence. He pulled the bolt on the door and stepped into the hall. Next to the door stood a soldier in black, carbine at his side, stiffly at attention. Doctor Svenson locked the door with a large iron key and returned the key to his jacket pocket. The soldier's attention did not waver as the Doctor walked past and down the hallway, nor did the Doctor think twice about the guard. He was used enough to these soldiers and their iron discipline—any question he had would be aimed at their officer, who was unaccountably still absent from the compound.

Svenson reached the end of the hall and stood on the landing, his gaze edging over the rail to the lobby three floors below. From above he could see the black and white checkerboard pattern of the marble floor—an optical illusion of staircases impossibly leading ever upwards and downwards to one another at the same time—with the crystal chandelier hovering above it. For Svenson, who did not like heights, just seeing the chandelier's heavy chain suspended in the air before him gave him a whiff of vertigo. Looking up to the high top of the stairwell, where the chain was anchored above the fourth floor landing—which he could not help but do, like an ass—made him palpably dizzy. He stepped away from the rail and climbed to the third floor, walking close to the wall, his eyes on the floor. He was still staring at his feet as he walked past the guards at the landing and outside the Envoy's door. With a quick grimace he squared his shoulders and knocked. Without waiting for an answer, he went in.

When Svenson had returned from the Institute with the Prince, Flaüss had not been present—nor could anyone say where he'd gone. The Envoy had burst into the Prince's room some forty minutes later—in the midst of the Doctor's squalid efforts to purge his patient of any poison or narcotic—and imperiously demanded what Doctor Svenson thought he was doing. Before he could reply, Flaüss had seen the revolver on the side table and then the marks on Karl-Horst's face and began screaming. Svenson turned to see the Envoy's face was white—with rage or fear he wasn't sure—but the sight had snapped the last of his patience and he'd savagely driven Flaüss from the room. Now, as he entered the office, he was keenly aware that of Conrad Flaüss he actually knew precious little. A provincial aristocrat with pretensions toward the cosmopolitan, schooled for the law, an acquaintance of a royal uncle at university—all the qualifications required to meet the diplomatic needs of the Prince's betrothal visit, and if a permanent embassy were to result from the marriage, as everyone hoped it would, to take over as the Duchy's first full ambassador. To Flaüss—to everyone—Svenson was a family retainer, a nurse-maid, essentially dismissible. Such perceptions generally suited the Doctor as well, creating that much less bother in his day. Now, however, he would be forced to make himself heard.

Flaüss was behind his desk, writing, an aide standing patiently next to him, and looked up as Svenson entered. The Doctor ignored him and sat in one of the plush chairs opposite the desk, plucking a green glass ashtray from a side table as he went past and cradling it on his lap as he smoked. Flaüss stared at him. Svenson stared back and flicked his eyes toward the aide. Flaüss snorted, scrawled his name at the base of the page, blotted it, and shoved it into the aide's hands. "That will be all," he barked. The aide clicked his heels smartly and left the room, casting a discreet glance at the Doctor. The door closed softly behind him. The two men glared at each other. Svenson saw the Envoy gathering himself to speak, and sighed in advance with fatigue.

"Doctor Svenson, I will tell you that I am not... *accustomed*... to such treatment, such *brutal* treatment, by a member of the mission staff. As the mission *Envoy*—"

"I am not part of the mission staff," said Svenson, cutting him off in an even tone.

Flaüss sputtered. "I beg your pardon?"

"I am not *part* of the mission staff. I am part of the Prince's household. I answer to that house."

"To the Prince?" Flaüss scoffed. "Between us, Doctor, the poor young man—"

"To the Duke."

"I beg your pardon—*I* am the Duke's Envoy. I answer to the Duke."

"Then we have something in common after all," Svenson muttered dryly.

"Are you *insolent*?" Flaüss hissed.

Svenson didn't answer for a moment, in order to increase what powers of intimidation he could muster. The fact was, whatever authority he claimed, he had no strength beyond his own body to back it up—all that rested with Flaüss and Blach. If either were truly against him—and realized his weakness—he was extremely vulnerable. His only real hope was that they were not outright villains, but merely incompetent. He met the Envoy's gaze and tapped his ash into the glass bowl.

"Do you know, Herr Flaüss, why a young man in the prime of his life would need a doctor to accompany him to celebrate his engagement?"

Flaüss snorted. "Of course I know. The Prince is unreliable and indulgent—I speak as one who cares for him deeply—and often unable to see the larger *diplomatic* implications of his actions. I believe it is a common condition among—"

"Where were you this evening?"

The Envoy's mouth snapped shut, then worked for a moment in silence. He could not believe what he had just heard. He forced a wicked, condescending smile. "I beg your pardon—"

"The Prince was in grave danger. You were not here. You were not in any position to protect him."

"Yes, and you will report to *me* concerning Karl-Horst's *medical* condition—his—his face—the strange *burns*—"

"You have not answered my question . . . but you are going to."

Flaüss gaped at him.

"I am here on the direct instructions of his father," continued Svenson. "If we fail further in our duties—and I do include you in this, Herr Flaüss—we will be held most strictly accountable. I have served the Duke directly for some years, and understand what that means. Do you?"

Doctor Svenson was more or less lying. The Prince's father, the Duke, was an obese feather-headed man fixated on military uniforms and hunting. Doctor Svenson had met him twice at court, observing what he could with a general sense of dismay. His instructions truly came from the Duke's Chief Minister, Baron von Hoern, who had become acquainted with the Doctor five years before, when Svenson was an officer-surgeon of the Macklenburg Navy and known primarily—if he was known at all—for treating the effects of frostbite among sailors of the Baltic fleet. A series of murders in port had caused a scandal—a cousin of Karl-Horst had been responsible—and Svenson had shown both acuity in tracing the deeds to their source and then tact in conveying this information to the Minister. Soon after he had been reassigned to von Hoern's household and asked to observe or investigate various circumstances—diseases, pregnancy, murder, abortion—as they might arise at court, always without any reference to his master's interest. To Svenson, for whom the sea was almost wholly associated with sorrow and exile, the opportunity to devote himself to such work—indeed, to the rigorous distractions of patriotism—had become a welcome sort of self-annihilation.

His presence in Karl-Horst's party had been attributed to the Duke easily enough, and Svenson had until this day remained in the background, reporting back as he could through cryptic letters stuffed into the diplomatic mail and from subtly insinuating cards sent through the city post, just in case his official letters were tampered with. He had done this before—brief sojourns in Finland, Denmark, and along the Rhine—but was really no kind of spy, merely an educated man likely, because of his position, both to gain access where he ought not and to be underestimated by those he observed. Such was the case here, and the tennis match of pettiness between Flaüss and Blach had livened what otherwise seemed to be trivial child-minding. What troubled him, however, was that in the three weeks since their arrival—and despite regular dispatches to Flaüss from court—Svenson had received no word whatsoever in return. It was as if Baron von Hoern had disappeared.

The idea of marriage had been considered after a continental tour by Lord Vandaariff, where the search for a sympathetic Baltic port had brought him to Macklenburg. His daughter had been a part of the entourage—her first time abroad—and as is so often the case when elders speak business, the children had been thrown together. Svenson had no illusions that any woman smitten to any degree by Karl-Horst retained her innocence—unless she was blindingly stupid or blindingly ugly—but he still could not understand the match. Lydia Vandaariff was certainly pretty, she was extremely wealthy, her father had just been given a title—though his financial empire spanned well beyond the borders of mere nations. Karl-Horst was but one of many such princelings in search of a larger fortune, growing less attractive by the day and never anyone's idea of a wit. The unlikely nature of it all made actual love a more real possibility, he had to admit—and he had dismissed this part of the affair with a shrug, a foolish mistake, for his attention had been set on preventing Karl-Horst from misbehaving. He now saw that his enemies were elsewhere.

In the first week he had indeed tended to the Prince's excessive drinking, his excessive eating, his gambling, his whoring, intervening on occasion but more generally tending to him once he had returned from each night's pursuit of pleasure. When the Prince's time had gradually become less occupied with the brothel and the gaming table—at dinners with Lydia, diplomatic salons with Flaüss and people from the Foreign Ministry, riding with foreign soldiers, shooting with his future father-in-law—Svenson had allowed himself to pass more time with his reading, with music, with his own small jaunts of tourism, content with looking in on the Prince when he returned in the evenings. He had suddenly realized his folly at the engagement party—could it be only last night?—when he'd found the Prince alone in Vandaariff's great garden, kneeling over the disfigured body of Colonel Trapping. At first he'd no idea what the Prince was doing—Karl-Horst on his knees usually meant Svenson digging out a moist cloth to wipe away the vomit. Instead, the Prince had been staring down, quite transfixed, his eyes strangely placid, even peaceful. Svenson had pulled him away and back into the house, despite the idiot's protests. He'd been able to find Flaüss—now he wondered how coincidentally nearby the Envoy was—gave the Prince over to his care and rushed back to the body. He found a crowd around it—Harald Crabbé, the Comte d'Orkancz, Francis Xonck, others he didn't know, and finally Robert Vandaariff himself arriving with a crowd of servants. He noticed Svenson and took him aside, questioning him in a low voice, rapidly, about the safety of the Prince, and his condition. When Svenson informed him that the Prince was perfectly well, Vandaariff had sighed with evident relief and wondered if Svenson might be so kind as to inform his daughter—she had guessed some awkward event had happened, but not its exact nature—that the Prince was unscathed and, if it were possible, allow her to see him. Svenson of course obliged the great man, but found Lydia Vandaariff in the company of Arthur Trapping's wife, Charlotte Xonck, and the woman's older brother, Henry Xonck, a man whose wealth and influence were surpassed only by Vandaariff and—perhaps, Svenson was dubious—the aging Queen. As Svenson stood stammering out some sort of veiled explanation—an incident in the garden, the Prince's lack of involvement, no clear explanation—both Xonck siblings began questioning him, openly competing with each other to expose his obvious avoidance of some truth. Svenson fell by habit into the pose of a foreigner who only poorly understood their language, requiring them to repeat as he fruitlessly strove for some story that might satisfy their strangely suspicious reaction, but this only increased their irritation. Henry Xonck had just imperiously stabbed Svenson's chest with his forefinger when a modestly dressed woman standing behind them—whom he had assumed to be a companion of the mutely smiling Lydia—leaned forward to whisper into Charlotte Xonck's ear. At once the heiress looked past Svenson's shoulder, her eyes widening—through her feathered mask—with a sudden glare of dislike. Svenson turned to see the Prince himself, escorted by the smiling Francis Xonck, who ignored his siblings and called gaily for Lydia to rejoin her intended.

The Doctor took this moment to quickly bow to his betters and escape, allowing himself one brief glance at the Prince to gauge his level of intoxication, and another for the woman who had whispered in Charlotte Xonck's ear, who he saw was now studying Francis Xonck rather closely. It was only upon walking from their parlor that Svenson realized that he'd been deftly prevented from examining the body. By the time he returned to the garden, the men and the body were gone. All he saw, from a distance, were three of Major Blach's soldiers, spaced several yards apart, walking across the grounds with their sabers drawn.

He'd been unable to interrogate the Prince further, and neither Flaüss nor Blach would answer his questions. They'd heard nothing of Trapping, and indeed openly doubted that such an important figure—or indeed, anyone—had been dead in the garden at all. When he demanded in turn to know why Blach's soldiers had been searching the grounds, the Major merely snapped that he was responding prudently to Svenson's own exaggerated claims of danger, murder, mystery, and sneered that he would hardly waste time with the Doctor's fears again. For his part, Flaüss had dropped the matter completely, saying that even if anything untoward had occurred, it was hardly their affair—out of respect to the Prince's new father-in-law, they must remain disinterested and apart. Svenson had no answer to either (save a silent growing contempt) but wanted very much to know what the Prince had been doing alone with the body in the first place.

But time alone with Karl-Horst had not been possible. Between the Prince's schedule, as arranged by Flaüss, and the Prince's own wish to remain undisturbed, he had managed to keep clear of Svenson all the next morning, and then to leave the compound with the Envoy and Blach while Svenson was tending to the suppurated tooth of one of Blach's soldiers. When they had not returned by nightfall, he had been forced into the city to find them. . . .

He exhaled and looked up at Flaüss, whose hands were tightened into fists above his desk top. "We have spoken of the vanished Colonel Trapping—" he began. Flaüss snorted, but Svenson ignored him and kept on, "of whom you will believe what you want. What you cannot avoid is that tonight your Prince has been attacked. What I am going to tell you is that I have seen the marks on his face before—on the face of that missing man."

"Indeed? You said yourself you did not examine him—"

"I saw his face."

Flaüss was silent. He picked up his pen, then peevishly threw it down. "Even if what you claim is true—in the garden, in the dark, from a distance . . ."

"Where were you, Herr Flaüss?"

"It is none of your affair."

"You were with Robert Vandaariff."

Flaüss smiled primly. "If I was, I could hardly tell you about it. As you imply, there is a delicacy about the whole affair—the need to preserve the reputation of the Prince, of the engagement, of the principals involved. *Lord* Vandaariff has been kind enough to make time to discuss possible *strategies*—"

"Is he paying you?"

"I will not answer insolence—"

"I will no longer suffer idiocy."

Flaüss opened his mouth to reply but said nothing, affronted into silence. Svenson was worried he'd gone too far. Flaüss dug out a handkerchief and mopped his forehead.

"Doctor Svenson—you are a military man, I do forget it, and your way is to be frank. I will overlook your tone this time, for we must indeed *depend* upon one another to protect our Prince. For all your questions, I confess I am most curious to know how *you* came to find the Prince tonight, and how you came to 'rescue' him—and from whom."

Svenson pulled the monocle from his left eye and held it up to the light. He frowned, brought it near his mouth and breathed on it until the surface fogged. He rubbed the moisture off on his sleeve and replaced it, peering at Flaüss with undisguised dislike.

"I'm afraid I must get back to my patient."

Flaüss snapped to his feet behind the desk. Svenson had not yet moved from the chair.

"I have decided," declared the Envoy, "that from now on the Prince will be accompanied by an armed guard at all times."

"An excellent suggestion. Has Blach agreed to this?"

"He agreed it was an excellent suggestion."

Svenson shook his head. "The Prince will never accept it."

"The Prince will have no choice—nor will you, Doctor. Whatever claim to care for the Prince you may have had before this, your failure to prevent this evening's incident has convinced both myself and Major Blach that *he* will from this point be managing the Prince's needs. Any medical matters will be attended to in the company of Major Blach or his men."

Flaüss swallowed and extended his hand. "I will require that you give me the key to the Prince's room. I know you have locked it. As Envoy, I will have it from you."

Svenson stood carefully, replacing the ashtray on the table, not moving his gaze from Flaüss, and walked to the door. Flaüss stood, his hand still open. Svenson opened the door and walked into the hallway. Behind he heard rushing steps and then Flaüss was beside him, his face red, his jaw working.

"This will not do. I have given an order."

"Where is Major Blach?" asked Svenson.

"Major Blach is under my command," answered Flaüss.

"You consistently refuse to answer my questions."

"That is my privilege!"

"You are quite in error," Svenson said gravely and looked at the Envoy. He saw that instead of any fear or reproach, Flaüss was smirking with ill-concealed triumph.

"You have been distracted, Doctor Svenson. Things have changed. So many, many things have changed."

Svenson turned to Flaüss and shifted his grip on his coat, slinging it from his right arm to his left, which had the effect of moving the pocket with the pistol-butt sticking out of it into the Envoy's view. Flaüss's face whitened and he took a step back, sputtering. "W-when M-Major Blach returns—"

"I will be happy to see him," Svenson said.

He was certain that Baron von Hoern was dead.

He walked back to the landing and turned to the stairs, startled to see Major Blach leaning against the wall, just out of sight from the corridor. Svenson stopped.

"You heard? The Envoy would like to see you."

Major Blach shrugged. "It is of no importance."

"You've been told of the Prince's condition?"

"That is of course serious, yet I require your services elsewhere immediately." Without waiting for an answer he walked down the stairs. Svenson followed, intimidated as always by the Major's haughty manner, but also curious as to what might be more important than the Prince's *crise.*

Blach led him across the courtyard to the mess room in the soldiers' barracks. Three of the large white tables had been cleared, and on each lay a black-uniformed soldier, with another two soldiers standing at each table's head. The first two soldiers were alive; the third's upper body was covered by a white cloth. Blach indicated the tables and stepped to the side, saying no more. Svenson draped his coat over a chair and saw that his medical kit had already been fetched and laid out on a metal tray. He glanced at the first man, grimacing in pain, his left leg probably broken, and absently prepared an injection of morphine. The other man was in more serious distress, bleeding from his chest, his breath shallow, his face like wax. Svenson opened the man's uniform coat and peeled back the bloody shirt beneath. A narrow puncture through the ribs—perhaps through the lungs, perhaps not. He turned to Blach.

"How long ago did this happen?"

"Perhaps an hour . . . perhaps more."

"He may die from the delay," observed Svenson. He turned to the soldiers. "Bind him to the table." As they did, he went to the man with the injured leg, pulled up his sleeve, and gave him the injection. He spoke softly as he pushed on the syringe. "You will be fine. We will do our best to straighten your leg—but you must wait until we work on your fellow. This will make you sleep." The soldier, a boy really, nodded, his face slick with sweat. Svenson gave him a quick smile and turned back to Blach, speaking as he peeled off his jacket and rolled up his shirtsleeves. "It's very simple. If the blade touched his lungs, they're full of blood by now and he'll be dead in minutes. If it didn't, he may die in any case—from the blood loss, from rot. I will do my best. Where will I find you?"

"I will remain here," Major Blach answered.

"Very well."

Svenson glanced over to the third table.

"My Lieutenant," said Major Blach. "He has been dead for some hours."

Svenson stood in the open doorway, smoking a cigarette and looking out into the courtyard. He wiped his hands with a rag. It had taken two hours. The man was still alive—apparently the lungs had been spared—though there was fever. If he lasted the night he would recover. The other man's knee had been broken. While he had done what he could, it was unlikely the man would walk without a limp. Throughout his work, Major Blach had remained silent. Svenson inhaled the last of the cigarette and tossed the butt into the gravel. The two men had been moved to the barracks—they could at least sleep in their own beds. The Major leaned against a table, near the remaining body. Svenson let the smoke out of his lungs and turned back into the room.

For all the savage nature of the Lieutenant's wounds, it was obvious the death had been quick. Svenson looked up at the Major. "I'm not sure what I can tell you that you cannot see yourself. Four punctures—the first, I would say, here: into the ribs from the victim's left side, a stabbing across . . . it would have been painful, but not a mortal blow. The next three, within an inch of each other, driving under the ribs and into the lungs, perhaps even touching the heart—I cannot say without opening the chest. Heavy blows—you can see the force of impact around the wound, the indentation—a knife or dagger driven to the hilt, repeatedly, to kill."

Blach nodded. Svenson waited for him to speak, but the Major remained silent. Svenson sighed and began to unroll and button his sleeves. "Do you wish to tell me how these injuries occurred?"

"I do not," muttered the Major.

"Very well. Will you at least tell me if it had to do with the attack on the Prince?"

"What attack?"

"Prince Karl-Horst was burned about the face. It is entirely possible he was a willing participant, nevertheless, I consider it an attack."

"This is when you escorted him home?"

"Exactly."

"I assumed he was drunk."

"He was drunk, though not, I believe, from alcohol. But what do you mean, you 'assumed'?"

"You were observed, Doctor."

"Indeed."

"We observe many people."

"But apparently not the Prince."

"Was he not with reputable figures of his new acquaintance?"

"Yes, Major, he was. And—I'll say this again if you did not understand it—in such company, indeed, at the behest of such company, he was scarred about the eyes."

"So you have said, Doctor."

"You may see for yourself."

"I look forward to it."

Svenson gathered his medical kit together. He looked up. Major Blach was still watching him. Svenson dropped his catling into the bag with an exasperated sigh. "How many men do you presently have under your command, Major?"

"Twenty men and two officers."

"Now you have eighteen men and one officer. And I assure you that whoever did this—whatever man or gang of men—had nothing to do with observing me, for my business was entirely occupied with preventing an idiot from disgracing himself."

Major Blach did not answer.

Doctor Svenson snapped his bag shut and scooped his coat from the chair. "I can only hope you observed the Envoy as well, Major—he was quite absent through all of this, and refuses to explain himself." He turned on his heels and strode to the door where he turned and called back, "Will you be telling him about the bodies or shall I?"

"We are not finished, Doctor," hissed Blach. He flipped the sheet back over his Lieutenant's face and walked toward Svenson. "I believe we must visit the Prince."

They walked up the stairs to the third floor, where they found Flaüss waiting with two guards. The Envoy and the Major exchanged meaningful looks, but Svenson had no idea what they meant—the men obviously hated each other, but could nevertheless be cooperating for any number of reasons. Flaüss sneered at Svenson and indicated the door.

"Doctor? I believe you have the key."

"Have you tried knocking?" This was from Blach, and Svenson suppressed a smile.

"Of course I have tried," answered Flaüss, unconvincingly, "but I am happy to try again." He turned and banged savagely on the door with the heel of his fist, after a moment calling sweetly, "Your Highness? Prince Karl-Horst? It is Herr Flaüss, here with the Major and Doctor Svenson."

They waited. Flaüss turned to Svenson and nearly spit, "Open it! I insist you open it at once!"

Svenson smiled affably and dug the key from his pocket. He handed it to Flaüss. "You may do it yourself, Herr Envoy."

Flaüss snatched the key and shoved it into the lock. He turned the key and the handle, but the door would not open. He turned the handle again and shoved the door with his shoulder. He turned back to them. "It will not open—something is against it."

Major Blach stepped forward and jostled Flaüss away, placing his hand over the handle and driving his weight against the door. It gave perhaps half an inch. Blach signaled to the two troopers and together all three pushed as one—the door lurched another inch or so, and then slowly ground open enough for them to see that the large bureau had been moved against the door. The three pushed again and the gap widened so a man could fit through. Blach immediately did so, followed by Flaüss, shoving his way past the troopers. With a resigned smile, Svenson followed them through, dragging his medical kit after him.

The Prince was gone. The bureau had been dragged across the room to block the doorway, and the window was open.

"He's escaped! For a second time!" Flaüss whispered. He wheeled upon Svenson. "You helped him! You had the key!"

"Don't be an idiot," muttered Major Blach. "Look at the room. The bureau is solid mahogany—it took the three of us to shift it. It's impossible that the Prince himself moved it alone and impossible for the Doctor to have helped him—the Doctor would have had to leave the room *before* the bureau was blocking the doorway."

Flaüss was silent. Svenson met the gaze of Blach, who was glaring at him. The Major barked out to the men in the hall, "One of you to the gate—find out if the Prince has left the compound, and if he was alone!"

Svenson stepped to the bureau and opened it up, glancing at the contents. "The Prince is wearing his infantry uniform—I do not see it—dark green, a colonel of grenadiers. He fancies it because the badge is of a flaming bomb. I believe it has a sexual significance for him." They stared at him as if he were speaking French. Svenson stepped to the window and leaned out. Below the window, three stories down, was a raked bed of gravel. "Major Blach, if you'll send a trusted man to examine the gravel below this window—it will tell us whether a ladder was used—there will be heavy indentations. Of course, a three-story ladder should have attracted attention. Tell me, Herr Flaüss, does the compound possess such a ladder?"

"How should I know?"

"By asking the *staff*, I expect."

"And if there is no such ladder?" asked Major Blach.

"Then either one was brought—which should have excited notice at the gate—or some other means were used—a grappling hook. Of course"—he stepped back and examined the plaster around the window frame—"I see no identations, nor any rope remaining by which they may have climbed down."

"Then how *did* they get down?" asked Flaüss. Svenson stepped back to the window, leaning out. There was no balcony, no wall of ivy, no nearby tree—indeed, the room had been chosen for this very reason. He turned and looked upwards—it was but two stories to the roof.

As they climbed the stairwell word came to Blach from the gate—the Prince had not been seen, nor had anyone passed in either direction in the last three hours, since the arrival of the Major. Svenson barely took in the trooper's report, so much was he dreading the inevitable trip to the building's rooftop. He walked on the inside wall, clutching the rail as casually as possible, his guts positively seething. Ahead of them another trooper was unfolding a staircase from the ceiling of the sixth-floor hallway. Above it was a narrow attic and within the attic a hatchway to the roof. Major Blach strode forward—somewhere a pistol had appeared in his hand—and climbed rapidly, disappearing in the darkness above, followed quickly by Flaüss, more nimble than his stout frame would suggest. Svenson swallowed and climbed deliberately after them, one hand gripping each side of the ladder, choking a heave of nausea as the hinges of the ladder bounced with the shifting weight of each footfall. Feeling like a child, he crawled on his hands and knees onto the rough timbers of the attic floor and looked around him. Flaüss was just pulling himself through the narrow hatchway, his body framed against the sickly glow of the city lights within the fog. With a barely suppressed groan, Doctor Svenson forced himself after them.

When he reached the roof, first on his knees and then, swaying, onto his feet, he saw Major Blach crouching near the edge that must be above the Prince's bedroom. The Major turned back and called, "The moss on the stone is worn away in several places—the rubbing of a rope or a rope ladder!" He stood and crossed to Flaüss and Svenson, looking around them as he did. He pointed to the nearby rooftops. "What I don't understand is that none of these seem close enough. I don't deny the Prince was pulled to the rooftop—but this building rises at least a story above any neighbor. Beyond this, it is a full street's width in distance in every direction. Unless they employed a circus, I do not see how anyone might have traversed from this rooftop to escape."

"Perhaps they didn't," suggested the Envoy. "Perhaps they merely re-entered the building from above."

"Impossible. The stair to the attic is bolted from inside."

"Unless someone helped them," offered the Envoy, slightly peevishly, "from inside."

"Indeed," admitted Blach. "In which case, they have still not passed through the gate. My men will search the entire compound at once. Doctor?"

"Mmn?"

"Any *thoughts*?"

Svenson swallowed, and inhaled the cool night air through his nose, trying to relax. He forced his gaze away from the sky and the open spaces around him, down to the black tarred surface of the roof. "Only . . . what is that?" he asked.

Flaüss followed his pointing finger and stepped to a small white object. He picked it up and brought his find over to the others.

"That is the butt of a cigarette," said Major Blach.

Thirty minutes had passed. They had returned to the Prince's room, where the Major was systematically rooting through each drawer and closet. Flaüss sat in the armchair, brooding, while Svenson stood near the open window, smoking. A complete search of the compound had produced nothing, nor were there any footprints or indentations to be seen in the gravel below the window. Blach had gone back to the rooftop with lanterns, but had found no footprints other than their own—though there were several marks on the side of the building, near where the ropes had worn into the slippery grime along the gutters.

"Perhaps he has merely escaped for an evening of pleasure," offered the Envoy. He looked darkly at Svenson. "Because of your hounding him earlier—he does not trust us—"

"Do not be a fool," snapped Major Blach. "This was planned, with or without the Prince's help—most likely without, if he was insensible as the Doctor describes. At least two men entered the room from above, possibly more—the guard did not hear the bureau being moved, which makes it more likely to be four men—and took the Prince with them. We must assume he has been taken, and must decide how to recover him."

Major Blach slammed the last drawer closed and turned his gaze to Svenson.

"Yes?" the Doctor asked.

"You found him earlier."

"I did."

"So, you will tell me where and how."

"I applaud your eventual concern," replied Svenson, his voice tight with disdain. "Do you think it is the same collection of people? Because if so you know who they are—you both know. Will you challenge them? Will you go to Robert Vandaariff in force? To Deputy Minister Crabbé? To the Comte d'Orkancz? To the Xonck ironworks? Or does one of you already know where he is—so we may end this ridiculous charade?"

Svenson was gratified to see that at this both he and the Major were looking at Flaüss.

"I do not know anything!" the Envoy cried. "If we must ask for the help of these august people you name—if they are *able* to help us—" Doctor Svenson scoffed. Flaüss turned to Major Blach for aid. "The Doctor still has not told us how he located the Prince before. Perhaps he can find him again."

"There is no mystery to it," lied Svenson. "I sought out the brothel. Someone in the brothel was able to assist me. The Prince was right around the corner. Apparently Henry Xonck's generous donations to the Institute provide a certain level of access for his younger brother's friends."

"How did you know the brothel?" asked Flaüss.

"Because I know the Prince at least that well—that is not the point! I have told you who he was with. If anyone knows what has happened, it will be they. I cannot confront these figures. It must be you—Herr Flaüss supported by the Major's men—that is the only way."

Svenson ground his cigarette into the china cup that had held his coffee so long ago. "This gets us nowhere," he told them. He picked up his coat and strode from the room.

With no other thought than that he had not eaten in hours, Svenson walked down the stairs to the great kitchen, which was unoccupied. He dug through the cupboards to find a hard cheese, dry sausage, and a loaf of that morning's bread. He poured himself a glass of pale yellow wine and sat alone at the large work table to think, methodically slicing off a hunk of cheese, a matching thickness of sausage, and piling them onto a piece of bread. After the first bite, realizing the bread was too dry, he got up and found a pot of mustard. He opened it and spooned more than he would normally favor onto the bread and re-stacked the sausage and cheese. He swallowed, and took a sip of wine. A routine established, he ate—the sounds of activity brewing about him in the compound—and tried to decide what to do. The Prince had been taken once, rescued, then taken again—it only followed it was by the same people, for the same reasons. Yet in the front of the Doctor's mind was the cigarette butt.

Flaüss had given it to him and, after the barest glance, he had handed it back and turned to climb off of the roof with what dignity he could muster—but the glance confirmed the idea that had already formed in his mind. The tip of the butt was crimped in a specific way he'd seen the night before—by a woman's lacquered cigarette holder—at the St. Royale Hotel. The woman—he took another sip of wine, slipped the monocle from his eye into his breast pocket and rubbed his face—was shockingly, derangingly lovely. She was also dangerous—obviously so—but in such a complete way as to almost be beside notice, as if one were discussing a particular cobra—a description that might include length or color or markings, but never the possession of deadly venom, which was an *a priori* feature that one could not, he found, take exception to . . . on the contrary. He sighed and pushed his tired mind to focus, to connect that woman at the hotel to her possible presence on the rooftop. He could not make sense of it, but knew that doing so would lead him to the Prince, and began to meticulously recomb his memory.

Much earlier in the day, when he had realized the Prince had not returned, and then that Flaüss and Blach were gone as well, Svenson had let himself into the Prince's room and searched it for any possible clue to the Prince's plans for the evening. In general Karl-Horst was about as cunning as a fairly clever cat or small child. If things were hidden, they were hidden under the mattress or in a shoe, but more likely to be simply tucked into the pocket of the coat he had been wearing and forgotten. Svenson had found embossed books of matches, theatre programs, calling cards, but nothing of any particular, striking nature. He sat on the bed and lit a cigarette, looking around the room, for the moment out of ideas. On the side table next to the bed was a blue glass vase with perhaps ten white lilies stuffed inside, drooping with various degrees of health over the rim. Svenson stared at it. He'd never seen flowers in the Prince's room before, nor were any similar touches of feminine decoration present in the diplomatic compound. He was unaware of any woman's presence in the compound at all, now that he thought of it, nor had Karl-Horst ever shown a preference for flowers or, for that matter, beauty. Perhaps they were a gift from Lydia Vandaariff. Perhaps some shred of affection had actually penetrated Karl-Horst's pageant of appetite.

Svenson frowned and scooted closer to the side table, peering at the vase. He wiped his monocle and looked closer—the glass was somewhat artistic, with a slightly irregular surface and occasional deliberate flaws, whorls, or bubbles. He frowned again—was there something *in* it? He snatched a towel from the Prince's shaving table and laid it on the bed, and then gathered the lilies with both hands and placed them dripping on the towel. He picked up the vase and held it to the light. There *was* something in it, another piece of glass perhaps, deflecting the light passing through, though it itself seemed invisible. Svenson put the vase down and pushed up his sleeve. He reached in, groped for a moment—the thing was quite slippery—and extracted a small rectangle of blue glass, approximately the size of a calling card. He wiped it and his hand on the towel and studied it. Within seconds, as if he had been struck with a hammer, Svenson was on his knees—shaking his head, dizzy, having nearly dropped the glass card in surprise.

He looked again.

It was like entering someone else's dream. After a moment the blue cast of the glass vanished as if he had pierced a veil... he was staring into a room—a dark, comfortable room with a great red sofa and hanging chandeliers and luxurious carpets—and then, which was why he had nearly dropped it the first time—the image *moved,* as if he was walking, or standing and turning his gaze about the salon—and he saw *people,* people who were looking right at him. He could hear nothing save the sound of his own breath, but his mind had otherwise fully entered the space of these images—*moving* images—like photographs but not like them also, at once more vivid and less sharp, more fully dimensional and incomprehensibly infused with *sensation,* with the feel of a silken dress, petticoats bunched up around a woman's legs, her satin flesh beneath the petticoats and then of a man stepping between her legs, sensing her smile somehow as his body fumblingly found its position. Her head leaned back over the top of the sofa—for he saw the ceiling and felt her hair hanging around her face and throat—a face that was masked, he realized—and then the sensation in her loins—luscious, exquisite—as, quite clearly—from the liquid sensations shuddering through Svenson's own body—the man was penetrating her. Then the image turned slightly, as the woman's head turned, and just visible against the wall behind her was part of a large wall mirror. For a sharp second, Svenson saw the reflection of the man's face and the back of the room beyond him. The man, perfectly plainly, was Karl-Horst von Maasmärck.

The woman was not Lydia Vandaariff, but someone with brown hair. In the glimpse of the room beyond the Prince, Svenson had been shocked to see other people—spectators?—and something else beyond them—an open door? a window?—but he let it be and with more effort than he expected wrenched his gaze from the card. What was he looking at? He looked down at himself with a spasm of shame—he had become quite aroused. What's more—he forced his mind to think clearly—he had been aware of moments within the interaction that he had not actually seen . . . the woman touching herself, both for pleasure and to gauge her lubrication, Karl-Horst fumbling with his trousers, and the moment of penetration itself . . . all of these, he realized, came from the point of view, the *experiential* point of view, of the woman—though the moments themselves had not been seen at all. With a breath of preparation he fixed his eyes again on the glass card, sinking into it as if he was entering a deep pool: first the bare sofa, then the woman pulling up her dress, then the Prince stepping between her legs, the coupling itself, the woman turning her head, the mirror, the reflection, and then, a moment later, the view was again the bare sofa—and then the entire scene was repeated . . . and then repeated again.

Svenson put down the card. His breath was rapid. What was he holding? It was as if the essence of this woman's feeling had been captured and somehow infused into this tiny window. And who was the woman? Who were the spectators? When had this happened? And who had instructed the Prince on where and how to hide it? He watched it again and found that he was able, with intense concentration, to slow the progress of movement, to dwell in a particular instant, with almost unbearably delicious results. With a firm resolve he pushed himself on to the moment with the mirror, studying the reflection closely. He was able to discern that the figures—perhaps ten men and women—were also masked, but he recognized none of them. He nudged himself onward and saw, in the last instants, an open doorway—someone must have been leaving the room—and through it a window, perhaps distant, with something written on it, in reverse, the letters *E-L-A*. At first, this made him think he was looking out from a tavern—the word "ale" being an advertisement—but the more he thought of the luxury of the room, and the elegance of the party, and the distance between the door and the lettered window the less a tavern or even restaurant seemed likely.

His thinking stalled for a moment and then he suddenly had it. A *hotel.* The St. Royale.

Within five minutes Svenson was in a coach, wheeling toward what was perhaps the most esteemed hotel in the city, in the heart of the Circus Garden, the card and his revolver in separate pockets of his coat. He was no creature of luxury or privilege—he could only adopt the haughty manner of those he knew from the Macklenburg court and hope he found people able to help, either through natural sympathy or by intimidation. His initial intention was merely to locate the Prince and assure himself of the fool's safety. Beyond this, if he could gain any insight into the origin and construction of the glass card, he would be very interested, for it confirmed how yet again Karl-Horst was mixing with figures whose ambitions he did not comprehend. While Svenson had an immediate carnal appreciation for the lurid possibilities of such an invention, he knew the true import was more far-reaching, well beyond his own too deliberate imagination.

He entered the St. Royale's bright lobby and casually glanced at the front windows, locating the letters he had seen reflected. They were to his left, and as he walked toward them he attempted to place the doorway through which the window had been seen. He could not. The wall where it ought to have been was flush and apparently seamless. He crossed to it, leaned against the wall, and took his time digging out a cigarette and lighting it, looking closely but to no avail. Hanging on the wall near him was a large mirror in a heavy gold frame. He stood in front of it, seeing his own frustration. The mirror itself was large, but it did not reach closer than three feet to the floor—it could hardly conceal an entrance. Svenson sighed and looked around him in the lobby—guests walked in and out or sat on the various leather banquettes. Not knowing what else to do, he crossed toward the main desk. As he passed the large stairwell to the upper stories he stepped out of his way to allow two women to more easily descend, nodding to them politely. As he did so his mind suddenly reeled with the fragrance of sandalwood. He looked up in shock, taking in one woman's light brown hair, the delicate nape of her neck as she passed. It was the woman from the glass card—he was sure of it—so strong was the resonance of her perfume, despite the fact that Svenson knew he had never smelled it before, and certainly did not smell it within the card. Nevertheless, the precise interaction of that perfume and this woman's body was something he was as intimately familiar with—he could not say how—as the woman must be herself.

The two women had continued toward the hotel's restaurant. Doctor Svenson darted after them, catching up just before they reached the entrance, and cleared his throat. They turned. He was taken aback to see the woman with brown hair's face was disfigured by a thin looping burn that wrapped around both of her eyes and onto each temple. She wore an elegant dress of pale blue, her skin was quite fair and otherwise unblemished, her lips were painted red. Her companion was shorter than she, hair a darker brown, face a trifle more round; in her own way equally appealing, yet bearing the same distressing scars. She wore a striped dress of imperial yellow and pale green, with a high lace collar. Under the full beam of their attention, Svenson abruptly began to grope for his words. He had never been married, he had never lived around women at all—it was a sad fact that Doctor Svenson was more comfortable at the side of a corpse than a living female.

"I beg your pardon, ladies—if I might intrude upon a moment of your time?"

They stared at him without speaking. He plunged on. "My name is Abelard Svenson—I am hoping you may assist me. I am a doctor. I am presently searching for a person under my care—a very important person, about whom, you will understand, all inquiries must be discreet."

They persisted in staring. The woman from the card smiled slightly, a brief flicker of interest at the corner of her mouth. Her gaze dropped to his greatcoat, the epaulettes and high collar.

"Are you a soldier?" she asked.

"I am a doctor, as I say, though I am an officer in the Macklenburg Navy—Captain-Surgeon Svenson, if you insist—detailed to special duties for"—his voice lowered—"*diplomatic* reasons."

"Macklenburg?" asked the other woman.

"Indeed. It is a German principality on the Baltic coast."

"You do have an accent," she said, and then giggled. "Is there not such a thing as Macklenburg Pudding?"

"Is there?" asked the Doctor.

"Of course there is," the first woman said. "It has raisins, and cream, and a particular blend of spice—aniseed and cloves—"

"And ground-up hazelnuts," said the other. "Sprinkled on the top."

The Doctor nodded at them, at a loss. "I'm afraid I do not know it."

"I should not worry," said the first woman, indulgently patting his arm. "Doesn't your eye get tired?"

They were looking at his monocle. He smiled quickly and adjusted it. "I suppose it must," he said. "I am so used to the thing, I no longer notice." They were still smiling, though Lord knows he had not been witty or charming—for some reason they had decided to accept him—he did his best to seize the opportunity. He nodded to the restaurant. "I presume you were about to dine. If I might share a glass of wine with you, it would be more than enough time to aid me on my quest."

"A *quest*?" said the woman from the card. "How diverting. I am Mrs. Marchmoor, my companion is Miss Poole."

Svenson offered an arm to each of the ladies and stepped between them—despite himself enjoying the feelings of physical contact, shifting his step slightly so the pistol in his pocket did not grind against Miss

Poole. "I am most grateful for your kindness," he said, and led them forward.

Once inside, however, the women guided *him* past several available tables to the far side of the restaurant, where a line of discreet doors concealed private dining rooms. A waiter opened a door for them, the women disengaging themselves from Svenson's arms and entering one after the other. Svenson nodded to the waiter and followed. As the door clicked shut behind him he realized that the room was already occupied. At the far end of a table elegantly laid with linen, china, silver, crystal, and flowers sat—or more accurately presided—a tall woman with black hair and piercing violet eyes. She wore a small black jacket over a red silk dress, subtly embroidered in yellow thread with Chinese scenes. She looked up at Svenson with a smile he recognized as neutrally polite but which nevertheless caused his breath to catch. He met her gaze and nodded respectfully. She took a sip of wine, still gazing at him. The two others had moved to either side of the table to sit adjacent to the woman in red. Svenson stood awkwardly at his end—the table was large enough for at least three people on each side—until Mrs. Marchmoor leaned forward to whisper into the woman in red's ear. The woman nodded and smiled at him more broadly. Svenson felt himself blushing.

"Doctor Svenson, please sit, and avail yourself of a glass of wine. It is very good, I find. I am Madame Lacquer-Sforza. Mrs. Marchmoor tells me you are on a *quest.*"

Miss Poole passed a bottle of wine on a silver dish to Svenson. He took the bottle and poured for himself and the other ladies.

"I am very sorry to intrude—as I was about to explain to these two ladies—"

"It is very strange," wondered Madame Lacquer-Sforza, "that you should choose to ask them. Was there a reason? Are you *acquainted*?"

The ladies giggled at the thought. Svenson was quick to speak. "Of course not—you will understand that in asking them for help I am revealing the desperate nature of my search. In brief—as I have said—I am in the diplomatic service of the Duchy of Macklenburg, specifically to my Duke's son and heir, Prince Karl-Horst von Maasmärck. He is known to have patronized this hotel. I am looking for him. It is perhaps foolish, but if any of you ladies—for I know the Prince has a great appreciation for such beauty—had perhaps seen him, or heard of his passage, and could direct me toward his present location, I should be very much obliged."

They smiled at him, sipping their wine. His face was flushed, he felt hot, and took a drink himself, gulping too much at once and coughing. He wiped his mouth with a napkin and cleared his throat, feeling like a twelve-year-old.

"Doctor, please, sit down." He'd no idea he was still standing. Madame Lacquer-Sforza smiled at him as he did, stopping half-way to stand again and remove his coat, laying it over the chair to his right. He raised his glass again. "Thank you once more for your kindness. I have no wish to intrude any more than necessary into your evening—"

"Tell me, Doctor," asked Mrs. Marchmoor, "is it often that you lose the Prince? Or is he such a man who needs... *minding*? And is such an office fitting for an officer and a surgeon?"

The women chuckled. Svenson waved his hand, drinking more wine to steady himself—his palms were slick, his collar hot against his neck. "No, no, it is an extraordinary circumstance, we have received a particular communication from the Duke himself, and at this moment neither the Mission Envoy nor our military attaché happens to be present—nor, of course, is the Prince. With no other knowledge of his agenda, I have taken it upon myself to search—as the message requires swift reply." He wanted urgently to mop his face but did not. "May I ask if you know of the Prince? He has spoken often of dining at the St. Royale, so you may have seen him—or you may have become acquainted with him yourselves; indeed, he is—if I may be so bold—a man for—excuse me—lovely women."

He took another drink. They did not answer. Miss Poole had leaned over and was whispering into Madame Lacquer-Sforza's ear. She nodded. Miss Poole sat back and took another sip of wine. Mrs. Marchmoor was watching him. He could not help it—as he looked into her eyes he felt a flicker of pleasure, recalling—from his own memory!—the inside of her thighs. He swallowed and cleared his throat. "Mrs. Marchmoor, do *you* know the Prince?"

* * *

Before she could answer, the door behind them opened and two men entered. Svenson shot to his feet, turning to face them, though neither spared him a glance. The first was a tall, lean man with a high forehead and close-cropped hair in a red uniform with yellow facing and black boots, the rank of a colonel marked by his epaulettes sewn into his collar. He had handed the waiter his coat and brass helmet and crossed directly to Madame Lacquer-Sforza, taking her hand and bending over to kiss it. He nodded to each of the other women and took a seat next to Mrs. Marchmoor, who was already pouring him a glass of wine. The second man walked to the other side of the table, past Svenson, to sit next to Miss Poole. He took Madame Lacquer-Sforza's hand after the Colonel, but with less self-importance, and sat. He poured his own glass and took a healthy swig without ceremony. His hair was pale but streaked with grey, long and greasy, combed back behind his ears. His coat was fine enough but unkempt—in fact the man's whole appearance gave the impression of a once-cherished article—a sofa, for example—that had been left in the rain and partially ruined. Svenson had seen men like him at his university, and wondered if this man was some kind of scholar, and if so what he was possibly doing among this party.

Madame Lacquer-Sforza spoke. "Colonel Aspiche and Doctor Lorenz, I am pleased to introduce you to Doctor Svenson, from the Duchy of Macklenburg, part of Prince Karl-Horst von Maasmärck's diplomatic party. Doctor Svenson, Colonel Aspiche is the new commander of the 4th regiment of Dragoons, recently made the Prince's Own—it is quite a promotion—and Doctor Lorenz is an august member of the Royal Institute of Science and Exploration."

Svenson nodded to them both and raised his glass. Lorenz took it as another opportunity to drink deeply, finishing his glass and pouring another. Aspiche fixed Svenson with a particularly searching eye. Svenson knew he was looking at Trapping's replacement—he had recognized the uniform at once—and knew the man must feel self-conscious for the circumstances of his promotion—if not, considering the missing body, for other more telling reasons as well. Svenson decided to probe the wound.

"I have had the honor of meeting Colonel Aspiche's unfortunate predecessor, Colonel Trapping, in the company of my Prince—on the very evening the Colonel seems to have vanished. I do hope for the sake of his family—if not a grateful nation as well—that the mystery of his disappearance will soon be solved."

"We are all quite grieved by the loss," muttered Aspiche.

"It must be difficult assuming command in such circumstances."

Aspiche glared at him. "A soldier does what is necessary."

"Doctor Lorenz," interrupted Madame Lacquer-Sforza easily, "I believe you have visited Macklenburg."

"I have," he answered—his voice was sullen and proud, like a once-whipped dog caught between rebellion and fear of another lashing. "It was winter. Cold and dark is all I can say for it."

"What brought you there?" asked Svenson, politely.

"I'm sure I don't remember," answered Lorenz, speaking into his glass.

"They have excellent puddings," giggled Miss Poole, her laugh echoed across the table by Mrs. Marchmoor. Svenson took the moment to study that woman's face. What had seemed at first to be burns struck him now as something else—the skin was not taut like a scar, but instead strangely discolored, as if eaten by a delicate acid perhaps, or scorched by a particularly harsh sunburn, or even a kind of impermanent tattoo—something with diluted henna? But it could not have been intentional—it was quite disfiguring—and he immediately pulled his eyes away, not wishing to stare. He met the gaze of Madame Lacquer-Sforza, who had been watching him.

"Doctor Svenson," she called. "Are you a man who likes games?"

"That would depend entirely on the game, Madame. I am not one for gambling, if that is what you mean."

"Perhaps it is. What of you others—Colonel Aspiche?"

Aspiche looked up, he had not been listening. With shock, Svenson realized that Mrs. Marchmoor's right hand was not visible, but that the angle of her arm placed it squarely in the Colonel's lap. Aspiche cleared his throat and frowned with concentration. Mrs. Marchmoor—and for that matter, Madame Lacquer-Sforza—watched him with a blithely innocent interest.

"Gambling is part of a man's true blood," he announced. "Or at least a soldier's. Nothing can be gained without the willingness to lose—all or part. Even in the greatest victory lives will be spent. At a certain level of *practice,* refusal to gamble becomes one with cowardice." He took a sip of wine, shifted in his seat—pointedly not looking at Mrs. Marchmoor, whose hand had not returned above the table top—and turned to Svenson. "I do not cast aspersions on you, Doctor, for your point of emphasis must be the saving of life—on *preservation.*"

Madame Lacquer-Sforza nodded gravely and turned to the other man. "Doctor Lorenz?"

Lorenz was attempting to see through the table top, staring at the point above Aspiche's lap, as if by concentration he might remove the barrier. Without averting his gaze the savant took another drink—Svenson was impressed by the man's self-absorption—and muttered, "In truth, games are an illusion, for there are only percentages of chance, quite predictable if one has the patience, the mathematics. Indeed there may be risk, for possibility allows for different results, but the probabilities are easily known, and over time the intelligent game player will accrue winnings exactly to the degree that he—or indeed, she"—and here he cast a glance at Madame Lacquer-Sforza—"acts in conjunction with rational knowledge."

He took another drink. As he did, Miss Poole blew into his ear. Doctor Lorenz choked with surprise and spat wine across the table top. The others burst into laughter. Miss Poole picked up a napkin and wiped Lorenz's blushing face. Madame Lacquer-Sforza poured more wine into his glass. Svenson saw that Colonel Aspiche's left hand was no longer visible, and then noted Mrs. Marchmoor shifting slightly in her seat. Svenson swallowed—what was he doing here? Again he met the eyes of Madame Lacquer-Sforza, watching him take in the table with a smile.

"And you, Madame?" he said. "We have not heard your opinion. I assume you raised the topic for a reason."

"Such a German, Doctor—so direct and 'to zee business.'" She took a sip of wine and smiled. "For my part, it is very simple. I never gamble with anything I care for, but will gamble to fierce extremes with everything that I don't. Of course, I am fortunate in that I care for very little, and thus the by far greater part of the world becomes for me infused with a sense of... for lack of a better word, *play*. But *serious* play, I do assure you."

Her gaze was fixed on Svenson, her expression placid, amused. He did not understand what was happening in the room. To his left, Colonel

Aspiche and Mrs. Marchmoor were openly groping each other beneath the table. To his right, Miss Poole was licking Doctor Lorenz's ear, the Doctor breathing heavily and sucking on his lower lip, both hands clutching his wineglass so hard it threatened to crack. Svenson looked back at Madame Lacquer-Sforza. She was ignoring the others. He realized that they had already been dealt with—they had been dealt with before they'd even arrived. Her attention was on him. He had been allowed to enter for a reason.

"You know me, Madame, . . . as you know my Prince."

"Perhaps I do."

"Do you know where he is?"

"I know where he might be."

"Will you tell me?"

"Perhaps. Do you care for him?"

"Such is my duty."

She smiled. "Doctor, I'm afraid I require you to be honest."

Svenson swallowed. Aspiche had his eyes shut, breathing heavily. Miss Poole had two of her fingers in Lorenz's mouth.

"He's an embarrassment," he said rapidly. "I would pay money to thrash him raw."

Madame Lacquer-Sforza beamed. "Much better."

"Madame, I do not know what your intent is—"

"I merely propose an exchange. I am looking for someone—so are you."

"I must find my Prince at once."

"Yes, and if—afterwards—you are in a position to help me, I will take it very kindly."

Svenson's mind rebelled against the entire situation—the others seemed nearly insensible—but could find no immediate reason to refuse. He searched her open violet eyes, found them perfectly impenetrable, and swallowed.

"Who is it you wish to find?"

The air in the Institute laboratory had been pungent with ozone, burning rubber, and a particular odor Svenson did not recognize—a cross between sulfur, sodium, and the iron smell of scorched blood. The Prince had been slumped in a large chair, Crabbé to one side of him, Francis Xonck to the other. Across the room stood the Comte d'Orkancz, wearing a leather apron and leather gauntlets that covered his arms to the elbow, a half-open metal door beyond him—had they just carried Karl-Horst from there? Svenson had brandished the pistol and removed the Prince, who was conscious enough to stand and stumble, but apparently unable to talk or—to Svenson's good fortune—protest. At the base of the stairs he had seen the strange figure in red, who had motioned him on his way. This man had seemed to be intruding as much as Svenson—he had been armed—but there had been no time to spare. The guards had followed to the courtyard, even to the street where he'd been lucky enough to find a coach. It was only back at the compound, in the bright gaslight of the Prince's room—away from the dim corridors and the dark coach—that he'd seen the circular burns. At the time he'd been too occupied with determining the Prince's condition, then with Flaüss's interruption, to work through the connections between the private room at the St. Royale and the Institute laboratory—much less to Trapping's disappearance at the Vandaariff mansion. Now, sitting at the kitchen table, hearing around him the preparations for an expedition into the city, he knew it could no longer wait.

He had said nothing more to Blach or Flaüss—he didn't trust them, and was only happy they were leaving together, as they didn't trust each other either. Obviously Madame Lacquer-Sforza was connected to Mrs. Marchmoor, who had undergone the same process of scarring as the Prince. Then why had Svenson been allowed to break up the procedure? And if Madame Lacquer-Sforza was not in league with the men at the Institute, then what of the blue glass card—depicting a scene clearly taking place at the St. Royale, which must tie her to the plot. Svenson rubbed his eyes, forcing himself back to the immediate point. Which of these two—Crabbé's cabal or Madame Lacquer-Sforza—had the reason or the means to extract the Prince immaculately from the compound rooftop?

He finished the wine in a swallow and pushed his chair from the table. Above him the compound seemed quiet. Without thinking he returned the food to its locker and placed the glass and knife on the counter to be cleaned. He took out another cigarette, lit it with a kitchen match, and threw the match into the stove. Svenson inhaled, then frowned as he picked a bit of tobacco off of his tongue. The name she had given him, Isobel Hastings, was unknown to him. He knew nothing of the habits of this city's whores—aside from those met in the process of fetching the incapacitated Prince—but he didn't think that mattered. If she was choosing to enlist a man like him it must be in addition to others searching who knew the city and its people. This also meant these searchers had failed, and her information was wrong. He pushed the matter aside—it was hardly something she could expect him to waste time on at the moment—no matter what he had bargained.

Svenson walked up into the courtyard, slipping on his coat as he walked, transferring his medical bag from hand to hand as he inserted his arms. He stood in the open air and buttoned it with one hand, looking up. The compound was quiet. They had left without a word to him. He knew he must search on his own, but could not decide where to go. The Prince would not be at the St. Royale—if only because Svenson had openly searched there the night before—nor would he be at the Institute for the same reason. He shook his head, knowing that equally the St. Royale or the Institute might indeed be the perfect place to hide him—both were enormous—precisely *because* they had been searched. Further, if the cabal had taken him, the Prince could be anywhere—between them Crabbé and Xonck must have hundreds of places a man could be housed unseen. Svenson could not search for the Prince himself and hope to find him. He must find one of these people and force them to speak.

He walked to the gate, nodded to the guard and stood in the street, waiting to flag an empty coach, running the options through his mind. He rejected Vandaariff—Blach and Flaüss were already seeing him—as he rejected Madame Lacquer-Sforza. He frankly could not trust himself to confront her with the violence he worried would be necessary. This left Crabbé, Xonck, and the Comte d'Orkancz. He dismissed others on the periphery—the other women, Aspiche, Lorenz, Crabbé's aide. Any attempt with these would take more time, and he had no idea where to find them. The Prince, however, had dined at the homes of Crabbé, the Comte, and Xonck, and Svenson had scrupulously memorized his calendar and thus their addresses. The Doctor sighed and fastened his topmost button around the collar. It was well after midnight, cold, and the road was empty. If he had to walk it would be to the nearest of the three: Harald Crabbé's house at Hadrian Square.

It took him half an hour, walking quickly to keep warm. The fog was thick, the surface of the city cold and moist, but Svenson found it comforting, for this was the weather of his home. When he reached Hadrian Square the house was dark. Svenson climbed the steps and rapped on the door knocker, number 14. He stuck his right hand into his coat pocket, closing his fingers around the revolver. No one answered. He knocked again. Nothing. He walked back to the street and then around the nearest corner. There was an alley providing service access to the square's back entrances, fronted by a barred, locked gate. The lock was undone. Svenson stepped through and crept down the narrow lane.

Crabbé's house was the middle of three. The fog forced Svenson to walk slowly and approach ridiculously close to the buildings before he could tell where one stopped and the other started, much less locate the rear door. There were no lights. Gazing up at the windows, Svenson nearly tripped over an abandoned wheelbarrow, biting back a cry of surprise. He rubbed his knee. Beyond the wheelbarrow was a set of stone steps leading down to a cellar, or perhaps to a kitchen. He looked up—it ought to be Crabbé's house. He gripped the revolver in his pocket and crept down to the door, which was ajar. He silently pulled out the gun and lowered himself to a crouch. He swallowed, and pushed the door open. No one shot him, which he considered a good start to a new career of house-breaking.

The room beyond was dark and silent. Svenson crept in, leaving the door open. He replaced the pistol in his pocket and reached into another for matches. He struck one off his thumb—the flaring match head extremely loud in the quiet night—and quickly looked around him. He stood in a storage room. On the walls were jars and boxes and tins and bales, around his feet were crates, casks, barrels—on the far side of the room was another set of stairs. Svenson blew out the match, dropped it, and padded toward them. He once more removed the revolver from his coat, and climbed the stairs, one painful step at a time. They did not creak. At the top of the stairs was another door, wide open. As his head rose on the steps he looked through it, but saw nothing—the match had destroyed his night vision. He listened, and took a moment to assess what he was doing—how foolish and perilous it seemed. If he could have thought of another path, he would have taken it. As it was, he dearly hoped he would not be forced to shoot any heroic servants, or cause Mrs. Crabbé—was there a Mrs. Crabbé?—to scream. He stepped from the staircase into a hallway, walking forward slowly, debating whether or not to risk another match. He sighed and once more stuffed away the pistol—the last thing he wanted to do was blunder into some porcelain lamp or display of china—and fished out another match.

He heard voices, below him in the storage room.

Moving quickly, Svenson struck the match, shielding it as well as he could with his other hand—which held the medical bag—and strode quietly and directly down the hall to the nearest door and through it. He was in the kitchen, and on the table in front of him was a dead man he did not recognize, covered save for his livid face by a cloth. Svenson spun behind him—footsteps coming up the stairs—and saw on the other side of the kitchen another door. The match was burning his fingers. He dodged around the table and through a swinging doorway. He just saw a quick glimpse of a dining table before he shook out the match. He dropped it, stuck the burned finger into his mouth, stilled the door, and crept to the far side of the table, sinking to the floor. He pulled out the pistol. The footsteps reached the kitchen. He heard the voices of two men, and then the distinct pop of a bottle being uncorked.

"There we are," said the first voice, one that seemed eminently pleased with itself. "I told you he'd have something worthwhile—where are glasses?" In answer there was clinking, more clinking, and then the *dook dook* sounds of wine being poured—a substantial amount of wine. The first man spoke again. "Do you think we can risk a light?"

"The Deputy Minister—" began the second voice.

"Yes, I know—all right—and it's just as well. I don't want to look at this fellow any more than I already have. What a waste of time. When is he supposed to be here?"

"The messenger said he had a prior errand before he could meet us."

The first man sighed. Svenson heard the sound of a match—an orange glow flickering under the door—and then the puffing of a man lighting a cigar.

"Do you want one, Bascombe?" the first man asked. Svenson searched his memory. He'd met or overheard the introductions of so many people in the last weeks—had there been a Bascombe? Perhaps, but he couldn't place him—if he could just *see* the man...

"No, thank you, Sir," replied Bascombe.

"I'm not 'Sir'," the first man laughed. "Leave that for Crabbé, or the Comte, though I daresay you'll be one of them soon enough. How does *that* feel?"

"I'm sure I don't know. It's happening very quickly."

"The best temptations always do, eh?"

Bascombe did not respond, and they were silent for a time, drinking. Svenson could smell the cigar. It was an excellent cigar. Svenson licked his lips. He wanted a cigarette desperately. He did not recognize either of the voices.

"Have you had much experience with corpses?" asked the first voice, with a trace of amusement.

"This is actually my first, in such close quarters," answered the second, with an air that told Svenson the man knew he was being goaded, but must make the best of it. "My father died when I was much younger—"

"And your uncle of course. Did you see *his* body?"

"I did not. I have not yet—I will of course—at the funeral."

"You grow used to it like anything. Ask any doctor, or soldier." Svenson heard more sounds of pouring. "All right, what's after corpses... what about women?"

"Beg pardon?"

The man chuckled. "Oh, don't be such a boiled trout—no wonder Crabbé favors you. You're not married?"

"No."

"Engaged?"

"No." The voice hesitated. "There was—but no, never so significant an attachment. As I say, all of these changes have come quickly—"

"Brothels, then, I assume? Or schoolgirls?"

"No, no," Bascombe said, with a professionally patient tone that Svenson recognized as the hallmark of a skilled courtier, "as I say, my own feelings have always, well, always been in service to obligation—"

"My goodness—so it's boys?"

"Mr. Xonck!" snapped the voice, perhaps less appalled than exasperated.

"I am merely asking. Besides, when you've traveled as much as I have, things stop surprising you. In Vienna for example, there is a prison you may visit for a small fee, as one would visit a zoo, you know—but for only a few more silver *pfennigs*—"

"But, Mr. Xonck, surely—I beg your pardon—our present business—"

"Didn't the Process teach you anything?"

Here the younger man paused, taking in that this might be a more serious question than the bantering tone implied.

"Of course," he said, "it was *transforming*—"

"Then have some more wine."

Had this been the right answer? Svenson heard the gurgling bottle as Francis Xonck began to hold forth. "Moral perspective is what we carry around with us—it exists nowhere else, I can promise you. Do you see? There is liberation and responsibility—for what is natural depends on where you are, Bascombe. Moreover, vices are like genitals—most are ugly to behold, and yet we find that our own are dear to us." He sniggered at his own wit, drank deeply, exhaled. "But I suppose you have no vices, do you? Well, once you've changed your hat and become Lord Tarr, sitting on the only deposit of indigo clay within five hundred miles, I daresay you'll find they appear soon enough—I speak from experience. Find yourself some tuppable tea cozy to marry and keep your house and then do what you want elsewhere. My brother, for example..."

Bascombe laughed once, somewhat bitterly.

"What is it?" asked Xonck.

"Nothing."

"I do insist."

Bascombe sighed. "It is nothing—merely that, only last week, I was still—as I said, not *significant*—you see, one can only smile at how easy it is to believe—believe so *deeply*—"

"Wait, wait—if you're going to tell a *story*, then we need another bottle. Come on."

* * *

Their footsteps moved out of the kitchen, to the hall, and soon Svenson heard them descending the cellar stairs. He didn't feel he could risk slipping past—he had no idea where the wine cellar actually was, or how long they would be. He could try to find the front door—but knew he was in the perfect position to learn more where he was, as long as he wasn't discovered. Suddenly Svenson had it. Bascombe! He was Crabbé's aide—a thin, youngish fellow, never spoke, always paying attention—he was about to be a *Lord*? Chiding himself Svenson realized he was wasting the most immediate source of information of all. He dug out another match and pushed silently through the swinging door. He listened—they were well out of hearing—struck the match and looked down at the dead man on the table.

He was perhaps forty years old, hair thin, clean-shaven, with a sharp pointed nose. His face was covered with red blotches, vivid despite the pallor of death, lips stretched back in a grimace, revealing a mouth half-full of tobacco-stained teeth. Working quickly as the match burned, Svenson pulled back the sheet and could not help but gasp. The man's arms, from the elbows down, were riven with veins of lurid, jagged, gleaming blue, bulging out from the skin, cutting through it. At first glance the veins looked wet, but Svenson was shocked to realize that they were in fact *glass*—and that they ran down through the man's forearms, thickening, seething into and stiffening the flesh around them. He pulled the cloth farther and dropped the match with surprise. The man had no hands. His wrists were completely blue, starred, and broken—as if the hands below them had *shattered.*

The footsteps returned below. Svenson whipped the cloth into place and retreated to the dining room, carefully stilling the swinging door, his mind reeling at what he'd just seen. Within moments he heard the men in the hall and then entering the kitchen.

"Another glass there, Bascombe," called Xonck, and then to a third man, "I'm assuming you will join us—or me, at least—Bascombe doesn't quite share my thirst. Always watching from a distance, aren't you, Roger?"

"If you insist," muttered the new voice. Svenson stopped breathing. It was Major Blach. Svenson slowly slipped his right hand around the butt of the revolver.

"Excellent." Xonck extracted the cork from the new bottle with a pop and poured. He drank, and Svenson could hear him emit little noises of pleasure as he did. "It's very good—isn't it? Damn—my cigar seems to have gone out." Svenson saw the light of a match flare. While it burned, Xonck chatted on. "Why don't we give him a peek—get the cloth, Bascombe. There you go—in all his glory. Well, Major, what do you say?"

There was no response. After a moment the match went out. Xonck chuckled. "That's more or less what we said too. I think old Crabbé said 'bloody hell!' Except of course it's not *bloody* at all." Xonck cackled. "Find relief where you can, that's what I say."

"What has happened to him?" asked Blach.

"What do you think? He's dead. He was rather valuable, don't you know—rather skilled in the technical mechanics. It's a good thing there's still Lorenz—if there is still Lorenz—because, Major, I'm not quite certain you understand exactly who's responsible for this damned outright *catastrophe.* It is *you,* Major. It is *you* because *you* could not locate one disreputable ruffian who was thus free to disrupt our work at its most delicate moment. Just as *you* could not control the members of your own diplomatic mission—I assume you know the man who took back the Prince, waving a pistol in our faces—which would be laughable if it didn't create problems for everyone *else* to solve!"

"Mr. Xonck—" began Major Blach.

"Shut your foul foreign mouth," snarled Xonck coldly. "I don't want excuses. I want thoughts. Think about your problems. Then tell us what you're going to do about them."

Except for the clink of Xonck's glass, there was silence. Svenson was astonished. He'd never heard Blach spoken to in such a way, nor could he have imagined Blach reacting with anything but rage.

Blach cleared his throat. "To begin—"

"First, Major," and it was Bascombe speaking, not Xonck, "there is the man from your compound, the Prince's Doctor, I believe?"

"Yes," hissed Blach. "He is not a factor. I will go back tonight and have him smothered in his bed—blame it on anything—no one will care—"

"Second," interrupted Bascombe, "the disruptive man in red."

"Chang—he is called Cardinal Chang," said Blach.

"He is Chinese?" asked Bascombe.

"No," snarled Blach—Svenson could hear Xonck snickering. "He has been—he is called that because of scars—apparently—I have not seen them. He escaped from us. He has killed one of my men and seriously injured two more. He is nothing but a vicious criminal without imagination or understanding. I have men posted across his usual haunts as they have been described to us—he will be taken soon, and—"

"Brought to me," said Xonck.

"As you wish."

"Third," continued Bascombe, "the female spy, Isobel Hastings."

"We have not found her. No one has found her."

"She must be somewhere, Major," said Bascombe.

"She is unknown at the brothels I was directed to—"

"Then try a hotel!" cried Xonck. "Try the rooming houses!"

"I do not know the city as you do—"

"Next!" barked Xonck.

"And fourth," continued Bascombe smoothly—Svenson had to admire the man's coolness of manner, "we must arrange for the return of your Prince."

Svenson listened—this would be what he was waiting for—but there was only silence . . . and then Blach's sputtering rage.

"What are you talking about?" he fumed.

"It is quite simple—there is a great deal of work yet to be done. Before the marriage, before anyone may return to Macklenburg—"

"No, no—why are you saying this? You have already taken him—without notifying me! You have taken him hours ago!"

No one spoke. Blach rapidly explained what had happened at the compound—the escape to the roof, the furniture against the door—then how he and Flaüss had just now left complaints and a request for aid with Lord Vandaariff, who had promised to do what he could. "Of course, all the time I assumed he had been taken by you," said Blach, "though I have no idea how it was done."

Once more there was silence.

"We do not have your Prince," said Xonck, in a quiet, calm voice. "All right—fifth, Blach, you will continue in your efforts to find this Chang and this Hastings woman. We will find the Prince. Bascombe will be in touch. Sixth . . . yes, and sixth . . ." He took a moment to toss off the last of his wine. "You can help us get poor Crooner out of Mrs. Crabbé's kitchen. They should have something ready by now at the river. We will take your coach."

Twenty minutes later Svenson stood in the kitchen alone, looking down at the now empty table, smoking a cigarette. He opened his medical kit and rummaged inside for an empty glass jar and pulled out the cork. He lit a match and leaned over the table, looking closely. It took several matches until he found what he wanted, a small flaking of what looked like blue glass. Using a tiny swab he brushed the glass bits into the jar, inserted the cork and stowed it back into his bag. He had no idea what it was, but was certain that a comparison with the Prince's glass card would be useful. He snapped the medical kit shut. He could not return to the compound. He did not know how long he could stay where he was—he should probably be gone already. At least he knew who his enemies were, or some of them—neither Xonck nor Bascombe had mentioned Madame Lacquer-Sforza. Svenson wondered if she could be responsible for taking the Prince. Yet she had been searching for the Hastings woman as well—the different figures overlapped maliciously. Indeed, for these men had mentioned Doctor Lorenz as if he were one of their own, while Svenson had seen with his own eyes the man's attendance to Madame Lacquer-Sforza. Perhaps they were all intent on betraying each other, but up to this point had been in league. Somewhere in the house, a clock chimed three. Svenson picked up his bag and walked out.

The alley gate was now locked, and he climbed over it with the stiffness of a man not used to this kind of exertion at such an hour. The fog was still thick, the street still dark, and Svenson still had no firm destination in mind. He walked away from the compound—generally toward the Circus Garden and the heart of the city—keeping to the shadows and forcing his increasingly tired mind to work. While the Prince was certainly in danger, Svenson doubted it was immediately mortal. At the same time, he'd felt a chill when Xonck had referred to "the Process." Could this be related to the facial burns? It almost sounded like a pagan ritual, like a tribal marking ceremony, or—he thought darkly—like branding one's cattle. The dead man, Crooner, had obviously been involved—

there was science behind it, which was why it was taking place at the Institute, and why Lorenz was part of it as well. Who *wasn't* part of it, aside from Svenson himself? The answer came quickly enough: Isobel Hastings and the menacing man in red, this "Chang." He had to find them before Major Blach. They might even know how to locate the Prince.

Svenson kept walking, his boots grinding on the wet cobblestones. His thoughts began to wander, the wet chill of the fog taking him back to his time in Warnemünde, the cold rail of the pier, the snow falling silently into the sea. He remembered, as a boy, walking into the winter forest—wanting to be alone, in despair once again—and sitting in his thick coat under a pine tree, pressing the snow around him into a soft burrow, laying back and looking up into the high branches. He didn't know how long he'd lain there, his mind drifting, perhaps even close to dangerous sleep, when he became aware that he was cold, that the heat from his body had been steadily leeched away by the snow and frosted air. His face was numb. It had happened so gradually, his mind had been elsewhere—he could no longer remember the girl's name—but as he forced his frozen limbs to work, rolling first to his knees and then to a shambling walk, he had a moment of insight, that he had just seen in miniature his own life—and every human life—a process where heat slowly, relentlessly dissipated in the face of unfeeling and beautiful ice.

He stopped and looked around him. The great park entrance of the Circus Garden was just to his right, and to his left the marble pools. He had to make a decision. If he looked for the man in red, Chang, and was lucky enough to locate his haunts, he would in all likelihood only find one of Major Blach's troopers. To look for Isobel Hastings would require knowledge of the city's hotels and rooming houses that he simply didn't possess. The cabal of Crabbé, Xonck, and d'Orkancz did not, by their own words, have the Prince. As much as he dreaded it, as much as his nerves fluttered at the idea, as little as he trusted himself, the best choice that came to mind was Madame Lacquer-Sforza and the St. Royale Hotel. He was only minutes away—perhaps brandishing his doctor's bag would get them to open the door at such an hour.

The windows of the hotel still streamed light, but the street outside was still and empty. Svenson walked to the door. It was locked. Before he could knock on the glass he saw a uniformed clerk walking toward him with a ring of keys, alerted by his pulling on the handle. The man unlocked the door and opened it a few narrow inches.

"May I help you?"

"Yes, excuse me—I realize the hour is late—or early—I am looking for—I am a doctor—it is very necessary that I speak with one of your guests, a Madame Lacquer-Sforza."

"Ah. The Contessa."

"Contessa?"

"That is not possible. You are a doctor?"

"Yes—my name is Svenson—I'm sure she will see me—"

"Doctor Svenson, yes. No, I am afraid it is not possible."

The clerk looked past Svenson to the street and called out with a brisk clicking of his tongue—the sound one makes to move a horse. Svenson wheeled to see who he was addressing. From the shadows across the street, in answer, stepped four men. Svenson recognized them by their cloaks—they were the guards from the Institute. He turned back to the door—the clerk had pulled it closed and was locking it. Svenson knocked his fist on the glass. The clerk ignored him. Svenson spun to face the men in the street. They stood in a loose semi-circle in the middle of the road, blocking his escape. His hand dug for his coat pocket, feeling for the revolver.

"No need for that, Doctor," hissed a low rasping voice to his right. He looked up to see the broad daunting figure of the Comte d'Orkancz standing in the shadows beyond the window front. He wore a top hat and a heavy fur coat, and held his silver-topped stick in his right hand. He looked at Svenson with a cold appraising eye.

"It may serve you later . . . for the moment there are more pressing matters to discuss, I assure you. I had hoped you might arrive, and you did not disappoint—such *agreement* is a good way to start our conversation. Will you walk with me?"

Without waiting for an answer, the Comte turned and strode into the fog. Svenson glanced at the men, swallowed uncomfortably, and hurried after him.

"Why would you be waiting for me?" he asked, once he had caught up.

"Why would you be calling on the Contessa at such an improper hour?"

Svenson's mouth worked to find a response. He glanced back to see the four men following some yards behind them.

"You need not answer," d'Orkancz whispered. "We each have our mysteries—I do not doubt that your reasons are real. No, when it came to my attention that you were of the Prince's party, I remembered your name—you *are* the author of a valuable pamphlet on the effects of frostbite?"

"I am the author of such a pamphlet—whether or not it has value . . ."

"A chief point of interest, if I recall, was the ironic similarity between the damage inflicted by certain types of extreme cold, and certain kinds of burns."

"Indeed."

The Comte nodded gravely. "And *that* is why I was waiting for you."

He led Svenson down an elegant side lane, bordered on the east by a walled garden. They stopped at a wooden door, set into an alcove vaulted as if it was part of a church, which d'Orkancz unlocked and led him through. They stepped into the garden, walking across thick, springing turf—behind them Svenson heard the guards enter and close the door. Around him he saw great empty urns and beds, and hanging leafless trees. Above was the fog-shrouded sky. He hurried to keep up with the Comte, who was striding toward a large glowing greenhouse, the smeared windows diffusing the lantern light within. The Comte unlocked a glass-paned door and entered, holding it open for Svenson. Svenson walked through and into a wave of moistly cloying hot air. D'Orkancz shut the door behind, leaving the four guards in the garden. He nodded to a nearby hat stand.

"You will want to take off your coat."

The Comte pulled off his fur as he crossed the greenhouse—which Svenson realized was carpeted—to a large canopied bed, the curtains drawn tight around it. He placed the coat, his hat, and his stick on a small wooden work table and delicately peeked through a gap in the curtains. He stared in for perhaps two minutes, his face impassive. Already Svenson could feel the sweat prickling over his body. He put his medical kit down and peeled off his greatcoat, feeling the weight of the pistol in the pocket, and hung it on the rack. He disliked being apart from the weapon, but he didn't expect he could shoot his way past d'Orkancz and all of the guards in any case. With a glance, d'Orkancz gestured him to the bed. He held the curtain aside as Svenson drew near.

On the bed lay a shivering woman, wrapped in heavy blankets, her eyes closed, her skin pale, her breathing shallow. Svenson glanced at the Comte.

"Is she sleeping?" he whispered.

"I don't believe so. If she were not cold, I should say it is a fever. As she is cold, I cannot say—perhaps you can. Please . . ." He stepped away from the bed, pulling apart the curtains as he did.

Svenson leaned forward to study the woman's face. Her features struck Svenson as slightly Asiatic. He pulled up her eyelid, felt the pulse in her throat, noted with unease the cobalt cast of her lips and tongue, and with an even greater distress the impressions across her face and throat—similar to the kind of marks a corset (or an octopus) might imprint on a woman's skin. He reached under the blankets for her hand, felt the cold of it, and listened to her pulse there as well. He saw that on the tip of each finger the skin had been worn away. He reached across the bed to find the other hand, where the fingers were identical. Svenson pulled the blankets back to her waist. The woman was nude, and the bluish impressions on her skin ran the length of her torso. He felt a movement at his side. The Comte had brought over the medical kit. Svenson fished out his stethoscope, and listened to the woman's lungs. He turned to the Comte. "Has she been in water?"

"She has not," rasped the Comte.

Svenson frowned, listening to her labored breathing. It sounded exactly like a person half-drowned. He reached back into the bag for a lancet and a thermometer. He would need to know her temperature, and then he was going to need some of her blood.

Some forty minutes later, Svenson had washed his hands and was rubbing his eyes. He looked out to see if the sun was coming up, but the sky was still dark. He yawned, trying to remember when he had last been up through an entire night—when he was more resilient, in any case. The Comte appeared at his side with a white china cup.

"Coffee with brandy," he said, handing the cup to Svenson and walking back to the table to pick up his own. The coffee was hot and black, almost burned, but perfect. Along with the brandy—a rather large amount of brandy for so small a cup—it was exactly what he needed. He took another deep drink, finishing the cup, and set it down.

"Thank you," he said.

The Comte d'Orkancz nodded, then turned his gaze to the bed. "What is your opinion, Doctor? Is it possible she will recover?"

"It would help if I had more information."

"Perhaps. I will tell you that her condition is the result of an accident, that she was not in water—I can only assure you of this, not explain it convincingly—yet water was permeating her person. Nor was this mere water, Doctor, but a liquid of special properties, an energetically *charged* liquid. The woman had laid her person open to this procedure. To my great regret the procedure was interrupted. The direction of the liquid was reversed and she was—how to say this—both depleted and flooded at the same time."

"Is this—I have heard—I have seen, on the Prince—the scarring—the Process—"

"Process?" d'Orkancz snapped in alarm, but then as quickly his voice became calm. "Of course, the Prince... you would have spoken to him, he would have been in a state to hold back nothing. It is regrettable."

"You must understand that my interests here are my duty to protect him, and my duty as a doctor—in good faith—and if *this*"—Svenson gestured to the woman, her pale flesh almost luminous in the lantern glow—"is the danger you have exposed Karl-Horst to—"

"I have not."

"But—"

"You do not know. The woman, if you please, Doctor Svenson."

The sharpness of his tone stopped further protest in Svenson's throat. He wiped the sweat from his face.

"If you've read my pamphlet enough to remember my name you know yourself already. She bears all the evidence of having been rescued after prolonged immersion in freezing water—the winter Baltic, for example. At certain temperatures the bodily functions slow precipitously—this can be both deadly and a preservative. She is alive, she breathes. Whether this has irreparably damaged her mind, I cannot say. Whether she will ever awake from this—this winter sleep—I cannot say either. Yet, I—I must ask about the marks across her body—whatever has been done to her—"

D'Orkancz held up his hand. Svenson stopped talking.

"Is there anything to be done *now,* Doctor—that is the question."

"Keep her warm. Force her to drink warm fluids. I would suggest some kind of massage to encourage circulation—all peripheral—either the damage has been done or it hasn't."

The Comte d'Orkancz was silent. His cup of coffee lay untouched beside him. "One more question, Doctor Svenson, . . . perhaps the most crucial of all."

"Yes?"

"Do you think she's dreaming?"

Svenson was taken aback, for the Comte's tone was not entirely one of sympathy—within the body of his concern ran a vein of iron inquiry. He answered carefully, glancing back to the now-curtained bed.

"There is inconstant movement of the eyes . . . it might be ascribed to some kind of fugue state . . . it is not catatonia . . . she is not aware, but perhaps . . . within her own mind . . . perhaps dreams . . . perhaps delirium . . . perhaps peace."

The Comte d'Orkancz did not reply, his eyes lost for a moment in thought. He came back to the present, looked up. "And now . . . what shall I do with you, Doctor Svenson?"

Svenson's eyes flicked over to his coat, hanging on the stand, the pistol buried in the pocket. "I will take my leave—"

"You'll stay where you are, Doctor," he whispered sharply, "until I say otherwise. You have assisted me—I would prefer to reward such cooperation—and yet you stand quite clearly opposed to other interests that I must preserve."

"I must recover my Prince."

The Comte d'Orkancz sighed heavily.

Svenson groped for something to say, but was unsure what to reveal—he could mention Aspiche or Lorenz, or Madame Lacquer-Sforza or Major Blach, he could mention the blue glass card, but would this make him more valuable in the Comte's mind, or more dangerous? Was he more likely to be spared the more ignorantly loyal to the Prince he appeared? He could not see clearly out of the greenhouse due to the glaring lantern light reflecting on the glass—he could not place any of the guards. Even if he were able to reach his pistol and somehow overcome d'Orkancz—by his size an extremely powerful man—how could he elude the others? He didn't know where he was—he was exhausted—he had no safe place to hide—he still knew nothing about the Prince's location.

He looked up at the Comte. "Would you mind if I had a cigarette?"

"I would."

"Ah."

"Your cigarettes are in your coat, are they not?"

"They are—"

"Most likely quite near to the service revolver you brandished earlier this evening. Does it not seem like a great deal has happened since then? I have grappled with death and disruption, with intrigue and retribution—and you have done the same. And you have lost your Prince *again.* We would both be nearly comic, were not these consequences so steeped in blood. Have you ever killed anyone, Doctor?"

"I'm afraid many men have died under my hands..."

"On the table, yes, but that is different—however you may rack yourself with accusation, it is entirely different—as you well know. You do know exactly what I am asking."

"I do. I have."

"When?"

"In the city of Bremen. A man who had—it seemed—corrupted a young niece of the Duke—he was intractable, my instructions... I—I forced him to drink poison, at pistol-point. I am not proud of the incident. Only an idiot would be."

"Did he know what he was drinking?"

"No."

"I'm sure he had his suspicions."

"Perhaps."

Svenson remembered the fellow's red face, the hacking rattle in his throat, his rolling eyes, and then recovering the incriminating letters from his pocket as he lay on the floor, the sharp smell of the man's bile. The memory haunted him. Svenson rubbed his eyes. He was hot—even more hot than he had been—the room was truly stifling. His mouth was so dry. He felt a sudden prickle of adrenaline. He looked at the Comte, then at the empty cup of coffee, then—how long did it take him to turn his head—at the Comte's untouched cup on the table. The table was above him. He had dropped to his knees, realizing dimly that he did not feel the impact. His head swam. The fibers of the carpet pressed into his face. Dark warm water closed over him, and he vanished within it.

He opened his eyes in shadow, goaded by a nagging shapeless urgency, through a warm woolen veil of sleep. He blinked. His eyelids were extremely heavy—impossibly heavy—he closed them. He was jolted awake again, his entire body jarred, and now he took in more of what his senses told him: the rough grain of wood against his skin, the smell of dust and oil, the sound of wheels and hoofbeats. He was in the back of a cart, staring up at a cloth canopy in the near dark. The wagon rattled along—they were traveling across uneven cobbles, the jolts waking him before he otherwise would have. He reached with his right hand and touched the canvas cover, some two feet above him. His mouth and throat were parched. His temples throbbed. He realized with a certain distant pleasure that he was not dead, that for some reason—or so far—the Comte had spared his life. He felt carefully around him, his limbs aching but responsive. Crumpled near his head was his coat—the revolver no longer in the pocket, though he still possessed the glass card. He groped farther, at his arm's length, and flinched as his hand found a booted foot. Svenson swallowed and rolled his eyes. How many corpses—or near-corpses, if he counted the woman and the soldiers—had been thrown Svenson's way this day alone? It would be ridiculous if it were not also sickening. With a grim determination the Doctor felt farther—the body was oppositely laid in the cart, the feet near his head—moving down the boots to the trousers, which had a heavy side seam, braid or frogging—a uniform. He followed the leg until he came to, next to it, a hand. A man's hand, and icy cold.

The cart lurched again and Svenson pushed his exhausted mind to determine in which direction they moved—was his head at the front of the cart or the rear? He couldn't tell—the vehicle was moving so slowly and over such an uneven surface that all he felt were the shakes up and down. He reached above his head and touched a wooden barrier. He felt along the corner, where this piece joined the side of the cart, and found no brackets, no bolts . . . could it be the rear? If so, it was bolted closed on the outside—to get out he would have to climb over it, perhaps even cutting through the canvas cover—if he had anything to cut it with. He felt for his medical kit, but it was nowhere to be found. With a grimace, he reached again toward the body and groped for the pockets in the man's uniform coat, and then his trousers—all had been emptied. With distaste his fingers found the man's collar, and felt his badge of rank. A colonel. Svenson forced himself to touch the man's face: the heavy neck, the moustache, and then, ever so faintly, the curved ridge of flesh around the eyes. He was next to Arthur Trapping.

Doctor Svenson rolled onto his back, facing up, his eyes squeezed shut, his hand over his mouth. He inhaled through his nose and exhaled, slowly, against his hand. He needed to think. He had been drugged and was en route—undoubtedly for disposal—with a deliberately hidden corpse. He was without weapons or allies, in a foreign country, with no knowledge of where he was—though from the cobblestones he was still in the city at least. He tried to think clearly—his mind was fogged, he was still so very tired—and forced his hands to go through his own pockets: a handkerchief, banknotes, coins, a pencil stub, a folded-over scrap of paper, his monocle. He rolled over toward Trapping and searched the man again, this time more thoroughly. In the jacket, between the layers of fabric over the left breast where it would be covered by dangling medals, he felt something hard. He crawled closer to the body and awkwardly pulled himself up onto his elbows, gripping the seam of Trapping's coat with both hands. He yanked at the fabric and felt it give. Another jolt knocked him off balance. He got a better grip and pulled with all his strength. The seam split open. Svenson inserted a finger into the gap and felt a hard, slick surface. He wedged his thumb into the hole and pulled the object free. He didn't need any light to know it was another glass card. He stuffed it into his coat pocket next to the first. He was suddenly still. The cart had stopped moving.

He felt it jostle as the drivers jumped off, and then heard footsteps on either side of him. He gathered up his coat and shut his eyes—he could at least feign sleep. If the opportunity came to run or knock someone on the head, all the better if they thought him asleep or incapable—though he was far from his best, and even at his best no great fighter. At his feet he heard the sharp metallic clanks of the bolts being shot, and then the back panel was lowered. The canvas cover was flung back and Svenson felt the cooler, damp air of the morning—for the glow through his closed eyelids told him there was light. Before he could fully decide whether or not to open his eyes, he felt a shocking blow in his stomach—a sharp poke from a wooden pole—that doubled him over with gasping pain. His eyes popped open, his mouth strained to take in breath, his hands clutched feebly at his abdomen, the pain lancing the full length of his body. Above he heard the laughter of several men, pitiless and shrill.

With a great effort, to prevent another blow, Doctor Svenson hauled himself up with his arms, rolled to his side and forced his legs underneath him one at a time, so he could kneel. His lank blond hair had fallen into his eyes and he brushed it away stiffly. He pulled his monocle from its pocket and screwed it into position, taking in the scene around him. The cart was stopped in a closed cobbled yard, morning fog clinging to the rooftops around it. The yard was littered with barrels and crates bristling with jagged, rusted pieces of metal. To his other side was an open double doorway, and beyond it a forge. He was at a blacksmith's. Two of the Comte d'Orkancz's ruffians stood at the end of the cart, one with a long pole with a sharp grapple on the end. The other, more practically, held Svenson's own pistol. Svenson looked down at Trapping's body in the light. The grey face was marked with the now-purpled scarring around the eyes. There was no obvious cause of death—no wound, no evidence of trauma, no particular discoloration. Svenson noticed that Trapping's other hand was gloved, and that the tip of the index finger was torn. He leaned down and wrestled the glove off. The tip of the finger was a striking indigo, the skin punctured by some kind of needle or thin blade, the flesh around the incision crusted with a blue-white powder. At a noise from the forge, Svenson looked up to see Francis Xonck and Major Blach walking into the courtyard. He dropped the glove back over the hand.

* * *

"At last, at last," called Francis Xonck. "We are ready down at the portage." He smiled at Svenson. "We were, however, only prepared for two. We must innovate. This way—use the barrow." He nodded at a wheelbarrow, and walked over to a wooden wall, which slid to the side on a track at his push. Beyond was a slanted, paved path. Xonck marched down it. Blach fixed Svenson with a glare of hatred and snapped his fingers. From the forge behind him emerged two of his black-coated troopers. Svenson did not recognize them, but he was bad at faces. Major Blach barked at them, "Escort the Doctor!" and followed Xonck. Svenson hobbled off the cart, clutching his coat, and with a trooper on either side walked from the yard. He glanced back once to see the Comte's men lugging Trapping to the barrow.

As they walked, Svenson struggled into his coat, for it was very cold. The path was lined on either side by rough, gapped, plank fencing, and wound between decaying buildings and heaps of refuse. He knew they were walking to the river. The pain in his stomach had eased and his immediate fear was edging into cold, reckless implacability. He called ahead to Major Blach, with as much of a sneer as he could muster.

"Did you find the Prince, Major? Or have you spent the night drinking other men's wine... and licking other men's... boots?"

Blach stopped where he was and turned. Svenson did his best with a dry mouth and launched a gob of spit in the Major's direction. It traveled only a few feet but still made its point. Major Blach flushed and took a stride toward Svenson. Behind Blach, Francis Xonck called out to him sharply. "Major!" Blach stopped, gave Svenson another murderous look and continued down the path. Xonck looked over the Major's shoulder for a moment, meeting Svenson's gaze, and chuckled. He waited for Blach to reach him, took hold of his arm and shoved him forward, so Xonck was now between them and Major Blach in the lead. Svenson looked back. The Comte's men were bringing down the body, covered by a tarp—one holding the barrow, one in the rear with the pistol. There was no clear way for him to run, should he be foolish enough to try. Instead he called ahead to Blach in an even louder voice.

"Is it an easy thing to betray your country, Major? I am curious—what was your price? Gold? New uniform? Women? Athletic young men? A sheep farm?"

Major Blach wheeled, his hand digging for his pistol. Xonck took hold of his uniform with both hands and with difficulty—Xonck was stronger than he seemed—restrained Blach where he was. Once the Major had stopped his charge, Xonck again turned him around—whispering into his ear—and shoved him forward. When the Major had advanced a few paces, Xonck turned to Svenson, nodding to the troopers. Svenson felt a shove and began again to walk, now with Xonck right ahead of him. Xonck looked back at him with a smile.

"I should have said suckling pigs instead of sheep, but I believe he took your point. I am Francis Xonck."

"Captain-Surgeon Abelard Svenson."

"Rather more than that, I think." Xonck smiled. "You have the distinction of actually impressing the Comte d'Orkancz, which is a rare enough event that there really ought to be a parade." He smiled again and took in the troopers and the men behind them with the wheelbarrow. "Perhaps it is a parade after all."

"I should have preferred more bunting," said Svenson, "and some trumpets."

"Another time, I am sure." Xonck chuckled.

They walked on. Ahead Svenson could see the river. They were actually quite close to it, the fog and the buildings around them having obscured the view.

"Did you locate the Prince?" asked Svenson, as airily as possible.

"Why, did you?" answered Xonck.

"I'm afraid I did not," admitted Svenson. "Though I do know who has taken him."

"Indeed?" Xonck studied him for a moment, his eyes twinkling. "How *satisfying* for you."

"I am not sure you know those responsible. Though I believe you—or your companions—have tried to apprehend them."

Xonck did not reply, but Svenson thought his smile had become that much more fixed on his lips, and disconnected from his searching eyes. Xonck turned his gaze ahead, and saw that they approached the end of the path. "Ah—the splendid waterfront. We are arrived."

The path opened onto a slippery portage way, sloping under the grey surface of the river. To either side was a raised stone pier, where cargo or passengers might more easily be lowered. Tied to the left-hand pier was a flat, featureless barge with one high oar in the rear like a gondola's. In its bow was a latched section that could be let down as a gangplank, as it presently was. In the center of the narrow barge was a closed metal coffin. Another, unsealed, lay on the pier. Svenson realized that once on the water, the ramp could be lowered again and the coffins slipped into the river to sink. If they had tried to push the coffins over the side the entire craft would be dangerously unbalanced. Two more of the Comte's men were in the barge, and they stepped forward to help the others bundle Arthur Trapping into the waiting coffin. As Svenson stood to the side between the troopers, he watched them install the body and secure the lid with a series of clamps and screws. With a small surge of something vaguely like hope he noticed that, under Trapping's body in the wheelbarrow, one of the men had thrown his medical kit. He looked up to see Major Blach on the pier, glaring at him. The Major snarled to Xonck, who had crossed to stand near him.

"What of him?" He nodded toward Svenson. "There are only two coffins."

"What would you suggest?" asked Xonck.

"Send back to the forge—weight him down with scrap metal and chain."

Xonck nodded and turned to the Comte's men who'd brought down the body. "You heard. Metal and chain, quickly." To Svenson's relief they tossed the medical kit on the ground before turning the barrow around and jogging back up the path. Major Blach removed his pistol from his holster and—staring at Svenson—barked at his men. "Help with the loading. I will watch him."

Xonck gestured to Blach's pistol with a smile, and then took in the riverside around them with a wave of his arm. "You will notice how peaceful the morning is, Doctor Svenson. And as a thinking man you will understand how the Major's pistol might shatter that peace and draw unwelcome attention to our efforts. In fact, since such a *thinking* man might also assume a well-placed cry for help might accomplish the same, I am obliged to point out that, were such a cry to occur, preserving this lovely silence would no longer *matter*—which is to say that if you make any noise you will be shot with less hesitation than if you were a foam-spitting cur."

"It is of course kind of you to explain things so nicely," muttered Svenson.

"Kindness costs very little, I find." Xonck smiled.

The troopers crossed to the coffin, but one of them glanced back at the Doctor with an expression of curiosity, if not doubt. Svenson watched as they manhandled the coffin onto the barge. When they were at the exact moment of balance—two of them knee-deep in water on the sides, one in the barge, one shoving from the rear—he called up to Major Blach.

"Tell me, Major, is Herr Flaüss a traitor like you, or merely incompetent?"

Blach cocked his pistol. Xonck sighed audibly and placed his hand on the Major's arm.

"Really, Doctor, you must desist."

"If I'm going to be murdered, I am at least curious whether I leave my Prince in the hands of two traitors or one."

"But presently he is in no one's hands."

"None of *their* hands."

"Yes yes," snapped Xonck. "As you have already told me. Careful there!"

The men had shoved the coffin too far, to the side of the barge, and the entire craft tilted perilously. One man flung himself onto the barge to balance the weight while the other three dragged the coffin back into position. The Comte's two men carefully took up their places on the barge—one at the rear oar, the other readying shorter paddling oars for each side.

"Why go to the bother of transporting the Colonel here?" asked Svenson. "Why not just sink him in a canal near Harschmort?"

Xonck cast a side glance at the Major. "Call it Germanic thoroughness," he said.

"The Comte examined his body," replied Svenson, suddenly knowing it was true. "In his greenhouse." They didn't know something... or had something to hide—but hidden from someone at Harschmort? Hidden from Vandaariff? Were they not all allies?

"We need to kill him," snarled Blach.

"Not with *that*," answered Xonck, nodding at Blach's pistol.

Svenson knew he should act before the others came back with the wheelbarrow, when there were that many fewer of them. He pointed to his medical kit.

"Mr. Xonck, I see there my own medical kit. I know I am to die, and I know that you may not shoot me for making too loud a noise. This leaves any number of more hideous options—strangling, stabbing, drowning, all of them slow and painful. If you will allow, I can quite easily prepare an injection for myself that will be swift, silent, and painless—it will perform a service to us all."

"Afraid, are you?" taunted Major Blach.

"Indeed, I admit it freely," answered Svenson, "I am a coward. If I must die—as it seems I must, for the credulous Prince you have abused and kidnapped—then I would prefer oblivion to agony."

Xonck studied him and called to one of the troopers. "Hand me the bag."

The nearest trooper did so. Xonck snapped it open, rummaged inside, and fixed Svenson with a searching, skeptical eye. He snapped the bag shut and threw it back to the trooper. "No needles," he said to Svenson, "and no attempt to throw acid or anything else you may have on hand. You will drink your medicine, and do it quietly. If there is the slightest trouble, I will merely gag you and let the Major do his worst—I assure you no one will hear the difference." He nodded to the trooper. The trooper clicked his heels by instinct and brought the medical kit to Svenson.

"I am grateful to you, I'm sure," he said, snapping the kit open.

"Hurry up," answered Xonck.

Svenson's mind was racing. He had said anything he could think of to try and muddle the loyalty of the two troopers, to cast Blach as a traitor—it hadn't worked. For a moment he wondered at his own loyalty—how far he had come, what desperate straits he had braved—all so beyond his normal character, and for what? He knew then it was not the Prince—a source of constant frustration and disappointment—nor his father, unthinking and proud. Was it for von Hoern? Was it for Corinna? Was it because he must dedicate his life to something, to stay true, no matter what that was, in the face of her loss? Svenson stared into his medical kit, not needing to counterfeit his shaking hands. The fact was, the oblivion of poison *was* a damned sight better than trying some foolhardy escape and failing—as he was bound to do. He had no illusions of the brutal lengths to which Blach would go—especially to quell any doubts in the minds of his men—to render Svenson a gibbering, pleading mess. Such an exit was tempting, and for a brief moment his searching logic was overtaken by an impulsive reverie of his lost past—the high meadows in flower, coffee in an autumn café, the opera box in Paris, Corinna as a girl, her uncle's farm. It was impossible, overwhelming—he could not surrender in such a rush. He plunged his hand into the case, brought out a flask, then deliberately bobbled it out of his grasp so it shattered on the pier. He looked up at Xonck pleadingly.

"No matter—no matter—there are other things to use—let me just find it—a moment, I beg you..." He set the kit on the pier and knelt over it, rummaging. He glanced quickly at the trooper to his right. The man carried a saber in a scabbard but no other weapon. Svenson was sane enough to realize that he could not hope to seize the hilt by surprise and draw it cleanly—the angle was all wrong. He was at best likely to have it half-out and be grappling with the trooper when Major Blach shot him cleanly in the back. Xonck was watching him. He selected a flask, looked at it in the light, shook his head, and replaced it, digging for another.

"What was wrong with that one?" called Blach impatiently.

"It was not quick enough," answered Svenson. "Here—this one will do."

He stood, a second glass flask in his hand. The troopers were on either side of him, and together they stood at the corner of one of the piers and the portage. Across from them on the other pier, some five yards away, were Xonck and Blach. Between them was the portage itself and the barge with the two coffins and the Comte's two men.

"What did you select?" called Xonck.

"Arsenic," answered Svenson. "Useful in small doses for psoriasis, tuberculosis, and—most pertinently for princes—syphilis. In larger doses, immediately fatal." He removed the stopper and looked around him, gauging the distances as closely as possible. The men were not yet back from the forge. The men on the barge were watching him with undisguised curiosity. He knew he had no choice. He nodded to Xonck. "I thank you for the courtesy." He turned to Major Blach, and smiled. "Burn in hell."

Doctor Svenson tossed back the contents of the flask in a gulp. He swallowed, choked hideously, his throat constricting, his face turning crimson. He dropped the flask, clutching at his throat, and staggered back into the trooper to his right, pawing for balance. An unearthly rattle rose out of his chest, his mouth worked, his tongue protruded horribly over his lips, his eyes rolled, his knees wobbled—all eyes were upon him. His entire body tensed, as if suspended over a precipice, poised at the very passage into death. In that moment, Svenson became strangely aware of the quiet of the city, that so many people could be so near to them and the only sound the dull lap of the river against the barge and somewhere far away the cry of gulls.

Svenson heaved his weight into the trooper. With a sudden pivot he took hold of the soldier's jacket with both hands and hurled him off the pier toward the barge. The momentum carried the trooper over the gap so he landed with a crash exactly on the side of the barge, causing it to lurch horribly. A sickening moment later, his arms flailing above, his legs thrashing in the water, the coffins slid toward the helpless man. He raised his arms as the first crashed into him, sweeping him viciously from the barge and into the water. Then the second coffin crashed into the first, tipping the entire barge at such a sudden angle that both of the Comte's men were thrown off their feet and into the coffins. Their extra weight tipped the angle even farther, and the shallow barge rolled up and then fully over, all three men and the coffins disappearing below the upended craft.

Svenson ran for the path. The remaining trooper took hold of Svenson's coat with both hands as he went past. Svenson turned, grappling with the trooper, furiously trying to wrench himself free. He could hear the splashes from the water, cries from Blach. The soldier was younger, stronger—they struggled, twisting each other in a circle. For a moment the soldier held Svenson in place and took hold of his throat. In the corner of his eye Svenson saw Blach raise the pistol. Svenson lurched desperately away, pulling the trooper into Blach's line of sight. A loud flat crack erupted into his ear and his face was wet, warm. The trooper fell at his feet—the side of his head a seething mess. Svenson swept the blood from his eyes to see Francis Xonck slap Major Blach savagely across the face. Blach's pistol was smoking.

"You idiot! The noise! You infernal fool!"

Svenson looked down—his feet tangled in the trooper's legs. He seized the fallen man's saber and swept it clear, causing Xonck to hastily step back. Svenson turned at the sound of Blach cocking the pistol.

"If the damage is done," he snarled, "it's no matter to do more . . ."

"Major! Major—there is no need," Xonck hissed in a fury.

Svenson could see Blach was going to fire. With a yell he heaved the saber like an awkward knife—end over end, directly toward them—and ran. He heard both men cry out and the loud clang of the blade striking the stone—he'd no idea whether they'd thrown themselves aside or not. His only thought was to charge up the path. He ran on—the uneven stones slick from the morning, his own footsteps obscuring the sound of any pursuit—and was perhaps half-way to the top when he saw the two men with the wheelbarrow coming toward him from the top. The barrow was piled with metal and the men each held one of the handles, balancing it between them. He didn't dare slow his pace, but his heart sank as they saw him and instantly began to trot forward, each man with a broad smile breaking over his face. As they picked up speed scraps of metal bounced out of the pile, clanging on the ground and against the fence. They were perhaps five yards away when they let it go. Svenson flung himself toward the top of the fence to his left, raising his legs. The barrow smashed beneath him, bounced off the wall, and continued recklessly down the slope. With a bestial surge of effort he hauled himself over the fence and dropped into a tangle of boxes and debris.

He had not hurt himself in the fall, though he was on his back and thrashing to rise. On the other side of the fence he could hear the crash of the barrow tipping over and more cries—could it have run into Xonck or Blach? Svenson rolled to his knees as, above him, the fence wobbled back and forth and one of the two barrow men vaulted over it. As the man landed—the drop causing him to double over for just a moment—Svenson snatched a thick wooden board from the mud with both hands and swung. The blow caught the man's near hand—holding a pistol—and hammered it cruelly—Svenson could feel the cracking small bones. The man screamed and the pistol flew across the ground. Svenson swung again, rising up, across the man's face. The man grunted at the impact and crumpled, curled and moaning, at the base of the fence. The fence wobbled again—another man was coming over. Svenson leapt at the pistol—it was his own—and still on his knees turned to the fence above him. The second barrow man was balanced on the fence top, an arm and a leg hooked over, looking down with alarm. Svenson snapped off a shot—missing the man but splintering the wood—and the fellow dropped from sight. A moment later the gleaming length of a saber shot through the fence at the level of Svenson's head, missing him by a matter of inches. He scrabbled away on his back like a crab as the blade scissored back and forth through the slats, probing for him. He could just see the shadows of bodies through the gaps between fence slats and fired again. In reply someone fired back, three shots in rapid succession that tore up the mud around him. Svenson returned fire twice, blindly, and hurled himself away, doing his best to run.

For the first time he saw that the yard was the back of a ruined house, the windows broken and the roof gone, the rear door off its frame and lying broken in the mud. The doorway and the open window frames were lined with faces. Svenson careened toward them even as he tried to take in who they were—children, an older man, women—their skin the color of milky tea, hair black, clothes colorful but worn. He raised the pistol, not at them but toward the sky. "Excuse me—I beg your pardon—please—look out!" He rushed through the door, the bodies around him skittering clear, and glanced back just long enough to see the fence in movement, bodies coming over. He dove ahead into the darkened rooms, leaping cooking pots, pallets, piles of clothing, doing his best not to step on anything or anyone, his senses assailed by the smell of so many persons in such a tangled space, by the open fire, and by pungent spices—he could not even name what they were. Behind him a shot rang out and a splinter of wood whipped into his face. He winced, knew he was bleeding, and nearly ran down a small child—where the hell was the door to the street? He stepped through doorway after doorway—as close as he could come to a dead run—dodging all the occupants—a room of goats?—jumping over an open cooking fire. He heard screams—the other men were in the house—just as he entered what had to be the main hallway, and directly in front of it a ruined set of double doors. He rushed to them, only to find they had been thoroughly nailed shut—of course, the house was condemned. He rushed back, looking for a window to the street. Another shot rang out—he didn't know from where—and he felt a hideous *snip* of air as the bullet traced past his ear. He kicked through a hanging curtain and into someone's occupied bed—a screaming woman, an outraged man—his feet caught up in their sheets but his gaze fixed on another carpet nailed to the wall, hanging down. Svenson threw himself to it and whipped the carpet aside. The window beyond was blessedly clear of glass. He hurdled the frame, tucking his hands around his head, and landed in an awkward sprawl that ended with him facedown on the paving, his pistol bouncing away on the stones.

Svenson thrust himself to his feet—his hands felt raw, his knee bruised, ankle complaining. As he bent to recover the pistol another shot rang out from the window. He turned to see Blach, one hand holding a bloody handkerchief to his face, the other with his smoking pistol, fixing Svenson in his sights. Svenson could not move fast enough. Blach squeezed the trigger, his eyes ablaze with hatred. The hammer landed on an empty chamber. Blach swore viciously and broke open the gun, knocking the empty shells out the window, digging for fresh cartridges. Svenson scooped up his weapon and ran.

He did not know where he was. He kept on until he was winded, doing his best to lose pursuit—dodging from street to street and cutting through what open lots and parks he could find. He finally collapsed in a small churchyard, sitting with his head in his hands on the ancient, cracked cover of a tomb, his chest heaving, his body spent. The light had grown—it was full morning—and the open space between objects struck him as almost shockingly clear. But instead of this making the events of his night seem unreal, Svenson found it was the day he could not trust. The weathered white stone, the worn letters spelling "Thackaray" under his fingers, the leafless branches above—none of these answered the relentless strange world he had entered. For a moment he wondered if he had eaten opium and was in that instant lying stupefied in a Chinaman's den, and all of this a twisting dream. He rubbed his eyes and spat.

Svenson knew that he was no real spy, nor any kind of soldier. He was lost. His ankle throbbed, his hands were scraped, he had not eaten, his throat was raw, and his head felt like a block of rotten cheese from the Comte's drug. He forced himself to remove his boot and palpate his tender ankle—it was not broken, nor probably even seriously sprained, he would simply have to treat it carefully. He scoffed at that unlikely prospect and pulled the revolver from his pocket, breaking it open. There were two cartridges left—he had no others with him. He stuffed it back in his pocket, and realized that the bulk of his money was still at the compound with his box of shells. He'd lost his medical kit, and was for the moment stuck in his uniform and greatcoat that, while a relatively restrained Prussian blue, nevertheless set him apart in a crowd.

His face stung. He brought up a hand to feel dried blood and a small splinter of wood still lodged below his right cheekbone. He delicately pulled it free and pressed a handkerchief to his face. Doctor Svenson realized that he desperately wanted a cigarette. He fished in his coat for his case, extracted one and then snapped a match alight off of his thumb. The smoke hit his lungs with an exquisite tug and he exhaled slowly. Taking his time, he worked his way to the butt, concentrating only on his breathing and on each successive plume of smoke sent over the gravestones. He tossed the butt into a puddle and lit another. He didn't want to be light-headed, but the tobacco was restoring some of his resolve. As he replaced the case his hand bumped the glass cards in his pocket. He had forgotten the second card, from Trapping. He looked around him—the churchyard was still quite abandoned and the buildings around it void of any visible activity. Svenson pulled out the card—it looked identical to the one he had taken from the Prince's chamber. Would he be looking into the mind of Arthur Trapping and see some clue about how he had died? He set his burning cigarette down on the tomb next to him and looked into the card.

It took a moment for the blue veil to part, but once it had Svenson found himself amidst a confusing swirl of images, moving rapidly from one to another without any logic he could discern. It was less as if he occupied another's actual experience—as with Mrs. Marchmoor's encounter with the Prince—so much as their free-floating mind, or even perhaps their dreams. He pulled his gaze up from the card and exhaled. He was shaking, it was just as involving, he had been as much outside of himself as before. He tapped the growing cylinder of ash from his cigarette and took a long drag. He set it down again and gathered himself for a second, more focused visit.

The first images were in a fussy, well-appointed interior—a carpeted room of dark wood and glass lamps, delicate Chinoiserie and thickly upholstered furniture—and a woman sitting on a sofa, a young woman only a part of whose body Svenson could see—her bare forearms and her small hands as they clutched the upholstery, and then her shapely calves just emerging from under her dress as she stretched her legs, and then to her charming green ankle boots . . . each glimpse imbued with a particular proprietary hunger from the gaze he was inhabiting.

From here the card jumped abruptly to a rocky scene, a high view into a pit of grey stone—a quarry?—below an only slightly less grey sky. Suddenly Svenson was *in* the pit, the feel of gravel against his knee—kneeling, bending over a seam of colored stone within the rock—a dark stubbled indigo. An arm—his arm, which was young, strong, in a black coat—and a hand in a black leather glove reached forward to touch the seam of blue, digging a finger into it and crumbling out a loose chunk, as if it were a chalky sort of clay.

The next movement began as one of standing up in the quarry, but as his point of vision rose, the scene around him changed, so that when he was fully upright he was in a winter orchard—apple trees, he thought—the base of each trunk packed with straw. His gaze moved to his left and he saw a high stone wall and a weathered hedgerow, and behind them both the peaked rooftop of a country manor.

He turned farther to his left and found himself facing Harald Crabbé, who was smirking, leaning back and looking out the window of a coach—the window beyond it showing a country wood racing past. Crabbé turned to him—to whomever this was—and quite clearly mouthed the words "your decision" . . . and turned back to the window.

The window now opened onto another room, a curving stone hallway, ending in a metal-banded door. The door swung open and revealed a cavernous chamber, ringed with machinery, a massive man leaning over a table, his broad back obscuring the identity of the woman strapped to it, a woman . . . Svenson suddenly recognized the room—at the Institute, where he had rescued the Prince.

He looked up from the card. There was more—in the gaps, almost like a window streaming with rain—that he could not clearly see. His cigarette had gone out. He debated lighting another, but knew that he must really decide what to do. He had no idea if they were still searching. If so, they would reach the churchyard eventually. He had to find somewhere he could stay in safety. Or, he countered, he had to seize the bull by the horns. At what point was the Prince beyond aid? Svenson could not in conscience abandon him. He could not go back to the compound—he did not trust Flaüss—and he still had no idea where to find the man in red or Isobel Hastings. If he was not going to simply find a place to hide, the only avenue he had left, however foolish it seemed, was to try once more to confront Madame Lacquer-Sforza. Surely during the busy scramble of morning it would be safe to approach the St. Royale. There were two bullets left in his pistol—more than enough to convince her, if he could just gain entry.

He looked down and saw that he had not replaced his boot, and did so, gingerly pulling it up around his still-throbbing ankle. He stood and took a few steps. Now that the rush of adrenalized fear had faded, he felt the pain more keenly, but he knew he could walk on it—indeed, that he had no choice. All it needed was rest. He would exhaust this last possibility for information and then find some place to sleep—whether he could return safely to Macklenburg he did not know. Svenson sighed heavily and limped from the churchyard, retracing his steps to a narrow alley that ran next to the church. The sun was behind clouds—he had no real idea which direction was which. At the alley's end he looked around him, and then back at the church with its open doors. He entered the dark interior and made his way down the aisle, nodding to the few figures at worship, walking steadily to the base of the bell tower, which must have a staircase. He strode past the puzzled priest with his best scowl of medical authority and snapped a brusque "Good day to you, Father—your bell tower?" He nodded gravely as the man pointed in the direction of a small door. Svenson walked to it and stepped through, inwardly groaning at the number of steps he was going to climb with his injured ankle. He did his best to trot briskly until he was out of the priest's view, and then favored the foot by hopping on the other and holding the rail. He was perhaps seventy galling steps into the climb when he came to a narrow window covered with a wooden shutter. He pushed it open, dislodging an accretion of pigeon droppings and feathers, and smiled. From this height he could see the curving silver loop of the river, the green of

Circus Garden, the white stone mass of the Ministries, and the open plaza of St. Isobel's Square. Between them all, its high red-tiled roof spires tipped with black and gold pennants, he found the St. Royale.

He descended as quickly as possible and dropped a coin into the collection box. Once on the street, he traveled through narrow alleys and residential lanes, keeping close to the walls. He passed a block of warehouses, swarming with men loading crates of all shapes onto carts. In the middle of it all was a small canteen, tucked between a storehouse of grain and another of raw fabric, rolling past in colorful bales. Svenson purchased a cup of boiled coffee and three fresh rolls. He tore them apart as he walked, the pith steaming, and drank the coffee as slowly as he could make himself, so as not to burn his mouth. He began to feel a bit more human as he neared the merchants' district near St. Isobel's—so much that he became self-conscious of his gashed face and disheveled greatcoat. He smoothed his hair back and swatted the dust from his coat—it would have to do—and strode ahead with what bluster he could manage. He imagined himself as Major Blach, which was at least entertaining.

Svenson skirted the hotel by a curving path of service alleys behind a row of fashionable restaurants, at this time of day thronged with deliveries of produce and slaughtered fowl. He had been careful, and perhaps lucky, to progress so far unobserved. Any attempt to take him would be swift and unforgiving. At the same time, his enemies were powerful enough to sway any mechanism of law. The slightest infraction—let alone shooting one of the Comte's men in the street—could send him to prison, or straight to the gallows. He stood at the alley's end, facing onto Grossmaere, the broad avenue that, two blocks away, ran past the St. Royale. He first looked in the opposite direction (it was possible that their line of sentries was farther away) but saw no one, or at least saw none of the Comte's men or Blach's troopers. With the involvement of Crabbé—or, heaven forbid, Vandaariff—there could be any number of other minions enlisted to find and kill him.

He looked toward the hotel. Could they be watching from above? The traffic was thick—it was by now well after nine o'clock—and the morning's business in full throng. Svenson took a breath and stepped out, keeping across the street from the hotel, walking close to the walls and behind other pedestrians, his right hand on the revolver in his pocket. He kept his gaze on the hotel, glancing quickly into each shop front or lobby that he passed. At the corner he trotted across and leaned casually against the wall, peering around. The St. Royale was across the avenue. He still saw no one he could place as a sentry. It made no sense. He had already been found here once, trying to see her. Why would they not, even as a contingency, consider he would do the same again? He wondered if the real trap lay inside—perhaps in another private room—where he could be dealt with outside the public view. The possibility made his errand more dangerous, for he would not know until the last moment whether he was safe or not. Still, he'd made his choice. Grimly resolved, Svenson continued down the sidewalk.

He was nearly opposite the hotel when his view became blocked by two delivery carts whose horses had run afoul of each other. The drivers cursed loudly as men jumped from each cart to disentangle the harnesses and carefully back up each team. This caused the coaches behind to stop in turn—with another eruption of curses from each newly inconvenienced driver. Svenson could not help being distracted—his attention on the two carts as they finally worked themselves free and passed by, their drivers each offering one last particularly foul epithet—and so he found himself directly across from the hotel's front entrance when the avenue had cleared. Before him, splendidly arrayed in a violet dress brilliantly shot with silver thread, black gloves, and a delicate black hat, stood Madame Lacquer-Sforza. Next to her, once more in a striped dress—now of blue and white—stood Miss Poole. Svenson immediately shrank away, pressing against the windows of a restaurant. They did not see him. He waited—scanning the street in either direction—ecstatic that he might be able to speak to her without entering the hotel, without being trapped. He swallowed, glanced for an opening in the coach traffic, and stepped forward.

His foot had just left the paved sidewalk for the cobbled street when he froze and then instantly scrambled backwards. From behind the two women had emerged Francis Xonck—now wearing an elegant yellow morning coat and top hat—tugging on a pair of yellow kidskin gloves. With a handsome smile he bent and whispered something that spurred Miss Poole to blush and giggle and Madame Lacquer-Sforza to wryly smile. Xonck extended an arm for each woman and stepped between them as they hooked their arms in his. He nodded toward the street and for a horrified moment Svenson thought he had been seen—he was more or less in plain sight—but saw that Xonck referred to an open coach that was even then drawing to them, blocking Svenson's view. In the coach sat the Comte d'Orkancz, in his fur, his expression dark. The Comte made no effort to speak or acknowledge the others as they entered the coach, Xonck assisting each woman and climbing in last. Madame Lacquer-Sforza sat next to the Comte. She leaned to whisper in his ear. He—grudgingly, but as if he too were unable to resist—smiled. At this Xonck grinned, showing his white teeth, and Miss Poole burst into another fit of giggles. The coach pulled away. Svenson turned and reeled down the street.

She was gone—she was with them. No matter what other webs she might be spinning, Madame Lacquer-Sforza was their ally. If he could have spoken to her alone—but he had no longer any idea where or when or how that might happen. Svenson looked back at the hotel and saw that two of the Comte's men were lounging by the main entrance. He walked steadily away, his face down, seized by the realization of just how close he had come to suicide. At the end of the block he again ducked around the corner and pressed himself against the wall. What could he possibly do? Where could he possibly go? What leverage could he acquire against such a powerful cabal? He looked up and saw across Grossmaere Avenue . . . was it? It was—the road he had taken so long ago with the Comte, toward the secret garden and the greenhouse. The woman. He could find her—he could take her—he could ransack the greenhouse for information—he might even lay in ambush for the Comte himself. What did he have to lose? He peered back at the hotel entrance—the men were laughing together. Svenson gauged the traffic and darted out, ducking behind one coach and then another, and was across the avenue. He looked back. No one was following. He was clear of them, and moved with a new purpose.

He tried to remember the exact route to the garden. It had been dark and the streets thick with fog, and his attention elsewhere—on the men following and on the Comte's conversation. The streets looked so very different in the day and full of people. Still, he could find it—a turn here, along the next block, across that lane—and then around another corner. He found himself at a broad intersection, feeling as if he had mistaken part of the path, when he saw the entrance to a narrow lane across and farther down the street. Could that be it? He walked rapidly along his side of the street until he could gaze down the lane... it was different, but he thought he could see the church-like alcove where the Comte had unlocked the door. Could that be the high wall that lined the garden? Would there be men guarding it? Could he force the lock? Though the alley itself was empty of traffic, he knew all these questions would have to be answered with the crowded avenue only a stone's throw away. Before he crossed the street toward it, he gave one last look around him to make sure he had not been followed.

Svenson froze. Behind him, through the glass double doors of what had to be another hotel, he saw a young woman sitting on a plush settee, her chestnut hair falling in sausage curls over her face, bent seriously over an open journal, scribbling notes, surrounded by books and newspapers. One of her legs was folded under her on the settee, but on the other—her dress riding up just enough to reveal her shapely calf—she wore a darling green ankle boot. Without another thought Doctor Svenson opened the door to the hotel and went in.

FOUR

Boniface

Naturally enough, Miss Temple's first reaction was one of annoyance. She had abandoned her rooms to avoid the mute searching gaze of her maids, silently following her about like a pair of cats, and the far more insistent presence of her Aunt Agathe. She had slept nearly all of the previous day, and when she finally opened her eyes the sky was once again dark. She had bathed and eaten in silence, then slept again. When she woke for the second time in the early morning her aunt had installed herself at the foot of the bed in an armchair dragged by the maids from another room. It had been made clear to Miss Temple the distress she had caused, starting with her unforeseen absence at afternoon tea, and then at dinner, and finally her (characteristically stubborn and reckless) refusal to appear throughout the whole of the evening, to the point that the hotel staff had been alerted—a point of no return, to put it bluntly. This notoriety within the Boniface could only have been inflamed by Miss Temple's own bloody unexplained arrival (only minutes, Agathe insisted, after she herself had fallen asleep from the exhaustion of worry and waiting).

Agathe was the older sister of Miss Temple's father, and had lived in the city all of her life. She had been married once to a man who died young and without money, and Agathe had spent her extended widowhood drawing meagerly upon the fortune of a distant grudging sibling. Her hair was grey and at all times tightly kept beneath a hat or wrap or kerchief, as if exposure to the air might breed disease. Her teeth were whole but discolored where her gums had pulled away, which made them appear rather long and giving the rare smiles she was able to bestow onto her niece an unwholesome predatory aspect.

Miss Temple accepted there had been cause for worry and so she had done all she could to allay the aged woman's fear, even going so far as to answer aloud the delicately pressing question that obviously loomed unvoiced behind her aunt's every euphemistic query—did her niece still possess her virtue? She had assured her aunt that indeed, she had returned intact, and all the more determined to remain so. She did not, however, go into any great detail about where she had been or what she had endured.

The bloody silk underthings and the filthy topcoat had been burnt in the room's coal heater while she'd been asleep—the maids hesitantly bringing them to her aunt's attention when they'd found them littering the floor. Miss Temple herself had refused any suggestion that she see a doctor, a refusal Aunt Agathe had accepted without protest. This acquiescence had surprised Miss Temple, but then she realized her aunt believed that the smaller the circle of knowledge, the smaller the prospect for scandal. They had managed to find a potent salve for the still-raw scoring above her left ear. She would retain a scar, but her hair, once washed and re-curled, hung down to cover it perfectly well, save for a small cherry-red flick the size of a baby's thumbnail that extended, glistening with salve, onto the unblemished skin of her cheekbone. However, as Miss Temple sat in bed eating her breakfast, she found her aunt's investiture in the armchair increasingly odious, watching her every bite like an animal hoping for scraps—in this case hoping for some further explanation, some crumb of surety that her position and pension were not to be obliterated by the foolish, wanton urges of a naïve girl thrown over by her ambitious cad of a sweetheart. The problem was that Agathe said nothing. Not once did she challenge Miss Temple's actions, not once did she trumpet the young lady's reckless irresponsibility or upbraid her for an unlikely escape, which was surely the result of some undeserved divine intervention. All of this Miss Temple could have dealt with, but the silence—the somehow *puling* silence—vexed her extremely. Once the tray had been removed she announced in a voice of unquestionable clarity that, while she again regretted any inconvenience caused, she had become involved in an adventure, she was unharmed and, far from being finished with the matter, had every intention to pursue it most keenly.

Her aunt did not answer, but merely cast her disapproving gaze away from Miss Temple and toward the tidy work desk, upon which the large oiled revolver lay like some kind of loathsome stuffed reptile, a gift brought from some strange uncle's journey to Venezuela. Her aunt looked back at Miss Temple. Miss Temple announced that she would also be needing a box of the appropriate cartridges.

Her aunt did not respond. Miss Temple took this as an opportunity to end the discussion—or non-discussion—and left the bed for her dressing room, locking the door behind her. With a sigh of frustration she balled her nightdress over her waist and squatted on the chamber pot. It was still early morning, but there was light enough to see her green boots on the floor where the maids had placed them. She winced with discomfort as she wiped herself and stood, replacing the lid. When she had taken her bath it had been dark, mere candle light. She walked to the mirror and understood why the others had stared so. On her throat, above the collar of her nightdress, were bruises—the exact purpled impressions of fingertips and a thumb. She leaned her face closer to the glass and touched them gingerly: it was a ghost of Spragg's hand. She took a step back and pulled the nightdress over her head. She felt her breath catch, fear dancing along the length of her spine, for it was as if she looked at a different body than her own. There were so many bruises and scratches, the narrow margin of her survival was abruptly, horribly vivid. She ran her fingers over each point of discolored, tender flesh, finally cupping herself where his fingers had most cruelly marked her.

She shut her eyes and sighed heavily, unable to quite expel her unease along with her breath. It was not a feeling Miss Temple could easily tolerate. She reminded herself sternly that she had escaped. The men were dead.

Miss Temple emerged some minutes later in her dressing gown, calling for the maids, and sat at her desk. She pushed up her sleeves—making a firm point not to glance at her aunt, who was staring at her—and picked up the revolver with as much confidence as she could muster. It took her longer than she would have liked—long enough that both maids were now watching as well—but finally she was able to open the cylinder and empty the remaining shells onto the blotter. This done, she quickly wrote a list—again, in the writing taking more time than she would have liked, simply because with each item details emerged that she must make plain. When she was finished she blew on the paper to dry the ink, and turned to the maids. They were two country girls, near enough to her own age that the gaps in respective experience and education became so obvious as to be unbridgeable. To the older, who could read, she handed the folded piece of paper.

"Marie, this is a list of items I will require both from the hotel management and from shops in the city. You will present the management with items one, two, and three, and then from them receive directions as to the shops best suited to satisfy items four and five. I will give you money"—and here Miss Temple reached into the desk drawer and removed a leather notebook with a small pile of crisp banknotes tucked into it. She deliberately peeled off two—then three—notes and handed them to Marie, who bobbed her head as she took them—"and you will make the purchases. Do not forget *receipts*, so I will know exactly how much money has been spent."

Marie nodded gravely, and with some reason, for Miss Temple was habitually watchful with her money and did not allow odd small sums to disappear where others might, or at least not without due acknowledgment of her generosity.

"The first item is a collection of newspapers, the *World*, the *Courier*, the *Herald*, for today, for yesterday, and for the day before. The second item is a map of the local railway lines. The third item is a geographical map, specifically as it relates to the coastal fen country. The fourth item, which you must find, is a box of *these*." Here she handed Marie one of the bullets from the revolver. "The fifth item, which will most likely take the longest, for you must be extremely exacting, are three sets of undergarments—you know my sizes—in the finest silk: one in white, one in green, and one... in black."

With the other maid, Marthe, she retreated into her dressing room to finish her hair, tighten her corset, and apply layers of powder and cream over the bruises on her throat. She emerged, in another green dress, this with a subtle sort of Italian stitchwork across the bodice, and her ankle boots, which Marthe had duly polished, just as a knock on the door brought the first wave of newspapers and maps. The room clerk explained that they had been forced to send out for some of the previous days' editions, but that these should arrive shortly. Miss Temple gave him a coin, and as soon as he was gone placed the pile on the main dining table and began to sort through it. She did not exactly know what she was looking for, only that she was finished with the frustration of not knowing what she had stepped into. She compared the rail map with the topographical atlas, and began to meticulously plot the route from Stropping Station to Orange Canal. Her finger had progressed as far as De Conque when she became particularly aware of Marthe and Agathe staring at her. She briskly asked Marthe to make tea, and merely gazed steadily at her aunt. Far from taking the hint, Aunt Agathe installed herself in another chair and muttered that a cup of tea would suit her very well.

Miss Temple shifted in her chair, blocking her aunt's view with her shoulder, and continued to trace the line to Orange Locks, and from there to the Orange Canal itself. She took a particular pleasure in plotting the progress from station to station, having a visual reference for each one in her memory. The rail map had no further detail about roads or villages, much less particularly great houses, so she pulled the atlas toward her and found the page with the greatest detail of the area. She marveled at the distance she had traveled, and suppressed another shiver at how isolated and in peril she had actually been. The country between the final two stations seemed uninhabited—there were no villages on the map that she could find. She knew the great house had been near the sea, for she remembered the smell of salt in the air, though she well knew that the sea breeze travels far over land as flat as the fen country, so it could have been farther than it seemed. She tried to work out a reasonable radius of possibility, given the time the coach took to reach the house from the station, and looked for any landmark whatsoever on the map. She saw an odd symbol near the canals themselves, which a quick check with the map's legend told her signified "ruin". How old was the map—could a house that size be so new? Miss Temple looked up at her aunt.

"What is 'Harschmort'?"

Aunt Agathe took in a sharp breath, but said nothing. Miss Temple narrowed her eyes. Neither spoke (for in some ways at least the older lady partook of a familial stubbornness) and after a full silent minute Miss Temple slammed the atlas shut and, brusquely rising from the table, strode to her inner room. She returned, to her aunt's great alarm, with the open revolver, reloading the bullets as she went, and making a great effort at slamming the cylinder home. Miss Temple looked up to see the two women gaping at her and sneered—did they think she was going to shoot them?—snatching up a clutch handbag and dropping the revolver into it. She wound the strap around her wrist and then proceeded to gather her pile of papers with both arms. She snapped at Marthe without the least veil over her irritation. "The *door,* Marthe." The servant girl darted to the front door and pulled it open so Miss Temple, her arms full, was free to sail through. "I will be working where I can find *peace,* if not *cooperation.*"

Walking down the thickly carpeted corridor, and then down to the lobby, Miss Temple felt as if she were re-entering the world, and more importantly that she was confronting the events that had overtaken her. As she walked past various maids and porters, she knew that—because it was the morning shift—these were the same that had seen her blood-soaked arrival. Of course they had all spoken of it, and of course they all cast inquiring glances her way as she walked by. Miss Temple's resolve was firm, however, and she knew if anything had changed, it was only that she needed to be even more self-reliant. She knew how fortunate she was to have her independence, and to have a disposition that cared so little for the opinions of others. Let them talk, she thought, as long as they also saw her holding her head high, and as long as she possessed the whip-hand of wealth. At the main desk she nodded at the clerk, Mr. Spanning—the very man who had opened the door upon her bloody return. Society manners were not so different than those among her father's livestock, she knew, or his pack of hounds—and so Miss Temple held Spanning's gaze longer than normal, until he obsequiously returned her nod.

She had installed herself on one of the wide plush settees in the empty lobby, a quick, hard glare alerting the staff that she required no assistance, spreading the papers into organized stacks. She began by going back to "Harschmort", jotting down her observations—its status as a ruin, its location. She then turned first to the *Courier,* whose pages would be more likely to follow social affairs. She was determined to learn all she could about the gala evening—first as it was understood by the populace at large, and then, by way of any comments she might find about murdered men in the road or missing women, about its true insidious nature. She read through headlines without any immediate idea of what might be most important: scanning the large black type announcing colonial skirmishes, cunning inventions, international ballooning, society balls, works of charity, scientific expeditions, reforms in the navy, infighting amongst the Ministries—it was clear that she was going to have to *delve.* It had not been ten minutes before she sensed the shadow falling over her work and then heard—had someone come in the main doors?—the vaguely insistent clearing of a throat. She looked up, fully ready to audibly snarl if her Aunt Agathe or Marthe had presumed to follow, but Miss Temple's eyes saw someone quite different.

He was a strange sort of man, tall, crisply rumpled in the way only a neat-minded person can be, wearing a blue greatcoat with pale epaulettes and silver buttons and scuffed black boots. His hair was almost white, parted in the center of his head and plastered back, though his exertions had caused some of it to break free and fall over his eyes, one of which held a monocle on a chain. He had not shaved, and it seemed to her that he was not especially well. She could not tell his age, partly because of his obvious fatigue, but also because of the way his hair, which was long on the top of his head, had been shaved on the back and sides, almost like some medieval lord—though perhaps he was merely German. He was staring at her, his gaze moving from her face down to her boots. She looked down at them, then up at his face. He was having difficulty with his words. There was a sparsity about the fellow she found nearly touching.

"Excuse me," he began. His voice was accented, which caused his phrasing to seem more formal than it actually was. "I—I apologize—I have seen you—I did not realize—but now—somehow—through the window—" He stopped, took a breath, swallowed, and opened his mouth to start again and then snapped it shut. She realized that he was staring at her head—the wound above her cheekbone—and then, with rising discomfort, that his eyes had dropped lower, over her neck. He looked up at her, speaking with surprise.

"You have been injured!"

Miss Temple did not reply. While she had not truly expected her cosmetics could hide the bruises for long, she was not prepared to be so soon discovered, much less confront the spectacle of her mauling, reflected in the man's expression of concern. And yet, who was this man? Could agents of the woman in red have found her so soon? As slowly as she could make her hand do it, she reached for the clutch bag. He saw the movement and put up his hand.

"Please—no—of course. You do not know who I am. I am Captain-Surgeon Abelard Svenson, of the Macklenburg Navy, in diplomatic service to his majesty Prince Karl-Horst von Maasmärck, who at this very moment is missing. I am your ally. It is of the utmost importance that we speak."

As he spoke Miss Temple slowly completed her reach for the bag, bringing it back to her lap. He watched in silence as she inserted her hand, clearly understanding that she took hold of a weapon.

"You said you had . . . seen me?"

"Indeed," he said, and then smiled, chuckling strangely. "I cannot even explain it—for truly, we have never to my knowledge been in each other's presence!"

He glanced behind her, and took a step back—obviously the staff at the desk had taken notice. For Miss Temple this was too much, too quickly—she did not trust it. Her thoughts were spinning back to the terrible evening—Spragg and Farquhar—and who knew how many other minions in service to the woman in red.

"I do not know what you mean," she said, "or indeed, what you *think* you mean, seeing that by your accent you are a foreigner. I assure you that we have never met."

He opened his mouth to speak, then closed it, then opened it again.

"That may be true. Yet, I have seen you—and I am sure you can assist me."

"Why would you possibly think that?"

He leaned toward her and whispered. "Your *shoes*."

To this, Miss Temple had no answer. He smiled and swallowed, glancing back out to the street. "Is there perhaps another place where we might discuss—"

"There is not," she said.

"I am not mad—"

"You do look it, I assure you."

"I have not slept. I have been hunted through the streets—I offer no danger—"

"Prove it," said Miss Temple.

She realized that with her sharp tone there was a part of her that was trying to drive him away. At the same time, another part of her realized that, far from wading through maps and newspapers, she had in his person been presented with the exact advantage she would have wished for in her investigation. She balked because the circumstance was so real, so immediate, and because the man was so obviously stricken with fatigue and distress—qualities from which Miss Temple instinctively withdrew. By continuing these inquiries, what might she herself endure in the future—or endure *again*? No matter how much she might steel herself to it in the abstract, the corporeal evidence shook Miss Temple's resolve.

She looked up at him and spoke quietly. "I should appreciate it if you could . . . in some fashion . . . please."

He nodded, gravely. "Then—permit me." He sat on the end of the settee and reached into his coat pocket. He pulled out two gleaming blue cards, quickly glanced at each and then returned one to the pocket. The other, he held out to her.

"I do not understand what this is. I only know what it shows me. As I say, there is a great deal to talk about and, if my fears are correct, very little time. I have been awake all night—I apologize for my desperate appearance. Please, look into this card—as if you were looking into a pool—take it with both hands or you will surely drop it. I will stand apart. Perhaps it will tell you more than it has told me."

He gave her the card and stepped away from the settee. With shaking hands he took a dark foul-looking cigarette from a silver case and lit it. Miss Temple studied the card. It was heavy, made of a kind of glass she had never seen, brilliant blue that shifted in hue—from indigo to cobalt to even bright aqua—depending on the light passing through. She glanced once more at the strange doctor—he *was* a German, by his accent—and then she looked into the card.

* * *

Without his warning she would have certainly dropped it. As it was, she was happy to be sitting down. She had never experienced the like, it was as if she were swimming, so *immersive* were the sensations, so tactile the images. She saw herself—*herself*—in the parlor of the Bascombe house, and knew that her hands were clutching the upholstery because, out of his mother's sight, Roger had just leaned forward to blow softly across her nape. The experience was not unlike seeing herself in the mirror wearing the white mask, for here she somehow appeared through the eyes of another—lustful eyes that viewed her calves and bare arms with hunger, almost as if they were rightful possessions. Then the entire location shifted, somehow seamlessly, as if in a dream . . . she did not recognize the pit or the quarry, but then gasped to see the country house of Roger's uncle, Lord Tarr. Next was the coach and the Deputy Minister—"your decision?"—and finally the eerie curving hallway, the banded metal door, and the terrifying chamber. She looked up and found herself once again in the lobby of the Boniface. She was panting for breath. It was Roger. She knew that all of this had been the experience—in the mind—of Roger Bascombe. Her heart leapt in her chest, surging with anguish that was swiftly followed by rage. Decision? Could that mean what she thought? If it did—and of course it must—it *must*!—Harald Crabbé became in that instant Miss Temple's particular, unpardonable enemy. She turned her flashing eyes to Svenson, who stepped back to the settee.

"How—how does this *work*?" she demanded.

"I don't know."

"Because . . . well . . . because it is *very* queer."

"Indeed, it is most disquieting—an—ah—unnatural *immediacy.*"

"Yes! It is—it is . . ." She could not find the words, and then stopped trying and merely blurted, ". . . *unnatural.*"

"Did you recognize anything?" he asked.

She ignored him. "Where did you get this?"

"If I tell you—will you assist me?"

"Possibly."

He studied her face with an expression of concern that Miss Temple had seen in her life before. Her features were pretty enough, her hair fine and her figure, if she were permitted to have an opinion, reasonably appealing, but Miss Temple knew by now and was no longer disquieted by the knowledge that she was only truly remarkable in the way an animal is remarkable, in the way an animal so fully and purely inhabits its *self* without qualm. Doctor Svenson, when faced with her strangely elemental presence, swallowed, then sighed.

"I found it sewn into the jacket of a dead man," he said.

"Not"—she held up the card, her voice suddenly brittle, feeling completely caught out—"not *this* man?"

She was unprepared for the possibility that anything so serious could have happened to Roger. Before she could say more, Svenson was shaking his head.

"I do not know who *this* man is, the—the point of *vantage,* so to speak—"

"It is Roger Bascombe," she said. "He is at the Foreign Ministry."

The Doctor clucked his tongue, clearly annoyed at himself. "Of course—"

"Do you know him?" she inquired tentatively.

"Not as such, but I have seen—or heard—him this very morning. Do you know Francis Xonck?"

"O! He is a terrible rake!" said Miss Temple, feeling foolishly prim as soon as she said it, having so thoughtlessly parroted the gossip of women she despised.

"No doubt," agreed Doctor Svenson. "Yet Francis Xonck and this man—Bascombe—between them were disposing of a body—"

She indicated the card. "The man who had this?"

"No, no, someone else—though they are related, for this man's arms—the blue glass—excuse me, I am getting ahead of myself—"

"How many bodies are involved—to your own knowledge?" she asked, and then, before he could answer, added, "And if you might—if it were possible to—generally—*describe* them?"

"Describe them?"

"I am not merely morbid, I assure you."

"No . . . no, indeed—perhaps you too have merely witnessed—yet I can only hope you have not—in any event, yes—I myself have seen two bodies—there may be others—others in peril, and others I myself may have slain, I do not know. One, as I say, was a man I did not know, an older man, connected to the Royal Institute of Science and

Exploration—a fellow I am led to believe of some great learning. The other was a military officer—his disappearance was in the newspaper—Colonel Arthur Trapping. I believe he was poisoned. How the first man—well, the officer was actually the first to die—but how the *other* man, from the Institute, was killed, I cannot begin to understand, but it is part of the mystery of this blue glass—"

"Only those?" asked Miss Temple. "I see."

"Do you know of others?" asked Doctor Svenson.

She decided to confide in him.

"Two men," Miss Temple said. "Two horrible men."

She could not for the moment say more. On impulse she removed a handkerchief from her bag, moistened a corner and leaned forward to dab at a thin line of blood etched across the Doctor's face. He muttered apologies and took the cloth from her, stepping away, and stabbed vigorously at his face. After a moment, he pulled it away and folded it over, offering it back. She motioned for him to keep it, smiling grimly and offhandedly wiping her eye.

"Let me see the other card," said Miss Temple. "You have another in your pocket."

Svenson blanched. "I—I do not think, the time—"

"I do insist." She was determined to learn more about Roger's inner life—who he had seen, the bargains with Crabbé, his true feelings for *her*. Svenson was blathering excuses—did he want some kind of exchange?

"I cannot allow—a lady—please—"

Miss Temple handed him the first card. "The country house belongs to Roger's uncle, Lord Tarr."

"Lord Tarr is his uncle?"

"Of course Lord Tarr is his uncle."

Svenson did not speak. Miss Temple pointedly raised her eyebrows, waiting.

"But Lord Tarr has been murdered," said Svenson.

Miss Temple gasped.

"Francis Xonck spoke of this Bascombe's inheritance," said Svenson, "that he would soon be important and powerful—my thought—when Crabbé says 'decision'—"

"I'm afraid that is quite impossible," snapped Miss Temple.

But even as she spoke, her mind raced. Roger had *not* been his uncle's heir. While Lord Tarr (a gouty difficult man) had no sons, he did have daughters with male children of their own—it had been quite clearly and bitterly explained to her by Roger's mother. Moreover, as if to confirm Roger's peripheral status, on their sole visit to Tarr Manor, its ever-ailing Lord proved disinclined to see Roger, much less make the acquaintance of Roger's provincial fiancée. And now Lord Tarr had been murdered, and Roger somehow acclaimed as his heir to lands and title? She could not trust it for a minute—but what other inheritance could Roger have? She did not think Roger Bascombe a murderer—all the more since having herself recently met several of the species—but she knew he was weak and tractable, despite his broad shoulders and his poise, and she suddenly felt cold... the people he had fallen in with, the demonstration he had willingly witnessed in the operating theatre... within her vow to ruin him, her utter and complete disdain for all things Bascombe, it was with a tinge of sorrow that Miss Temple felt oddly certain that he was lost. Just as she had wondered, in the operating theatre at Harschmort, if Roger had truly understood with whom or what he had become entangled—and in that wondering felt a pang at being unable to protect him from his own blindness when it came to the powerful and rich—so Miss Temple felt suddenly sure that, one way or another and without it being his intention, these events would be his doom.

She looked up at Svenson. "Give me the other card. Either I am your ally or I am not."

"You have not even told me your name."

"Haven't I?"

"No, you have not," said the Doctor.

Miss Temple pursed her lips, then smiled at him graciously and offered her hand, along with her standard explanation.

"I am Miss Temple, Celestial Temple. My father enjoyed astronomy—I am fortunate not to be named for one of Jupiter's moons." She hesitated, then exhaled. "Though if we are to be true allies, then—yes—you must call me Celeste. Of course you must—though I am quite unable to call you, what is it—Abelard? You are older, foreign, and it would in any case be ridiculous." She smiled. "There. I am so very pleased to have made your acquaintance. I am sure I have never before met an officer of the Macklenburg Navy, nor a captain-surgeon of any kind."

Doctor Svenson took her hand awkwardly. He bent over to kiss it. She pulled it away, not unkindly.

"You needn't do that. It is not Germany."

"Of course... as you say." Miss Temple saw with some small satisfaction that Doctor Svenson was blushing.

She smiled at him, her gaze pointedly drifting to the pocket that held the second card. He noted this and hesitated, quite awkwardly. She did not see the difficulty—she had already seen the other—she would not be disoriented a second time.

"Perhaps you would prefer to view it in a more private room—"

"I would not."

Svenson sighed and fished out the card. He handed it to her with an evident wave of trepidation. "The man—it is not Bascombe—is my Prince—also a rake. It is the St. Royale Hotel. Perhaps you will know the woman—I know her as Mrs. Marchmoor... or the... ah... spectators. In this glass card—the, ah, vantage of experience—lies with the lady." He stood and turned away from her, making a fuss of finding and lighting another cigarette, refusing to meet her eye. She glanced at the desk clerks, who were still watching with interest, despite being unable to hear the intense conversation, then to Svenson, who she saw had discreetly stepped away and turned to study the leaves of a large potted plant. Her curiosity was thoroughly piqued. She looked into the card.

When she lowered the card some minutes later, Miss Temple's face was flushed and her breathing rapid. She looked nervously around her, met the idly curious eye of the desk clerk and immediately turned away. She was relieved and somewhat touched to see that Doctor Svenson still had his back to her—for he clearly knew what she had been experiencing, if only by virtue of another woman's body. She could not believe what had just happened—what had *not* happened, despite the intimacy, the utterly persuasive intimacy of the equally disquieting and delicious sensations. She had just—she could not believe—in *public,* for the first time, without warning!—and felt ashamed that she had so insisted, that she had not taken the Doctor's strong hint to withdraw—and so had been—a man she did not know, nor had feelings for—though she had sensed the lady's feelings for him, or for the experience—could those be separated? She shifted in her seat and straightened her dress, feeling to her dismay an undeniable, insistent itching tickle between her legs. If her aunt had at that moment asked again about her virtue, how should she answer? Miss Temple looked down at the glass rectangle in her hands, and marveled at the vast and thoroughly disquieting possibilities residing in such a creation.

She cleared her throat. Doctor Svenson turned at once, his gaze flickering across her, refusing for a moment to meet her eyes. He stepped closer to the settee. She handed him the glass card and smiled up at him quite shyly.

"My goodness . . ."

He returned it to his pocket, touchingly mortified. "I am desperately sorry—I'm afraid I did not make clear—"

"Do not trouble yourself—please, it is I who should apologize—though in truth I should prefer not to speak of it further."

"Of course—forgive me—it is vulgar of me to go on so."

She did not answer—for she could not answer without prolonging what she herself had just expressed a desire to curtail. There followed a pause. The Doctor looked at her with an uncomfortable expression. He had no idea what to say next. Miss Temple sighed.

"The lady, whose—as you say, whose *vantage* is conveyed—do you know her?"

"No, no—but did you . . . perhaps . . . recognize anyone?"

"I could not be sure—they were all masked, but I think the lady—"

"Mrs. Marchmoor."

"Yes. I believe I have seen her before. I do not know her name, nor even her face, for I have only seen her so masked."

She saw Doctor Svenson's eyes widen. "At the engagement party?" He paused. "At—at Lord Vandaariff's!"

Miss Temple did not answer at once, for she was thinking. "Indeed, at . . . ah—what is the name of his house?"

"Harschmort."

"That's right—it was once some kind of ruin?"

"So I am told," said Svenson, "a coastal fortification—Norman, perhaps—and then after that, with some expansion—"

Miss Temple recalled the plain, thick, forbidding walls and risked a guess. "A prison?"

"Exactly so—and then Lord Vandaariff's own home, purchased from the Crown and completely re-made at some great expense."

"And the night before last—"

"The engagement party, for the Prince and Miss Vandaariff! But—but—you were there?"

"I confess . . . I was."

He was looking at her with intense curiosity—and she knew that she herself was keenly hungry for more information, particularly after the revelations about Roger and his uncle—and even now, the prospect of another person's narrative of the masked ball was desperately appealing. But Miss Temple also saw the extreme fatigue in the face and frame of her newfound ally, and—especially as he persisted in glancing suspiciously out of the window to the street—thought it by far the wiser course to procure for him a place to rest and recover, so that once they had agreed on a course of action, he would be capable of following it. Also, she had to admit, she wanted more time to go through the newspapers—now she had a better sense of what to look for—so that, once they did fully hash through each other's stories, she could present herself as less a foolish girl. She felt that her own experiences ought not to be undermined by the absence of a handful of place names and perfectly obvious—once one thought of them—hypotheses. She stood up. In an instant, his automatic politeness somehow dog-like, Svenson was on his feet.

"Come with me," she said, rapidly collecting her papers and books. "I have been shamefully negligent." She marched across toward the hotel desk, her arms full, looking back at Doctor Svenson, who followed a step behind her, vague protests hovering about his mouth. "Or are you hungry?" she asked.

"No, no," he sputtered, "I—moments ago—in the street—coffee—"

"Excellent. Mr. Spanning?" This was to the sleek man behind the desk, who at once gave Miss Temple his every attention. "This is Doctor Svenson. He will need a room—he has no servants—a sleeping room and a sitting room should suffice. He will want food—some sort of broth, I expect—he is not completely well. And someone to clean his coat and boots. Thank you so much. Charge my account." She turned to face Svenson and spoke over his incoherent protest. "Do not be a fool, Doctor. You need help—there is an end to it. I am sure you will help me in your turn. Ah, Mr. Spanning, thank you so much. Doctor Svenson has no baggage—he will take the key himself."

Mr. Spanning held out the key to Svenson, who took it without a word. Miss Temple heaved her papers onto the counter, quickly signed the chit the clerk had placed in front of her, and then re-gathered her load. With a last crisp smile at Spanning—openly daring the man to find anything in the transaction to assail propriety or sully her reputation in the slightest—she led the way up the main curving flight of stairs, a small industrious figure, with the lanky Doctor bobbing uncertainly in her wake. They reached the second floor and Miss Temple turned to the right, down a wide, red-carpeted corridor.

"Miss Temple!" whispered Svenson. "Please, this is too much—I cannot accept such charity—we have much to discuss—I am content to find a less expensive room in an unobtrusive lodging house—"

"That would be most inconvenient," answered Miss Temple. "I am certainly not inclined to seek you out in such a place, nor—if your furtive looks are anything to judge—ought you to be wandering the streets until we fully understand our danger, and you have had some sleep. Really, Doctor, it is quite sensible."

Miss Temple was proud of herself. After so many experiences that seemed almost designed to demonstrate the profound degree of Miss Temple's ignorance and incapacity, the exercise of such decisive action was highly satisfying. She was also—though she had only known him for a matter of minutes—pleased with herself for making the choice to accept Doctor Svenson, and to extend what aid she could. It was as if the more she was able to do, the farther she removed herself from the painful isolation of her time at Harschmort.

"Ah," she said, "number 27." She stopped to the side of the door, allowing Svenson to open it. He did so and peered inside, then indicated that she should enter before him. She shook her head. "No, Doctor. You must sleep. I will return to my own rooms, and when you have restored yourself, alert Mr. Spanning and he will send word, and the two of us can properly confer. I assure you I am looking toward that time with great impatience, but until you are fully rested—"

She was interrupted by the sound of a door opening farther down the corridor. Out of habit she glanced toward the sound and then returned her gaze to Svenson . . . and then—her eyes widening in surprise, the words dying on her lips—turned back to the guest who had just stepped into the hallway from his room. The man stood watching her, his eyes shifting quickly between her and Svenson. Miss Temple saw the Doctor's own expression was one of shock, even as she felt him groping in the pocket of his greatcoat. The man in the corridor walked slowly toward them, his footsteps absorbed by the thick carpet. He was tall, his hair black, his deep red coat reaching nearly down to the floor. He wore the same round dark glasses she had seen on the train. His movements were gracefully muscular, like a cat's, exuding ease and menace equally. She knew she should be reaching in her bag for the revolver, but instead calmly placed her hand over the Doctor's, stilling his movement. The man in red stopped perhaps a yard or two away. He looked at her—she could not see his eyes—then looked at the Doctor, and then at the open door between them.

He whispered, conspiratorially. "No blood. No princes. Shall we send for tea?"

The man in red shut the door behind him, his masked, depthless eyes fixed on Miss Temple and the Doctor as they stood in the small sitting room. Each had managed to secure a firm grip on their respective weapons. For a long moment, all three glanced back and forth between each other in silence. Finally, Miss Temple spoke to Doctor Svenson.

"I take it you know this man?"

"We have not spoken . . . perhaps it is better to say that we overlapped. His name—correct me if I am wrong, Sir—is Chang."

The man in red nodded in acknowledgment. "I do not know your name, though the lady . . . it's a pleasure to formally meet the famous Isobel Hastings."

Miss Temple did not answer. Beside her, she could feel Svenson sputtering. He pulled away from her, his eyes goggling.

"Isobel Hastings? But you—you were with Bascombe!"

"I was," said Miss Temple.

"But... how did they not know you? I am sure he is looking for you as well!"

"She looks very different in the... daylight." Chang chuckled.

Svenson stared at her, taking in the bruises, the red line traced by the bullet.

"I'm a fool...." he whispered. "But... how—I beg your pardon—"

"He was on the train," she said to Svenson, her gaze fixed on Chang. "On my return from Harschmort. We did not speak."

"Did we not?" asked Chang. He looked to Svenson. "Did *we* not speak? You and I? I think we did. A man like me. A woman covered in blood—did she tell you that? A man brazening his way into and then away from a pack of enemies with a pistol. I think there was, in each instance... recognition."

No one spoke for a moment. Miss Temple took a seat on the small sofa. She looked up at the Doctor and indicated the armchair. He wavered, but then sat in it. They both looked at Chang, who drifted to the remaining chair, across from them both. It was only then that Miss Temple realized that something bright was tucked within his hand—his razor. From the way he moved, she had no doubt that he was far more dangerous with the razor than the two of them with their pistols put together—and if that was the case, then something entirely else was called for. She cleared her throat and very deliberately brought her hand out of her green clutch bag. She then took the bag from her lap and placed it to the side on the sofa. A moment later, Chang abruptly shoved the razor into his pocket. After another few seconds, Svenson removed his hand from his coat pocket.

"Were you in earnest about the tea?" Miss Temple asked. "I should like some very much. It is always best when discussing serious matters to do so around a teapot. Doctor—you are nearest—if you would be so kind as to ring the bell."

They did not speak in the minutes it took for the tea to be ordered and then arrive, nor again in the time spent pouring, aside from monosyllabic inquiries about lemon, milk, or sugar. Miss Temple took a sip from her cup, one hand on the saucer beneath—it was excellent—and so fortified decided that someone had better take charge—for the Doctor seemed in danger of falling asleep and the other man—Chang—was positively wolfish.

"Mr. Chang, you are clearly reticent—I am sure I do not misspeak when I say we all have good reason to be suspicious—and yet you are here. I will tell you that Doctor Svenson and I have been acquainted not above this hour, and that through a chance meeting in the lobby of this hotel, exactly as we have met you in its hallway. I can see that you are a dangerous man—I neither compliment nor criticize, it is merely plain enough—and so understand that if the three of us do come to some profound disagreement, there may be a violent outcome which will leave at least one faction, well, probably dead. Would you agree?"

Chang nodded, a smile playing about his lips.

"Excellent. Given this, I see no reason not to be candid—if any tales are told, it will not disturb the dead, and if we are to join forces, then we will be stronger for sharing our knowledge. Yes?"

Chang nodded again, and sipped his tea.

"You are very agreeable. I propose then—since I have already spoken to Doctor Svenson—this is Captain-Surgeon Abelard Svenson of the Macklenburg Navy"—here the men exchanged an archly formal nod—"I will briefly narrate my part in this affair. As the Doctor and I had not reached this level of frankness, I hope it will be of some interest to him as well. The Doctor has been awake all night, apparently the object of violent pursuit, and has lost his Prince—as you so astutely noted in the hall." She smiled. "If Doctor Svenson is *able* to continue . . ."

"By all means," Svenson muttered. "The tea has revived me powerfully."

"Mr. Chang?"

"I don't mean to be impertinent," observed Svenson, "but when I overheard men speaking of you—they called you 'Cardinal'."

"It is what some call me," said Chang. "It derives from the coat."

"And do you know," said Miss Temple, "that Doctor Svenson recognized me by the color of my boots? Already we have so many interests in common."

Chang smiled at her, cocking his head, trying to gauge whether she was serious. Miss Temple chuckled aloud, satisfied to have pushed the razor so far from his thoughts. She took another sip of tea and began.

"My name is not Isobel Hastings, it is Celestial Temple. But no one calls me that—they call me Miss Temple, or—in particularly rare circumstances—they call me Celeste. At this moment, in this city, having met the Doctor and extended to him that privilege, the number has risen to two—the other being my aunt. Some time after my arrival here, from well across the sea, I became engaged to marry Roger Bascombe, a Deputy Under-Secretary in the Foreign Ministry, working primarily for Harald Crabbé." She felt Svenson's reaction to this news, but did not look at him, for it was so much easier to speak of anything delicate or painful to someone she knew not at all—still more to a man like Chang whose eyes she could not see. "Some days ago, after perhaps a week where I did not see him for various but perfectly believable reasons, I received a letter from Roger severing our engagement. I wish to make very plain to you both that I harbor no further feelings—save those of disdain—for Roger Bascombe. However, his brusque and cruel manner prompted me to discover the true cause of his act, for he tendered no explanation. Two days ago I followed him to Harschmort. I disguised myself and saw many things and many people, none of which I was intended to see. I was captured and questioned and—I will be frank—given over to two men, to be first ravished and then killed. Instead, it was I who killed them—thus, Doctor, my question about *bodies.* On the return journey I made the acquaintance—the nodding acquaintance—of Cardinal Chang. It was during my interrogation that I gave the name Isobel Hastings . . . which seems to have followed me."

The two men were silent. Miss Temple poured more tea for herself, and then for the others, each man leaning forward with his cup.

"I'm sure there are many questions—the details of what and who I saw—but perhaps it would be better if we continued in the broadest vein of disclosure? Doctor?"

Svenson nodded, drank the whole of his cup and leaned forward to pour another. He took a sip of this, the fresh cup steaming around his mouth, and sat back.

"Would either of you object if I smoked?"

"Not at all," said Miss Temple. "I'm sure it will sharpen your mind."

"I am much obliged," said Svenson, and he took a moment to extract a dark cigarette and set it alight. He exhaled. Miss Temple found herself studying the visible structure of the man's jaw and skull, wondering if he ever ate at all.

"I will be brief. I am part of the diplomatic party of my country's heir, Prince Karl-Horst von Maasmärck, who will marry Lydia Vandaariff. It is a match of international significance, and I am attached to the party in a medical capacity only for the sake of appearance. My prime aim is to protect the Prince—from his own foolishness, and from those around him seeking to take advantage of it—figures of which there has never been short supply. The diplomatic Envoy and the military attaché have both, I believe, betrayed their duty and given the Prince over to a cabal of private interest. I have rescued the Prince from their hands once—after he had been subject, perhaps willingly, to what they called 'the Process'—which leaves a perhaps temporary facial scarring, a burn—"

Miss Temple sat up to speak, and saw Chang do the same. Svenson held up his hand. "I am sure we have all seen evidence of it. My first instance was at the ball at Harschmort, when I briefly viewed the body of Arthur Trapping, but there have since been many others—the Prince, a woman named Mrs. Marchmoor—"

"Margaret Hooke," said Chang.

"Beg pardon?"

"Her true name is Margaret Hooke. She is a whore of the highest *echelon.*"

"Ah," said Doctor Svenson, wincing with discomfort at the word being spoken in Miss Temple's hearing. While she was touched by his care, she found the impulse tiresome. If one was engaged in an adventure, an investigation, such delicacy was ridiculous. She smiled at Chang.

"There will be more about her later, for she figures elsewhere in our evidence," Miss Temple told him. "Is this not progress? Doctor, please go on."

"I say the scars may be temporary," continued Svenson, "because this very night I overheard Francis Xonck query Roger Bascombe about his own experience of this 'Process'—though I saw Bascombe's face myself when I was at the Institute—I am getting ahead of myself—and there was no such scarring."

Miss Temple felt a distant pang. "It was before he sent his letter," she said. "The days he claimed to be at work with the Deputy Minister . . . it was happening even then."

"Of course it was," said Chang, not unkindly.

"Of course it was," whispered Miss Temple.

"Harald Crabbé." Svenson nodded. "He is near the heart of it, but there are others with him, a cabal from the Ministry, the military, the Institute, other individuals of power—as I say, the Xonck family, the Comte d'Orkancz, the Contessa Lacquer-Sforza, even perhaps Robert Vandaariff—and somehow my country of Macklenburg is a part of their plan. In the face of indifference from my colleagues, I rescued the Prince from their twisted science at the Institute. It was there I saw Cardinal Chang. At our compound I was forced to attend to several of our soldiers—also, I believe, a result of Cardinal Chang"—again he held up his hand—"I make no judgments, they have since tried to kill *me.* In that time, the Prince was taken in secret from his room, I do not know how—from *above.* I set out alone to find him. In Harald Crabbé's house I heard Francis Xonck and Roger Bascombe discuss philosophy over the strangely disfigured body of an Institute savant—quantities of his blood had been turned to blue glass. They were joined by my own military attaché, Major Blach, who is part of their plans—the only bit of news being Blach's assumption that the cabal had taken the Prince, and Xonck's assurance that they had not. In any case, I escaped, and attempted to find Madame Lacquer-Sforza, but was taken by the Comte d'Orkancz—dragooned to consult on another medical matter, another of their experiments that had gone wrong—and then—it is a long story—given over to be killed, sent to the river bottom with the corpses of this dead scientist and Arthur Trapping. I escaped. I again tried to find Madame Lacquer-Sforza, only to see her with Xonck and d'Orkancz—she is one of them. In my flight from her hotel, I saw Miss Temple through the window—recognizing her from the card—I have not mentioned the cards—" He fumbled the cards onto the small table that held the tea tray. "One from the Prince, one from Trapping. As Miss Temple points out—they are valuable, if mysterious, evidence."

"You did not say where you heard the name Isobel Hastings," observed Chang.

"Didn't I? I'm sorry, from Madame Lacquer-Sforza. She asked that I help her find one Isobel Hastings in exchange for telling me where the Prince was—at the Institute. That was the curious thing, for she told me where he was, allowing me to take him away quite against the wishes of Crabbé and d'Orkancz. This was why I had thought to find her again—for while someone took the Prince from our rooftop tonight, at least some of these conspirators—Xonck and Crabbé—seemed ignorant of his whereabouts. I had hoped *she* might know."

Miss Temple felt the back of her neck tingle. "Perhaps it would help, Doctor, if you could describe the woman."

"Of course," he began. "A tall woman, black hair, curled about her face and gathered in the back, pale skin, exquisite clothing, elegant to an almost vicious degree, gracious, intelligent, wry, dangerous, and I should say wholly remarkable. She gave her name as Madame Lacquer-Sforza—one of the hotel staff referred to her as Contessa—"

"The St. Royale Hotel?" asked Chang.

"The same."

"Do you know her?" asked Miss Temple.

"Merely as 'Rosamonde'... she hired me—that is what people do, hire me to do things. *She* hired me to find Isobel Hastings."

Miss Temple did not speak.

"I assume you know the woman," said Chang.

Miss Temple nodded, her earlier poise slightly shaken; as much as she tried to deny it, the Doctor's description had conjured the woman, and the dread she inspired, freshly into her thoughts.

"I do not know her names," said Miss Temple. "I met her at Harschmort. She was masked. At first she assumed I was one of a party with Mrs. Marchmoor and others—as you say, a group of whores—but then it was she who questioned me... and it was she who gave me over to die." As she finished speaking, her voice seemed painfully small. The men were silent.

"What is amusing—genuinely amusing," said Chang, "is that for all they are hunting us, we are not at all what they assume. My own portion of this tale is simple. I am a man for hire. I also followed a man to Harschmort—the man you saw dead, Doctor—Colonel Arthur Trapping. I had been hired to kill him."

He took a sip of tea and watched their reactions over the rim of his cup. Miss Temple did her level best to nod with the same degree of polite detachment as when someone mentioned a secret keenness for growing begonias. She glanced at Svenson, whose face was blank, as if this new fact merely confirmed what he'd already known. Chang smiled, somewhat bitterly, she thought.

"I did *not* kill him. He was killed by someone else—though I did see the scars you mentioned, Doctor. Trapping was a tool of the Xonck family—I do not understand who killed him."

"Did he betray them?" asked Svenson. "Francis Xonck sunk his body in the river."

"Does that mean Xonck killed him, or that he didn't want the body found—that he could not allow it to be found with the facial scars? Or something else? You mentioned the woman—why would she betray the others and allow you to rescue your Prince? I have no idea."

"I was able to examine the Colonel's body briefly, and believe he was poisoned—an injection of some kind, in his finger."

"Could it have been an accident?" asked Chang.

"It could have been anything," answered the Doctor. "I was about to be murdered at the time, and had no mind to reason clearly."

"May I ask who hired you to kill him?" asked Miss Temple.

Chang thought for a moment before answering.

"Obviously it is a professional secret," Miss Temple said. "Yet if you do not wholly trust that person, perhaps—"

"Trapping's adjutant, Colonel Aspiche."

Svenson laughed aloud. "I met him yesterday in the presence of Madame Lacquer-Sforza at the St. Royale Hotel. By the end of the visit, Mrs. Marchmoor—" He glanced awkwardly at Miss Temple. "Let us say he is their creature."

Chang nodded and sighed. "The entire situation was wrong. The next day there was no body, no news, and Aspiche was useless and withdrawn, because—as you confirm—he was in the midst of being seduced. In short order, it was *I* who met seduction, in the form of this woman, who hired me to find one Isobel Hastings—a prostitute who had murdered her very dear friend."

Miss Temple snorted. They looked at her. She waved Chang on.

"With this description, I searched several brothels—never, for reasons that are now obvious, finding Isobel Hastings, but soon learning that two others—Mrs. Marchmoor and Major Black—"

"*Blach,* actually," said Svenson, providing the proper pronunciation.

"*Blach,* then," muttered Chang. "They were both searching for her as well, and in the Major's case at least, also searching for me. At Harschmort, I had been seen—and I am a figure some people know. When I returned to my own lodgings one of the Major's men tried to kill me. A trip to a third brothel led me to follow a small party—your Prince, Bascombe, Francis Xonck, a large fellow in a fur—"

"The Comte d'Orkancz," said Svenson.

"O!" said Miss Temple. "I have seen him as well!"

"He had taken Margaret Hooke from this same brothel, and was now taking another woman—I followed them to the Institute—saw you enter, Doctor, and followed you down. They are doing strange experiments with great amounts of heat and blue glass . . ." Chang picked up one of the blue cards from the tray. "It is the same glass, but instead of these small cards, here—and with great effort, with vast machinery—they had made a blue glass *book*—unfortunately the man making it was startled—by me—and dropped it. I am sure he is the man you saw on the Deputy Minister's table. In the confusion I escaped, only to meet your Major and his men. I escaped from them as well, and found my way here . . . quite entirely by chance."

He leaned forward and took up the pot, pouring another round of tea. Miss Temple cradled her fresh cup and allowed it to warm her hands.

"What did you mean when you said we are not what our enemies assume?" she asked Chang.

"I *mean,*" Chang said, "that they believe that we are agents of a larger power—a cabal opposing their interests that has hitherto existed without their knowledge. They are so arrogant as to think that such a body—a mighty union of insidious talents like themselves!—is all that could possibly threaten them. The idea that they have been attacked by the haphazard actions of three isolated individuals—for whom they have contempt? It is the last thing they could believe."

"Only because it does not flatter them," Miss Temple sniffed.

Doctor Svenson was in the other room, asleep. His coat and boots were being cleaned. For a time Miss Temple and Chang had spoken about his experience of the hotel, and the coincidence that had brought all three of them together, but the conversation had fallen into silence. Miss Temple studied the man across from her, trying to make palpable sense of the knowledge that he was a criminal, a killer. What she saw was a certain kind of animal elegance—or, if not elegance, efficiency—and a manner that seemed both brazen and restrained. She knew this was the embodiment of experience, and she found it an attractive quality—wanting it for herself—even as she found the man daunting and disquieting. His features were sharp and his voice was flat and raw, and direct to a point just before insolence. She was intensely curious to know what he thought of her—what he had thought when he saw her on the train, and what he thought now, seeing her normal self—but could not ask him any of these things. She felt he must somehow despise her—despise the hotel room, the tea, the entirety of her life—for if she herself were not born to privilege, she was sure she would carry with her a general hatred for it every day of her life.

Cardinal Chang watched her from his chair. She smiled at him, and reached into her green bag.

"Perhaps you will help me, for I am only now tackling the matter..." She pulled out the revolver and placed it on the table between them. "I have sent out for more ammunition, but have little sense of the weapon itself. If you are knowledgeable about it, I would appreciate any advice you can give me."

Chang leaned forward and took the revolver in his hand, cocking it, and then slowly easing the hammer down. "I am not one for firearms," he said, "but I know enough to load and fire and keep a weapon clean." She nodded with anticipation. He shrugged. "We will need a cloth..."

Over the next half an hour he showed her how to reload, to aim, to break the gun apart, to clean it, to put it back together. When she had done this for herself, to her own satisfaction, she put the pistol back on the table and looked up at him, finally broaching the question she had withheld all that time.

"And what about killing?" she asked.

Chang did not immediately respond.

"I would appreciate your advice," she prompted.

"I thought you were already a killer," observed Chang. He was not smiling at her, which she appreciated.

"Not with this," she said, indicating the revolver.

She realized that he was still trying to decide if she was serious. She waited, a firm expression in her eyes. When Chang spoke, he was watching her very closely.

"Get as close as you can—grind the barrel into the body—there's no reason to shoot unless you mean to kill."

Miss Temple nodded.

"And stay calm. Breathe. You will kill better—and you'll die better too, if it comes to that." She saw that he was smiling. She looked into his black lenses.

"You live with that possibility, don't you?"

"Don't we all?"

She took a deep breath, for all of this was going a bit too quickly. She put the revolver back into her bag. Chang watched her stow it away.

"If you didn't kill them with that, how did you kill them? The two men."

She found she could not easily answer him.

"I—well, one of them—I—it was very dark—I . . ."

"You do not need to tell me," he said quietly.

She took another heavy breath and let it out slowly.

It was after another minute that Miss Temple was able to ask Chang what his plans for the day had been, before seeing them in the corridor. She indicated the papers and maps and explained her own intentions, and then noted that she ought to return to her rooms, if only to allay the worries of her aunt. She also remembered the two glass cards that Doctor Svenson had placed on the table.

"You really should look at them, particularly as you have seen some of their strange glasswork for yourself. The experience is unlike anything else I have known—it is both powerful and diabolical. You'll think I am foolish, but I promise you I know enough to see that in these cards is another kind of opium, and in the books you describe—an *entire* book—well, I cannot imagine it is anything but a splendid—or indeed, horrid—prison."

Chang leaned forward to pick up one of the cards, turning it over in his hand.

"One of them shows the experience—I cannot explain it—of Roger Bascombe. I myself make an appearance. Believe me, it is most disquieting.

The other shows the experience of Mrs. Marchmoor—your Margaret Hooke—and is even *more* disquieting. I will say no more, only that it were better to view it in discreet solitude. Of course, to view either, you will really have to remove your spectacles."

Chang looked up at her. He pulled the glasses from his face and folded them into his pocket. She did not react. She had seen similar faces on her plantation, though never sitting across the tea table. She smiled at him politely, then nodded to the card in his hand.

"They really are the most lovely color blue."

Miss Temple left Cardinal Chang with the instruction that he should call for whatever meal the Doctor required upon waking, for which she would sign upon her return. She had her arms full of newspapers and books as she reached her own rooms, and kicked on the door three times instead of shifting her burdens to find her key. After a moment of rustling footsteps, the door was opened by Marthe. Miss Temple entered and dropped the pile of papers on the main table. Her aunt sat where she had left her, sipping a cup of tea. Before she could voice a reproof, Miss Temple spoke to her.

"I must ask you several questions, Aunt Agathe, and I will require your honest replies. You may be able to help me, and I will be very grateful for the assistance." She fixed her aunt with a firm look at the word "grateful" and then turned back to Marthe, to ask for Marie. Marthe pointed to Miss Temple's dressing room. Miss Temple entered to see Marie quickly folding and arranging a row of silk underthings on top of the ironing table. She stepped back as Miss Temple swept in and was silent as her mistress examined her purchases.

Miss Temple was extremely pleased, going even so far as to give Marie a congratulatory smile. Marie then pointed out the box of cartridges that sat by the mirror, and gave Miss Temple the receipts and leftover money. Miss Temple quickly scrutinized the figures and, satisfied, gave Marie an extra two coins for her efforts. Marie bobbed in surprise at the coins and again as Miss Temple motioned her out of the room. The door shut behind her, Miss Temple smiled again and turned to her purchases. The silk felt delicious between her fingers. She was happy to see that Marie had been smart enough to select a green that matched the dress she was wearing, and her boots. In the mirror, Miss Temple saw her own beaming face and blushed, looking away. She composed herself, cleared her throat, and called for her maids.

After the two young women had taken apart her dress and corset, helped her into the green silk undergarments, and then restored her outer layers, Miss Temple—her entire body tickling with enjoyment—carried the box of cartridges to the main table. With all the casual efficiency she could muster, recalling each step of Chang's instruction, she struck up a conversation with her aunt, and as she spoke, spun the cylinder, snapped it open, and smoothly loaded each empty chamber with a shell.

"I have been reading the newspapers, Aunt," she began.

"It seems you have enough of them."

"And do you know what I have learned? I saw the most astonishing announcement about Roger Bascombe's uncle, Lord Tarr."

Aunt Agathe pursed her lips. "You should not be bothering with—"

"Did you see the announcement?"

"Perhaps."

"Perhaps?"

"There is so much that I do not remember, my dear—"

"That he has been *murdered,* Aunt."

Her aunt did not reply at once. When she did, it was merely to say, "Ah."

"Ah," echoed Miss Temple.

"He was quite gouty," observed her aunt, "something dire was bound to happen. I understand it was wolves."

"Apparently not. Apparently the wound was altered to *implicate* wolves."

"People will do anything," muttered Agathe.

She reached to pour more tea. Miss Temple slapped the cylinder back into position and spun it. At the noise, her aunt froze in position, eyes wide in alarm. Miss Temple leaned forward and spoke as deliberately and patiently as she could.

"My dear Aunt, you must accept that the money you need is in my possession, and thus, despite our difference in age, that I am your mistress. These are facts. Your position will not be helped by frustrating me. On the contrary, the more we work in concert, the more I promise your situation will improve. I have no wish to be your enemy, but you must see that your previous sense of what was best—my marriage to Roger Bascombe—is no longer appropriate."

"If you were not so *difficult*—" her aunt burst out, stopping herself just as quickly.

Miss Temple glared at her with unmitigated rage. Aunt Agathe recoiled as if from a snake.

"I am sorry, my dear," whispered the frightened woman, "I merely—"

"I do not care. *I do not care!* I am not asking about Lord Tarr because I *care*! I am asking because—though you do not know it—others have been murdered as well, and Roger Bascombe is in the thick of it—and now he will be the next Lord Tarr! I do not know how Roger Bascombe has become his uncle's heir. But you do, I am sure—and you are going to tell me this minute."

Miss Temple stalked down the corridor toward the stairwell, the clutch bag around her wrist, heavy with the revolver and an extra handful of cartridges. She snorted with annoyance and tossed her head—*difficult*—and cursed her aunt for a small-minded old fool. All the woman thought of was her pension and her propriety, and the number of parties she might be invited to as the relation of a rising Ministry official like Roger. Miss Temple wondered why she should even be surprised—her aunt had only known her for three months, but had been acquainted with the Bascombes for years. How long she must have planned, and how sharp had been her disappointment, Miss Temple sneered. But that her aunt held *her* at fault stung to the quick.

Yet under pressure she had answered her niece's questions, though her answers just added to the mystery. Roger's cousins—the over-fed Pamela and the younger but no less porcine Berenice—both had infant sons of their own, each of whom should have assumed Lord Tarr's title and lands before Roger. Yet both had signed a paper to waive their children's claims, to abdicate, and clear the way for Roger's inheritance and ennoblement. Miss Temple did not understand how Roger had managed this, for he was not especially wealthy, and she knew each woman well enough to be sure that no small sum would have satisfied either. The cash had been supplied by others, by Crabbé or his cohorts, that was obvious enough. But what was so important about Roger, and how did his advancement possibly relate to the various other plots and murders she had stumbled into? Further—though she told herself the question was merely academic—as Roger took up the rightful property of his cousins, what was he giving up of himself, and for what grand purpose?

In short order she had also learned—for her aunt followed the city's gossip with an evangelical fervor—the owner of Harschmort, the occasion of the masked ball, the reputations of Prince Karl-Horst and his bride (wretched and unsullied, respectively), and what she could about the various other names she had heard: Xonck, Lacquer-Sforza, d'Orkancz, Crabbé, Trapping, and Aspiche. The latter two her aunt did not know—though she was acquainted with the tragedy of Trapping's disappearance. Crabbé she knew by way of the Bascombes, but even that family concentrated their attention on the Chief Minister, and not his respected deputy—he was a figure in the government, but hardly public. As the Xonck family's fame was by way of business, it was significantly less interesting to her aunt—though she had *heard* of them—who was generally attracted to titles (indeed, Robert Vandaariff's elevation within Agathe's mind to the rank of a Man who Mattered had only occurred upon his becoming a Lord, though Miss Temple understood that at a certain point such a man *must* be made a Lord, lest the government appear peripheral to *him*). Francis Xonck was of course a figure of scandal, though no one knew exactly why—there were whispers about deviant tastes from abroad newly appeared—but his elder siblings were merely substantial. The Comte d'Orkancz her aunt only knew as a patron of the opera—apparently he was born in some dire Balkan enclave, raised in Paris, and inherited family titles and wealth after a particularly devastating series of house fires cleared the way. Beyond this, Agathe could merely say he was a man of serious refinement, learned and severe, who could have been at a university if those university people were not so very dreadful. The final name, which Miss Temple had put to her aunt with a quaver in her otherwise sure interrogation, met with a hapless shrug. The Contessa Lacquer-Sforza was of course *known,* but nothing seemed to be known *about* her. She had arrived in the city the previous autumn—Agathe smiled, and observed that it must have been very near to when Miss Temple herself had arrived. Agathe had never seen the lady, but she was said to rival Princess Clarissa or Lydia Vandaariff for beauty. She smiled and sweetly asked her niece if *she* had seen the Contessa, and if that were indeed the case. Miss Temple merely snapped that of course not, she had seen none of these people—she saw no one in society unless during her excursions with Roger—and certainly none of these figures from the very cream of the continent. She snorted that the Roger Bascombe *she* had known was hardly the type to mix with such company. Her aunt, with a rueful shake of her head, admitted this was true.

Miss Temple stopped on the landing between the third and second floors and, after looking around to see that she was not observed, sat on the stairs. She felt the need to order her thoughts before rejoining her new comrades—she needed to order her thoughts *about* her new comrades—and before advancing further into her adventure. The sticking point, to her great dismay, remained Roger, neck deep in whatever was taking place. The man was a fool, she knew that now without question—but she felt she was constantly brought up against her former feelings as she strove to move forward without them. Why could she not simply carve them from her thoughts, from her heart? For moments she was sure she had, and that the ache she felt, the pressure in her chest and at the catch of her throat, was not love for Roger, but in fact its absence, as the removal of anything substantial must leave behind it open space—a hole in her heart, so to speak, around which her thoughts were, temporarily at least, forced to navigate. But then without warning she would find herself worrying at how Roger had placed his entire life so thoughtlessly at risk, and craving just one minute of sharp speech to wake him to his folly. Miss Temple sighed heavily and had for some reason a vivid memory of the plantation's sugar works, the great copper pots and the spiraled coils that converted the raw cane into rum. She knew that Roger had allied himself with people who sanctioned murder—her own murder—and she feared, as cane was by rough science and fire reduced to rum, that this must inevitably lead to a mortal confrontation between Roger and herself. She felt the weight of the revolver in her clutch bag. She thought of Chang and Svenson—did they have any similar torment of feeling? They both seemed so sure—especially Chang, who was a type of man she had never before known. Then she realized that this was not true, that she had known other men with such open capacity for brutal action—in fact, her father was just such a man—but there the brutality had always been clothed in the guise of business and of ownership. With Chang, the truth of the work was worn openly. She struggled to find this refreshing—she told herself it was exactly that—but could not repress a shudder. Doctor Svenson seemed to her less formidable and more stricken by common fears and hesitancies, but then, so was she—and Miss Temple knew no one in her world would have granted her the capacity to survive what she already had. She trusted in the Doctor's resilience then, as she trusted in her own. Besides, she smiled to think it, many otherwise capable men were not at their best around a fetching woman.

She was at least confident that armed with her aunt's gossip she would be able to follow the conversation. So much of her comrades' accounts referred to a city she did not know—to brothels and institutes and diplomatic compounds—a mix of lower depths and exclusive heights quite apart from her middling experience. She wanted to feel that she brought to their partnership an equal third, and wanted that third to be something other than money to provide a room or a meal. If they were to continue in league against this—what was the Doctor's word?—*cabal,* then she must continue to expand her capacities. What she had done so far seemed a mix of actual investigation and mere tagging along, where even the killing of Spragg and Farquhar struck her as unlikely happenstance. The figures arrayed against her were beyond imagination, her few allies equally so—what did she possess besides her change purse? It was a moment when she could easily spiral into self-doubt and fear, assurance melting like a carnival ice. She imagined herself alone in a train compartment with a man like the Comte d'Orkancz—what could she possibly do? Miss Temple looked around her at the Boniface's stairwell wallpaper, painted with an intricate pattern of flowers and leaves, and bit her lip hard enough to draw blood. She wiped her eyes and sniffed. What she would *do* is to press the barrel of her revolver against his body and pull the trigger as many times as it took to bring his foul carcass to the floor. And then she would find the Contessa Lacquer-Sforza and thrash the woman until her arm was too tired to hold a whip. And then . . . Roger. She sighed. From Roger Bascombe she would merely walk away.

* * *

She stood and made her way down to the second floor, but paused at the final step, hearing voices in the corridor. She peered around the corner to see three men in black uniforms and another man in a dark brown cloak standing directly outside the door to room 27. The men muttered to each other (Miss Temple was a foe of muttering in general and always resented not hearing what other people said, even if it was not strictly her business) and then as a group marched away from her, to the main stairs at the far end of the hall. She crept into the corridor, moving as quickly as she could to the door. She gasped to see it was ajar—the men must have been inside—and with great trepidation pushed the door open. The sitting room was empty. What papers she had left behind had been scattered across the room, but she saw no token of Chang or Svenson, nor of any particular struggle. She crossed quickly to the bedchamber, but it too was empty. The bedclothes were pulled apart, and the window was open, but she saw no sign of either man. Miss Temple peered out of the window. The room was directly above the rear alley, with a sheer drop of some thirty feet to the paving. She tightened her grip on the clutch bag and made her way back to the corridor. Both Chang and Svenson had been chased by soldiers—but which had drawn them here? She frowned with thought—it could not have been Chang, for as far as anyone knew, Chang was not in room 27. She raced to the door she had seen him leave—number 34—to find it also open. The room was empty. The window was locked. She returned to the hall, more agitated—somehow the soldiers had known of Svenson's room and of Chang's. With a sudden bolt of horror she thought of her own, and her aunt.

Miss Temple charged up the stairs, feverishly digging the revolver from her bag. She rounded the landing, cocking the pistol and taking a breath. She strode into the corridor and saw no one. Were they already inside? Or about to arrive any moment? This door was shut. Miss Temple banged on it with the heel of her fist. There was no sound from beyond the door. She knocked again. Still there was no answer, and her mind was assailed by images of her aunt and her maids slaughtered, the room running with blood. Miss Temple dug her key from her bag and, using her left hand, which made it awkward, unlocked the door. She shoved it open and threw herself to the side. Silence. She peeked around the corner. The entryway was empty. She held the revolver with both hands and walked slowly through the doorway. The outer parlor was empty as well, with no signs of disturbance. She turned to the inner parlor door, which was closed. It was never closed. She crept toward it, looked about her and reached her left hand toward the knob. She slowly turned it and, hearing the click of the bolt, thrust it open. She shrieked—a small shriek, she later hoped—for before her, his revolver extended to Miss Temple's face, stood Doctor Svenson in his stockinged feet. Sitting next to him, trembling and white with terror, was her aunt. Behind them sat the two maids, frozen with fright. A sudden prickling caused Miss Temple to wheel. Behind her, a long double-edged knife in his hand, stood Cardinal Chang, having just stepped out from the maids' room. He smiled at her grimly.

"Very good, Miss Temple. Would you have shot me before I'd cut your throat? I do not know, which is the profoundest of compliments."

She swallowed, unable quite yet to lower the pistol.

"The front door, I'd suggest," called Doctor Svenson from behind her.

Chang nodded. "Indeed." He turned and walked to the door, glancing quickly into the hall before stepping back and closing it, turning the lock. "And perhaps a chair..." he said to no one in particular, and selected one of the inner parlor chairs to wedge beneath the knob. This done, he turned to them and smiled coolly. "We have made the acquaintance of your aunt."

"We were extremely worried when you were not here," said Svenson. He had pocketed his pistol, and was looking uncomfortable to be standing among the openly terrified women.

"I used the other stairs," said Miss Temple. She saw both men were watching her closely and followed their gaze to her hands. She forced herself to slowly release the hammer of the revolver, and to exhale. "There are soldiers—"

"Yes," said Chang. "We were able to escape."

"But how—they were on one staircase and you did not pass me on the other. And how did you know which room was mine?"

"The chit you signed for the tea," said Svenson. "It noted your room—we did not leave it for them to find, do not worry. As for the escape—"

"Doctor Svenson is a sailor." Chang smiled. "He can climb."

"I can climb when I am pushed," said Svenson, shaking his head.

"But—I looked out the window," cried Miss Temple, "there was nothing to climb but brick!"

"There was a metal pipe," said Svenson.

"But that was tiny!"

She saw that the Doctor's face had paled as they spoke. He swallowed awkwardly and wiped his brow.

"Exactly." Chang smiled. "He is a clambering marvel."

Miss Temple caught the gaze of her aunt, still trembling in her chair, and she was flooded with guilt for so endangering the woman. She looked up at the others, her voice sharp with urgency.

"It does not matter. They will know from the desk—from that vile Mr. Spanning, whose pomaded hair I shall set aflame. The Doctor's room is paid for by me. They will be here any moment."

"How many men did you see?" asked Chang.

"Four. Three soldiers and another, in a brown cloak."

"The Comte's man," said Svenson.

"We are three," said Chang. "They'll want to take us quietly, not force a pitched battle."

"There may be others in the lobby," warned Svenson.

"Even if there are, we can beat them."

"At what cost?" asked the Doctor.

Chang shrugged.

Miss Temple looked around her, at the comfort and security that had been her life at the Hotel Boniface, and knew that it was over. She turned to her maids. "Marthe, you will prepare a traveling bag—light enough for me to carry, with the barest essentials—the flowered carpet bag will do." The girl did not move. Miss Temple shouted at her. "At *once*! Do you think this is any time to shirk? Marie, you will prepare traveling bags for my aunt and for the two of you. You will be spending time at the seaside. Go!"

The maids leapt to their work. Her aunt looked up at her.

"Celeste—my dear—the *seaside*?"

"You must move to safety—and I apologize, I am so very, very sorry to have placed you in such danger." Miss Temple sniffed and gestured toward her own room. "I will see what ready money I have, of course you will have enough for travel, and a note to draw upon—you must take both maids—"

Agathe's gaze went, rather wide-eyed, from Miss Temple over to the figures of Chang and Svenson, neither of whom seemed anywhere near respectable enough for her niece to be alone with. "But—you cannot—you are a well-bred young lady—the *scandal*—you must come with me!"

"It is impossible—"

"You will not have a maid—*that* is impossible!" The aged lady huffed at the men, chiding them. "And the seaside will be so *cold*—"

"That is the exact point, my Aunt. You must go to a place no one would expect. You must tell no one—you must tell *no one.*"

Her aunt was silent as the maids bustled around them, studying her niece with dismay—though whether at the present predicament or at what her niece had become, Miss Temple was not sure. She was particularly aware that Svenson and Chang were watching the entire exchange.

"And what of you?" whispered her aunt.

"I cannot say," she answered. "I do not know."

At least twenty minutes had passed, and Miss Temple—idly tracing her fingers back and forth across one of the Doctor's blue glass cards—saw Chang at the main door, peering out into the hall. He stepped back, caught her eye, and shrugged. Marthe had brought the carpet bag for her to inspect. Miss Temple sent her to help Marie, tucked the blue card into her own clutch bag—without looking at the Doctor, who having given it to her again to examine had not perhaps agreed it was hers to *keep*—and carried the carpet bag over to an armchair, where she sat. Her attention elsewhere, she glanced through what the maid had chosen and tied the bag shut without finishing. Miss Temple sighed. Her aunt sat at the table, watching her. Chang stood by the door. Svenson leaned against the table near her aunt, his attempts to help pack having been rebuffed by the maids.

"If these men have not come," said her aunt, "then perhaps they are not coming at all. Perhaps there is no need to go anywhere. If they do not know Celeste—"

"Whether they know your niece is not the issue," said Svenson gently.

"They know who I am, at least, and also Chang. As they know we have been here, they will be watching the hotel. It will be a mere matter of time before they connect your niece to us—"

"They already have," said Chang, from the doorway.

"Then once they *act* on it," continued Svenson, "as your niece has said—you yourself are in danger."

"But," her aunt persisted, "if they are not here yet—"

"It is a blessing," said Miss Temple. "It means we may all get away unseen."

"That will be difficult," said Chang.

Miss Temple sighed. It would be very difficult. Each entrance would be watched from the street. The only question, and their only hope, was in what those men were watching *for*—and surely it was not two maids and an old woman.

"You had best accomplish it, Sir—and neatly!" sniffed Aunt Agathe, as if Chang were a workman whose expression of doubt was a prelude to an increase in his fee.

Miss Temple exhaled and stood.

"We must assume that the clerk who pointed the way to the Doctor's room has been paid to inform on us further. We must distract him while my aunt and the maids depart. The men in the street will not be looking for them, or at least not without some signal. Once you do leave," she said to her aunt, "you must go directly in a coach to the railway station, and from there to the shore, the southern shore—to Cape Rouge, there must be many inns—and I will send a letter to you, to the post office, once we are secure."

"What of yourself?" asked Agathe.

"Oh, we shall shift ourselves easily enough," she said, forcing a smile. "And this business will soon be over." She looked over to Svenson and Chang for confirmation, but neither man's expression would have convinced a credulous child. She called sharply for the maids to finish and gather their coats.

Miss Temple knew that she herself must go to Mr. Spanning, for the others would more profitably assist with the luggage—as well as best remaining concealed. She looked back to see them making their way to the rear stairs, Chang and Svenson each with an end of her aunt's clothes trunk, the maids on either side of Agathe, one hand on their own small bags, the other steadying the aged lady. Miss Temple herself made for the main staircase carrying a large satchel and the green purse, wearing as carefree an expression as she could produce and nodding cheerfully at the other guests she passed. At the second floor her path opened onto a large gallery above the splendid lobby and then to the great curve of the main stairs. She glanced over the railing and saw no black-coated soldiery, but directly outside the doors were two men in brown cloaks. She continued down the wide steps and saw Mr. Spanning behind his counter, his gaze snapping up to hers as she descended into view. She smiled brilliantly at him. Spanning's eyes darted about the lobby as she neared, and so before he could make any signal she gaily called to him.

"Mr. Spanning!"

"Miss Temple?" he answered warily, his normally sleek manner caught between distrust and pride in his own cunning.

She crossed to the desk—from the corners of her eyes seeing that no one lurked under the stairs—while watching the front door in the mirror behind Spanning's desk. The cloaked men had seen her, but were not coming in. Quite apart from her habit, Miss Temple stood on her toes and leaned her elbows playfully on the counter.

"I'm sure you know why I have come." She smiled.

"Do I?" replied Spanning, forcing an obsequious grin that did not suit him.

"O yes." She batted her eyes.

"I'm sure I do not..."

"Perhaps you have been so set upon by business that it has slipped your mind..." She looked around the vacant lobby. "Though it does not appear so. Tell me, Mr. Spanning, *have* you been so set upon with pressing duties?" She was still smiling, but a hint of steel had crept into her otherwise honeyed tone.

"As you know, Miss Temple, my *normal* duties are very—"

"Yes, yes, but you haven't had to bother with anyone *else*?"

Spanning cleared his throat with suspicion. "May I ask—"

"Do you know," continued Miss Temple, "I have always meant to inquire as to your brand of pomade, for I have always found your hair to be so very... *managed.* And slick—managed *and* slick. I have wanted to impart such grooming to any number of other men in the city, but have not known what to recommend—and always forget to ask!"

"It is Bronson's, Miss."

"*Bronson's.* Excellent." She leaned in with a suddenly serious expression. "Do you never worry about fire?"

"Fire?"

"Leaning too close to a candle? I should think—you know—*whoosh*!" She chuckled. "Ah, it is so pleasant to laugh. But I *am* in earnest, Mr. Spanning. And I do require an answer—no matter how you strive to charm me!"

"I assure you, Miss Temple—"

"Of what, Mr. Spanning? Of what do you—this day—*assure* me?"

She was no longer smiling, but looking directly into the man's eyes. He did not reply. She brought the green bag onto the counter top, allowing its weight to land with a *thump.* Its contents were not usual for a lady's purse. Spanning saw her deftly angle the bag in his direction and take hold of it through the fabric—her manner still casual but unaccountably menacing.

"How precisely may I help you?" he asked meekly.

"I will be traveling," she said. "As will my aunt, but to another destination. I wish to retain my rooms. I assume my note of credit will answer any worries?"

"Of course. You will be returning..."

"At some point."

"I see."

"Good. Do you know, earlier, that this hotel seemed absolutely full of foreign soldiers?"

"Did it?"

"Apparently they were directed to the second floor." She looked around them and then dropped her voice to a whisper. Despite himself Spanning leaned closer to hear. "Do you know, Mr. Spanning,... do you know the *sound* a person makes... when they're *thrashed*... to such an *extreme*... they can no longer even cry out... with pain?"

Mr. Spanning flinched, blinking his eyes. Miss Temple leaned even closer and whispered, "Because I do."

Spanning swallowed. Miss Temple stood up straight and smiled.

"I believe you have the Doctor's boots and his coat?"

She climbed back up the main staircase to the second floor and then dashed down the hallway to the rear stairs, her green bag in one hand, the boots in the other, and the Doctor's coat over her left arm. The satchel, thickly packed with unnecessary clothing, had been left in Spanning's care with the request for him to hold it until she was ready to leave, which she announced would most likely be after luncheon—thus making a point to inform Spanning (and the soldiers) that she (and by extension, via the boots, Svenson and Chang) could be found in her rooms for the next few hours. Once out of sight from the lobby, Miss Temple picked up her dress as best she could and briskly climbed. With luck the others had used her distraction to get her aunt and the maids out the service entrance. The porters would take the luggage and find a coach, allowing Svenson and Chang to remain hidden indoors. But were the soldiers marching into the lobby even then, men who moved much faster than she? She reached the fourth floor and stopped to listen. She heard no bootsteps and resumed her trotting pace upwards. At the eighth floor she stopped again, flushed with exertion and panting. She had never been to this topmost floor and had no idea where to find what Chang assured her was there. She walked along the corridor, past what looked like doors to normal rooms, until she rounded a corner and faced the end of the hall. She looked back the other way and saw an identical dead end. Hot and out of breath from her climb, Miss Temple worried about what next might follow her up the stairs. She whispered—or rather hissed—to the air around her with frustration. *"Psssssst!"*

She wheeled abruptly at a wooden squeak. A section of the red-flocked wallpaper swung forward on hinges she had not seen, revealing Doctor Svenson, and behind him, on a narrow staircase steep enough to be more like a ladder, Chang, silhouetted in an open doorway to the roof. Despite the distress of a moment before, she could not suppress her admiration at the cunningly concealed doorway.

"My goodness," she exclaimed, "whoever made that is as clever as five monkeys put together!"

"Your aunt is safely away," said Svenson, stepping into the hall to collect his things.

"I am relieved to hear it," replied Miss Temple. The Doctor struggled into his coat, which—after being brushed and steamed—did restore some of his military crispness. "I could not see this door at all," she continued, admiring the inset hinges. "I don't know how anyone should find it—"

"Are they following?" hissed Chang from inside the passage.

"Not that I have seen," Miss Temple whispered in return. "I could not see them in the lobby—O!" She turned sharply at Doctor Svenson's hand clutching her shoulder.

"I beg your pardon!" he said, bracing himself as he tried to put on his right boot. He could not do it with one hand and was reduced to trying with two while awkwardly hopping.

"We should hurry," called Chang.

"Half a moment," whispered Svenson—the first boot was nearly on. Miss Temple waited. His task remained difficult. She tried to find encouraging conversation.

"I have never been on a rooftop before, or not one so high. I'm sure we'll have quite a view—up with the birds!"

Somehow it seemed the wrong thing to say. Svenson looked up at her, his face more pale, and started in on the second boot.

"Are you perfectly well, Doctor? I know you did not find but a few hours' rest—"

"Go on ahead," he said, essaying a casual tone that did not persuade. The second boot was on half-way. He stumbled, stepping upon it, the excess flopping around like an odd fish attached to the base of his leg. "I shall follow—I assure you—"

"Doctor!" hissed Chang. "It will be fine. The roof is wide, and the climb will be nothing like the pipe!"

"The pipe?" asked Miss Temple.

"Ah—well—that—" said Doctor Svenson.

"I thought you managed it splendidly."

From the passage Chang scoffed.

"I have a difficulty with height. An excruciating difficulty—"

"I have the same with root vegetables." Miss Temple smiled. "We shall help one another—come!" She anxiously looked past his shoulder down the hallway, relieved to see it still empty, and took his arm. He thrust his foot down into the boot—fully in but for a last uncooperative inch. They stepped through the door.

"Pull it tight," whispered Chang, who had continued on above them. "It is better they not notice we have forced the lock."

The sky above was grey and so low as to seem palpably near, the sun well behind a thick bank of winter cloud. The air was cool and moist, and if there were only more wind Miss Temple might have told herself she was on the sea. She inhaled with pleasure. She looked down to see with a certain small wonder that under her feet was a crusty layer of tarred paper and copper sheathing—so this was walking on a roof! Behind her Doctor Svenson had knelt, concentrating closely on his left boot, eyes fixed to the ground. Chang secured the door with bits of broken wood, wedging them into the frame to prevent it from opening easily. He stepped away and wiped his hand on his coat. She saw that his other hand held her carpet bag—she had completely forgotten it, and reached to take it from him. He shook his head and nodded toward a nearby building.

"I believe we can go this way—north," he said.

"If we must," muttered Svenson. He stood, still keeping his eyes low. Miss Temple saw it was time for her to act.

"Excuse me," she said, "but before we travel further together, I believe—I am convinced—that we need to speak."

Chang frowned at her. "They may be coming—"

"Yes, though I do not think they are. I think they are waiting for us in the street, or waiting for Mr. Spanning to make sure the guests in the rooms near to mine will not be disturbed by any screams. I am confident we have at least some few minutes."

The two men looked at each other. She could sense the doubt in the glance that went between them. She pointedly cleared her throat, bringing their eyes back to her.

"To the great distress of my only available relative, I have been thrust into the company of two men at the very border—if that—of respectability. This morning we were strangers. In this instant all three of us are without sanctuary. What I want—in fact demand—is that we make quite clear what we each hope to achieve in this matter, what masters we serve—in short, what is our *agreement.*"

She waited for their reaction. The two men were silent.

"I do not find the request excessive," said Miss Temple.

Svenson nodded at her, looked to Chang and muttered, groping in his pocket. "Excuse me—a cigarette—it will distract from the altitude, this sea of vacant space—" He looked back at Miss Temple. "You are correct. It is most sensible. We do not know each other—chance has thrown us together."

"Can we not do this later?" asked Chang, his tone clinging to the merest edge of civility.

"When would that be?" answered Miss Temple. "Do we even know where we are going next? Have we decided how best to act? Who to pursue? Of course we haven't, because we have each made assumptions from our very different experiences."

Chang exhaled, vexed. After a moment, he nodded sharply, as if to invite her to begin. Miss Temple did so.

"I have been attacked and now uprooted. I have been misled, threatened, and lied to. I wish for justice... which means the *thorough* settling of each person involved." She took a breath. "Doctor?"

Svenson took the moment to actually light his cigarette, return the case to his coat pocket, and exhale. He nodded to her.

"I must recover my Prince—no matter this conspiracy, it remains my duty to *disentangle* him. I have no doubt that this entails a kind of war—but I have little choice. Cardinal?"

Chang paused, as if he found this a pointless, formal exercise, but then spoke quietly and quickly. "If this business is not answered I have no work, no place to live, and no good reputation. For these all being set at hazard, I will have revenge—I must, as I say, to preserve my name. Does that satisfy you?"

"It does."

"These figures are intertwined, and deadly," said Chang. "Are we to follow them all—to an end?"

"I would insist upon it, actually," said Miss Temple.

Doctor Svenson spoke. "I too. No matter what happens with Karl-Horst, the work must be finished. This conspiracy—this cabal—I cannot say *what* drives its members, but I know together they are like rot around a wound, like a cancer. If not removed in its entirety, what remains will only grow back, more virulent and vicious than ever. Not one of us or any that we care for shall be safe."

"Then it's agreed," said Chang.

He smiled wryly and put his hand out. Doctor Svenson stuck his cigarette into his mouth and, his hand free, took hold of Chang's. Miss Temple placed her small hand over theirs. She had no idea what this would portend—it was intrigue after all—but she did not think she had ever been happier in her life. As she had agreed to something exceedingly serious, she did her best not to giggle, but she could not prevent herself from beaming.

"Excellent!" announced Miss Temple. "I am happy to have it so directly spoken. And now, the other question—as I have said—is how to proceed. Do we find another place of refuge? Do we go on the attack—and if so, where? The St. Royale? The Ministry? Harschmort?"

"My first thought would be to move from the rooftop," said Chang.

"Yes, yes, but we can talk while we go—no one will overhear us."

"Then this way—stay with us, Doctor—to the north. The hotel is connected to the next building—I believe there is no gap at all."

"Gap?" asked Svenson.

"To jump across," said Chang.

Svenson did not reply.

"Surely," said Miss Temple, "we should look down to the street—to see the men arrayed around the Boniface."

Chang sighed, acquiescing, and looked to Svenson, who waved them toward the edge of the building. "I shall proceed to the next roof—so as not to detain you . . ." He walked slowly in that direction, looking down at his boots. Miss Temple marched to the edge and carefully looked down. The view was exquisite. Below her the avenue was laid out like a doll's house full of tiny creatures. She looked over to see Chang had joined her, kneeling in the cover of the copper moldings. "Do you see anyone?" she whispered. He pointed to the end of the street: behind a grocer's cart were two men in black, quite out of sight from the Boniface but able to view its entrance with ease. With growing excitement Miss Temple looked the other way and smiled, tugging Chang's coat. "The iron fence—at the corner!" Another two figures lurked behind it, just visible to them above but concealed from the street by the fence's veil of ivy.

"They are watching at each corner," Chang said. "Four men in uniform—already more than you saw in the hotel. Now they think we are trapped, they may bring every man at their command. They will be in your rooms even now. We must go."

They found Svenson advanced across the rooftops of two very fine town houses, connected to each other and the Boniface. He gestured vaguely to the far edge. "The drop is significant," he said, "and the distance across farther than any of us can leap. To the front of the building is the avenue, which is even wider, and to the rear is an alley, narrower, but still more than we can manage."

"I should quite like to see in any case," said Miss Temple, and walked smilingly to the rear edge. The town house roof was at least two stories taller than the building across the street, whatever it was—she could not tell, its few windows small and blackened by smoke. She looked down and felt a giddy pleasure. The Doctor was right, she could not imagine any person breasting it. She saw Chang crouched at the far edge looking down—more soldier-counting, she assumed.

Miss Temple returned to the Doctor, who she saw was having a hard time of it. In truth this was a comfort, for compared to the menacing capacity of Chang, her own feelings of ignorance and weakness were lessened by Svenson's obvious distress.

"We saw several pairs of soldiers watching the front of the hotel," she said to him. "More than were inside—Chang thinks they are *gathering.*"

Svenson nodded. He was digging out another cigarette.

"You consume those at quite a rate, don't you?" she said affably. "We shall have to find you more."

"That will be difficult," he said, smiling. "They are from Riga, from a man I know in a Macklenburg shop—I cannot get them otherwise *there,* and doubt anyone could find them *here.* I have a cedar box of them in my room at the compound—for all the good it does me."

Miss Temple narrowed her eyes. "Without them . . . will you become peevish and ill?"

"I will not," said Svenson. "What is more, the effects of tobacco are entirely beneficial to me—a restorative that both soothes and awakens."

"It is the chewing and spitting of tobacco I dislike," said Miss Temple. "Such usage is common where I come from, and fully abhorrent. Besides, tobacco of any kind stains the teeth most awfully." She noticed the Doctor's teeth were stained the color of new-cut oak.

"Where are you from?" asked Svenson, pressing his lips together self-consciously.

"An island," Miss Temple answered simply. "Where it is *warmer,* and one may eat fresh fruit on a regular basis. Ah, here is Chang."

"I can see soldiers in the main streets," he said, walking up to them, "but not at the alley. There is a chance we can go through this rooftop"—here he pointed to an undoubtedly locked door that led into the town house—"and out to the alley. I do not, however, see how we can hope to leave the alley itself, for each end of it will lead us to them."

"Then we are trapped," said Svenson.

"We can hide downstairs," said Chang.

They turned to Miss Temple for her opinion—which in itself was gratifying—but before she could answer, there was the sound of trumpets, echoing to the rooftops.

She turned to the sound, its clear call seemingly answered by a crisp low rumbling. "Horses," she said, "a great many of them!" All three, Miss Temple steadying the Doctor's arm, crept carefully to look over the main avenue. Below them, filling the street, was a parade of mounted soldiers in bright red tunics and shining brass helmets, each draped with a black horse's tail.

"Are they coming for us?" she cried.

"I do not know," said Chang. She saw him share a look with Svenson, and wished they would not do this so often, or at least so openly.

"The 4th Dragoons," said the Doctor, and he pointed to an important-looking figure whose epaulettes dripped with gold fringe. "Colonel Aspiche."

Miss Temple watched the man ride by, officers to either side, lines of troopers in front and behind—a stern figure, gaze unwavering, his finely groomed horse immaculately controlled. She tried to count his men but they moved too quickly—at least a hundred, perhaps more than twice that. Then there was a gap between the lines of horsemen, and Miss Temple squeezed Doctor Svenson's arm. "Carts!"

It was a train of some ten carts each driven by uniformed soldiers.

"The carts are empty," said Svenson.

Chang nodded toward the Boniface. "They are going past the hotel. This has nothing to do with us."

It was true. Miss Temple saw the red mass of uniforms continuing past the hotel and then winding toward Grossmaere.

"What is in that direction?" she asked. "The St. Royale is the other way."

Doctor Svenson leaned forward. "It is the Institute. They are going to the Institute with *empty* carts—the glass machinery—the—the—what did you say, both of you—the *boxes*—"

"Boxes in carts were delivered to Harschmort," said Chang. "Boxes were all over their Institute laboratory."

"The boxes at Harschmort were lined with orange felt, and had numbers painted on them," said Miss Temple.

"At the Institute . . . the linings were not orange," said Chang. "They were blue."

"I would bet my eyes they are collecting more," said Svenson. "Or relocating their workplace, after the death at the Institute."

Below them the trumpets sounded again—Colonel Aspiche was not one for a demure passage. Svenson tried to speak over them but the words were lost to Miss Temple. He tried again, leaning closer to them, pointing down. "Major Blach's men have entered the hotel." Miss Temple saw that he was right—a stream of black figures, just visible along the edges of the red horsemen, scurrying toward the Boniface like rats for an open culvert. "If I might suggest," the Doctor said, "it seems an excellent time to attempt to leave through the alley."

As they made their way down a luxuriously carpeted stairway, Miss Temple wondered that anyone thought themselves immune to housebreaking or burglary at all. It had taken Chang but a moment to effect their entry into a dwelling whose owners she was sure prided themselves on inviolable security. They were fortunate not to find anyone at home on the upper stories (for the servants who lived in those rooms were at work), and were able to creep quietly past the floors where they heard footsteps or clinking crockery or even in one case an especially repellent huffing. Miss Temple knew that the ground floor and the rear entrance itself would be the most likely places for a confrontation—these *would* be occupied by servants, if no one else—and so as they stepped free of the staircase she made a point to thrust herself in front of Chang and Svenson despite their looks of surprise. She knew full well that she could offer an appearance that was unthreatening but nevertheless imperious, where each of them would invite the outrage sparked by any interloping man. From the corner of her eye she saw a young housemaid stacking jars who out of instinct bobbed into a curtsey at her passing. Miss Temple acknowledged the girl with a nod and strode on into the kitchen, which held at least three servants hard at work. She smiled at them crisply. "Good afternoon. My name is Miss Hastings—I require your rear door." She did not pause for their reply. "I expect it is this way? I am obliged to you. What a well-kept room—the teapots are especially fine—" Within moments she was beyond them and down a short flight of stairs to the door itself. She stepped aside for Chang to open it, for behind him and over the Doctor's shoulder she saw the crowd of curious faces that had followed. "Have you seen the parade of cavalry?" she called. "It is the Prince's Own 4th Dragoons—my goodness, they are splendid! Such trumpets, and so many fine animals—remarkable. Good day!" She followed the Doctor through the door and exhaled with relief as Chang closed it behind them.

The sound of hoofbeats was fainter—the parade was already passing by. As they ran toward the alley's end, Miss Temple noted with alarm that Chang had drawn his long double-edged knife and Svenson his revolver. Miss Temple groped at her green bag, but needed one hand to hold up her dress to run and could not successfully open it with the other. If she was a cursing sort of girl she would have been cursing then, for the obvious urgency with which her companions treated the situation had caught her unawares. They were at the street. Svenson took hold of her arm as they walked rapidly away from the Boniface. Chang loped a pace or two behind, his eyes searching for enemies. There were no cries, no shots. They reached the next street and Svenson wheeled her around the corner. They pressed themselves against the wall and waited for Chang to follow a moment later. He shrugged, and the three of them continued away as quickly as they could. It seemed incredible to be free so easily, and Miss Temple could not help but smile at their success.

Before either of the men could set a path, Miss Temple picked up her pace so that they would be forced to follow her. They rounded the corner into the next broad avenue—Regent's Gate—where ahead of them, Miss Temple spotted a familiar awning. She steered them toward it. She'd had an idea.

"Where are you going?" asked Chang, brusquely.

"We must strategize," answered Miss Temple. "We cannot do it in the street. We cannot do it in a café—the three of us would be much talked of—"

"Perhaps a private room—" suggested Svenson.

"Then we would be even *more* talked of," interrupted Miss Temple. "But there is a place where no one will comment on our strange little band."

"What place?" asked Chang with suspicion.

She smiled at her cleverness. "It is an art gallery."

The artist presently exhibited was a Mr. Veilandt—a painter from somewhere near Vienna—whose work Roger had taken her to see as a way of showing favor to a visiting group of Austrian bankers. Miss Temple had been alone among the party to pay the art itself any attention—in her case, a negative interest, for she found the paintings unsettling and presumptuous. Everyone else had ignored them in favor of drinking schnapps and discussing markets and tariffs, as Roger had assured her they would. Reasoning that the gallery would not mind another such visit of ill-attention, she pulled Svenson and Chang into the outer lobby to speak to the attending gallery agent. She explained in a low tone that she had been part of the Austrian party and here brought a representative of the Macklenburg court, in search of wedding presents for his Prince—a figure of *taste*—surely the man had heard of the impending match? He nodded importantly that he had. The man's gaze drifted to Chang and Miss Temple noted with some tact that her second companion was also an *artist,* much impressed with Mr. Veilandt's reputation as a *provocateur.* The agent nodded in sympathy and ushered them into the main viewing room, delicately slipping a brochure with printed prices and titles into the hands of Doctor Svenson.

The paintings were as she remembered them: large, lurid oils depicting in an almost obscenely deliberate manner incidents of doubt and temptation from the lives of saints, each chosen for its thoroughly unwholesome spectacle. Indeed, without the establishing context within each composition of the single figure with a halo, the collection of canvases created a pure pageant of decadence. While Miss Temple perceived how the artist used the veil of the sacred to indulge his taste for the depraved, she was not sure whether, on a level deeper than cynical cleverness, the paintings were not more truthful than was ever intended. Indeed, when she had first seen them, among the throng of self-important financiers, her dismay had been not with the profligate and blasphemous carnality but, on the contrary, the precarious isolation, the barely persuasive presence, of virtue. Miss Temple led her companions down the length of the gallery, away from the agent.

"Good Lord," whispered Doctor Svenson. He peered at the small card to the side of a largely orange canvas whose figures seemed to slither from the surface fully fleshed into the air around them. *"St. Rowena and the Viking Raiders,"* he read, and turned up to the face that could perhaps charitably be said to be glowing with religious fervor. "Good *Lord.*"

Chang was silent, but equally transfixed, his expression unreadable behind the smoked-glass lenses. Miss Temple spoke in a low tone, so as not to attract the agent.

"So . . . now that we may speak without concern . . ."

"The Blissful Fortitude of St. Jasper," read the Doctor, glancing up at a canvas on the other wall. "Are those *pig snouts*?"

She cleared her throat. They turned to her, slightly abashed.

"Good Lord, Miss Temple," said Svenson, "these paintings do not take you aback?"

"In fact they do, yet I have already seen them. I had thought, since we have already shared the blue cards, we could weather their challenge."

"Yes—yes, I see," said Svenson, at once even more obviously awkward. "The gallery is certainly empty. And convenient."

Chang did not offer any opinion on the place or the paintings of Mr. Veilandt, but merely smiled—once more rather wolfishly, it seemed.

"My own idea . . . ," began Miss Temple. "You *did* look at the glass cards, Cardinal?"

"I did." The man was positively *leering.*

"Well, in the one with Roger Bascombe—and myself—" She stopped and frowned, gathering her thoughts—there were too many at wing inside her brain. "What I am trying to decide is where we ought to next direct our efforts, and most importantly whether it is best for us to remain together or if the work is more effectively accomplished in different directions."

"You mentioned the *card*?" prompted Chang.

"Because it showed the country house of Roger's uncle, Lord Tarr, and some kind of quarry—"

"Wait, wait," Svenson broke in. "Francis Xonck, speaking of Bascombe's inheritance . . . he referred to a substance called 'indigo clay'—have you heard of it?"

She shook her head. Chang shrugged.

"Neither had I," continued Svenson. "But he suggested that Bascombe would soon be the owner of a large deposit of the same. It has to be the quarry, which has to be on his uncle's land."

"*His* land," corrected Chang.

Svenson nodded. "And my thought is that it may be vital to making their glass!"

"Thus why Tarr was killed," said Chang. "And why Bascombe was chosen. They seduce him to their cause, and then this indigo clay is under their control."

Miss Temple saw the ease of it—a few words from Crabbé about the usefulness of a title to an ambitious man, the flattering company of a woman like the Contessa or even—she sighed with disappointment—Mrs. Marchmoor and cigars and brandy with a flattering rake like Francis Xonck. She wondered if Roger had any real idea of the value of this indigo clay, or if his allegiance was being purchased as cheaply as that of an Indian savage, with these people's equivalent of beads and feathers. Then she remembered that he too had borne the purple scars. Did he even retain his own unfettered mind, or had this *Process* transmuted him into their slave?

"He *is* a pawn after all . . . ," she whispered.

"I'd wager every preening member of this cabal sees every other as a pawn." Chang chuckled. "I would not single out poor Bascombe."

"No," said Miss Temple. "I'm sure you're correct. I'm sure he's only like them all."

She shrugged away the glimmer of sympathy. "But the question remains—should we direct our efforts to Tarr Manor?"

"There is another possibility," said Doctor Svenson. "I've been distracted. Not three minutes from here is the walled garden where the Comte d'Orkancz brought me to look at the injured woman—it was my destination when I saw you in the window."

"What woman?" asked Chang.

Svenson exhaled heavily and shook his head. "Another unfortunate caught up in the Comte's experiments, and another mystery. She bore all the features of drowning in frozen water, though the damage had apparently been inflicted by some machine—I assume it has to do with the glass, or the boxes—I could not say if she survived the night. But the location—a greenhouse, to keep her warm—must be a stronghold of the Comte, and it is very near. He sought me to treat her—"

"Sought you?" asked Miss Temple.

"He claimed to have seen a pamphlet I wrote, years ago, on the afflictions of Baltic seamen—"

"He is indeed widely read."

"It is ridiculous, I agree—"

"I do not doubt it, but *why*?" Miss Temple frowned, her thoughts quickening. "But wait... if the pamphlet is so old, then it means the Comte must have had cause, even then, to be mindful of such injuries!"

Svenson nodded. "Yes! Would this mean the Comte is the chief architect of these *experiments*?"

"At Harschmort it was quite clearly he who managed the boxes and the strange mechanical masks. It only follows he is master of the science itself..." She shivered at the memory of the large man's callous manipulation of the somnolent women.

"What did the woman look like?" interrupted Chang. "At this greenhouse?"

"Look like?" said Svenson, his train of thought jarred. "Ah—well—there were disfiguring marks across her body—she was young, beautiful—yes, and perhaps Asiatic. Do you know who she is?"

"Of course not," said Chang.

"We can see if she is still there—"

"So that is another possibility," said Miss Temple, attempting to keep the conversation clear. "I can also think of several destinations in search of particular people—back to Harschmort, to the St. Royale for the Contessa—"

"Crabbé's house on Hadrian Square," said Svenson.

They turned to Chang. He was silent, lost in thought. Abruptly he looked up, and shook his head. "Following an individual merely gives us a prisoner—at best, that is. It means interrogation, threats—it is awkward. True, we may find the Prince—we may find anything—but most likely we will catch Harald Crabbé at dinner with his wife and end up having to cut both their throats."

"I have not made Mrs. Crabbé's acquaintance," said Miss Temple. "I should prefer any mayhem be directly applied to those who we know have harmed us." She knew that Chang had raised the idea of murdering the woman just to frighten them, and she *was* frightened—a test, as she realized the paintings were a way for her to test the two of them. As they stood speaking, she saw that placing herself with two men amidst a room full of undulating flesh was actually a declaration of a certain capacity and knowledge that she did not in fact possess. It had not been her initial intention, but it made her feel more their equal.

"So you are not content to simply kill everyone." Chang smiled.

"I am not," replied Miss Temple. "In all this I have wanted to know *why*—from the first moment I decided to follow Roger."

"Do you suppose we should separate?" asked Svenson. "Some to visit the greenhouse—which may involve the throat-cutting you describe, if it is full of the Comte's men—and one to visit Tarr Manor?"

"What of your Prince?" asked Miss Temple.

Svenson rubbed his eyes. "I do not know. Even *they* did not know."

"Who did not?" asked Chang. "Specifically."

"Xonck, Bascombe, Major Blach, the Comte . . ."

"Did they rule out the Contessa?"

"No. Nor Lord Vandaariff. So . . . perhaps the Prince is in a room at the St. Royale, or at Harschmort—perhaps, if we *were* able to find him, it would accentuate the divisions between them, and who can say—thus provoke some rash action or at least reveal more of their true aims."

Chang nodded. He turned to Miss Temple and spoke quite seriously. "What is your opinion about dividing our efforts? About pursuing one of these choices alone?"

Before she could answer—as she knew she must answer—Miss Temple felt the whole of her mind relocated to the jolting coach with Spragg, the hot smell of his sweating, bristled neck, the suffocating weight of his body, the imperious force of his hands, the crush of fear that had taken such implacable hold over her body. She blinked the thought away and found herself again facing the woman in red, her piercing violet eyes sharper than any knife, her dismissive, lordly insolence of expression, her dark chuckling laugh that seemed to flay the nerves from Miss Temple's spine. She blinked again. She looked around her at the paintings, and at the two men who had become her allies—because she had chosen them, as she had chosen to place her very self at hazard. She knew they would do whatever she said.

"I do not mind at all." Miss Temple smiled. "If I should have the chance to shoot one of these fellows by myself, then all the better, I say."

"Just a moment . . . ," said Doctor Svenson. He was looking past her at the far wall and walked over to it, wiping his monocle on the lapel of his greatcoat. He stood in front of a small canvas—perhaps the smallest on display—and peered at the identifying card, then back at the painting with close attention. "Both of you need to come here."

Miss Temple crossed to the painting and abruptly gasped with surprise. How could she have not remembered this from before? The canvas—clearly cut from a larger work—showed an ethereal woman reclining on what one first assumed to be a sofa or divan, but which on further study was clearly an angled table—there even seemed to be straps (or was this merely the artist's conception of a Biblical garment?) securing her arms. Above the woman's head floated a golden halo, but on her face, around her eyes, were the same purpled looping scars they had all witnessed in the flesh.

Svenson consulted his brochure. "*Annunciation Fragment* . . . it is . . . a moment—" He flipped the page. "The painting is five years old. And it is the newest piece in the collection. Excuse me."

He left them and approached the agent, who sat making notes in a ledger at his desk. Miss Temple returned to the painting. She could not deny that it was unsettlingly lovely, and she noticed with horror that the woman's pale robe was bordered at the neck with a line of green circles. "The robes in Harschmort," she whispered to Chang, "the women under the Comte's power—they wore the same!"

The Doctor returned, shaking his head. "It's most bizarre," he hissed. "The artist—Mr. Oskar Veilandt—was apparently a mystic, deranged, a dabbler in alchemy and dark science."

"Excellent," said Chang. "Perhaps he's the one to tie these threads together—"

"He can lead us to the others!" Miss Temple whispered excitedly.

"My exact thought." The Doctor nodded. "But I am told that Mr. Veilandt has been dead for these five years."

All three were silent. Five years? How could that be possible? What did it mean?

"The lines on her face," said Chang. "They are definitely the same..."

"Yes," agreed Svenson, "which only tells us that the plot itself—the Process—is at least that old as well. We will need to know more—where the artist lived, where he died, who holds custody of his work—indeed, who has sponsored this very exhibition—"

Miss Temple extended her finger to point at the small card with the work's title, for next to it was a small blot of red ink. "Even more, Doctor, we will need to know who has *bought* this painting!"

The gallery agent, a Mr. Shanck, was happy to oblige them with information (after the Doctor had thoroughly inquired as to prices and delivery procedures for several of the larger paintings, in between mutters about wall space in the Macklenburg Palace), but unfortunately what Mr. Shanck knew was little: Veilandt himself was a mystery, school in Vienna, sojourns in Italy and Constantinople, *atelier* in Montmartre. The paintings had come from a dealer in Paris, where he understood Veilandt had died. He glanced toward the opulent compositions and tendered that he did not doubt it was due to consumption or absinthe or some other such destructive mania. The present owner wished to remain anonymous—in Mr. Shanck's view because of the *oeuvre*'s scandalous nature—and Shanck's only dealings were with his opposite number at a gallery in the Boulevard St. Germain. Mr. Shanck clearly relished the patina of intrigue around the collection, as he relished sharing his privileged information with those he deemed discerning. His expression faltered into suspicion however when Miss Temple, in a fully casual manner, wondered who had purchased the "odd little painting", and if he might have any others like it for purchase. She quite fancied it, and would love another for her home. In fact, he outright blanched.

"I . . . I assumed—you mentioned the wedding—the Prince—"

Miss Temple nodded in agreement, dispelling none of the man's sudden fear.

"Exactly. Thus my interest in buying one for myself."

"But none are available for purchase at all! They never were!"

"That seems no way to run a gallery," she said, "and besides, *one* has been sold—"

"Why—why else would you come?" he said, more to himself than to her, his voice fading as he spoke.

"To see the paintings, Mr. Shanck—as I told you—"

"It was not even *bought*," he sputtered, waving at the small canvas. "It was given, *for* the wedding. It is a gift for Lydia Vandaariff. The entire exhibition has been arranged for no other reason than to reunite each canvas with the others in a single collection! Anyone acquainted with the gallery—anyone suitable to be *informed*—surely, the union of the artist's themes . . . religion . . . morality . . . appetite . . . mysticism . . . you must be aware . . . the forces at work—the *dangerous* . . ."

Mr. Shanck looked at them and swallowed nervously. "If you did not know *that*—how did you—who did you—"

Miss Temple saw the man's rising distress and found she was instinctively smiling at him, shaking her head—it was all a misunderstanding—but before she could actually speak, Chang stepped forward, immediately menacing and sharp, and took up a fistful of Mr. Shanck's cravat, pulling him awkwardly over his desk. Shanck bleated in futile protest.

"I know nothing," he cried. "People use the gallery to meet—I am paid to allow it—I say nothing—I will say nothing about any of you—I swear it—"

"Mr. Shanck—" began Miss Temple, but Chang cut her off, tightening his grip on the man with a snarl.

"The paintings have been gathered together you say—by *whom*?"

Shanck sputtered, utterly outraged and afraid—though not, it seemed to her, of them. "By—*ah!*—by her *father*!"

Once released, the man broke away and fled across the gallery into a room Miss Temple believed actually held brooms. She sighed with frustration. Still, it gave them a moment to speak.

"We must leave at once," she said. There were noises from beyond the distant doorway. She reached out an arm and prevented Chang from investigating. "We did not yet decide—"

Chang cut her off. "This greenhouse. It may be dangerous enough that numbers will help our entry. It is also nearby."

Miss Temple bristled with irritation at Chang's peremptory manner, but then perceived a flicker of emotion cross his face. Though she could not, with his eyes so hidden, guess what feelings were at work, the very fact of their presence piqued her interest. Chang seemed to her then like a kind of finely bred horse whose strengths were at the mercy of any number of infinitesimal tempests at work in the blood—a character that required a very particular sort of managing.

"I agree," replied Svenson.

"Excellent," said Miss Temple. She noted with alarm a growing clamor from amongst the brooms. "But I suggest we leave."

"Wait...," called Doctor Svenson, and he dashed away from them toward Veilandt's *Annunciation.* With a quick glance after Mr. Shanck's closet, the Doctor snatched it from the wall.

"He's not going to *steal* it?" whispered Miss Temple.

He was not. Instead, the Doctor flipped the picture over to look at the back side of the canvas, the deliberate nodding of his face confirming that he'd found something there to see. A moment later the painting was returned to the wall and the Doctor running toward them.

"What was it?" asked Chang.

"Writing," exclaimed Svenson, ushering them toward the street. "I wondered if there might be any indication of the larger work, or—seeing as the man was an alchemist—some kind of mystical formula."

"And was there?" asked Miss Temple.

He nodded, groping for a scrap of paper and a pencil stub from his coat pocket. "Indeed—I will note them down, though the symbols mean nothing to me—but also, I cannot say what they portend, but there were words, in large block letters—"

"What words?" asked Chang.

" *'And so they shall be consumed',* " Svenson replied.

Miss Temple said nothing, recalling vividly the blackboard at Harschmort, for there was no time. They were on the avenue, the Doctor taking her arm as he led the way toward the greenhouse.

"In blood?" asked Chang.

"No," answered Doctor Svenson. "In *blue.*"

"The entrance to the lane that I know is directly opposite the Boniface," said Svenson, speaking low as they walked. "To reach the garden gate safely, we will have to walk some distance around the hotel and come at it from the opposite side."

"And even then," observed Chang, "you say it may be guarded."

"It was before. But of course, the Comte was there—without him, the guards may be gone. The problem is, I entered through the garden, that is, the back way—and it was dark and foggy, and I have no real idea whether there is a house connected to it—still less if the house is presently occupied."

Chang sighed. "If we must circle around it will be longer to walk, yet—"

"Nonsense," said Miss Temple. The men looked at her. She really would need to take a firmer hand. "We will hire a coach," she explained, and realized that neither of her companions even thought of hiring a coach as a normal part of their day. It was obvious that between the three of them were different sorts of strength, and different brands of fragility. As a woman, Miss Temple perceived how each of her companions felt sure about where *she* might fail, but lacked a similar sense of their own vulnerabilities. It was, she accepted, her own responsibility, and so she directed their attention down the avenue.

"There is one now—if one of you would *wave* to the man?"

Thus conveyed, each one pressing themselves into their seat and away from the windows, they were on the other side of the lane within minutes. Chang gave Miss Temple a nod to indicate he saw no soldiers. They climbed out and she sent the coach on its way. The trio entered the empty, narrow, cobbled lane, which Miss Temple saw was called Plum Court. The gate stood in the middle of the lane—as they neared it the sounds of the adjoining avenues faded before the deepening shadow, for the buildings around them blocked out whatever light did not fall from directly above, which from this clouded sky was very feeble. Miss Temple wondered how any kind of garden could thrive in such a dull and airless place. The entrance was a strange church-like arch set into the wall around a thick wooden door. The arch itself was decorated with subtle figures carved into the wood, a strange pattern of sea monsters, mermaids, and shipwrecked sailors who were smiling even as they drowned.

Miss Temple turned her gaze to the end of the lane and saw, in the brighter light of the avenue, as if it were a framed colored picture, the front of the Boniface. Standing at the door was Mr. Spanning, with a soldier to either side. Miss Temple tapped Chang on the shoulder and pointed. He stepped quickly to the doorway, set down Miss Temple's flowered bag and dug in his pocket for a heavy ring of many keys. He rapidly sorted through them, and muttered out of the side of his mouth, "Let me know if they see us . . . and you might step closer to the wall."

Miss Temple and the Doctor did press themselves against the wall, each of them readying their pistols. Miss Temple felt more than a little anxious—she had never fired any weapon in her life, and here she was, playing the highwayman. Chang inserted a key and turned. It did not work. He tried another, and another, and another, each time patiently flipping through the ring for a new one.

"If there is anyone on the other side of the door," whispered Svenson, "they will hear!"

"They already have," Chang whispered in reply, and Miss Temple noticed that he had casually insinuated himself—and they behind him—to the side of the door, clear of any shots that might be fired through it. He tried another key, and another, and another. He stood back and sighed, then looked up at the wall. It was perhaps ten feet tall, but the sheer face was broken around the door by the ornamental arch. Chang pocketed his keys and turned to Svenson.

"Doctor, your hands please . . ."

Miss Temple watched with some alarm and a certain animal appreciation as Chang placed his boot in the knitted hands of Doctor Svenson, and then launched himself at the overhanging archway. With the barest grip he slithered up to where he could wedge his knee onto the shingles, shift his weight, and then reach as high as the edge of the wall itself. Within moments, and by what Miss Temple felt to be a striking display of physical capacity, Chang had swung a leg over the wall. He looked down with what seemed to be a professional lack of expression, and dropped from her sight. There was silence. Svenson readied his revolver. Then the lock was turning, the door open, and Chang beckoning them to enter.

"We have been anticipated," he said, and reached out to take the bag from her.

Under its pall of shadow, the garden was a dreary place, the beds withered, the patches of lawn brown, the limbs of the delicate ornamental trees hanging limp and bare. Miss Temple walked between stone urns taller than her head, their edges draped with the dead fallen stalks of last summer's flowers. The garden bordered the rear of a large house that had once, she saw, been painted white, though it was now nearly black from a layered patina of soot. Its windows and rear door had been nailed shut with planks, effectively sealing it off from the garden. Before her, Miss Temple saw the greenhouse, a once-splendid dome of grey-green glass, streaked with moss and grime. The door hung open, dark as the gap of a missing tooth. As they walked toward it, she saw that Doctor Svenson was studying the garden beds and muttering under his breath.

"What do you see, Doctor?" she asked.

"I beg your pardon—I was simply noting the Comte's choice of plants. It is the garden of a dark-hearted herbalist." He pointed to various withered stalks that to Miss Temple looked all the same. "Here is black hellebore, here is belladonna . . . foxglove . . . mandrake . . . castor beans . . . bloodroot . . ."

"My goodness," said Miss Temple, not knowing the plants Svenson was listing, but willing to approve of his recitation. "One would think the Comte was an apothecary!"

"To be sure, Miss Temple, these are all, in their way, poisons." Svenson looked up and drew her eye to the door, where Chang had entered without them. "But perhaps there is time to study the flower beds later..."

The light in the greenhouse bore a greenish cast, as if one were entering an aquarium. Miss Temple walked across thick Turkish carpets to where Chang stood next to a large canopied bed. The curtains had been pulled from the posts and the bedding stripped away. She looked down at the mattress with rising revulsion. The thick padding was stained with the deep ruddy color of dried blood, but also, near the head, marked with strange vivid spatters of both deep indigo blue and an acid-tinged orange. Taking her rather aback, Doctor Svenson climbed onto the bed and bent over the different stains, sniffing. For Miss Temple, such intimacy with another person's bodily discharges—a person she did not even know—extended well beyond her present sphere of duty. She turned away and allowed her eyes to roam elsewhere in the room.

While it seemed like the Comte had vacated the greenhouse and taken with him anything that might have explained his use of it, Miss Temple could still see how the circular room had held different areas of activity. At the door was a small work table. Nearby were basins and pipes where water was pumped in, and next to the basins a squat coal stove topped by a wide flat iron plate for cooking either food or, more probably, alchemical compounds and elixirs. Past these was a long wooden table, nailed to the floor and fitted, she noted with a fearful shiver, with leather straps. She glanced back at the bed. Doctor Svenson was still bent over the mattress, and Chang was looking underneath it. She walked to the table. The surface was scored with burns and stains, as was—she noted when her foot snagged in an open tear—the carpet. In fact, the carpet was absolutely ruined with burns and stains along a small pathway running from the stove to the table, and then again from the stove to the basins, and then, finishing the triangle, from the basins to the table directly. She stepped to the stove, which was cold. Out of curiosity, she knelt in front of it and pried open the hatch. It was full of ash. She looked about her for some tongs, found them, and reached in, her tongue poking from her mouth in concentration as she sifted through the ashes. After a moment she stood up, wiped her hands, and turned quite happily to her companions, holding out a scrap of midnight blue fabric.

"Something here, gentlemen. Unless I am mistaken it is *shantung* silk—is it possible this was the woman's dress?"

Chang crossed to her and took the piece of burnt cloth. He studied it a moment without speaking and handed it back. He called to Svenson, his voice a trifle brusque.

"What can *you* tell us, Doctor?"

Miss Temple did not think the Doctor noticed Chang's tone, nor the distressed tapping of his fingertips against his thigh, for Svenson's reply was unhurried, as if his mind was still occupied with solving this newest puzzle. "It is unclear to me . . . for, you see, the bloodstains *here* . . . which do, to my experience with the varied colors of drying blood, seem to be relatively recent . . ."

He pointed to the center of the mattress, and Miss Temple found herself prodding Chang to join her nearer to the bed.

"It seems a lot of blood, Doctor," she said. "Does it not?"

"Perhaps, but not if—if you will permit the indelicacy—if the blood is the result of a *natural*—ah, monthly—process. You will see the stain *is* in the center of the bed—where one would expect the pelvis—"

"What about childbirth?" she asked. "Was the woman pregnant?"

"She was not. There are of course other explanations—it could be another injury, there could be violence, or even some kind of poison—"

"Could she have been raped?" asked Chang.

Svenson did not immediately reply, his eyes flitting to Miss Temple. She bore no expression, and merely raised her eyebrows in encouragement of his answer. He turned back to Chang.

"Obviously, yes—but the quantity of blood is prodigious. Such an assault would have had to be especially catastrophic, possibly mortal. I cannot say more. When I examined the woman, she was not so injured. Of course, that is no guarantee—"

"What of the other stains? The blue and the orange?" asked Miss Temple, still aware of Chang's restless tapping.

"I cannot say. The blue . . . well, firstly, the *smell* is consistent with a strange odor I have smelt both in the Institute and on the body in Crabbé's kitchen—mechanical, chemical. I can only hazard it is part of their glass-making. Perhaps it is a narcotic, or perhaps . . . I do not know, a preservative, a fixative—as it fixes memories into glass, perhaps there is some way in which d'Orkancz hoped to fix the woman into life. I am certain he sought to preserve her," he added, looking up into Chang's stern face. "As for the orange, well, it's very queer. Orange—or an essence of orange peel—is sometimes used as an insecticide—there is an acidity that destroys the carapace. Such is the smell of this stain—a bitter concentrate derived by steam."

"But, Doctor," asked Miss Temple, "do not the stains themselves suggest that the fluid has come—been expelled—*from* the woman? They are sprayed—spattered—"

"Yes, they are—very astute!"

"Do you suggest she was *infested*?"

"No, I suggest nothing—but I do wonder about the effects of such a solvent with regard to the possible properties of the blue fluid, the glass, within the human body. Perhaps it was the Comte's idea of a remedy."

"If it melts an insect's shell, it might melt the glass in her lungs?"

"Exactly—though, of course, we are ignorant of the exact ingredients of the glass, so I cannot say if it might have proven effective."

They said nothing for a moment, staring at the bed and the traces of the body that had lain there.

"If it worked," said Miss Temple, "I do not know why he has burnt her dress."

"No." Svenson nodded, sadly.

"No," snapped Chang. He turned from them and walked out to the garden.

Miss Temple looked to Doctor Svenson, who was still on the bed, his expression one of concern and confusion, as if they both knew something was not right. He began to climb off—awkwardly, his coat and boots cumbersome and his lank hair falling over his face. Miss Temple was quicker to the door, snatching up her flowered bag where Chang had left it—it was shockingly heavy, Marthe was an idiot to think she could carry the thing for any distance—and lurching into the garden. Chang stood in the middle of the lifeless lawn, staring up at the boarded windows of the house—windows that in their willful impenetrability struck Miss Temple as a mirror of Chang's glasses. She flung down the bag and approached him. He did not turn. She stopped, perhaps a yard from his side. She glanced back to see Doctor Svenson standing in the greenhouse doorway, watching.

"Cardinal Chang?" she asked. He did not answer. Miss Temple did not know if there was anything so tiresome as a person ignoring a perfectly polite, indeed sympathetic, question. She took a breath, exhaled slowly, and gently spoke again. "Do you know the woman?"

Chang turned to her, his voice quite cold. "Her name is Angelique. You would not know her. She is—she *was*—a whore."

"I see," said Miss Temple.

"Do you?" snapped Chang.

Miss Temple ignored the challenge and again held up the scrap of burnt silk. "And you recognize this as hers?"

"She wore such a dress yesterday evening, in the company of the Comte—he took her to the Institute." Chang turned to call over her shoulder to Svenson. "She was with him there, with his machines—she is obviously the woman you saw—and she is obviously dead."

"Is she?" asked Miss Temple.

Chang snorted. "You said it yourself—he has burnt the dress—"

"I did," she agreed, "but it really makes little sense. I do not see any freshly turned earth here in this garden, do you?"

Chang looked at her suspiciously, and then glanced around him. Before he could answer her, Svenson called out from the doorway, "I don't."

"Nor did—forgive the indelicacy—I find any *bones* in the stove. And I do believe that if one were to burn such a thing as a body—for I have seen the bodies of animals in such a fire—that at least some bones would remain. Doctor?"

"I would expect so, yes—the femur alone—"

"So my question, Cardinal Chang," continued Miss Temple, "is why—if she is dead and he is abandoning this garden—does he not bury or burn her remains right here? It truly is the sensible thing—and yet I do not see that he's done it."

"Then why burn the dress?" asked Chang.

"I've no idea. Perhaps because it was ruined—the bloodstains the Doctor described. Perhaps it was *contaminated*." She turned to Svenson. "Was she wearing the dress when *you* saw her, Doctor?"

Svenson cleared his throat. "I saw no such dress," he said.

"So we do not know," announced Miss Temple, returning to Chang. "You may hate the Comte d'Orkancz, but you may also yet hope to find this woman alive—and who can say, even recovered."

Chang did not reply, but she sensed something change in his body, a palpable shifting in his bones to accommodate some small admission of hope. Miss Temple allowed herself a moment of satisfaction, but instead of that pleasure she found herself quite unexpectedly beset by a painful welling of sadness, of isolation, as if she had taken for granted a certain solidarity with Chang, that they were alike in being alone, only to learn that this was not true. The fact of his feelings—that he *had* feelings, much less that they were of such fervor, and for this particular sort of woman—threw her into distress. She did not desire to be the object of such a man's emotions—of course she didn't—but she was nevertheless unprepared to face the depth of her loneliness so abruptly—nor by way of consoling someone else—which seemed especially unjust and was hardly Miss Temple's *forte* to begin with. She could not help it. She was pierced by solitude, and found herself suddenly sniffing. Mortified, she forced her eyes brightly open and tried to smile, making her voice as brisk and amiable as she could.

"It seems that we have each lost someone. You this woman, Angelique, the Doctor his Prince, and my own . . . my cruel and foolish Roger. While there is the difference that the two of you have some hope—and indeed the desire—to recover the one you have lost . . . for me I am content to assist how I can, and to achieve my share of understanding . . . and revenge."

Her voice broke, and she sniffed, angry with her weakness but powerless to fight it. Was this her life? Again she felt the gagging absence in her heart—how could she have been such a fool as to allow Roger Bascombe to fill it? How could she have allowed such feelings to begin with—when they had only left her with this unanswerable ache? How could she be still beset by them, still want to be somehow simply misunderstood by him and taken by the hand—her own weakness was unbearable. For the first time in her twenty-five years Miss Temple did not know where she was going to sleep. She saw Doctor Svenson stepping toward her and forced a smile, waving him away.

"Your aunt," he began, "surely, Miss Temple, her concern for you—"

"Pffft!" scoffed Miss Temple, unable to bear his sympathy. She walked to her bag and hefted it with one hand, doing her best to conceal the weight but stumbling as she made her way to the garden gate. "I will wait in the street," she called over her shoulder, not wanting them to see the emotion on her face. "When you are finished, I'm sure there is much for us to do . . ."

She dropped the bag and leaned against the wall, her hands over her eyes, her shoulders now heaving with sobs. Only moments ago she had been so proud to find the scrap of silk in the stove and now—and why? Because Chang had feelings for some whore?—the full weight of all she had suffered and sacrificed and stuffed aside had reappeared to rest on her small frame and tender heart. How did anyone bear this isolation, this desolated hope? In the midst of this tempest, Miss Temple, for her mind was restless and quick, did not forget the sharp fear inspired by her enemies, nor did she refrain from berating herself for the girlish indulgence of crying in the first place. She dug for a handkerchief in her green bag, her hand searching for it around the revolver, another sign of what she had become—what she had embraced with, if she was honest, typically ridiculous results. She blew her nose. She *was* difficult, she knew. She did not make friends. She was brisk and demanding, unsparing and indulgent. She sniffed, bitterly resenting this sort of introspection, despising the need for it nearly as much as she despised introspection itself. In that moment she did not know which she wanted more, to curl up in the sun room of her island house, or to shoot one of these blue-glass villains in the heart . . . yet were either of these the answer to her present state?

She sniffed loudly. Neither Chang, for all his hidden moods, nor Svenson, for all his fussy hesitance, were standing in the open street in tears. How could she face them as any kind of equal? Again, and relentlessly, she asked herself what she thought she was doing. She'd told Chang that she was willing to pursue her investigations alone, though in her heart she had not believed it. Now she knew that this was exactly what she must do—for at the moment *doing* seemed crucial—if she was ever going to scour this awful sense of being *subject* from her body. She looked back at the garden door—neither man had appeared. She snatched up the bag with both hands and walked back the way they had come, away from the Boniface. With each step she felt as if she were in a ship leaving its port to cross an unknown ocean—and the farther down Plum Court she went, the more determined she became.

At the avenue, she hailed a coach. She looked back. Her heart caught in her throat. Chang and Svenson stood in the garden doorway. Svenson called to her. Chang was running. She climbed into the coach and threw the bag to the floor.

"Drive on," she called. The coach pulled away and with an almost brutal swiftness she was beyond the lane and any vision of her two companions. The driver looked back at her, his face an unspoken inquiry for their destination.

"The St. Royale Hotel," said Miss Temple.

FIVE

Ministry

By the time Chang reached the end of the lane, the coach was out of sight and he could not tell in which direction it had vanished. He spat with frustration, his chest heaving with the wasted effort. He looked back to see Svenson catch up, the Doctor's face a mask of concern.

"She is gone?" he asked.

Chang nodded and spat again. He had no idea what had transpired in the girl's head, nor where the irresponsible impulses had carried her.

"We should follow—" began Svenson.

"How?" snapped Chang. "Where is she going? Is she abandoning her efforts? Is she attacking our enemies on her own? Which one? And when, between being taken and being killed, will she tell them all they need know to find us?"

Chang was furious, but in truth he was just as angry at himself. His display of bad temper with regard to Angelique had touched off the foolishness—and what was the point? Angelique had no feelings for him. If she were alive and he could find her, it would help his standing with Madelaine Kraft. That was the end of it, the only end. He turned to Svenson, speaking quickly.

"How much money do you have?"

"I—I don't know—enough for a day or two—to eat, find a room—"

"Purchase a train ticket?"

"Depending on how far the journey—"

"Here, then." Chang thrust his hand into his coat pocket and pulled out the leather wallet. It held only two small banknotes, change from his night at the Boniface, but he had a handful of gold coins in his trouser pocket to fall back on. He handed one of the notes to Doctor Svenson with a bitter smile. "I don't know what will befall us—and the change purse of our partnership has just walked away. How are you for ammunition?"

As if to reinforce his reply, Svenson hefted the revolver from his pocket. "I was able to reload from Miss Temple's supply—the weapons share a caliber—"

"That's a service .44."

"It is."

"As was hers?"

"Yes, though her weapon *was* deceptively small—"

"Has she ever fired it, do you know?"

"I do not think so."

The two men stood for a moment between thoughts. Chang attempted to shrug off his feelings of remorse and recrimination. How had he not realized the gun was so powerful—he'd helped her clean it, for God's sake. He wondered what he'd been thinking—but in truth knew exactly what had distracted him: the surprise at seeing her again in such different apparel than on the train, the curves of her throat marked by bruises instead of bloodstains, her small nimble fingers working to disassemble the black oiled metal parts of the revolver. He shook his head. The kick from such a weapon would knock her arm up back over her head—unless she pressed the barrel into her target's body, she would never hit a thing. She had no idea what she was doing, in any of this.

"It is senseless to consider what's done," the Doctor said. "Do we go after her?"

"If she is taken, she is dead."

"Then we must part to cover more ground. It really is unfortunate—it seems but a moment ago we were each running for our lives in isolation. I will miss someone to help me scale what water pipes I must." He smiled and extended his hand. Chang took it.

"You will scale them by yourself—I am sure."

Svenson smiled with a pinched expression, as if he appreciated Chang's encouragement but remained unpersuaded. "Where do we each go?" he asked. "And where shall we meet again?"

"Where would *she* go?" Chang asked. "Do you think she is running to her aunt? That would be easier for us all . . ."

"I do not think so," said Svenson. "On the contrary, whatever distress she has felt, I believe it has spurred her to direct action."

Chang frowned, thinking. What had she said to him in the garden, her face, the smile belied by her grey eyes.

"Then it has to be this Bascombe idiot."

Svenson sighed. "The poor girl."

Chang spat again. "Will she shoot him in the head or blubber at his feet—that's the question."

"I disagree," said Svenson quietly. "She is brave and resourceful. What do we know about anyone—very little. But we know Miss Temple has surprised any number of powerful people into thinking she was a deadly assassin-courtesan. Without her we both could have been taken in the hotel. If we can find her, I will wager you that she will save each of us in our turn before this is finished."

Chang did not answer, then smiled.

"What is your Macklenburg currency—gold shillings?"

Svenson nodded.

"Then I will happily wager you ten gold shillings that Miss Temple will not preserve our lives. Of course, it's a fool's bet—for if we are not so preserved, then neither shall we be in any position to profit."

"Nevertheless," said Svenson, "I accept the wager." They shook hands again. Svenson cleared his throat. "Now . . . this Bascombe—"

"There's the country house—Tarr Manor. He could well be there. Or he could be at the Ministry, or with Crabbé." Chang looked quickly up and down the avenue—they really ought not to be standing so long in the street so near to the Boniface. "The trip to Tarr Manor—"

"Where is it?"

"To the north, perhaps half a day by rail—we can find out easily enough at Stropping—we may even catch her at the station. But the trip will take time. The other possibilities—his home, the Ministry, Crabbé—these are in the city, and one of us can easily move from one to another as necessary."

Svenson nodded. "So, one to the country, one to stay here—do you have a preference? I am an outsider in either instance."

Chang smiled. "So am I, Doctor." He gestured to his red coat and his glasses. "I am not one for country gentry, nor for the drawing rooms of respectable townsfolk . . ."

"It is still your city—you are its animal, if you will forgive me. I will go to the country, where they may be more persuaded by a uniform and tales of the Macklenburg Palace."

Chang turned to flag another coach. "You should hurry—as I say, you may find her at Stropping. The path to the Ministry takes me the other way. We will part here."

They shook hands for a third time, smiling at it. Svenson climbed into the coach. Without another word Chang began to walk quickly in the opposite direction. Over his shoulder he heard Svenson's voice and turned.

"Where do we meet?" called the Doctor.

Chang called back, shouting through his hands. "Tomorrow noon! The clock at Stropping!"

Svenson nodded and waved before sitting back down in the coach. Chang doubted that either of them would be there.

As soon as he could, Chang left the avenue for a winding trail of alleys and narrow lanes. He had not decided where he ought to go first. More than anything he wanted to orient himself to his task in his normal manner and not rush headlong into circumstances he didn't understand—even though this was exactly what Celeste was doing. Celeste? He wondered how he used that name in his thoughts, but not to her face, nor when speaking to Doctor Svenson, when it was always "Miss Temple". It hardly mattered—it was undoubtedly because she was behaving like a child. With this thought, Chang resolved that if he were to try and enter the offices of the Foreign Ministry, or the house of Harald Crabbé, he needed to be better prepared. He increased his pace to a loping trot. He could not brave the Raton Marine, for it would certainly be watched—he had to believe Aspiche was now one with this Cabal. He would have very much liked to reach the Library. There were so many questions to answer—about indigo clay, about the Comte and the Contessa, about Bascombe and Crabbé, about the foreign travels of Francis Xonck, about Oskar Veilandt, even, he admitted, about Miss Celestial Temple. But the Library was where Rosamonde had found him, and they would certainly be waiting. Instead, his thinking more practical and dark, he made his way to Fabrizi's.

The man was an Italian ex-mercenary and weapons master who catered to a clientele drawn from all across the city and whose only shared characteristic was an elegant bloody purpose. Chang entered the shop, glancing to either side at the glass display cases with his usual surge of covetous pleasure. He was relieved to see Fabrizi himself behind the counter, a crisp suit covered by a green flannel apron.

"Dottore," said Chang, with a nod of greeting.

"Cardinale," answered Fabrizi, his tone serious and respectful.

Chang pulled out his dagger and placed it before the man. "I have had a misadventure with the rest of your splendid cane," he said. "I would like you to repair it, if possible. In the meantime, I would request the use of a suitable replacement. I will of course pay for all services in advance." He took the remaining banknote from the wallet and laid it on the counter. Fabrizi ignored it, instead picking up the dagger and studying the condition of the blade. He returned the blade to the counter, looked at the banknote with mild surprise, as if it had appeared there independently, and quietly folded it into the pocket of his apron. He nodded to one of the glass cases. "You may select your replacement. I will have this ready in three days."

"I am much obliged," said Chang. He walked to the case, Fabrizi following him behind the counter. "Is there one you would suggest?"

"All are superb," said the Italian. "For a man like you, I recommend the heavier wood—the cane may be used alone, yes? This one is teak... this one Malaysian ironwood."

He handed the ironwood to Chang, who held it with immediate satisfaction, the hilt curved like a black-powder pistol grip in his hand. He pulled out the blade—a bit longer than he was used to—and hefted the stick. It was lovely, and Chang smiled like a man holding a new baby.

"As always," he whispered, "the work is exquisite."

It was after three o'clock. Without the Library to tell him where Bascombe lived, the easiest thing would be to follow the man from the Ministry. Besides, if Celeste were truly intent on finding him quickly, she would certainly go to the Ministry herself, doing her best to meet him—kill him?—in his office. If he was not there... well, Chang would answer that when it became necessary. He weighed the coins in his pocket, decided against a coach, and began to jog toward the maze of white buildings. It took him perhaps fifteen minutes to reach St. Isobel's Square, and another five to walk—taking the time to ease his breathing and his countenance—to the front entrance. He made his way under the great white archway, through a sea of coaches and the throng of serious-faced people pursuing government business, and into a graveled courtyard, with different lanes—paved with slate and lined with ornamental shrubbery—leading off to different Ministries. It was as if he stood at the center of a wheel, with each spoke leading to its own discrete world of bureaucracy. The Foreign Ministry was directly before him, and so he walked straight ahead, boots crunching on the gravel and then echoing off the slate, to another smaller archway opening into a marble lobby and a wooden desk where a man in a black suit was flanked by red-coated soldiers. With some alarm, Chang noticed that they were troopers from the 4th Dragoons, but by the time he had realized this, they had seen him. He stopped, ready to run or to fight, but none of the soldiers stirred from their stiff postures of attention. Between them, the man in the suit looked up at Chang with an inquiring sniff.

"Yes?"

"Mr. Roger Bascombe," said Chang.

The man's gaze took in Chang's apparel and demeanor. "And . . . who shall I announce?"

"Miss Celeste Temple," said Chang.

"Excuse me—Miss Temple, you say?" The man was well enough trained in dealing with foreign manners not to sneer.

"I bring word from her," said Chang. "I am confident he will want to hear it. If Mr. Bascombe is unavailable, I am willing to speak to Deputy Minister Crabbé."

"I see, you are . . . *willing* . . . to speak to the Deputy Minister. Just a moment." The man jotted a few lines onto a piece of paper and stuffed it into a leather tube, which he fed into a brass opening in the desk, where it was sucked from sight with an audible hiss. Chang was reminded of the Old Palace, and found it somehow comforting that the highest levels of government shared the latest means of communication with a brothel. He waited. Several other visitors arrived and were either allowed to pass through or became the subject of another such message sent through the leather tubes. Chang glanced at the others waiting—a dark-skinned man in a white uniform and a hat with peacock feathers, a pale Russian with a long beard and a blue uniform of boiled wool with a line of medals and a sash, and two elderly men in run-down black tailcoats, as if they had been continuously attending the same ball for the last twenty years. He was not surprised to see all four of them staring at him in return. He casually looked around to make sure the exit behind was still clear, and to note the hallways and staircases on the other side of the desk, the better to anticipate any danger that might arrive. The troopers remained still.

It was five more minutes before an answering tube thumped into its receptacle near the desk. The clerk unfolded the paper, made a note in the ledger next to him, and handed the paper to one of the troopers. He then called to Chang.

"You're to go up. This man will show you the way. I will need your name, and your signature... here." He indicated a second ledger on the desk top, and held out a pen. Chang took it and wrote, and handed it back.

"The name is Chang," he said.

"Just 'Chang'?" the man asked.

"For the moment, I'm afraid so." He leaned forward with a whisper. "But I am hoping to win at the races... and then I shall purchase another."

The soldier led Chang along a wide corridor and up an austere staircase of polished black granite with a wrought iron rail. They moved among other men in dark suits walking up and down, all clutching thickly packed satchels of paper, none of whom paid Chang the slightest attention. At the first landing the soldier led the way across a marble corridor to another staircase blocked off with an iron chain. He unlatched the chain, stepped back for Chang to pass, and replaced it behind them. On this staircase there was no other traffic, and the farther they climbed the more Chang felt he was entering a labyrinth he might never escape from. He looked at the red-coated trooper ahead of him and wondered if it would be better to simply slip a knife between the man's ribs here, where they were alone, and then take his chances. As it was, he could only hope that he was indeed being taken to Bascombe—or Crabbé—and not into some isolated place of entrapment. He had mentioned Miss

Temple's name on a whim, to provoke a response—as well as to see if she had been there before him. That he had gained entry without any particular reaction left him mystified. It could mean that she was there, or that she wasn't—or that they merely wanted to find her, which he already knew. He had to assume that the people who had allowed him in did not ultimately plan for him to leave. Still, the impulse to kill the soldier was mere nervousness. All that would come soon enough.

They climbed past three landings but never a door or window. At the landing of the next floor, however, the soldier took a long brass key from his coat, glanced once at Chang, and stepped to a heavy wooden door. He inserted the key and turned it several times in the lock, the machinery echoing sharply within the stairwell, before pulling it open. He stepped aside and indicated that Chang should go in. Chang did so, his attention neatly divided between the instinctive suspicion about the man at his back and the room he was entering—a short marbled corridor with another door on the opposite side, some five yards away. Chang looked back to the soldier, who nodded him on toward the far door. When Chang did not move the soldier suddenly slammed the door shut. Before Chang could leap for the knob he heard the key being turned. The thing would not budge. He was locked in. He berated himself for a credulous fool and strode to the far door, fully expecting it to be locked as well, but the brass knob turned with a well-oiled *snick.*

He looked into a wide office with a deep green carpet, and a low ceiling made less oppressive by a domed skylight of creamy glass rising over the center of the room. The walls were lined with bookshelves stuffed with hundreds of massive numbered volumes—official documents no doubt, collected through the years and from around the world. The wide space of the room was divided between two great pieces of furniture—a long meeting table to Chang's left and an expansive desk to his right—that, like oaken planets, cast their nets of gravity across an array of lesser satellites—end tables, ashtrays, and map-stands. The desk was unoccupied, but at the table, looking up from an array of papers spread around him, sat Roger Bascombe.

"Ah," he said, and awkwardly stood.

Chang glanced around the office more carefully and saw a communication door—closed—in the wall behind Bascombe, and what might well be another hidden entrance set into the bookcases behind the desk. He pushed the main door closed behind him, turned to Bascombe and tapped the tip of his stick lightly on the carpet.

"Good afternoon," Chang said.

"Indeed, it is," Bascombe replied. "The days grow warmer."

Chang frowned. This was hardly the confrontation he had expected. "I believe I was announced," he said.

"Yes. Actually, Miss Celeste Temple was announced. And then your name of course, in turn." Bascombe gestured to the wall where Chang could see the sending and receiving apparatus for the message tubes. Bascombe gestured again toward the end of the table. "Please . . . will you sit?"

"I would prefer to stand," said Chang.

"As you wish. I prefer a seat, if it is all the same to you . . ."

Bascombe sat back at the table, and took a moment to rearrange the papers in front of him. "So . . . ," he began, "you are acquainted with Miss Temple?"

"Apparently," said Chang.

"Yes, apparently." Bascombe nodded. "She is—well—she is herself. I have no cause to speak of her beyond those terms."

It seemed to Chang that Bascombe was choosing his words very carefully, almost as if he were afraid of being caught out somehow . . . or being overheard.

"What terms exactly?" asked Chang.

"The terms she has set down by her own choices," answered Bascombe. "As you have done."

"And you?"

"Of course—no one is immune to the consequences of their own actions. Are you sure you will not sit?"

Chang ignored the question. He stared intently at the slim, well-dressed man at the table, trying to discern where in all the competing spheres of his enemies he might fit in. He could not help seeing Bascombe as he thought a woman must—his respectability, his refinement, his odd assumption of both rank and deference—and not any woman, but Miss Temple in particular. This man had been the object of her love—almost certainly was still, women being what they were. Looking at him, Chang had to admit that Bascombe possessed any number of attractive qualities, and was thus equally quite certain that he disliked the young man intensely, and so he smiled.

"Ambition . . . it does strange things to a fellow, would you not agree?"

Bascombe's gaze measured him with all the dry, serious purpose of an undertaker. "How so?"

"I mean to say . . . it often seems that until a man is given what he assumes he wants . . . he has no real idea of the cost."

"And why would you say that?"

"Why would I indeed?" Chang smiled. "Such an opinion would have to be derived from actual achievement. So how *could* I possibly know?" When Bascombe did not immediately respond, Chang gestured with his stick to the large desk. "Where are your confederates? Where is Mr. Crabbé? Why are you meeting me alone—don't you know who I am? Haven't you spoken to poor Major Blach? Aren't you just the slightest bit worried?"

"I am not," replied Bascombe, with an easy self-assurance that made Chang want to bloody his nose. "You have been *allowed* into this office for the specific purpose of being presented with a proposition. As I assume you are no idiot, as I assure you *I* am no idiot, I am in no danger until that proposition has been made."

"And what proposition is that?"

But instead of answering, Bascombe stared at him, running his gaze over Chang's person and costume, very much as if he were an odd kind of livestock or someone from a circus. Chang had the presence of mind to realize that the gesture was deliberate and designed to anger—though he did not understand why Bascombe would take the risk, being so obviously vulnerable. The entire situation was strange—for all that Bascombe spoke of plans and propositions, Chang knew his appearance at the Ministry must be a surprise. Bascombe was delaying him at personal risk so something else could happen—the arrival of reinforcements? But *that* made no sense, for the soldiers could have stopped him at any time on the way up. Instead, what they had accomplished was to divert Chang from the entrance. Was this all a performance—was Bascombe somehow demonstrating his loyalty, or was it possible that Bascombe played a double game? Or was the delay not to bring anyone *to* the room, but to get someone away *from* it?

In a swift movement Chang raised his stick and strode to Bascombe. Before the man could half-rise from his chair the end landed viciously against his ear. Bascombe slumped down with a cry, holding the side of his head. Chang took the opportunity to press the stick roughly across his neck. Bascombe choked, his face abruptly reddening. Chang leaned forward and spoke slowly.

"Where is she?"

Bascombe did not immediately answer. Chang shoved the stick sharply into his windpipe.

"Where is she?"

"Who?" Bascombe's voice was a rasp.

"Where is she?"

"I don't think he knows who you mean."

Chang whirled around and with a smooth motion pulled apart his stick. Behind the desk, leaning indolently against the bookcases, stood Francis Xonck, in a mustard yellow morning coat, his red hair meticulously curled, an unlit cheroot in his hand. Chang took a careful step toward him, risking a quick glance back to Bascombe, who was still laboring to breathe.

"Good afternoon," said Chang.

"Good afternoon. I hope you haven't hurt him."

"Why? Does he belong to you?"

Xonck smiled. "That's very clever. But you know, I'm clever too, and I must congratulate you—the mystery about the 'she' you so desperately seek is positively diverting. Is it Rosamonde? Is it little Miss Temple—or should I say Hastings? Or even better, the Comte's unfortunate, slant-eyed trollop? Either way, the idea that you're actually looking for any of them is richly amusing. Because you're so *manly,* don't you know, and at the same time such a *buffoon.* Excuse me."

He pulled a small box of matches from his waistcoat and lit the cheroot, looking over the glowing tip at Chang as he puffed. His eyes shifted to Bascombe. "Will you survive, Roger?" He smiled at Bascombe's reply—a hacking cough—and tossed the spent match onto the desk top.

Chang took another step closer to Xonck, who seemed as uncaring in his manner as Bascombe had been moments before, but oddly gay where Bascombe had been watchful. "Shall I ask you?" he hissed.

"You would do better to listen," Xonck replied dryly. "Or, in lieu of that, to think. The way behind you is locked, as is the door behind me. If you were able to make your way through the door behind Bascombe—which you won't—I promise you will be quickly lost within a dense maze of corridors with absolutely no chance of evading or surviving the very large number of soldiers even now assembling to kill you. You would die, Mr. Chang, in such a way as to serve no one—a dog run down by a coach in the dark." He frowned and picked a scrap of tobacco off his lower lip and flicked it away, then returned his eyes to Chang.

"And you would suggest I serve *you*?" asked Chang.

"Serve yourself," croaked Bascombe, from the table.

"He rallies!" laughed Xonck. "But you know, he is right. Serve yourself. Be reasonable."

"We're wasting time—" muttered Chang, moving for Xonck. Xonck did not move, but spoke very quickly and sharply.

"That is foolish. It will kill you. Stop and think."

Against his better judgment, Chang did. He was nearly within reach of the man, if he lunged with the long part of the stick. But he didn't lunge, partly because he saw that Xonck wasn't frightened . . . not in the slightest.

"Whatever reason brought you here," Xonck said, "your *search*—you must postpone. You were allowed up for the sole reason, as Mr. Bascombe has said, to make you a proposition. There is plenty of time to fight, or to die—there is always time for that—but there is no more time to find whichever woman you hoped would be here."

Chang wanted very much to leap over the desk and stab him, but his instincts—which he knew to trust—told him that Xonck was not like Bascombe, and that any attack on him needed to be as carefully considered as one on a cobra. Xonck did not seem to be armed, but he could easily have a small pistol—or for that matter a vial of acid. At the same time, Chang did not know what to make of the man's warning about escaping into the Ministry. While it might be true, it was in Xonck's every interest to lie. But why *had* they let him ascend without any soldiers to take him in hand? He had too many questions, but Chang knew that nothing revealed more about a man than his estimation of what your price might be. He stepped away from Xonck and sneered.

"What proposition?"

Xonck smiled, but it was Bascombe who spoke, clearly and coolly despite the hoarseness of his voice, as if he were describing the necessary steps in the working of a machine.

"I cannot give you details. I do not seek to convince, but to offer opportunity. Those who have accepted our invitation have and will continue to benefit accordingly. Those who have not are no longer our concern. You are acquainted with Miss Temple. She may have spoken of our former engagement. I cannot—for it is impossible to say how I was then, for that would be to say how I was a child. So much has changed—so much has become clear—that I can only speak of what I have become. It's true I thought myself to be in love. In love because I could not see past the ways in which I was subject, for I believed, in my servitude, that this love would release me. What view of the world had I convinced myself I understood so well? It was the useless attachment to another, to *rescue,* which existed in place of my own action. What I believed were solely consequences of that attachment—money, stature, respectability, pleasure—I now see merely as elements of my own unlimited capacity. Do you understand?"

Chang shrugged. The words were eloquently spoken, but somehow abstractly, like a speech learned by heart to demonstrate rhetoric... and yet, through it all, had Bascombe's eyes been as steady? Had they betrayed some other tension? As if responding to Chang's thought, Bascombe then leaned forward, more intently.

"It is natural that different individuals pursue different goals, but it is equally clear that these goals are intertwined, that a benefit to one will be a benefit to others. Serve yourself. You are a man of capacity—and even, it seems possible, of some intelligence. What you have achieved against our allies only certifies your value. There are no grievances, only interests in competition. Refuse that competition, join us, and be enriched with clarity. Whatever you want—wherever you direct your action—you will find reward."

"I have no uncle with a title," observed Chang. He wished Xonck was not there—it was impossible to read Bascombe's true intention apart from his master's presence.

"Neither does Roger, anymore." Xonck chuckled.

"Exactly," said Bascombe, with all the evident emotion of the wooden chair he sat in.

"I'm afraid I don't actually understand your proposition," said Chang.

Xonck sneered. "Don't be coy."

"You have desire," said Bascombe. "Ambition. Frustration. Bitterness. What will you do—struggle against them until one of your adventures goes wrong and you die bleeding in the street? Will you trust your life to the whims of a"—his voice stumbled just slightly—"a provincial *girl*? To the secret interests of a German spy? You have met the Contessa. She has spoken for you. It is at her urging you are here. Our hand is out. Take it. The Process will transform you, as it has transformed us all."

The offer was enormously condescending. Chang looked to Xonck, whose face wore a mild, fixed smile of no particular meaning.

"And if I refuse this proposition?"

"You won't," said Bascombe. "You would be a fool."

Chang noticed a smear of blood on Bascombe's ear, but whatever pain he had caused made no impression on the man's self-assurance, nor on the sharpness of his gaze, the meaning of which Chang could not discern. Chang glanced back to Xonck, who rolled the cheroot between his fingers and exhaled a jet of smoke toward the ceiling. The question was how best to learn more, to find Angelique, or Celeste—even, he had to admit, confront Rosamonde. But had he only come here to deliver himself into their hands so effortlessly?

About the Ministry at least, Xonck had been telling the truth. They walked down a twisting narrow hallway in the dark—Bascombe in the front with a lantern, Xonck behind. The rooms they passed—the flickering light giving Chang brief, flaring glimpses before they fell back into shadow—had been constructed without any logic he could see. Some were crammed with boxes, with maps, with tables and chairs, day beds, desks, while others—both large and small—were empty, or contained but a single chair. The only point of unity was the complete absence of windows, indeed of any light at all. With his poor eyesight, Chang soon lost any sense of direction as Bascombe led him this way and that, up short sets of stairs and then down odd curving ramps. They had allowed him to keep his stick, but he was deeper in their power with each step he took.

"This Process of yours," he said, ostensibly to Bascombe though hoping for a reply from Xonck. "Do you really think it will alter my desire to ruin you both?"

Bascombe stopped, and turned to face him, his gaze flicking briefly to Xonck before he spoke.

"Once you have experienced it yourself, you will be ashamed of your doubts and mockery, as well as the purposeless life you have so far pursued."

"Purposeless?"

"Pathetically so. Are you ready?"

"I suppose I am."

Chang heard a slight rustle from the darkness behind him. He was sure Xonck held a weapon.

"Keep walking," muttered Xonck.

"You swayed Colonel Aspiche to your cause, didn't you? The 4th Dragoons are a fine regiment—so helpful to the Foreign Ministry. Good of him to step into the breach." He clucked his tongue and called back to Xonck. "You're not wearing black. Trapping *was* your brother-in-law."

"And I am devastated, I do assure you."

"Then why did he have to die?"

He received no answer. Chang would have to do better than this to provoke them. They walked on in shuffling silence, the lantern light catching on what seemed to be chandeliers in the air above them. Their passageway had opened into some much larger room. Xonck called ahead to Bascombe.

"Roger, put the lantern on the floor."

Bascombe turned, looked at Xonck as if he didn't fully comprehend, and then placed the lantern on the wooden floor, well out of Chang's reach.

"Thank you. Now go ahead—you can find your way. Give word to prepare the machines."

"Are you quite sure?"

"I am."

Bascombe glanced once, rather searchingly, at Chang, who took the opportunity to sneer, and then disappeared into the dark. Chang heard his footsteps well after the man had passed from the light, but soon the room was silent once more. Xonck took a few steps into the shadow and returned with two wooden chairs. He placed them on the floor and kicked one over to Chang, who stopped its momentum with his foot. Xonck sat, and after a moment Chang followed his example.

"I thought it worthwhile to attempt a frank discussion. After all, in half an hour's time you will either be my ally or you will be dead—there seems little point in mincing words."

"Is it that simple?" asked Chang.

"It is."

"I don't believe you. I don't mean my decision to submit or die—that *is* simple—but your own reasons . . . your desire to speak without Bascombe . . . not simple in the slightest."

Xonck studied him, but did not speak. Chang decided to take a chance, and do exactly what Xonck asked—speak frankly.

"There are two levels to your *enterprise*. There are those who have undergone this Process, like Margaret Hooke . . . and then there are those—like you, or the Contessa—who remain free. And in competition, despite your *rhetoric*."

"Competition for what?"

"I do not know," Chang admitted. "The stakes are different for each of you—I imagine that's the problem. It always is."

Xonck chuckled. "But my colleagues and I are in complete agreement."

Chang scoffed. He was aware that he could not see Xonck's right hand, that the man held it casually to the side of his chair behind his crossed leg.

"Why should that surprise you?" Xonck asked. Chang scoffed again.

"Then why was Tarr's death so poorly managed? Why was Trapping killed? What of the dead painter, Oskar Veilandt? Why did the Contessa allow the Prince to be rescued? Where is the Prince now?"

"A lot of questions," Xonck observed dryly.

"I'm sorry if they bore you. But if I were you, and *I* didn't have those answers—"

"As I explained, either you'll be dead—"

"Don't you think it's amusing? You're trying to decide whether to kill me before I join you—so I won't tell your colleagues about your independent plans. And I'm trying to decide whether to kill you—or to try and learn more about your Process."

"Except I don't have any independent plans."

"But the Contessa does," said Chang. "And you know it. The others *don't.*"

"We're going to disappoint Bascombe if you don't show up. He's a keen one for *order.*" Xonck stood, his right hand still behind his body. "Leave the lantern."

Chang rose with him, his stick held loosely in his left hand. "Have you met the young woman, Miss Temple? She was Bascombe's fiancée."

"So I understand. Quite a shock to poor Roger, I'm sure—quite a good thing his mind is so *stable.* So much fuss for nothing."

"Fuss?"

"The search for Isobel Hastings," Xonck scoffed, "mysterious killer whore."

Xonck's eyes were full of intelligence and cunning, and his body possessed the easy, lithe athleticism of a hunting wolf—but running through it all, like a vein of rot through a tree, was the arrogance of money. Chang knew enough to see the man was dangerous, perhaps even his better if it came to a fight—one never knew—but all of this was still atop a foundation of privilege, an unearned superiority imposed by force, fear, disdain, by purchased experience and unexamined arrogance. Chang found it odd that his estimation of Xonck was crystallized by the man's dismissal of Celeste—not because she wasn't in part a silly rich girl, but because she was that and still managed to survive, and—more important than anything—accept that the ordeal had changed her. Chang did not believe Francis Xonck ever changed—in fact change was the exact quality he held himself above.

"I take it you haven't made her acquaintance then," Chang said.

Xonck shrugged and nodded at the door in the shadows behind Chang. "I will bear the loss. If you would..."

"No."

"No?"

"No. I've found what I meant to. I'll be going."

Xonck swung his hand forward and aimed a shining silver-plated pistol at Chang's chest. "To hell?"

"At some point, certainly. Why invite me to join you—your *Process*? Whose idea was that?"

"Bascombe told you. Hers."

"I'm flattered."

"You needn't be." Xonck stared at him, the lines of his face deeply etched in the flickering lantern light. His sharp nose and pointed chin looked positively devilish. Chang knew it was a matter of moments—either Xonck would shoot him or drive him along to Bascombe. He was confident that his guesses about the fissures within the Cabal were correct, and that Xonck was smart enough to see them too. Was Xonck arrogant enough to think they didn't matter, that he was immune? Of course he was. Then why had he wanted to talk? To see if Chang was still working for Rosamonde? And if he thought Chang was . . . did that mean he would kill him, or try to satisfy the Contessa and let him escape—thus the need to get rid of Bascombe . . .

Chang shook his head ruefully, as if he had been caught out. "She did say you were the smartest of them all, even smarter than d'Orkancz."

For a moment Xonck didn't respond. Then he said, "I don't believe you."

"She hired me to find Isobel Hastings. I did. Before I could contact her, I was waylaid by that idiot German Major—"

"I don't believe you."

"Ask her yourself." He suddenly dropped his voice, hissing with annoyance. "Is that Bascombe coming back?"

Chang turned behind him as if he'd heard footsteps, so naturally that Xonck would have been inhuman not to look, even for a moment. In that moment Chang, whose hand was on the back of the wooden chair, swept it up with all his strength and hurled it at Xonck. The pistol went off once, splintering the wood, and then once more, but by that time Xonck was flinching against the chair's impact and the shot went high. The chair hit his shoulder with a solid cracking sound, causing him to swear and stumble back against the possibility that Chang would rush him with his stick. The chair rebounded away and, his face a mask of fury, Xonck brought the pistol back to bear. His third shot coincided exactly with a scream of surprise. Chang had scooped up the oil lantern and flung it at him, the contents soaking Xonck's extended arm. When he fired, the spark from the gun set his arm ablaze. The shot missed Chang by a good yard. His last image of Xonck, screaming with rage, was the man's desperate attempt to rip off his morning coat, his fingers—the pistol dropped—roiling with flame and clutching in agony against the sizzling rush of the fire that swallowed his entire arm. Xonck thrashed like a madman. Chang dove forward into the darkness.

Within moments he was blind. He slowed to deliberate steps, hands held out to prevent walking into walls or furniture. He needed to put distance between himself and Xonck, but he needed to do it quietly. His hand found a wall to his left and he moved along it in what seemed to be another direction—had he entered a corridor? He paused to listen. He could no longer hear Xonck... could the man have put out the fire so quickly? Could he be dead? Chang didn't think so. His one comfort was that Xonck was now forced to shoot with his left hand. He crept along, pawing at a curtain in front of him until he found an opening. Behind it—he nearly twisted his ankle missing the first step—was an extremely narrow staircase—he could easily touch the walls on either side. He silently made his way down. At the landing, some twenty steps below, he heard noises above him. It had to be Bascombe. There would be lights, a search. He groped ahead of himself for the far wall, found a door, then the knob. It was locked. Chang very carefully dug in his pockets for his ring of keys and, clutching them hard to stop them jingling into one another, tried the lock. It opened with the second key, and he stepped through, easing the door closed behind him.

The new room, whatever it was, was still pitch black. Chang wondered how long before these corridors were full of soldiers. He felt his way forward, his hands finding a stack of wooden crates, and then a dusty bookcase. He worked his way past it, and to his great relief felt a pane of glass, a window undoubtedly painted black. Chang pulled the dagger from his cane and smartly rapped the butt into the glass, punching it clear. Light poured into the room, transforming it from formless dark to an unthreatening vestibule full of dusty unused furniture. He peered out through the broken pane. The window overlooked one of the wheel-spoke pathways, and was—he craned his neck—at least two floors below the roof. To his dismay he saw the outer wall was sheer, with no ledges or molding or pipes to cling to, going up or down. There was no exit this way.

Chang wheeled around at a sudden draft of cool air behind him—as if the door had been opened. The breeze came from a metal vent in the floor, the cool air—which with a sense of smell might well have made him nauseous—flowing out to the open window. Chang knelt at the vent. He could hear voices. He sighed with frustration—he could not make out the words for the echoing effect of the vent. The opening was wide enough for a man to crawl through. He felt inside and was gratified to find it was not moist. Keeping as quiet as possible, he pried apart the housing until it was wide enough for him to get at the hole. It was pitch black. He set his stick inside and wormed his way after it. There was just room for him to move on his hands and knees. He crawled forward as quietly as he could.

He'd gone perhaps five yards when the vent split three ways, to either side and angling upwards. He listened carefully. The voices were coming from above—from the floor he'd just escaped. He peered up, and saw a dim light. He climbed upwards, pressing his legs against both sides to keep himself from sliding back. As he rose, the vent leveled off again—where the light bled in. He kept climbing, finding it more and more difficult, for the surface of the vent was covered with a fine powder that prevented him from getting any solid purchase. Was it soot? He couldn't see in the dark—he cursed the fact that he was probably filthy—and kept struggling to reach the light. He reached up, his fingers finding a ledge and just beyond it, a metal grate over the opening. He laced his fingers over the grating and pulled his body up until he could see out the hole, but the only view was a slate-covered floor and a tattered dark curtain. He listened . . . and heard a voice he did not recognize.

"He is a protégé of my uncle's. Of course, I do not approve of my uncle, so this is not the highest recommendation. Is he quite secured? Excellent. You will understand that I am not—given these recent events—inclined toward the risks of *politesse*."

A woman chuckled politely in response. Chang frowned. The voice spoke with an accent quite like the Doctor's, but with an indolent drawl that announced its words one at a time without regard to conversational sense or momentum, so draining them of any possible wit.

"Excuse the interruption, but perhaps I should assist—"

"You will not."

"Highness." The word was followed by the clicking of heels. The second voice was also German.

The first voice went on, and obviously not to the second voice, but to the woman. "What people do not understand—who have not known it—is the great burden of obligation."

"Responsibility," she agreed. "Only a few of us can bear it well. Tea?"

"*Danke.* Is he able to breathe?"

It was a question from curiosity, not from concern, and it was answered—to Chang's ears—with a swift meaty impact followed by a violent expulsion of coughing discomfort.

"He should not expire before the Process re-makes him," continued the voice rather pedantically. "He will know what it means to be faithful, yes? Is there a lemon?"

The voices were still some distance away, perhaps across the room, he could not tell. He reached out and tentatively exerted pressure on the grated covering. It gave, but not enough to come loose. He pushed again, steadily and with more force.

"Who is this man they have with them?" asked the first voice.

"The criminal," answered the second man.

"Criminal? Why should we be joined by such a fellow?"

"I would not agree that we should—"

"Different walks of life bear different cares, Highness," said the woman smoothly, cutting into the second man's words. "Truly when we have nothing more to learn, we have stopped living."

"Of course," the voice agreed eagerly. "And by this logic you're very much alive, Major—for you have obviously very much to learn about sensible thinking!"

Chang's brain took in the fact that the second voice must be Major Blach and the first voice—though his manner contradicted the sense-drugged dissipation as described by Svenson—Karl-Horst von Maasmärck, but these were hardly the crux of his attention. The woman was Rosamonde,

Contessa Lacquer-Sforza. What she was doing here he could not say. He was too much stirred at the knowledge she was speaking of *him.*

"The Major is angry, Highness, for this man has caused him much discomfort. But yet, that is exactly why Mr. Bascombe, at my suggestion, has importuned him to join our efforts."

"But will he? Will he see the sense of it?" The Prince slurped his tea.

"We can only hope he is as wise a man as you."

The Prince chuckled indulgently at this *ridiculous* suggestion. Chang pressed again against the grate. He knew it was foolish, but he very much wanted to see her, and to see—for he recognized the particular sounds—who was being kicked on the floor. He could feel the grate giving way, but had no idea what sound it would make when it pulled free. Then the room's door was kicked open with a bang, the commotion of a man violently swearing, and another calling for aid. He heard Bascombe shouting for help and the room was an uproar—Xonck's vitriolic profanity, Rosamonde sharply issuing commands for water, towels, scissors, the Prince and Blach bawling contradictory orders to whoever else was present. Chang slipped backwards from the grate, for the commotion had driven his enemies into view.

The cries had faded to fierce muttering as Xonck was attended to. Bascombe attempted to explain what had happened in the office, and then that he had gone ahead.

"Why did you do that?" snapped Rosamonde.

"I—Mr. Xonck asked that—"

"I told you. I told you and you did not pay attention."

But her words were not addressed to Bascombe.

"I *did* pay attention," Xonck hissed. "You were wrong. He would not have submitted."

"He would have submitted to *me.*"

"Then next time you can get him yourself... and pay the consequences," Xonck replied malevolently.

They stared at each other and Chang saw the others watching with various degrees of discomfort. Bascombe looked positively stricken, the Prince—the scars still visible on his face—looked curious, as if not sure he should be concerned, while Blach viewed them all with a poorly masked disapproval. On the floor behind them, trussed and gagged, was a short stocky man in a suit. Chang did not know him. Kneeling to the other side of Xonck was another man, balding with heavy glasses, wrapping the burned arm with gauze.

Xonck sat on a wooden table, his legs between dangling leather straps. Around them on the floor were several of the long boxes. Covering one wall were large maps stuck with colored pins. Hanging over the table from a long chain was a chandelier. Chang looked up. The ceiling was very high, and the room itself was round—they were in one of the building's corner cupolas. Just under the ceiling beams was a row of small round windows. He knew from his view on the street that these were just above the rooftop, but he saw no way to reach them. He returned his gaze to the maps. With a start he realized that they were of northern Germany. The Duchy of Macklenburg.

Xonck rolled off of the table with a snarl and strode for the door. His face was drawn and he was biting his lip against what must have been excruciating pain.

"Where are you going?" Bascombe asked.

"To save my bloody hand!" he cried. "To find a surgeon! To prevent myself from *killing one of you*!"

"You see what I mean, Highness," Rosamonde said lightly to the Prince. "Responsibility is like courage. You never know you possess it until the test. At which point, of course, it is too late—you succeed or fail."

Xonck stopped in the doorway, doing his best not to whimper—Chang had just seen the livid blistering flesh of his arm before they'd wrapped it—while he spoke. "Indeed . . . *Highness*," he snarled dangerously, as if his very words were smoking vitriol. "Abdicating *responsibility* can be mortal—one is scarcely in more peril than when trusting those who promise all. Was not Satan the most beautiful of angels?" Xonck staggered away.

Bascombe appealed to the Contessa. "Madame—"

She nodded tolerantly. "Make sure he doesn't hurt anyone." Bascombe hurried out.

* * *

"Now we are alone," said the Prince, in a satisfied tone that was meant to be charming. The Contessa smiled, looking around the room at the other men.

"Only a Prince thinks of himself 'alone' with a woman when there are merely no other women in the room."

"Does that make Francis Xonck a woman—as he's just left us?" laughed Major Blach. He laughed like a crow.

The Prince laughed with him. Chang felt a twinge of empathy for Xonck, and was tempted to simply step out and attack them—as long as he killed Blach first, the others would be no trouble. Then Rosamonde was speaking again, and he found her voice still fixed him where he was.

"I would suggest we place Herr Flaüss on the table."

"Excellent idea," agreed the Prince. "Blach—and you there—"

"That is Mr. Gray, from the Institute," said Rosamonde patiently, as if she had said this before.

"Excellent—pick him up—"

"He is very heavy, Highness . . . ," muttered Blach, his face red with exertion. Chang smiled to see Blach and the older Mr. Gray futilely struggling with the awkward, kicking mass of Herr Flaüss, who was doing his best to avoid the table altogether.

"Highness?" asked the Contessa Lacquer-Sforza.

"I suppose I must—it is ridiculous—stop struggling, Flaüss, or indeed it will go the worse for you—this is all for your benefit, and you will thank me later!"

The Prince shoved Gray to the side and took the writhing man's legs. The effort was not much more successful, but with much grunting they got him aboard. Chang was pleased to see Rosamonde smiling at them, if discreetly.

"There!" gasped Karl-Horst. He gestured vaguely to Gray and returned to his seat and his tea. "Tie him down—prepare the—ah—apparatus—"

"Should we question him?" asked Blach.

"For what?" replied the Prince.

"His allies in Macklenburg. His allies here. The whereabouts of Doctor Svenson—"

"Why bother? Once he has undergone the Process he will tell us of his own accord—indeed, he will be one of our number."

"You have not undergone the Process yourself, Major?" asked the Contessa in a neutral tone of polite interest.

"Not as of yet, Madame."

"He will," declared the Prince. "I insist upon it—all of my advisors will be required to partake of its . . . *clarity*. You do not know, Blach—you do not *know*." He slurped his tea. "This is of course why you have failed to find Svenson, and failed with this—this—*criminal*. It is only by the grace of the Contessa's wisdom that you were not relied on to effect changes in Macklenburg!"

Blach did not answer, but less than deftly tried to change the subject, nodding to the door. "Do we need Bascombe to continue?"

"Mr. Gray can manage, I am sure," said the Contessa. "But perhaps you will help him with the boxes?"

Chang watched with fascination as the long boxes were opened and the green felt packing pulled onto the floor. While Blach secured Flaüss to the table—without the slightest scruple for tightening the straps—the elderly Mr. Gray removed what looked to be an oversized pair of eyeglasses, the lenses impossibly thick and rimmed with black rubber, the whole apparatus—for indeed, it was part of a machine—run through with trailing lengths of bright copper wire. Gray strapped the glasses over the struggling man's face—again, viciously tight—and then stepped back to the box. He removed a length of rubber-sheathed cable with a large metal clamp at either end, attaching one end to the copper wire and then kneeling for the box with the other. He attached it there—Chang could not see exactly to what—and then, with some effort, turned some kind of switch or nozzle. Chang heard a pressurized hiss. Gray stood, looking to Rosamonde.

"I suggest we all step away from the table," she said.

Blue light began to radiate from inside the box, growing in brightness. Flaüss arched his back against his bonds, snorting breath through his nose. The wires began to hiss. Chang realized that this was his moment. He shoved the grate forward and to the side, slithering quickly into the room. He felt a pang for Flaüss—especially if he was indeed an ally of Svenson, though Svenson had mentioned no ally—but this was the best distraction he was likely to find, as all four of them were watching the man's exertions as if it were a public hanging. Chang gathered his stick, stood, took three quick steps and swung his fist as hard as he could against the base of Blach's head. Blach staggered forward with the force of the blow before his knees buckled and he crumpled to the floor. Chang turned to the Prince, whose face was a gibbering mask of surprise, and backhanded him savagely across the jaw, so hard the man sprawled over his chair and into the tea table. Chang spun to Gray, who'd been on the other side of Blach, and stabbed the blunt end of his stick into the man's soft belly. Gray—an old man, but Chang was not one for taking chances—doubled up with a groan and sat down hard on the floor, his face purpling. Chang wheeled toward Rosamonde and pulled his stick apart, ready to answer whatever weapon she had drawn. She had no weapon. She was smiling at him.

Around them the ringing wires rose to a howl. Flaüss was vibrating on the table hideously, foam seeping around the gag in his mouth. Chang pointed to the box. "Stop it! Turn it off!"

Rosamonde shouted back, her words slow and deliberate. "If you stop now it will kill him."

Chang glanced at Flaüss with horror, and then turned quickly to the other men. Blach was quite still, and he wondered if the blow had broken his neck. The Prince was on his hands and knees, feeling his jaw. Gray remained sitting. Chang looked back at Rosamonde. The noise was deafening, the light flaring around them brilliantly blue, as if they were suspended in the brightest, clearest summer sky. It was pointless to speak. She shrugged, smiling still.

He had no real idea how long they stood there, minutes at least, looking into each other's eyes. He did force himself to check the men on the floor, and once snapped the stick into Karl-Horst's hand as the Prince attempted to palm a knife from the scattered tea tray. The roaring Process made it all seem as if it occurred in silence, for he could not hear any of the normal sounds of reality—the tinkling of the knife on the stone floor, the Prince's profanity, the groans of Mr. Gray. He returned to Rosamonde, knowing she was the only danger in the room, knowing that to look into her eyes as he was doing was to cast the whole of his life up for judgment where it must be found desolate, wanting, and mean. Steam rose up from Flaüss's face. Chang tried to think of Svenson and

Celeste. They were both probably dead, or on their way to ruin. He could do nothing for them. He knew he was alone.

With a sharp cracking sound the Process was complete, the light suddenly fading and sound reduced to echo. Chang's ears rang. He blinked. Flaüss lay still, his chest heaving—he was alive at least.

"Cardinal Chang." Rosamonde's voice sounded unsettlingly small in the shadow of such a din, as if he wasn't hearing correctly.

"Madame."

"It seemed as if I would not see you. I hope I am not forward to say that was a disappointment."

"I was not able to accompany Mr. Xonck."

"No. But you are here—I'm sure through some very cunning means."

Chang glanced quickly to the Prince and Gray, who were not moving.

"Do not trouble yourself," she said. "I am intent that we should have a conversation."

"I am curious whether Major Blach is dead. A moment . . ." Chang knelt at the body and pressed two fingers into the man's neck. The pulse was there. He stood again, and restored the dagger to the stick. "Perhaps next time."

She nodded politely, as if she understood how that could be a good thing, then gestured to the older man. "If you will permit—as long as we are interrupted—perhaps Mr. Gray can attend to Herr Flaüss? Just to make sure he has not injured himself—sometimes, the exertions—it is a violent transformation."

Chang nodded to Gray, who rose to his feet unsteadily and moved to the table.

"May we sit?" asked Rosamonde.

"I must ask that you . . . behave," replied Chang.

She laughed, a genuine burst of amusement he was sure. "O Cardinal, I would never dream of anything else . . . here—" She stepped to the two chairs she'd shared with the Prince—who was still on his hands and knees. She sat where she had, and Chang picked up the Prince's upended chair and extended his stick toward Karl-Horst. The Prince, taking the hint, scuttled away like a sullen crab.

"If you will give Cardinal Chang and me a moment to discuss our situation, Highness?"

"Of course, Contessa—as you desire," he muttered, with all the dignity possible when one is crouched like a dog.

Chang sat, pushing his coat to the side, and looked to the table. Gray had removed the restraints and was detaching the mask of glass and wire, peeling it away from what looked to be a pink gelatinous residue that had collected where the mask touched the skin. Chang was suddenly curious to see the fresh scarring firsthand, but before the mask was pulled completely free Rosamonde spoke, drawing his attention away from the spectacle.

"It seems a long time since the Library, does it not?" she began. "And yet it was—what—but little more than a day ago?"

"A very full day."

"Indeed. And did you do what I asked you?" She shook her head with a mocking gravity.

"What was that?"

"Why, find Isobel Hastings, of course."

"That I did."

"And bring her to me?"

"That I did not."

"What a disappointment. Is she so beautiful?" She laughed, as if she could not keep the pretense of it being a serious question. "Seriously, Cardinal—what is it that prevents you?"

"Now? I do not know where she is."

"Ah . . . but if you did?"

He had not remembered the color of her eyes correctly, like petals of the palest purple iris flower. She wore a silk jacket of the precise same color. Dangling from her ears were beads of Venetian amber, fitted with silver. Her exquisite throat was bare.

"I still could not."

"Is she so remarkable? Bascombe did not think so—but then, I would not ask a man like Bascombe for the truth about a woman. He is too . . . well, 'practical' is a kind word."

"I agree."

"So will you not describe her?"

"I believe you have met her yourself, Rosamonde. I believe you consigned her to rape and murder."

"Did I?" Her eyes widened somewhat coyly.

"So she says."

"Then I'm sure I must have."

"So perhaps *you* should describe her."

"But you see, Cardinal, that is exactly the trouble. For—and perhaps this is obvious—in my own interaction with the lady I judged her to be an insignificant insolent chit of no value whatsoever. Is there any more tea?"

"The pot is on the floor," Chang said. He glanced to the table. Gray was still bent over Flaüss.

"Dommage," Rosamonde smiled. "You have not answered me."

"Perhaps I'm unsure of the question."

"I would think it evident. Why have you insisted on choosing her over me?"

If it was possible her smile became even more engaging, adding a tinge of sensuality to her lips, teasingly revealed as the first hint of explicit temptations to follow.

"I did not know it *was* my choice."

"Really, Cardinal, . . . you will disappoint me."

It was an odd conversation to have in the midst of toppled bodies, crouching princelings, and the trappings of scientific brutality—all in a secret room in the maze of the Foreign Ministry. He wondered what time it was. He wondered if Celeste was in another room nearby. This woman was the most dangerous of anyone in the Cabal. Why was he behaving like her suitor?

"Perhaps it had to do with your associates trying to kill me," he replied.

She dismissed this with a wave. "But *did* they kill you?"

"Did you kill Miss Temple?"

"Touché." She studied him. "Is it merely that? That she survived?"

"Perhaps it is. What else am I, but survival?"

"A provocative question—I shall inscribe it in my diary, I assure you."

"Xonck knows, by the way," he said, desperate to shift the conversation.

"Knows what?"

"That there are diverging interests."

"It's very charming of you to get ahead of yourself like this, but—and please do not take this as in any way a criticism—you were best to concentrate on mayhem and rooftops. What Mr. Xonck knows is my affair. Ah, Herr Flaüss, I see you are with us."

Chang turned to see the man on his feet next to the table, Gray at his side, his face livid with looping burns, the skin around them drawn and slick, his collar moist with sweat and drool. His eyes were disturbingly, utterly, vacant.

"I do admire you, Cardinal," said Rosamonde.

He turned to her. "I'm flattered."

"Are you?" She smiled. "I admire very few people, you know . . . and tell even fewer."

"Then why are you telling me?"

"I do not know." Her voice dropped to a provocatively intimate whisper. "Perhaps what has happened to your eyes. I can glimpse the scars, and I can only imagine how terrible they are without your glasses. I expect they would repulse me, and yet at the same time I have imagined myself running my tongue across them with pleasure." She gazed at him closely, then seemed to restore her composure. "But there it is, you see, now I am ahead of my own self. I do apologize. Mr. Gray?"

She turned to Gray, who had walked Flaüss quite near to them. Chang was sickened by the man's dead eyes, as if he were an example of ambulatory taxidermy. He turned away with discomfort, wishing he had been able to intervene more quickly—what had happened to Flaüss was somehow worse than if he had been killed. A rattling choking snapped Chang's gaze back—Gray's hands were around Flaüss's neck from behind, throttling him. Chang half-rose from his chair, turning to Rosamonde. Hadn't they done enough?

"What is he—"

The words died on his lips. Both of Flaüss's hands had shot forward and wrapped around Chang's windpipe, squeezing horribly. He pulled at Flaüss's arms, tried to pry apart his grip. It was like steel, the man's face still expressionless, the fingers digging into his neck. Chang could not breathe. He drove his knee into Flaüss's stomach, but there was still no reaction. The vise of his hands tightened. Black spots swam before Chang's eyes. He wrenched apart his stick. Gray's face was staring at him, over Flaüss's shoulder, Gray's hands were still squeezing Flaüss . . . Flaüss was reacting to Gray! Chang drove the dagger into Gray's forearm. The old man screamed and flung himself away, blood pouring from his wound.

Released, Flaüss immediately relaxed, his hands still in place around Chang's neck but loosened. Chang thrashed free of his grip, sucking in air. He did not understand what had happened. He turned to Rosamonde. There was something in her gloved hand. She blew on it. A puff of blue smoke burst into Chang's face.

The sensation was instantaneous. His throat clenched and then felt bitterly cold, as if he was swallowing ice. The bitter feeling flowed into his lungs and up through his head, wherever he had breathed in the powder. His stick and dagger fell from his hands. He could not speak. He could not move.

"Do not be alarmed," said Rosamonde. "You are not dead." She looked past Chang to the Prince, still on the floor. "Highness, if you would assist Mr. Gray with his bleeding?" She turned her violet gaze back to Chang. "What you are, Cardinal Chang, . . . is my own." She reached out to take hold of Karl-Horst's arm, stopping him on his way to Gray. "Actually, why doesn't the Cardinal help Mr. Gray? I'm sure he has more experience staunching wounds than the Crown Prince of Macklenburg."

He helped them with everything, his body answering her commands without question, his mind watching from within, as if from a terrible distance, through a frost-covered window. First he effectively bound Gray's wound, then lifted Blach onto the table so Gray could examine his head. How long had this taken? Bascombe returned with several red-coated Dragoons and spoke to the Contessa. Bascombe nodded and whispered earnestly in the Prince's ear. He then called to the others—the Dragoons lifted Blach, Gray took Flaüss by the arm—and led them all from the circular room. Chang was alone with Rosamonde. She crossed to the door and locked it. She returned to him and pulled up a chair. He could not move. Her face bore an expression he had never seen, as if deliberately purged of the barest trace of kindness.

"You will find that you can hear me, and that you can respond in a rudimentary way—the powder in your lungs makes it impossible to speak. The effects will fade—unless I desire them to be permanent. For now I will be satisfied with a yes or no answer—a simple nod will suffice. I had hoped to sway you with conversation, or barring that give you over to the Process, but now there is no time and no one to properly assist—and I should be very annoyed to lose all of your information in a mishap."

It was as if she was asking someone else. He felt himself nod in agreement, that he understood. Resistance was impossible—he could barely follow her words, and by the time he made sense of them his body had already answered.

"You have been with the Temple girl, and the Prince's Doctor."

Chang nodded.

"Do you know where they are now?"

He shook his head.

"Are they coming here?"

He shook his head.

"Do you have plans to meet them?"

Chang nodded. Rosamonde sighed.

"Well, I'm not going to spend all my time guessing where . . . you spoke to Xonck. He is suspicious—of me in particular?"

Chang nodded.

"Did Bascombe hear you speak?"

Chang shook his head. She smiled.

"Then there is ample time . . . it is true that Francis Xonck carries some of his older brother's great power, but only a very little, for he is so rebellious and rakish that there is no intimacy of friendship between them, and little prospect of inheritance. But of course *I* am a friend to Francis no matter what—so he truly has nowhere else to go. So, enough of that—imagine, *you* trying to scare *me*—what about what *you* know, from your *investigations* . . . do you know who killed Colonel Trapping?"

Chang shook his head.

"Do you know why we have chosen Macklenburg?"

Chang shook his head.

"Do you know of Oskar Veilandt?"

Chang nodded.

"Really? Good for you. Do you know of the blue glass?"

Chang nodded.

"Ah . . . not so good—for your survival, I mean. What have you seen . . . wait, were you at the Institute?"

Chang nodded.

"Breaking in—that was you, when that idiot dropped the book—or did you perhaps *cause* him to drop the book?"

Chang nodded.

"Incredible—you're an unstoppable force. He's dead, you know—and then of course what happened to the Comte's girl because of it—but I don't suppose that would bother you?"

In the prison of his mind Chang was wrenched by the confirmation that his actions had doomed Angelique. He nodded. Rosamonde cocked her head.

"Really? Not for the man. Wait—wait, the girl . . . she was from the brothel—I did not think you so chivalrous—but wait, could you *know* her?"

Chang nodded. Rosamonde laughed.

"It is the coincidence of a novel for ladies. Let me guess . . . did you love her terribly?"

Chang nodded. Rosamonde laughed even louder.

"Oh, that is priceless! Dear, dear Cardinal Chang . . . I believe you have just given me the nugget of information I require to make friends again with Mr. Xonck—an unintended prize." She attempted to compose her face but was still grinning. "Have you seen any glass other than the broken book?"

Chang nodded.

"I *am* sorry, for your sake. Was it—yes of course, the Prince had one of the Comte's novelty cards, didn't he? Has there ever been a man who likes more to watch himself? Did the Doctor find it?"

Chang nodded.

"So the Doctor and Miss Temple know of the blue glass as well?"

Chang nodded.

"And they know of the Process—never mind, of course they do—she saw it for herself, and the Doctor examined the Prince . . . do you know the significance of Lydia Vandaariff's marriage?"

Chang shook his head.

"Have you been to Tarr Manor?"

Chang shook his head. Her eyes narrowed.

"Miss Temple has been there, I expect, with Roger . . . but so long ago it would not signify. All right. One last question for the moment . . . am I the most exquisite woman you've ever known?"

Chang nodded. She smiled. Then, slowly, like a sunset slipping over the horizon, her smile faded and she sighed. "It is a sweet thought to end on, perhaps for both of us. The end itself is regrettable. You are an exotic dish for me... quite raw... and I would have preferred to linger over you. I am sorry." She reached into the tiny pocket of her fitted silk jacket and came up with another dose of fine blue powder on the tip of her gloved finger. "Think of it as a way to join your lost love..."

She blew the powder into his face. Chang's mouth was closed but he could feel it enter through his nose. His head felt as if it was freezing then and there, his blood stiffening, splitting the veins within his skull. He was in agony but could not move. His ears echoed with an audible crack. His eyes swam. He was staring at the floor tiles. He had fallen. He was blind. He was dead.

The chandelier was formed of three concentric large iron rings, each ring set with forged-metal sockets to hold candles... in all three rings perhaps a hundred sockets. Chang looked up to the high ceiling above him and saw perhaps eight of them still lit. How much time had passed? He had no idea. He could barely think. He rolled over to be sick and found that he had already done so, perhaps many times. The discharge was blue and—even to him—stinking. He rolled in the other direction. He felt as if someone had cut off his head and packed it in ice and straw.

It was his nose that had saved him, he was sure. The damage inside, the scars, the blockages—somehow the powder, or enough of the powder to kill, had not fully penetrated. He wiped his face—blue smears of mucus ran from his mouth and each nostril. She had intended to kill him with an overdose but his scarred passages had prevented the fatal concentration from taking effect, absorbing the vile chemicals more slowly and allowing him the time to survive. How long had it taken? He looked up at the round windows. It was after nightfall. The room was cold, with wax spattered on the floor in a sloppy ring where it had dripped to the floor. He tried to sit up. He could not. He curled up away from the vomit and shut his eyes.

* * *

He woke feeling distinctly better, if still only slightly more spry than a slaughtered pig on a hook. He rolled to his knees, working his tongue in his mouth with revulsion. He dug for a handkerchief and wiped his face. There did not seem to be any water in the room. Chang stood, shutting his eyes. The darkness weaved about him, but he did not fall. He saw the teapot, on its side on the floor. He picked it up and shook it gently—the dregs were still there sloshing. Taking care not to cut himself on the broken spout, he poured the bitter tea into his mouth, worked it around and then spat it on the floor. He took another sip and swallowed, then set the broken pot on the tea tray. With no small feeling of wonder, he saw his stick underneath the table. He understood that leaving it was a gesture of contempt—mainly so his body would be found with a weapon. As weak and sick as he felt, Chang was more than willing to make them regret it.

The room had a lantern and, after some minutes of search, matches to light it. The door opened into darkness as before, but now Chang was able to navigate clearly, if not with any knowledge of where he should go. He wandered for some minutes, finding no other person, nor hearing any noise, through various storage rooms, meeting rooms, and hallways. He did not see any of the rooms he remembered passing through with Bascombe and Xonck, and instead simply forged ahead, alternating left and right turns in an attempt to keep a straight line. This eventually brought him to a dead end: a large door without lock or knob. It would not budge. It was either sealed or barred from the other side. Chang shut his eyes. He felt sick again, his weakened body overtaxed by the walking. In frustration, he pounded on the door.

A muffled voice answered him from the other side. "Mr. Bascombe?"

Instead of calling out, Chang pounded again on the door. He heard the bar being shifted. He did not know what to prepare for—whether he should fling the lantern, ready his stick, or retreat. He was without the energy for any of them. The door was pulled back. Chang was faced with a red-coated Dragoon private.

He took in Chang. "You're not Mr. Bascombe."

"Bascombe's gone," said Chang. "Hours ago—you didn't see him?"

"I've just been on watch since six." The trooper frowned. "Who are you?"

"My name is Chang. I was part of Bascombe's party. I became sick.

Would you . . ." Chang shut his eyes for a moment and strained to finish the sentence. "Would you have some water?"

The trooper relieved Chang of the lantern and took his arm, leading him to a small guardroom. This, like the hallway, was fitted with gaslight fixtures and had a warm, hazy glow to it. Chang could see that they were near a large staircase—perhaps the main access for this floor, as opposed to Bascombe's secret lair where he had been taken. He was too tired to think. He sat on a simple wooden chair and was given a metal mug of tea with milk. The trooper, who offered that his name was Reeves, put a metal plate of bread and cheese on Chang's lap, and nodded that he should eat something.

The hot tea stung his throat as it went down, but he could feel it restoring him all the same. He pulled off a hunk of the white loaf with his teeth and forced himself to chew, if only to stabilize his stomach. After the first few bites however he realized how hungry he was and began to steadily devour everything the man had given him. Reeves refilled his mug and sat back with one of his own.

"I am much obliged to you," said Chang.

"Not at all." Reeves smiled. "You looked like death, if you don't mind me saying. Now you just look like hell." He laughed.

Chang smiled and drank more tea. He could feel the rawness of his throat and the roof of his mouth, where the powder had burned him. Each breath came with a twinge of pain, as if he'd broken his ribs. He could only speculate about the true state of his lungs.

"So you said they all left?" asked Reeves.

Chang nodded. "There was an accident with a lantern. One of the other men, Francis Xonck—do you know him?" Reeves shook his head. "He spilled oil on his arm and it caught fire. Mr. Bascombe went with him for a surgeon. I was left, and unaccountably became ill. I thought he might return, but find I have been asleep, with no idea of the time."

"Near nine o'clock," said Reeves. He eyed the door a bit nervously. "I need to finish rounds—"

Chang put out his hand. "Do not let me disturb you. I will leave—just point me the way. The last thing I would want is to be more of a bother—"

"No bother to help a friend of Mr. Bascombe." Reeves smiled. They stood, and Chang awkwardly put his mug and plate on the sideboard.

He looked up to see a man in the doorway, a polished brass helmet under his arm and a saber at his side. Reeves snapped to attention. The man stepped in. The rank of captain was in gold on the collar and the epaulettes of his red uniform.

"Reeves . . . ," he said, keeping his gaze on Chang.

"Mr. Chang, Sir. An associate of Mr. Bascombe's."

The Captain did not reply.

"He was inside, Sir. When I was on my rounds, I heard him knocking on the door—"

"Which door?"

"Door five, Sir, Mr. Bascombe's area. Mr. Chang's been sick—"

"Yes. All right, off with you. You're overdue to relieve Hicks."

"Sir!"

The Captain stepped fully into the room and motioned for Chang to sit. Behind them, Reeves snatched up his helmet and dashed from the room, pausing at the door to nod to Chang behind the Captain's back. His hurried steps clattered down the hallway, and then down the stairs. The Captain filled a mug with tea and sat. Only then did Chang sit with him.

" 'Chang', you say?"

Chang nodded. "It's what I am called."

"Smythe, Captain, 4th Dragoons. Reeves says you were unwell?"

"I was. He was most kind."

"Here." Smythe had reached into his coat and removed a small flask. He unscrewed the cap and handed it to Chang. "Plum brandy," he said, smiling. "I have a sweet tooth."

Chang took a sip, feeling reckless and very much wanting a drink. He felt a sharp spasm of pain in his throat, but the brandy seemed to burn through the blue dust's residue. He returned the flask.

"I am obliged."

"You're one of Bascombe's men?" asked the Captain.

"I would not go so far. I was calling upon him at his request. Another man of the party had an accident involving lantern oil—"

"Yes, Francis Xonck." Captain Smythe nodded. "I hear he was quite badly burned."

"It does not surprise me. As I told your man, I became ill waiting for their return. I must have slept, perhaps there was fever . . . it was some hours ago—and I woke to find myself alone. I expected Bascombe to return. Our business was hardly finished."

"Undoubtedly the trials of Mr. Xonck demanded his attention."

"Undoubtedly," said Chang. "He is an . . . important figure."

He took the liberty of pouring more tea for himself. Smythe did not seem to notice. Instead, he stood and crossed to the door, pulled it shut, and turned the key. He smiled somewhat ruefully at Chang.

"One can never be too careful in a government building."

"The 4th Dragoons are newly posted to the Foreign Ministry," observed Chang. "I believe it was in the newspaper. Or was it to the Palace?"

Smythe drifted back to his chair and studied Chang for a moment before answering. He took a sip of tea and leaned back, cradling the mug in both hands. "I believe you are acquainted with our Colonel."

"Why would you say that?"

Smythe was silent. Chang sighed—there was always a cost to idiocy.

"You saw me yesterday morning," he said. "At the dockside, with Aspiche."

Smythe nodded.

"It was a stupid place to meet."

"Will you tell me the reason for it?"

"Perhaps . . ." Chang shrugged. He could sense Captain Smythe's suspicion and defensiveness, but decided to test him further. "If you tell me something first."

Smythe's mouth tightened. "What is that?"

Chang smiled. "Were you with Aspiche and Trapping in Africa?"

Smythe frowned—it was not the question he expected. He nodded.

"I ask," Chang went on, "because Colonel Aspiche made much of the moral and professional differences between Trapping and himself. I have no illusions about the character of Colonel Trapping. But—if you will forgive me—the insistence on our meeting place was just one example, in our dealings together, of Aspiche's thoughtless *arrogance*."

Chang wondered if he'd gone too far—one never knew how to read loyalty, especially with an experienced soldier. Smythe studied him closely before speaking.

"Many officers have purchased their commissions—to serve with men who are not soldiers save by money paid is not unusual." Chang was aware that Smythe was picking his words with exceptional caution. "The Adjutant-Colonel was not one of those . . . but . . ."

"He is no longer the man he once was?" suggested Chang.

Smythe studied him for a moment, measuring him with a hard professional acuity that was not entirely comfortable. After a moment he sighed heavily, as if he had come to a decision he did not like but could not for some reason avoid.

"Are you acquainted with opium eating?" he asked.

It was all Chang could do not to smile, instead offering a disinterested, knowing nod. Smythe went on.

"Then you will know the pattern whereby the first taste can corrupt, can drive a man to sacrifice every other part of his life for a narcotic dream. So it is with Noland Aspiche, save the opium is the example of Arthur Trapping's position and success. I am not his enemy. I have served him with loyalty and respect. Yet his envy for this man's undeserved advancement is consuming—or has consumed—all that was dutiful and fair in his character."

"He *does* now command the regiment."

Smythe nodded in brusque agreement. His face hardened. "I've said enough. What was your meeting?"

"I am a man who *does* things," said Chang. "Adjutant-Colonel Aspiche engaged me to find Arthur Trapping, who had disappeared."

"Why?"

"Not for love, if that's what you mean. Trapping represented powerful men, and their power—their interest—was why the regiment had been transferred from the colonies to the Palace. Now he was gone. Aspiche wanted to take command, but was worried about the other forces at work."

Smythe winced with disgust. Chang was happy with his decision to withhold the whole truth.

"I see. Did you find him?"

Chang hesitated, and then shrugged—the Captain seemed plain enough. "I did. He is dead, murdered. I do not know how, or by whom. The body has been sunk in the river."

Smythe was taken aback. "But why?" he asked.

"I truly don't know."

"Is that why you were here—reporting this to Bascombe?"

"Not . . . exactly."

Smythe stiffened with wariness. Chang raised his hand.

"Do not be alarmed—or rather, be alarmed, but not by me. I came here to speak to Bascombe—what is your impression of the man?"

Smythe shrugged. "He is a Ministry official. No fool—and without the superior airs of many here. Why?"

"No reason—his is a minor role, for my errand truly lay with Xonck, and with the Contessa Lacquer-Sforza, because *they* were in league with Colonel Trapping—Xonck especially—and for reasons I do not understand, one of them—I don't know which, nor, perhaps, do they—arranged for him to die. You know as well as I that Aspiche is now in their pocket. Your operations today, taking the boxes of machinery from the Royal Institute—"

"To Harschmort, yes."

"Exactly," said Chang, not missing a beat but elated at what Smythe had revealed. "Robert Vandaariff is part of their plan, likely its architect, along with the Crown Prince of Macklenburg—"

Smythe held up his hand to stop him. He dug out his flask, unscrewed it with a frown and took a deep drink. He held it to Chang, who did not refuse. The swig of brandy set off another fire in his throat, but in some determined self-punishing way he was sure it was for the better. He returned the flask.

"All of this . . ." Smythe spoke almost too low to hear. "So much has felt wrong—and yet, promotions, decorations, the Palace, the Ministries—so we can spend our time escorting carts, or socialites stupid enough to set themselves on fire—"

"Whom do you serve at the Palace?" asked Chang. "Here it is Bascombe and Crabbé—but even they must receive some approval from above."

Smythe was not listening. He was lost in thought. He looked up, his face marked by a fatigue that Chang had not previously seen. "The Palace? A nest of impotent Dukes posing around an unloved, fading hag." Smythe shook his head. "You should go. The guard will be changing, and the Colonel may be with them—he often meets with the Deputy Minister late in the evening. They are making plans, but none of the other officers know what they are. Most, as you can imagine, are as full of arrogance as Aspiche. We should hurry—they may have been given your name. I take that your story of being ill was a fabrication?"

Chang stood with him. "Not at all. But it was the result of being poisoned—and having the dreadful manners to survive."

Smythe allowed himself a quick smile. "What has come of the world when a man won't obey his betters and simply die when they ask him?"

Smythe led him quickly down the stairs to the second floor, and then through several winding corridors to the balcony above the rear entrance. "It is relieved later than the front, and my men will still be here," he explained. He studied Chang closely, glancing over his clothing and ending at his impenetrable eyes. "I fear that you are a scoundrel—or so I would normally find you—but strange times make for strange meetings. I believe you are telling the truth. If we can help each other . . . well, we're that much less alone."

Chang extended his hand. "I'm sure I *am* a scoundrel, Captain. And yet I am these people's enemy. I am much obliged for your kindness. I hope some time to return it." Smythe shook his hand and nodded to the gate.

"It is half-past nine. You must go."

They walked down the stairs. On a whim, Chang whispered to him. "We are not alone, Captain. You may meet a German doctor, Svenson, of the Prince's party. Or a young woman, Miss Celeste Temple. We are together in this—mention my name and they will trust you. I promise they are more formidable than they appear."

They were at the gate. Captain Smythe gave him a curt nod—anything more would have been noticed by the troopers—and Chang walked out into the street.

He made his way to St. Isobel's Square and sat at the fountain, where he could easily see anyone approaching him from any direction. The moon was a scant pale glow behind the murky clouds. The fog had risen from the river and crawled toward him across the bricks, its moist air tickling his raw throat and lungs. With a nagging dismay he wondered how badly he'd been injured. He had known consumptives, hacking their life away into bloody rags—was this the first stage of such a misery?

He felt another twinge as he inhaled, as if he had glass in his lungs, cutting into the flesh with the movement of each breath. He hawked up a gob of thick fluid from his throat and spat on the paving. It seemed darker than normal, but he could not tell if it was more of the blue discharge or if it was blood.

The boxes were sent to Harschmort. Because there was more room? More privacy? Both were true, but a further thought arose to him—the canals. Harschmort was the perfect location to send the boxes away to sea . . . to Macklenburg. He berated himself for not studying the maps in the cupola room when he'd had the chance. He could have at least described them to Svenson—now he only had the barest sense of where they had placed a few colored pins. He sighed—a lost opportunity. He let it go.

The time he'd been insensible had spoiled his hope to find Miss Temple, for wherever she might have reasonably gone, it was doubtful she would still be there—no matter what had happened. The obvious possibility was Bascombe's house, but he resisted it, as much as thrashing Bascombe might have pleased him, no matter what the man's true loyalties. For the first time he questioned whether Celeste might not have the same resistance—was it possible that Bascombe hadn't been her destination? She had left them churning with emotion, after speaking of what she had lost. If that didn't mean Bascombe, then who could it mean? If he took her at her word—which he realized he never had—Bascombe was no longer anchored to her heart. Who else had so punctured her happiness?

Chang cursed himself for a fool and walked as quickly as he could to the St. Royale Hotel.

He ignored the front and instead went directly to the rear alley, where white-jacketed men from the night kitchen were dragging out metal bins heaped with the evening's scraps and refuse. He strode to the nearest, gestured to the growing collection of bins and snapped at him. "Who told you to leave these here? Where is your manager?"

The man looked up at him without comprehension—clearly they *always* put the bins there—but stuttered when faced with Chang's harsh, strange demeanor. "M-Mr. Albert?"

"Yes! Yes—where is Mr. Albert? I will need to speak to him at once!"

The man pointed inside. By this time the others were watching. Chang turned to them. "Very well. Stay here. We'll see about this."

He stalked inside along a service corridor, taking the first turn he could find away from the kitchen and Mr. Albert. This led him, as he had hoped, to the laundry and storage rooms. He hurried on until he found what he wanted: a uniformed porter loafing with a mug of beer. Chang stepped in—amidst mops and buckets and sponges—and shut the door behind him. The porter gulped with surprise, backing up instinctively into a clattering array of broom-handles. Chang reached out and took him by the collar, speaking quickly and low.

"Listen to me. I am in haste. I must get a message—in person, discreetly—to the rooms of the Contessa di Lacquer-Sforza. You know her?" The man nodded. "Good. Take me there now, by the rear stairs. We cannot be seen. It is to preserve the lady's reputation—she must have my news." He reached into his pocket and pulled out a silver coin. The man saw it, nodded, and then in one movement Chang pocketed the coin and pulled the man out of the room. He'd get it once they were there.

It was on the third floor, in the rear, which made sense to a suspicious mind like Chang's—too high to climb to or jump from, and away from the crowds on the avenue. The porter knocked on the door. There was no answer. He knocked again. There was no answer. Chang pulled him away from the door, and gave him the coin. He took out a second piece of silver. "We have not met," he said, and flipped the coin into the porter's hand, doubling his fee. The porter nodded, and backed away. After a few steps—Chang staring at him fiercely—he turned and ran from sight. Chang took out his ring of keys. The bolt snapped clear and he turned the knob. He was in.

The suite was everything that Celeste's suite at the Boniface had not been—exuding the excess that defined the St. Royale, from the carpets to the crystal, the monstrously over-carved furniture, the profusion of flowers, the luxurious draperies, the painfully delicate pattern of the wallpaper, to the truly expansive size of the suite itself. Chang shut the door behind him and stood in the main parlor. The suite seemed empty of life. The gaslight had been lowered, but the dim glow was enough for him to see. He smiled wryly at another difference. Clothes—admittedly, laces and silks—were strewn haphazardly over the arms of the chairs and sofas, even on the floor. It was impossible for him to imagine such a thing under the tight scrutiny of Aunt Agathe, but here, the occupant's decadent experience extended a casual disregard for so naïve a sense of order. He stepped to a lovingly fashioned writing desk cluttered with empty bottles and took its equally elegant wooden chair back to the front door, wedging it under the handle. He did not want to be interrupted as he searched.

He turned up the gaslight and returned to the main parlor. There were open doorways to either side and a closed door at the far end. He quickly glanced to each side—maids' rooms and second parlor, equally strewn with clothing and in the case of the parlor, glasses and plates. He stepped to the closed door, and pushed it open. It was dark. He fumbled for the gaslight sconce and illuminated another elegant sitting room, this with a handsome pair of chaise longues and a mirror-topped tray full of bottles. Chang stopped where he stood, a twinge of dread at his heart. Under one chaise was a tumbled pair of green ankle boots.

His gaze swept the room for any other signs. The drinks tray held four glasses, some half-empty and smeared with lipstick, and there were two more glasses on the floor beneath the other chaise. High on the wall across from him was a large mirror in a heavy frame pointing to his doorway at a looming angle. Chang looked into it with distaste—he disliked seeing himself at any time—but his eye was caught by something else in the reflection—on the wall next to him, a small painting that could only have been executed by the hand of Oskar Veilandt. He reached up and took it from the wall, and flipped it over to examine the rear of the canvas. In what he assumed was the artist's own hand, in blue paint, he read "*Annunciation Fragment,* 3/13", and then beneath it a series of symbols—like a mathematical formula incorporating Greek letters—which were in turn followed by the words, *"And so they shall be Reborn."*

He turned the canvas to the painted image and found himself astonished by its bluntly lurid nature. Perhaps it was the contrast between the image and its luxurious gold frame, the subsequent isolation—the *fragmentary* nature, its *containment*—of the subject matter that made the whole seem such a transgression, but Chang could not turn his eyes away. It was not so much pornographic—indeed it was not precisely explicit—as it was, somehow, palpably monstrous. He could not even say why, but the stark tremor of revulsion was as undeniable and as simultaneous as the stirring in his groin. This portion of the painting did not seem to be adjacent to the one they had seen in the gallery, of the woman's—the very idea of thinking of her as "Mary" was appalling—rapturous scarred face. This section showed her naked pelvis from the side, her splendid thighs wrapped around the hips of a figure in blue who had quite obviously mounted her. On a second glance however, Chang saw the hands of the blue figure clutching the woman's hips . . . the hands were blue as well, and decorated with many rings, as the wrists glittered with many bracelets of different metals—gold, silver, copper, iron—the man was not wearing a blue garment, *the blue was his skin.* Perhaps he was an angel—blasphemy enough—but the work's unnatural quality was compounded by the perfectly realized corporeality of the bodies, the sensual immediacy of the weight of the woman's haunches in the man's grip, the twisting angle of their conjoinment, fixed for a moment, but directly evocative of the writhing exquisite union that would continue—in the mind of the viewer if nowhere else.

Chang swallowed and clumsily replaced the painting on its hook. He glanced at it again, mortified at his reaction, compelled and disturbed anew at the long nails at the tip of each blue finger and the tenderly rendered impressions they made in the woman's flesh. He turned away to the chaise and collected the green boots from beneath it. They had to belong to Celeste. It was rare enough that Chang felt any obligation to another soul that to have formed such a bond—to so unlikely a person—and then find it so swiftly broken gnawed terribly at his conscience. The poignance of the empty boots—the very idea that her feet could be so small, could fit within such a space and yet enable her willful marching, was suddenly unbearable. He sighed quite bitterly, stricken with regret, and dropped them back on the chaise. The room had one door, which was ajar. He forced himself to push it with the tip of his stick. It opened silently.

This was clearly Rosamonde's bedroom. The bed itself was massive, with high mahogany pillars at each corner and a heavy purple damask curtain drawn across each side. The floor was littered with clothing, mainly underthings, but also here and there pieces of a dress, or a jacket, or even shoes. He recognized none of them as belonging to Celeste, but knew that he wouldn't in any case. The very idea of Celeste's underthings forced his mind to a place it had not formerly been, which seemed somehow—now that he feared she was dead—transgressive. Perhaps it was just the residual impact of Veilandt's painting, but Chang found his thoughts—indeed, he wondered, his heart—punctured by the idea of his hands around her slim ribcage . . . sliding down to her hips, hips unencumbered by a corset or petticoats, the unquestionably creamy texture of her skin. He shook his head. What was he thinking? For all he knew, he was about to part the purple curtains and find her corpse. He forced himself grimly back to the task, to the room and away from his insistent fantasies. Chang took a deliberately deep breath—his chest seizing in pain—and stepped to the bed. He pulled the curtain aside.

The bedclothes were heavy and tangled, kicked into careless heaps, but Chang could see a woman's pale arm extending from beneath them. He looked to the pillows piled over the woman's head and pulled the topmost away. It revealed a mass of dark brown hair. He pulled away another and saw the woman's face, her eyes closed, her lips delicately parted, the skin around her eyes displaying the nearly vanished looping scars. It was Margaret Hooke—Mrs. Marchmoor. Chang realized that she was naked at about the same moment she opened her eyes. Her gaze flickered as she saw him above her, but her face betrayed no lapse in composure. She yawned and lazily rubbed the sleep from her left eye. She sat up, the sheets slipping to her waist before she absently pulled them up to cover herself.

"My goodness," she said, yawning again. "What is the time?"

"It must be near eleven," answered Chang.

"I must have slept for *hours*. That is very bad of me, I'm sure." She looked up at him, her eyes dancing with coy pleasure. "You're the Cardinal, aren't you? I was told you were dead."

Chang nodded. At least she had the manners not to sound disappointed.

"I am looking for Miss Temple," he said. "She was here."

"She *was* . . . ," answered the woman somewhat dully, her attention elsewhere. "Is there no one else you can ask?"

He resisted the impulse to slap her. "You're alone, Margaret. Unless you'd prefer that I take you to Mrs. Kraft—I'm sure she's worried sick over your disappearance."

"No thank you." She looked at him as if she was seeing him clearly for the first time. "You're unpleasant." She spoke as if it were a surprise.

Chang reached out and took hold of her jaw, wrenching her eyes to face his. "I haven't *started* to be unpleasant. What have you done with her?"

She smiled at him, fear fretting at the edges of her expression. "What makes you think she didn't do it to herself?"

"Where is she?"

"I don't know—I was so sleepy—I am always so sleepy... afterwards... but some people find they want something to eat. Did you ask in the kitchens?"

Chang didn't reply to her vulgar implication—he knew she was lying to provoke him, to buy time, but her words were nevertheless a spur to lurid thoughts flickering impulsively across his inner eye... the image of this woman's mouth flinching with surprise at her own pleasure—and then with disturbing ease that face became Celeste's, her lips curled in a desperate mixture of anguish and delight. Chang was startled and stepped away from Mrs. Marchmoor, releasing his grip. She threw back the covers and stood, walking toward a pile of discarded clothes on the floor. She was tall and more graceful than he would have thought. Quite deliberately she turned her back to him and bent over at the waist for a robe—rather like a dancer—exposing herself lewdly in the process. As she stood—glancing back to confirm Chang's appreciation with a smile—he noticed a lattice-work of thin white scars across her back, whip marks. She slipped into her robe—pale silk with a great red Chinese dragon across the back—and tied the sash with a practiced gesture, as if her hands were marking the well-known end, or the start, of some arcane ritual.

"I see your face is healing," said Chang.

"My face is of no consequence," she answered, nudging her foot through the pile of clothes, finding a single slipper as she spoke and stuffing her foot into it. "The change takes place within, and is sublime."

Chang scoffed. "I only see you've left the service of one brothel for another."

Her eyes became sharp—he had offended her, he saw with great satisfaction.

"You have no idea," she said, affecting a lightness he knew was false.

"I've just watched another undergo your hideous Process—quite against his wishes—and I can tell you now, if you've done that to Miss Temple—"

She laughed—contemptuously. "It is no *punishment.* It is a *gift*—and the very notion—the very ridiculous notion that—*that* person—your precious Miss Inconsequent—"

Chang felt a moment of profound relief, a reprieve from a fear he hadn't realized was with him—that Celeste would become one of them... almost as if he would rather she were dead. But Mrs. Marchmoor was still speaking. "... cannot appreciate the capacity, the reserves of power..." It was a quality of pride, he knew, especially in those who in their lives have been subject and then elevated—years of withheld speech turned their mouths into arrogant floodgates, and her quick turn from coy seductress to haughty lady made Chang sneer. She saw the sneer. It inflamed her.

"You think I do not know what you are. Or who *she* is—"

"I know you hunted us both through the brothels—without skill or success."

"Without success?" She laughed. "You are here, aren't you?"

"As was Miss Temple. Where is she now?"

She laughed again. "You truly do not *understand*—"

Chang stepped forward quickly, took a handful of the front of her robe and threw the woman bodily onto the bed, her white legs kicking free as she fell. He stood over her, giving her a moment to shake the hair from her face and look up into his depthless eyes.

"No, Margaret," he hissed. "*You* do not understand. You have been a whore. Giving up your body is no longer cause for delicacy, thus you will understand, given *my* profession... well, just imagine what no longer causes *me* to hesitate. And I am hunting *you,* Margaret. This day I have set Francis Xonck on fire, I have defeated the Prince's Major, and I have survived the trickery of your Contessa. She will not trick me again—do you understand? In these things—and I know these things—there are rarely second chances. Your people have had their chance to kill me—the only one of you that could—and I survived. I am here to find—quickly—whether you are of the slightest—*the slightest*—use to me whatsoever. If you are not, then I assure you I don't have the *slightest* qualm in exterminating you as if you were just one more rat in a filthy *infestation* that I am—believe me—going to destroy."

He pulled his stick apart as dramatically as he could—hoping the speech hadn't been too much—and allowed his voice to become more conversationally reasonable.

"Now, as I have asked... Margaret,... where is Miss Temple *now*?"

It was then that Chang first took in the severity of the Process. The woman was not stupid, she was alone, she possessed reason and experience, and yet, even though her eyes had widened in terror when he had taken out his blade, she began to rant at him, as if the words themselves were weapons to drive him away.

"You're a fool! She is gone—you'll never find her, she is beyond rescue—she will be beyond your comprehension! You live like a child—you are all children—the world was never yours, and it never will be! I have been consumed and reborn! I have surrendered and been renewed! You cannot harm me—you cannot change anything—you are a worm in the mud—get away from me! Get out of this room—cut your own throat in the gutter!"

She was screaming and Chang was suddenly furious—the deep disdain in her voice pricking his composure like a venomous fang. He dropped his stick and with his left hand took hold of her kicking ankle and yanked her body sharply toward him. She sat up, screaming still, her face quite mad now, not even bothering to fend him off with her arms, spittle flying from her lips. The dagger was in his right hand. Instead of stabbing her, he forced himself to drive a punch into her jaw, his fist bolstered by the cane-hilt. Her head snapped back—his fingers were jarred cruelly—but she did not fall. Her words became more disjointed, there were tears at the corners of her eyes, her hair was ragged.

"—worth nothing! Ignorant and abandoned—alone in rooms—pathetic rooms of pathetic bodies—kennels—the rutting of dogs—"

He dropped the dagger and struck her again. She sprawled across the bed with a grunt, her head hanging over the other side, silent. Chang shook his hand, wincing, and sheathed the dagger. His fury was gone. Her contempt for him was so clearly one with her contempt for herself—he remembered Mrs. Kraft saying Margaret Hooke had been the daughter of a mill owner—that he let it pass. He wondered if anyone else in the hotel had heard, and hoped that such screams—judging perhaps by the profusion of empty bottles—were not unusual in the rooms of Rosamonde, Contessa Lacquer-Sforza. He looked down at Margaret Hooke's body—the gapping robe showed the softness of her belly and the open tangle of her legs, somehow strangely poignant. She was a handsome woman. Her ribs rose and fell with each still-ragged breath. She was an animal like anyone else. He thought of the scars on her back, so different perhaps from the scars on her face—both testament to her submission to the desires of others more powerful, yet each also the mark of some inarticulate groping on her part, for peace of mind. Her vitriolic eruption told Chang she had not found it yet, but merely imprisoned her discontent beneath layers of control. It was perhaps more poignant than anything. He straightened her robe, allowing himself a moment to run his hand along her hips, and made his way unseen from the hotel.

As he walked in the darkened streets, Chang ran over the words of Mrs. Marchmoor in his mind . . . "beyond rescue" . . . which either meant that something had already happened to Celeste, or was so certain to happen that he would be unable to alter it. Her arrogance made him think the latter. He felt the clumping weight of Celeste's ankle boots in each side pocket of his coat. It was likely, he felt, that they had taken her to some concentration of power—perhaps to convert her with the Process, perhaps to merely kill her—but if that were so, why not already do it? With a sickening thought, his mind went to Angelique and the glass book. Would they dare to repeat that ritual with Celeste? Their attempt with Angelique had been spoiled by his interruption—but what would be a successful outcome? He had no doubt that it was somehow even more monstrous.

The first question was where they would take her. It would be either Harschmort—where they had taken the boxes—or Tarr Manor—which Rosamonde had asked him about. Both places would offer solitude and space, without any outside interference. He assumed Svenson had reached the Manor, and so perhaps he ought to go to Harschmort . . . but if such forces were in fact in play, could he rely on the Doctor to effect a rescue? He had an image of that earnest man, an inert Celeste over one shoulder, trying to walk while firing the pistol at a pursuing gang of

Dragoons . . . utterly doomed. He had to know where they had taken her. A wrong guess could destroy them all. He would have to risk a visit to the Library.

Like most great buildings, the Library was of a size to be without adjacent rooftops that might have removed the problem altogether. The high front double doors and the rear staff entrance both had regular postings of guards inside, even during the night. From a vantage point of forty yards away, Chang could also see the black Macklenburg troopers slouching in the shadow of the columns that lined the front steps. He assumed they were at the rear as well—presenting him with guards within and without. Neither mattered. Chang jogged to a squat stone structure perhaps fifty yards away from the main edifice. The door had a crude wooden bolt, but a minute of concerted effort with the dagger—sliding it through the gap, digging into the bolt, pushing it a fraction of an inch to the side, again and again—had the door open. He stepped in and closed it behind him. In the dim light from the one barred window he saw a stack of lanterns, selected one and checked the oil, and then carefully struck a match. He turned the wick low, allowing just enough of a glow to find the hatch in the floor. He set the lamp down and with all his strength pulled on the handle. The heavy metal hatch creaked on its hinges, but swung open. He picked up the lantern again and stared into the pit below. For the second time in the day he thanked fate for his damaged nose. He descended into the sewers.

He had done it before during a protracted disagreement with a client unwilling to pay. The man had sent agents into the Library and Chang had been forced to use this most loathsome bolt-hole. He was still dripping sewage when he kicked in the client's window later that evening—resolving the disagreement at razor's edge—but that had been in late spring. Chang hoped it was close enough to winter and the water levels still low so he could pass without getting soaked in filth. The hatch led to a slimy set of stone steps, without any kind of rail. He walked down, stick in one hand and lantern in the other, until he reached the sewage tunnel itself. The fetid stream had shrunk since his last visit and he was relieved to see a slippery yard of stone to the side where he could walk. He bent his shoulders beneath the overhang and stepped very carefully.

It was very dark, and the lantern wick sputtered and sparked in the foul air. He was under the street, and then soon enough—counting his steps—under the Library itself. It was another twenty paces to another set of stairs and another hatch. He climbed up, heaved on the hatch with his shoulder, and entered the lowest Library basement—three floors below the lobby. He scraped his boots as best he could and shut the hatch behind him.

Keeping the lamp wick low, Chang made his way up to the main floor and darted across the corridor into the stacks. The building itself he knew intimately—indeed, like a blind man. There were three floors of hidden book stacks for each spacious floor of the Library that was open to the public. The stack aisles were crammed, dusty, and narrow, stuffed with seldom used books that could nevertheless never be disposed of. The walls—and floors and ceilings—were no more than iron scaffolding, and during the day one could look up through the gaps, as if through a strange sort of kaleidoscope, to the very top of the building, some twelve levels above. Chang climbed quickly up six narrow flights of stairs to what was the third floor of the Library proper, pushed open the door with his shoulder—it always stuck—and entered the vaulted map room, where he had so recently been hired by Rosamonde.

Now Chang turned up the wick, knowing there was no chance the guards would see—the map room was well away from the main staircase where light might be glimpsed from below. He set the lantern on one of the great wooden cases and searched for a particular volume on the curator's desk—the massive *Codex of Royal Surveyor's Maps,* and the easiest source for a detailed view of Harschmort and Tarr Manor. He did not, however, know where each of them was exactly located—or not precisely enough to guess the map that would contain them. He braced himself for the small print of the *Codex* and found his way to the index of place names, squinting painfully. It took him several minutes to find each, with grid references to the main master map in the front of the *Codex.* By locating them on the grid-marked master map that unfolded awkwardly from the front of the *Codex,* he would then have the citation numbers for the detailed surveyor maps, of which there were hundreds and hundreds in the Library's collection. It was another matter of minutes, closely poring over the master map, and he was off to the surveyor maps, kept in a high bureau of wide, thin drawers. Again, with his face inches from their identifying numbers, he located the two maps in question and pulled them from the bureau. He dragged the maps—each of them easily six feet square—over to one of the wide reading tables and collected the lantern. He rubbed his eyes and began the next step of his search.

The map of Tarr Manor—and Lord Tarr's quite expansive grounds—showed it to be in the county of Floodmaere. It was easy enough to find the quarry, some five miles from the main house, where the Lord's estate claimed a low range of craggy hills. The manor house itself was large but not abnormally so, and the immediate grounds did not strike any particularly suspicious chord: orchards, pasture, stables. The land seemed generally wild, without notable cultivation or building. The map did show a number of small outlying structures at the quarry itself, but were they large enough to contain the Comte's experiments?

The map of Harschmort was similarly inconclusive. The house was larger, certainly, and there were the nearby canals, but the surrounding land was fen and flat pasture. He had been in the house itself—it was not especially high. He was looking for any place where they might replicate the great sunken building at the Institute, which had been set well into the earth, but in these places must mean some kind of high tower. He could see no such location on either map. Chang sighed and rubbed his eyes. He was running out of time. He returned his attention to the map of Harschmort, for that had been where Aspiche's Dragoons had taken the Cabal's boxes, looking for anything he might have missed. He could not see the far edge of the map, and rotated it on the table to bring it closer to the light. In his haste, his fingers tore at the lower corner. He swore with annoyance and glanced at the damage. There was something there, something written. He peered closer. It was a citation to another map, a second map of the same area. Why another map? He noted the number in his head and crossed back to the *Codex,* searching quickly for the reference. He did not immediately make sense of it. The second map was part of a survey of buildings. Chang rushed to the bureau, hurriedly dug for it and spread it onto the table. He had forgotten. For his great house, Robert Vandaariff had purchased and re-made a prison.

It was only a moment before he found the clue he sought. The present house was a ring of buildings around an open center occupied by a substantial formal garden in the French geometrical style. In the prison map, this center was dominated by a circular structure that—Chang's mind raced to take it in—descended many floors, a panopticon of prison cells arranged around a central observation tower, all of it sunk under the earth. He looked again at the map of Vandaariff's Harschmort... there was no visible trace of it at all. Chang knew in an instant that it was still there, underground. He thought of the Institute chamber, the mass of pipes running down the walls to the table where Angelique had lain. The prison panopticon could be easily re-made for the same purpose. There could be nothing like it at Tarr Manor—the expense would be well beyond the income of such a middling estate. He left the maps where they were and strode back to the stacks with the lantern. For all he knew Celeste was in that table's embrace at Harschmort even then.

By the time he descended into Stropping it was after midnight. If anything, the spectacle of the place was even more infernal than he remembered (for Chang disliked leaving the city and so the station was invariably colored by annoyance and resentment)—the shrieking whistles, the fountains of steam, the glowering angels to either side of the awful clock, and below them all a desperate handful of driven souls, even at this hour, isolated under the vast iron canopy. Chang raced toward the large board that detailed the trains and their platforms and destinations, forcing his eyes to focus as he ran. He was half-way across the floor when the blurred letters congealed into a shape he could read—platform 12, leaving at 12:23 for Orange Canal. The ticket counter was closed—he would pay the conductor—and he dashed for the platform. The train was there, steam rising from the stack of its red engine.

As he came nearer he noted with a stab of wariness a line of finely dressed figures—men and women—boarding at the rear car. He slowed to a walk. Could it be another ball? After midnight? They would not be arriving at Harschmort until nearly two o'clock in the morning. He loitered until the last of the line had boarded—he recognized none of them—and approached the rear carriage himself, unseen. Perhaps twenty people had entered. He looked up at the clock—it was 12:18—and allowed another minute for them to clear the rear car before he climbed the steps and entered. The conductor was not there. Had he escorted the others forward? Chang took a few steps farther in and looked around. No one was in the rear-most compartments. He turned back to the door and froze. Advancing toward the train across the marble floor of Stropping Station was the unmistakable form of Mrs. Marchmoor, in a dress of dramatic black and yellow, and marching behind her a group of some fifteen red-coated Dragoons, their officer at her side. Chang spun on his heels and dashed forward into the car.

The compartments were empty. At the far end of the corridor Chang pulled open the door and closed it behind him, moving steadily ahead. This car seemed to be empty as well. It wasn't surprising for so late an hour, especially since the people boarding seemed to make up a single large party. They would undoubtedly be seated together—and Chang had little doubt that Mrs. Marchmoor would be joining them, once she had established to her satisfaction he was not to be found. He reached the end of the second car and plunged on into the third. He looked back with a start, for through the glass doors and down the length of two corridors, he could see the reddish shapes of the Dragoons. They were aboard. Chang broke into a run. These compartments were equally empty—he was barely bothering to look into them as he passed. He reached the end of the third car and stopped dead. This door was different. It opened onto a small open platform with a handrail of chain on either side. Beyond it, just a short step away, was another car, different from the others, painted black with gold fittings, with a forbidding doorway of black-painted steel. Chang reached out for the handle. The door was locked. He turned to see red coats at the far end of the corridor. He was trapped.

With a lurch the train began to move. Chang looked to his right and saw the ground of the station drop away. Without another thought he vaulted the chain and landed heavily in a crouch on the gravel; the wind was knocked from his lungs with a wickedly sharp wrench. He forced himself up. The train was still picking up speed. He stumbled after it, driving his body to move, fighting the sensation that he had just inhaled a box full of needles. He broke into a tormented run, legs pumping, catching up to the platform where he had jumped and then racing to reach the front of the black car. Ahead the track disappeared into a tunnel. He looked up at the black car's windows, dark, covered by curtains—or was it paint? Or steel? His lungs were in agony. He could see the gap at the front of the car, but even if he reached it, had he the strength to pull himself up? The vision of dropping under the train's wheels flashed hideously into his mind—legs sheared off in an instant, the gouts of blood, his last glimpse of life the filthy soot-covered slag of a Stropping railway track. He pushed himself harder. The whistle sounded. They were nearing the tunnel. With a surge of relief he saw a ladder bolted to the far end of the car. Chang leapt for it and caught hold, legs swinging near the rails, and clawed his way madly up hand over hand—somehow not dropping his stick—until he could hook a knee into the lowest rung. He panted desperately, his lungs and throat on fire. The train swept into the tunnel and he was swallowed by the dark.

Chang held on for his life, working both legs through the rungs to take the burden from his arms. His chest heaved. He hawked and spat repeatedly into the darkness, away from the train, the taste of blood in his mouth. His head was swimming and he felt dangerously close to a faint. He tightened his grip on the iron rungs and took deep, agonizing breaths. With a sickening thought he realized that if anyone had seen him, he was utterly unable to defend himself. He cursed Rosamonde and her blue powder. His lungs were being ground up like sausage-meat. He spat again and squeezed his eyes shut against the pain.

He waited until the end of the tunnel, which was at least fifteen minutes. No one emerged from the car. The train raced through the city to the northeast, past desolate yards and crumbling brick houses, to the wood and tar-paper hovels that lined the tracks at the city's edge. The hidden moon still gave Chang enough light to see another platform with a chain rail connecting the black car to the next, which had no door at all, only another ladder rising to its upper edge. With a slowness that revealed how spent he had become, he understood. This was the coal wagon, and ahead of it the engine. He worked his legs free and, wedging his foot tightly, reached across the empty space toward the coal wagon's ladder. His arm was perhaps three inches short. If he threw himself, he was almost sure to make it, and it was another sign of his fatigue that he even thought twice. But he couldn't stay where he was, and he trusted himself to leap over the chain rail even less. He stretched out his arm and one leg, glancing once at the gravel track rattling past beneath him, the rail ties a flickering blur. He turned his gaze solely to the ladder, took a breath and jumped... and landed perfectly, his heart pounding. He looked over at the metal door from this better angle. It seemed exactly like its counterpart on the opposite side: heavy, steel, windowless—as welcoming as the front of any bank safe. Chang turned his gaze to the top of the ladder and began to climb.

The coal wagon had been recently filled, so the drop from the top of the ladder into the bed of coal was perhaps two feet—just enough to conceal Chang from anyone on the platform between cars. More than this, the level of coal was higher in the center, where it had been poured into the wagon, creating a hillock between Chang and the engineers and stokers on the other side. He lay on his back, looking up into the midnight fog as the train raced through it, the sound of the wheels and the steam loud in his ears, but so constant as to become soothing. He rolled over and spat onto the wall of the wagon. From the taste in his mouth there was no question, this was blood. He felt a thin primal vibration of fear running up his spine, recalling the terrible year when he'd first felt the crop across his eyes—damned to a poorhouse sickroom, and lucky to survive the fever, his every thought trapped in the fearful space between the person he remembered himself being and the person he was terrified to become—weak, dependent, contemptible. If anything, once he'd left the sickroom and attempted to reclaim his life, the reality had been worse than his fear—after the first day he had abandoned everything for a new existence fueled by bitterness and rage and the desperation of the destitute. As for the young nobleman who had struck him... Chang hadn't known who he was at the time—the blow had come in the common room of a university drinking hall in the midst of a larger, tangled disagreement between gangs of students—and still didn't. The glimpse had been very, very brief—a sharp jaw, a rictus of vicious glee, mad green eyes. For all he knew—or hoped—the man had succumbed to syphilis years ago... he had left that kind of impression.

In the coal wagon however, it was all starting again. If his lungs were ruined, then so was his livelihood. He could wheeze through his work at the Library, but actually settling the business—which he both enjoyed and found a source of self-defining pride—would be beyond him. He thought of his impromptu adventures over the past days and knew that he never would have escaped the soldier in his room—or from the

Institute, or the Major, or Xonck, or survived Rosamonde... none of them with his body in such a state. He had re-made himself by an assertion of will, learning to survive, learning his business (when and who and to what degree to trust, when and how and who to kill or merely thrash) and most importantly where to safely locate, in a life of apportioned areas—work and peace, action and oblivion—some semblance of human contact. Whether it was chatting about horses with Nicholas the barman between drinks at the Raton Marine, or allowing himself the painful leisure to approach Angelique (the clacking rush of the train brought to mind her native tongue—he'd said that someone speaking Chinese sounded like an articulate cat, and she'd smiled, because he knew she liked cats), the space for all of these interactions depended on his place in the world, on his ability to take care of himself. What if this was gone? He shut his eyes, and exhaled. He thought of dying in his sleep, choking on the blood in his chest and being found whenever the stokers reached this far into the coal for fuel. When would that be—days? His body would go to a pauper's grave, or simply into the river. His mind drifted to Doctor Svenson, and he saw him stumbling away from pursuit—limping, as Chang realized dimly the Doctor had done throughout their time together, though he had not mentioned it—out of shells, dropping the pistol... he would die. Chang would die. The stability of Chang's thoughts drifted, and without him noticing, as if in a dream, his sympathy for the Doctor's plight caused his gaze to transpose itself into the struggle—he saw his own hands throw down the pistol and fumble for and draw apart his stick (somewhere in the back of his mind he wondered that the Doctor would have such a weapon) and flail at the many men who followed him through the fog (or was it falling snow—he must have lost his glasses)—sabers everywhere, surrounded by soldiers in black and in red... swinging helplessly, his weapons knocked away... the blades flashing toward him like starving bright fish darting up from the depths of the sea, their hideous punctures in his chest—or was he merely breathing?—and then behind him, from far away yet insistently in his ear, the whispered voice of a woman, her moist, warm breath. Angelique? No... it was Rosamonde. She was telling him that he was dead. Of course he was... there was no other explanation.

* * *

When Chang opened his eyes the train was no longer moving. He could hear the desultory hiss of the engine in repose, like a muttering, tamed dragon, but nothing else. He sat up, blinking, and dug out a handkerchief to wipe his face. His breath was easier, but there was a dark crust at each corner of his mouth and around both nostrils. It did not exactly look like dried blood—he couldn't be certain in the dark—but rather like blood that had been crystallized, as if seeped into sugar, or ground glass. He peered over the lip of the coal wagon. The train was at a station. He could see no one on the platform. The black car was still closed—or re-closed, he had no idea if it had been vacated or not. The station house itself was dark. As the train did not seem about to move on, he reasoned they had to be at the end of the line, at Orange Canal. Chang laboriously swung his leg over the side of the wagon and climbed down, tucking the stick under his arm. His joints were stiff, and he looked up at the sky, trying to judge by the moon how long he'd been asleep. Two hours? Four? He dropped onto the gravel and brushed himself off as best he could—he knew the back of his coat was blackened with coal dust. There would be no chance to brazen his way past servants looking like this, but it made no difference. The situation was beyond disguise.

As so often happens, the return trip to Harschmort seemed much shorter than his flight away from it. Small landmarks—a dune, a break in the road, the stump of a tree—appeared one after the other with almost dutiful dispatch, and it was a very brief half an hour before Chang found himself standing on a hillock of knee-high grass, gazing across a flat fennish pasture at the brightly lit, forbidding walls of Robert Vandaariff's mansion. As he advanced he weighed different avenues of approach, based on the parts of the house he knew. The gardens in the rear were bordered by a number of glass doors which would offer easy entry, but the garden was above the hidden chamber—the inverse tower—and might be closely watched. The front of the house was sure to be well-occupied, and the main wings only had windows high off the ground, as per the original prison. This left the side wing, where he'd smashed through a lower window to escape, which also seemed to be where much of the secret activity had been found before—Trapping's body, at any rate. Should he try there? He had to assume Mrs. Marchmoor had warned them of his possible arrival, despite not finding him on the train. They would expect him, to be sure.

The fog broke apart at a rise in the wind, laying the ground before him more open to the moonlight. Chang stopped, a pricking of suspicion at the back of his neck. He was mid-way across the pasture, and could suddenly see that in front of him the grass had been flattened in narrow trails. People had been here recently. He stepped slowly forward, his eyes noting where these trails might cross his path. He stopped again and sank to one knee. He extended his stick ahead of him and pushed aside the grass. Just visible in the sandy dirt was a length of iron chain. Chang dug the stick under it and lifted, pulling the chain free of the sand. It was only two feet long, with one end bolted to a metal spike driven deep into the earth. The other end, he noted with a weary kind of dread, was attached to a metal bear trap—or in this case, man trap, the vicious circle of iron teeth stretched apart and ready to shatter his leg. He looked up at the house, then behind him. He had no idea where else they had placed these—he didn't even know if this was their beginning or his progress so far just luck. The road was well away—and getting to it didn't offer any safer route than going forward. He would have to take a chance.

Not wanting it broken, he wormed the tip of his stick under the rim of the trap's teeth and edged it within reach of the small sensitive plate. He rapped with the tip on the plate and the trap went off with vicious speed, snapping savagely through the air. Even though he expected it, Chang was still startled and chilled—the trap's action was just shockingly brutal. He screamed, cupping his hand around his mouth to propel the sound toward the house. He screamed again, desperately, pleadingly, allowing it to trail off in a moan. Chang smiled. He felt better for the release of tension, like an engine venting built-up steam. He waited. He screamed a third time, still more abjectly, and was rewarded by a new chink of light in the nearest wall, an opened doorway and then an exiting line of men carrying torches. Keeping low, Chang scuttled back whence he had come, aiming for a part of the pasture where the grass was high. He threw himself down and waited for his breath to settle. He could hear the men, and very slowly raised his head enough to watch them approach. There were four men, each with a torch. With a sudden thought he pulled off his glasses, not wanting the lenses to reflect the torchlight. The men came nearer, and he noted with satisfaction the very deliberate path they walked, one after another, marking it clearly in the grass. They reached the sprung trap, perhaps twenty yards from where he watched, and it quite visibly dawned on them that they saw no writhing man in the grass, nor heard any further screaming. They looked around with suspicion.

Chang smiled again. The coal dust absorbed the light and made him nearly invisible. The men were speaking low to each other. He couldn't hear them. It didn't matter. Three were Dragoons, in brass helmets that caught the torchlight, but the one in front was from the household, his head bare, his coat flapping about his knees. The soldiers had torches in one hand and sabers in the other. The man held a torch and a carbine. He planted the torch in the sandy ground and inspected the trap, looking for blood. The man stood up, collected his torch, and quite deliberately scanned the pasture around him. Chang slowly lowered himself—there was no point botching it now—and waited, following the man's thoughts as clearly as if he saw into his mind. The man knew he was being watched, but had no idea from where. Chang was abstractly sympathetic, but whoever's idea the traps actually were, this was obviously the man who had set them. While Chang was a killer, he did not admire those whose traffic was agony. He made a point of fixing the man's face—a wide jaw with grizzled side whiskers and a balding pate—in his mind. Perhaps they would meet indoors.

After another minute, when it became clear that they were not willing to blunder around searching amongst the unsprung traps, they retreated to the house. Chang let them go, and then very cautiously followed in the safe pathway of their steps, crouching low. At the edge of the grass and the end of his cover, he waited—for all he knew they were watching from a darkened window. He was facing the same side wing, but could not place the window he'd broken through only two nights before. It had already been reglazed. Chang smiled wickedly, and felt around him for a stone. With Mrs. Marchmoor having arrived before him, the only way he was going to get inside was by creating a bit of fuss.

He rolled to one knee and threw—it was a lovely, smooth stone, and sailed very well—as hard as he could at the window to the right of the doorway where the men had emerged, which shattered with a gratifying crash. Chang ran toward the house, vaulting a border of flower beds, to the left of the door, reaching the wall as he heard cries within and saw answering light flooding out from the broken window. The door opened. He pressed himself flat. An arm appeared holding a torch, and just after it the man with the grizzled whiskers. The torch was between his face and Chang, and the man's attention—naturally—was toward the broken window, in the other direction.

Chang snatched the torch from his astonished grasp and kicked him soundly in the ribs. The man went down with a grunt. Behind, through the door, Chang saw a crowd of Dragoons. He thrust the torch in their faces, driving them back until the handle of the door was in reach. Before they could react he threw the torch into the room, against what he hoped was drapery. He slammed the door shut, turned to the grizzled man, who was rising, and slashed the stick against his head. The man cried out, with shock at the impropriety as much as pain, and raised his arms to block another blow. This allowed Chang to kick him again in the ribs, and shoulder him aside, knocking him off balance and down with another squawk of outrage. Chang bolted past him along the wall. With luck the Dragoons would prevent the house from catching fire before giving chase.

He rounded the corner and kept running. Harschmort was a kind of nearly closed horseshoe, and he was on the far right end. In the center was the garden, and he quickly raced for the depths of its ornamental trees and hedges, putting as much distance as he could between himself and any pursuers. During the day, he was sure the garden gave the impression of being rigid and arid, nature subdued to the strictures of geometry. Now, in his headlong rush to escape, it seemed to Chang a murky labyrinth fabricated solely to provoke collision, as benches, fountains, hedges, and pedestals loomed abruptly up at him through the fog and the night. But if he could elude pursuit here they would be forced to re-group and look for him *everywhere,* which would mean fewer enemies in any single place—it would give him a chance. He stopped in the shadow of boxed shrubbery, pain rising damnably in his lungs like an undeterred creditor. There were bootsteps somewhere behind. He drove himself forward, keeping low, making a point to tread on the grass paths instead of the gravel. It occurred to him that he was even then moving across the great submerged chamber. Could there be any entrance left through the garden? He had no leisure to look—in any case the fog was too thick—and continued to creep across the garden to the opposite wing. That was where he had first met Trapping, where the great ballroom was. If tonight's events were indeed of a more secretive nature, perhaps it would be unoccupied.

The bootsteps were growing unpleasantly closer. Chang listened carefully, waiting, trying to determine how many men there were. Fighting two or three Dragoons with sabers in the open air was suicidal, even without his lungs seething blood. He padded rapidly along a waist-high hedge, bent double, and then across a gravel lane into another ornamental thicket. The few steps on the gravel would draw them like a pack of hounds, and Chang immediately changed direction, angling toward the house and the nearest of the glass garden doors. He reached the cover of another low hedge and listened to the boots converge behind him, gratified that they had not thought to send men around the borders of the garden to trap him from the sides. It was just as he congratulated himself that Chang heard the unmistakable rattle of a scabbard-belt, somewhere *ahead* of him. He swore silently and drew apart his stick—had he been seen? He didn't think so. He took a bead on the man's location . . . near a short conical pine tree . . . Chang crept toward it, quiet as a corpse. He inched around the tree and the back of a red coat came into view.

Whether it was his rasping breath or the smell of the blue crystals that signaled his presence, or merely his own fatigue, Chang knew as soon as his arms shot out for the man that there would be a struggle. His left hand clamped over the Dragoon's mouth and stifled any scream, but his right arm didn't cleanly clear the man's shoulder and so his blade was not at once in position. The man thrashed, his brass helmet falling onto the grass and his saber waving for some kind of purchase. In the next moment Chang pulled him off balance and dug the edge of the dagger into the man's throat . . . but in that same moment he also saw that the man whose life he held in his hands was Reeves.

What did it matter? The 4th Dragoons were his enemies, paid lackeys of the corrupt and wicked. Did he care whether Reeves was merely duped into their service? Chang recalled the man's kindness in the Ministry and knew the answer, just as he knew any alliance with Smythe would crumble to nothing if he started killing Dragoons. All this went through Chang's mind—along with an estimate of where the other Dragoons might be and how much noise he was making—in the time it took to place his mouth next to Reeves's ear.

"Reeves," he whispered, "do not move. Do not speak. I am not your enemy." Reeves stopped struggling. Chang knew there were perhaps seconds before they were found. "It is Chang," he hissed. "You have been lied to. A woman is in the house. They are going to kill her. I am telling you the truth."

He released his hold and stepped away. Reeves turned, his face pale and his hand drifting up to his throat. Chang whispered urgently.

"Is Captain Smythe at Harschmort?"

Their attention was drawn by a sharp noise. Reeves wheeled. Over his shoulder Chang saw the grizzled bald man with the carbine step from the shadow of the hedges, along with a knot of Dragoons. They were well away—some twenty yards distant.

"You there!" the man shouted. "Stand clear!"

The man whipped the carbine to his shoulder and took aim. Reeves turned to Chang, his face a mask of confusion, just as the shot of the carbine echoed across the garden. Reeves arched his body with a hideous spastic clench and jackknifed into Chang, his face twisting with pain. Chang looked up to see the man with the carbine eject the shell and advance another into the chamber. He slammed the bolt home and raised the weapon. Chang dropped Reeves—whose legs kicked feebly, as if their action might yet undo the damage of the bullet—and dove behind the tree.

The next shot carried past him into the night. Chang ran, tearing his way into the hedges, trying to reach the house. He had no illusion it would be any safer, but there would at least be less room for shooting. A third shot rang out, whistling near him and then a fourth, sent he didn't know where... had he slipped them for a moment? He heard the man's voice, barking to the soldiers. He reached the far edge of the garden and stopped, gasping. Between where he crouched and the nearest glass door was an open band of grass perhaps five yards across. He would be entirely visible for the time it took to gain the door and—somehow—force it open. It was a fool's risk. He'd be shot where he stood. He glanced behind him—he could feel the Dragoons getting closer. There had to be another way.

But Chang's mind was blank. He was spent with pain, with fatigue, and with the sudden murder of Reeves. He looked at the glass doors, tensing himself—ridiculously—for a reckless, suicidal dash. They were waiting for him to show himself. Above the glass doors the wall rose two stories of sheer granite before there was an elegant bay window set out over the garden. There was no way to reach it. He imagined the view from that window was delightful. Perhaps it was Lydia Vandaariff's own room. Perhaps it was covered with pillows and silk. She was a lovely young woman, he remembered from his visit to Harschmort. He wondered idly if she was a virgin, and felt a ripple of disgust at the subsequent image of Karl-Horst climbing aboard and crowing like a peacock. The thought brought him instantly, horribly, back to Angelique, the ever-piercing distance between them and his failure to preserve her. He shut his eyes as the final words of DuVine's *Christina* rose to his scattered mind:

What is the pull of a planet to the gravity of care?
What the flow of time to her unfathomable heart?

Chang shrugged off his despair—he was drifting again—and found himself staring at the window. Something was wrong with the reflection. Because of the odd angle of the glass he could see part of the garden behind him . . . and the scraps of fog billowing in the wind. He frowned. There was no wind in the garden that he could feel, or not to cause such billowing. He turned behind him, trying to place the reflected ground. Hope rose in his heart. The wind was coming from *below.*

Chang crept quietly along the edge of the garden, on the bordering band of grass, until he could see the wisps of fog shifting, and stepped in to find a row of four large stone urns, each as tall as himself. Three were topped by the withered stalks of seasonal flowers. The fourth was empty and quite obviously the source of a steady exhalation of warm air. He placed his hands on the rim and went on his toes to peer inside. The hot air was foul and set off the raw flesh in his mouth and lungs. He winced and stepped back—his hands now covered in a pale crust of crystalline powder left by the chemical exhaust. Chang kneeled and pulled out his handkerchief. He tied it tightly across his face, stood again, and took a last glance around the garden. He saw no one—they were still waiting for him to run for the house. Tucking the stick under his arm he hoisted himself up and threw a leg over the lip of the urn. He looked down into it. Just below his boot was a wooden lattice-work across the urn, also covered with chemical accretions, in place to prevent the leaves and twigs from the garden that were trapped against it—and now dusted an icy blue—from blowing into the pipe. Chang leaned down and kicked once, very hard, on the lattice. His foot went through with an audible crack. He kicked again, knocking in the entire thing. Behind him there were sounds from the Dragoons—he had been heard, they were converging on the sound. He dropped completely inside, disappearing from their view, pulling apart the last bits of the lattice with his arms. He slid to the base of the urn, pressing against each side of it with his legs to stop himself from sliding down into the dark hole. He had no idea how far it went, if it was a sheer drop, or if it led into a furnace, but he knew it was better than being shot in the back. He lowered himself into the pipe—the steel sides warm to the touch—until he hung by his hands from the bottom edge of the urn.

Chang let go.

SIX

Quarry

As he stepped from the coach outside the yawning entrance to Stropping Station, Doctor Svenson's attention was elsewhere. During his ride from Plum Court he had allowed his thoughts to drift, spurred by the poignant quality of Miss Temple's reckless pursuit of lost love, to the sorrows and vagaries of his own existence. As he descended the crowded staircase his eyes mechanically scanned the crowds for a diminutive figure with chestnut sausage curls and a green dress, but his mind was awash with a particular astringent quality of Scandinavian reproach he had inherited from a disapproving father. What had he made of his life? What more than unnoticed service to an unworthy Duke and his even less worthy offspring? He was thirty-eight years old. He sighed and stepped onto the main station floor. As always, his regrets were focused on Corinna.

Svenson tried to recall when he had last been to the farm. Three winters? It seemed the only season he could bear to visit. Any other time, when there was life or color in the trees, it reminded him too painfully of her. He had been at sea and returned to find her dead from an epidemic of "blood fever" that had swept the valley. She'd been ill for a month before, but no one had written. He would have left his ship. He would have come and told her everything. Had she known how he felt? He knew she had—but what had been in her heart? She was his cousin. She had never married. He had kissed her once. She'd stared up at him and then broken away... there wasn't a day he did not find a moment to torment himself... not a day for the past seven years. On his last visit there were new tenants (some disagreement with his uncle had driven Corinna's brother off the land and into town) and though they greeted Svenson politely and offered him room when he explained his relation to the family, he found himself devastated by the fact that the people living in her house no longer knew—had no memory of, no celebration in their hearts for—who was buried in the orchard. A profound sense of abandonment took hold of him and he had not, even in the depths of this present business, been able to shake himself free. His home—no matter where he had been—had lain with her, both living and in the ground. He had ridden back to the Palace the next day.

He had since traveled to Venice, to Berne, to Paris, all in the service of Baron von Hoern. He had performed well—well enough to merit further tasks instead of being sent back to a freezing ship—and even saved lives. None of it mattered. His thoughts were full of her.

He sighed again, heavily, and realized that he had no earthly clue where to find Tarr Manor. He walked to the ticket counter and joined one of the lines. The station buzzed with activity like a wasps' nest kicked by a malicious child. The faces around him were marked with impatience, worry, and fatigue, people unified in their desperate rushing to make whichever train they sought, relentlessly flowing in awkward clumps back and forth, like the noisome circulatory system of a great distended creature of myth. He saw no trace of Miss Temple, and the place was so thronged that his only real hope was to find the train she sought and search there. In the time it took to light and smoke the first third of another cigarette, he reached the front of the line. He leaned forward to the clerk and explained he needed to reach Tarr Manor. Without pause the man scribbled a ticket and shot it toward him through the hole in the glass and announced the price. Svenson dug out his money and pushed it through the hole, one coin at a time as he counted. He picked up the ticket, which was marked "Floodmaere, 3:02", and leaned forward again.

"And at which stop do I get off?" he asked.

The clerk looked at him with undisguised contempt. "Tarr *Village,*" he replied.

Svenson decided he could wait to ask the conductor how long the journey would be, and walked onto the station floor, looking around for the proper platform. It was at the other end of the great terminal hall. He looked up at the hideous clock and judged he did not need to run. His ankle was behaving itself, and he had no desire to aggravate it without reason. He made a point to look in the various stalls as he passed—food, books, newspapers, drink—but in none of them saw the slightest sign of Miss Temple. By the time he got to the train itself, it was clear that Floodmaere was not the most illustrious of destinations. There were only two cars attached to a coal wagon and an engine that had certainly seen better days. Svenson looked around once more for any woman in green—for a glimpse of green anywhere—but saw no one. He flicked away his cigarette butt and entered the rear of the train, resigned that his was a fool's errand and that she would be located by Chang. He caught himself. Why the flicker of jealousy, of—he had to admit—peevish possessiveness? Because he'd met her before Chang? But he hadn't—they'd seen each other on the train . . . he shook his head. She was so young . . . and Chang—an absolute rogue—practically feral—not that he or Chang presented any kind of match—not that he even could consider—or in conscience desire . . . it really was too ridiculous.

A greying, unshaven conductor, his face looking as if it had been stippled with paste, snatched Svenson's ticket and brusquely indicated he should walk forward. Svenson did so, reasoning that he could speak to the man later about arrival times, return trips, and other passengers. It would be better to find her himself without drawing attention, if possible. He walked down the aisle of the first car peering into each compartment as he passed. They were empty, save for the rear-most, which held the many members of a family of gypsies, and at least one crate of indeterminate fowl.

He entered the second and last car, which was more crowded, with each compartment occupied, but none by Miss Temple. He stood at the end of the corridor and sighed. It seemed a futile errand—should he get off the train? He went back to the conductor, who watched him approach with a reptilian expression of cold dislike. Svenson screwed in his monocle and smiled politely.

"Excuse me. I am taking this train to Tarr Village, and had hoped to meet an acquaintance. Is it possible they could have taken an earlier train?"

"Of course it's possible," the conductor spat.

"I am not clear. What I mean to ask is when was the last train, the previous train, which my acquaintance might have taken?"

"2:52," he spat again.

"That is but ten minutes before this one."

"I see you're a professor of mathematics."

Svenson smiled patiently. "So another train stopping at Tarr Village left as recently as that?"

"As I have said, yes. Was there anything else?"

Svenson ignored him, weighing his choices. It was possible, if her coach had made good time, that Miss Temple could have caught the 2:52. If that were so, then he needed to follow her on this train, with hope to catch her at the Tarr Village station. But if she hadn't come here at all—if she were still in town—he should go to Roger Bascombe's house, or to the Ministry, to do what he could to help Chang. The conductor watched his indecision with evident pleasure.

"Sir?"

"Yes, thank you. I shall require information about my return tomorrow—"

"Best to get that from the station master himself, I usually find."

"The Tarr Village station master?"

"Exactly so."

"Then that is excellent. Thank you."

Svenson wheeled and strode down the corridor toward the second car, the conductor audibly snorting behind him. He was hardly confident in his choice, but if there was even a chance she'd come this way, he needed to follow. He could ask for her at the station—they would have to notice her—and if she had not appeared, take the next train directly back. At most it would be only a few hours' delay. And at the worst, he would still find Chang at Stropping the next morning—if he was lucky, with Miss Temple on his arm.

He glanced into the first compartment and saw it held a man and a woman, sitting next to each other on one side. As the opposite row of seats was empty, he pulled the door open, nodded to them, and installed himself by the window. He slipped the monocle into his pocket and rubbed his eyes. He had not slept above two hours. His heavy mood was now compounded by the likely pointless nature of his journey, and a vague gloomy disapproval of the reckless danger Miss Temple had thrown herself—indeed, all of them—into without any larger plan or understanding. He wondered when their descriptions would be given to the constabulary. Was this Cabal so confident as to involve the power of the law? He scoffed—for all practical purposes they *were* the law... Crabbé had a regiment at his call, Blach had his troopers... Svenson could only hope that a train to the country would take him free of their immediate influence. The whistle blew and the train began to move.

It took perhaps a minute to clear the station and enter a tunnel. Once they emerged into a narrow trough of soot-stained brick buildings, Svenson availed himself of the opportunity to examine his traveling companions. The woman was young, perhaps even younger than Miss Temple, her hair the color of pale beer, stuffed under a blue silk bonnet. Her skin was white and her cheeks pink—she could have been from Macklenburg—and her slightly plump fingers held a black volume tightly in her lap. He smiled at her. Instead of returning the smile, she whipped her eyes to the man, who in turn gazed at Doctor Svenson with a glaring suspicion. He was also fair—Svenson wondered if they could be siblings—and had the antic, rawboned look of an underfed horse. His arms were long and his hands large, gripping his knees. He wore a brown striped suit and a cream-colored cravat. On the seat next to him he had placed a tall brown beaver hat. Svenson could not help noticing, as the man studied him openly, that the fellow's complexion was poor and there were circles under his eyes—most probably from self-abuse.

As someone who was generally tolerant and at least conversationally kind, it took Doctor Svenson a moment to realize that the pair stared at him with unfeigned hatred. He glanced again at their faces and was confident that he had never before made their acquaintance... could it be merely that his presence interrupted their privacy? Perhaps the fellow had planned to propose? Or perhaps an explanation more *louche*... in Venice he'd once bought a battered volume of lurid stories celebrating the physical pleasures associated with different modes of transport—trains, ships, horse-carts, horseback, dirigibles—and despite his fatigue he was just recalling the particular details of a caravan of camels (something about the unique rhythm of that animal's gait . . .) when the young woman across from him snapped open her book and began to read aloud.

"In the time of redeeming the righteous shall be even as lanterns in the night, for by their light will be told the faithless from the true. Look well into the hearts of those around you and traffic only with the holy, for the cities of the world are realms of living sin, and shall suffer in reclamation the scouring of the Lord. Corrupted vessels shall be smashed. The unclean house will be burned. The tainted beasts will be put to slaughter. Only the blessed, who have already opened themselves to purifying flame, shall survive. It is they who shall re-make the world a Paradise."

She closed the book and, once more holding it tightly with both hands, looked at the Doctor with narrowed disapproving eyes. Her voice, which held all the charm of broken crockery, made it that much easier for him to now see the signs of rigid stupidity in her features, where before he had been willing to assume a neutral bovine placidity. Her companion was gripping his knees even more tightly, as if to release them would be cause for damnation. Svenson sighed—he really could not help himself—but in this mood he could not be fully answerable.

"What a *gratifying* homily," he began. "Yet . . . when you say *Paradise*"—the woman's mouth pursed with shock that he could presume to answer—"would that refer back to the conditions of life *before* the Fall, when shame was unknown and the course of desire without stain? That *would* be exquisite. It has always seemed a cunning part of God's wisdom that he offers to each of us who are saved the innocence and joy of beasts rutting in the road—or, who knows, in a train car. The point, of course, being the *purity* of experience. I thank the Lord each minute of the day. I could not agree with you *more*."

He reached in his pocket for another cigarette. They did not answer, though he noted with some satisfaction their eyes had widened with discomfort. He replaced his monocle and nodded. "I *do* beg your pardon . . ." and made his way to the corridor.

Once there Svenson found a match and lit his cigarette, breathing deeply and attempting to gather his scattered mind after this ridiculous interruption. The train was racing north, the trackside lined with hovels and debris and tattered stunted trees. He could see clustered figures around cooking fires, and ragged children running, followed by excited dogs. Moments later these were gone and the train shot through a luxuriant royal park, then past a small square of white stone monuments that reminded him of France. He exhaled, blowing smoke against the glass, and noted the differences between traveling by land and by sea—the relative density and variety of spectacle one saw on the land versus the sparse nature of even the richest seascape. It was an irony, he noted, that the relative plenty of the land absolved him of thought—he was content to watch it flow by—whereas the sameness of the sea drove him inward. Life on land—though he welcomed it, in some northern sort of self-criticism—struck him as somehow lazy and distracted from the higher goals of ethical scrutiny, of philosophical contemplation that the sea enforced upon a man. The couple in the compartment—apes, really—were a perfect example of land-bound self-satisfaction. His mind drifted painfully to Corinna, and her life in the country—though she had read so voraciously that it seemed to him she carried an ocean in her mind—for they had spoken of this very thing... she had always promised to visit him and sail... Doctor Svenson pushed his thoughts elsewhere, to Miss Temple. He reflected that her own experience of the sea, on an island and on her passage over, must inform the part of her character he found most remarkable.

He forced himself to walk down the corridor, glancing again into the compartments—perhaps there was a more hospitable place for him to sit. The other passengers certainly represented a variety—merchants and their wives, a party of students, laborers, and several better-dressed men and women that Svenson did not recognize, but could not help (for such was the world of Lacquer-Sforza, Xonck, and d'Orkancz) but view with great suspicion. What was more, it seemed that in every compartment there were couples of men and women—sometimes more than one—but never another single traveler, except possibly in one compartment, which held a single man and woman, sitting on opposite sides and apparently not speaking to each other. Svenson crushed his cigarette on the corridor floor and entered their compartment, nodding as each looked up at the sound.

* * *

Both were in the window seats of their respective row, so Doctor Svenson installed himself on the man's side, nearest the door. Upon sitting he was at once markedly aware of his fatigue. He removed his monocle, rubbed his eyes with a forefinger and thumb, and replaced it, blinking like a dazed lizard. The man and woman were looking at him discreetly, not with the hostility of the couple in the first compartment, but rather with the mild civilized rebuke of suspicion that is natural when one's relative solitude on public transport has been disturbed by a stranger. Svenson smiled deferentially and asked, by way of a conversational olive branch, if they were familiar with the Floodmaere line.

"Specifically," he added, "if you might know the distance to Tarr Village, and the number of stops in between."

"You are bound for Tarr Village?" asked the man. He was perhaps thirty and wore a crisp suit of indifferent quality, as if he were clerk to a lawyer of middling importance. His black hair was parted in the center and plastered flat to either side, the rigid grooves from his comb revealing furrows of pale flaking scalp contrasting with the flushed pink of his face. Was it hot in the compartment? Svenson did not think so. He turned to the woman, a lady of perhaps his own age, her brown hair braided into a tight bun behind her head. Her dress was simple but well-made—governess to some high-placed brats?—and she wore her age with a handsome frankness Svenson found immediately compelling. Where were his thoughts? First Corinna, then Miss Temple, the rutting dogs of Paradise, now he was ogling every woman he saw—and the Doctor chided himself for, even within that moment, examining the tightly bound swell of her bosom. And then in that same instant, he looked at the woman and felt a vague prick of recognition. Had he met her before? He cleared his throat and answered briskly.

"Indeed, though I have never been before."

"What draws you there, Mr. . . . ?" The woman smiled politely. Svenson returned the smile with pleasure—he'd no idea where he might have seen her, perhaps in the street, perhaps even just then in the station—and opened his mouth to reply. In that very moment, when he felt it was just possible for his heavy mood to shift, his eyes took in the black leather volume she held in her lap. He glanced at the man. He had one as well, poking out from the side pocket of his coat. Was this a train of Puritans?

"Blach—Captain Blach. You will know from my accent that I am not from this land, but indeed, the Duchy of Macklenburg. You may have read of the Macklenburg Crown Prince's engagement to Miss Lydia Vandaariff—I am attached to Prince Karl-Horst's party."

The man nodded in understanding—the woman did not seem to Svenson to react at all, her face maintaining its friendly cast while her mind seemed to work behind it. What could *that* mean? What might either of them know? Doctor Svenson decided to investigate. He leaned forward conspiratorially and dropped his voice.

"And what draws me are dire events . . . dire events in the world—I'm sure I have no need to elaborate. The cities of the world . . . well, they are realms of living sin. Who indeed shall be redeemed?"

"Who indeed?" echoed the woman quietly, with a certain deliberate care.

"I was traveling with a woman," Svenson went on. "I was prevented—perhaps I should say no more about her—from meeting this lady. I believe she may have been forced to take an earlier train. In the process, I was deprived of my"—he nodded to the book in the woman's lap—"that is, my *guide*."

Was this too thick? Doctor Svenson felt ridiculous, but was met by the man shifting his position to face him fully, leaning forward in earnest concern.

"Prevented how? And by whom?"

This type of intrigue—play-acting and lies—was still awkward for Doctor Svenson. Even in his work for Baron von Hoern, he preferred discretion and leverage and tact over any outright dissembling. Yet, faced with the man's open desire for more information, he had—as a doctor—enough experience with conjuring credible authority when he felt helpless and ignorant (how many doomed men had asked him if they were going to die? To how many had he lied?) to frame his immediate hesitation—trying to think of *something*—as the troubled moment of choice where he *decided* to trust them with his tale. He glanced at the corridor and then leaned forward in his turn, as if to imply that perhaps their compartment alone was safe, and spoke just above a whisper.

"You must know that several men have died, and perhaps a woman. A league has been organized, working in the shadows, led by a strange man in red, a half-blind Chinaman, deadly with a blade. The Prince was attacked at the Royal Institute, the powerful work there disrupted . . . the glass . . . do you know . . . have you seen . . . the blue glass?"

They shook their heads. Svenson's heart sank. Had he completely misjudged them?

"You do know of Lord Tarr . . . that he—"

The man nodded vigorously. "Has been redeemed, yes."

"Exactly." Svenson nodded, more confident again—but was the man insane? "There will be a new Lord Tarr within days. The nephew. He is a friend of the Prince . . . a friend to us all—"

"Who prevented you from meeting your lady?" the woman asked, somewhat insistently. The nagging sense he had seen her persisted . . . something about the slight tilt of her head when she asked a question.

"Agents of the Chinaman," Svenson answered, feeling an idiot even as he said the words. "We were forced to take separate coaches. I pray she is safe. These men have no decency. We were—as you well know—to travel together—as arranged . . ."

"To Tarr Village?" asked the man.

"Exactly."

"Could any of these agents have boarded the train?" the woman asked.

"I do not believe so. I did not see them—I believe I was the last to board."

"That is good at least." She sighed with a certain small relief, but did not relax her shoulders, nor her cautious gaze.

"How should we know these agents?" asked the man.

"That is just the thing—they have no uniform, save duplicity and cunning. They have penetrated even to the Prince's party and turned one of our number to their cause—Doctor Svenson, the Prince's own physician!"

The man inhaled through his teeth, a disapproving hiss.

"I am telling you," Svenson went on, "but I fear no one else should know—it may be all is fine, and I should hesitate to agitate—or, that is, make public—"

"Of course not," she agreed.

"Not even to . . . ?" the man began.

"Who?" asked Svenson.

The man shook his head. "No, you are right. We have been invited—we are guests, after all, guests to a *banquet*." With this he smiled again, shaking off the Doctor's tale of dread. His hand went to the book in his pocket and patted it absently, as if it were a sleeping puppy. "You look very tired, you know, Captain Blach," he said kindly. "There will be time enough to find your friend. Tarr Village is at least another hour and a half away. Why not rest? We will all need our strength for the *climb*."

Svenson wondered what he meant—the quarry? The hills? Could it mean the manor house? Svenson could not say, and he was exhausted. He needed to sleep. Was he safe with them? The woman interrupted his thoughts.

"What is your lady's name, Captain?"

"Beg pardon?"

"Your friend. You did not say her name."

Svenson caught a worried glance from the man to the woman, though her face remained open and friendly. Something was wrong.

"Her name?"

"You did not say what it was."

"No, you didn't," confirmed the man, somewhat after the fact and a touch more insistent for it, as if he'd been caught out.

"Ah. But you see . . . I do not know it. I only know her clothes—a green dress with green shoes. We were to meet and travel together. Why . . . did you know each other's name before this journey?"

She did not immediately answer. When the man answered for her, he knew he had guessed correctly. "We do not know each other's names even now, Captain, as we were indeed instructed."

"Now you really should rest," the woman said, genuinely smiling for perhaps the first time. "I promise we will wake you."

Within his dream, a part of Doctor Svenson's mind was aware that he'd not had a regular stretch of sleep in at least two days, and so expected turbulent visions. This sliver of rational distance might contradict but did not alter the successive waves of vivid engagement thrust upon him. He knew the visions were fed by his feelings of loss and isolation—more than anything by his helplessness in the face of Corinna's death and then his own chronic reticence and cowardice in life—and then all of this regret swirling together with a world of cruelly unquenched desire for other women. Was it merely that, so exhausted, even in sleep, his guard was so much lowered? Or was it, could he admit, that his feelings of guilt provoked in turn a secret pleasure in the act of dreaming with such erotic fervor in an open train compartment? What he knew was the deep warm embrace of sleep, twisting effortlessly in his mind into the embrace of pale soft arms and sweet caressing fingers. He felt as if his body were refracted in a jewel, seeing—and feeling—multiple instances of himself in hopelessly delicious circumstances... Mrs. Marchmoor stroking him under a table... Miss Poole with her tongue in his ear... his nose buried in Rosamonde's hair, inhaling her perfume... on his hands and knees on the bed, licking each circular indentation on the luscious flesh of the bed-ridden Angelique... his hands—O shamefully!—cupping Miss Temple's buttocks beneath her dress... his eyes closed, nursing tenderly, hungrily, at the bared breast of the brown-haired governess, who had moved to sit next to him, to ease his torment, offering herself to his lips... the incomparably soft sweet pillow of flesh... her other hand stroking his hair... whispering to him gently... shaking his shoulder.

He snapped awake. She was sitting next to him. She was shaking his arm. He sat up, painfully aware of his arousal, thankful for his greatcoat, his hair in his eyes. The man was gone.

"We are near Tarr Village, Captain," she said, smiling. "I am sorry to wake you."

"No, no—thank you—of course—"

"You were sleeping very soundly—I'm afraid I had to shake your arm."

"I am sorry—"

"There is no reason to be sorry. You must have been tired."

He noticed that the top button of her dress was now undone. He felt a smear of drool on his lip and wiped it with his sleeve. What had happened? He nodded at where the man had been.

"Your companion—"

"He has gone to the front of the train. I am about to join him, but wanted to make sure you were awake. You were... in your dream, you were speaking."

"Was I? I do not recall—I seldom recall any dream—"

"You said 'Corinna'."

"Did I?"

"You did. Who is she?"

Doctor Svenson forced a puzzled frown and shook his head. "I've no idea. Honestly—it's most strange." She looked down at him, her open expression, along with the insistent pressure in his trousers, inspiring him to speak further. "You have not told me your name."

"No." She hesitated for just a moment. "It is Elöise."

"You're a governess, for the children of some Lord."

She laughed. "Not a Lord. And not a governess either. Perhaps more a *confidante,* and for my salary a tutor, in French, Latin, music, and mathematics."

"I see."

"I do not begin to know how you could have guessed. Perhaps it is your military training—I know that officers must learn to read their men like books!" She smiled. "But I do not mind my pupils all the day. They have another lady for that—*she* is their proper governess, and enjoys children much more than I."

Svenson had no reply, for the moment happy enough to look into her eyes. She smiled at him and then stood. He struggled to stand with her, but she put a hand on his shoulder to dissuade him. "I must get to the front of the train before we arrive. But perhaps we shall see each other in the Village."

"I should like that," he said.

"So should I. I do hope you find your lady friend."

In that moment Doctor Svenson knew where he had seen her, and why he could not place her face, for this Elöise had worn a mask—leaning forward to whisper into the ear of Charlotte Trapping at Harschmort, the night Colonel Trapping had been killed.

Then she was gone, and the compartment door latched shut behind her. Svenson sat up and rubbed his face, and then, with self-conscious reproach, adjusted his trousers. He stood, shrugging his coat more comfortably onto his shoulders, the weight of the pistol in the pocket, and exhaled. He worked to reconcile the instinctive warmth he felt toward the woman with the knowledge that she had been amongst his enemies at Harschmort, and was now here on the train, unquestionably in the service of them still. He did not want to believe that Elöise was aware of the dark forces at work and yet how could it be otherwise? They all had a black book, and responded easily to his spun story . . . and it was *she* who had worked to make sure of him, asking questions . . . and yet . . . he thought of her role in his dream with simultaneous spasms of sympathy and discomfort. With another breath he pushed her from his mind entirely. Whatever the purpose of the other passengers' pilgrimage to Tarr Village, Doctor Svenson's only goal was to find Miss Temple before any further mischance. If the station agent had not seen her, then he would return at once—wherever she was, she would need his help.

He stepped to the window, looking out on the passing landscape of county Floodmaere: low scrubby woods clinging to worn rolling hills, with here and there between them a stretch of meadow and, breaking through like damaged teeth, crags of reddish stone. Doctor Svenson had seen such stone before, in the hills near his home, and knew it meant iron ore. He recalled the taste of it in the winter snow-melt, ruddying the water as it flowed down the valley. No wonder there was mining here. He was amused to notice the clear sky—he'd spent so many days in the clouds and fog that he could not remember when he'd last seen it so open—smiling that it must be nearing five o'clock, for the sun was already going down, as if he were journeying to a blue sky merely to be denied it. At least—as opposed to earlier in the day—he could laugh at the irony. Beneath his feet, the train's momentum shifted, and he felt it slow. They were arriving. He dug out another cigarette—how many did he have left?—and stuck it in his mouth, lit it and shook out the match, dreading a return journey without tobacco. The train came to a stop. He'd have to find some other brand in the village.

By the time he stepped onto the platform, the party of couples was well ahead of him, walking toward the station house. As near as he could figure—save perhaps for the gypsies—the train had emptied. He did not see Elöise or the clerk she was apparently paired with, though he did spy the hateful couple from his first compartment. The young blonde woman turned back, saw him, and tugged on the arm of her companion, who turned as well. They quickened their pace, her plump bottom moving in a way that Svenson might have normally—surreptitiously—enjoyed but now made him only want to thrash it. He let them all go ahead, through the wooden archway of the station and out into the Village proper, while he stepped into the small station house. There were perhaps three waiting benches, all empty, and a cold metal stove. He walked over to the ticket counter, but found the window shuttered. He knocked on it and called out. There was no answer. At the end of the counter was a door. He knocked on it as well, again received no answer, and then tried the handle, which was locked. If Miss Temple had been here, which he doubted, she was not here now.

On the wall was a blackboard with a painted grid of train departures and arrivals. The next return train was, he was exasperated to read, at eight o'clock the next morning. Svenson sighed with annoyance. He would be wasting hours and hours of time—who knew where she was, and what help he might have offered to Chang had he stayed with him. He looked around the room, as if by remaining there he might find some reprieve, but Doctor Svenson had to accept that his only real recourse was to walk into the Village and find a room for the night. Perhaps he should catch up to Elöise and her mysterious party, all with their black books. Were they Bibles? He had no idea what else they could be, especially with the hectoring specter of redemption and sin, but who could take such a thing seriously? He felt sure the answer was more insidious and complicated . . . or did he merely prefer to associate Elöise with villains rather than with fanatics?

He walked from the station onto the road. By now, the others were gone from his view. The road was lined on either side with an overgrown tangle of black briar, the hard thorns casting wicked shadows onto the road. Shadows? There was a rising moon, and Svenson looked up at it with pleasure. Above the briars, in the distance, he could see the thatched rooftops of Tarr Village. He walked toward them with a brisk purpose, and it was only another minute before the road opened up onto a small square with a common green in the center and a cobbled lane running around it. On the far side was a church with a white steeple, but—happily—the building nearest to him announced itself by a hanging wooden sign, painted with a picture of a crow wearing a silver crown.

Svenson stopped at the door, one foot on the step, and looked around the square. There were lights here and there in the buildings he could see, but no people in the street, nor any sound in the air. If there had been visible sentries, Tarr Village would have reminded him of nothing more than a military camp after nightfall. He went into the tavern.

As a foreigner, Doctor Svenson knew he was no knowledgeable judge, but the King Crow struck him as a decidedly odd village pub, adding—with the excessively orderly nature of the town itself and the apocalyptic halo of the party from the train—to his growing suspicion that Tarr Village might in fact be one of those *communities,* purposely organized around religious or moral principles (but what was the doctrine, and who its charismatic—or stern—leader?). For one, the King Crow did not smell like a tavern at all, of beer and smoke and the sour pungence of sweat and human grease. Indeed, the air was all soap and vinegar and wax, and the main room scrubbed and sparse as the bare, clean insides of a ship, with the walls whitewashed and a fire in its modest hearth. For another, the only two occupants were wearing crisp black suits with high white shirt collars and black traveling cloaks. Each man stood near the fire with a glass of red wine, not even, or no longer, speaking to each other, but obviously waiting for some word, or someone. Both turned swiftly at his entrance.

One cleared his throat and spoke. "Excuse me. Are you just arrived . . . on the 3:02 train?"

Svenson nodded politely, his face impassive. "I am."

They were examining him, or waiting for him to speak . . . so, he did not.

"That is a Macklenburg uniform coat, if I am not mistaken?" asked the other man.

"It is."

One whispered into the other's ear. The listener nodded. They continued to look at him, as if they could not come to a decision. Svenson turned his gaze to the bar, behind which a porcine fellow in a spotless white shirt stood silently.

"I require a room for the night," Svenson told him. "Do you have any?"

The man looked at his two customers—whether to receive instruction or to simply see if they needed anything before he left, Svenson could not say—and then walked out around the bar, wiping his hands. He continued past Svenson, muttering, "This way..."

Svenson looked once more to the two men by the fire, and turned to follow the innkeeper's heavy steps up the stairs.

The room was simple, the price fair. After a moment of looking at it—a narrow bed, a stand with a basin, a hard chair, a mirror—Svenson said it would do well and asked where he might find some food. Once more, the man muttered, "This way..." and led him back down to the fire. The other two were still there—it could only have been two minutes—and continued to watch him as he removed his greatcoat and sat at the small table his host indicated before disappearing through a door behind the bar, into what Svenson assumed was the kitchen. That there was no discussion of what the food might be did not trouble him. He was used to traveling in the country and doing with what he could find. But when had he last eaten—tea at the Boniface with Miss Temple and Chang? And before that? His bread and sausage the night before... two sparse meals in as many days. It was no way to manage an adventure.

The two men were still studying him, now with the barest pretense of manners.

"Was there something you wanted to say?" he asked.

They shuffled and muttered and cleared their throats to no great purpose. It was his turn to stare at them, so he did. Beyond the room he could hear gratifying noises of pots and crockery. Fortified by the mere prospect of a meal, Svenson spoke again.

"I take it you are here to meet a traveler from the 3:02 train from Stropping Station. I also take it that you do not know the traveler you are meeting. Thus, I take your habit of studying my person as if I were a zoo animal to be not so much a personal affront as an admission of your own foolish predicament. Or—you must tell me, please—am I in error? Is there an offense that, as gentlemen"—he lowered his voice meaningfully—"we need to settle out-of-doors?"

Svenson was not normally given to such arrogant posturing, but he felt sure that the two were not men of violence—that indeed, they were educated and accustomed to clean cuffs and uncalloused hands... rather like himself, actually. Perhaps Chang was rubbing off on him. After a moment the one who had spoken first, who was taller and with a sharper nose, held up his open palm.

"We are sorry to have disturbed you—it was never our intent. It is merely that such a uniform—and accent—is understandably rare around these parts—"

"You are *from* these parts?" asked Svenson. "I would find that a surprise. I would think it much more likely that you came today on the train—on the 2:52 train, though I suppose you could have come earlier. The person you now seek was supposed to travel with you, but did not appear. You then hoped he would appear on the next train. That you at all entertained the possibility it might be me confirms, as I say, that you have never met this person. One cannot help wondering if the purpose of the meeting is entirely savory."

At this, the door to the kitchen banged open and their host appeared carrying a wooden platter with both hands, loaded with several plates—roasted meat, thick bread, steaming boiled potatoes, a pot of gravy, and a plate of buttered mashed turnips. He laid it down on Svenson's table, his hand then drifting half-heartedly toward the bar.

"Drink..." he muttered.

"A mug of beer, if you will."

"He does not have beer," announced the second man, whose hair was receding and brushed hopefully forward in the old Imperial fashion.

"Wine then," said Svenson. The innkeeper nodded and stepped behind the bar. Doctor Svenson returned to the two men. He breathed in the smells of the food before him, feeling the intensity of his hunger. "You have not answered my... hypothesis," he said.

The two men exchanged one quick look, set their wineglasses on the hearth, and strode abruptly from the King Crow without another word.

The clock in the entryway of the King Crow chimed seven. Doctor Svenson lit the first of his remaining cigarettes, inhaled deeply, and then slowly blew smoke across the remains of his meal. He swirled the contents and tossed off the last of his second glass of wine—a meaty, country claret—then set down his glass and stood. The innkeeper was behind the bar, reading a book. Svenson shrugged on his greatcoat and called to the man.

"I should like to take a walk across the green. Will there be any difficulty getting back inside? When do you retire?"

"Doors are not locked in Tarr Village," the man replied, and went back to his book. Svenson saw he was to get no further communication, and walked to the front door.

Outside, the night was clear and cool, with bright moonlight casting a pale, silvered sheen over the grassy common, as if it had just rained. Across the square, he could see light through the windows of the church. No other building seemed to be so occupied, again as if an order had been given to extinguish all candles by a particular hour. In possible confirmation, the light vanished behind him in the windows of the King Crow, its proprietor closing down for the night. It could not be much past seven! When did these villagers wake—before dawn? Perhaps the puritanical nature of the train party was not so out of place after all—perhaps his recent time in the sin-filled city (he could hardly deny it was so) had overly influenced his skeptical views. Svenson set off across the grass toward the church, to see if he could discover what kept these particular people awake.

In the center of the common was a very large, old oak tree, and Svenson made a point of walking beneath it and looking up at the moon through its enormous, tangled network of leafless branches, just to torment himself with the subsequent whiff of vertigo. As he turned down to his boots to steady himself, he heard across the square the unmistakable sound of a horse-drawn coach rattling into Tarr Village. It was small and efficient, drawn by two black horses and driven by a well-wrapped coachman who reined the horses directly in front of the King Crow. Svenson knew instantly this was the party, arriving late, who was to meet the two men. The coachman went to the door, knocked, waited, knocked again much more loudly, and several minutes later—receiving no response—returned to the coach. Svenson could not but admire the pugnacious reticence on the part of the innkeeper. After another word with his master, the coachman climbed back into place. With a sharp whistle and a snap of the reins the coach pulled forward along the square and then disappeared into the heart of the village. Soon it had passed beyond Svenson's hearing, and in the re-gathering of the night's quiet it was as if the coach had never been.

In construction, the church in Tarr Village was quite plain: white-painted wood with a boxy steeple in the rear more like a watchtower than a pinnacle rising to heaven. The front of the church was more of a mystery. The double doors were closed, but they were also, he realized as he neared them, bolted shut with a heavy chain wound through each handle and held fast with a blockish padlock. Svenson ambled onto the cobbled lane and looked up at the doorway. He saw no one, and walked quietly up the three stone steps and put his ear to the door. Something . . . a sound that, the more he took it in, set his nerves on edge . . . a low, undulating sort of buzz. Was it chanting? A queer, dyspeptic drone from a pipe organ? He stepped back again, got no other clue from anything he could see. The church was bordered by an open lot, so he walked quietly through untended grass that rose above his ankles and, with the evening dew, wetted his boots. A row of tall windows ran along the side of the church. The glass bore the knotted surface of elaborate leaded detail, without any particular colors to make plain the illustration. It made him wonder if the images were merely decoration—a geometrical pattern, say—as in a mosque, where any depiction of a man or woman, much less the Prophet, would be a blasphemy. Looking up, all he could see was a dim glow from within—there was *some* kind of light, but nothing more than a modest lantern or small collection of candles. Suddenly, Svenson saw a blue flash like a bolt of azure lightning snap out of the windows. Just as instantly it was gone. There was no accompanying sound, and no sound of reaction from within . . . had he truly seen it? He had. He raced to the back of the church, for another door, rounded the corner—

"Captain Blach!"

It was the man from the train, Elöise's ostensible partner, the lawyer's clerk. He stood in the open rear door of the church, in one hand a lit cigarette and in the other—incongruously—a heavy cast iron wrench, for use on only the most unwieldy of machines. Before Svenson could speak, the man stuck the cigarette between his lips and offered the Doctor his hand.

"You arrived after all—I was worried you would not. Did you ever find your lady friend?"

"I'm afraid I did not—"

"Not to worry—I'm sure she went ahead to the house with the others."

"The light." Svenson gestured behind him to the windows. "A blue flash, just moments ago—"

"Yes!" The man's eyes lit up. "Isn't it splendid? You really are just in time!"

He took another drag on his cigarette, dropped it to the stone porch and ground it beneath his shoe. Svenson's gaze went to the wrench—it was perhaps as long as the man's forearm. The man noticed his look and chuckled, hefting the hunk of iron as if it were a prize. "They are letting us help with the works, you see—it really is just as engaging as I hoped! Come, everyone will be delighted to see you!"

He turned and went into the church, holding the door open for Svenson to follow. The blue flash made him think of d'Orkancz and the Institute. He'd given this man a false name—but any member of the Cabal, if present, would know him instantly. Further—his mind raced, gesturing for the man to go first, and closing the door behind them—were the women at Tarr Manor? What other house could be meant? If that was so, there was no hiding the connection of this group—the black books, the Puritan brimstone—with Bascombe and his Cabal. But—he must decide, he must do something (even then the man was leading him into a dressing vestibule hung with church robes). Lord Tarr had been killed to gain control of the quarry and the deposits of indigo clay. What did that have to do with this religious nonsense? And what religious ceremony involved that size of... wrench?

The man abruptly stopped, one hand on Doctor Svenson's chest, the other—with the wrench, which could not but look foolish—held over his mouth to indicate silence. He nodded ahead of them at an open door, and then stepped quietly ahead until they could see into the next room. Svenson followed, apprehensive and curious in equal measure, craning his head over the man's shoulder.

They were to the side of the altar, looking past it into the nave of the church, where the pews had been pushed away and stacked against either side wall. In the center of the open floor was an impromptu table made of stacked wooden boxes . . . boxes like those Chang described from the Institute, or that Colonel Aspiche's men had taken away in carts that morning. Atop the table was a . . . machine—an interlocking conglomeration of metal parts sticking out of a central casket not unlike a visored medieval helmet, and trailing bright twists of copper wire that ran into an open box on the floor (which Svenson could not see into). The air was sharp with that same mechanical smell—ozone, cordite, burnt rubber, oil—that he'd known on the bodies of Trapping and Angelique and the man in Crabbé's kitchen, only now so intense that his nostrils wrinkled in protest, even from this far away. Around the machine, in a circle, was a collection of men—the same mix of classes and types he'd seen on the train, including the tall horse-ish fellow from his first compartment. Most had taken off their coats and rolled up their sleeves, some held tools, some oily rags, some merely rested their hands on their hips with satisfaction, and all of them gazed lovingly at the machine between them. At the circle's head was another man, in an unkempt but elegantly cut black coat, his streaked hair pushed back behind his ears, his sharp face dominated by a pair of dark goggles, and his hands magnified—like a giant's—by a pair of padded leather gauntlets that went up to his elbows. It was Doctor Lorenz.

Svenson stepped away from the door. His companion felt him move and turned with a look of concern. Svenson held up his hand and began to silently gag, motioning that there was some trouble with his breathing, with his throat—he took another step back and waved the man forward, as if this would only take a moment, he would be right with him. Instead of going ahead, the man stepped after him—forcing Svenson to gag still more theatrically—and then to the Doctor's dismay turned to the room, as if to call for help. Svenson took hold of the man's arm and tugged him along back toward the rear door of the church. They reached the far side of the dressing room before Svenson allowed himself to audibly cough and gag.

"Captain Blach, are you all right? Are you unwell? I'm sure Doctor Lorenz—"

Svenson charged through the rear door and bent over on the paved portico, hands on his knees, sucking in great gasps of air. The man followed him outside, clucking with concern. Svenson could not go in. Lorenz would know him. And now, whatever else happened, this man was sure to mention him—perhaps he had already?—in such a way that would leave little mystery to those who already marked him as an enemy. He felt a comforting hand on his back and tilted up his head.

"I hope we are not disturbing them," Svenson rasped.

"O no," the man answered. "I'm sure they did not even know we were there—"

As he had hoped, the man instinctively turned his head toward the door as he spoke. Svenson stood up swiftly, the butt of the pistol in his right hand, and brought it down hard behind the man's ear. The man grunted with surprise and staggered into the doorframe. Svenson hesitated—he did not want to hit him again. He was no judge on giving blows to the head, though he knew well enough they could kill. The man groaned and tried to stand, wobbling. Svenson cursed and struck him once more, feeling the sickening thud of impact through his entire arm. The man went down in a heap. Svenson quickly stowed the pistol and dragged him into the church. He listened—he heard nothing from within—and quietly snatched several of the robes from the inner room. He spread these over the body, leaving him in a sitting position behind the propped-open door, so he was quite hidden to any casual eye. Doctor Svenson felt the back of the man's head. It was swollen, pulpy, but he did not think there was a fracture—though he could hardly tell for sure, leaning over the fellow in the dark. The man was alive—he told himself perhaps that was enough, though it did not ease his guilt. Svenson picked up the wrench. He then rolled his eyes at his own forgetfulness and knelt again, digging through the layers of robe, and came up with the man's black book. He stuffed this into his greatcoat and crept again to the inner doorway. The buzzing sound had returned.

The machine vibrated on the table top with an escalating whine that seemed—by the reactions of the men around it—to indicate that it was nearing the successful achievement of whatever process it performed. Lorenz held a pocket watch in his hand, his other hand raised, with the men around him alertly poised for his signal. To Svenson, it looked like nothing more than a group of overgrown boys waiting for their schoolmaster's permission to start a scrimmage. The machine kicked, shaking the boxes beneath it with a dangerous rattle. Was it going to explode?

Lorenz had not moved. The men were still clustered close around. At once the scientist dropped his arm and the men leapt to the machine, holding it firmly in place. The restraint seemed to drive the machine's energy inward, and Svenson could detect first thin plumes of smoke and then a rising glow. He saw that the men had all screwed their eyes shut and faced away from the machine and, realizing what this meant just before it happened, Svenson spun from the door, his back to the wall, eyes shut. A bright blue flash erupted from the other room that he could feel through his eyelids, seeing a floating after-flash in the air without even having opened them. He placed a hand over his mouth and nose—the smell was intolerable. He could hear the men in the other room choking and laughing in equal measure, congratulating themselves. He rolled his head back to the door, risking a peek.

Lorenz bent over the machine. He'd pulled back a metal plate on a hinge, like the cover of a stove, and was reaching inside with his heavily gloved hand, into a bright blue light that washed all color from his already pallid face. The attention of the men was fixed on Lorenz's hand as it penetrated the open chamber and then returned with a ball of pulsing blue (stone? glass?) in his palm. He held it up for them all to see and the men erupted with a ragged, exuberant cheer. The faces of the men were flushed and crazed. The chemical smell had Svenson feeling light-headed already, he could just imagine what it was doing to all of them. Lorenz flipped back his cloak. Slung across his chest he bore a heavy leather bandolier, from which hung many capped metal flasks, like the powder charges of an old musketeer. He carefully unscrewed one of the flasks and then squeezed—as if it was glowing, malleable clay—the ball in his hand into the narrow flask opening. When it was completely in, he replaced the cap and with a small flourish flipped his cloak back into place.

Doctor Lorenz looked up at the men around him and asked, with an even-toned curiosity, "Where is Mr. Coates?"

Svenson wheeled from sight, his back against the wall. In two long silent strides he was through the dressing room and then, now running, out of the church entirely. He crossed the empty lot and ducked behind the next building, back to the cobbled road and across it onto the common. He did not stop until he had reached the trunk of the oak tree, running low and as quietly as he could, where he knelt and finally looked back, his heart pounding. There were men standing in the grassy lot, and one who had walked as far as the front of the church, looking across its steps and onto the common. Svenson ducked back. Had they seen him running? With any luck, their discovery of the unfortunate Coates slowed any pursuit long enough for him to make his way. Of course, given the high spirits of the group, it could just as well fire them up for immediate vengeance. Would Coates revive? What could he tell them? Svenson dared not risk running across the open ground to the King Crow. He glanced above him. Any other man might cleverly climb the tree and rest undetected. Svenson shuddered. He was not Cardinal Chang.

The man in front of the church gave another long look to the grassy common and then retreated back to the rear door, collecting the men in the lot on his way. Svenson heard the rear door close. Now was the time for him to dash to cover, but he remained behind his tree, watching. It was another fifteen minutes of gnawing cold before the door opened again, and a line of men emerged, carrying the boxes between them. Last of all came Lorenz, no longer with the gauntlets and goggles, holding his cloak closely about him. The line vanished from Svenson's view, along the same road the coach had followed earlier. He could only assume it went to Tarr Manor.

Svenson gave them another two minutes before leaving the oak tree and walking back to the church. He had no idea what he thought to find, but anything was better than another ignorant walk in the dark. Coates was no longer in the corner where he placed him—hopefully he'd been able to walk away upon being revived—and Svenson picked his way through the dressing room into the darkened church. Moonlight still poured in through the windows, but without the machine's blue glow the room had a different feel, more mournful and abandoned—though the pews had been hastily restored to their places. Svenson glanced over to the altar, which had acquired a peculiar shadow beneath it. He looked at the windows but did not see what could be blocking the light—some kind of smudge or deposit on the glass—soot from the machine? He crossed to the altar itself and saw his mistake. The shadow was a pool. Svenson pulled back the white cloth and saw, beneath it, the crumpled figure of Mr. Coates, whose throat had been quite cleanly cut.

Svenson bit his lip. He dropped the cloth and turned, reaching into his pocket for the service revolver. He checked the cartridges and the hammer, spun the chamber, and stuffed it away. He looked around him with a rising urge to kick over the pews and forced himself to breathe evenly. He could do nothing for Coates except remember him as affable and attentive. He walked out of the church and made for the road.

Because the line of men carried the boxes of machinery, Svenson half-thought he might overtake them—or at least come within sight—on the way, but he had walked a mile on the country road, briar hedges to his left and barren winter fields to his right, without doing so. At the mile marker the road forked, and he stood under the moonlight trying to decide. There was no delineating sign, and each road seemed equally traveled. Looking ahead, the left fork sloped up a gentle rise, which made him recall Coates's reference to a climb. With nothing else to go on, Svenson turned his steps that way.

At the top, he saw that the road dipped and then continued to rise in a gentle winding path around an escalating series of scrubbish hills. As he crested each new height, the Doctor saw his destination more clearly, and by the time he faced it directly—still without trace of the men—he could see an estate house of such size that it must be Tarr Manor: orchards in the surrounding fields, a tall windbreak of leafless poplars, and fronted by an old-fashioned stone fence and high iron gate. The outbuildings were few and small, and the house itself, though nothing compared to a monstrosity like Harschmort, was a great, crenellated cube bristling with gables and pipes and brickwork, more than half smothered in ivy whose leaves looked to Svenson, under the insidious moonlight, like the scales of a reptile's skin.

The ground-floor windows of the house were blazing with light. With a prick to his curiosity, the Doctor saw that the only other so lit was a gable window in the highest attic, which made, as he counted the windows, four completely dark stories in between. He approached the gate with caution—being shot for trespassing would be a particularly stupid way to die—and found it chained. He called out to the small guard's hut on the other side of the wall, but received no answer. He looked up—the gate was very high—and shuddered at the prospect of climbing. He preferred to find another, less egregious point of entry, and remembered from Bascombe's blue glass card an image near an orchard, of a crumbled wall that, could he find it, would be simple to scramble over. He set off around the side, tramping through the high, dry grass drifting—from the wind, he supposed—up against the stone—like sand.

Svenson tried to form a plan of action, a task at which he never felt particularly skilled. He enjoyed studying evidence and drawing conclusions, even confronting those he had managed to entrap with facts, but all of this activity—running through houses, climbing drainage pipes, rooftops, *shooting,* being shot *at*... it was not his *métier.* He knew his approach to Tarr Manor ought to be an order of battle—he tried to imagine Chang's choices, but this didn't help at all: it only spelled out the degree to which he found Chang utterly mysterious. Svenson's trouble was contingency. He was searching for several things at once, and depending on what he found, all of his goals would shift. He hoped to find Miss Temple, though he did not think he would. He hoped to find the women from the train, which was also to say that he wanted to know if Elöise was corrupt as he feared, or perhaps a duped innocent like Coates. He hoped to find some information about Bascombe and the previous Lord Tarr. He hoped to find the true nature of the work at the quarry. He hoped to find the truth behind Lorenz and his machinery, and what it had to do with these men from the city. He hoped to find who was in the coach and thus more about the two men who had journeyed from the city themselves to meet it. But all these goals were a jumble in his head, and all he could think to do was to enter the house and skulk about with as much secrecy as possible—and what, his stern skeptical logic demanded, would he do if he found someone from the Cabal who could name him directly, aside from Lorenz? What if he were to be brought before the Contessa, or the Comte d'Orkancz? He stopped and sighed heavily, a dry pinch in his throat. He had no idea what he would do at all.

When he found the crumbled gap in the wall, Svenson peered over it first to make sure the path was safe. He was much closer to the house here—it seemed that there were only a few small fruit trees and fallow garden beds between him and the nearest windows. He recalled the newspaper report of Lord Tarr's death—had he not been discovered in his garden?

Svenson heaved his body up and over the wall, scraping his hands just a little, and dropped onto grass. The nearest windows were actually dark; perhaps this was the old Lord's study, which no one was presently using (did that mean Bascombe was not in residence?). Svenson padded quietly across, stepping on the grass to avoid boot prints in the earthen beds. He reached the windows; the inner two were actually a pair of French doors—from the wall he had not seen the stairs that rose from the garden to meet them. Svenson leaned forward and adjusted his monocle. One of the doors was broken, a whole pane of glass missing near the handle. He looked on the steps below him and found no glass—of course, it would have been cleaned up—but then turned again to the missing pane. Around the wooden frame small flicks of wood had broken away. If he read the signs correctly, the blow had come from within, punching the glass outward. Even if Svenson credited that it was an animal that slew the old Lord (which he did not)—and why should an animal break open the door in such a way to reach through to the lock?—he would expect the assailant to come from outside. If he were already on the inside, why break the door at all? Could perhaps Lord Tarr have broken it himself, in his hurry to escape? But that only made sense if the door had been locked from the *outside*... if Lord Tarr had been confined to his room...

The door was locked now, from the inside, and Svenson reached in carefully and opened it. He stepped into the darkened room and closed the glass door behind him. In the moonlight he could see a desk and long walls completely fitted with bookshelves. He fumbled a match from his pocket, struck it on his nail and located a candle in an old copper holder on a side bookshelf. With this much light, he carefully went through each drawer of the desk, but at the end all he knew was that Lord Tarr had a keen interest in medicine, and next to none in his estate. For the single ledger—completely written in what Svenson assumed was his overseer's hand—detailing Lord Tarr's business, there were many, many notebooks and banded stacks of receipts from different physicians. Svenson had seen this enough before to realize that the Lord's own ebbing health had been itself a pursuit of pleasure beyond any particular restorative or cure—indeed, the man seemed to record the failures with as much satisfaction in his journal. This was a neat volume Svenson had found in the top drawer, under another larger ledger of receipts for potions and procedures. He flipped through it idly, just ready to put it down when his eye caught a reference to "Doctor Lorenz: Mineral Treatment. Ineffective!" He turned the page and found two more entries, identical save for a growing number of exclamation points, the last also describing Lord Tarr's bilious reaction and the subsequent forceful voiding of many chambers in his body. This was the final page in the journal, but Svenson saw a small ridge of paper between this and the journal's back cover... there had been another page, several, but someone had carefully cut them out with a razor. He frowned with frustration. The entries were undated—the egotism of the patient assumed no need to record what he already knew—so Svenson had no idea how long this had been going on. No matter. He dropped the journal back in the drawer and slid it shut. The Cabal had made its attempt to swing Lord Tarr to their party long before they settled on Bascombe's succession... and murder.

Svenson knelt at the keyhole and looked unhelpfully onto a bare wall some three or four feet away. He sighed, stood, and very, very slowly turned the knob, feeling the latch release with a far-too-audible *click*. He did not move, ready to shoot the bolt and run back for the garden. Apparently, no one had heard. He took a breath and just as slowly eased the door open, his eye against the growing gap. He desperately wanted a cigarette. The hallway was empty. He opened the door enough to poke his head and look in the other direction. The hall itself was dim, illuminated only from lighted rooms at either end. He could not see what those rooms were, nor could he hear. Svenson's nerves were fraying. He forced himself to step into the hallway and close the door—he didn't want anyone to come across it ajar and start investigating—even though he was afraid of getting lost in the house and not recognizing it again when he was trying to escape. He steeled himself—he did not need to escape. *He* was the predator. The people in the house should be afraid of *him*. Svenson stuck his hand into the pocket of his greatcoat and took hold of his revolver. It was foolish for a weapon to reassure him—either he had courage or he didn't, he chided himself, anyone can carry a gun—but he nevertheless felt better able to walk to the end of the hallway and peer around the corner.

He whipped his head back and brought his hand up over his face. The smell—that sharp sulfurous mechanical smell—assaulted his nostrils and his throat as if he had inhaled the fumes of an iron works. He wiped his nose and eyes with his handkerchief and looked again, the handkerchief held over his face. It was a large room, a reception parlor, ringed with elegant old-fashioned sitting chairs and sofas, all with wide seats to accommodate women with bustles or hoops. Around the chairs were small end tables, the tops of each punctuated with half-empty tea cups and small plates bearing crusts and demurely unfinished slices of cake. Doctor Svenson made a quick count and came up with a total of eleven cups—enough to supply the women from the train? But where were they now—and who was their host? He crept across the parlor and peeked out the opposite doorway—directly into a small ante-room that housed a dauntingly steep staircase and, beyond it, an archway to another parlor. Peeking in from this archway at that exact instant was a short, well-fed woman dressed in black. As one they both recoiled in surprise, the woman with a squeak, Svenson with his open mouth inaudibly groping for an explanation. She held up a hand to him and swallowed, using her other to fan her reddening face.

"I do beg your pardon," she managed. "I thought they—you—had all gone! I would have never—I was merely looking for the cake. If any is left. To put away. To bring to the kitchen. The cook will have retired—and it is a very large house. There may very well be rats. Do you see?"

"I am terribly sorry to surprise you," replied Doctor Svenson, his voice tender with concern.

"I thought you all had gone," she repeated, her own voice reedy and wheezing.

"Of course," he assured her. "It's most understandable."

She cast an apprehensive glance up the staircase before looking back to Svenson. "You're one of the Germans, aren't you?"

Svenson nodded and—because he thought it would appeal to her—clicked his heels. The woman giggled, and immediately covered her mouth with a pudgy pink hand. He studied her face, which reminded him of nothing more than a smirking child's. Her hair was elaborately arranged but without any particular style. In fact—he realized he was desperately slow at this kind of observation—it was a rather ambitious wig. The black dress meant mourning, and it occurred to him that her eyes were the same color as Bascombe's, and that her eyes and her mouth bore his same elliptical shape . . . could she be his sister? His cousin?

"May I ask you something, Madame?"

She nodded. Svenson stepped aside and with his hand indicated the parlor behind him. "Do you apprehend the *smell*?"

She giggled again, this time with a wild uncertain gleam at work in her vaguely porcine eyes. She was nervous, even frightened, by the question. Before she could leave, he spoke again.

"I merely mean, I did not expect them to be . . . working . . . *here*. I assumed it would be elsewhere. I speak for us all when I hope it does not too much *infuse* your upholstery. May I ask if you spoke to any of the women?"

She shook her head.

"But you saw them."

She nodded.

"And you *are* the present Lady of the house."

She nodded.

"Can you—I am merely making sure of *their* work, you understand—tell me what you saw? Here, please, come in and take advantage of a chair. And perhaps there is some cake left after all . . ."

She installed herself on a settee with striped upholstery and pulled a plate of untouched cake slices onto her lap. With impulsive relish the woman crammed the whole of a slice into her mouth, giggled with her mouth full, swallowed with practiced determination, picked up another slice—as if having it in her hand was a comfort. She spoke in a rush.

"Well, you know, it is the sort of thing that seems, well, it seems awful, just *awful*—but then so many things seem that way at first, so many things that are good for one, or actually—eventually—delicious—" She realized what she had just said, and to whom, and erupted in another shrill laugh, stifled only by another bite of cake. She choked it down, her full bosom heaving with the effort beneath the bodice of her dress. "And they did seem happy—these women—alarmingly so, I must say. If it wasn't so frightening I would have been envious. Perhaps I still am envious—but of course I have no reason to be. Roger says it will do wonders for the family—all of this—which perhaps I shouldn't tell you, but I do believe he is right. My boy is a child—he can do nothing for his family for years—and Roger has promised, aside from every other generosity, that Edgar will inherit from him, that Roger—who has no children, but even if he did—he had a fiancée, but doesn't any longer—not that *that* matters—she was a wicked girl, I always said, never mind her money—he's quite eligible—and most impressively connected—he will pass it all back when the time comes. Fair is fair! And do you know—it is nearly certain—we shall be invited to the Palace! I cannot say it should have happened with Edgar on his own!"

Doctor Svenson nodded encouragingly.

"Well, Mr. Bascombe's work is very important."

She nodded vigorously. "I know it!"

"Though it must—I can only imagine, of course—surely some would find it a touch . . . unsettling . . . to have such *intrusions* into their house."

She did not answer, but smiled at him stiffly.

"May I also inquire—the recent loss of your father—"

"What of that? There is no sense—no decent sense to dwell on—on—on—*tragedy*!"

She persisted in smiling, though once more her eyes were wild.

"Were you with him in the house?"

"No one was with him."

"No one?"

"If there'd been anyone with him, they'd have been killed by wolves as well!"

"Wolves?"

"What's worse is that the creature's not been found. It could happen again!"

Svenson nodded gravely. "I should stay indoors."

"I do!"

He stood, gesturing to the ante-room with the staircase. "The others . . . are they . . . upstairs?"

She nodded, then shrugged, and finished the second slice.

"You've been very helpful. I shall inform Roger when I see him . . . and Minister Crabbé."

The woman giggled again, blowing crumbs.

* * *

Svenson walked up the stairs, realizing that he was searching for Elöise. He knew Miss Temple was not here. In all likelihood, Elöise did not want to be found—that is, she was his enemy. Was he such a sentimental fool? He looked back down the stairs and saw the Bascombe woman cramming another piece of cake into her mouth, tears streaming down her face. She met his gaze, cried out with dismay and dashed awkwardly from sight like a silk-wrapped scuttling dog. Svenson thought about stopping to find her for perhaps one second and then continued up the stairs. His hand drifted again to his revolver. His other hand absently bounced against the black book in his other pocket. Was he an idiot? He'd forgotten completely about it—the lack of light to read, probably—but it was the surest thing to explain what Elöise—and everyone else—was doing there.

He reached a dark landing and remembered that this and the following floors were completely dark from outside. Tarr Manor was an old house, subsisting solely on lanterns and candles, which meant there was always a near sideboard with a drawer of tallow stubs for contingencies. The Doctor stumped down the hallway until he found the very thing, and snapped a match to the candle. Now for some place to read. Svenson glanced at the labyrinthine passages and doorways and decided to stay where he was. Even taking this long went against a nagging fear that something might be happening to the women even now. He remembered Angelique. What if Lorenz, who clearly lacked the Comte d'Orkancz's esthetic scruples, was upstairs even then, unscrewing one of his glass-packed metal flasks?

Svenson controlled his thoughts—he was working himself up to no purpose. Two minutes. He would give the book that much.

It was all the task required. On the first page was the quotation he'd had read to him on the train. And on the second page, and the next, and throughout the entirety of the book, printed again and again in small script, one great continuous flow of the identical passage. He looked on the inside and back covers, to see if Coates had written anything... and saw that he had, a series of numbers, jotted in pencil and then ineffectively erased. Svenson held the candle close, and turned to the first of the pages listed, 97... it seemed like any other page, with no special sign or significance that he could see. An idea gnawed at him . . . he looked at the first word at the top of the page—could these add up to a message? Some kind of basic code? Svenson took a pencil stub from his pocket and began to jot notes on the inner flap of the book. The first word of page 97 was "the" . . . he looked at the next number in Coates's list, page 132 . . . the first word was "already" . . . Svenson quickly flipped the pages.

He frowned. "The already remake realms vessels into . . ." did not seem like anything sensible. Perhaps it was itself a code—he tried to puzzle it out: "already" meant the past . . . so "already remake" might mean their progress so far . . . but why bother with "the" at the beginning? Weren't coded messages supposed to be economical? Svenson sighed, looking at the book with as much insight as if it were a Hungarian newspaper, but feeling just within reach of the solution . . . he tried the last words of each page, but this gave him "of Lord will their night only". It sounded like a dire prediction of some kind, but wasn't right . . .

The letters! He looked at the list of first words—if he only took the first letters he got . . . "T-A-R-R-V-I" . . . he anxiously looked for the next page—the first word was "look"—it meant Tarr Village! He kept going and got as far as "Tarr Vill" when the next page, page 30, began with a blank line . . . as did the next, page 2. It came in an instant—3:02!—it was the time of the train! It was the matter of another minute before Svenson had nearly the whole of it done—there was only the last number, whose page started with the letter *p* . . . which gave him a last word of "bravep" . . . which could not be correct. He double-checked Coates's numbering, and noticed that this last number was underlined. Could it mean something different? He chuckled and had it—it indicated the whole word! He jotted it down and looked at what he'd written:

Tarr Vill. 3:02. Who offers sin shall brave Paradise

Doctor Svenson snapped the book closed and picked up the candle. These people—in ignorance of one another—had been invited to come, to submit "sin" in exchange for "Paradise". He knew enough to shudder at what this Paradise might actually be. Did any of them know with whom they trafficked? Had Coates? He walked back to the stairs, wondering *why*—why these people? Karl-Horst, Lord Tarr, Bascombe, Trapping—suborning *them* made mercenary sense, they were perfect well-placed tools. He thought of the stupid woman on the train and he thought of Elöise. He thought of Coates under the altar, and knew exactly how little these people were worth to those who had seduced them. At the base of the stairs Doctor Svenson took the pistol out of his coat and blew out his candle. He climbed into the darkness.

He heard nothing until he stepped onto the fourth floor. Above were the gabled attics, where he'd seen the light. His steps climbing were as light as he could make them, but anyone listening would have heard the creaks and groans of the old wood well in advance of his arrival. As he ascended the steps he also met a thicker concentration of the mechanical smell—perversely, as if he were in the thinning alpine air, his breath more shallow and his head dizzied. He stopped and put his handkerchief over his nose and mouth, sweeping across the shadowed landing with the pistol.

The silence was broken by a footstep above him in the attic. Svenson cocked the pistol and searched for the way up, nearly tripping on it: a ladder, flat on the floor. Whoever it was above him, they'd been marooned.

Svenson eased back the hammer and stuffed the pistol into his pocket. He picked up the ladder and looked above him for the hatch, only noticing it—the thing was quite flush with the ceiling—because of the bolt that held it shut. There was a wooden lip to rest the ladder against, and Svenson wedged it securely in place and began his tentative climb, eased by the darkness—he could not exactly see how high he was, nor thus how far there was to fall. He kept his gaze resolutely above him and reached out—nerves dancing with dismay at holding on with but a single hand—to undo the bolt. He pushed back the hatch and nearly lost his balance recoiling from the chemical stench. This was a good thing, as his instinctive shrinking from the smell caused his head to duck just out of the path of a sharp wooden heel. A moment later—taking in the swinging heel and the woman swinging it—Doctor Svenson's foot slipped on the rung and dropped through it—a sudden descent of two feet until his hands caught hold (and his jaw smacked into a rung of its own). He looked up with distress, rubbing his stinging face. Looking down at him, hair in her face and a shoe in her hand, was Elöise.

"Captain Blach!"

"Have they hurt you?" he rasped, working to restore his dangling leg on the ladder.

"No . . . no, but . . ." She looked to something he could not see. She had been crying. "Please—I must come down!"

Before he could protest, she was out of the hatch and nearly on top of him. He half-caught, half-hung on to her legs as they descended, finding the floor himself just in time to help her do the same. She turned and buried her face in his shoulder, hugging him tightly, her body shaking. After a moment, he put his arms around her—timidly, without exerting any untoward pressure, though even this much contact set off a wondrous appreciation that her shoulder blades could be so small—and waited for her emotions to subside. Instead of subsiding, she began to sob, his greatcoat muffling the sounds. He looked past her, up into the open hatch. The light in the room was not from a candle or lantern—it was somehow more pale and cold, and did not flicker. Doctor Svenson took it upon himself to pat the woman's hair and whisper "It's all right now . . . you're all right . . ." into her ear. She pulled her face away from him, out of breath, swallowing, her face streaked. He looked at her seriously.

"You can breathe? The smell—the chemicals—"

She nodded. "I covered my head—I—I had to—"

Before she could erupt once more he indicated the hatch. "Is there anyone else—does anyone need help?"

She shook her head and shut her eyes, stepping away. Svenson had no idea what to think. Dreading what he would find, he climbed the ladder and looked in.

It was a narrow gabled room with the roof slanted on each side—perhaps a child of seven could have stood without stooping in the very center. Across the floor near the window were the slumped shapeless forms of two women, obviously dead. Equally clear, though he possessed no explanation, was that their bodies were the source of the unnatural blue glow animating the grisly attic. He crawled into the room. The smell was unbearable and he paused to replace the handkerchief over his face before continuing on his hands and knees. They were from the train—one was well-dressed, and the other probably a maid. Both had bled from the ears and nose, and their eyes were filmed over and opaque, but from within, as if the contents of each sphere had become scrambled and gelatinous under extreme pressure. He thought of the Comte d'Orkancz's medical interests and recalled men he had seen pulled from the winter sea, whose soft bodies had been unable to withstand the crushing tons of ice water above them. The women were of course completely dry—nothing of the kind could explain their conditions... nor could any disease of the arctic account for the unearthly blue glow that arose from every visible discolored inch of their skin.

Svenson bolted the hatch behind him and climbed down, laying the ladder on the floor. He coughed into his handkerchief—his throat was unpleasantly raw, he could only imagine what hers felt like—and then tucked it away. Elöise had crept to the stairs, sitting so she could look into the shadow of the floor below. He sat next to her, no longer presuming to place an arm around her, but—as a physician—scrupling to take one of her hands in both of his.

"I woke up with them. In the room," she said, her voice a whisper, ragged but under her control. "It was Miss Poole—"

"Miss Poole!"

Elöise looked up at Svenson. "Yes. She spoke to us all—there was tea, there was cake—all of us from so many places... come for our different reasons, for our *fortunes*—it was all so congenial."

"But Miss Poole is not in the attic—"

"No. She had the book." Elöise shook her head, covering her eyes with a hand. "I'm not making any kind of sense, I'm sorry."

Svenson looked back at the attic. "But those women—you must know them, they were on the train—"

"I don't know them any more than I know you," she said. "We were told how to get here, not to speak of it—"

Svenson squeezed her hand, fighting down each impulse of sympathy, knowing he must determine who she really was. "Elöise... I must ask you, for it is very important—and you must answer me truthfully—"

"I am not *lying*—the book—those women—"

"I am not asking about them. I must know about you. To whom are you a *confidante*? Whose children is it that you tutor?"

She stared at him, perhaps unsure in the face of his sudden insistence, perhaps calculating her best response, and then scoffed, bitterly and forlorn. "For some reason I thought everyone knew. The children of Charlotte and Arthur Trapping."

"There is too much to tell," she said, straightening her shoulders and pushing the loosened strands of hair from her eyes. "But you will not understand unless I explain that, upon the disappearance of Colonel Trapping"—she looked at him to see if he required more information but Svenson merely nodded for her to go on—"Mrs. Trapping had taken to her rooms, receiving the calls of no one save her brothers. I say brothers, for it is the habit of the family, but in truth the brother she wanted to hear from, to whom she sent card after card—Mr. Henry Xonck—did not once respond, and the brother with whom her relations are strained—Mr. Francis Xonck—called upon her throughout the day. On one visit, he sought me out in the house, for he is enough of a family presence to know who I am, and my relation to Mrs. Trapping." She looked up again at Svenson, who opened his expression into one of gentle questioning. She shook her head, as if to gather her thoughts. "Who of course you don't know—she is a difficult woman. She has been shut out of her family business by her older brother—she gets money, understand, but not the work, the power, the sense of place. It haunts her—and it is why she was so determined her husband should rise to importance, and why his absence was so distressing... indeed, perhaps more than the loss of her man was the loss of her, if you will permit me... *engine.* In any case, Francis Xonck took me aside and asked if I should like to help her. He knows my devotion to Mrs. Trapping—as I say, he has seen her reliance on my advice, and he is a man who misses nothing—of course I said yes, even as I wondered at this sudden attention to his sister, a woman who despised him as a corrupting influence on her already corrupted husband. He told me there would be secrecy and intrigue, there would even—and here he looked into my eyes—I would not be telling this to a soul, Captain, were it not—what has occurred—" She gestured to the darkened house around her.

Svenson squeezed her hand. She smiled again, though her eyes were unchanged.

"He looked at me—looked *into* me—and whispered that I might find advantage in the affair myself, that I might find it... a revelation. He *chuckled.* And yet even as he played at seducing me, the story he told was very dark and horrid—he was convinced Colonel Trapping was being held against his wishes—because of scandal it was impossible to go to the authorities. Mr. Xonck had only heard rumors but was too visible himself to attend to them. It was part of a much larger set of events, he said. He informed me that I would be expected to reveal secrets—compromising information—of the Trappings, of the Xonck family—and he authorized me to do so. I refused, at least without first consulting Mrs. Trapping, but he insisted in the gravest terms that to alert her to even this much of her husband's predicament was to strain the marriage to the breaking point, to say nothing of what it must do to the poor woman's nerves. Still, it seemed shameful—what I knew, I knew only because of her trust. Again I refused, but he pressed me—flattering me as he praised my devotion, only to insinuate a deeper devotion lay in doing as he asked. Finally I agreed, telling myself I had no choice—though of course I had. We always do... but when someone praises us, or calls us beautiful, how easy it is to believe them." She sighed. "And then this morning instructions arrived to take the train and come here."

"Who offers sin shall brave Paradise," said Svenson. Elöise sniffed, nodding.

"The others were all like me—relations or servants or partners or associates of the very powerful. All of us bearing secrets. One at a time, Miss Poole led us from the parlor to another room. Several men were there, wearing masks. When my turn came I told them what I knew—about Henry Xonck and Arthur Trapping, about Charlotte Trapping's hunger and ambition—I am ashamed of it, and I am ashamed that while part of my mind did this in earnest hope to save the missing man, another part—the truth of this is bitter to me—was greedy to see what Paradise I'd find. And now... now I cannot even recall what I said, what might have been so important—the Trappings are not scandalous people. I am a fool—"

"Do not—do not," whispered Svenson. "We are all so foolish, believe me."

"That cannot be an excuse," she answered him flatly. "We are all also given the chance to be strong."

"You were strong to come so far alone," he said, "and you were even stronger... in the attic."

She shut her eyes and sighed. Svenson tried to speak gently. He felt utterly convinced by her story, and yet wished he was not so predisposed to believe it. She had been at Harschmort—with the Trappings, as explained—but still, he needed more before he could trust her fully.

"You said that Miss Poole had a book..."

"She laid it on the table, after I'd told them what I thought they wanted to hear. It was wrapped in silk, like—like some kind of Bible, or the Jewish Torah—and when she revealed it—"

"It was made of blue glass."

She gasped at the word. "It was! And you had mentioned glass on the train—and I hadn't known, but then—I thought of you—and I knew I did not understand my situation—and just at that moment I had the most vivid recollection of the chill of Mr. Francis Xonck's eyes—and then Miss Poole opened the glass book... and I read... or should I say that it read me. That makes no sense—but *it* made no sense at all. I fell into it like a pool, like falling into another person's body, only it was more than one—there were dreams, desires, such thrills that I blush to recall them—and such visions... of power... and then—Miss Poole—she must have placed my hand on the book, for I remember her laughing... and then... I cannot convey it... I was deep... so deep, and so cold, drowning—holding my breath but finally I had to breathe and gulped in—I don't know what—freezing liquid glass. It... felt like dying." She paused and wiped her eyes and glanced back at the hatch. "I woke up there. I am lucky—I know that I am lucky. I know I should have perished like the others, my skin glowing blue."

"Can you walk?" he asked.

"I can." She stood, and smoothed out her dress, still holding his hand, and reached down to replace her shoes. "After all the trouble to gather me here they have cast me aside without a care, with so little thought! If you had not come, Captain Blach—I shudder to think—"

"Do not," said Svenson. "We must leave this house. Come... the next floors are dark—the house seems to be abandoned, at least for now. I have followed the party of men, who I believe went elsewhere on the estate. Perhaps Miss Poole and the other ladies have gone to join them."

"Captain Blach—"

He stopped her. "My name is Svenson. Abelard Svenson, Captain-Surgeon of the Macklenburg Navy, attached to the service of a very foolish young Prince who I, also a fool, yet retain a hope of saving. As you say, there is not enough time to tell the necessary tale. Arthur Trapping is dead. Earlier this morning Francis Xonck tried to sink me in the river, in the same iron casket as Colonel Trapping's corpse. It may well be that he schemes to undo both of his siblings as his own part of these machinations—and indeed, damn it all, there is too much to say—we have no time—they could return. The man you sat with on the train, Mr. Coates—"

"I did not know—"

"His name, no, nor he yours—but he is dead. They have killed him for as little cause as can be imagined. They are all dangerous, without scruple. Listen to me—I do recognize you, I have seen you among them—I must say this—at Harschmort House, not two nights past—"

Her hand went to her mouth. "You! You brought word of the Prince to Lydia Vandaariff! But—but it wasn't about that at all, was it? It was Colonel Trapping—"

"Found dead, yes—murdered, for what and by whom I've no idea—but what I am saying, what—I am deciding to trust you, despite your connection to the Xonck family, despite—"

"But you have seen them try to kill me—"

"Yes—though apparently some among them are happy to kill each other—no matter, please, what I need to tell you—should we escape, as I hope we shall, but if we are separated . . . Oh, this is ridiculous—"

"What? What?"

"There are two people you may trust—though I don't know how you should find them. One is the man I described on the train—in red, dark glasses, very dangerous, a rogue—Cardinal Chang. I am to meet him tomorrow at noon under the clock at Stropping Station."

"But why—"

"Because . . . Elöise . . . if the last days have taught me anything it is that I do not know where I shall be tomorrow at noon. Perhaps you will be there instead . . . perhaps we have met one another for just that purpose."

She nodded. "And the other? You said two people."

"Her name is Celeste Temple. A young woman, very . . . *determined,* chestnut hair, of small stature—she is the ex-fiancée of Roger Bascombe—a Ministry official who figures in this—who owns this house! Oh, this is foolish, there is no time. We must be off."

Svenson led her by the hand down the successive flights, a nagging anxiety rising along his spine. They had taken too long. And even if they escaped the house—where to go? The two men knew he was at the King Crow—it could not be safe if they were part of the Cabal, as of course they must be—but the train was not until next morning. Could he sleep in someone's shed? Could Elöise? He flushed at the very idea, and squeezed her hand in instinctive assurance that the thoughts in his head would not be succumbed to—a certainty challenged by her squeeze of his own hand in return.

At the top of the last staircase—leading down to the brightly lit first floor and the parlor where he'd left the Bascombe woman—he stopped again, indicating they should be especially silent. Svenson listened . . . the house was still. They crept down one stair at a time until Svenson could step to the parlor door itself and peer in. It was empty, the dishes still there (but not the cake). He looked the other direction—another parlor, also empty. He turned back to Elöise and whispered.

"No one. Which way is the door?"

She finished descending the stairs and crossed to him, standing close and leaning past his chest to look for herself. She stepped back, still quite close, and whispered in return. "I believe it is through that room and one other, not far at all."

Svenson barely took in her words. In her exertions in the attic, her dress had opened another button. Looking down at her—she was not so very short, but still his was a lovely view—he could see the determination in her face and eyes, the naked skin of her throat and then, through the opened collar of her dress, the join of her clavicles to her sternum—bones that always made him think with a strange sensual stirring of bird skeletons. She looked up at him. Without moving her eyes he knew she saw him looking at her body. She said nothing. Around Doctor Svenson time had slowed—perhaps it was all this talk of ice and freezing—and he drank in the sight of her and her acceptance of his gaze equally. He was as helpless as he had been before the Contessa. He swallowed and attempted to speak.

"This afternoon... do you know... on the train... I had... such a dream..."

"Did you?"

"I did... goodness, yes..."

"Do you remember it?"

"I do..."

He had no idea what lay behind her eyes. He was about to kiss her when they heard the screaming.

It was a woman, somewhere in the house. Svenson spun his head toward either parlor but could not tell in which direction to go. The woman screamed again. Svenson snatched hold of Elöise's hand and pulled her back through the tea cups and cake plates to the corridor where he'd first arrived, his hand digging at his greatcoat as they went. He quickly opened the door and thrust her into the study. She tried to protest, but her words were stopped as he placed the heavy service revolver in her hands. Her mouth opened with shock, and Svenson gently forced her fingers around the butt of the gun, so she was holding it correctly. This got her attention enough that he could whisper and know she would understand him. Behind them the woman screamed again.

"This is Lord Tarr's study. The garden door"—he pointed to it—"is open, and the stone wall is low enough to climb. I will be right back. If I am not, go—do not hesitate. There is a train at eight o'clock tomorrow morning to the city. If anyone accosts you—anyone who is not a man in red or a woman wearing green shoes—shoot them dead."

She nodded. Doctor Svenson leaned forward and placed his lips on hers. She responded fervently, emitting the softest small moan of encouragement and regret and delight and despair all together. He stepped back and pulled the door closed. He walked down the hallway to the other end, passed through a small service room. Svenson availed himself of a heavy candlestick, twisting it in his hand to get a firm grip. The woman was no longer screaming. He strode forward to his best estimate of where the sound had been with five pounds of brass in his hand.

Another hallway fed Svenson into a large carpeted dining room, the high walls covered with oil paintings, the floor dominated by an enormous table surrounded by perhaps twenty high-backed chairs. At the far end stood a knot of men in black coats. Curled into a ball on her side, on top of the table, was the Bascombe woman, her shoulders heaving. As he walked toward them—the carpet absorbing the sound of his step—Svenson saw the man in the middle take hold of her jaw and bend her head so she must face him. Her eyes were screwed shut and her wig dislodged, revealing the poignantly thin, lank, dull hair beneath. The man was tall, with iron grey hair worn down to his collar—and Svenson saw with alarm the medals on the chest of his tailcoat and the scarlet sash that crossed his shoulder, signs of the highest levels of nobility. If he were a native he felt sure he would have known the man . . . could he be *Royal*? To his left were the two men from the tavern. To his right was Harald Crabbé, who—pricked by some presentiment—looked up, eyes widening, at Svenson's grim-faced approach.

"Get away from her," Svenson called coldly. No one moved.

"It is Doctor Svenson," said Crabbé, for the benefit of his superior.

Svenson saw that the Royal's other gloved hand held a lozenge of blue glass above the struggling woman's mouth. At Svenson's call she had opened her eyes. She saw the lozenge and her throat gurgled in protest.

"Like this?" the man idly asked Crabbé, taking the lozenge between two fingers.

"Indeed, Highness," replied the Deputy Minister, with all deference, his widening eyes on Svenson's approach.

"Get away from her!" Svenson cried again. He was perhaps ten feet away and approaching fast.

"Doctor Svenson is the Macklenburg *rebel* . . . ," intoned Crabbé.

The man shrugged with indifference and stuffed the glass into her mouth, snapping the woman's jaw between his two hands, holding it tight, her voice rising to a muted scream as the effects within intensified. He met Svenson's hot gaze with disdain and did not move. Svenson raised the candlestick—for the first time the others saw it—fully intending to dash the fellow's brains out, no matter who he was, never breaking stride.

"Phelps!" Crabbé snapped, a sudden, desperate imperative in his voice. The shorter of the two men—with the Empire hairstyle—rushed forward, a hand out toward Svenson in reasonable supplication, but the Doctor was already swinging and the candlestick caught the man across the forearm, snapping both bones. He screamed and dropped to the side with the momentum of the blow. Svenson kept coming and now Crabbé was between him and the Royal—who still had not moved.

"Starck! Stop it! Stop him! *Starck!*" Crabbé barked, backing up, exerting his full authority. Over his shoulder dove the other man from the tavern—Mr. Starck—reaching for Svenson with both hands. Svenson met him with his own outstretched left arm. For a moment they grappled at such arm's length, which left Svenson's other hand, with the candlestick, free to swing. The blow caught Starck squarely on the ear with a sickening, pumpkin-thwacking thud, dropping him like a stone. Crabbé stumbled into the Royal personage, who was finally taking note of the mayhem around him. He had released the woman's jaw—the bubbles at her mouth a foaming mix of blue and pink. Svenson prepared to strike over the shorter diplomat's head directly at the offending aristocrat—Prince, Duke, whoever—and realized, somewhere in the periphery of his mind, that he was acting just like Chang. He was astonished at how *good* it felt, and how much *better* it would feel as soon as he'd broken the face of this monster into pulp . . . but it was just then that the ceiling of the room—he did not know, as he fell, what else could have been so heavy—collapsed without warning on the back of Doctor Svenson's head.

He opened his eyes with the distinct memory of having been in this exact lamentable situation before, only this time he was not in a moving horse-cart. The back of his head throbbed mercilessly and the muscles of his neck and right shoulder felt as if they'd been set aflame. His right arm was numb. Svenson looked over to see it shackled above his head to a wooden post. He was sitting in the dirt, leaning against the side of a wooden staircase. He squinted his eyes, trying to focus through the pain in his head. The staircase wound back and forth many times above him, climbing close to a hundred feet. Finally the truth dawned on his dimmed intelligence. He was in the quarry.

He struggled to his feet, desperately craving a cigarette despite the bitter dryness of his throat. Doctor Svenson squinted and shaded his eyes against the glaring torchlight and the quite oppressive heat. He had awoken into a very hive of activity. He fished for his monocle and attempted to take it all in.

The quarry itself was deeply excavated, its sheer orange stone walls betraying an even higher concentration of iron than he had seen from the train. The density of the reddish color made his scattered mind wonder if he had been transported in secret to the Macklenburg mountains. The floor was a flattened bed of gravel and clay, and around him he could see piles of different mineral substances—sand, bricks, rocks, slag heaps of melted dross. On the far side was a series of chutes and grates and sluices—the quarry must have some supply of water, native or pumped in—and what might have been a shaftway descending underground. Near this—far away but still close enough to bring sweat to Svenson's collar—was a great bricked kiln with a metal hatch. At the hatch crouched Doctor Lorenz, intent as a wicked gnome, once again wearing his goggles and gauntlets, a small knot of similarly garbed assistants clustered around him. Opposite these actual mining works of the quarry, and sitting on a series of wooden benches that reminded Svenson of an open-air schoolroom, were the men and women from the train. Facing them and giving some sort of low-voiced instruction was a short, curvaceous woman in a pale dress—it could only be Miss Poole. Installed alone on the backmost bench, Svenson was startled to see the Bascombe woman, her wig restored and her face—if perhaps a little pale and drawn—almost ceramically composed.

He heard a noise and looked up. Directly above him on the wide, first landing of the staircase, which made a balcony from which to overlook the quarry, stood the party of black-coated men: the Royal personage, Crabbé, and to the side, his complexion the color of dried paste, Mr. Phelps, his arm in a sling. Behind them all, smoking a cheroot, stood a tall man with cropped hair in the red uniform of the 4th Dragoons, the rank of a colonel at his throat. It was Aspiche. Svenson had not attracted their notice. He looked elsewhere in the quarry—not daring to hope that Elöise had escaped—scanning for any sign of her capture. On the other side of the stairs was an enormous, stitched-together amalgamation of tarps, covering something twice the size of a rail car and taller, some kind of advanced digging apparatus? Could it being covered mean they were *done* with digging, that the seam of indigo clay was exhausted? He looked back to the kiln for a better sense of what Lorenz was actually doing, but his eyes were stopped by another single tarp, thrown over a small heap, near the large stacks of wood used to stoke the oven. Svenson swallowed uncomfortably. Sticking out from the tarp was a woman's foot.

"Ah . . . he has awakened," said a voice from above.

He looked up to see Harald Crabbé leaning over the rail with a cold, vengeful gaze. A moment later he was joined by the Royal, whose expression was that of a man examining livestock he had no intention to buy. "Excuse me for a moment, Highness—I suggest you keep your attention on Doctor Lorenz, who will no doubt have something of great interest to demonstrate momentarily." He bowed and then snapped his fingers to Phelps, who slunk after his master down the stairs. After another taste of his cheroot, Aspiche ambled after them, allowing his saber to bang on each step as he went. Svenson wiped his mouth with his free left hand, did his best to hawk the phlegm from his throat and spat. He turned to face them as Crabbé stepped from the stairs.

"We did not know if you would revive, Doctor," he called. "Not that we cared overmuch, you understand, but if you did it seemed advantageous to try and speak with you about your actions and your confederates. Where are the others—Chang and the girl? Who do you all serve in this persistently foolish attempt to spoil things you don't comprehend?"

"Our conscience, Minister," answered Svenson, his voice thicker than he'd expected. He wanted very much to sleep. Blood was creeping into his arm, and he knew abstractly that he was going to be in agony very soon as the nerves flooded back to life. "I cannot be plainer than that."

Crabbé studied him as if Svenson could not possibly have meant what he said, and therefore must be speaking in some kind of code.

"Where are Chang and the girl?" he repeated.

"I do not know where they are. I don't know if they're alive."

"Why are you here?"

"And how's the back of your head?" chortled Aspiche.

Svenson ignored him, answering the Minister. "Why do you think? Looking for Bascombe. Looking for you. Looking for my Prince so I can shoot him in the head and save my country the shame of his ascending its throne."

Crabbé twitched the corners of his mouth in a sketch of a smile.

"You seem to have broken this man's arm. Can you set the bones? You *are* a doctor, yes?"

Svenson looked at Phelps and met his pleading eyes. How long had it been? Hours at least, with the raw fractures cruelly jarred with each step the poor fellow took. Svenson raised his shackled wrist. "I will need out of this, but yes, certainly I can do something. Do you have wood for a splint?"

"We have plaster, actually—or something like it, Lorenz tells me—they use it for mining, or for shoring up crumbling walls. Colonel, will you escort the Doctor and Phelps? If Doctor Svenson diverges from his task in the slightest, I'll be obliged if you would hack off his head directly."

They walked across the quarry, past the impromptu schoolroom, toward Lorenz. As they passed, Svenson could not help but glance at Miss Poole, who met his eyes with a dazzling smile. She said something to her listeners to excuse herself and a moment later was walking quickly to catch him.

"Doctor!" she called. "I did not think to meet you again, or not so soon—and certainly not here. I am *told*"—she glanced wickedly at Aspiche—"that you have made yourself a most deadly nuisance, and have nearly slain our guest of honor!" She shook her head as if he were a charmingly disobedient boy. "They say that enemies are often closest in character—what separates them is but an attitude of mind, and as I think we all must see, those are eminently flexible. Why not join us, Doctor Svenson? Forgive me for being blunt, but when I first saw you in the St. Royale, I had no idea of your status as an adventurer—your legend grows by the day, even to the heights of your unfortunate friend Cardinal Chang, who I am led to understand is, well, no longer your competition in heroic endeavors."

Svenson could not help it, but at her words he flinched. To the obvious anger of Colonel Aspiche, Miss Poole draped her arm in Svenson's and clucked her tongue, leaning in to his face. Her perfume was sandalwood, like Mrs. Marchmoor's. Her soft hands, the overwhelmingly delicate scent, the sweat around his neck, the hammering in his skull, the woman's galling *blitheness*: Doctor Svenson felt as if his brain would boil. She chuckled at his discomfort.

"*Next* of course you will tell me you are a rescuer and defender of women—I have heard as much this very evening. But look"—she turned and waved to the Bascombe woman, sitting on the bench, who immediately waved back with the hopeful vigor of a whipped dog's wagging tail—"there is Pamela Hawsthorne, the present Lady of Tarr Manor, and happy as can be, despite the unpleasant *misunderstanding*."

"She has undergone your Process?"

"Not yet, but I'm sure she will. No, she has merely been exposed to our powerful science. Because it *is* science, Doctor, which I hope as a scientific man you will credit. Science advances, you know, just as must the moral fiber of our society. Sometimes it is dragged forward by the actions of those more knowledgeable, like a recalcitrant child. You *do* understand."

He wanted to offend her, call her a whore, to crassly violate this pretense of companionable flirtation, but he lacked the presence of mind to form the appropriate insult. Perhaps he could vomit from dizziness. Instead, he tried to smile.

"You are very persuasive, Miss Poole. May I ask you a question—as I am a foreigner?"

"Of course."

"Who *is* that man?"

Svenson turned and nodded to the tall figure next to Crabbé on the stair landing, looking over the quarry as if he were a Borgia Pope sneering down from a Vatican balcony. Miss Poole chuckled again and patted his arm indulgently. It occurred to him that she had not possessed this sort of power before the Process, and still searched for its proper expression—was he a child to her, a pupil, an ignorant tool, or a trainable dog?

"Why, that is the Duke of Stäelmaere. He is the old Queen's natural brother, you know."

"I did not know."

"Oh yes. If the Queen and her children were to perish—heaven forbid—the Duke would inherit the throne."

"That's a lot of perishing."

"Please don't misunderstand me. The Duke is Her Majesty's most trusted sibling. As such he works most *intimately* with the present government."

"He seems intimate with Mr. Crabbé."

She laughed and was about to make a witticism when she was brusquely interrupted by Aspiche.

"That's enough. He's here to fix this man's arm. And then he's going to die."

She bore the intrusion gracefully and turned to Svenson.

"Not much of a prospect, Doctor. I would consider a switch in alliances, if I were you. You truly do not know what you are missing. And if you never do, well . . . won't that be too sad?"

Miss Poole gave him a smiling, teasing nod of her head and returned to her benches. Svenson glanced at Aspiche, who watched her with evident relish. Had she been groping Aspiche or Lorenz in the private dining room at the St. Royale? Lorenz, he was fairly sure—though it looked as if Lorenz was quite occupied with his smelting and could not be bothered. Svenson saw the man empty one of the bandolier flasks into a metal cup that his assistants were preparing to stuff into the raging kiln. He wondered what the chemical process really was—there seemed to be several distinct steps of refinement . . . were these for different purposes, to convert the indigo clay to distinct uses? He looked back at Miss Poole, and wondered where her glass book was now. If he could manage to capture that . . .

He was interrupted again by Aspiche, tugging his tingling arm toward Mr. Phelps, who was painfully attempting to take off his black coat. Svenson looked up at Aspiche, to ask for splints and for some brandy at least for the man's pain, when he saw, looming in the orange kiln-light like the tattoos of an island savage, the looping scars of the Process scored across his face. How had he not noticed them before? Svenson could not help it. He laughed aloud.

"What?" snarled the Colonel.

"You," answered Svenson boldly. "Your face looks like a clown's. Do you know that last time I saw Arthur Trapping—which was in his coffin, mind you—his face was the same? Do you think, just because they have expanded your *mind,* that you are any less their contingent tool?"

"Be quiet before I kill you!" Aspiche shoved him toward Phelps, who began to move out of the way and then flinched with pain.

"You'll kill me anyway. Listen—Trapping was a man with powerful friends, he was someone they needed. You can't pretend to that—you're just the man with the soldiers, and your own elevation should demonstrate how easily you too could be replaced. You mind the hounds when they need to hunt—it's servitude, Colonel, and your expanded mind ought to be *broad* enough to see it."

Aspiche backhanded Doctor Svenson viciously across the jaw. Svenson sprawled in a heap, his face stinging. He blinked and shook his head. He saw that Lorenz had heard the sound and turned to them, his expression hidden behind the black goggles.

"Fix his arm," said Aspiche.

In fact the "plaster" was some kind of seal for the kiln, but Svenson thought it would work well enough. The breaks were clean, and to his credit Phelps did not pass out—though to Svenson this always seemed a dubious credit indeed. For, if he *had* passed out it certainly would have gone easier for them all. As it was, the man was left trembling and spent, sitting on the ground with his arm swathed in his cast. Svenson had curtly apologized for the inconvenience of breaking his arm—assuring him that it was the Duke he had wanted to strike—and Phelps had answered that, of course, given the circumstances, it was entirely understandable.

"Your companion . . . ," Svenson began, wiping his hands on a rag.

"I'm afraid you have done for him," replied Phelps, his voice somehow distant for all the pain, with the delicate, whispered quality of dried rice paper. He nodded to the tarp. Now that they were closer, Svenson saw that in addition to the woman's foot, there was also a man's black shoe. What had been his name—Starck? The weight of the killing settled heavily on the Doctor's shoulders. He looked to Phelps, as if he should say something, and saw the man's eyes had already drifted elsewhere, biting his lip against the grinding of his broken bones.

"It's what happens in war," Aspiche sneered with contempt. "When you made the choice to fight, you made the choice to die."

Svenson's gaze returned to the hidden stack of bodies, trying desperately to recall Elöise's shoes. Could that be her foot? How many people—dear God—were under the tarp? It had to be at least four, judging by the height, perhaps more. He hoped that, with him captured, they would not bother to search the inn or the train platform in the morning, that she might somehow get away.

"Is he going to live?" This was the arch, mocking call of Doctor Lorenz, walking over from the kiln, the goggles pulled down around his neck. He was looking at Phelps, but did not even wait for an answer. His eyes roamed over Svenson once, a professional estimation that revealed nothing save an equally professional depth of suspicion, and then moved on to Aspiche. Lorenz gestured to his assistants, who had followed him over from the kiln.

"If we're to dispose of this evidence, then now is the time. The kiln is at its hottest, and will only burn lower from this point on—for all that we wait, the remains shall be more legible."

Aspiche looked across the quarry and raised his arm, getting the attention of Crabbé. Svenson saw the Minister peer, then realize what the Colonel was pointing to and give him an answering wave of approval. Aspiche called to Lorenz's men.

"Go ahead."

The tarp was whipped away and the men stepped to either side, each pair picking up a body between them. Svenson staggered back. On top of the pile were the two women from the attic room, their flesh still glowing blue. Beneath them were Coates and Starck and another man who he recalled but vaguely from the train, his skin also aglow (apparently the men had been shown the book as well). He watched in horror as the first two bodies were taken to the kiln and the wider stoking panel kicked open, revealing a white-hot blaze within. Svenson turned away. At the smell of burning hair his stomach heaved. Aspiche grabbed his shoulder and shoved him back across the quarry to Crabbé. He was dimly aware of Phelps stumbling along behind. At least Elöise had not been there... at least she'd been spared that...

As they again passed Miss Poole and her charges, he saw her amongst the benches, handing out books—these with a red leather cover instead of black, whispering something to each person. He assumed it was a new code, and the key for new messages. She saw him looking and smiled. To either side of Miss Poole were the man and woman he'd first sat with on the train. He barely recognized them. Though their garments had changed—his were smeared with grease and soot, and hers were noticeably loosened—it was more for the transformation of their faces. Where before had been tension and suspicion, now Svenson saw ease and confidence—it truly was as if they were different people entirely. They nodded to him as well, smiling brightly. He wondered who they were in the world, who in their lives they had just betrayed, and what they had found in the glass book to be so altered.

Svenson tried to make sense of it all, to force his tired brain to think. He ought to be drawing one conclusion after another, but nothing followed in his dulled condition. What was the difference between the glass book and the Process? The book could obviously kill—though this seemed almost cruelly arbitrary, like a toxic reaction to shellfish, as he doubted the deaths were intentional or planned. But what did the book *do*? Elöise spoke of falling into it, of visions. He thought of the compelling nature of the blue glass card, and then extrapolated that to the experience of a *book*... but what else... he felt near to something... *writing*... a book must be written in, the thoughts must be recorded... was that what they were doing? He recalled Chang's description of the Institute, the man dropping the book as it was being made—made somehow *from* Angelique—the same man from Crabbé's kitchen. What was the difference between using a person to *make* the book, and then using these people here to *write* in it... or be drawn into its clutches like a spider's web? And what of the Process? That was simple conversion, he felt—a chemical-electric process using the properties of the refined indigo clay—indigo clay melted somehow into glass—to affect the character: to lower inhibitions and shift loyalties. Did it merely erase moral objections? Or did it re-write them? He thought how much a person could accomplish in life without scruples, or one hundred such people working together, their numbers growing by the day. Svenson rubbed his eyes as he walked—he was getting confused again, which merely returned him to the first question: what was the difference between the Process and the book? He looked back at Miss Poole and her little schoolroom in the slag heaps. It was a question of direction, he realized. In the Process, the energy went *into* the subject, erasing inhibitions and converting them to the cause. With the glass book, the energy was sucked *out* of the subject—along with (or in the form of—was memory energy?) specific experiences in their lives. Undoubtedly this was the blackmail: the secrets these bitter underlings had to tell were now *secreted* within Miss Poole's book, and that book—like the cards—would allow anyone else to *experience* those shameful episodes. There would be no denial, and no end to the Cabal's power over those so implicated.

It was making more sense to him now—the books were tools and could, like any other book, be used for a variety of purposes, depending on what was in them. Furthermore, it might be that they were constructed in different ways, for different reasons, some written whole and some with a different number of empty pages. He could not but recall the vivid, disturbing paintings of Oskar Veilandt—the compositions explicitly depicting the Process, the reverse of each canvas scrawled with alchemical symbols. Did that man's work lie at the root of the books as well? If only he was still alive! Was it possible that the Comte—clearly the master within the Cabal of this twisted science—had pillaged Veilandt's secrets and then had him killed? As he thought of books and purposes, Svenson suddenly wondered if d'Orkancz had been intending to make a book of Angelique alone—the vast adventures of a lady of pleasure. It would be a most persuasive enticement for his cause, offering the detailed experience of a thousand nights in the brothel without ever leaving one's room. Yet that would be but one example . . . the limit was sensation itself—what adventures or travels or thrills that one person had known could not be imprinted onto one of these books for anyone to consume, which was to say, to experience *bodily* for themselves? What sumptuous banquets? What quantities of wine? What battles, caresses, what witty conversations . . . there truly was no end . . . and no end to what people would pay for such oblivion.

He looked back to Miss Poole and the smiling couple. What had changed them? What had killed the others, but spared these two? It was somehow important to know—for this was a wrinkle, something that did not flow cleanly. If there was only a way to find out—yet any idea of who those people were or what might have killed them was even now disappearing into ash. Svenson snorted with anger—perhaps there was enough after all. Their skin had been infused with blue—this hadn't happened to the ones who had survived. He thought of the couple, changed from suspicious resentment to open amity... Svenson stumbled with the sudden impact of his thoughts. Aspiche took hold of his shoulder and shoved him forward.

"Get along there! You'll be resting soon enough!"

Doctor Svenson barely heard him. He was recalling Elöise—how she could not remember what scandals she might have revealed about the Trappings or Henry Xonck. She had said it in a way to mean there had been nothing to reveal... but Svenson knew the memories had been *taken* from her, just as the memories of spite and injustice and envy had been taken from the venal young couple—all to be inscribed in the book. And the ones who had died... what had d'Orkancz said about Angelique? That the energy had "regrettably" gone the other direction... this must have happened here too... the book's energy must have entered deeper into the people who died, leaving its mark as it drained them utterly. But why them and not the others? He looked back at the smiling people around Miss Poole. None of them could remember exactly what they had revealed—indeed, did they even know why they were here? He shook his head at the beauty of it, for each could be safely sent back to their life, lacking any knowledge of what had been done, aside from a trip to the country and a few strange deaths. But when was there not a way to explain deaths of those considered to be insignificant? Who would protest—who would even remember those killed?

For a moment Svenson's thoughts stabbed toward Corinna—the degree to which her true memory was retained in his breast alone—and he felt within him a sharpening rage. The death of Starck weighed heavily, but he took the words of the simpleton Aspiche (why must such men always reduce the complexity of the world to single-syllable thinking—an empire of grunts?) as a reminder of who his enemies truly were. He was not Chang—he could not feel good about killing, nor kill well enough to preserve his life—but he was Abelard Svenson. He knew what these villains were doing, and which of them were truly doing it: above him on the platform balcony, Harald Crabbé and the Duke of Stäelmaere. If he could kill them, then Lorenz and Aspiche and Miss Poole did not matter—whatever mischief they made in the world would be limited to the reach of their own two arms and would land them in the same undoubted discontent they knew before their glorious redemption in the Process. The Process depended on the organization of the Cabal—on these two, on d'Orkancz, Lacquer-Sforza, and Xonck. And Robert Vandaariff... he must be the leader. Doctor Svenson suddenly knew that even if he did escape he would not be meeting Chang or Miss Temple at Stropping Station. Either they were dead, or they would be at Harschmort.

But what could he hope to do? Aspiche was tall, strong, armed, and vicious—perhaps even a match for Chang. Doctor Svenson was unarmed and spent. He looked back to the kiln. Lorenz walked toward them, shucking his gauntlets as he came. Above, Crabbé and the Duke chatted quietly—or Crabbé was chatting and the Duke nodding at what he heard, his face glacially impassive. Svenson counted fifteen wooden steps to their platform. If he could make a dash for it, reach them ahead of Aspiche—Crabbé would again throw himself in front of the Duke... Svenson thought of his pockets—was there any kind of weapon? He scoffed—a pencil stub, a cigarette case, the glass card... the card, perhaps if he could snap it in his hands as he ran, and use the jagged edge, one sharp cut into Crabbé's throat, and then to take the Duke hostage—to drag him up the steps, somehow—would he have his coach above?—making it back to the train, or all the way to the city. Lorenz was nearing them. It was the perfect distraction. He casually slipped a hand into his pocket and groped for the card. He shifted his feet, ready to run.

"Colonel Aspiche," called Doctor Lorenz, "we are nearly—"

Aspiche swung his forearm savagely across the back of Svenson's head, knocking him to his knees, his skull near to bursting with pain, his stomach heaving, tasting the vomit in his throat, blinking tears from his eyes. Somewhere behind him—it seemed miles away—he could hear Lorenz's thin laughter and then the dark hiss of Aspiche at his ear.

"Don't even *think* of it."

Svenson knew he would probably die, but he also knew that if he did not get off his knees he would lose whatever infinitesimal chance he had. He spat and wiped his mouth on his sleeve, noticing with vague surprise that his hand held the blue card still. With a terrible effort he braced his other arm on the grimy clay and raised one knee. He pushed off, wobbled, and then felt Aspiche take hold of his greatcoat collar and yank him up to his feet. He let go and Svenson staggered, nearly falling again. Again he heard Lorenz laugh, and then Crabbé call out from above.

"Doctor Svenson! Any new thoughts about the location of your comrades?"

"I am told they are dead," he called back, his voice hoarse and weak.

"Perhaps they are," responded Crabbé. "Perhaps we have taken enough of your time."

Behind him he heard the metal swish of Colonel Aspiche drawing his saber. He must turn and face him. He must snap the card and drive the sharp edge into his neck, or his eyes, or . . . he could not turn. He could only look up at Crabbé's satisfied face, leaning over the railing. Svenson pointed to the quarry walls and called up to the Deputy Minister.

"Macklenburg."

"I beg your pardon?"

"Macklenburg. This quarry. I understand the connection, your indigo clay. This can only be a small deposit. The Macklenburg mountains must be full of it. If you control its Duke, there is no end to your power . . . is that your plan?"

"*Plan,* Doctor Svenson? I'm afraid that is already the *case.* The *plan* is what to do with the power we've managed to achieve. With the help of wise men like the Duke here—"

Svenson spat. Crabbé stopped mid-sentence.

"Such *vulgarity*—"

"You've insulted my country," called Svenson. "You've insulted this one. You're going to pay, each arrogant one of you—"

Crabbé looked past Svenson's shoulder to Colonel Aspiche. "Kill him."

The shot took him by surprise, as he was expecting a blow from a saber—and it took him another moment to realize that it wasn't he who had been hit by the bullet. He heard the scream—again, wondering that it wasn't coming from his own mouth—and then saw the Duke of Stäelmaere reel into the railing, clutching his right shoulder, quite cleanly punctured, blood pouring through his long white fingers clutching the wound. Crabbé wheeled, his mouth working, as the Duke dropped to his knees, his head slipping through the rails. Above and behind them, both hands tightly gripping the smoking service revolver, stood Elöise.

"God be damned, Madame!" shouted Crabbé. "Do you know who you have shot? It is a capital offense! It is treason!" She fired again, and this time Svenson saw the shot blow out through the Duke's chest, a thick quick fountain of blood. Stäelmaere's mouth opened with surprise at the impact, at the shocking scope of his agony, and he collapsed to the planking.

Svenson whirled, drawing new energy from his rescue, and—recalling something he'd once seen in a wharf-side bar—stomped on Colonel Aspiche's boot in the same moment he shoved the man straight back sharply with both hands. As the Colonel fell back, Svenson's weight fixed his foot to the ground so that he was both unable to rebalance himself and to prevent his own weight from being thrown against his pinned ankle. Svenson heard the cracking bones as the Colonel landed with a cry of rage and pain. He leapt away—Aspiche, even so down, was swinging the saber, face reddened, tears at the corners of his eyes—and dashed to the stairs. Elöise fired again—apparently missing Crabbé, who had retreated into the corner of the landing, arms over his face, hunched away from the gun. Svenson charged and struck him in his exposed stomach. Crabbé doubled forward with a grunt, his hands clutching his belly. Svenson swung again at the Deputy Minister's now-exposed face, and the man went down in a heap. Svenson gasped—he had no idea how such a blow would hurt his hand—and staggered toward his rescuer.

"Bless you, my dear," he breathed, "for you have saved my life. Let us climb—"

"They are coming!" she said, her voice rising with fear. He looked back down to see Lorenz's assistants and the gang of men from the benches all running. Lorenz had helped Aspiche to his feet and the limping, hopping Colonel was waving his saber and bawling orders.

"Kill them! Kill them! They have murdered the Duke!"

"The Duke?" whispered Elöise.

"You did right," Svenson assured her. "If I may, for there are many of them—"

He reached for the pistol and took it, pulling back the hammer, and jumped down to the cowering Crabbé. The men charged up the stairs as Svenson took the Minister by his collar and raised him to his knees, grinding the gun barrel against Crabbé's ear. They surged to the very edge of the platform, eyeing Svenson and Elöise with hatred. Svenson looked over the rail to the quarry floor to where Lorenz stood supporting Aspiche. He shouted down to them.

"I will kill him! You know I will do it! Call your fellows off!"

He looked back to the crowd and saw it part to allow Miss Poole to pass through. She stepped onto the platform, smiling icily.

"Are you quite all right, Minister?" she asked.

"I am alive," muttered Crabbé. "Has Doctor Lorenz finished his work?"

"He has."

"And your charges?"

"As you can see, quite well—enthusiastic to protect you and avenge the Duke."

Crabbé sighed. "Perhaps it is best this way, perhaps it can be better worked. You will need to prepare his body."

Miss Poole nodded, and then looked up beyond Svenson to Elöise. "It seems we have underestimated you, Mrs. Dujong!"

"You left me to die!" shouted Elöise.

"Of course she did," called Crabbé, rubbing his jaw. "You failed your test—it seemed as if you *would* die, like the others. It cannot be helped—you are wrong to place blame with Elspeth. Besides, look at you now—so bold!"

"Do you think we were hasty with our decision, Minister?" asked Miss Poole.

"Indeed I do. Perhaps Mrs. Dujong will be joining our efforts after all."

"Join you?" cried Elöise. "*Join* you? After—after all—"

"You forget," called Miss Poole. "Even if you do not remember why you came, *I* remember it quite well—every noisome little secret you offered up in exchange for your *advancement*."

Elöise stood, her mouth open, looking to Svenson, then back at Miss Poole. "I did not—I cannot—"

"You wanted it before," said Miss Poole. "And you want it still. You've proven yourself quite bold."

"There's barely a choice, my dear," observed Crabbé with a sigh.

Svenson saw the confusion on Elöise's face and jabbed the gun hard into Crabbé's ear, stopping the man's speech. "Did you not hear what I said? We will be going at once!"

"O yes, Doctor Svenson, you were heard quite clearly," Crabbé muttered, wincing. He looked up at Miss Poole. "Elspeth?"

The woman retained her icy smile. "Such *chivalry,* Doctor. First it is Miss Temple, and now Mrs. Dujong—a veritable collector of hearts you seem, I never would have thought it."

Svenson ignored her, and yanked Crabbé back toward the stairs.

"We will be taking our leave—"

"Elspeth!" the Deputy Minister croaked.

"You will not," Miss Poole announced.

"I beg your pardon?" asked Svenson.

"You will not. How many shots remain in your gun?"

Aspiche called back to her from below, a disembodied voice. "She fired three times, and it is a six-shot cylinder."

"So there you are," continued Miss Poole, indicating the crowd of men around her. "Three shots. We are at least ten, and you at the very most can shoot three. We will take you."

"But the first I shoot shall be Minister Crabbé."

"It is more important that our work proceed, and your escape may endanger it. Do you agree, Minister?"

"Unfortunately, Svenson, the woman is correct—"

Svenson cracked him sharply on the head with the gun butt. "Stop talking!"

Miss Poole spoke to the gang of men behind her. "Doctor Svenson is a *German* agent. He has succeeded in causing the death of the Queen's own noble brother—"

Doctor Svenson looked up at Elöise, whose eyes were wide with fear. "Run now," he told her. "Escape—I will hold them off—"

"Do not bother, Mrs. Dujong," called Miss Poole. "We cannot allow either of you to leave—really we can't. And I do promise, Doctor, however much time your bravery does buy your ally, she will not in that dress outrun these gentlemen across three miles of open road."

Svenson was at a loss. He did not believe they would sacrifice Crabbé so easily—yet could he risk Elöise's life on the chance? But, if he were to surrender—impossible, surely—what hope would they have of surviving? None! They'd be ash in Lorenz's oven—it was an appalling thought, unconscionable—

"Doctor . . . Abelard . . ." Elöise whispered to him from above. He looked up at her, helpless, sputtering.

"You will not join them—you will not stay—"

"What if she wants to stay?" asked Miss Poole, wickedly.

"She does not—she cannot—be quiet!"

"Doctor Svenson!" It was Lorenz, shouting from below. Svenson edged closer to the rail—pulling his hostage with him—and looked down. The man had walked over to the large conglomeration of tarps, covering the hidden train car. "Perhaps this will convince you of our great purpose!"

Lorenz pulled on a rope line and the tarps were released. At once the great shape beneath them rose some twenty feet in a lurch, thrusting up clear of the covering. It was an enormous cylindrical gasbag, an airship, a dirigible. As it ascended to the limits of its tethering cables, he could see propellers, engines, and the large cabin underneath. The entire thing was even larger than he'd thought, expanding like an insect coming out of its cocoon, an iron skeleton of supporting struts snapping into place as it rose—and the whole painted to perfectly match the deepest midnight sky. Traveling at night the craft would be near invisible.

Before Svenson could say a word, Elöise screamed. He wheeled to see her off balance, a man's hand incongruously holding onto her leg through the gap in the stairs—an arm in a red sleeve, Aspiche, reaching up from below while he'd been distracted by Lorenz's spectacle like a gullible fool. Svenson watched helplessly as she tried to pull herself free, to step on his wrist with her other foot—it was all that was needed for the spell to be broken. The men around Miss Poole surged forward, cutting Svenson off from Elöise. Crabbé dropped into a ball on the planking, pulling Svenson off balance. Before he could re-position the pistol the men were upon him—a fist across his jaw, a forearm clubbing him across the head and he staggered back into the rail. Elöise screamed again—they were all around her—he had failed her completely. The men scooped him up bodily and threw him over the rail.

He came to his senses with the cloudless black night sky in motion above him and the steady bumping of gravel and dirt beneath his skull. He was being dragged by his feet. It took the Doctor a moment to realize that his arms were over his head and his greatcoat tangled up behind, scooping up loose earth like a rake as he was pulled along. Toward the oven, he knew. He craned his head and saw a man at each leg, two of Lorenz's fellows. Where was Elöise? He felt the pain in his neck and aches everywhere, but nowhere the sharp jarring agony that must mean a broken bone—and the way they carried his legs and his arms dragged, he would certainly know. His hands were empty—what had happened to his revolver? He cursed his pathetic attempts at heroism. Rescued by a woman only to betray her trust with incompetence. As soon as the men saw he was awake they would simply dash his brains out with a brick. And what could he possibly do, unarmed, against both of them? He thought of everyone he had failed... how would this be any different?

The men dropped his legs without ceremony. Svenson blinked, still groggy, as one of them looked back at him with a knowing smile, and the other stepped to the oven.

"He's awake," said the smiling one.

"Hit him with the shovel," called the other.

"I will at that," said the first, and began to look around him for it.

Svenson tried to sit up, to run, but his body—awkward, aching, stiff—did not respond. He rolled onto his side and forced his knees up beneath him, pushing off and then up into a stumbling tottering attempt to walk away.

"Where do you think you're going, then?" called the laughing voice behind him. Svenson flinched, fearing any moment to feel the shovel slicing across the back of his skull. His eyes searched for some answer, some idea—but only saw the dirigible hovering across the quarry and above it a pitiless black sky. Could this be the finish? So pedestrian and brutal, cut down like a beast in a farmyard? With a sudden impulse Svenson spun around to face the man, extending his open hand.

"A moment, I beg of you."

The man had indeed picked up the shovel and held it ready to swing. His companion stood some feet behind him, with a metal hook he'd clearly just used to pry open the oven hatch—even this far from the glowing furnace Svenson could feel the increase in heat. They smiled at him.

"Will he offer us money, do you reckon?" said the one with the hook.

"I will not," said the Doctor. "First, because I have none, and second, because whatever money I have will be yours in any case, once you knock me on the head."

At this the men nodded, grinning that he had guessed their unstoppable plan.

"I cannot offer you anything. But I can ask you—while I have breath—for I know you will be curious, and it would pain me to leave such honest fellows—for I know you merely do what you must—in such very, very grave danger."

They stared at him for just a moment. Svenson swallowed.

"What danger's that?" asked the man with the shovel, shifting his grip in anticipation of swinging it rather hard into Svenson's face.

"Of course—of course, no one has told you. Never mind—I'm not one to interfere—but if you would, for the sake of my conscience—promise to throw this, this *article* straight into the oven after—well, after *me*—" His hand reached into a pocket and pulled forth his remaining blue card—he'd no idea which—and held it out for them to see. "It seems a mere bit of glass, I know—but you must, for your own safety, put it straight into the fire. Do it now—or let me do it—"

Before he could say another word the one with the shovel stepped forward and snatched the card from Svenson's hand. He took two steps back, eyeing the Doctor with a sullen suspicion, and then looked down into the card. The man went still. His companion looked at him, then at Svenson, and then lunged over the other man's shoulder to look at the card, reaching for it with a large calloused hand. Then he stopped as well, his own attention hooked into place.

Svenson watched with disbelief. Could it be so simple? He took a gentle step forward, but as he extended his hands to take the shovel the card came to the end of its cycle and both men emitted a small sigh that stopped his movement cold. Then they sank into the next repetition, jaws slack, eyes dull. With a brutal determination, Svenson snatched the shovel cleanly away and swept it down twice, slamming the flat blade across each man's head, one after the other, as they looked up at him, still dazed. He dropped the shovel, collected the blue glass card, and turned away as quickly as he could. He had not used the edge—with luck each man would live.

* * *

A chopping roar echoed off the stone walls—such an encompassing din that he'd barely noticed it, assuming it was inside his battered skull. It must be the dirigible—its engine and propellers! What would drive such a thing, he wondered—coal? steam? The iron-framed cabin had looked woefully fragile. Had anyone heard his conversation with the men? Had anyone seen? He looked up, squinting—what had happened to his monocle?—at the demonic airship. It had risen to the height of the iron-red stone walls, tethered to the quarry bed only by a few small cables. There were figures in the window of the gondola, too far away to see clearly. He didn't care about them—what had happened to Elöise? If she had not been taken to the oven with him—if she was not dead—then what had they done with her?

The tall staircase seemed empty save at the very top, where a cluster of figures had gathered on a level equal to the suspended dirigible's cabin. On the quarry floor he saw only three men minding the last ropes, their attention focused upwards. Doctor Svenson limped toward the stairs, his right leg dragging, his neck and shoulders and head feeling as if they'd been wrapped in plaster and then set aflame. He wiped his mouth on his filthy sleeve and spat, having put more dust into his mouth than he'd wiped away. There was blood on his face—his own? He'd no idea. The figures on the giant staircase had to be the men and women from the train. Would Miss Poole be with them? No, he reasoned—no one would be with them. They'd served their purpose. Miss Poole would be waving from the gondola, off to Harschmort with the others. Where was Elöise?

Svenson walked more quickly, pushing against the objections of his body. His fingers dug into his coat and came out with his cigarette case. There were three left, and he stuffed one into his bloody face as he hobbled forward, and then exclaimed with pain when he tried to strike a match on a split thumbnail. He changed hands, lit the cigarette, and drew in an exquisitely taxing lungful of smoke, shaking the pain out of his hand, dragging his right foot forward, and finally heaving a thick bolus of phlegm and blood and dust from the back of his throat. His eyes were watering but the smoke pleased him nevertheless, somehow recalling himself to his task. He was becoming relentless, unstoppable, an adversary of legend. He spat again and in another stroke of luck happened to glance down at where he was spitting—to see if there was any visible blood—and saw something in the dirt catching the light. It was glass—it was his monocle! The chain had snapped when he was being dragged, but the glass was whole! He wiped it off as best he could, smiling stupidly, then pulled out his shirt-tail to wipe it again, his sleeve having hopelessly smeared things. He screwed it in place.

Crabbé stood framed in the small opened window, shouting to someone on the stairs. It was Phelps, evidently enough recovered to travel on his own. Next to Crabbé in the window was indeed Miss Poole, waving away. He did not see Lorenz—perhaps Lorenz was flying the craft. Doctor Svenson knew absolutely nothing about how these things worked, indeed, how they stayed in the air at all. Aspiche had to be inside. Where was the body of the Duke? Would that be in a cart, going back to the city with Phelps? Would that be where he found Elöise—dead or alive? It seemed likely—he would need to climb the stairs and follow them into Tarr Village.

He was half-way across the quarry, the airship looming larger above him with each step. Still no one had seen him, not even to look for the two stupefied men. Someone would have to turn—the fellows minding the cable would release it any moment. He'd never make the stairs—he couldn't outrun a child. He needed to hide. Svenson stopped and looked around for some niche in the rock when something fell in the dirt some ten yards away. He looked at it—couldn't tell what it was—and then turned his gaze to where it might have possibly come from. Above him, through the back window of the dirigible's gondola, he saw a hand against the glass and a pale, half-obscured face. He looked again at what had fallen. It was a book... a black book... leather-bound... he looked up again. It was Elöise. He was an idiot.

The Doctor charged forward just as the nearest of the men minding the cables finally happened to look his way, but his cry of alarm at the strange, running figure emerged as an inarticulate shout. Svenson lowered his shoulder and cannoned into his midsection, knocking them both sprawling and the cable loose from the grounded spike that had held it. The rope began to snake around them as the dirigible surged against its moorings. The other two men released their own lines, thinking this had been the signal—only realizing their error once the lines had actually been slipped. Svenson struggled to his feet and dove for the whipping cable—he was insane, nearly gibbering with terror—and thrust his arm through the knotted loop at its end. The dirigible lurched upwards and with a shriek Svenson was pulled off his feet, some three feet in the air. The craft surged into the black sky, Doctor Svenson kicking his legs and holding to the rope more tightly than he ever imagined human beings could do. He swept past the crowd on the steps, swinging like a human pendulum. At once he was out of the quarry and over a meadow, the soft grass close beneath him for a sudden tempting moment. Could he drop and survive? His hand was tangled in the rope. Fear had made his grip hard as steel and before he could push another thought through his paralyzed mind the craft rose again, the meadow spiraling farther and farther away.

Black night above and around him, mocked by a chilling wind, Doctor Svenson looked helplessly at the impossibly distant gondola and began to climb, hand over bloodied hand, gasping, sobbing, all the terrors of hell screaming below his feet, his eyes now screwed shut in agony.

SEVEN

Royale

Once she made a decision, Miss Temple considered it an absolutely ridiculous waste of time to examine the choice further—and so from the vantage of her coach she did not debate the merits of her journey to the St. Royale Hotel, instead allowing herself the calming pleasure of watching the shops pass by to either side and the people of the city all about their day. Normally, this was not a thing she cared for—save for a certain morbid curiosity about what flaws could be deduced from a person's dress and posture—but now, as a consequence of her bold separation from the Doctor and Cardinal Chang, she felt empowered to observe without the burden of judgment, committed as she was to action, an arrow in mid-flight. And the fact was, she did feel that merely being in motion had stilled the tempest of feeling that had overtaken her in the Comte's garden and, even worse, in the street. If she was not up to the challenge of braving the St. Royale Hotel, then how could she consider herself any kind of adventurer? Heroines did not pick their own battles—the ones they knew they could win. On the contrary, they managed what they had to manage, and they did not lie to themselves about relying on others for help instead of accomplishing the thing alone. Would she be safer to have waited for Chang and Svenson—however much of the plan was her own devising—so they could have entered the place in force? It was arguable at the very least (stealth, for one) that she alone was best suited for the task. But the larger issue was her own opinion of herself, and her level of loss, relative to her companions. She smiled and imagined meeting them outside the hotel—she chuckled at how long it would take them to find her—vital information in hand and perhaps the woman in red or the Comte d'Orkancz, now utterly subject, in tow.

Besides, the St. Royale held her destiny. The woman in red, this Contessa Lacquer-Sforza (simply another jot of proof, as if any were needed, of the Italian penchant for ridiculous names) was her primary enemy, the woman who had consigned her to death and worse. Further, Miss Temple could not help wonder at the woman's role in the seduction—there was no other word—of Roger Bascombe. She knew objectively that the primary engine must be Roger's ambition, manipulated with ease by the Deputy Minister, to whose opinions, as a committed climber, Roger would slavishly adhere. Nevertheless, she could not but picture the woman and Roger in a room together . . . like a cobra facing a puppy. She had seduced him, obviously, but to what actual—which is to say literal, physical—degree? One perfect raised eyebrow and a single purse of her rich scarlet lips would have had him kneeling. And would she have taken Roger for herself or passed him along to one of her minions—one of the other ladies from Harschmort House—that Mrs. Marchmoor—or was it Hooke? There were really too many names. Miss Temple frowned, for thinking of Roger's idiocy made her cross, and thinking of her enemies turning him to their usage with such evident ease made her even crosser.

The coach pulled up outside the hotel and she paid off the driver. Before the man could jump from his box to help her, a uniformed doorman stepped forward to offer his hand. Miss Temple took it with a smile and carefully climbed down to the street. The coach rattled away as she walked to the door, nodding her thanks to a second doorman as he opened it, and into the grand lobby. There was no sign of any person she recognized—all the better. The St. Royale was openly sumptuous, which didn't quite appeal to Miss Temple's sense of *order.* Such places did the work *for* a person, which she recognized was part of the attraction but disapproved of—what was the point of being seen as remarkable when it was not really you being seen at all, but your surroundings? Still, Miss Temple could admire the display. There were scarlet leather banquettes and great gold-rimmed mirrors on the wall, a tinkling fountain with floating lotus flowers, large pots of greenery, and a row of gold and red columns supporting a curving balcony that hung over the lobby, the two colors twisting around the poles like hand-carved ribbons. Above, the ceiling was more glass and gold mirrors, with a crystal chandelier whose dangling end point, a multifaceted ball of glittering glass, was quite as large as Miss Temple's head.

She took all of this in slowly, knowing there was a great deal to see, and that such sights easily dazzled a person, encouraging them to ignore what might be important details: like the row of mirrors against the oddly curving left wall, for example, which were strange in that they seemed placed not so much for people to stand before as to reflect the entirety of the lobby, and even the street beyond it—almost as if they were a row of windows rather than mirrors. Miss Temple immediately thought of the odious comment of the still more odious Mr. Spragg, about the cunning Dutch glass—about her own unintentional display in the Harschmort dressing room. Doing her best to shrug off twin reactions of mortification and thrill, she turned her thoughts more directly to her task. She imagined herself still standing in the lobby, trying to get up her nerve, when Chang and Svenson entered behind her, catching up before she had even done anything—she would feel every bit the helpless fool she was trying not to be.

Miss Temple strode to the desk. The clerk was a tall man with thinning hair brushed forward with a bit too much pomade, so the normally translucent hair tonic had creamed over the skin beneath his hair—the effect being not so much offensive as unnatural and distracting. She smiled with the customary crispness that she brought to most impersonal dealings and informed him she had come to call on the Contessa Lacquer-Sforza. He nodded respectfully and replied that the Contessa was not presently in the hotel, and indicated the door to the restaurant, suggesting that she might desire to take a little tea while she waited. Miss Temple asked if the Contessa would be long in arriving. The man answered that, truthfully, he did not know, but that her normal habit was to meet several ladies for a late tea or early aperitif at this time. He wondered if Miss Temple was acquainted with those ladies, for indeed one or more of them might well be in the restaurant already. She thanked him, and took a step in that direction. He called to her, asking if she wanted to leave her name for the Contessa. Miss Temple told him that it was *her* habit to remain a surprise, and continued into the restaurant.

Before she could even scan the tables for a familiar or dangerous face, a black-coated fellow was standing far too close and asking if she was meeting someone, if she had come for tea or supper or perhaps, his brow twitching in encouragement, an aperitif. Miss Temple snapped—for she did not like to be pestered under any circumstances—that she would prefer tea and two scones and a bit of fruit—fresh fruit, and peeled—and walked past him, looking around the tables. She proceeded to a small table that faced the doorway but was yet some distance into the restaurant, so that she would not be immediately visible from the doorway—or the lobby—and could herself scrutinize anyone who happened to enter. She placed her bag, holding the revolver, onto the next chair, making sure it was beneath the starched tablecloth and unapparent to any passing eye, and sat back to wait for her tea, her mind wandering again to the question of her present solitude. Miss Temple decided that she liked it perfectly well—in fact, it made her feel quite free. To whom was she obliged? Chang and Svenson could take care of themselves, her aunt was packed away—what hold could any enemy now place over her, aside from a threat to her own bodily safety? None at all—and the idea of drawing the revolver and facing down a host of foes right there in the restaurant became increasingly appealing.

She picked at the weave of the tablecloth—it was of quite a high quality, which pleased her—and found she was equally impressed with the St. Royale's tableware, which, while displaying an elegance of line, did not abjure a certain necessary *weight,* especially important in one's knife, even if all one were to do with that knife was split a scone and slather cream into the steaming crease. Despite Miss Temple having had tea that very morning, she was looking keenly forward to having tea again—indeed, it was her favorite meal. A diet of scones, tea, fruit, and, if she must, some beef consommé before bedtime and she would be a happy young lady. Her tea arrived first, and she was busily occupied with scrutinizing her waiter's handling of the teapot and the hot water pot and the cup and saucer and the silver strainer and the silver dish in which to set the strainer and the little pitcher of milk and the small plate of fresh-cut wedges of lemon. When all had been arranged before her and the man departed with a nod, Miss Temple set about to deliberately re-arrange everything according to her taste and reach—the lemon going to the side (for she did not care for lemon in her tea, but often enjoyed sucking on one or two slices after she had eaten everything else, as a kind of astringent meal-finisher—apart from which, as she had *paid* for the lemon slices, it always seemed she might as well sample them), the strainer near it, the milk to the other side, and the pot and hot water positioned to allow her to easily stand—which was often, due to their weight, the length of her arms, and the leverage involved with her chair (whether or not its height allowed her feet to touch the floor, as hers presently did just with the toes) required of her in order to pour. Finally, she made sure there was ample space left for the soon-to-arrive scones, fruit, jam, and thick cream.

She stood and poured just a touch of tea into her cup to see if it was dark enough. It was. She then poured in a bit of milk and took up the teapot again, tipping it slowly. For the first cup, if one was careful, it was usually possible to forego the strainer, as most of the leaves would be sodden and at the bottom of the pot. The tea was a perfect pale mahogany color, still hot enough to steam. Miss Temple sat down and took a sip. It was perfect, the kind of hearty, savory brew that she imagined really ought to be somehow cut up with a knife and fork and eaten in bites. Within another two minutes, passed affably with sipping, the rest of her dishes had arrived and she was again pleased to find that the jam was a deeply colored blackberry conserve and that the fruit was, of all things in the world, a lovely orange hothouse mango, arranged on its plate in finger-thick, length-wise slices. She wondered idly how much this tea was going to cost, and then shrugged away her care. Who knew if she would even be alive in the morning? Why begrudge the simple pleasures that might unexpectedly appear?

Though she did make a point, when she remembered, to glance at the restaurant doorway and scrutinize whoever might be entering, Miss Temple spent the next twenty minutes assiduously focused on slicing and preparing the scones with just the right thickness to each half, applying an under-layer of jam, and then on top of that slathering the proper amount of cream. This done, she set these aside and indulged in two strips of mango, one after the other, spearing each with her silver fork on one end and eating her way from the other, bite by bite, down to the tines. After this, she finished her first cup of tea and stood again to pour another, this time using the strainer and also pouring in a nearly equal amount of hot water to dilute the brew that had been steeping all this time. She sampled this, added a bit more milk, and then sat once more and essayed the first half of the first scone, alternating each bite with a sip of tea until it had disappeared. Another slice of mango and she went back to the second half of the first scone, and by the time she had finished that it was also time for another cup of tea, this one requiring just a touch more of the hot water than before. She was down to the final half of her second scone, and the final slice of mango—and trying to decide which of the two to demolish first—when she became aware that the Comte d'Orkancz stood on the opposite side of her table. It was to Miss Temple's great satisfaction that she was able to smile at him brightly and through her surprise announce, "Ah, it seems you have finally arrived."

It was clearly not what he had expected her to say. "I do not believe we have been introduced," replied the Comte.

"We have not," said Miss Temple. "You are the Comte d'Orkancz. I am Celeste Temple. Will you sit?" She indicated the chair near him—which did not hold her bag. "Would you care for some tea?"

"No thank you," he said, looking down at her with both interest and suspicion. "May I ask why you are here?"

"Is it not rude to so interrogate a lady? If we are to have a *conversation*—I do not know where you are from, they say Paris, but my understanding is even in Paris they are not so rude, or not rude in such an ignorant fashion—it would be much better if you would *sit*." Miss Temple grinned wickedly. "Unless of course you fear I will *shoot* you."

"As you would have it," answered the Comte. "I have no wish to be... ill-mannered."

He pulled out the chair and sat, his large body having the odd effect of placing him both near to her and far away at the same time, his hands on the table but his face strangely distant beyond them. He was not wearing his fur coat, but instead an immaculate black evening jacket, his stiff white shirt held with gleaming blue studs. She saw that his fingers, which were disturbingly strong and thick, wore many rings of silver, several of them set with blue stones as well. His beard was heavy but neatly trimmed, mouth arrantly sensual, and his eyes glittering blue. The entire air of the man was strangely powerful and utterly, disturbingly, masculine.

"Would you care for something *other* than tea?" she asked.

"Perhaps a pot of coffee, if you will not object."

"There is no evil in coffee," answered Miss Temple, a bit primly. She raised her hand for the waiter and gave him the Comte's order when he arrived at the table. She turned to the Comte. "Nothing else?" He shook his head. The waiter darted to the kitchen. Miss Temple took another sip of tea and leaned back, her right hand gently gathered the strap on her bag and pulled it onto her lap. The Comte d'Orkancz studied her, his eyes flicking at her hidden hand with a trace of amusement.

"So . . . you were expecting me, it seems," he offered.

"It did not particularly matter who it was, but I knew one of you would arrive, and when you did, that I would meet you. Perhaps I preferred another—that is, perhaps I have more personal *business* elsewhere—but the substance remains unchanged."

"And what substance is that?"

Miss Temple smiled. "You see, that is the kind of question one might ask a foolish young woman—it is the kind of question an idiot suitor would ask *me* when he is convinced that the path to groping my body on a sofa leads through flatteringly earnest conversation. If we are going to get anywhere, Comte, it will aid us both to be reasonable and clear. Do you not think?"

"I do not think too many men have groped you on a sofa."

"That is correct." She took a bite of her scone—she had been regretting the interruption for some minutes—and then another sip of tea. "Would it be better if I asked questions of you?"

He smiled—perhaps in spite of himself, she could not tell—and nodded. "As you prefer."

But here his coffee arrived and she was forced to hold her tongue as the waiter set down the cup, the pot, the milk, the sugar, and their requisite spoons. When he was gone, she gave the Comte time to sample his drink, and was gratified to see that he consumed it black, minimizing the delay. He set down the cup and nodded to her again.

"The woman—I suppose for you there are so *many* women," she said, "but the woman I refer to was from the brothel, one Angelique. I understand from Doctor Svenson that you might have been genuinely troubled—even surprised—at the unfortunate results of your . . . procedure, with her, at the Royal Institute. I am curious—and it is not an idle curiosity, I promise you, but *professional*—whether you possessed any genuine feeling for the girl, either before or after your work destroyed her."

The Comte took another sip of coffee.

"Would you object if I smoked?" he asked.

"If you must," replied Miss Temple. "It is a filthy habit, and I will have no spitting."

He nodded to her gravely and fished a silver case from an inner pocket. After a moment spent considering its contents, he removed a small, tightly wrapped, nearly black cheroot and snapped the case shut. He stuck the cheroot in his mouth and the case in his pocket and came back with a box of matches. He lit the cheroot, puffing several times until the tip glowed red, and dropped the spent match on his saucer. He exhaled, took another sip of coffee, and looked into Miss Temple's eyes.

"You ask because of Bascombe, of course," he said.

"I do?"

"Certainly. He has dashed your plans. When you ask of Angelique, someone from the lower orders we have taken up to join our work, to whom we have offered *advancement*—social, material, *spiritual*—you also inquire about our feeling for *him,* another, if not from such a dubious social stratum, we have embraced. And equally you speculate, indeed are ferociously hungry to know, what reciprocal feeling our work receives *from* him."

Miss Temple's eyes flashed. "On the contrary, Monsieur le Comte, I ask out of curiosity, as the answer will likely dictate whether your fate is a more perfunctory retribution at the hand of objective justice, or lingering, stinging, relentless *torment* at the hands of vengeance."

"Indeed?" he replied mildly.

"For my own part—well, it matters only that your intrigue fails and you are powerless to further pursue it—which could equally mean the law, a bullet, or fierce persuasion. Roger Bascombe is nothing to me. And yet, as I must feel about your lady friend who has profoundly wronged *me*—this, this *Contessa*—so others feel about *you*—concerning this very

Angelique. Because it is rash to assert there are no consequences when a 'mere' woman is at stake."

"I see."

"I do not believe you do."

He did not answer, taking a sip of coffee. He set down the cup and spoke with a certain weariness, as if expanding his opinion even this far involved physical effort. "Miss Temple, you *are* an interesting young lady."

Miss Temple rolled her eyes. "I'm afraid it means very little to me, coming from a murderous cad."

"I have so gathered your opinion. And who is it I have so foully wronged?"

Miss Temple shrugged. The Comte tapped his ash onto the edge of his saucer and took another puff, the cheroot tip glowing red.

"Shall I guess, then? It could well be the Macklenburg Doctor, for indeed through my efforts he was to die, but I do not see him as your sort of wild revenger—he is too much the *raisonneur*—or perhaps this other fellow, whom I have never met, the rogue-for-hire? He is most likely too cynical and grim. Or someone else still? Some distant wrong from my past?" He sighed, almost as if in acceptance of his sinful burden, and then inhaled again—Miss Temple's eyes fixed to the spot of glowing tobacco as it burned—as if to re-embrace the infernal urge that drove him.

"Why exactly have you come to the St. Royale?" he asked her.

She took another bite of scone—quite relishing this serious banter—and another sip of tea to wash it down, and then while she was swallowing shook her head, the chestnut-colored curls to either side of her face tossed into motion. "No, I will not answer your questions. I have been interrogated once, at Harschmort, and that was more than enough. If you want to talk to me, we will do so on my terms. And if not, then please feel free to leave—for you will find out why I am here only exactly when I have planned to show you." She speared the last slice of mango without waiting for his reply and took a bite, licking her lips to catch the juice. She could not help but smile at the exquisite taste of it.

"Do you know," she asked, swallowing just enough of the fruit to speak clearly, "this is quite nearly as delicious as the mangos one can find in the garden of my father's house? The difference—though this is very good—is due, I should think, to the different quality of sunlight, the very positioning of the planet. Do you see? There are great forces at play around us, each day of our lives—and who are we? To what do we pretend? To which of these masters are we in service?"

"I applaud your metaphorical thought," said the Comte dryly.

"But do you have an answer?"

"Perhaps I do. What about . . . art?"

"Art?"

Miss Temple was not sure what he meant, and paused in her chewing, narrowing her eyes with suspicion. Could he have followed her to the art gallery (and if so, when? During her visit with Roger? More recently? Had he been contacted so quickly by the gallery agent, Mr. Shanck?), or did he mean something else . . . but what? To Miss Temple, art was a curiosity, like a carved bone or shrunken head one found at a village market—a vestige of unknown territories it did not occur to her to visit.

"Art," repeated the Comte. "You are acquainted with it . . . with the *idea*?"

"What idea in particular?"

"Of art as alchemy. An act of transformation. Of re-making and rebirth."

Miss Temple held up her hand. "I'm sorry, but do you know . . . this merely prompts me to ask about your relations with a particular painter, a Mr. Oskar Veilandt. I believe he is also from Paris, and most well known for his very large and provocative composition on the theme of the Annunciation. I understand—perhaps it is merely a cruel rumor—that this expressive *masterwork* was cut up into thirteen pieces and scattered across the continent."

The Comte took another drink of coffee.

"I'm afraid I do not know him. He is from Paris, you say?"

"At some point, like so very many people one finds disagreeable."

"Have you seen his work?" he asked.

"O yes."

"What did you think of it? Were you provoked?"

"I was."

He smiled. "*You?* How so?"

"Into thinking you had caused his death. For he *is* dead, and you seem to have stolen a great deal from him—your ceremonies, your Process, and your precious indigo clay. How odd for such things to come from a painter, though I suppose he was also a mystic and an *alchemist*—strange you should just mention *that* too—though I am told it is the usual way of things in that garret-ridden, absinthe-soaked community. You carry yourself so boldly, and yet one wonders, Monsieur, if you have ever had an original thought at all."

The Comte d'Orkancz stood up. With his cigar in his right hand he extended his left to her and as a matter of instinctive response Miss Temple allowed her own hand to be taken—her other groping for purchase on the pistol butt. He raised her hand up to kiss it, an odd moist, brushing whisper across her fingers, released her hand, and stepped back.

"You leave abruptly," she said.

"Think of it as a reprieve."

"For which one of us?"

"For you, Miss Temple. For you will persist . . . and such persistence will consume you."

"Will it indeed?" It was not much of a tart reply as those things go, but the way his eyes glowered it was the best she could do in the moment.

"It will. And that's the thing," he said, placing both hands on the table and leaning close to her face, whispering. "When it comes, you will submit of your own accord. Everyone does. You think you battle monsters—you think you battle us!—but you only struggle with your fear . . . and that fear will shrivel before desire. You think I do not sense your hunger? I see it clearly as the sun. You are already mine, Miss Temple—just waiting for the moment when I choose to take you."

The Comte stood again and stuck the cheroot in his mouth, his tongue flashing wet and pink against the black tobacco. He blew smoke through the side of his mouth and turned without another word, striding easily from the restaurant and Miss Temple's view.

She could not tell if he left the hotel or climbed the great stairs to the upper floors. Perhaps he was going to the Contessa's rooms—perhaps the Contessa had already returned and she had not seen her because of the Comte. But why had he left so abruptly—and after threatening her? She had spoken of the artist, Veilandt. Had that touched a nerve? Did the Comte d'Orkancz *have* nerves? Miss Temple did not know what she ought to do next. Any plan she might have once imagined had vanished in her moment-by-moment desire to frustrate and best the Comte in conversation—yet what had that achieved? She pursed her lips and recalled her first impression of the man, on the train to Orange Canal, his fearsome bulk seemingly doubled by the fur, his harsh, stark penetrating gaze. He had filled her with dread, and after the strange ritualistic presentation in the medical theatre with a darker dread still. But she was quite satisfied with his reaction to the subject of Oskar Veilandt. Despite the Doctor's ruthless tale of the stricken woman and of poison, Miss Temple felt that the Comte d'Orkancz was but another man after all—horrid, arrogant, brutal, powerful to be sure, but with his own architecture of vanity that, once studied, would show the way to bring him down.

Thus assured, she used the next minutes to call for her bill and finish what remained of her meal, sucking on a lemon wedge as she dug into her bag for the proper amount of coin. She had contemplated signing the cost over to the Contessa's rooms, but decided such a mean trick was beneath her. What was more, she felt a profound disinclination to owe the woman for anything (an attitude evidently not shared by the Comte, who had allowed Miss Temple to buy his coffee). Miss Temple stood, collected her bag, and dropped the husk of lemon onto her plate, wiping her fingers on a crumpled napkin. She walked from the restaurant, which was beginning to fill for the early evening service, with a trace of rising anxiety. Chang and Svenson had not arrived. This was good, in that she had not yet accomplished anything of substance and she did truly want to be free of them to work, and yet, did this mean something had happened to them? Had they attempted some particularly foolish scheme without her? Of course they hadn't—they were merely pursuing their own thoughts, about this Angelique, no doubt, or Doctor Svenson's Prince. Their not showing up was entirely to the good of their larger mutual goals.

She returned to the main desk, where the same clerk informed her the Contessa was still to arrive. Miss Temple cast a sly look about her and leaned closer to him. With her eyes, she indicated the curved wall with the mirrors, and she asked if anyone had engaged the private rooms for the evening. The clerk did not immediately reply. Miss Temple brought her voice nearer to a whisper, while at the same time adopting an idle innocent tone.

"Perhaps you are acquainted with other ladies in the Contessa's party of friends, a Mrs. Marchmoor, for one. Or—I forget the others—"

"Miss Poole?" asked the clerk.

"Miss Poole! Yes! Such a sweet creature." Miss Temple grinned, her eyes conveying to the best of her ability innocence and depravity at the same time. "I wonder if either of them will attend the Contessa, or perhaps the Comte d'Orkancz . . . in one of your private rooms?"

She went so far as to bite her own lip and blink at the man. The clerk opened a red leather ledger, ran his finger down the page, and then closed it, signaling for one of the men from the restaurant. When the fellow arrived, the clerk indicated Miss Temple. "This lady will be joining the Contessa's party in room *five*."

"There is one other young lady," the waiter said. "Arrived some minutes ago—"

"Ah, well, even better," said the clerk, and turned to Miss Temple. "You will have company. Poul, please show Miss . . ."

"Miss Hastings," said Miss Temple.

"Miss *Hastings* to room five. If you or the other lady need anything, simply ring for Poul. I will inform the Contessa when she arrives."

"I am most grateful to you," said Miss Temple.

She was led back into the restaurant, where she noticed for the first time a row of doors whose knobs and hinges were cunningly hidden by the patterns in the wallpaper, so they were all but invisible. How had she not seen the previous woman enter—could she have been speaking to the Comte? Could her entry have been what sparked the Comte's exit—could he have done it just to distract her? Miss Temple was intensely curious as to whom it might be. There had been three women in the coach with her at Harschmort, two of whom she took to be Marchmoor and Poole—though who knew, there could be any number of so-swayed female minions—but she had no idea as to the third. She then thought of the many people who had been in the audience in the theatre—like the woman with the green-beaded mask in the corridor. The question was whether it could be anyone who would know her by sight. Most of the time at Harschmort she had worn a mask—and those who had seen her without it were either dead or known figures like the Contessa . . . or so she hoped—but who could say? Who else had been behind the mirror? Miss Temple blanched. Had Roger? She held tightly to her bag, reaching into it for a coin to give the waiter and leaving it open so she could take hold of the revolver.

He opened the door and she saw a figure at the end of the table, wearing a feathered mask that matched the brilliant blue-green of her dress—peacock feathers, sweeping up to frame her gleaming golden hair. Her mouth was small and bright, her face pale but delicately rouged, her throat swanishly long, her small fine hands still wearing her blue gloves. She reminded Miss Temple of one of those closely-bred Russian dogs, thin and fast and perpetually querulous, with the unsettling habit of showing their teeth at anything that set off their uninsulated nerves. She pressed the coin into the waiter's hand as he announced her: "Miss Hastings." The two women nodded to one another. The waiter asked if they required anything. Neither answered—neither *moved*—and after a moment he nodded and withdrew, shutting the door tightly behind him.

"Isobel Hastings," said Miss Temple, and she indicated a chair on the opposite end of the table from the masked blonde woman. "May I?"

The woman indicated that she should sit with a silent gesture and Miss Temple did so, flouncing her dress into a comfortable position without her gaze leaving her companion. On the table between them was a silver tray with several decanters of amber-, gold-, and ruby-colored liquors, and an array of snifters and tumblers (not that Miss Temple knew which glass was for which, much less what the bottles held to begin with). In front of the blonde woman was a small glass, the size of a tulip on a stiff clear stem, filled with the ruby liquid. Through the crystal it gleamed like blood. She met the woman's searching gaze, the shadowed eyes a paler blue than the dress, and tried to infuse her voice with sympathy.

"I am told that the scars fade within a matter of days. Has it been long?"

Her words seemed to startle the woman to life. She picked up her glass and took a sip, swallowed, and just refrained from licking her lips. She set her drink back on the tablecloth, but kept hold of it.

"I'm afraid you are . . . mistaken." The woman's voice was tutored and precise, and Miss Temple thought a trifle bereft, as if a life of constraint or routine had over time encouraged a certain narrowness of mind.

"I'm sorry, I merely assumed—because of the mask—"

"Yes, of course—that is quite obvious—but no, that is not why—no . . . I have not—I am here . . . in secret."

"Are you an intimate of the Contessa?"

"Are you?"

"I should not say so, no," said Miss Temple airily, forging ahead. "I am more an acquaintance of Mrs. Marchmoor. Though I have of course spoken to the Contessa. Did you—if I may speak of it openly—attend the affair at Harschmort House, when the Comte made his great *presentation*?"

"I was there . . . yes."

"May I ask your opinion of it? Obviously, you are *here*—which is an answer in itself—but beyond that, I am curious—"

The woman interrupted her. "Would you care for something to drink?"

Miss Temple smiled. "What are *you* drinking?"

"Port."

"Ah."

"Do you disapprove?" The woman spoke quickly, an eager peevishness entering her voice.

"Of course not—perhaps a small taste—"

The woman dramatically shoved the silver tray toward her, some several feet down the table, clinking the glasses together and jostling the bottles—though nothing fell or broke. Despite the effect of this strange gesture, Miss Temple still needed to stand to reach the tray and did so, pouring a small amount of the ruby port into an identical glass, replacing the heavy stopper, and sitting. She breathed in the sweet, medicinal odor of the liquor but did not drink, for something about the smell made her throat clench.

"So . . . ," Miss Temple continued, "we were *both* at Harschmort House—"

"What of the Comte d'Orkancz," the woman said, interrupting her *again*. "Do you know *him*?"

"Oh, certainly. We were just speaking," replied Miss Temple.

"Where?"

"Just here in the hotel, of course. Apparently he has other urgent business and cannot join us."

For a moment she thought the woman was going to stand, but she could not tell if her desire was to find the Comte or run away, startled at his being so near. It was the sort of moment where Miss Temple felt the strange injustice of being a young woman of perception and intelligence, for the more deeply her understanding penetrated a given situation, the more possibilities she saw and thus the less she knew what to do—it was the most unfairly frustrating sort of "clarity" one could imagine. She did not know whether to leap up and stop the woman from leaving or launch into a still more nauseating celebration of the Comte's masculine authority. What she wanted was for the woman to do some of the talking instead of her, and to have an easy minute in which to sample the port. The very name of the beverage had always appealed to her, as an islander, and she had never before tasted it, as it was always the province of men and their cigars after a meal. She expected to find it as vile as it smelled—she found most liquors of any kind vile on principle—but nevertheless appreciated that this one's name suggested travel and the sea.

The woman did not stand, but after a poised second or two re-settled herself on her seat. She leaned forward and—as if reading Miss Temple's frustrated mind—took up her delicate glass and tipped it to Miss Temple, who then took up her own. They drank, Miss Temple appreciating the ruby sweetness but not at all liking the burn in her mouth and throat, nor the queasy feeling she now felt in her stomach. She set it down and sucked on her tongue with a pinched smile. The masked woman had consumed her entire glass and stood up to reach for more. Miss Temple slid the tray back to her—more elegantly than it had been sent—and watched as her companion pulled the decanter from the tray and poured, drank without replacing the decanter, and then to Miss Temple's frank surprise poured yet again. The woman left the decanter where it was and only then resumed her seat.

Feeling cunning, Miss Temple realized with a sly smile that her disapproval was misplaced, for on the contrary, the drunker and more free-speaking her quarry became the better her inquisition would proceed.

"You have not told me your name," she said sweetly.

"Nor will I," snapped the woman. "I am wearing a mask. Are you a fool? Are all of you people fools?"

"I do beg your pardon," said Miss Temple demurely, repressing the urge to throw her glass at the lady's face. "It sounds as if you have had a rough time of things today—is there another who has caused you annoyance? I do hope there is something I can do to help?"

The woman sighed tremblingly, and Miss Temple was again surprised—even dismayed a little—at the ease with which even a false kindness can pierce the armor of despair.

"I beg your pardon," the woman said, her voice just over a whisper—and it seemed then that her companion was a person who very rarely in her life had need to say those words, and that she only voiced them now out of utter desperation.

"No no, please," insisted Miss Temple, "you must tell me what has happened to make your day so trying, and then together we shall find an answer."

The woman tossed off the rest of her port, choked for a moment, swallowed with difficulty, then poured again. This was getting alarming—it was not even time for supper—but Miss Temple merely wetted her own lips on her glass and said, "It *is* very delicious, isn't it?"

The woman did not seem to hear, but began to speak in a low sort of mutter, which when combined with her brittle, sharp voice gave the effect of some circus marvel, one of those disquieting carnival automaton dolls that "spoke" through a strange breathy mix of bladders of air and metal plates from a music box. The sound was not exactly the same, but the spectacle was similar in the way the blonde woman's voice was disturbingly at odds with her body. Miss Temple knew this was partially because of the mask—she had done a great deal of thinking about masks—and was oddly stirred by the movement of the woman's coral-pink lips as they opened and shut within a proscenium of vivid feathers... the unsettling spectacle of her pale face, the puffed fleshy lips—though they were thin, they were still quite evidently tender—the glimpse of white teeth and the deeper pink of her gums and tongue. Miss Temple had a sudden impulse to shove two fingers into the woman's mouth, just to feel how warm it was. But she caught her wandering mind and shook away that shocking thought, for the lady *was* finally speaking.

"I am actually most agreeable, even tractable, that is the thing of it—and when one is of such a temperament, one is *known* and thus gets no credit for being so, people take it as assumed and then want more—they always want more, and such is my nature, for I have always strived within the boundaries of polite society to provide what I can to anyone I can, for I have tried not to be proud, for I could be proud, I could be the proudest girl in the land—I have every right to be whatever I want, and it is vexing, for there are times when I feel that I ought to be, that I ought to be another Queen, more than the Queen, for the Queen is old and horrid-looking—and the worst part is that if I just chose to be that way, if I just did start ordering and screaming and demanding, I would get it, I would get exactly that—but now I wonder if that is really true, I wonder if it's all gone on so long that no one would listen, that they would laugh in my face, or at least behind my back, the way they all laugh behind my back—even though I am who I am—and they would simply do what they are doing already, save more openly and without pretense, with disdain which I do not think I could bear, and my father is the worst of them, he has always been the worst and now he does not see me at all, he does not even attempt to care—he has never cared—and I am expected without question to accept a future chosen for me. No one knows the life I lead. None of you care—and this man, this vulgar *man*—I am expected—a foreigner—it is appalling—and my only solace is that I have always known that he—whoever he turned out to be—would prove the utter ruin of my heart."

The woman drank off her fourth glass of port—and who knew how many she'd consumed before Miss Temple's arrival?—grimaced, and reached at once for the decanter. Miss Temple thought of her own father—craggy, full of rage, impossibly distant, only arbitrarily kind. Her only way of understanding her father was to consider him a natural force, like the ocean or the clouds, and to weather sunny days and storms alike without being personally aggrieved. She knew he had fallen ill, that he would most likely not be living once she returned—if she ever did return—to her island home. It was a thought to prick her conscience with sorrow if she let it, but she did not let it, for she did not really know if the sadness was any different from that she felt at missing the tropical sun. Miss Temple believed that change brought sorrow as a matter of course. Was there particular sadness in her father's absence—either on account of distance or death? Was there sorrow in the fact that she could not for certain say? Her mother she had never known—a young woman (younger than Miss Temple was now, which was a strange thought) slain by the birth of her child. So many people in the world were disappointing, who was to say the lack of any one more was a loss? Such was Miss Temple's normal waspish response to the expression of sympathy at her mother's absence, and if there did exist a tiny deeply set wound within her heart, she did not spend time excavating it for the benefit of strangers, or for that matter anyone at all. Nevertheless, for some reason she could not—or chose not to—name, she found her sympathies touched by the masked woman's jumbled ranting.

"If you were to see him," she asked kindly, "what do you guess the Comte d'Orkancz would advise you to do?"

The woman laughed bitterly.

"Then why don't you leave?"

"And where am I to go?"

"I'm sure there are many places—"

"I cannot *leave*! I am *obliged*!"

"Refuse the obligation. Or if you cannot refuse, then turn it to your advantage—you say you ought to be a queen—"

"But no one will *listen*—no one *imagines*—"

Miss Temple was growing annoyed. "If you truly want to—"

The woman snatched up her glass. "You all sound the same, with your prideful *wisdom*—when it only serves to justify your place at my table! 'Be free! Expand your perceptions!' A load of mercenary rubbish!"

"If you are so assailed," replied Miss Temple patiently, "then how have you managed to come here, masked and alone?"

"Why do you think?" The woman nearly spat. "The St. Royale Hotel is the only place I *can* go to! With two coachmen to make sure I am delivered and collected with no other stop in between!"

"That is ridiculously dramatic," said Miss Temple. "If you want to go elsewhere, *go*."

"How can I?"

"I am sure the St. Royale has many exits."

"But then what? Then where?"

"Any place you want—I assume you have money—it is a very large city. One simply—"

The woman scoffed. "You have no *idea*—you cannot know—"

"I know an insufferable child when I see one," said Miss Temple.

The woman looked up at her as if she had been struck, the port dulling her reactions, her expression tinged with both incomprehension and a growing fury, neither of which would do. Miss Temple stood and pointed to the somewhat isolated swathe of red drapery on the left-hand wall.

"Do you know what that is?" she asked sharply.

The woman shook her head. With a huff, Miss Temple walked over to the curtain and yanked it aside—her ingenious plan momentarily crushed by the flat section of wall that was revealed. But before the woman could speak, Miss Temple saw the indented spots in the painted wood—that it *was* painted wood and not plaster—where one could get a grip, and then the deftly inset hinges that told her how it opened. She wedged her small fingers into the holes and pried up the wooden shutters to reveal a darkened window, the reverse of the golden-framed Dutch mirror, offering the two of them an unobstructed view of the lobby of the St. Royale Hotel and the street front beyond.

"Do you see?" she said, herself distracted with the strangeness of the view—she could see people who were only three feet away who could not see her. As she looked, a young woman stepped directly to the window and began to nervously pull at her hair. Miss Temple felt a discomfiting shiver of familiarity.

"But what does it *mean*?" asked the blonde woman in a whisper.

"Only that the world is not measured by your troubles, and that you are not the limit of the intrigue that surrounds you."

"What—what nonsense—it is like looking into a fish tank!"

Then the woman's hand went to her trembling mouth and she looked anxiously for the decanter. Miss Temple stepped to the table and pushed the tray from her reach. The woman looked up at her with pleading eyes.

"Oh, you do not understand! In my house there are mirrors *everywhere*!"

The door behind them opened, causing both to turn toward the waiter Poul as he escorted another lady into their private room. She was tall, with brown hair and a pretty face marred by the dimming traces of a ruddy looping scar around both eyes. Her dress was beige, set off by a darker brown fringe, and she wore a triple string of pearls tied tightly to her throat. In her hand was a small bag. She saw the women and smiled, slipping a coin to Poul and nodding him from the room as she merrily addressed them.

"You are here! I did not know you would each be free to come—an unhoped-for pleasure, and this way you've had time to get acquainted by yourselves, yes?"

Poul was gone, the door shut behind him, and she sat at the table, in Miss Temple's former spot, moving the port glass to the side as she settled her dress. Miss Temple did not recognize her face, but she remembered the voice—in the coach to Harschmort, the woman who'd told the story of the two men undressing her. The scars on her face were fading—she'd been the one in the medical theatre talking of her changed existence, her newfound missions of power and pleasure... this was Mrs. Marchmoor... Margaret Hooke.

"I wondered if we would meet again," Miss Temple said to her, somewhat icily, intending to alert the blonde woman to the obvious peril this newcomer presented to them both.

"You didn't wonder at all, I am sure," Mrs. Marchmoor replied. "You knew, because you knew you would be hunted down. The Comte tells me you are... of *interest*." She turned to the masked woman in blue, who had drifted back to the table, though she had not resumed her seat. "What do you think, Lydia—from your observation, is Miss Temple a person worth the time? Is she worthy of our investment, or should she be destroyed?"

Lydia? Miss Temple looked at the blonde woman. Could this be the daughter of Robert Vandaariff, the fiancée of the Doctor's drunken

Prince, the heiress to the largest fortune imagined? The object of her gaze did not respond, save to search again for the decanter, this time catching it, pulling out the stopper, and pouring another glass.

Mrs. Marchmoor chuckled. Lydia Vandaariff downed the contents—her fifth glass?—and positively bleated, "Shut up. You're late. What are the two of you talking about? Why am I talking to you two when it's Elspeth I'm supposed to see? Or even more—the Contessa! And why are you calling her Temple? She said her name was Hastings."

Miss Vandaariff wheeled to Miss Temple, squinting with suspicion. "Didn't you?" She looked back to Mrs. Marchmoor. "What do you mean, 'hunted down'?"

"She is making a poor joke," said Miss Temple. "I have not been *found*—on the contrary, it is I who have come here. I am glad you spoke to the Comte—it saves me time explaining—"

"But who *are* you?" Lydia Vandaariff was becoming drunker by the minute.

"She is an enemy of your father," answered Mrs. Marchmoor. "She is undoubtedly armed, and intends some mayhem or ransom. She killed two men the night of the ball—that we know of, there may be more—and her confederates have plans to assassinate your Prince."

The blonde woman stared at Miss Temple. *"Her?"*

Miss Temple smiled. "It is ridiculous, is it not?"

"But . . . you *did* say you were at Harschmort!"

"I was," said Miss Temple. "And I have tried to be kind to you—"

"What were you doing at my masked ball?" Miss Vandaariff barked at her.

"She was killing people," said Mrs. Marchmoor tartly.

"That soldier!" whispered Lydia. "Colonel Trapping! They told me—he seemed so fit—but why would anyone—*why would you want him dead*?"

Miss Temple rolled her eyes and exhaled through her teeth. She felt as if she had become marooned in a ridiculous play made up of one rambling conversation after another. Here she had before her a young woman whose father surely sat at the heart of the entire intrigue, and another who was one of its most subtle agents. Why was she wasting time confirming or denying their trivial questions, when it was in her own power to take control? So often in her life Miss Temple was aware of the frustration that built up when she allowed other people their own way of action when she very clearly knew that their intentions were absolutely not her own. It was a pattern followed endlessly with her aunt and servants, and again now as she felt herself a shuttlecock knocked between the two women and their annoyingly at-odds nattering. She thrust her hand into her bag and pulled out the revolver.

"You will be silent, both of you," she announced, "except when answering my questions."

Miss Vandaariff's eyes snapped wide at the sight of the gleaming black pistol, which in Miss Temple's small white hand seemed fearsomely large. Mrs. Marchmoor's reaction was, on the contrary, to adopt an expression of placid calm, though Miss Temple doubted the depths of its serenity.

"And what questions would those be?" Mrs. Marchmoor replied. "Sit *down,* Lydia! And stop drinking! She has a weapon—do try and concentrate!"

Miss Vandaariff sat at once, her hands demurely in her lap. Miss Temple was surprised to see her so responsive to command, and wondered if such discipline had come to be the only kind of attention she recognized and thus, though her entire rambling rant would seem to contradict the idea, what she craved.

"I am looking for the Contessa," she told them. "You will tell me where she is."

"Rosamonde?" Miss Vandaariff began. "Well, she—" She stopped abruptly at a look from the end of the table. Miss Temple glared at Mrs. Marchmoor and then turned back to Lydia, who had placed a hand over her mouth.

"I beg your pardon?" asked Miss Temple.

"Nothing," whispered Miss Vandaariff.

"I should like you to finish your sentence. 'Rosamonde?' "

Miss Temple received no answer. She was particularly annoyed to see a small curl of satisfaction at the corner of Mrs. Marchmoor's mouth. She turned back to the blonde woman with an exasperated snarl.

"Did you not just exclaim to me about the injustice of your position, the predatory nature of those around you, and around your father, the loathsome quality of your intended husband, and the degree to which you—despite your position—are accorded no respect? And here you defer to—to whom? One who has only these weeks shifted her employment from a brothel! One who is an utter minion of the very people you despise! One who quite obviously bears you no good will at all!"

Miss Vandaariff said nothing.

Mrs. Marchmoor's expression devolved into a grim smile. "I believe the girl plays tricks upon us both, Lydia—it is well known she has been thrown over by Roger Bascombe, the prospective Lord Tarr, and no doubt it is some pathetic attempt to regain his affection that brings this person to our door."

"I am not here for Roger Bascombe!" spat Miss Temple, but before she could continue, or wrench the conversation back into her control, the mention of Roger had prompted Miss Vandaariff to carom back to her pose of condescending superiority.

"Can it be any surprise he has dropped her? Just look at her! Pistols in a hotel restaurant—she's a savage! The type that would do well with a whipping!"

"I cannot disagree," replied Mrs. Marchmoor.

Miss Temple shook her head at this scarcely credible idiocy.

"This is nonsense! First you say I am a murderer—an *agent* in league against you—and *now* I am a deluded heartsick girl! Pray make up your mind so I can scoff at you with precision!" Miss Temple confronted Miss Vandaariff directly, her voice rising near to a shout. "Why do you listen to her? She treats you like a servant! She treats you like a child!" She wheeled again to the woman at the end of the table, who was idly twirling a lock of brown hair around a finger. "Why is Miss Vandaariff here? What did you intend for her? Your *Process*? Or merely the thralldom of debauchery? I have seen it, you know—I have seen you—and *him*—in this very room!"

Miss Temple thrust a hand into her green bag. She still had one of the Doctor's glass cards—was it the right one? She took it out, glanced at it and stumbled to her feet—causing Mrs. Marchmoor to menacingly half-rise from the table. Miss Temple recovered her wits—pulling herself out of the blue depths—and brought the revolver to bear, motioning the woman back into her seat. It was the wrong card, with Roger and herself—still the sinister immersion itself might be enough. Miss Temple set the card in front of Miss Vandaariff.

"Have you seen one of these?" she asked.

The querulous blonde looked to Mrs. Marchmoor before answering and then shook her head.

"Pick it up and look into it," said Miss Temple, sharply. "Be prepared for a shock! An unnatural insinuation into the very mind and body of another—where you are helpless, trapped by sensation, subject to their desires!"

"Lydia—do not," hissed Mrs. Marchmoor.

Miss Temple raised the revolver. "Lydia... *do*."

There was something curious, Miss Temple found, in the ease with which one could impose on another an experience that one knew—first hand—to be disquieting, or frightening, or repugnant, and at the grim satisfaction one took in watching the person undergo it. She had no idea of Miss Vandaariff's intimate experience, but assumed, from her childish manner, that she had been generally sheltered, and while she was not thrusting her brusquely into the carnal union of Karl-Horst and Mrs. Marchmoor on the sofa—though she would have been happy to do so—she still felt a little brutal in forcing even this less transgressive card upon her at all. She remembered her own first immersion—the way in which she had naïvely assured Doctor Svenson it was nothing she could not bear (though she had been unable to fully meet his eyes afterwards)—and the shocking sudden delicious troubling rush of sensation she'd felt as the Prince had stepped between his lover's open legs, the lover whose undeniably sweet experience she had herself then shared for that exquisite instant. As a young lady, the value of her virtue had been drilled into her like discipline into a Hessian soldier, yet she could not exactly say where her virtue presently stood—or rather could not separate the knowledge of her body from that of her mind, or the sensations she now knew. If she allowed herself the room to think—a dangerous luxury, to be sure—she must face the truth that her confusion was nothing less than the inability to distinguish her thoughts from the world around her—and that by virtue of this perilous glass her access to ecstasy might be as palpable a thing as her shoes.

Miss Temple had taken out the card as a way to prove to Miss Vandaariff in one stroke the wicked capacity of her enemies and the seductive dangers they might have already offered, to warn her by way of frightening her and so win the heiress to her side, but as she watched the girl gaze into the card—biting her lower lip, quickening breath, left hand twitching on the table top—and then glanced to the end of the table to see Mrs. Marchmoor studying the masked woman with an equally intent expression—she no longer knew if the gesture had been wise. Faced with Lydia's intensity of expression, she even wondered if somehow she had done it to gain perspective on her own experience, as if watching Miss Vandaariff might be watching herself—for she could too readily, despite the need to pay attention, the obvious danger, imagine herself again in the lobby of the Boniface, eyes swimming into the depths of blue glass, hands absently groping her balled-up dress, and all the time Doctor Svenson knowing—even as he turned his back—what was passing with a shudder through her body.

Miss Temple recalled with shock the words of the Comte d'Orkancz—that she would fall prey to her own desire!

Her hand darted forward and she snatched the card away. Before Miss Vandaariff could do anything but sputter in mortified confusion, it had been stuffed back in the green bag.

"Do you see?" Miss Temple cried harshly. "The unnatural science—the feeling of another's experience—"

Miss Vandaariff nodded dumbly, and looked up, her eyes fixed on the bag. "What . . . how could it be possible?"

"They plan to use your place of influence, to seduce you as they have seduced this man, Roger Bascombe—"

Miss Vandaariff shook her head with impatience. "Not them . . . the glass—the *glass*!"

"So, Lydia . . ." chuckled Mrs. Marchmoor from the end of the table, relief and satisfaction in her voice, "you weren't frightened by what you saw?"

Miss Vandaariff sighed, her eyes shining, an exhalation of intoxicated glee. "A little . . . but in truth I don't care about what I saw at all—only for what I *felt* . . ."

"Was it not *astonishing*?" hissed Mrs. Marchmoor, her earlier concern quite forgotten.

"O Lord . . . it *was*! It was the most *exquisite* thing! I was inside his hands, his hunger—groping her—" She turned to Miss Temple. "Groping *you*!"

"But—no, no—" began Miss Temple, her words interrupted by a glance to Mrs. Marchmoor, who was beaming like a lighthouse. "There is another—with *this* woman! And your Prince! Far more intimate—I assure you—"

Miss Vandaariff snapped at Miss Temple hungrily. "Let me see it! Do you have it with you? You must—there must be many, many of them—let me see this one again—*I want to see them all*!"

Miss Temple was forced to step away from Miss Vandaariff's grasping hands.

"Do you not *care*?" she asked. "*That* woman—*there*!—with your *intended*—"

"Why should I care? He is nothing to me!" Miss Vandaariff replied, flapping her hand toward the end of the table. "*She* is nothing to me! But the *sensation*—the submersion into such *experience*—"

The woman was drunk. She was troubled, damaged, spoiled, and now yanking at Miss Temple's arm like a street urchin, trying to get at her bag.

"Control yourself!" she hissed, taking three rapid steps away, raising the pistol—though here she made the realization (and in the back of her mind knew that this was exactly the kind of thing that made a man like Chang a professional, that there *were* things to learn and remember about, for example, threatening people with guns) that whenever one used a gun as a goad to enforce the actions of others, one had best be prepared to use it. If one was not—as, in this moment, Miss Temple recognized she was not prepared to do against Miss Vandaariff—one's power vanished like the flame of a blown-out candle. Miss Vandaariff was too distracted to take in anything save her strangely insistent hunger. Mrs. Marchmoor, however, had seen it all. Miss Temple wheeled, her pistol quite thrust at the woman's smiling face.

"Do not move!"

Mrs. Marchmoor chuckled again. "Will you shoot me? Here in a crowded hotel? You will be taken by the law. You will go to prison and be hanged—we will make sure of it."

"Perhaps—though you shall die before me."

"Poor Miss Temple—for all your boldness, still you comprehend nothing."

Miss Temple scoffed audibly. She had no idea why Mrs. Marchmoor would feel empowered to say such a thing, and thus took refuge in defiant contempt.

"What are you talking about?" whined Lydia. "Where are more of these *things*?"

"Look at that one again," said Mrs. Marchmoor soothingly. "If you practice you can make the card go more slowly, until it is possible to suspend yourself within a single moment as long as you like. Imagine *that,* Lydia—imagine what moments you can drink in again and again and again."

Mrs. Marchmoor raised her eyebrows at Miss Temple and cocked her head, as if to urge her to give up the card—the implication being that once the heiress was distracted the two of them—the adults in the room—could converse in peace.

Against all her better instincts, perhaps only curious to see if what Mrs. Marchmoor had just said might be true, Miss Temple reached into her bag and withdrew the card, feeling as her fingers touched its slick cool surface the urge to look into it herself. Before she could fully resolve not to, Miss Vandaariff snatched it from her grasp and scuttled away to her seat, eyes fixed on the blue rectangle cupped reverently in her hands. Within moments Lydia's tongue was flicking across her lower lip . . . her mind riveted elsewhere.

"What has it done to her?" Miss Temple asked with dismay.

"She will barely hear us, and we can speak clearly," answered Mrs. Marchmoor.

"She seems not to care about her fiancé."

"Why should she?"

"Do *you* care for him?" she demanded, referring to the explicit interaction held fast within glass. Mrs. Marchmoor laughed and nodded at the blue card.

"So *you* are held within that card . . . and on another *I* am . . . *encaptured* with the Prince?"

"Indeed you are—if you think to deny it—"

"Why should I? I can well imagine the situation, though I confess I don't remember it—it is the price one pays for immortalizing one's experience."

"You do not *remember*?" Miss Temple was astonished at the lady's decadent disregard. "You do not remember—*that*—with the Prince—before *spectators*—"

Mrs. Marchmoor laughed again. "O Miss Temple, it is obvious you would benefit from the clarity of the Process. Such foolish questions should nevermore pass your lips. When you spoke to the Comte, did he ask that you join us?"

"He did not!"

"I am surprised."

"He in fact threatened me—that I should submit to you, being so defeated—"

Mrs. Marchmoor shook her head with impatience. "But that is the same. Listen, you may wave your pistol but you will not stop me—for I am no longer of such a foolish mind to be so occupied with *grievance*—from asking again that you recognize the inevitable and join our work for the future. It is a better life, of freedom and action and satisfied desire. You *will* submit, Miss Temple—I can promise you it is the case."

Miss Temple had nothing to say. She gestured with the revolver. "Get up."

If Mrs. Marchmoor had convinced her of one thing, it was that the private room was too exposed. It had served her purpose to pursue her inquiries but was truly no place to linger—unless she was willing to risk the law. With the revolver and the card both in her bag, she drove the women before her—Mrs. Marchmoor cooperating with a tolerant smile, Miss Vandaariff, still masked, making furtive glances that revealed her flushed face and glassy eyes—up the great staircase and along to the Contessa Lacquer-Sforza's rooms. Mrs. Marchmoor had answered the inquiring look of the desk clerk with a saucy wave and without any further scrutiny they passed into the luxurious interior of the St. Royale.

The rooms were on the third floor, which they reached by a second only slightly less grand staircase, the rods and banisters all polished brass, that continued the curve of the main stair up from the lobby. Miss Temple realized that the winding staircases echoed the red and gold carved ribbons around the hotel's supporting pillars, and found herself gratified by the depth of thought put into the building—that one *could* expend such effort, and that she had been clever enough to note it. Miss Vandaariff glanced back at her again, now with a more anxious expression—almost as if some idea had occurred to her as well.

"Yes?" asked Miss Temple.

"It is nothing."

Mrs. Marchmoor turned to her as they walked. "Say what you are thinking, Lydia."

Miss Temple marveled at the woman's control over the heiress. If Mrs. Marchmoor still bore the scars of the Process, she could only have been an intimate of the Cabal for a short time, before which she was in the brothel. But Lydia Vandaariff deferred to her as to a long-time governess. Miss Temple found it entirely unnatural.

"I am merely worried about the Comte. I do not want him to come."

"But he may come, Lydia," replied Mrs. Marchmoor. "You do well know it."

"I do not like him."

"Do you like me?"

"No. No, I don't," she muttered peevishly.

"Of course not. And yet we are able to get along perfectly well." Mrs. Marchmoor threw a smug smile back to Miss Temple, and indicated a branching hallway. "It is this way."

The Contessa was not in the suite. Mrs. Marchmoor had opened it with her key, and ushered them inside. Miss Temple had removed her revolver in the hallway, once they were off the staircase and out of view, and she followed them carefully, her eyes darting about in fear of possible ambush. She stepped on a shoe in the foyer and stumbled. A shoe? Where were the maids? It was a very good question, for the Contessa's rooms were a ruin. No matter where Miss Temple cast her gaze it fell across uncollected plates and glasses, bottles and ashtrays, and ladies' garments of all kinds, from dresses and shoes to the most intimate of items, petticoats, stockings, and corsets—draped over a divan in the main receiving room!

"Sit down," Mrs. Marchmoor told the others, and they did, next to each other on the divan. Miss Temple looked around her and listened. She heard no sound from any other room, though the gaslight lamps were lit and glowing.

"The Contessa is not here," Mrs. Marchmoor informed her.

"Has the place been pillaged in her absence?" Miss Temple meant it as a serious question, but Mrs. Marchmoor only laughed.

"The Lady is not one for particular order, it is true!"

"Does she not have servants?"

"She prefers that they occupy themselves with other tasks."

"But what of the smell? The smoke—the drink—the plates—does she desire *rats*?"

Mrs. Marchmoor shrugged, smiling. Miss Temple scuffed at a corset on the carpet near her foot.

"I'm afraid *that* is mine," whispered Mrs. Marchmoor, with a chuckle.

"Why would you remove your corset in the front parlor of a noble lady?" Miss Temple asked, little short of appalled, but already wondering at the answer, the possibilities disorientingly lurid. She looked away from Mrs. Marchmoor to compose her face and saw herself in the large mirror above her on the wall, a determined figure in green, her chestnut curls, pulled to the back and each side of her head, a darker shade in the warm gaslight, and all around her the tattered litter of decadent riot. But behind her head in the reflection, a flash of vivid blue caught her eye and she turned to see a framed canvas that could only be the work of Oskar Veilandt.

"Another *Annunciation*..." she whispered aloud.

"It is," whispered Mrs. Marchmoor in reply, her voice hesitant and cautious behind her. Hearing it, Miss Temple had the feeling of being watched carefully, like a bird stalked by a slow-moving cat. "You've seen it elsewhere?"

"I have."

"Which fragment? What did it portray?"

She did not want to answer, to acknowledge the woman's interrogation, but the power of the image drove her to speak. "Her head . . ."

"Of course—at Mr. Shanck's exhibition. The head is beautiful . . . such a heavenly expression of peace and pleasure lives in her face—would you not say? And here . . . see how the fingers hold into her hips . . . you see, in the artist's interpretation, how she has been *mounted* by the Angel . . ."

Behind them, Miss Vandaariff whimpered. Miss Temple wanted to turn to her but could not shift her gaze from the near-seething image. Instead, she walked slowly to it . . . the brushstrokes immaculate and smooth, as if the surface more porcelain than pigment and canvas. The flesh was exquisitely rendered, though the fragment itself—so out of context of the whole, with neither face seen, just their hips and the two blue hands—struck her as at once compelling and somehow dreadful to imagine. She wrenched her eyes away. Both women watched her. Miss Temple forced her voice to a normal tone, away from the sinister intimacy of the painting.

"It is an allegory," she announced. "It tells the story of your intrigue. The Angel stands for your work with the blue glass, the lady for all those you would work upon. It is the Annunciation, for you believe that the birth—what your plans conceive—will—will—"

"Redeem us all," finished Mrs. Marchmoor.

"I've never seen such blasphemy!" Miss Temple announced with confidence.

"You have not seen the *rest* of the painting," said Miss Vandaariff.

"Hush, Lydia."

Miss Vandaariff did not answer, but then suddenly placed both hands over her abdomen and groaned with what seemed to be sincere discomfort . . . then doubled over and groaned again, rocking back and forth, a rising note of fear in her moaning, as if this feeling were something she knew.

"Miss Vandaariff?" cried Miss Temple. "What is wrong?"

"She will be fine," said Mrs. Marchmoor mildly, her hand reaching up to gently pat the stricken woman's rocking back. "Did you perchance drink any of the port?" she asked Miss Temple.

"No."

"I *did* note a second glass . . ."

"A taste to wet my lips, nothing more—"

"That was very prudent."

"What was *in* it?" Miss Temple asked.

Miss Vandaariff groaned again, and Mrs. Marchmoor leaned forward to take her arm. "Come, Lydia, you must come with me—you will feel better—"

Miss Vandaariff groaned more pitifully still.

"Come, Lydia . . ."

"What is wrong with her?" asked Miss Temple.

"Nothing—she has merely consumed too much of the preparatory *philtre.* How many glasses did you see her drink?"

"Six?" answered Miss Temple.

"My goodness, Lydia! It is a good thing I am here to help you void the excess." Mrs. Marchmoor helped Miss Vandaariff to her feet, smiling indulgently. She ushered the young blonde woman in an unsteady shuffle toward an open doorway and paused there to turn back to Miss Temple. "We will return in a moment, do not worry—it is merely to the suite's convenience. It was known she would drink the port—so the preparatory *philtre* was added to it in secret. The mixture is necessary for her—but not to such excess."

"Necessary for what?" asked Miss Temple, her voice rising. "Preparatory for *what*?"

Mrs. Marchmoor did not seem to have heard her and reached up to smooth Miss Vandaariff's hair.

"It will do her good to marry, I daresay, and be past such independent revels. She has no head for them at all."

Miss Vandaariff groaned again, perhaps in protest to this unfair assessment, and Miss Temple watched with annoyance and curiosity as the pair disappeared into the next room—as if she had no revolver and they were no sort of prisoner or hostage! She stood where she was, utterly affronted, listening to the clanging lid of a chamber pot and the determined rustling of petticoats, and then decided it was an excellent opportunity to investigate the other rooms without being watched. There were three doors off of the main parlor she was in—one to the chamber pot, which seemed a maid's room, and two others. Through one open archway she could see a second parlor. In it was set a small card table bearing the half-eaten remains of an uncleared meal, and against the far wall a high sideboard quite crowded with bottles. As she stared in, trying to piece together some sense of the display—how many people had been at the table, how much had they been drinking—as she presumed a real investigating adventurer ought to do, Miss Temple worried she'd had at least one complete mouthful of the port—had it been enough to inflict the insidious purpose of their horrid *philtre* onto her body? What fate was Miss Vandaariff being prepared *for*? Marriage? But it could hardly be that—or not in any normal sense of the word. Miss Temple was reminded of livestock being readied for slaughter and felt a terrible chill.

With a hand against her brow she stepped back into the main room and quickly to the third door, which was ajar, the sounds of groans and scuffling feet still insistent behind her. This was the Contessa's bedroom. Before her was an enormous four-poster bed shrouded in purple curtains, and across the floor was strewn more clothing—but these objects, large and small, seemed to float in a room where the walls were far away and, like the floor, dark with shadow like the surface of a black, dead-placid pool, the discarded garments floating like clumps of leaves. She pulled aside the bed curtains. With a primitive immediacy Miss Temple's nostrils flared . . . a delicate scent the Contessa's body had left in the bedclothes. Part of it was frangipani perfume, but underneath that flowered sweetness lay something else, steeped gently between the sheets, close to the odor of freshly baked bread, of rosemary, of salted meat, even of lime. The scent rose to Miss Temple and brought to her mind the human quality of the woman, that however fearsome or composed she was a creature of appetite and frailties after all . . . and Miss Temple had penetrated her lair.

She breathed in again and licked her lips.

Miss Temple quickly wondered if, in such ruinous disorder, the Contessa might have hidden anything of value, some journal or plan or artifact that might explain the Cabal's secret aims. Behind, the complaining groans of Miss Vandaariff persisted. What *had* been done to the woman—it was practically as if she was giving birth! Anxiety gnawed at Miss Temple anew, and she felt a glow of perspiration rise upon her brow and between her shoulder blades. Her truest adversaries—the Contessa and the Comte d'Orkancz—must eventually arrive at these rooms. Was she prepared to meet them? She had brazened out her tea with the Comte well enough, but was much less satisfied by her extended interaction with the two ladies, by any estimation less formidable opponents (if opponent was even the proper word for the distressingly unmoored Miss Vandaariff). Somehow a confrontation that ought to have been taut, antagonistic, and thrilling had become mysterious, distracted, sensual, and lax. Miss Temple resolved to find what she could and leave as quickly as possible.

She first swept her hand beneath the voluminous feather pillows at the head of the bed. Nothing. This was to be expected—a quick lift of the mattress and a look under the bed frame revealed the same result—and it was only with the smallest increase of hope that Miss Temple marched to the Contessa's armoire in search of the drawer containing her intimates. A foolish sort of woman might hide things there, with an idea that somehow the personal nature of the drawer's contents would ward off inquiry. Ever an enemy to the inquisitive, Miss Temple knew the opposite was true—that such silks and stays and hose and whalebone inspired a feral curiosity in almost anyone—who *wouldn't* want to paw through them?—and so the idea of stashing, for example, a tender diary in such a place was tantamount to leaving it in the foyer like a newspaper or, still worse, on the servants' dining table at mealtime. As she expected, no such items of worth were to be found amongst the Contessa's undergarments—though she perhaps dallied a moment running her fingers through the quantities of silk and may have also, with a furtive blush, pressed a luscious delicacy or two to her nose—and she shut the drawer. The best hiding places were the most banal—cunningly in plain sight, or cluttered amongst, say, one's jumbled shoes. But she found nothing save a truly astonishing and expensive range of footwear. Miss Temple turned—did she have time to ransack the entire armoire? Was Miss Vandaariff still groaning?—looking for some ostensibly clever hiding place she could *see.* What she saw was discarded clothing everywhere... and Miss Temple smiled. There to the side of the armoire, against the dark wall in shadow, was a pile of blouses and shawls that struck her as quite deliberately set aside from any possible foot traffic. She knelt before it and rapidly sorted apart the layers. In no time at all, its glow nested in a yellow Italian damask wrap like an infant in straw, she had uncovered a large book crafted entirely of blue glass.

It was the size of a middling volume from an encyclopedia—"N" or "F", perhaps—over a foot in height and slightly under that in width, and perhaps three inches thick. The cover was heavy, as if the glass-maker had emulated the embossed Tuscan leather Miss Temple had seen in the market near St. Isobel's, and opaque, for even though it seemed as if she ought to have been able to see clearly into it, the layers were in fact quite dense. Similarly, at first glance the book appeared to be one color, a deep vivid indigo blue, but upon staring Miss Temple perceived it was riven with rippling streaks where the color fluctuated through an enticing palette, from cerulean to cobalt to aquamarine, every twisting shade delivering a disturbingly palpable impact to her inner eye, as if each bore an emotional as well as a visual signature. She could see no words on the cover, nor, when she looked—placing a hand on the book to shift it—on the spine.

At its touch Miss Temple nearly swooned. If the blue card had exerted a seductive enticement upon a person, the book provoked a maelstrom of raw sensation set to swallow her whole. Miss Temple yanked her hand free with a gasp.

She looked to the open door—beyond it the other women were silent. She really ought to return to them—she ought to *leave*—for they would no doubt enter the room after her any second, and on their heels must soon be the Comte or the Contessa. She dug her hand under the damask shawl, so to touch the book with impunity, and prepared to wrap it up and take it with her—for surely here was a prize to amaze the Doctor and Chang. Miss Temple looked down and bit her lip. If she opened the book without touching the glass... surely that would protect her... surely then she should have even more understanding to share with the others. With another glance behind her—had Miss Vandaariff fallen into a faint?—she carefully lifted up the cover.

The pages—for she could see down through them, each thin layer overlapping the next with its unique formless pattern of swirling blues—seemed as delicate as wasp wings—square wasp wings the size of a dish plate—and were strangely hinged into the spine so that she could indeed turn them like a normal book. She could not tell at once, but there seemed to be hundreds of pages, all of them imbued, like the cover, with a pulsing blue glow that cast the whole of the room in an unnatural spectral light. She was frightened to turn the page for fear of snapping the glass (just as she was frightened to stare at it too closely), but when she gathered her nerves to do so she found the glass was actually quite strong—it felt more like the thick pane of a window than the paper-thin sheet it was. Miss Temple turned one brilliant page and then another. She stared into the book, blinked, and then squeezed her eyes—could the formless swirls be *moving*? The worry in her head had transformed into a heaviness, an urge toward sleep, or if not sleep outright a relaxation of intention and control. She blinked again. She should close the book at once and leave. The room had become so hot. A drop of sweat fell from her forehead onto the glass, the surface clouding darkly where it landed, then swirling, the dark blot expanding across the page. Miss Temple gazed into it with sudden dread—an indigo knot opening like an orchid or blood blossoming from a wound... it was perhaps the most beautiful thing she had ever seen, though she was filled with fear at what would happen when the dark unfurling had covered the entirety of the page. But then it was done, the last bit of shimmering blue blotted out and she could no longer see through to the lower pages... only into the depths of the indigo stain. Miss Temple heard a gasping sound—dimly aware that it came from her own mouth—and was swallowed.

The images writhed around her mind and then with a rush passed through it, the singular point, both terrifying and delicious, being that *she* did not seem to be present at all, for just as with Mrs. Marchmoor and the card, her awareness was subsumed within the immediacies of whichever sensation had entrapped her. It felt to Miss Temple that she had plunged into the experience of several lifetimes piled up in delirious succession, so wholly persuasive and in such number that they threatened the very idea of Celeste Temple as any stable entity... she was at a masked ball in Venice drinking spiced wine in winter, the smell of the canal water and the dank stone and the hot tallow candles, the hands groping her from behind in the dark and her own delighted poise while she somehow maintained a conversation with the masked churchman in front of her, as if nothing untoward was happening... creeping slowly through a narrow brick passage, lined with tiny alcoves, holding a shuttered lantern, counting the alcoves to either side and then at the seventh on her right stepping to the far wall and slipping aside a small iron disk on a nail and pressing her eye to the hole beneath it, looking into the great bedchamber as two figures strained against each other, a young muscular man, his naked thighs pale as milk, bent over a side table and an older man behind him, face reddened, frothing like a bull... she was riding a horse, her legs gripping the animal with strength and skill, one hand on the reins and another waving a wickedly curved saber, charging across an arid African plain at a flying wedge of horsemen in white turbans, faces dark, she was screaming with fear and pleasure, the redcoated men to either side of her screaming as well, the two lines racing at each other fast as a cracking whip, lowering her body over the neck of her surging mount, saber extended, squeezing the horse between her knees and then one split second of slamming impact—the Arab's blade lancing past her shoulder and her tip digging into his neck, a quick jet of blood and the hideous wrench on her arm as the horses pulled past, the saber yanked free, another Arab in front of her, screaming with exhilaration at the kill... an ecstatic waterfall the size of two cathedrals, she stood among squat red-skinned Indians with their bows and arrows, black hair cut like a medieval king's... mountains of floating ice, the smell of fish and salt, a fur collar tickling her face, behind her voices speaking of skins and ivory and buried metals, in her large gloved hand an unsettling carved figure, squat with a leering mouth and one great eye... a dark marble chamber gleaming with gold, small pots and jars and combs and weapons, all golden, and then the casket itself, little more than the body of the boy-king close-shrouded in a thick hammered sheet of gold and knotted with jewels, then her own hand snapping open a clasp knife and bending down to pry out a singularly fetching emerald... an artist's studio, naked on a divan, reclining shamelessly, looking up into an open skylight, the pearl-grey clouds above her, a man with his skin painted blue between her legs, playfully holding her bare feet in his hands, raising one to his shoulders and then turning, as she also turned, to ask the artist himself about the pose, a figure behind an enormous canvas she could not see as she could not see his face, just his strong hands holding the palette and brush, but before she could hear his answer her attention was drawn pleasantly back to her posing partner who had reached down to luxuriously drag two fingers, just barely making contact, across the length of her shaven labia . . . a stinking sweltering room crowded with dark, slick bodies in clanking chains, striding back and forth, her boots against the planking of a ship, making notes in a ledger . . . a banquet amongst tall, pale, bearded uniformed men and their elegant ladies, dripping with jewels, the great silver trays of tiny glasses rimmed with gold leaf, each one with a clear, fiery, licorice-tinged cordial, tossing down glass after glass, a curtain of violins behind the polite conversation, crystal dishes of black roe in ice, platters of black bread and orange fish, a nod to a functionary wearing a blue sash who casually passed her a black leather volume with one page folded down, she would read it later and smiled, wondering which of the assembled guests it would instruct her to betray . . . crouched before a campfire ringed with stones, the black shadow of a castle dark against the moonlit sky, its high walls rising up from sheer red stone cliffs, feeding piece after piece of parchment to the flames, watching the pages blacken and curl and the red wax seals bubble into nothing . . . a stone courtyard in the hot evening, surrounded by fragrant blooming jasmine and the sounds of birds, on her back on a silken pallet, others around her unconcerned, drinking and speaking and glancing mockingly at the muscled shirtless turbaned guards, her legs apart and her fingers entwined in the long braided hair of the adolescent girl bent over her pelvis, lips and tongue flicking with a measured dreamy insistence, the rise of sensation gathering across her body, an exquisite wave preparing to break, rising, rising, her fingers gripping harder, the knowing chuckle of the girl who chose at that moment to pull back, the tip of her tongue alone slipping across the fervid, yearning flesh and then plunging forward again, the wave that had dipped surging up, higher, fuller, promising to break like the bloom of a thousand blue orchids over and within every inch of her body . . .

At this very exquisite moment, in the distant reaches of her mind Miss Temple was aware that she had become lost, and with some difficulty located in her memory—or the memories of so many others—a thin voice against the ecstatic roar, the words of Mrs. Marchmoor to Miss Vandaariff about the card, about concentrating on a moment to relive it, to take control of the sensation, of the experience itself. The girl's nimble tongue sparked another spasm of pleasure within her loins and Miss Temple—through the eyes of whoever had given her experience to this book—looked down and with excruciating effort focused her mind on the feeling of the girl's hair between her hands, her fingers pushing against the braids, studded with beads, and then the beads alone, the color . . . they were blue, of course they were blue . . . blue glass . . . she made herself stare into it, deeply, gasping again, thrusting her hips despite herself but somehow pushing her attention past the sweetly searching tongue, driving all other thoughts and sensations from her mind until she saw and felt nothing save the surface of glass and then, in that clear moment, with the force of her entire being, she willed herself elsewhere, pulling free.

Miss Temple gasped again and opened her eyes, surprised to see that her head was against the floor, pressed into the pile of fabric to the side of the book. She felt weak, her skin hot and damp, and pushed herself to her hands and knees, looking behind her. The Contessa's suite of rooms was silent. How long had she been looking at the book? She could not begin to recall all of the stories she had seen—been a part of. Had it taken hours, lifetimes?—or was it like a dream, where hours could transpire within minutes? She rolled back on her heels and felt the unsteadiness of her legs and, to her discomfort, the slickness between them. What had happened to her? What thoughts were now embedded in her mind—what *memories*—of ravaging and being ravaged, of blood and salt, male and female? With a dull irony, Miss Temple wondered if she had become the most thoroughly debauched virgin in all of history.

Forcing her drained body to move, Miss Temple carefully wrapped the damask shawl around the book and tied it. She looked around her for her green bag. She did not see it. Had it not been wrapped around her hand? It had been, she was sure . . . but it was gone.

She stood, taking up the wrapped book, and turned her attention to the still half-open door. As quietly as possible she peered through the gap into the parlor. For a moment she was unsure whether she had truly left the book, so strange was the sight before her, so wholly *composed,* as if she gazed into a Pompeian grotto recreated in the modern world. Mrs. Marchmoor sat reclining on the slope of a divan, her beige dress unbuttoned and pushed to her hips and her corset removed, upper body naked save for the triple row of pearls that tightly spanned her throat. Miss Temple could not help but look at her left breast, heavy and pale, the fingers of the woman's left hand idly teasing the nipple, for her right was quite blocked by Miss Vandaariff's head. Miss Vandaariff, no longer wearing the mask, blonde hair undone down the length of her back, lay fully on the divan next to Mrs. Marchmoor, eyes closed, legs curled, one hand closed in a soft fist in her lap, the other softly supporting the second breast, from which she nursed dreamily, for comfort, like a satiated milk-drunk babe.

Across from them, in an armchair, a cheroot in one hand and his pearl-tipped ebony stick in the other, once more in his fur, sat the Comte d'Orkancz. Behind him, standing in a half-circle, were four men: an older man with his arm in a sling, a short, stout man with a red complexion and livid scars around his eyes, and then two men in uniforms that, from her contact with Doctor Svenson, she knew must be from Macklenburg. One was a severe, hard-looking man with very short hair, a weathered, drawn face, and bloodshot eyes. The other she knew—from the card, she realized, she knew him most intimately—was Karl-Horst von Maasmärck. Her first corporeal impression of the Prince was less than favorable—he was tall, pale, thin, depleted, *and* epicene, lacking a chin, and with eyes reminiscent of uncooked oysters. But past all of these figures her gaze moved quickly to the second divan, upon which sat the Contessa Lacquer-Sforza, her cigarette holder poised perfectly, a thin thread of smoke curling up to the ceiling. The lady wore a tight violet silk jacket with a fringe of small black feathers to frame her pale bosom and throat, and dangling amber earrings. Below the jacket her dress was black and it seemed, as if she were some elemental magic being, to flow down her body and directly into the dark floor . . . where the previous litter of garments had been joined by the wholly savaged contents of Miss Temple's slashed and ruined carpet bag.

With the exception of Miss Vandaariff's, every set of eyes stared at Miss Temple in complete silence.

"Good evening, Celeste," said the Contessa. "You have returned from the book. Quite impressive. Not everyone does, you know."

Miss Temple did not reply.

"I am happy you are here. I am happy you have had the opportunity to exchange views with the Comte, and with my companion Mrs. Marchmoor, and also to acquaint yourself with dear Lydia, with whom you must of course have much in common—two young ladies of property, whose lives must appear to be the very epitome of an endless horizon."

The Comte exhaled a plume of blue smoke. Mrs. Marchmoor smiled into Miss Temple's eyes and slowly turned the ruddy tip of her breast between her thumb and forefinger. The row of men did not move.

"You must understand," the Contessa went on, "that your companion Cardinal Chang is no more. The Macklenburg Doctor has fled the city in fear and abandoned you. You have seen the work of our Process. You have looked into one of our glass books. You know our names and our faces, and the relation of our efforts to Lord Vandaariff and the von Maasmärck family in Macklenburg. You even"—and here she smiled—"must know the facts behind the impending elevation of a certain Lord Tarr. You know all of these things and can, because I'm sure you are as clever as you are persistent, guess at many more."

She raised the lacquered holder to her lips and inhaled, then her hand floated lazily away to again rest on the divan. With a barely audible sigh her lips parted in a wry, wary smile and she blew a stream of smoke from the side of her mouth.

"For all of this, Celeste Temple, it is certain you must die."

Miss Temple did not reply.

"I confess," the Contessa continued, "that I may have misjudged you. The Comte tells me I have, and as I'm sure you know the Comte is rarely wrong. You are a strong, proud, determined girl, and though you have caused me great inconvenience... even—I will admit it—*fury*... it has been suggested that I tender to you an offer... an offer I would normally not make to one I have determined to destroy. Yet it has been suggested... that I allow you to become a willing, valuable part of our great work."

Miss Temple did not reply. Her legs were weak, her heart cold. Chang was dead? The Doctor gone? She could not believe it. She refused to.

As if sensing defiance in her quivering lip, the Comte took the cheroot from his mouth and spoke in his low, rasping, baleful manner.

"It could not be simpler. If you do not agree, your throat will be cut straightaway, in this room. If you do, you will come with us. Be assured that no duplicitous cunning will avail you. Abandon hope, Miss Temple, for it will be expunged . . . and replaced by *certainty*."

Miss Temple looked at his stern expression and then to the forbidding beauty of the Contessa Lacquer-Sforza, her perfect smile both warmly tempting and cold as stone. The four men gazed at her blankly, the Prince scratching his nose with a fingernail. Had they all been transformed by the Process, their bestial logic released from moral restraints? She saw the scars on the Prince and on the stout man. It seemed that the older fellow shared their glassy-eyed hunger—perhaps his marks had already faded—only the other soldier bore a normal expression, where certainty and doubt were both at play. On the face of the others was only an inhuman, uncomplicated confidence. She wondered which of them would be the one to kill her. She looked finally to Mrs. Marchmoor, whose blank expression masked what Miss Temple thought was a genuine curiosity . . . as if she did not know what Miss Temple would do, nor what, once she did submit, might possibly come of it.

"It seems I have no choice," Miss Temple whispered.

"You do not," agreed the Contessa, and she turned to the large man seated next to her and raised her eyebrows, as if to signal her part in the matter was finished.

"You will oblige me, Miss Temple," said the Comte d'Orkancz, "by removing your shoes and stockings."

She had walked in her bare feet—a simple stratagem to prevent her from running away with any speed through the ragged filthy streets—down the stairs and out of the St. Royale Hotel. Mrs. Marchmoor remained behind, but all of the others descended with her—the soldier, the stout scarred fellow, and the older man going ahead to arrange coaches, the Comte and Contessa to her either side, the Prince behind with Miss Vandaariff on his arm. As she walked down the great staircase, Miss

Temple saw a new clerk at the desk, who merely bowed with respect at a gracious nod from the Contessa. Miss Temple wondered that such a woman had need of the Process at all, or of magical blue glass—she doubted that anyone possessed the strength or inclination to deny the Contessa whatever she might ask. Miss Temple glanced to the Comte, who gazed ahead without expression, one hand on his pearl-topped stick, the other cradling the wrapped blue book, like an exiled king with plans to regain his throne. She felt the prickling of the carpet fibers between her toes as she walked. As a girl her feet had once been tough and calloused, used to running bare throughout her father's plantation. Now they had become as soft and tender as any milk-bathed lady's, and as much a hindrance to escape as a pair of iron shackles. With a pang of desolating grief she thought of her little green boots, abandoned, kicked beneath the divan. No one else would ever again care for them, she knew, and could not but wonder if anyone would ever again care for her either.

Two coaches waited outside the hotel—one an elegant red brougham and the other a larger black coach with what she assumed was the Macklenburg crest painted on the door. The Prince, Miss Vandaariff, the soldier, and the scarred stout man climbed inside this coach, with the older man swinging up to sit with the driver. A porter from the hotel held open the door of the brougham for the Contessa, and then for Miss Temple, who felt the textured iron step press sharply into her foot as she went in. She settled into a seat opposite the Contessa. A moment later they were joined by the Comte, the entire coach shuddering as it took on his weight. He sat next to the Contessa and the porter shut the door. The Comte rapped his stick on the roof and they set forth. From the time of the Comte's demand for her shoes to the coach moving, they had not spoken a word. Miss Temple cleared her throat and looked at them. Extended silence nearly always strained her self-control.

"I should like to know something," she announced.

After a moment, the Comte rasped a reply. "And what is that?"

Miss Temple turned her gaze to the Contessa, for it was she at whom the question was truly aimed. "I should like to know how Cardinal Chang died."

The Contessa Lacquer-Sforza looked into Miss Temple's eyes with a sharp, searching intensity.

"I killed him," she declared, and in such a way that dared Miss Temple to speak again.

Miss Temple was not yet daunted—indeed, if her captor did not want to discuss this topic, it now constituted a test of Miss Temple's will.

"Did you really?" she asked. "He was a formidable man."

"He was," agreed the Contessa. "I filled his lungs with ground glass blown from our indigo clay. It has many effective qualities, and in such amounts as the Cardinal inhaled is mortal. 'Formidable' of course is a word with many shadings—and physical prowess is often the simplest and most easily overcome."

The ease of speech with which the Contessa described Chang's destruction took Miss Temple completely aback. Though she had only been acquainted with Cardinal Chang for a very short time, so strong an impression had he made upon her that his equally sudden demise was a devastating cruelty.

"Was it a quick death, or a slow one?" Miss Temple asked in as neutral a voice as she could muster.

"I would not call it *quick*. . . ." As the Contessa answered, she reached into a black bag embroidered with hanging jet beads, pulling out in sequence her holder, a cigarette to screw into the tip, and a match to light it. "And yet the death itself is perhaps a generous one, for—as you have seen yourself—the indigo glass carries with it an affinity for dream and for . . . sensual experience. It is often observed that men being hanged will perish in a state of extreme tumescence—" she paused, her eyebrows raised to confirm that Miss Temple was following her, "if not outright spontaneous eruption, which is to say, at least for the males of our world, such an end might be preferable to many others. It is my belief that similar, perhaps even more expansive, transports accompany a death derived from the indigo glass. Or such at least is my hope, for indeed, your Cardinal Chang was a singular opponent . . . truly, I could scarcely wish him ill, apart from wishing him dead."

"Did you confirm your hypothesis by examining his trousers?" huffed the Comte. It was only after a moment that Miss Temple deduced he was laughing.

"There was no time." The Contessa chuckled. "Life is full of regrets.

But what are those? Leaves from a passing season—fallen, forgotten, and swept away."

The specter of Chang's death—one that despite the Contessa's lurid suggestion she could not picture as anything but horrid, with bloody effusions from the mouth and nose—had spun Miss Temple's thoughts directly to her own immediate fate.

"Where are we going?" she asked.

"I'm sure you must know," answered the Contessa. "To Harschmort House."

"What will be done to me?"

"Dreading what you cannot change serves no purpose," announced the Comte.

"Apart from the pleasure of watching you writhe," whispered the Contessa.

To this Miss Temple had no response, but after several seconds during which her attempts to glance out of the narrow windows—placed on either side of their seat, not hers, assumedly to make it easier for someone in her position to either remain unseen or, on a more innocent planet, fall asleep—revealed no clear sense of where in the city she might now be, she cleared her throat to speak again.

The Contessa chuckled.

"Have I done something to amuse you?" asked Miss Temple.

"No, but you are about to," replied the Contessa. "'Determined' does not describe you by half, Celeste."

"Very few people refer to me with such intimacy," said Miss Temple. "In all likelihood, they can be counted on one hand."

"Are we not sufficiently intimate?" asked the Contessa. "I would have thought we were."

"Then what is *your* Christian name?"

The elegant woman chuckled again, and it seemed that even the Comte d'Orkancz curled his lip in a reluctant grimace.

"It is Rosamonde," declared the Contessa. "Rosamonde, Contessa di Lacquer-Sforza."

"Lacquer-Sforza? Is that a *place*?"

"It was. Now I'm afraid it has become an idea."

"I see," said Miss Temple, not seeing at all but willing to appear agreeable.

"Everyone has their own plantation, Celeste, . . . their own island, if only in their heart."

"What a pity for them," declared Miss Temple. "I find an *actual* island to be far more satisfactory."

"At times"—the Contessa's warm tone grew just perceptibly harder—"such is the only way those locations may be visited or maintained."

"By not being *real,* you mean?"

"If that is how you choose to see it."

Miss Temple was silent, knowing that she did not grasp the Contessa's larger point.

"I don't intend to lose mine," she said.

"No one ever does, darling," replied the Contessa.

They rode on in silence, until the Contessa smiled as kindly as before and said, "But you were going to ask a question?"

"I was," replied Miss Temple. "I was going to ask about Oskar Veilandt and his paintings of the Annunciation, for you had another in your rooms. The Comte and I discussed the artist over tea."

"Did you *really*?"

"In fact, I pointed out to the Comte that, as far as I am concerned, he seems to be suspiciously in this fellow's debt."

"Did you indeed?"

"I should say so." Miss Temple did not fool herself that she was capable of angering or flattering either of these two to a point of distraction that might allow her to throw herself from the coach—a gesture more likely than anything to result in her death under the wheels of the coach behind them—and yet, the paintings were a topic that might well produce useful information about the Process that she might use to prevent her ultimate subversion. She would never understand the science or the alchemy—were science and alchemy the same thing?—for she had always been indifferent to theoretical learning, though she knew the Comte at least was not. What was more, Miss Temple knew he was *sensitive* about the question of the missing painter, and as a rule she was not above being a persistent nuisance.

"And how exactly is that?" asked the Contessa.

"*Because,*" Miss Temple responded, "the *Annunciation* paintings themselves are clearly an allegorical presentation of your Process, indeed of your intrigue as a whole—that the imagery itself is a brazen blasphemy is beside the immediate point, save to convey a scale of arrogance—as you see it, of *advancement* provoked by the effects of your precious blue glass. Of course," she went on with a side glance at the unmoving Comte, "it seems that all of this—for on the back of the paintings are imprudently scrawled the man's alchemical secrets—has been taken by the Comte for his own—taken by all of you—at the expense of the missing Mr. Veilandt's life."

"You said this to the Comte?"

"Of course I did."

"And how did he respond?"

"He left the table."

"It *is* a serious charge."

"On the contrary, it is an obvious one—and what is more, after all the destruction and violence you have put into motion, such an accusation can hardly strike any of you as either unlikely or unprovoked. As the work itself is monstrous, and the murder of its maker even more so, I would not have thought the murderer himself so . . . *tender.*"

For an answer that perhaps too fully fulfilled Miss Temple's hopes of agitation, the Comte d'Orkancz leaned deliberately forward and extended his open right hand until he could place it around Miss Temple's throat. She uselessly pressed her body back into her seat and tried to convince herself that if he was going to hurt her out of anger he would have seized her more quickly. As the strong fingers tightened against her skin she began to have her doubts, and looked with dismay into the man's cold blue eyes. His grip held her fast but did not choke her. At once she was assailed by hideous memories of Mr. Spragg. She did not move.

"You looked at the paintings—two of them, yes?" His voice was low and unmistakably dangerous. "Tell us . . . what was your *impression*?"

"Of what?" she squeaked.

"Of *anything.* What thoughts were provoked?"

"Well, as I have said, an allegorical—"

He squeezed her throat so hard and so suddenly she thought her neck would snap. The Contessa leaned forward as well, speaking mildly.

"Celeste, the Comte is attempting to get you to *think*."

Miss Temple nodded. The Comte relaxed his grip. She swallowed.

"I suppose I thought the paintings were unnatural. As the woman in them has been given over to the angel—she is given over to—to sensation and pleasure—as if nothing else might exist. Such a thing is impossible. It is dangerous."

"Why is that?" asked the Comte.

"Because nothing would get done! Because—because—there is no border between the world and one's body, one's mind—it would be unbearable!"

"I should have thought it delicious," whispered the Contessa.

"Not for me!" cried Miss Temple.

With a swift rush of fabric the Contessa shifted across the coach next to Miss Temple, her lips pressed close to the young woman's ear.

"Are you sure? For I have seen you, Celeste, . . . I have seen you through the mirror, and I have seen you bent over the book . . . and do you know?"

"Do I know what?"

"That when you were in my room . . . kneeling over so sweetly . . . I could *smell* you . . ."

Miss Temple whimpered but did not know what she could do.

"Think of the book, Celeste," hissed the Contessa. "You remember what you saw! What you did, what was done to you—what you *became*!—through what exquisite realms you traveled!"

At these words Miss Temple felt a burning in her blood—what was happening to her? She sensed her memories of the book like a stranger's footprints in her mind. They were everywhere! She did not want them! But why could she not thrust them aside?

"You are wrong!" Miss Temple shouted. "It is not the same!"

"Neither are you," snarled the Comte d'Orkancz. "You've already taken the first step in your *process* of transformation!"

The coach had become too warm. The Contessa's hand found Miss Temple's leg and then quickly vanished beneath her dress, the knowing fingers climbing up her inner thigh. Miss Temple gasped. These were not the blunt, stabbing, rude fingers of Spragg but—if still invasive—playful, teasing, and insistent. No one had ever touched her this way, in that place. She could not think.

"No—no—" she began.

"What did you see in the book?" The Comte pressed at her with his insistent, terrifying rasp. "Do you know the taste of death and power? Do you know what lovers feel in their blood? You do! You know all of it and more! It has taken root in your being! You feel it as I speak! Will you ever be able to turn away from what you've seen? Will you ever be able to reject these pleasures, having tasted their full intoxicating potency?"

The Contessa's fingers pushed through the slit of her silken pants and slid across her liquid flesh with a practiced skill. Miss Temple shrank from her touch, but the coach seat was so small and the sensation so delicious.

"I don't think you will, Celeste," whispered the Contessa. She softly nuzzled the tips of two fingers, then wetly slipped them deeper while rubbing gently above them with her thumb. Miss Temple did not know what she was supposed to do, what she was fighting against save the imposition of their will upon her—but she did not want to fight, the pleasure building in her body was heavenly, and yet she also longed to hurl herself away from their openly predatory usage. What did her pleasure matter to them? It was but a goad, a tool, an endless source of thralldom and control. The Contessa's fingers worked slickly back and forth. Miss Temple groaned.

"Your mind is set on fire!" hissed the Comte. "You cannot evade your *mind*—we hold you, you must give in—your body will betray you, your heart will betray you—you are already abandoned, utterly given over—your new memories are rising—surrounding you completely—your life—your *self*—has changed—your once-pure soul has been stained by my glass book's *usage*!"

As he spoke she felt them, doors opening across her spinning mind directly into her fevered body—the masked ball in Venice, the two men through the spy hole, the artist's model on the divan, the heavenly seraglio, and then so many, many more—Miss Temple was panting, the Contessa's fingers deftly plying her most intimate parts, the woman's lips against her ear, encouraging her pleasure with little mocking moans that nevertheless—the very provocative sound of that woman even counterfeiting ecstasy—served as a concrete spur to further delight . . . Miss Temple felt the sweetness gathering in her body, a warm cloud ready to burst . . . but then she shut her eyes and saw herself, in the coach between her enemies, beset, and then Chang dead, his pale face streaked with blood, the Doctor running and in tears, and finally, as if it were the answer she'd been seeking, the hot, clear, open view of barren white sand bordering a blue indifferent sea . . . she pulled herself from the brink—*their* brink she decided, not her own—

And in that exact moment, in such a way that Miss Temple knew they had not perceived her interior victory, the Contessa snatched away her hand and returned in smirking triumph to the other seat. The Comte released her neck and leaned back. She felt the sudden ebb of the pleasure in her body and its instinctive protest against the loss of stimulation—and met their eyes, seeing that they had brought her to the edge only to demonstrate her submission. They looked at her with a condescending disdain that seconds earlier might have been shattering—and before she could say a word, the Contessa's hand—the same hand that had been under her dress—slapped her hard across the face. Miss Temple's head spun to the side, burning. The Contessa slapped her again just as hard, knocking her bodily into the corner of the coach.

"You killed two of my people," she said viciously. "Do not ever believe it is forgotten."

Miss Temple touched her numbed face, shocked and dizzied, and felt the wetness from the Contessa's hand—which was to say from herself. The spike of rage at being struck was dampened by her mortified realization that the close air in the coach was heavy with the smell of her own arousal. She yanked her dress down over her legs and looked up to see the Contessa wiping her fingers methodically on a handkerchief. Their attempt to demonstrate her helplessness had only solidified Miss Temple's defiance. She sniffed again, blinking back tears of pain and further emboldened by the glimpse of her green clutch bag poking out of the side pocket of the Comte d'Orkancz's voluminous fur.

Their coach ride ended at Stropping Station, where once more Miss Temple was made to walk in her bare feet, down the stairs and across the station hall to their train. She was quite certain that her soles would be blackened by the filth of so many travelers and she was not wrong, pausing to scoff at the dirty result with open disgust before she was again pushed forward. Again she was placed between the Comte and the Contessa, the Prince and his fiancée behind them, and the other three men bringing up the rear. Various people they passed gave a polite nod—to the Prince and Miss Vandaariff, she assumed, for they were often recognized—but were nonplussed by the sight of the barefoot young lady who could apparently afford a maid to dress her hair but not even the simplest footwear. Miss Temple gave them no thought at all, even when their questioning looks slipped into open disapproval. Instead, she gazed persistently around her for possible methods of escape but located nothing, dismissing even a pair of uniformed constables—in the company of such elegant nobility, there was no way anyone would credit her account of capture, much less the larger intrigue. She would have to escape from the train itself.

She had just so resolved on this plan when Miss Temple noted with sharp dismay two figures waiting with the conductor on the platform, at the open door of the rearmost car. One, based on the description of Doctor Svenson, she took to be Francis Xonck, sporting a tailcoat worn only on his left arm and buttoned across—the other sleeve hanging free—for his right arm was thickly bandaged. The other, standing tall in a crisp black topcoat, was a man she would no doubt recognize from across the entire station floor until the end of her days. Miss Temple actually stopped walking, only to have her shoulder gently seized by the Comte d'Orkancz and her body carried along for several awkward steps until she had resumed her pace. He released her—never once deigning to look down—and she glanced at the Contessa in time to see her smiling with cruel amusement.

"Ah, look—it is Bascombe and Francis Xonck! Perhaps there will be time on the journey for a lovers' reunion!"

Miss Temple paused again and again the Comte's hand shot out to shove her forward.

Roger's gaze passed over her quite quickly, but she saw, no matter how he hid it behind the fixed face of a government functionary, her presence was no more welcome to him than his to her. When had they spoken last? Nine days ago? Ten? It had still been as engaged lovers. The very word caused Miss Temple to wince—what word could possibly be more changed by the events of her last hours? She knew that they were now separated by a distance she could never have previously imagined, discrepancies of belief and experience that were every bit as vast as the ocean she had crossed to first enter Roger Bascombe's world. She must assume that Roger had given himself over to the Cabal and its Process, to amoral sensation—to one only imagined, if the book were any indicator, what depravities. He must have conspired in the murder of his uncle—how else would he have the title? Had he even stood by—or, who knew, participated?—while murders and worse were enacted, perhaps even that of Cardinal Chang? She did not want to believe it, yet here he was. And what of her own changes? Miss Temple thought back to her night of distress, weeping in her bed over Roger's letter—what was this compared to Spragg's attack, or the Contessa's menace, or the fiendish brutality of the Process? What was this compared to her own discovered reserves of determination and cunning, of authority and choice—or standing as an equal third with the Doctor and the Cardinal, an adventuress of worth? Roger's gaze fell to her dirty feet. She had never allowed herself to be less than immaculate in his presence, and she watched him measure her in that very moment and find her wanting—as he must by necessity find her, something he had cast off. For a moment her heart sank, but then Miss Temple inhaled sharply, flaring her nostrils. It did not matter what Roger Bascombe might think—it would never matter again.

Francis Xonck occupied her interest for a brief glance of estimation and no more. She knew his general tale—the wastrel rakish brother of the mighty Henry Xonck—and saw all she needed of his preening peacock wit and manner in his overly posed, wry expression, noting with satisfaction the apparently grievous and painful injury he had suffered to his arm. She wondered how it had happened, and idly wished she might have witnessed it.

The two men then stepped forward to pay their respects to the Contessa. Xonck first bowed and extended his hand for hers, taking it and raising it to his lips. As if Miss Temple had not been enough abased, she was aghast at the discreet wrinkling of Francis Xonck's nose as he held the Contessa's hand—the same that had been between her legs. With a wicked smile, looking into the Contessa's eyes—the Contessa who exchanged with him a fully wicked smile of her own—Xonck, instead of kissing the fingers, ran his tongue deliberately along them. He released the hand with a click of his heels and turned to Miss Temple with a knowing leer. She did not extend her hand and he did not reach out to take it, moving on to nod at the Comte with an even wider smile. But Miss Temple paid him no more attention, her gaze fixed despite herself on Roger Bascombe's own kiss of the Contessa's hand. Once more she saw her scent register—though Roger's notice was marked by momentary confusion rather than wicked glee. He avoided looking into the Contessa's laughing eyes, administered a deft brush of his lips, and released her hand.

"I believe you two have met," said the Contessa.

"Indeed," said Roger Bascombe. He nodded curtly. "Miss Temple."

"Mr. Bascombe."

"I see you've lost your shoes," he said, not entirely unkindly, by way of conversation.

"Better my shoes than my soul, Mr. Bascombe," she replied, her words harsh and childish in her ears, "or must I say Lord Tarr?"

Roger met her gaze once, briefly, as if there were something he did want to say but could not, or could not in such company. He then turned, directing his voice to the Comte and Contessa.

"If you will, we ought to be aboard—the train will leave directly."

Miss Temple was installed alone in a compartment in a car the party seemed to claim all for itself. She had expected—or feared—that the Comte or Contessa would use the journey to resume the abuses of her coach ride, but when the Comte had slid open the compartment door and thrust her into it she had turned to find him still in the passageway shutting it again and walking impassively from sight. She had tried to open the door herself. It was not locked, and she had poked her head out to see Francis Xonck standing in conversation some yards away with the Macklenburg officer. They turned at the sound of the door with expressions of such unmitigated and dangerous annoyance that Miss Temple had retreated back into the compartment, half-afraid they were going to follow. They did not, and after some minutes of fretful standing, Miss Temple took a seat and tried to think about what she might do. She was being taken to Harschmort, alone and unarmed and distressingly unshod. What was the first stop on the way to Orange Canal—Crampton Place? Gorsemont? Packington? Could she discreetly open the compartment window and lower herself from the train in the time they might be paused in the station? Could she drop from such a height—it was easily fifteen feet—onto the rail bed of jagged stones without hurting her feet? If she could not run after climbing out she would be taken immediately, she was sure. Miss Temple exhaled and shut her eyes. Did she truly have any choice?

She wondered what time it was. Her trials with the book and in the coach had been extremely taxing and she would have dearly loved a drink of water and even more a chance to shut her eyes in safety. She pulled her legs onto her seat and gathered her dress around them, curling up as best she could, feeling like a transported beast huddling in a corner of its cage. Despite her best intentions Miss Temple's thoughts wandered to Roger, and she marveled again at the distance they had traveled from their former lives. Before, in accounting for his rejection of her, she had merely been one element among many—his family, his moral rectitude—thrown to the side in favor of ambition. But now they were on the same train, only yards away from one another. Nothing stopped him from coming to her compartment (the Contessa was sure to allow it out of pure amusement) and yet he did not. For all that he too must have undergone the Process and was subject to its effects, she found his avoidance demonstrably cruel—had he not held her in his arms? Had he not an ounce remaining of that sympathy or care, even so much as to offer comfort, to ease his own heart at the fate that must befall her? It was clear that he did not, and despite all previous resolve and despite her hidden victories over both the book and her captors—for did these change a thing?—Miss Temple found herself once more alone within her barren landscape of loss.

The door of her compartment was opened by the Macklenburg officer. He held a metal canteen and extended it to her. For all her parched throat she hesitated. He frowned with irritation.

"Water. Take it."

She did, uncorking the top and drinking deeply. She exhaled and drank again. The train was slowing. She wiped her mouth and returned the canteen. He took it, but did not move. The train stopped. They waited in silence. He offered the canteen again. Miss Temple shook her head. He replaced the cork. The train pulled forward. With a sinking heart she saw the sign for Crampton Place pass by her window and recede from sight. When the train had resumed its normal speed, the soldier gave her a clipped nod and left the compartment. Miss Temple tucked her legs beneath her once again and laid her head against her armrest, determined that she would rather sleep than give in again to tears.

She was woken by the officer's reappearance as the train stopped at Packington, and again at Gorsemont, De Conque, and Raaxfall. Each time he brought the steel canteen of water and each time remained otherwise silent until the train resumed its full forward momentum, after which he left her alone. After De Conque Miss Temple was no longer inclined to sleep, partially because it annoyed her to be awoken so relentlessly, but more because the impulse had gone. In its place was a feeling she could not properly name, gnawing and unsettling, which caused her to shift in her seat repeatedly. She did not know where she was—which was to say, she realized with the impact of a bullet, she did not know *who* she was. After having become so accustomed to the dashing tactics of adventure—shooting pistols, escaping by rooftop, digging clues from a stove as if this were the natural evolution of her character (and for a wistful moment Miss Temple occupied herself with a recounting of all the adventurous tasks she had managed in the past few days)—it seemed as if her failure had thrust forward another possibility, that she was merely a naïve and willful young woman without the depth to understand her doom. She thought of Doctor Svenson on the rooftop—the man had been petrified—and yet while she and Chang had leaned over the edge to look into the alley, he had driven himself to walk alone across the top of the Boniface Hotel and the next two buildings—even stepping across the actual (negligible, it was true, but such fear was not born of logic) gaps between structures. She knew what it had cost him, and that the look on his face showed the exact sort of determination recent events had proven she did not possess.

However harsh her judgment, Miss Temple found the clarity helpful, and she began with a clear-eyed grimness—in the irritating absence of a notebook and pencil (oh, how she wished for a pencil!)—to make a mental accounting of her probable fate. There was no telling if she would again be mauled and traduced, just as there was no telling if, despite the Contessa's words, she would finally be slain, before or after torment. Again she shivered, confronting the full extent of her enemies' deadly character, and took a deep breath at a likelihood more dire still—her transformation by the Process. What could be worse than to be changed into what she despised? Death and torment were at least actions taken against *her*. With the Process, that sense of *her* would be destroyed, and Miss Temple decided there in the compartment she could not allow it. Whether it meant throwing herself into a cauldron or inhaling their glass powder like Chang, or simply provoking some guard to snap her neck—she would never give in to their vicious control. She remembered the dead man the Doctor had described—what the broken glass from the book had done to his body . . . if she could just get to the book and smash it, or hold it in her arms and leap headlong to the floor—it must shatter and her life be ended with it. And perhaps the Contessa was right, that death from the indigo glass carried with it a trace of intoxicating dreams.

She began to feel hungry—despite her love for tea, it was not an overly substantial meal—and after an idle five minutes where she was unable to think about anything else, she opened her compartment door and again looked into the passage. The soldier stood where he had before, but instead of Francis Xonck, it was the scarred stout man that stood with him.

"Excuse me," called Miss Temple. "What is your name?"

The soldier frowned, as if her speaking to him was an unseemly breach of etiquette. The scarred man—who it seemed had recovered his sensibilities somewhat, being a bit less glassy about the eyes and more fluid in his limbs—answered her with a voice that was only a little oily.

"He is Major Blach and I am Herr Flaüss, Envoy to the Macklenburg diplomatic mission accompanying the Prince Karl-Horst von Maasmärck."

"*He* is Major Blach?" If the Major was too proud to speak to her, Miss Temple was happy enough to speak about him as if he were a standing lamp. She knew that this was the nemesis of both the Doctor and Chang. "I had no idea," she said, "for of course I have heard a great deal about him—about you both." She really had heard nothing much at all about the Envoy, save that the Doctor did not like him, and even this not in words so much as a dismissive half-distracted shrug—still she expected everyone liked to be talked of, Process or no. The Major, of course, she knew was deadly.

"May we be of service?" asked the Envoy.

"I am hungry," replied Miss Temple. "I should like something to eat—if such a thing exists on the train. I know it is at least another hour until we reach the Orange Locks."

"In truth, I have no idea," said the Envoy, "but I will ask directly." He nodded to her and padded down the passageway. Miss Temple watched him go and then caught the firm gaze of the Major upon her.

"Get back inside," he snapped.

When the train stopped at St. Triste, the Major entered with a small wrapped parcel of white waxed paper along with his canteen. He gave them both to her without a word. She did not move to open it, preferring to do it alone—there was precious little entertainment else—and so the two of them waited in silence for the train to move. When it did he reached again for the canteen. She did not release it.

"May I not have a drink of water with my meal?"

The Major glared at her. Clearly there was no reason to deny her save meanness, and even that would betray a level of interest that he did not care to admit. He released the canteen and left the compartment.

The contents of the waxed paper parcel were hardly interesting—a thin wedge of white cheese, a slice of rye bread, and two small pickled beets that stained the bread and cheese purple. Nevertheless she ate them as slowly and methodically as she could—alternating carefully small bites of each in succession and chewing each mouthful at least twenty times before swallowing. So passed perhaps fifteen minutes. She drank off the rest of the canteen and re-corked it. She balled up the paper and with the canteen in her hand poked her head back into the passageway. The Major and the Envoy were where they had been before.

"I have finished," she called, "if you would prefer to collect the canteen."

"How kind of you," said Envoy Flaüss, and he nudged the Major, who marched toward her and snatched the canteen from her hand. Miss Temple held up the ball of paper.

"Would you take this as well? I'm sure you do not want me passing notes to the conductor!"

Without a word the Major did. Miss Temple batted her eyelashes at him and then at the watching Envoy down the passageway as the Major turned and walked away. She returned to her seat with a chuckle. She had no idea what had been gained except distraction, but she felt in her mild mischief a certain encouraging return to form.

At St. Porte, Major Blach did not enter her compartment. Miss Temple looked up to the compartment door as the train slowed and no one had appeared. Had she annoyed him so much as to give her a chance to open the window? She stood, still looking at the empty doorway, and then with a fumbling rush began her assault on the window latches. She had not even managed to get one of them open before she heard the clicking of the compartment door behind her. She wheeled, ready to meet the Major's disapproval with a winning smile.

Instead, in the open door stood Roger Bascombe.

"Ah," she said. "Mr. Bascombe."

He nodded to her rather formally. "Miss Temple."

"Will you sit?"

It seemed to her that Roger hesitated, perhaps because she had been found so evidently in the midst of opening the window, but equally perhaps because so much between them lay unresolved. She returned to her seat, tucking her dirty feet as far as possible beneath her hanging dress, and waited for him to stir from the still-open door. When he did not, she spoke to him with a politeness only barely edged with impatience.

"What can a man fear from taking a seat? Nothing—except the display of his own ill-breeding if he remains standing like a tradesman . . . or a marionette Macklenburg soldier."

Chastened and, she could tell from the purse of his lips, pricked to annoyance, Roger took a seat on the opposite side of the compartment. He took a preparatory breath.

"Miss Temple—Celeste—"

"I see your scars have healed," she said encouragingly. "Mrs.

Marchmoor's have not, and I confess to finding them quite unpleasant. As for poor Mr. Flaüss—or I suppose it should be *Herr* Flaüss—for *his* appearance he might as well be a tattooed aboriginal from the polar ice!"

With satisfaction, she saw that Roger looked as if a lemon wedge had become lodged beneath his tongue.

"Are you finished?" he asked.

"I don't believe I am, but I will let you speak, if that is what you—"

Roger barked at her sharply. "It is not a surprise to see you so relentlessly fixed on the trivial—it has always been your way—but even *you* should apprehend the gravity of your situation!"

Miss Temple had never seen him so dismissive and forceful, and her voice dropped to a sudden icy whisper.

"I apprehend it very fully . . . I assure you . . . Mr. Bascombe."

He did not reply—he was, she realized with a sizzling annoyance, allowing what he took to be his acknowledged rebuke to fully sink in. Determined not to first break the silence, Miss Temple found herself studying the changes in his face and manner—quite in spite of herself, for she still hoped to meet his every attention with scorn. She understood that Roger Bascombe offered the truest window into the effects of the Process she was likely to find. She had met Mrs. Marchmoor and the Prince—her pragmatic manner and his dispassionate distance—but she had known neither of them intimately beforehand. What she saw on the face of Roger Bascombe pained her, more than anything at the knowledge that such a transformation spoke—and she was sure, in her unhappy heart, that it did—to his honest desire. Roger had always been one for what was ordered and proper, paying scrupulous attention to social niceties while maintaining a fixed notion of who bore what title and which estates—but she had known, and it had been part of her fondness for him, that such painstaking alertness arose from his own lack of a title and his occupation of yet a middling position in government—which is to say from his naturally cautious character. Now, she saw that this was changed, that Roger's ability to juggle in his mind the different interests and ranks of many people was no longer in service to his own defense but, on the contrary, to his own explicit, manipulative advantage. She had no doubt that he watched the other members of the Cabal like an unfailingly deferential hawk, waiting for the slightest misstep (as she was suddenly sure Francis Xonck's bandaged arm had been a secret delight to him). Before when Roger had grimaced at her outbursts or expressions of opinion, it had been at her lack of tact or care for the delicate social fabric of a conversation he had been at effort to maintain—and his reaction had filled her with a mischievous pleasure. Now, despite her attempts to bait or provoke him, all she saw was a pinched, unwillingly burdened *tolerance,* rooted in the disappointment of wasting time with one who could offer him no advantage whatsoever. The difference made Miss Temple sad in a way she had not foreseen.

"I have presumed to briefly join you," he began, "at the suggestion of the Contessa di Lacquer-Sforza—"

"I am sure the Contessa gives you all manner of suggestions," interrupted Miss Temple, "and have no doubt that you follow them eagerly!"

Did she even believe this? The accusation had been too readily at hand not to fling . . . not that it seemed to find any purchase on its target.

"Since," he continued after a brief pause, "it is intended that you undergo the Process upon our arrival at Harschmort House, it will arise that, although we have been in the last days *sundered,* after your ordeal we shall be reconciled to the same side—as allies."

This was not what she had expected. He watched her, defensively expectant, as if her silence was the prelude to another childish eruption of spite.

"Celeste," he said, "I do urge you to be rational. I am speaking of facts. If it is necessary—if it will clarify your situation—I will again assure you that I am well beyond all feelings of attachment . . . or equally of resentment."

Miss Temple could not credit what she had heard. Resentment? When it was *she* who had been so blithely overthrown, she who had borne for how many evenings and afternoons in their courtship the near mummifying company of the condescending, starch-minded, middling-fortuned Bascombe family!

"I beg your pardon?" she managed.

He cleared his throat. "What I mean to say—what I have come to say—is that our new alliance—for your loyalties will be changed, and if I know the Contessa, she will insist that the two of us continue to work in concert—"

Miss Temple narrowed her eyes at the idea of what *that* might mean.

"—and it would be best if, as a rational being, you could join me in setting aside your vain affection and pointless bitterness. I assure you—there will be less *pain*."

"And I assure *you*, Roger, I have done just that. Unfortunately, recent days having been so very busy, I've yet had a moment to set aside my virulent *scorn*."

"Celeste, I speak for your good, not mine—truly, it is a generosity—"

"A *generosity*?"

"I do not expect you to see it," he muttered.

"Of course not! I haven't had my mind re-made by a *machine*!"

Roger stared at her in silence and then slowly stood, straightening his coat and, by habit, smoothing back his hair with two fingers, and even then in her heart she found him to be quite lovely. Yet his gaze, quite fixed upon her, conveyed a quality she had never seen in him before—undisguised contempt. He was not angry—indeed, what hurt her most was the exact lack of emotion behind his eyes. It truly made no sense to her—in Miss Temple's body, in her memory, all such moments were rooted in some sort of *feeling*, and Roger Bascombe stood revealed to her as no kind of man she had ever met.

"You will see," he said, his voice cool and low. "The Process will remake you to the ground, and you will see—for the very first time in your life, I am sure—the true nature of your shuttered mind. The Contessa suggests you possess reserves of character I have not seen—to which I can only agree that I have *not* seen them. You were always a pretty enough girl—but there are many such. I look forward to finding—once you've been burned to your bones and then *re-made* by the very 'machine' you cannot comprehend—if any actually remarkable parts exist."

He left the compartment. Miss Temple did not move, her mind ringing with his biting words and a thousand unspoken retorts, her face hot and both of her hands balled tight into fists. She looked out the window and saw her reflection on the glass, thrown up between her and the darkened landscape of salty grassland racing past outside the train. It occurred to her that this dim, transparent, second-hand image was the perfect illustration for her own condition—in the power of others, with her own wishes only peripherally related to her fate, insubstantial and half-present. She let out a trembling sigh. How—after *everything*—could Roger Bascombe still exert any sway over her feelings? How could he make her feel so *desperately* unhappy? Her agitation was not coherent—there was no point from which she could begin to untangle answers—and her heart beat faster and faster until she was forced to sit with a hand over each eye, breathing deeply. Miss Temple looked up. The train was slowing. She pressed her face to the window, blocking the light from the passageway with her hand, and saw through the reflection the station, platform, and white painted sign for Orange Locks. She turned to find Major Blach opening the door for her, his hand inviting her to exit.

Beyond the platform were two waiting coaches, each drawn by a team of four horses. To the first, his fiancée on his arm, went the Prince, followed as before by his Envoy and the older man with the bandaged arm. The Major escorted Miss Temple to the second coach, opened the door, and assisted her climb into it. He nodded crisply to her and stepped away—undoubtedly to rejoin the Prince—to be replaced by the Comte d'Orkancz, who sat across from her, and then the Contessa, who stepped in to sit next to her opposite the Comte, then Francis Xonck, who sat next to the Comte with a smile, and finally, with no expression in particular on his face, Roger Bascombe, hesitating only an instant when he saw that, due to the size of the Comte and the room accorded Xonck's thickly wrapped arm, the only seat was on the other side of Miss Temple. He climbed into place without comment. Miss Temple was firmly lodged between the Contessa and Roger—their legs pressing closely against hers with a mocking familiarity. The driver shut the door and climbed to his perch. His whip snapped and they clattered on their way to Harschmort.

The ride began in silence, and after a time Miss Temple, who initially assumed this was because of her presence—an interloper spoiling their usual plots and scheming, began to wonder if this was wholly the case. They were wary enough not to say anything revealing, but she began to sense levels of competition and distrust... particularly with the addition of Francis Xonck to the party.

"When can we expect the Duke?" he asked.

"Before midnight, I am sure," replied the Comte.

"Have you spoken to him?"

"Crabbé has spoken to him," said the Contessa. "There is no reason for anyone else to do so. It would only confuse things."

"I know everyone got to the train—the various parties," added Roger. "The Colonel was collecting the Duke personally, and two of our men—"

"Ours?" asked the Comte.

"From the Ministry," clarified Roger.

"Ah."

"They rode ahead to meet him."

"How thoughtful," said the Contessa.

"What of your cousin Pamela?" asked Xonck. "And her disenfranchised brat?"

Roger did not reply. Francis Xonck chuckled wickedly.

"And the little *Princess*?" asked Xonck. *"La Nouvelle Marie?"*

"She will perform admirably," said the Contessa.

"Not that she has any idea of her part," Xonck scoffed. "What of the Prince?"

"Equally in hand," rasped the Comte. "What of his transport?"

"I am assured it sails to position tonight," answered Xonck. Miss Temple wondered why he of all people would be the one with information about ships. "The canal has been closed this last week, and has been prepared."

"And what of the mountains—the Doctor's scientific marvel?"

"Lorenz seems confident there is no problem," observed the Contessa. "Apparently it packs away most tidily."

"What of the... ah... Lord?" asked Roger.

No one answered at once, exchanging subtle glances.

"Mr. Crabbé was curious—" began Roger.

"The *Lord* is agreeable to everything," said the Contessa.

* * *

"What of the *adherents*?" asked the Contessa. "Blenheim sent word that they have arrived throughout the day discreetly," answered Roger, "along with a squadron of Dragoons."

"We do not need more soldiers—they are a mistake," said the Comte.

"I agree," said Xonck. "Yet Crabbé insists—and where government is concerned, we have agreed to follow him."

The Contessa spoke to Roger across Miss Temple. "Has he any new information about... our departed brother-in-law of Dragoons?"

"He has not—that I know of. Of course we have not recently spoken—"

"Blach insists that it's settled," said Xonck.

"The Colonel was poisoned," snapped the Contessa. "It is not the method of the man the Major wishes to blame—aside from the fact that man assured his employer that he did *not* do it, when having done so would have meant cash in hand. Moreover, how would *he* have known when to find his victim in that vulnerable period after undergoing the Process? He would not. That information was known to a select—a *very* select—few." She nodded to Xonck's bandaged arm and scoffed. "Is *that* the work of an elegant schemer?"

Xonck did not respond.

After a pause, Roger Bascombe cleared his throat and wondered aloud mildly, "Perhaps the Major is overdue for the Process himself."

"Do you trust Lorenz to have everything aboard?" asked Xonck, to the Comte. "The deadline was severe—the large quantities—"

"Of course," the Comte replied gruffly.

"As you know," continued Xonck, "the invitations have been sent."

"With the wording we agreed upon?" asked the Contessa.

"Of course. Menacing enough to command attendance... but if we do not have the *leverage* from our harvest in the country—"

"I have no doubts." The Contessa chuckled. "If Elspeth Poole is with him, Doctor Lorenz will strive mightily."

"In exchange for her joining *him* in strenuous effort!" Xonck cackled. "I am sure the transaction appeals to his mathematical mind—sines and tangents and bisected spheres, don't you know."

* * *

"And what about our little magpie?" asked Xonck, leaning forward and cocking his head to look into Miss Temple's face. "Is she worthy of the Process? Is she worthy of a *book*? Something else entirely? Or perhaps she cannot be swayed?"

"Anyone can be swayed," said the Comte. Xonck paid no attention, reaching forward to flick one of Miss Temple's curls.

"Perhaps . . . something *else* will happen . . ." He turned to the Comte. "I've read the back of each painting, you know. I know what you're aiming at—what you were trying with your Asiatic whore." The Comte said nothing and Xonck laughed, taking the silence as an acknowledgment of his guess. "That is the trick of banding with clever folk, Monsieur le Comte—so many people are *not* clever, those who *are* sometimes grow into the habit of assuming no one else will ever divine their minds."

"That is enough," said the Contessa. "Celeste has done damage to *me*, and so—by all our agreements—she is indisputably *mine*." She reached up and touched the tip of Miss Temple's bullet-scar with a finger. "I assure you . . . no one will be disappointed."

The coach clattered onto the cobblestone plaza in front of Harschmort House and Miss Temple heard the calls of the driver to his team, pulling them to a halt. The door was opened and she was handed down to a pair of black-liveried footmen, the cobbles cold and hard beneath her feet. Before Miss Temple had scarcely registered where she was—from the second coach she saw the Prince and his party descending, Miss Vandaariff's expression a shifting series of furtive smiles and frowns—the Comte's iron grasp directed her toward a knot of figures near the great front entrance. Without any ceremony—and without even a glance to see if the others were following—she was conveyed roughly along, doing her best to avoid a stubbed toe on the uneven stones, only coming to a stop when the Comte acknowledged the greetings of a man and woman stepping out from the larger group (a mixture of servants, black-uniformed soldiers of Macklenburg, and red-coated Dragoons). The man was tall and broad, with grizzled and distressingly thick side whiskers and a balding pate that caught the torchlight and made his entire face seem like a primitive mask. He bowed formally to the Comte. The woman wore a simple dark dress that was nevertheless quite flattering, and her affable face bore the recognizable scars around her eyes. Her hair was brown and plainly curled and gathered behind her head with black ribbon. She nodded at Miss Temple and then smiled up at the Comte.

"Welcome back to Harschmort, Monsieur," she said. "Lord Vandaariff is in his study."

The Comte nodded and turned to the man. "Blenheim?"

"Everything as ordered, Monsieur."

"Attend to the Prince. Mrs. Stearne, please escort Miss Vandaariff to her rooms. Miss Temple here will join you. The Contessa will collect both ladies when it is time."

The man nodded sharply and the woman bobbed into a curtsey. The Comte drew Miss Temple forward and shoved her in the direction of the door. She looked behind her to see the woman—Mrs. Stearne—dipping again before the Contessa and Miss Vandaariff, rising to kiss each of the younger woman's cheeks and then take her hand. The Comte released Miss Temple from his grip—his attention turned to the words passing between Xonck, Blach, and Blenheim—as Mrs. Stearne took up her hand, Lydia Vandaariff stepping into place on the woman's other side. The three of them walked—with four liveried footmen falling in place behind them—into the house.

Miss Temple glanced once at Mrs. Stearne, sure that she had finally located the fourth woman from her first coach ride to Harschmort. This was the pirate, who had undergone the Process in the medical theatre, screaming before the audience dressed in their finery. Mrs. Stearne caught her look and smiled, squeezing Miss Temple's hand.

Lydia Vandaariff's rooms overlooked a massive formal garden in the rear of the house, what Miss Temple assumed was once the prison's parade ground. The entire idea of living in such a place struck her as morbid, if not ridiculously affected, all the more when the rooms one lived in were so covered in lace as to seem one great over-flounced pillow. Lydia immediately retreated to an inner closet with two of her maids to change clothes, muttering at them crossly and tossing her head. Miss Temple was installed on a wide lace-fringed settee. This had served to expose her filthy feet, prompting Mrs. Stearne to call for another maid with a basin and a cloth. The girl knelt and washed Miss Temple's feet carefully one at a time, drying them on a soft towel. Throughout, Miss Temple remained silent, her thoughts still a-swim at her situation, her heart alternating between anger and despondence. She had committed their path from the front door to Lydia's apartments to memory as best she could, but with only the barest hope of escape for that way was lined with servants and soldiers, as if the entire mansion had become an armed camp. Miss Temple could not but notice that nowhere around her was a single thing—a nail file, a crystal dish for sweets, a letter opener, a candlestick—she might have snatched up for a weapon.

When the girl had finished, collecting her things and nodding first to Miss Temple and then Mrs. Stearne before backing from the room, the two remained for a moment in silence—or near silence, the hectoring comments of Miss Vandaariff to her maids reaching them despite the distance and closed doors.

"You were in the coach," Miss Temple said at last. "The pirate."

"I was."

"I did not know your name. I have since met Mrs. Marchmoor, and heard others speak of Miss Poole—"

"You must call me Caroline," said Mrs. Stearne. "Stearne is my husband's name—my husband is dead and not missed. Of course, I did not know your name either—I knew no one's name, though I think we each assumed the others were old hands. Perhaps Mrs. Marchmoor was an old hand, but I am sure she was as frightened—and thrilled—as the rest of us."

"I doubt she would admit it," replied Miss Temple.

"So do I." Caroline smiled. "I still do not know how you came to be in our coach—it shows a boldness, to be sure. And what you must have done since . . . I can only guess how hard it was."

Miss Temple shrugged.

"Of course." Caroline nodded. "What choice did you have? Yet, to most people, your path would have been plagued with choice—while to you it seems inexorable—quite like my own. However much our characters may be fixed, they are only revealed to us one test at a time. And so we are here together after all, with perhaps more in common than any of us would care to admit—though only a fool does not admit the truth once it is plain to her."

* * *

The woman's dress was simpler than Mrs. Marchmoor's, less ostentatious—less like an actor's idea of how the wealthy dressed, she realized—and she was pained that her heart's impulse was to think of her captor kindly (this being rare enough in Miss Temple's life to be a surprise in itself, captor or no). No doubt the woman had been placed for that very purpose, for a natural sympathy that had somehow survived the Process or could at least be readily counterfeited, to worm Miss Temple's determination that much further from its sticking place.

"I watched you," she said accusingly, "in the theatre . . . you were . . . *shrieking*—"

"I'm sure I was," said Caroline. "And yet, perhaps it is most like having a troubling tooth pulled. The act itself is so distressing as to seem in no way justified . . . and yet, after it is done, the peace of mind . . . the ease of being—and I speak of a former life of no great difficulty, you understand, merely the fraying worries that are part of every day—I cannot now imagine being without this . . . well, it is a kind of bliss."

"Bliss?"

"Perhaps that sounds foolish to you."

"Not at all—I have seen Mrs. Marchmoor—her sort of—of—*spectacle*—and I have seen the book—one of your glass books—I have been inside, the sensation, the debauchery—perhaps 'bliss' *is* an applicable word," said Miss Temple, "though I assure you it is not my choice."

"You mustn't judge Mrs. Marchmoor harshly. She does what she must do for her larger purpose. As we all are guided. Even you, Miss Temple. If you have peered into these extraordinary books then you must know." She gestured toward Miss Vandaariff's dressing closet. "So many are so tender, hungry, so deeply in need. How much of what you read—or indeed, what you remember—was most singularly rooted in painful loneliness? If a person could rid themselves of such a source of anguish . . . can you truly find fault?"

"Anguish and loss are part of life," Miss Temple retorted.

"They are," Caroline agreed. "And yet . . . if they need not be?"

Miss Temple tossed her head and bit her lip. "You present kindness . . . where others . . . well, they are a nest of vipers. My companions have been killed. I am compelled here by force . . . I have been and will be *violated*—as surely as if your finely dressed mob were a gang of Cossacks!"

"I hope that is not the case, truly," said Caroline. "But if the Process has made anything clear to me, it is that what happens here is only the expression of what you yourself have decided—indeed, what you have asked for."

"I beg your pardon?"

"I do not say it to anger you." She held up a hand to forestall Miss Temple's announcement that she was *already* angry. "Do you think I cannot see the bruises on your pretty neck? Do you imagine I enjoy the sight? I am not a woman who dreams of power or fame, though I know there have been deaths—I do not presume to understand their cause—as a result of those dreams. I know there has been murder, around me and within this house. I know that I do *not* know what those above me plan. And yet I also know that these dreams—theirs and mine—bring with them . . . the opposite side of their coin, if you will—a bliss of purpose, of simplicity, and indeed . . . Celeste . . . of surrender."

Miss Temple sniffed sharply and swallowed, determined not to give way. She was not used to hearing her name so freely used and found it unnerving. The woman presented the Cabal's goals in terms of reason and care—indeed, she seemed a higher level of antagonist altogether for not seeming one at all. The room was unbearable—the lace and the perfumes—so many and so thick—were smothering.

"I would prefer it if you referred to me as Miss Temple," she said.

"Of course," said Caroline, with what seemed a gentle, sad sort of smile.

As if by some rotation of the gears of a clock, they no longer spoke, the room settling into silence and subsequently into contemplation. Yet Miss Temple could only think of the oppressive vacuity of the furnishings around her—though she had no doubt they were the heartfelt expression of Miss Vandaariff—and the low ceiling that, despite the luxurious cherry wood, still bespoke confinement. She looked at the walls and decided at least four prison cells had been opened up together for this room alone. Was it inevitable that *this* luxuriously impersonal lodging was her final refuge as a whole-minded person? As if her burdens had become at once too much to bear, Miss Temple's tears broke suddenly forward, quite dissolving her face, her small shoulders shaking with emotion, blinking, her pink cheeks heedlessly streaked, her lips quivering. So often in her life, tears were the consequence of some affront or denial, an expression of frustration and a sense of unfairness—when those with power (her father, her governess) might have acceded to her wishes but out of cruelty did not. Now Miss Temple felt that she wept for a world without any such authority at all . . . and the kind face of Caroline—however much she knew it to represent the interests of her captors—only reinforced how trivial and unanswered her complaints must remain, how insignificant her losses, and how fully removed from love, or if not love, primacy in another's thoughts, she had become.

She wiped her eyes and cursed her weakness. What had happened she had not already known in her heart to expect? What revelations had challenged her pragmatic, grim determination? Had she not hardened herself to this exact situation—and was not that hardness, that firmness of mind, her only source of hope? Still the tears would not cease, and she covered her face in her hands.

No one touched her, or spoke. She remained bent over—who knew how long?—until her sobbing eased, eyes squeezed shut. She was so frightened, in a way even more than in her deathly struggle with Spragg, for that had been sudden and violent and close and this . . . they had given her time—so much time—to steep in her dread, to roil in the prospect that her soul—or *something,* some fundamental element that made Miss Temple who she was—was about to be savagely, relentlessly changed. She had seen Caroline on the stage, limbs pulling against the leather restraints, heard her animal groans of uncomprehending agony. She recalled her own earlier resolve to jump from a window, or provoke some sudden mortal punishment, but when she looked up and saw Caroline waiting for her with a tender patience, she understood that no such rash gesture would be allowed. Standing next to Caroline were Miss Vandaariff and her maids. The young woman was dressed in two white silk robes, the outer—without sleeves—bordered at the collar and the hem with a line of embroidered green circles. Her feet were bare and she wore a small eye-mask of densely laid white feathers. Her hair had been painstakingly worked into rows of sausage curls to either side of her head and gathered behind—rather like Miss Temple's own. Miss Vandaariff smiled conspiratorially and then put a hand over her mouth to mask an outright giggle.

Caroline turned to the maids. "Miss Temple can change here."

The two maids stepped forward and for the first time Miss Temple saw another set of robes draped over their arms.

Caroline walked between them, black feathered mask across her eyes, holding hands with each, the three followed by another trio of black-coated Macklenburg troopers with echoing black boots. The marble floor of the corridor—the same great corridor of mirrors—was cold against Miss Temple's still bare feet. She'd been stripped to her own silk pants and bodice and, as before, given first the short transparent robe, then the longer robe without sleeves, and finally the white feathered mask—all the time aware of the eyes of Miss Vandaariff and Caroline frankly studying her.

"Green silk," said Lydia approvingly, as Miss Temple's undergarments were revealed.

Caroline's eyes met Miss Temple's with a smile. "I'm sure they must be specially made."

Miss Temple turned her head, feeling her desires—foolish and naïve—on display every bit as much as her body.

The maids had finished tying the string and then stepped away with a deferent bob. Caroline had dismissed them with a request to inform the Contessa that they awaited her word, and smiled at her two women in white.

"You are both so lovely," said Caroline.

"We are indeed." Miss Vandaariff smiled, and then shyly glanced at Miss Temple. "I believe our bosom is the same size, but because Celeste is shorter, hers looks larger. For a moment I was jealous—I wanted to *pinch* them!" She laughed and flexed her fingers wickedly at Miss Temple. "But then again, you know, I am quite happy to be as tall and slender as I am."

"I suppose you prefer Mrs. Marchmoor's bosom above all," said Miss Temple, her voice sounding just a bit raw, attempting to rally her caustic wit. Miss Vandaariff shook her head girlishly.

"No, I don't like her one jot," she said. "She is too coarse. I prefer people around me to be smaller and fine and elegant. Like Caroline—who pours tea as sweetly as anyone I have ever met, and whose neck is pretty as a swan's."

Before Caroline could speak—a response that surely would have been an answering praise of Miss Vandaariff's features—they heard a discreet tap at the door. A maid opened it to reveal three soldiers. It was time to depart. Miss Temple tried to will herself to run at the window and hurl herself through. But she could not move—and then Caroline was taking her hand.

They were not half-way down the mirrored corridor when behind them erupted a clatter of bootsteps. Miss Temple saw the whiskered man, Blenheim, whom she took to be Lord Vandaariff's chamberlain, racing toward them with a group of red-coated Dragoons in his wake. He carried a carbine, and all of the Dragoons held their saber-sheaths so they would not bounce as they ran.

In a moment his group had passed them by, running ahead to one of the doors on the far right side . . . a room—she had tried to maintain Harschmort's geography in her head as they walked—that bordered the exterior of the house. Caroline pulled on her hand, walking more quickly. Miss Temple could see that they were nearing the very door she had gone through with the Contessa, where she had previously found her robes, the room that led to the medical theatre . . . it seemed a memory from another lifetime. They kept walking. They had reached it—should she try to run?—Caroline did not release her hand but nodded to one of the soldiers to get the door. Just then the door ahead of them—where Blenheim's party had gone—burst open, spewing a cloud of black smoke.

A Dragoon with a soot-smeared face shouted to them, "Water! Water!"

One of the Macklenburg men turned at once and ran back down the hall. The Dragoon disappeared back through the open door, and Miss Temple wondered if she dared dash toward it, but again before she could move, her hand was squeezed by Caroline and she was pulled along. One of the remaining Macklenburg troopers opened the door to the inner room and the other anxiously shepherded them inside away from the smoke. As the door shut behind them Miss Temple was sure she heard an escalation of shouts and the echoing clamor of more bootsteps in the marble hall.

It was once more silent. Caroline nodded to the first soldier and he crossed to the far door, the one cunningly set into the wall, and vanished through it. The remaining man installed himself at the hallway entrance, hands behind his back, and his back square against the door. Caroline looked around, to make certain all was well, and released her grip on their hands.

"There is no need to worry," she said. "We will merely wait until the disturbance is settled."

But Miss Temple could see that Caroline *was* worried.

"What do you think has happened?" she asked.

"Nothing that Mr. Blenheim has not dealt with a thousand times before," Caroline replied.

"Is there really a *fire*?"

"Blenheim is horrid," said Lydia Vandaariff, to no one in particular. "When I have my way he will be *sacked*."

Miss Temple's thoughts began to race. On the far side of the theatre was another waiting room—perhaps that was where the soldier had been forced to go . . . she remembered that her own first visit had revealed the theatre to be empty. What if she were to run to the theatre now? If it was empty again might not she climb into the gallery and then to the spiral staircase, and from there—she knew!—she could retrace the path of Spragg and Farquhar across the grounds and through the servants' passage back to the coaches. And it was only running on floors and carpets and the grassy garden—she could do it with bare feet! All she needed was a momentary distraction. . . .

Miss Temple manufactured a gasp of shock and whispered urgently to Miss Vandaariff. "Lydia! Goodness—do you not see you are most lewdly exposed!"

Immediately Lydia looked down at her robes and plucked at them without finding any flaw, her voice rising in a disquieting whimper. Caroline's attention of course went the same way, as did the Macklenburg trooper's.

Miss Temple darted for the inner door, reaching it and turning the handle before anyone even noticed what she was doing. She had the door open and was already charging through before Caroline called out in surprise...and then Miss Temple cried out herself, for she ran headlong into the Comte d'Orkancz. He stood in heavy shadow, fully blocking the doorway with his massive frame, somehow even larger for the thick leather apron over his white shirt, the enormous leather gauntlets sheathing his arms up to each elbow, and the fearsome brass-bound helmet cradled under one arm, crossed with leather straps, great glass lenses like an insect's eyes and strange metal boxes welded over the mouth and ears. She flung herself away from him and back into the room.

The Comte glanced once, disapprovingly, at Caroline, and then down to Miss Temple.

"I have come myself to collect you," he said. "It is long past time you are redeemed."

EIGHT

Cathedral

Chang made a conscious effort to bend his knees—knowing that a rigid leg could easily mean a shattered joint—and did so just as he collided hard with a curving, hot wall of filthy, slippery metal. The actual time in the air, undoubtedly brief, was enough to allow a momentary awareness of suspension, a rising in his stomach which, due to the total darkness in the shaft, was exceptionally disorienting. His mind made sense of the fall—he'd struck a curve in the pipe, after a drop of perhaps ten or fifteen feet—as his body crumpled and rolled, losing all pretense of balance or control, and then dropped again as the pipe straightened into vertical once more. This time he slammed down even harder, knocking the breath from his lungs on a welded corner—he'd struck a gap where his pipe was joined by another, his upper body striking the seam and his legs continuing past, dragging him downwards. He scrabbled for a grip, couldn't get one on the slick metal—covered with the same slimy deposit caked onto the lattice in the urn—and slid down into the darkness, just keeping hold of his stick as it clattered from under his coat. But the impact had slowed his descent, and he was no longer falling but sliding—this pipe was set at an angle. The air rising up to Chang was more noxious and becoming hotter—it seemed grimly probable that this path would feed him into their furnace. He pressed his legs and his arms to the side of the pipe, grudgingly but surely slowing his descent. By the time he slammed into the next junction he was able to catch hold of the lip and stop himself completely, legs swinging below him in the dark. He pulled himself up with an effort and wedged his torso into the opening, so he was nearly balanced and could relax his arms. Chang caught his breath, wondering how far down he had come, and what in the utter world he had been thinking.

He shut his eyes—he couldn't see anything anyway—and forced himself to focus on what he could hear. From the pipe below came a steady, metallic rattle, in time with regularly spaced gusts of steaming, chemically fouled air. He leaned into the second, joining pipe, which was not as large—large enough to hold him?—and cooler to the touch. He waited, allowing time for a longer cycle, but heard no such rattle from its depths nor felt any such toxic exhalations. He realized absently that his head hurt. The first tendrils of bilious nausea were rising in his stomach. He had to get out. He wrenched himself around in the narrow space and slipped his feet into the narrower pipe. There was just room to fit, and Chang pushed from his mind the prospect of the pipe getting thinner mid-way down—he did not want to think about trying to claw his way back against the slippery interior. He tucked his stick under his coat and pinned it with his left arm, and eased himself down as slowly as he could, pressing his legs against the side of the shaft. There was less of the greasy accretion and Chang found that he could more or less manage his descent, for the pipe went down at a milder angle. The farther he sank from the main shaft, the clearer became the air, and the less he worried about being dropped into a cauldron of molten glass. The pipe continued for some distance—he stopped even trying to guess—and then flattened out, blessedly without narrowing, so that he was on his back (and doing his best to keep his mind from tales of coffins and live burial). The pipe still curved, but now horizontally...as if, he thought with a smile, it traveled around the floor of a circular room. He inched along feet first—unable to turn—trying to make as little noise as he could, though he was forced to stop once, preventing by sheer force of will the voiding of his stomach—jaw clenched against the rising bile, huffing like a wounded horse through his scarred nasal passages. He pushed himself on until, so suddenly it took his fogged mind a moment to make sense of what he was seeing—that he was seeing anything at all—the blackness above him was punctuated by a chink of light. He reached up to it carefully and felt the underside of a metal clasp, and then by delicately searching around it sketched out the borders and sweetly welcome hinges of some sort of panel.

Chang turned the clasp to the side, slipping the bolt clear, and then brought both hands beneath the panel and slowly pushed. The hinges gave way with a rusted groan. He stopped, listened, and forced himself to listen more, another whole agonizing minute. A dim light poured into the shaft and he could see with disgust how rusted and filthy it was. He pushed again, and with a longer squeal of protest the panel swung clear. Chang gasped at the cleaner air and sat up. Only his head and the tip of one shoulder fit with ease through the gap. He was in some sort of brick-walled machine room—a secondary one, perhaps, thankfully not in use—with several similarly sized pipes coming through the walls from different directions, all converging at an enormous riveted metal boiler, clotted with dials and smaller hoses. He shifted back inside the pipe and extricated his right arm and once again his head and then, over the course of an awkward, desperate minute, he was able to force his left arm and torso through the gap, gouging his ribs and his shoulder in the process. Feeling like an insect emerging from its sticky cocoon—and just as feeble—Chang inched his way onto the floor and took in the room around him. It was really quite small. Hanging from a row of hooks was a collection of syringes and stoppered glass tubes, a pair of leather gloves and one of the infernal brass and leather helmets. Undoubtedly his escape hatch was employed to test whatever liquid or gaseous concoctions would be steeped in the iron cauldron. Next to the hooks was an inset sconce with the lower third of a fat, guttering tallow candle—the source of the dim light that had wormed through the latched panel. That it was alight told Chang that someone had been in the room recently... and would be coming back.

At that moment he did not care about them, the machine, or its purpose. Under the rack of pipes was a dirty leather fire bucket. Chang crawled to it and vomited without any effort at all until his stomach had nothing more to give and his throat was raw. He sat back and dug out a shirt-tail to wipe his mouth, then pulled it out farther to smear the filth of the furnace pipes from his face. Chang forced himself to his feet and looked at his red leather coat with bitter resignation. The pride of his wardrobe was most assuredly ruined. The coal dust could have been cleaned, but as he wiped at the caked chemical deposits he saw the red leather beneath had been discolored and blistered, almost as if the coat itself was burned and bleeding. He scooped away as much of the mess as he could with his fingers and then wiped his hands on his filthy pants, feeling as if he'd just swum through a demonic mire. He took a deep breath. He was still light-headed, pain pounding behind his eyes like a hammer—the kind of pain he knew, barring opium, he would be carrying with him for days. He expected that some sort of pursuit must even now be working its way to these depths of the house, if only to confirm that his bones were cracking and popping in a furnace, or he was choked to death in the pipes above it, stuck like a dead squirrel in a chimney. Chang felt the parch of his throat and the desperate dizziness in his head. He needed water. Without it he would die on the blade of the first Dragoon that found him.

The door was locked, but the lock was old and Chang was able to force it with his skeleton keys. It opened into a narrow, circular corridor of brick lit by a sputtering torch bolted into a metal bracket above the door. He could not see another torch in either direction. He quickly walked into darkness to his right. Just around the curve the way ended at a bricked-in wall whose mortar was noticeably fresher than the side walls or the ceiling. Chang walked back past the boiler room in the other direction, looking up at the oppressive ceiling and the circular path of his corridor. He was sure it corresponded to the side of the larger chamber. It was vital—to give himself some breathing room, and to find Miss Temple—that he find some way to climb.

The next torch was bracketed near an open doorway. Inside was a spiral staircase of stone with a bright iron rail on the inner wall. Chang looked up, but could only see a few yards ahead because of the curving stairs. He listened... there was a sound, a low roar, like the wind, or heavy distant rain. He began to climb.

It was twenty steps to another open doorway and another circular corridor. He poked out his head and saw its ceiling was banked as if it were the underside of a stadium. Chang stepped back into the stairwell and shut his eyes. His throat was burning. His chest felt as if it was being squeezed from within—he could just imagine the grains of glass boring into his heaving lungs. He forced himself into the hall, looking for some kind of relief, following the path back to where, on the floor below, his boiler room had been. There was another door in the exact spot, and he forced the lock just as easily. The room was dark. Chang worked the torch from its bracket and thrust it inside: another boiler with another set of metal pipes coming through the walls—perhaps this was the juncture where he'd been unable to hold his grip. His eye saw another leather fire bucket on the floor. He stepped to it and with relief saw that it held water—filthy, brackish, unwholesome, but he did not care. Chang dropped the torch, pulled off his glasses and splashed it onto his face. He rinsed the filthy taste from his mouth and spat, and then drank deeply, gasping, and drank again. He sat back, leaning against the pipe, and looped his glasses back into place. He hawked up another gob of who knew exactly what and let it fly into a dark corner of the room. It was not a night at the Boniface, but it would do.

Chang was back in the hallway, returning to the stairs. He wondered that no one had come down to search for him—either they were sure he was dead . . . or he'd fallen farther than he'd thought . . . or they were concentrating on the most important places he might have landed first . . . all of which made him smile, for it told him his enemies were confident, and that confidence was giving him time. But perhaps they were only making sure he didn't reach a particular room to interrupt some particular event—after which it would not matter if they hunted him down at their leisure. It was possible—and it could only mean Celeste. He was a fool. He ran for the stairway and charged up it two steps at a time. Another door. He stepped out—another narrow, dusty hallway with a banked ceiling—and listened. The dull roar was louder, but he was convinced that these were only service corridors, that he was still below the main access. Would he have to go to the absolute top before he could find a way inside? There had to be another way—the path above was sure to be swarming with soldiers. Chang sprinted down the corridor in each direction, first to the right, where his boiler had been—another door to an empty room whose boiler had either been removed or not yet installed—and another dead end. He turned and jogged to the left. The roar became louder, and when he reached its dead end—no door at all in this part of the corridor—he placed his hand on the brick, and felt a faint vibration in time with the rumbling sound.

He raced up another rotation of the circular stairs—how far *had* he fallen?—and this time came not to an open doorway but a locked metal door. He looked above him, saw no one, and again strained to hear any sort of useful sound. Were those voices? Music? He could not be sure—if so, it told him he was only a few of these levels below the main house itself. He turned his attention to the door. This must be the access he wanted. He nearly laughed out loud. Some idiot had left the key in the lock. Chang took the handle and turned it in the exact instant it was turned from the opposite side. Seizing the opportunity, he kicked at the door with all his strength, driving it into whoever stood on the other side, and charged through, whipping apart his stick. Staggering away from him with a puling cry, clutching his bandaged arm—which had taken the brunt of the door—was the aged Mr. Gray, Rosamonde's creature who had administered the Process to the unfortunate Mr. Flaüss. Chang slashed him across the face with the haft of the stick, spinning him to the floor, and glanced quickly to either side. Gray was alone. This hallway was wider, the ceiling still banked, but lit with gaslight sconces instead of torches, and Chang could see doors—or niches?—lining the inner walls. Before Gray could raise his head and bleat for help—which Chang could see he was about to do—he dropped onto the man's chest, pinning Gray's arms cruelly under his knees, and pressed the haft of his stick hard across his throat. With a venomous hiss that caught Gray's full attention, Chang laid the tip of his dagger on the old man's face, pointing directly at his left eye.

"Where is Miss Temple?" he whispered.

Gray opened his mouth to respond but nothing came out. Chang eased up his pressure on the fellow's windpipe.

"Try again," he hissed.

"I—I do not *know*!" pleaded Mr. Gray.

Chang doubled up his fist holding the dagger and slammed it into Mr. Gray's cheek, knocking his head brutally against the stone.

"Try again," he hissed. Gray began to weep. Chang raised his fist. Gray's eyes widened in desperate fear and his mouth began to move, groping for words.

"I—don't!—I don't—I have not seen her—she's to be taken to the theatre—or the chamber—elsewhere in the house! I do not know! I am only to prepare the works—the great works—"

Chang slammed his fist once more into Mr. Gray's head.

"Who is with her?" he hissed. "How many guards?"

"I cannot *tell* you!" Gray was weeping openly. "There are many Macklenburgers, Dragoons—she is with the Comte—with Miss Vandaariff—they will be processed together—"

"Processed?"

"Redeemed—"

"Redeemed?" Chang felt the natural pleasure of violence blooming directly into fury.

"You are too late! By now it will be started—to interrupt it will kill them both!" Mr. Gray looked up and saw his own reflection in the smoked black lenses over Cardinal Chang's eyes and wailed. "O—they all said you were!—why are you not *dead*?"

His eyes opened even wider, if that were possible, in shock, as Chang drove the dagger into Mr. Gray's heart, which he knew would be quicker and far less bloody than cutting the man's throat. In a matter of seconds Gray's body had relaxed and gone forever still. Chang rolled back onto his knees, still breathing hard, wiped the dagger on Gray's coat, and sheathed it. He spat again, felt the stab of pain in his lungs, and muttered darkly.

"How do you know I am not?"

He dragged the body back to the stairwell and down one full curve before propping it up and tipping it over, doing his best to send the unregretted Mr. Gray all the way to the bottom—wherever it had landed, it was at least out of sight to anyone coming to this door. He pocketed the key Gray had stupidly left in the lock and returned to the corridor, trying to guess what Gray had been doing. Chang sighed. There had been more information to glean from the man, but he was in a hurry, and itching, after being hunted and assailed, to strike some blow in answer. That it was against an aged, wounded man was to Cardinal Chang no matter at all. Every last one of these people was his enemy, and he would not scruple to excuse a single soul.

The niches in the inner wall were old cell doors—heavy metal monstrosities whose handles had been hacked off with a chisel and sealed shut with iron bolts driven into the brick. Chang laced his fingers in the small barred window and strained but could not shift it at all. He peered into the cell. The far wall of bars was draped with canvas. On the other side of the canvas, he knew, was the great chamber, but this was no way for him to reach it. He paced rapidly down the length of the curving hallway. Gray was another fool from the Institute, like Lorenz and the man he'd surprised making the book. As a reader of poetry, Chang believed that learning was dangerous and best suited for private contemplation, not something to put in the service of the highest bidder—as the Institute did, in thrall to the patronage of men with blind dreams of empire. Society was not bettered by such men of "vision"—though, if Chang was honest, was it bettered by anyone? He smiled wolfishly at the thought that it *was* better without the corrupted Mr. Gray, amused at the notion that he himself might be seen as an engine of civic progress.

At the end of the corridor was another door. Gray's key turned sharply in the lock and Chang peered into a room scarcely larger than a closet, with seven large pipes running vertically from the ceiling to disappear through the floor, each one set with an access panel similar to the one he'd emerged through downstairs. The room was stiflingly hot and reeking—even to him—with the acrid, chemical excrescence of indigo clay. To the side was another rack of pegs, dangling another collection of flasks, vials, and unsettlingly large syringes. The roar of the machines echoed in the tiny chamber as if he were near the humming pipes of a massive church organ. Chang noticed a narrow slice of light between two pipes, and then, looking closely, saw similar small gaps elsewhere in the wall they formed . . . and realized that this was literally true—the far wall of the closet *was* the pipes, and beyond them, its brilliant illumination shining through, lay the great chamber. Chang crouched and removed his glasses, pressing his face to the nearest chink of light he could find. The pipes were hot against his skin, and he could only see the smallest view, but what he saw was astonishing: an opposite wall, high as a cliff-face, thick with more pipes flowing the entire height of a gigantic, vaulted chamber, and then, just on the edge of his sight, what looked like the central tower, like the hub of a wheel, whose sheer face of riveted steel was dotted with tiny vents from which the interior of every cell in the old prison could have been viewed. Chang shifted to another gap on his hands and knees, searching for an angle that showed him more. From here he saw a different segment of the opposite wall. Between the banks of pipes lay a tier of exposed cells—actually several tiers—bars still in place, looking for all the world like viewing galleries in a theatre. He sat back and brushed himself off by habit, wincing at how smeared with filth he was. Whatever was going to happen in the chamber, it was designed to have an audience.

He was back in the spiral staircase, climbing quietly, both hands on his stick. The next and final door did not appear until double the usual number of stairs, and when it did, he was surprised to see it was wood, with a new brass doorknob and lock—consistent with the formal decor of Harschmort. Chang had ascended to the—probably lowest—level of the house proper. Gray had said they thought he was dead—but did that mean back at the Ministry or just now in the furnace pipes? Surely he had been recognized in the garden—did it matter? He was more than happy to play the role of avenging ghost. He opened the door a narrow crack and peered, not into the hallway he expected, but a small dark room, blocked by a drawn curtain, under which he saw flickers of light—flickers matching audible footfalls on the curtain's other side. Chang eased through the doorway and crept close to the curtain. He delicately pinched the fabric between two fingers, making a gap just wide enough to peek through.

The curtain merely masked an alcove in a large storeroom, the walls lined with shelves and the bulk of the open floor taken up with free-standing racks stuffed full of bottles and jars and tins and boxes. While he watched, two porters shifted a wooden crate of clinking brown bottles onto a wheeled cart and pushed it from sight, pausing to make conversation with someone Chang couldn't see. After they left, the room was silent . . . save for bootsteps and a metallic knocking Chang had heard too many times before—the jostling of a saber scabbard as a bored guard paced back and forth. But the guard was hidden on the opposite side of the racks. To reach him Chang would have to leave the curtained alcove and only then decide on his angle of attack—while exposed.

Before he could begin he heard approaching steps and a harsh commanding voice he recognized from the garden.

"Where is Mr. Gray?"

"He hasn't returned, Mr. Blenheim," answered the guard—by his accent not one of the Macklenburgers.

"What was he doing?"

"Don't know, Sir. Mr. Gray went downstairs—"

"Damn him to hell! Does he not know the time? The schedule?"

Chang braced himself—they were certain to search. Without the covering noise of the servants there was no way to slip back through the door without them hearing. Perhaps it was better. Mr. Blenheim would pull the curtain aside and Chang would kill him. The guard might sound the alarm before he fell as well—or the guard might kill Chang—either way it was an additional helping of revenge.

But Blenheim did not move.

"Never mind," he snapped irritably. "Mr. Gray can hang himself. Follow me."

Chang listened to their bootsteps march away. Where had they gone—what was so important?

Chang chewed on a handful of bread torn from an expensive fresh white loaf purloined from the storeroom as he walked, recognizing nothing around him from his previous travels through the back passages of Harschmort House. This was a lower story, finely appointed but not opulent. The pipes could have landed him at any point of the house's horseshoe arc. He needed to work his way to the middle—there he would find the entrance to the panopticon tower, to the great chamber—and do it quickly. He could not remember when he'd eaten such delicious bread—he should have stuffed another loaf in his pocket. This caused Chang to glance down at his pocket, where he felt the knocking weight of Miss Temple's green ankle boot. Was he a sentimental fool?

Chang stopped walking. Where *was* he? The truth of his situation penetrated his thoughts as abruptly as a blade: he was in Robert Vandaariff's mansion, the very heart of wealth and privilege, of a society from which he lived in mutually contemptuous exile. He thought of the very bread he was eating, his very enjoyment of it feeling like a betrayal, a spike of hatred rising at the endless luxury around him, a pervasive ease of life that met him no matter where he turned. In Harschmort House Cardinal Chang suddenly saw himself as he must be seen by its inhabitants, a sort of rabid dog somehow slipped through the door, already doomed. And why had he come? To rescue an unthinking girl from this very same world of wealth? To slaughter as many of his enemies as he could reach? To avenge the death of Angelique? How could any of this scratch the surface of this world, of this inhuman labyrinth? He felt he was dying, and that his death would be as invisible as his life. For a moment Chang shut his eyes, his rage hollowed out by despair. He opened them with a sharp, slicing intake of breath. Despair made their victory easier still. He resumed his pace and took another large bite of bread, wishing he'd found something to drink as well. Chang snorted; that was exactly how he needed to collide with Blenheim, or with Major Blach, or with Francis Xonck—with a bottle of beer in one hand and a wad of food in the other. He stuffed the last of the loaf into his mouth and pulled apart his stick.

As he went he dodged two small parties of Dragoons and one of the black-coated Germans. They all traveled in the same direction and he altered his course to follow them—assuming that whatever event had called Blenheim was calling them as well. But why was no one searching for him? And why did no one look for Mr. Gray? Gray had been doing something with the chemical works, the content of the pipes... and none of the soldiers seemed to care. Was Gray doing something for Rosamonde that none of the others knew about—some secret work? Could that mean division within the Cabal? This didn't surprise him—he would have been surprised by its absence—but it explained why no one had come. It also meant that Chang had, without intending it, spoiled Rosamonde's scheme. She would only know that Gray had not returned, but never why, and—he smiled to imagine it—be consumed with doubt and worry. For what if it was the Comte or Xonck who had interrupted her man, men who would know in a moment how she planned to betray them? He smiled to imagine that lady's discomfort.

Chang shifted his thoughts to the great chamber, recalling the tier of cells, where prisoners—or spectators—could see the goings-on below which must, he assumed, be where he would find Celeste. He estimated how far he'd climbed—*that* row of cells might be on this level... but how to find it? The curtained alcove had so casually hidden the entrance to the spiral staircase... the door to these cells might be hidden in the same offhand manner. Had he already passed it by? He trotted down the hallway, opening every interior-facing door and peering into blind corners, finding nothing and feeling very quickly as if he was wasting time.

Shouldn't he follow the soldiers and Blenheim—wouldn't they be guarding the Comte and his ceremony? Couldn't Celeste be with them just as easily? He'd give his search another minute and then run after them. That minute passed, and then five more and still Chang could not pull himself from what he felt was the right path, rushing on through room after room. This entire level of the house seemed deserted. He unheedingly spat on the pale, polished wooden floor and winced at the gob's scarlet color, then turned yet another out-of-the-way corner. Where was he? He looked up.

He sighed. He was an idiot.

Chang was in a sort of workroom, set with many tables and benches, racks of wood, shelves stuffed with jars and bottles, a large mortar and pestle, brushes, buckets, large tables whose surfaces were scarred with burns, candles and lanterns and several large free-standing mirrors—to reflect light?—and everywhere stretched canvases of different dimensions. He was in an artist's studio. He was in the studio of Oskar Veilandt.

There was no mistaking the paintings' author, for they bore the same striking brushwork, lurid colors, and disquieting compositions. Chang walked into the room with the same trepidation as if he were entering a tomb . . . Oskar Veilandt was dead . . . were these his works—more that had been salvaged from Paris? Had Robert Vandaariff made it his business to gather the man's entire *oeuvre*? For all the brushes and bottles, none of the paintings seemed obviously in mid-composition—as if the artist was alive and working. Was someone else restoring or cleaning the canvases to Vandaariff's specifications? On impulse Chang stepped to a small portrait leaning against one of the tables—of a masked woman wearing an iron collar and a glittering crown—and turned it over. The back of the canvas was scrawled, just as Svenson had described, with alchemical symbols and what seemed like mathematical formulae. He tried to locate a signature or a date, but could not. He set the painting down and saw, across the room, a large painting, not leaning but hanging in place, its lowest edge flush with the floor—a life-size portrait of none other than Robert Vandaariff. The great man stood against a dark stone battlement, behind him a strange red mountain and behind that a bright blue sky (these compositional elements reminding Chang of nothing more than a series of flat, painted theatrical backdrops), holding in one hand a wrapped book and in the other a pair of large metal keys. When would it have been painted? Vandaariff had known Veilandt personally—which meant the Lord's involvement went back at least to Veilandt's death.

But standing in the midst of so many of the man's unsettling works, it was hard to believe he was dead at all, so insistent was the air of knowing, insinuating, exultant menace. Chang looked again at the portrait of Vandaariff, like an allegorical emblem of a Medici prince, and realized that it was hung lower than the paintings around it. He crossed and hefted the thing from its hook and set it none-too-gently aside. He shook his head at the obviousness of it. Behind the painting was another narrow alcove and three stone steps leading down to a door.

It opened inward, the hinges recently greased and silent. Chang entered another low curving hallway, light bleeding in through small chinks on the inner wall, like the interior of an old ship, or—more accurately—like the depths of a prison. The inner wall was lined with cells. Chang stepped to the nearest: here too the handles had been chiseled off and the doors bolted to their frames. He pulled aside the viewing slot and gasped.

The far wall of the cell, though blocked off with bars, revealed the entirety of the great chamber. Chang doubted he'd ever seen a place—so ambitiously a monument to its master's dark purpose—that so filled him with dread, an infernal cathedral of black stone and gleaming metal.

In the center of the room was the massive iron tower, running from the closed ceiling (the chamber's brilliant light came from massive chandeliers of dangling lanterns suspended on chains) all the way to a floor that was tangled and clotted with the bright pipes and cables that flowed down the walls to the base of the tower like a mechanical sea breaking at the foot of a strangely land-bound lighthouse. The slick surface of the tower was pock-marked with tiny spy holes. As a prisoner in the insect-hive of open cells, it would be impossible to know if anyone inside was watching or not. Chang knew that in such circumstances the incarcerated began to act, despite themselves, as if they *were* being watched at all times, steadily amending their behavior, their rebellious spirit inexorably crushed as if by an invisible hand. Chang snorted at the perfect ideological *aptness* of the monstrous structure to its current masters.

He could not see the base of the tower from his vantage point and was about to seek a better view when he heard a metallic clang and spied, in one of the cells opposite him, a flicker of movement . . . legs . . . a man was descending into the cell by way of a ladder. Abruptly he heard another clang much nearer, to his right. Before he could see where it exactly was he heard a third directly above his head, from the very cell he peered into. A hatch in the ceiling had been heaved open and the legs of a man in a blue uniform slithered through, feeling for a metal ladder bolted to the wall that Chang hadn't noticed. All sorts of men and women were climbing into the cells across the chamber, usually a man first who then assisted the ladies, sometimes being handed folding camp chairs, setting up the prison cells as if they were private boxes at the theatre. The air around Chang began to buzz with the excited anticipation of an audience before an unrisen curtain. The man in the blue uniform—a sailor of some sort—called merrily up through the hatch for the next person. Whatever was about to start, Chang wasn't going to do anything about it where he was. However much he'd just discovered, he'd made the wrong decision as far as locating Celeste. Whatever the Comte had arranged for all of the people to watch, Chang was sure she would be part of it—for all he knew she could be descending the central tower that very minute.

As he ran his lungs met each breath with a crest of small sharp pains. Chang spat—more blood this time—and again cursed his stupidity for not killing the Contessa outright when he had the chance. He drove himself forward—looking for a staircase, some way up to the main level, it had to be near—and saw it at the same time as he heard the sound of steps descending straight toward him. He could not get away quickly enough. He pulled apart his stick and waited, breathing deeply, lips flecked with red.

He did not really know who he expected to see, but it was definitely not Captain Smythe. The officer saw Chang and stopped dead on the stairs. He glanced once above him and then stepped quickly forward.

"Good Lord," he whispered.

"What's happening?" hissed Chang. "Something's happening upstairs—"

"They think you are dead—*I* thought you were dead—but no one could find a body. I took it upon myself to make sure."

Smythe drew his saber and strode forward from the stairs, the blade floating easily in his hand.

Chang called to him. "Captain—the great chamber—"

"I trusted you like a fool and you've killed my man," Smythe snarled, "the very man who saved your treacherous life!"

He lunged forward and Chang leapt away, stumbling into the corridor wall. The Captain slashed at his head—Chang just ducking down and rolling free. The blade bit into the plaster with a pale puff of dust.

Smythe readied his blade for another lunge. In answer—there was no way he could possibly fight him with any hope of survival—Chang stood tall and stepped into the center of the corridor, snapping his arms open wide, cruciform, in open invitation for Smythe to run him through. He hissed at Smythe with fury and frustration.

"If you think that is so—do what you will! But I tell you I did not kill Reeves!"

Smythe paused, the tip of his blade a pace or so from Chang's chest, but within easy range.

"Ask your own damned men! They were there!" snapped Chang. "He was shot with a carbine—he was shot by—by—what's his name—the overseer—*Blenheim*—the chamberlain! Don't be a bloody idiot!"

Captain Smythe was silent. Chang watched him closely. They were close enough that he might conceivably deflect the saber with his stick and get to the Captain with the dagger. If the man persisted in being stupid, there was nothing else for it.

"That was not what I was told . . ." said Smythe, speaking very slowly. "You used him as a shield."

"And who told you that? Blenheim?"

The Captain was silent, still glaring. Chang scoffed.

"We were speaking—Reeves and I. Blenheim saw us. Did you even look at the body? Reeves was shot in the *back*."

The words landed like a blow, and Chang could see Smythe thinking, restraining his anger by force of will, his thoughts at odds. After another moment the Captain lowered his sword.

"I will go examine the body myself." He looked back at the stairs and then again to Chang, his expression changing, as if he were seeing him freshly without the intervening veil of rage.

"You're injured," said Smythe, fishing out a handkerchief and tossing it to Chang. Chang snatched it from the air and wiped his mouth and face, seeing the dire nature of his wounds reflected in the officer's concern. Once again the notion that he was truly dying pressed at his resolve to keep on—what was the point, what had ever been the point? He looked at Smythe, a good man, no doubt, bitter himself, but bolstered by his uniform, his admiring men—who knew, a wife and children. Chang wanted to suddenly snarl that he desired none of those things, loathed the very idea of such a prison, loathed the kindness of Smythe himself. Just as he loathed himself for loving Angelique or having come to care for Celeste? He looked quickly away from the Captain's troubled gaze and saw everywhere around him the luxurious, mocking fittings of Harschmort. He was going to die at Harschmort.

"I am, but nothing can be done. I am sorry about Reeves—but you must listen. A woman has been taken—the woman I spoke of, Celeste Temple. They are about to *do* something to her—an infernal ceremony, I have seen it—it is beyond deadly—I assure you she would rather die."

Smythe nodded, but Chang could see that the man was still goggling at his appearance.

"I look worse than I am—I have come through the pipes—the smell cannot be helped," he said. He offered the handkerchief back, saw Smythe's reaction, and then wadded it into his own pocket. "For the last time, I beg you, what is happening above?"

Smythe glanced once up the stairs as if someone might have followed and then spoke quickly. "I'm afraid I barely know—I have just now come in the house. We were outside, for the Colonel's arrival—"

"Aspiche?"

"Yes—it is quite a disaster—they arrived from the country, some sort of accident, the Duke of Stäelmaere—"

"But people are entering the great chamber to watch the ceremony!" said Chang. "There is no time—"

"I cannot speak to that—there are parties of people everywhere and the house is very large," answered the officer. "All of my men are occupied with the Duke's party—after they landed—"

"Landed?"

"I cannot begin to explain. But the whole household has been turned over—"

"Then maybe there's still hope!" said Chang.

"For what?" asked Smythe.

"All I need is to get upstairs and be pointed in the right direction."

He could see that Smythe was torn between helping him and confirming his story. He suspected that the presence of Aspiche had done as much as anything to spur the officer toward mutiny.

"Our transfer to the Palace..." began Smythe quietly as if this were an answer to Chang's request, "was accompanied by a significant rise in pay for all officers... life-saving for men who had spent years abroad and were swimming in debt... it should be no surprise when a reward—the money being now spent—turns out instead to be... an entrapment."

"Go to Reeves," Chang said quietly, "and talk to your men who were there. They will follow you. Wait and stay ready... when the time comes, believe me, you will know what to do."

Smythe looked at him without any confidence whatsoever. Chang laughed—the dry croak of a crow—and clapped the man on the shoulder.

"The house is confusing at first," Smythe whispered to him as they climbed the stairs and crept into the main-floor hallway. "The left wing is dominated by a large ballroom—now quite full of people—and the right by a large hallway of mirrors that leads to private rooms and apartments—again, now quite full of people. Also in the right wing is an inner corridor that takes one to a spiral staircase—I have not climbed it. When I saw it the corridor was lined with Macklenburg guards."

"And the center of the house?" asked Chang.

"The great reception hall, the kitchens, the laundry, staff quarters, the house manager—that's Blenheim—and his men."

"Where is Lord Vandaariff's study?" asked Chang suddenly, his mind working. "At the rear of the house?"

"It is"—Smythe nodded—"and on the main floor. I have not been there. The whole left wing has been restricted to special guests and a very few trusted staff. No Dragoons."

"Speaking of that," said Chang, "what are you doing here? When did you come from the Ministry?"

Smythe smiled bitterly. "The story will amuse you. As my men were relieved from their posts, I received urgent word—from my Colonel I assumed—that we were needed at the St. Royale Hotel. Upon hurrying there—though domestic quarrels are not our usual duty—I was met by an especially presumptuous woman, who *informed* me that I must accompany her at once to this house by train."

"Mrs. Marchmoor, of course."

Smythe nodded. "Apparently she had been agitated by a certain fellow in red—an absolute villain, I understand."

"I believe we took the same train—I was hiding in the coal wagon."

"The possibility occurred to me," said Smythe, "but I could not send a man forward without sending him on the roof—we were forbidden to pass through the iron-bound black railcar."

"What was in it?" asked Chang.

"I cannot say—Mrs. Marchmoor had the key and went in alone. Upon our arrival at Orange Locks we were met by Mr. Blenheim, with carts and a coach. He went into the black car with his men, under Mrs. Marchmoor's eye, and they brought out—"

"What was it?" hissed Chang, suddenly impatient to know, yet fearing to hear the words.

"Again, I cannot say—it was covered with canvas. It could have been another of their boxes, or it could have been a coffin. But as they were loading it I distinctly heard Blenheim order the driver to go slow—so as not to break the *glass*—"

They were interrupted by the sound of approaching bootsteps. Chang pressed himself flat against the wall. Smythe stepped forward and the hallway rang with the unmistakable and imperious voice of Mr. Blenheim.

"Captain! What are you doing apart from your men? What business, Sir, can you have in this portion of the house?"

Chang could no longer see Smythe but heard the tightening of his voice.

"I was sent to look for Mr. Gray," he answered.

"Sent?" snapped Blenheim with open skepticism. "By whom *sent*?"

The man's arrogance was appalling. If Chang were in Smythe's place, knowing the overseer had just murdered one of his men, Blenheim's head would already be rolling on the floor.

"By the Contessa, Mr. Blenheim. Would you care to so interrogate *her*?"

Blenheim ignored this. "Well? And did you *find* Mr. Gray?"

"I did not."

"Then why are you still here?"

"As you can see yourself, I am *leaving*. I understand that you've moved my trooper's body to the stables."

"Of course I have—the last thing the master's guests want to see is a corpse."

"Indeed. Yet I, as his officer, must attend to his effects."

Blenheim snorted with disdain at such petty business. "Then you will *oblige* me by vacating this part of the house, and assuring me that neither you nor your men will return. By the wish of Lord Vandaariff himself, it is for his guests alone."

"Of course. It is Lord Vandaariff's house."

"And I manage that house, Captain," said Blenheim. "If you will come with me."

Chang struck out as best he could for the Lord of the manor's study. His look at the prison plans had not been so detailed as he might like, but it made sense that the warden might have personal access to the central viewing tower. Had Vandaariff simply adopted—and no doubt expanded and layered with mahogany and marble—the previous despot's lair for his own? If Chang's guess was right, Vandaariff's study could then get him to Celeste. It was the thought he kept returning to in his mind, her rescue. He knew there were other tasks—to revenge Angelique, to find the truth about Oskar Veilandt, to discover what falling-out between his enemies had led to Trapping's death—and normally he would have relished the idea of juggling them all together, to carry their evolving solutions in his head as he carried the sifted contents of the Library. But tonight there was no time, no room to fail, no second chances.

He could not risk being seen by anyone, and so was reduced to painful dashes across open corridors, creeping to corners, and scuttling back into cover when guests or servants happened by. With a scoff Chang thought of how nearly everyone in the pyramid of Harschmort's inhabitants was some sort of servant—by occupation, by marriage, by money, by fear, by desire. He thought of Svenson's servitude to duty—duty to *what,* Chang could not understand—and his own doomed notions of obligation and, even if he disdained the word, honor. Now he wanted to spit on them all, just as he was spitting blood on these white marble floors. And what of Celeste—had she been a servant to Bascombe? Her family? Her wealth? Chang realized he did not know. For a moment he saw her, wrestling to reload his pistol at the Boniface . . . a remarkable little beast. He wondered if she had shot someone after all.

The guests, he saw, were once again masked and in formal dress, and their snatches of conversation all carried a buzzing current of anticipation and mystery.

"Do you know—it is said they will be married—tonight!"

"The man in the cape—with the red lining—it is Lord Carfax, back from the Baltic!"

"Did you notice the servants with the iron-bound chests?"

"They will give us a signal to come forward—I had it myself from Elspeth Poole!"

"I'm sure of it—a shocking vigor—"

"Such dreams—and afterwards such peace of mind—"

"They will come like trusting puppies—"

"Did you see it? In the air? Such a machine!"

"Fades in a matter of days—I have it on the highest authority—"

"I have heard it from one who has been before—a particular *disclosure*—"

"No one has seen him—Henry Xonck himself was refused!"

"I've never heard such screaming—nor right after, witnessed such ecstasy—"

"Such an unsurpassed collection of *quality*!"

"Spoken in front of everyone, 'is not history best written with a whip mark?' The Lady is superb!"

"No one has spoken to him for days—apparently he will reveal all tonight, his secret plans—"

"He's going to speak! The Comte as much as promised it—"

"And then . . . the work will be revealed!"

"Indeed . . . the work will be revealed!"

* * *

This last was from a pair of thin rakish men in tailcoats and masks of black satin. Chang had penetrated well into the maze of private apartments and presently stood behind a marble pillar upon which was balanced an ancient and delicate amphora of malachite and gold. The chuckling men walked past—he was in a middling-sized sitting room—toward a sideboard laid with bottles and glasses. The men poured themselves whiskies and sipped them happily, leaning against the furniture and smiling at one another, for all the world like children waiting for permission to unwrap birthday presents.

One of them frowned. He wrinkled his nose.

"What is it?" asked the other.

"That smell," said the first.

"My goodness," agreed the other, sniffing too. "What could it be?"

"I've no idea."

"It's really quite horrid..."

Chang shrank as best he could behind the pillar. If they continued toward him he would have no choice but to attack them both. One of them would surely have a chance to scream. He would be found. The first man had taken an exploratory step in his direction. The other hissed at him.

"Wait!"

"What?"

"Do you think they might be *starting*?"

"I don't understand—"

"The smell! Do you think they're *starting*? The alchemical fires!"

"O my goodness! Is that what they smell like?"

"I don't know—do you?"

"I don't know! We could be late!"

"Hurry—hurry—"

Each tossed back his whisky and slammed down his glass. They rushed unheedingly past Chang, straightening their masks and smoothing their hair.

"What will they make us do?" asked one as they opened the door to leave.

"It does not matter," the other barked urgently, "you must do it!"

"I will!"

"We will be redeemed!" one called with a giddy chuckle as the door closed. "And then *nothing* shall stop us!"

Chang stepped from his spot. With a shake of his head, he wondered if their reaction would have been any different had he not traveled through the furnace pipes, but merely arrived at a Harschmort drawing room bearing the normal odors of his rooming house. *That* smell they would have recognized, he knew—it had been settled into their social understanding. The hideous smells of Harschmort and the Process carried the possibility of advancement, suspending all natural judgment. Similarly, he saw now the Cabal could be as blunt and open as it wished about its aims of power and domination. The beauty was that none of these aspirants—crowding together in their finery, as if they'd managed an invitation to court—saw themselves as people dominated, though their desperate fawning made it obvious that they were. The unreality of the evening—their *induction*—only served to flatter them more, thrilling themselves with the silks and the masks and scheming—enticing trappings that Chang saw were nothing but the distractions of a circus mountebank. Instead of looking up at the Contessa or the Comte with any suspicion, these people were turned gleefully the other way, looking at all the people—from within their new "wisdom"—they might now dominate in turn. He saw the brutal sense of it. Any plan that trusted for success on the human desire to exploit others and deny the truth about one's self was sure to succeed.

Chang cracked open the far doors and looked into the corridor Smythe had described, the whole of its length lined with doors. One of these doors had led him to Arthur Trapping's body. At one end he could see the spiral staircase. He was convinced that Vandaariff's study must lay in the other direction if it held a way down into the great chamber.

But where to start? Smythe had said the house was full of guests—as he had said the hallway was full of guards . . . but for this moment it was unaccountably empty. Chang could not expect it to stay so while he tried each of what—at a quick glance—seemed to be at least thirty doors. All this time . . . was there any hope that Celeste was alive?

He stepped boldly into the hall, striding away from the staircase. He passed the first doors, one after another, with a rising sense of anticipation. If whatever had happened to Aspiche and the Duke (it was difficult for Chang to think of a more loathsome member of the Royal Family) had indeed served to disrupt the ceremony in the great chamber, then Chang was committed to causing as many additional disturbances as he could. He whipped apart his stick—still no one intruded—he was halfway down the hallway. Could everything have already started in spite of what Smythe had said? Chang stopped. To his left one of the doors was ajar. He crept to it and peered through the crack: a narrow slice of a room with red carpet and red wallpaper and a lacquered stand upon which balanced a Chinese urn. He listened... and heard the unmistakable sounds of rustling clothing and heavy breathing. He stepped back, kicked in the door with a crash, and charged forward.

Before him on the carpet was a Macklenburg trooper with his trousers around his knees, desperately trying to pull them up at the same time he hopelessly groped for his saber—the belt and scabbard tangled around his ankles. The man's mouth was opened in fearful protest and there was just time for Chang to register his expression shifting, from shame to incomprehension as he saw who had surprised him, before driving the dagger to the hilt into the trooper's throat, choking off any cry of alarm. He yanked the blade free, stepping clear like a bullfighter of the attending spray of blood, and let the man topple to the side, his pale buttocks uncovered by his dangling shirt-tails.

Was there anything that more signified the helplessness of humanity than the exposed genitals and buttocks of the dead? Chang did not think so. Perhaps a single discarded child's shoe... but that was mere sentiment.

Beyond the dead soldier, lying on the carpet with her dress above her waist was a richly clad woman, hair askew, her face aglow with perspiration around a green beaded mask. Her eyes were wild, blinking, and her breathing coarse and drawn... but the rest of her body seemed unresponsive, as if she were asleep. The man had clearly been about her rape, but Chang saw that her undergarments were yet only half-lowered—he had been surprised in the midst of his attack. Yet the woman's vacant expression suggested her utter unconcern. He stood for a moment over her, his gaze drawn both to her beauty and by the twitches and spasms that rippled across her frame, as if she lay in the midst of a distended fit. He wondered how long it had taken the soldier to advance from hearing her heavy breathing in the hall, through cautious entry and voyeuristic observation, to outright violation. Chang shut the door behind him—the hall was still empty—and then bent down to restore the woman's dress. He reached up to pull the hair away from her face and revealed, beneath her head like a pillow, what her apparently unseeing eyes so greedily devoured . . . a gleaming blue glass book.

The woman's exhalations rose into a moan, her skin as hot and red as if she had fever. Chang looked at the book and licked his lips. With a decisiveness he did not wholly feel he took hold of the woman beneath her arms and lifted her from it, his eyes flinching from the bright gleam of the uncovered glass. As he pulled her away she whimpered in protest like a drowsing puppy separated from its teat. He set her down and winced—the light from the book stabbed to the center of his head. Chang snapped it closed, his lips stretched back in a grimace, feeling even through his leather gloves a strange pulsing as he touched it and a protesting energetic resistance when he pushed it shut. The woman did not make another sound. Chang watched her, idly wiping his dagger on the carpet—it was already red, what was the harm?—as her breath gradually calmed and her eyes began to clear. He gently pushed aside the hanging mask of beads. He did not recognize her. She was merely another of the great ladies and gentlemen drawn into the insidious web of Harschmort House.

Chang stood and snatched a pillow from the nearby settee. He ripped open one end with the dagger and he brusquely turned the lining inside out, dumping yellowed clumps of cotton wadding onto the floor. He inserted the book carefully into the pillowcase and stood. The lady could take care of herself as she woke—her fingers fitfully groped against the carpet—and forever wonder about her mysterious delivery . . . and if she started to scream, it would cause the disturbance he wanted. He stepped back to the door and paused, looking behind him at the room. There was no other door . . . and yet something caught his eye. The wallpaper was red, with a circular decoration of golden rings that looked vaguely Florentine. Chang crossed the room to a section of wallpaper, perhaps as high as his head. In the middle of one of the golden rings the pattern appeared to be frayed. He pressed at it with his finger and the interior of the ring popped through, leaving a hole. A spy hole. Chang strode past the woman—dreamily shaking her head and struggling to raise herself to one elbow—and out to the corridor.

Once more, Chang's notion that most things are only effectively hidden because no one ever thinks to look for them was confirmed. Once he knew what he sought—a narrow corridor between rooms—it was easy enough to identify what door might lead to it. While it was possible that the other side of the spy hole was in another normal room, Chang felt this went against the entire idea—as he understood it—of Harschmort House, which was the *integrated* nature of the establishment. Why have a spy hole into one room, when one might construct an inner passage that spanned the length of many apartments to either side, so one man with patience and soft shoes could effectively gain the advantage on a whole collection of guests? He chuckled to think that he had here explained Robert Vandaariff's famed success at business negotiation, his uncanny aptitude for knowing what his rivals were planning—a reputation side by side with his renown as a generous host (especially—Chang shook his head at the cunning—to those with whom he most bitterly strove). Not three yards from the one he'd entered Chang found two doors quite closely set together—or more accurately, one door in the space that, elsewhere in the corridor, was only blank wall.

Chang dug out his keys—first Gray's and then his own—and struggled to open the lock. It was actually rather tricky, and differed from others he'd found in the house. He looked around him with growing alarm, trying a second key and then fumbling for a third. He thought he heard a rising noise from the far end, near the staircase... applause? Was there some sort of performance? The key did not work. He felt for the next. With a click that echoed down the length of the corridor, a door was opened in the balcony above the staircase—and then the sound of steps, many people... they would be at the railing any instant. His key caught, the lock turned, and without hesitation Chang slipped the door open and darted through into the bitter dark. He closed it as quickly and silently as he could, with no idea if he'd been seen or heard.

There was nothing for it. He turned the lock behind him and felt his way deeper into the blackness. The walls were narrow—his elbows rubbed the dusty brick on either side as he went—but the floor was smoothly laid stone (as opposed to wood that might warp and in time begin to creak). He felt his way along, hampered by his restored stick in one hand and the wrapped book in the other, and by Miss Temple's boots jostling the walls from his pockets. The spy hole in the woman's room had been at head height, so he placed his hands there as he walked, to feel for any depression in the brick. Surely it had to be near . . . his impatience nearly caused him to pitch headlong into the dark as his foot struck a step in the blackness below him and he tripped forward—only saved from falling outright, despite a cruel barking on his knee, by another two steps on top of that. He found himself kneeling on what was effectively a small stepladder spanning the width of the passage. Chang carefully set down his stick and the book, and then felt the wall for the hole, finding it by the small half-circle of light caused by his partial dislodging of its plug from the room. He silently pulled the plug free and peered in. The woman had crawled away from the dead soldier, and crouched kneeling on the carpet. Her hands were under her dress—restoring her undergarments or perhaps attempting to see how far along the dead soldier's obvious intentions had proceeded. She still wore her mask, and Chang was curious to see that despite the tears on her cheeks she seemed calm and determined in her manner . . . was this a result of her experience with the book?

He replaced the plug in the wall and wondered that the stair-step should be built across the entire passage . . . was there another spy hole on the opposite wall? Chang shifted his position and felt for it, finding the plug easily. He worked it free as gently as he could and leaned forward to gaze into the second room.

A man sprawled with his head and shoulders on a writing table. Chang knew him despite the black band across his eyes—as he came to know any man he'd followed through the street, identifying him from behind or within a crowd merely by his size and manner of being. It was his former client, the man who had apparently recommended his talents to Rosamonde, the lawyer John Carver. Chang had no doubt the secrets Carver held in his professional possession would open many a door to the Cabal across the city—he wondered how many of the law had been seduced, and shook his head at how simple those seductions must have been. Carver's face was as red as the woman's, and a pearling bead of drool connected his mouth to the table top. The glass book lay flickering under Carver's hand. The upper part of his face lay pressed against it, eyes twitching with an idiot rapture, transfixed by its depths. Chang noted with some curiosity that the lawyer's face and fingertips—the ones touching the glass—had taken on a bluish cast to the skin . . . almost as if they'd been frozen, though his sweat-sheened face belied that explanation. With distaste he noticed Carver's other hand clutched at his groin with a spastic, dislocated urgency. Chang looked around the room for any other occupant, or any other useful sign, but saw nothing. He was not sure what such exposure to the book actually gained the Cabal—apart from this insensibility on the part of the victim. Did it re-make them like the Process? Was there something *in* the book they were supposed to learn? He felt the weight of the book tucked under his own arm. He knew—from the glass in his lungs and Svenson's description of that man's shattered glass arms—that the object itself could be deadly, but as a tool, as a *machine* . . . he hadn't even a glimpse into its true destructive power. Chang replaced the plug and felt with his stick for the next set of stairs.

When it came he looked again, prying the plug first from the left, the side where he'd seen the woman. Chang's conscience gnawed at him—should he not ignore the holes and move directly for the office? Yet to do so was to pass up information about the Cabal he would never be afforded again . . . he would go more quickly. He peered into the room and suddenly froze—there were two men in black coats helping an elderly man in red onto a sofa. The churchman's face was obscured—could it be the Bishop of Baax-Saornes? Uncle to the Duke of Stäelmaere and the Queen, he was the most powerful cleric in the land, an advisor to government, a curb to corruption, . . . and here having the spittle wiped from his chin by malevolent lackeys. One of the men wrapped a parcel in cloth—assuredly another book—while the other took the Bishop's pulse. Then both turned to a knock at a door Chang could not see and rapidly walked from the room.

Without a further thought for the ruined Bishop—what could he do for him anyway?—Chang turned to the opposite hole. Another man slumped over a book—how many of these hellish objects had been made?—his red face and twitching eyes pressed down into the glowing surface. It was without question Henry Xonck, his customary aura of power and command quite fully absent . . . indeed, it seemed to Chang that the man's normal attributes had been drained away . . . drained *into* the book? The thought was absurd, and yet he recalled the glass cards—the manner in which they became imprinted with memories. If the books managed the same trick on a larger scale . . . suddenly Chang wondered if the memories were simply imprinted from the victim's mind . . . or actually removed. How much of Henry Xonck's memories—indeed his very soul—had here been stripped away?

The following spy holes revealed more of the same, and even though Chang didn't recognize every slumped figure, those he did were enough to reveal a naked assault on the powerful figures of the land: the Minister of Finance, the Minister of War, a celebrated actress, a Duchess, an Admiral, a high court judge, the publisher of the *Times*, the president of the Imperial Bank, the widowed Baroness who ran the most important, opinion-setting *salon* in the city, and finally, tempting him to postpone his search even further and intervene, Madelaine Kraft. Each one discovered in the throes of a fitful, nearly narcotic state of possession, utterly absent of mind and unresponsive of body—their only point of attention being the book that had been set before their eyes. In several cases Chang saw masked figures—men and women—monitoring a stricken victim, sometimes collecting the book and starting to wake them, sometimes allowing more time to steep in those blue glowing depths. Chang recognized none of these functionaries. He was certain that but a few days ago their tasks would have been performed by the likes of Mrs. Marchmoor or Roger Bascombe—and a few days before that by the Contessa or Xonck themselves. Now their organization had grown—had absorbed so many new adherents—that they were all freed for more important matters. It was another spur to Chang that something else was happening in the house, perhaps as cover for the subjugation of these particular, spectacularly placed figures, but important enough to draw the Cabal's leaders. He rushed ahead into the dark.

He ignored the remaining spy holes, driving on to the end of the passageway and hoping that when he got there he would find a door.

Instead, he found a painting. His stick struck something with a light exploratory touch that was not stone and his hand reached gingerly forward to find the heavy carved frame. It seemed similar in size to the portrait of Robert Vandaariff that had masked the door to the tier of cells, though the passage was so dark that he'd no idea what it actually portrayed. Not that Chang wasted any time on the matter—he was on his knees groping for a catch or lever that might open the hidden door. But why was the painting on the inside? Did that mean the door rotated fully on each usage and someone had already come through? That was unlikely—a simple concealed hinge, opening and closing normally, would be far easier to use and to hide. But then what was on the canvas that it should remain unseen in the dark?

He sat back on his haunches and sighed. Injuries, fatigue, thirst... Chang felt like a ruin. He could keep on fighting—that was instinctive—but actual cleverness felt beyond him. He shut his eyes and took a deep breath, exhaling slowly, thinking about the other side of the door—the catch would be concealed... perhaps it was not *around* the frame, but *part* of it. He ran his fingers along the inside border of the ornately (overly, really) carved frame, concentrating first on the area where a normal doorknob might be... when he found the curved depression, he realized the only trick was the knob being on the left side rather than the right—the kind of silly misdirection that could have easily flummoxed him for another half hour. He dug his fingers around the odd-shaped knob and turned it. The well-oiled lock opened silently and Chang felt the weight of the door shift in his hands. He pushed it open and stepped through.

He knew it was Vandaariff's study immediately, for the man himself sat before him at an enormous desk, scratching earnestly away at a long page of parchment with an old-fashioned feathered quill. Lord Robert did not look up. Chang took another step, still holding the door open with his shoulder, his eyes darting around at the room. The carpets were red and black and the long room was sub-divided into functional areas by the furniture: a long meeting table lined with high-backed chairs, a knot of larger, more upholstered armchairs and sofas, an assistant's desk, a row of tall locked cabinets for papers, and then the great man's desk, as large as the meeting table and covered with documents, rolled-up maps, and a litter of glasses and mugs—all driven to the edge of his present work like flotsam on a beach.

No one else was in the room.

Still, Lord Vandaariff did not acknowledge Chang's presence, his face gravely focused on his writing. Chang remembered his main errand, a secret way to the great chamber. He couldn't see it. On the far wall beyond the table was the main entrance, but it seemed like the only one.

As he stepped forward something caught Chang's attention at the corner of his eye . . . it was the painting behind him—he hadn't looked at it in the light. He glanced again at Vandaariff—who gave Chang no attention at all—and opened the door wide. Another canvas by Oskar Veilandt, but no similar sort of image . . . instead its front was like the back of the *Annunciation* fragments and other paintings—what at first glance seemed mere cross-hatched lines was in truth a densely wrought web of symbols and diagrams. The overall shape of the formulae, Chang saw more with instinct than with understanding, was a horseshoe . . . mathematical equations made in the shape of Harschmort House. It was also, he realized with a certain self-consciousness, wondering if the insight was merely the product of his own low mind, perversely anatomical—the curving U of the house and the peculiarly shaped cylindrical figure, longer than he had imagined, of the great chamber clearly inserted within it . . . whatever else Veilandt's alchemy intended, it was quite clear that its roots lay as much in sexual congress as any elemental transmutation—or was the point that these were the same? Chang did not know what this had to do with the ceremony in the chamber, or with Vandaariff. And yet . . . he tried to remember when Vandaariff had purchased and re-fitted Harschmort Prison—at most a year or two previously. Hadn't the gallery agent told them Veilandt had been dead *five* years? That was impossible—the alchemical painting on the door was definitely the same man's work. Could it be that Veilandt hadn't died at all? Could it be that he was here—perhaps willingly, but given the degree to which Vandaariff and d'Orkancz were exploiting his every discovery it seemed suddenly more likely he was a prisoner, or even worse, fallen victim to his own alchemy, his mind drained into a glass book for others to consume.

And yet—even within his exhaustion and despair Chang could not prevent himself from indulging this tendril of hope—if Veilandt were alive he could be *found*! Where else might they learn how to resist or overturn the effects of the glass? With a stab into his heart Chang realized this was even a chance to save Angelique. At once his heart was torn—his determination to save Celeste, this last prayer to preserve Angelique—it was impossible. Veilandt could be anywhere—shackled in a cage or drooling in a forgotten corner... or, if he retained his sanity and his mind, where he could best aid the Cabal... with the Comte d'Orkancz at the base of the great tower.

Chang looked again at the painting. It *was* a map of Harschmort... as it was equally an alchemical formula of dazzling complexity... and also distinctly pornographic. Focusing on the map (for he had no knowledge of alchemy and no time for the lurid), he located to the best of his ability the spot where, within the house, he presently stood. Was there any obvious path depicted to the great chamber and the panopticon column tower within it?

The room itself was signified—he'd had enough Greek to name them—by an alpha and then just above it, as if it were its multiplying power, a tiny omega... and from the omega ran one clear scoring line of paint down to the nest of symbols representing the chamber. Chang looked up from the canvas, feeling foolishly literal. If the room was the alpha—where in it might he find the omega? To his best estimate it lay just beyond Vandaariff's desk... where the wall was covered by a heavy hanging curtain.

Chang crossed quickly to the spot, watching Vandaariff closely. The man *still* did not stir from his writing—he must have covered half a long page in the time Chang had been there. This was perhaps the most powerful man in the nation—even on the continent—and Chang could not resist his curiosity. He stepped closer to the desk—by all rights his reeking clothes alone should have shattered a saint's concentration—to get a look at Vandaariff's unchangingly impassive face.

It did not seem to Cardinal Chang that Robert Vandaariff's eyes saw anything at all. They were open, but glassy and dull, the thoughts behind them entirely elsewhere, facing down at the desk top but quite to the side of his writing, as if he were instead inscribing thoughts from memory. Chang leaned even closer to study the parchment—he was nearly at Vandaariff's shoulder and still there was no reaction. As near as he could tell, the man was documenting the contents of a financial transaction—in amazingly complicated detail—referring to shipping and to Macklenburg and French banking and to rates and markets and shares and schedules of repayment. He watched Vandaariff finish the page and briskly turn it over—the sudden movement of his arms causing Chang to leap back—continuing mid-phrase at the top of the fresh side. Chang looked on the floor behind the desk and saw page after long page of parchment completely covered with text, as if Robert Vandaariff was emptying his mind of every financial secret he had ever possessed. Chang looked again at the working fingers, chilled by the inhuman insistence of the scratching pen, and noticed that the tips were tinged with blue... but it was not cold in the room, and the blue was more lustrous beneath the pale flesh than Chang had ever seen on a living man.

He stepped away from the automaton Lord and felt behind him for the curtain, swept it aside to expose a simple locked door. He fumbled with his ring of keys, sorting out one, and then dropped them all—suddenly full of dread at being in Vandaariff's unfeeling presence, the pen scratching along behind him. Chang scooped up the keys and with an abrupt, anxious impatience simply kicked the wood by the lock as hard as he could. He kicked again and felt it begin to split. He did not care about the noise or any trail of destruction. He kicked once more and cracked the wood around the still-fixed bolt. He hurled himself against it, smashing through, and staggered into a winding stone tunnel whose end sloped downward, out of view.

Apart from his relentless spidery hand, Lord Vandaariff did not move. Chang rubbed his shoulder and broke into a run.

The tunnel was smoothly paved and bright from regularly placed gas-lit globes above his head. The passage curved gently over the course of some hundred paces, at the end of which Chang was forced to reduce his speed. It was just as well, for as he paused to steady his breath—leaning against the wall with one hand and allowing the gob of bloody spit to drop silently from his mouth—he heard the distant sound of many voices raised in song. Ahead the tunnel took a sharp bank to his right, toward the great chamber. Would there be any kind of guard? The singing drowned out any other noise. It came from below... from the occupants of the overhanging cells! Chang sank to his knees and cautiously peered around the corner.

The tunnel opened into a narrowed walkway, little more than a catwalk, with railings of chain to either side, extending to a black, malevolent turret of iron that rose into the rock ceiling above him. Through the metal grid of the catwalk rose the sound of singing. Chang peered down, but between the dim light and his squinting eyes, could get no true sense of the chamber below. On the far side of the catwalk was an iron door, massive with a heavy lock and iron bar, that had been left ajar. Chang stopped just to his side of it, waiting, listening, heard no one, and slipped into the dark... and onto another spiral staircase, this one welded together from cast iron plates.

The staircase continued up to the roof of the cavern, toward what must be the main entrance to the tower. But Chang turned downwards, his boots' tapping on steps more sensed than audible over the chorus of voices. He could hear them more clearly, but it was the kind of singing where even if one did know the language the words might well have been those of an Italian (or for all he knew Icelandic) opera, so distended and unnatural was the phrasing imposed by the music. Still, the lyrics he did manage to pick out—"impenetrable blue"... "never-ending sight"... "redemption kind"—only drove him to descend more quickly.

The interior of the tower was lit by regular sconces, but their light was deliberately dim, so as not to show through the open viewing slots. Chang slowed. The step below him was covered by a tangled shape. It was a discarded coat. He picked it up and held it to the nearest sconce... a uniform coat, dark blue at some point but now filthy with dirt and, he saw with interest, blood. The stains were still damp, and soaked the front of the coat quite completely. He did not, however, see any wound or tear *in* the coat—was the blood from the wearer, or from, perhaps, the wearer's enemy? Whoever had worn it might have bled from the head or had their hand cut off and clutched the stump to their chest—anything was possible. It was then that—his mind moving so slowly!—Chang noticed the bars of rank on the coat's stiff collar... he looked again at the cut, the color, the silver braid around each epaulette... he damned himself for a fool.

It was Svenson's coat, without question, and covered in gore.

He quickly searched around him in the stairwell, and on the wall saw the dripping remains of a wide spray of blood. The violence had happened here on the stairs—perhaps only moments ago. Was Svenson dead? How had he possibly reached Harschmort from Tarr Manor? Chang crab-walked another few steps, face close against the iron. There *was* a descending trail of blood, but the trail was smeared . . . not made by a wounded man walking, but a wounded—or dead—man dragged.

Chang threw the coat aside—if the Doctor had dropped it, he hardly needed to carry it himself—and clattered down as quickly as he could. He knew the distance was roughly what he'd previously climbed—two hundred steps, perhaps? What in the world would he find at the base? Svenson's corpse? What was d'Orkancz possibly doing? And why were there no guards?

Chang's foot slipped on a splash of blood and he clutched at the rail. It would be all too simple for one mistake to land him at the bottom with a broken neck. He forced himself to concentrate—the voices still soared in song, though he had descended past the tiers of viewing cells and the chorus was above him. But when had Svenson arrived? It had to be with Aspiche! Could the Doctor be the cause of Smythe's disturbance? Chang smiled to think of it, even as he winced at the likely retribution the Colonel would have delivered to anyone crossing his path. He did not relish the image of the Doctor standing alone against these men—he was no soldier, nor was he an unflinching killer. That was Chang's place—and he knew he must reach Svenson's side.

And if Svenson *was* dead? Then perhaps Chang's place was to die with him . . . and with Miss Temple.

He raced down another thirty steps and stopped at a small landing. His lungs were laced with stabbing pains and he knew it was better not to reach the bottom in a state of collapse. One of the viewing slots was near him on the wall and he pulled it aside, grinning with sinister appreciation. The slot was covered with a plate of smoked glass. From the inside, he could see through it, but to any prisoner the glass would mask whether the metal slat had been opened at all. Chang pulled off his spectacles and pressed his face to the glass at the very moment the singing stopped.

Above and opposite him were the viewing cells, full of finely dressed people, all masked, faces pressed to the bars, for all the world like inmates in an asylum. He shifted his gaze down, but could not see the tables. He was still too high.

As he stepped away a voice echoed up from below—unnatural, strangely amplified, deepened, and unquestionably mighty. He did not recognize it immediately . . . he'd only heard the man speaking a very few words, and those in a rasping whisper to Harald Crabbé, an enormous fur-clad arm enfolding Angelique. But Chang knew . . . it was the Comte d'Orkancz. Damning his lungs, he began to run, recklessly, his feet flying two and even three steps at a time, hand on the rail with his stick, the other hand holding the wrapped book safely free of collision, his soiled coat flapping behind him, its heavy pockets knocking against his legs. All around him the chamber rang with the Comte's inhuman voice.

"You are here because you believe . . . in yourselves . . . in giving yourselves over to a different dream . . . of the future . . . of possibility . . . transformation . . . revelation . . . redemption. Perhaps there are those among you who will be deemed worthy . . . truly worthy and truly willing to sacrifice their illusions . . . sacrifice the entirety of their world . . . *which is a world of illusion* . . . for this final degree of wisdom. Beyond redemption is *designation* . . . as Mary was made apart from every other woman . . . as Sarah was made pregnant after a barren lifetime . . . as Leda was implanted with twin seeds of beauty and destruction . . . so these vessels before you all have been chosen . . . *designated* to a higher destiny . . . a transformation you will witness. You will feel the higher energies . . . you will taste this greatness . . . this ethereal ambrosia . . . before known only to those creatures who were named gods by shepherds . . . and by the children we all once were . . ."

Chang toppled off balance into the rail and was forced to stop, clutching with both hands to prevent a fall. He spat against the wall and groped, gasping, for the viewing slat, ripping off his glasses to look. Below him he saw it all, like an iron cathedral from hell laid out for an infernal mass. At the base of the tower was a raised platform—seemingly suspended on a raft of the silver tubing—holding three large surgical tables, each surrounded by racks and trays and brass boxes of machinery. The tables each bore a woman, held with leather straps just as Angelique had been at the Institute, naked, bodies obscured by a sickening nest of slick black hoses. Each woman's face was completely covered by a black mask fitted with smaller hoses—for each ear, each eye, the nose and mouth—and their hair completely wrapped in a dark cloth, so that despite their nudity Chang could not begin to guess who might be on which table. Only the woman nearest to the turret, who he could barely glimpse from his angle of sight, was distinguished from the others, for the soles of her feet were discolored blue in an identical manner to Robert Vandaariff's hands.

Next to her stood d'Orkancz, with the same leather apron and gauntlets he'd worn at the Institute and the same brass-bound helmet, to which he'd attached another hose, hooking it into the metal box that made the mask's mouth. Into this hose the Comte was speaking, and somehow through its engine his voice was magnified, like a very god's, to crash against every distant corner of the vast chamber. Behind d'Orkancz stood at least four more men, identically dressed, their faces hidden. Men from the Institute, like Gray and Lorenz? Or could one of these be Oskar Veilandt—present either as prisoner or slave? Chang could not see the very base of the tower. Where were the guards? Where was Svenson? Which table held Celeste? None of the women seemed awake—how could he carry her away?

Chang spun at a sound behind him—a clanking from the staircase itself. The stairs wound around an iron pillar—the noise came from within it. He reached across and felt a vibration. The clanking made him think at once of a hotel's dumbwaiter . . . could the pillar be hollow? How else to get things quickly from the top to the bottom? But what was being delivered? This was his chance. When whatever was being sent reached the bottom, someone was going to have to open the tower door to get it—and that would be his moment to break through. He shoved his glasses back into place, set the pillowcase down against the wall and threw himself forward.

The Comte was still speaking. Chang didn't care—it was all the same nonsense—another stage of the circus act to dazzle the customers. Whatever the real effects of this "transformation", he didn't doubt it was but a veil for another unseen web of exploitation and greed. The clanking stopped. As Chang swept around the final curve he saw two men wearing the aprons and gauntlets and helmets bending over the open dumbwaiter, just sliding an iron-bound crate from it and into a wheeled cart. Behind them was the open door to the chamber platform, to either side of it a Macklenburg trooper. Chang ignored the men and the cart and vaulted from the steps at the nearest Macklenburger with a cry, slamming the man across the jaw with his forearm and driving a knee into his ribs, knocking him sprawling. Before the second man could draw his weapon Chang stabbed the stick into his stomach, doubling him over (the man's face falling near enough to Chang that he heard the brusque click of the fellow's teeth). He drove the dagger up under the man's open jaw and just as quickly wrenched it free. He stood—the dead trooper sinking like a timed counterweight—and wheeled back to the first man, planting a deliberate kick to the side of his head. Both troopers were still. The two men in the masks stared at him with the dumb incomprehension of inhabitants from the moon first witnessing the savagery of mankind.

Chang spun to the open door. The Comte had stopped speaking. He was staring at Chang. Before Chang could react he heard a noise behind and without looking threw his body forward out the door—just as the two men in helmets shoved the trolley at his back. The corner clipped him sharply across his right thigh—drawing blood, but not enough to run him down. Chang stumbled onto the platform, the sudden enormity of the cathedral-like void above staggering him with a spasm of vertigo. He groped for his bearings. The platform held four more Macklenburgers—three troopers, who as he watched swept out their sabers in one glittering movement, and Major Blach, calmly drawing his black pistol. Chang glanced wildly around him—absolutely no sign of Svenson or which, if any, of the brass-masked men might be Veilandt—and then up to the dizzying heights and the clustered ring of masked faces peering down in rapt attention. There was no time. Chang's only path away from the soldiers led to the tables and—striding quite directly to cut him off from the women—d'Orkancz.

The troopers rushed forward. Chang in turn charged directly at the Comte before dodging to the left and ducking beneath the first table, swatting through the dangling hoses to reach the other side. The soldiers careened to either side of d'Orkancz. Chang kept going, crouched low, until he was under and past the second table. He emerged on the other side as the Comte shouted to the soldiers not to move.

Chang stood and looked back. The Comte faced him from the far side of the first table, still wearing the mechanical mask, the first woman swathed in hoses before him. At the Comte's side stood Blach, his pistol ready. The troopers waited. Svenson was not here. Nor, as best as he could tell, was Veilandt—or not with his own mind, for the two masked men behind the Comte had not stopped in their working of the brass machinery, looking for all the world like a pair of insect drones. Chang looked at the platform's edge. Below it, on every side, was a steaming sea of metal pipes, hissing with heat and reeking sulphurous fumes. There was no escape.

"Cardinal Chang!"

The Comte d'Orkancz spoke in the same projected, amplified tones that Chang had heard in the tower. Heard this close the words were impossibly harsh, and he winced despite himself.

"You will not move! You have trespassed a place you do not comprehend! I promise you do not *begin* to understand the penalties!"

Without a thought for the Comte, Chang reached out to the woman on the second table and ripped the dark cloth free that held her hair.

"Do not touch them!" screamed the Comte d'Orkancz.

The hair was too dark. It was not Celeste. He scuttled at once to the far side of the third table. The troopers advanced with him, up to the second table. The Comte and Blach remained on the far side of the first, the Major's pistol quite clearly aimed at Chang's head. Chang ducked behind the third woman and pulled the cloth from her hair. Too light and less curled... Celeste must be on the first table. He'd charged past her like a fool and left her in the direct control of d'Orkancz.

He stood. Upon seeing him the troopers stepped forward and Chang detected the briefest flicker of movement from Blach. He dropped again as the shot crashed out. The bullet spat past his head and punched into one of the great pipes, spitting out a jet of gas that hung flickering in the air like a blue-white flame. The Comte screamed again.

"Stop!"

The soldiers—nearly at the third table—froze. Chang risked a slow peek over the raft of black hoses—glimpsing between them pale damp flesh—and met the Major's baleful gaze.

The chamber was silent, save for the dull roar of the furnace and the high note of hissing gas behind him. He needed to overcome nine men—counting the two with the cart—and get Celeste from the table. Could he do that without harming her? Was that harm possibly worse than what would happen to her if he didn't? He knew what she would want him to do—as he knew how meaningless any notion of preserving his own life had become. He felt the seething lattice of cuts inside his chest. This exact moment was why he had come so far, this very effort the last defiant, defacing mark he could inflict upon this privileged world. Chang looked up again to the mass of masked faces staring down in suspenseful silence. He felt like a beast in the arena.

The Comte detached the black speaking hose from the mask and draped it carefully over a nearby pedestal box bristling with levers and stops. He faced Chang and nodded—with the mask on it was the gesture of an inarticulate brute, of a storybook ogre—to the woman nearest Chang, whose hair he had exposed.

"Looking for someone, Cardinal?" he called. His voice was less loud, but issuing from the strange mouth box set into the mask, it still struck Chang as inhuman. "Perhaps I can assist you..."

The Comte d'Orkancz reached out and pulled away the cloth that wrapped the final woman's hair. It cascaded out in curls, dark, shining, black. The Comte reached out with his other hand and swept away the hoses hanging across her feet. The flesh was discolored, sickly lustrous, even more so than Vandaariff's hand or John Carver's face when it had lain against the book—pale as polar ice, slick with perspiration, and beneath it, where he had before known a color of golden warmth, was now the cool indifference of white ash. On the third toe of her left foot was a silver ring, but Chang had known from the first glimpse of her hair... it was Angelique.

"I believe you are... acquainted with the lady," continued d'Orkancz. "Of course you may be acquainted with the others as well—Miss Poole"—he nodded at the woman in the middle—"and Mrs. Marchmoor." The

Comte gestured to the woman directly in front of Chang. He looked down, trying to locate Margaret Hooke (last seen on a bed in the St. Royale) in what he saw—the hair, her size, the color of what flesh he could see beneath the black rubber. He felt the urge to be sick.

Chang spat a lozenge of blood onto the platform and called to the Comte, his hoarse voice betraying his fatigue.

"What will you do to them?"

"What I have planned to do. Do you search for Angelique, or for Miss Temple? As you see she is not here."

"Where is she?" cried Chang hoarsely.

"I believe you have a choice," said the Comte in reply. "If you seek to rescue Angelique, there is no human way—for I read the effects of the glass in your face, Cardinal—for you to bear her from this place and *then* do the same for Miss Temple."

Chang said nothing.

"It is, of course, academic. You ought to have died ten times over—is that not correct, Major Blach? You will do so now. But it is perhaps fitting that it take place at the feet—if I am correctly informed—of your own hopeless love."

Staring directly at the Comte, Chang gathered hold of as many of the hoses rising from Mrs. Marchmoor's body as he could and prepared to rip them free.

"If you do that, you kill her, Cardinal! Is that what you desire—to destroy a helpless woman? At this distance I cannot stop you. The forces at work have been committed! None of these may retreat from their destiny—truly their lot is transformation or death!"

"What transformation?" shouted Chang above the rising roar of the pipes, and the hissing gas behind him.

In answer d'Orkancz reached for the speaking hose and jammed it sharply back into the mask. His words echoed through the vaulted heights like thunder.

"The transformation of *angels*! The powers of heaven made flesh!"

The Comte d'Orkancz yanked hard on one of the pedestal's brass levers, and brought his other hand down like a hammer on a metal stop. At once the hoses around Angelique, which had been hanging and lank, stiffened with life as they were flooded with gas and boiling fluid. Her body arched on the table, and the air was filled with a hideous rising whine. Chang could not look away. The Comte pulled a second lever and her fingers and toes began to twitch . . . a third, and to Chang's growing terror their color began to change even more, a deadening, freezing blue. D'Orkancz pushed in two stops at once, and shifted the first lever back. The whine redoubled its intensity, ringing within every pipe and echoing throughout the vaulted cathedral. The crowd above them gasped and Chang heard voices shouting from the cells—cries of excitement and delight, hoots of encouragement—that grew into a second buzzing chorus. Her body arched again and again, rippling the hoses like a dog shaking off the rain, and then within the screams and roars Chang heard another tone that pierced his heart like a spike: the rattle of Angelique's own voice, an insensate moan from the very depths of her lungs, as if the final defenses of her body were expending themselves against the vast mechanical assault. Tears flowed unheeded down the Cardinal's face. Anything he did would kill her—but was she not being destroyed before his eyes? He could not move.

The whining roar snapped at once to nothing, silencing the entire chamber like a gunshot. With a sudden rippling shimmer that Chang could scarce credit he was seeing, a wave of fluid rushed beneath her skin along each limb from her feet and hands, flooding up to her hips and torso and finally enveloping her head.

Angelique's flesh was transformed to a brilliant, shining translucent blue, as if she herself . . . her very body . . . had been before them all transmuted into glass.

The Comte pulled up his stops and pushed in his final lever. He turned up to the throng of spectators and raised his hand in triumph.

"It has been done!"

The crowd erupted into ecstatic cheering and applause. D'Orkancz nodded to them, raised his other hand, and then turned to Blach, for a moment pulling the speaking hose from its place.

"Kill him."

The obscenity of what d'Orkancz had perpetrated on Angelique—was it not a rape of her *essence*?—at once spurred Chang into action and turned his heart to ice. He launched himself around the third table at the two Macklenburg guards at Miss Poole's head, the lessons of a thousand battles pouring into each relentless, bitter blow. Without the slightest pause he swung at them, a feint—their sabers rising to his chest with the unison of German training—and then swept both blades aside with his stick. He slashed his dagger at the nearest man's face, laying it open from the tip of the jaw to the nose—a spray of blood against the silver pipes—the trooper wheeled away. The other riposted, stabbing hard at Chang's body. Chang broke his stick deflecting the thrust past his shoulder, and knew the lunge had brought the trooper too close. He jabbed the dagger beneath the young man's ribs and ripped it free, already—for each second seemed to arrive from a great distance as he watched—dropping to his knees. Above his head, another bullet from Blach flew into the wall of pipes. The third trooper came around from Miss Poole's feet, stepping over his fallen companions. Chang turned and dove forward to Angelique. Blach stepped near Angelique's head to give himself room to shoot. The Comte d'Orkancz stood at Angelique's feet. Chang was boxed in—the trooper was right behind him. Chang wheeled and cut through a handful of hoses. The hideous, reeking gas, spitting out like a polar flame, flew into the trooper's face. Chang wheeled, knocked the saber aside, and drove a fist into the fellow's throat, stunning him where he stood. Before Blach could shoot, he bull-rushed the trooper around the head of the table directly at the Major. A shot crashed out and Chang felt the trooper lurch. Another shot and he felt a burn—the bullet (or was it bone?) blowing through the soldier to graze his shoulder. He shoved the dying man at Blach and immediately dove for the door.

But Blach had done the same thing and they faced each other directly, perhaps two feet apart. Blach swept the gun to bear, firing as Chang slashed at the Major's hand. The shot went wide as the dagger bit into Blach's fingers and the pistol fell to the floor. Blach cried out in a rage and leapt after it. The door was still blocked by the metal cart and the two helmeted men behind. Chang shoved with all his strength, driving them several steps—but they caught themselves and pushed back, stranding him within the chamber. Blach scooped up the pistol with his left hand. The Comte was urgently tying off the steaming hoses with rope. Blach raised the pistol. With a sudden shock Chang saw what the cart held, for the top of the metal casket had become dislodged in the commotion.

Without a thought he dropped his dagger, seized the nearest object, and whipped it behind him at the Major, flinging himself into the cart as soon as the thing left his hand.

The glass book lanced toward Blach at the same time he pulled the trigger, shattering it in flight. Half of the shards sprayed back at the tower with the force of the bullet, into the iron walls and through the doorway at the two helmeted men, who threw themselves desperately aside. But half kept flying with the momentum of the book itself. The Comte d'Orkancz was shielded by the table, as Angelique—if in her present state the glass could even have had any effect upon her—was shielded by the hoses, and by the Major himself who stood most directly in the way. His unprotected face and body were instantly savaged by gashes small and large.

Chang raised his head from the cart to see the man shaking with spasms, his mouth open and a hideous hoarse croaking scream rising from his lungs like smoke from a catching fire. Patches of blue began to form around each laceration, spreading, cracking, flaking free. The rattle died in his throat with a puff of pink dust. Major Blach fell to his knees with a snapping crunch and then forward onto his face, the front of which shattered on impact like a plate of lapis-glazed terra cotta.

The great chamber was silent. The Comte rose slowly behind the table. His eyes fell upon Chang, clambering awkwardly free of the cart. The Comte *screamed* with an amplified rage that shook the entire cathedral. He rushed at Chang like a giant rabid bear. Without his dagger (it had fallen somewhere under the iron chest) Chang hurtled the cart—the two men were on their hands and knees, shaken but not in the Major's straits, their leather aprons having saved them—and shoved the cart behind him into the Comte. Without looking to see its effect he raced to the stairs and began to climb.

Almost immediately, on the seventh step, he slipped on a smear of blood, fell, and looked back, his hand digging into his coat for his razor. The two aproned men were crouched low, still flinching away from the doorway that framed the Comte d'Orkancz, who had snatched up Blach's pistol and was even then aiming it at Chang. Chang knew there was only one bullet left and that with two steps more he would be out of the Comte's line of fire, but behind the Comte, on the table, Cardinal Chang's gaze was fixed on Angelique's glassy blue right arm . . . which had begun to move. Chang screamed. Angelique's hand was flexing, groping. She caught a handful of the hoses and tore them from their seals, shooting blue steam. The Comte turned as she let go and wrenched another handful, pulling at them like weeds in a garden. As d'Orkancz dove for her hand, crying out for his assistants, Chang caught a hideous glimpse, over the large man's shoulder, of Angelique's face, eyes still covered by the partially dislodged mask, twisting with fury, her open mouth, tongue, and lips a glistening dark indigo, her blue-white teeth snapping like an animal. Chang ran up the stairs.

It was another turn before he saw the book he'd set against the wall in the pillowcase. Chang snatched it up as he ran, his right hand finally pulling the razor from his pocket. Below he heard a commotion of voices and a slamming door, and then the lurching clank of the dumbwaiter come again to life. In moments it had reached him—Chang's energy was already beginning to flag—and then sped past. Whoever stood at the upper end would receive warning of his arrival well before Chang could climb. Was it only a matter of moments before he met Blenheim and his men coming down? Chang doggedly kept on. If he could just reach the gangway to Vandaariff's office . . .

His thoughts were interrupted by the voice of d'Orkancz, echoing through the chamber to the assembled crowds above.

"Do not be alarmed! As you know yourselves, our enemies are many and desperate—dispatching this assassin to disrupt our work. But that work has not been stopped! Heaven *itself* could not forestall our efforts! Behold what has been done before your eyes! Behold the *transformation*!"

Chang paused on the stairs, despite himself, his mind seared with the image of Angelique's face and arm. He looked behind him down the winding metal depths of the tower and heard outside it, like a rush of wind, a collected gasp of astonishment from the Comte's audience in the cells.

"You see!" the Comte continued. "She lives! She walks! And you see yourselves . . . her extraordinary *powers* . . ."

The crowd gasped again—a hissing whisper punctuated by several screams—of fright or joy, he could not say. Another gasp. What was happening? Tears for Angelique were still hot on his face but Chang could not help it. He lurched to a viewing slot and pulled it aside. It was ridiculous to stay—his enemies would be gathering above him any minute—and yet he had to know . . . was she alive? Was she still *human*?

He could not see her—she must be too close to the base of the tower—but he could see d'Orkancz. The Comte was facing where Angelique must be, and had stepped back to the second table to stand next to another box of levers and stops. Each table had such a box attached to it by way of the black hoses, and Chang was just realizing on a visceral, sickening level that each of the other two women were about to be so transfigured. He looked down at the inert form on the third table and found his heart pricked by the image of Margaret Hooke, savage, wounded, and proud, writhing in agony as her flesh was boiled away to glass. Had she chosen such a fate, or had she merely given herself over to d'Orkancz out of desperate ambition—trusting, because of the first few crumbs of power he had shown her, that his final ends lay in her interest?

The crowd gasped again and Chang felt his knees give, grabbing at the rail to keep balance. His mind spun as sharply as if he'd been kicked in the head, then the moment of nausea passed and he felt himself moving—but it was movement of the mind, a swift restless rushing, as if in a dream, through different scenes—a room, a street, a bed, a crowded square, one after another. Then the momentum of thought eased, settling on one sharp instant: the Comte d'Orkancz in a doorway in his fur, his gloved hand extended and offering a shining rectangle of blue glass. Chang felt his own hand reach out to the Comte, even as he knew it fiercely gripped the iron rail, and saw it touch the glass—the small delicate fingers he knew so well—and felt the sudden rush of erotic power as he—as she—was swept into the memory held within, a rising, impossibly vivid stimulation, irresistible as opium and just as addictive, then quickly, cruelly withdrawn before he could grasp whose sweet memory it had been or even the circumstance. The Comte tucked the card back into his coat and smiled. This had been the villain's introduction to Angelique, Chang knew, and Angelique was now, somehow, projecting her own experience of that intimate moment into the mind and body of every person within a hundred yards.

The image departed from his mind with another spasm of dizziness and he felt himself abruptly empty and cruelly, cruelly alone—her sudden presence in his mind had seemed a harsh intrusion, but once withdrawn there was a part of him that wanted more—for it was her, and he could *feel* it was her, Angelique, with whom he had so long desired this exact sort of impossible intimacy. Chang looked again down the twisting stairs, fighting an impulse to return, to fling himself away to an embrace of love and death. A part of his mind insisted that neither mattered, so long as it came from her.

"You feel the power for yourselves! You experience the truth!"

The Comte's voice broke the spell. Chang shook his head and turned, climbing as quickly as he could. He could not make sense of all he felt—he could not decide what he must do—and so Cardinal Chang retreated, as he often did, into action alone, driving himself on until he found an object for his desolated rage, looking for mayhem to once more clarify his heart.

The rising, grating whine began again, escalating to the heights of the chamber. The Comte d'Orkancz had moved on to the next woman, Miss Poole, pulling the levers to begin her metamorphosis. The sound of screaming machinery was bolstered by cries from the gallery of cells, for now that they knew what they were going to see, the crowd was even more willing to voice encouragement and delight. But Chang was assailed by the image of the woman's arched back, like a twig bent to its limit before snapping, and he ran from their approval as if he ran from hell itself.

He still had no idea where to find Svenson or Miss Temple, but if he was going to help them, he needed to remain free. The screaming of the pipes abruptly ceased, answered after a hanging moment of rapt attention by another eruption from the crowd. Once again the Comte crowed about power and transformation and the truth—each fatuous claim echoed by another bout of applause. Chang's lips curled back with rage. The whining rise in the pipes resumed—d'Orkancz had moved on to Margaret Hooke. There was nothing Chang could do. He ascended two more turns of the stairs and saw the door to the gangway and Lord Vandaariff's office.

Chang stood, breathing hard, and spat. The iron door was closed and did not move—barred from the other side. Chang was to be driven like a breathless stag to the top of the tower. For a final time the roar of the pipes dropped suddenly away and the crowd erupted with delight. All three of the women had undergone the Comte's ferocious alchemy. They would be waiting for him at the top. He had not found Celeste. He had lost Angelique. He had failed. Chang tucked the razor back into his coat and resumed his climb.

The upper entrance was fashioned from the same steel plates, held together with the heavy rivets of a train car. The massive door swung silently to reveal an elegant bright hallway, the walls white and the floor gleaming pale marble. Some twenty feet away stood a shapely woman in a dark dress, her hair tied back with ribbon and her face obscured by a half-mask of black feathers. She nodded to him, formally. The line of ten red-coated Dragoons behind her, sabers drawn and clearly under command, did not move.

Chang stepped from the turret onto the marble floor, glancing down. The tiles were marked by a wide stain of blood—quite obviously pooled from some violent wound and then smeared by something (the victim, he assumed) dragged through it. The path led straight beneath the woman's feet. He met her eyes. Her expression was open and clear, though she did not smile. Chang was relieved—he had not realized how sick he'd become of his enemies' sneering confidence—but perhaps her demeanor had less to do with him than with the bloody floor.

"Cardinal Chang," she said. "If you will come with me."

Chang pulled the glass book from the pillowcase. He could feel its energy push at him through the tip of each gloved finger, an antagonistic magnetism. He clutched it more firmly and held it out for her to see.

"You know what this is," he said, his voice still hoarse and ragged. "I am not afraid to smash it."

"I'm sure you are not," she said. "I understand you are afraid of very little. But nothing will be settled here. I do not criticize to say you truly do not know all that has happened, or hangs in the balance. I'm sure there are many of whom you want to hear, as I know there are many who would like to see you. Is it not better to avoid what violence we can?"

The bright blood-smeared marble beneath the woman's feet seemed the perfect image for this hateful place, and it was all Chang could do not to snarl at her gracious tone.

"What is your name?" Chang asked.

"I am of no importance, I assure you," she said. "Merely a messenger—"

A harsh catch in Chang's throat stopped her words. His brief sharp vision of Angelique—the unnatural color of her skin, its glassy, gleaming indigo depths and brighter transparent cerulean surface—was seared into Chang's memory but its suddenly overwhelming impact was beyond his ability to translate to sense, to mere words. He swallowed, grimacing with discomfort, and spat again, diving into anger to override his tears. He gestured with his right hand, the fingers clutching with fury at the thought of such an abomination undertaken for the entertainment of so many—so many *respectable*—spectators.

"I have seen this *great work,*" he hissed. "Nothing you can say will sway my purpose."

In answer, the woman stepped aside and indicated with her hand that he might follow along. At her movement the line of Dragoons split and snapped crisply into place to either side, forming a gauntlet for him to pass through. Some ten yards beyond them Chang saw a second line dividing itself with the same clean stamping of boots to frame an open archway leading deeper into the house.

Behind in the turret he heard a muted roar—the crowd in the cells crying out—but before he could even begin to wonder why, Chang's knees buckled with the sudden visceral impact of another vision thrust into his mind. To his everlasting shame, he was presented with *himself,* stick in hand, his appearance fine as he could make it—a threadbare vanity, with an expression of poorly veiled hunger, reaching to take the small hand extended to him—extended, he now knew (and now *felt*), with disinterest and disdain. He saw himself for one flashing, impossibly sharp moment through the eyes and heart of Angelique, and stood revealed within her mind as a regretted relic of a former life that she had at all times loathed with every fiber of her being.

The vision snapped away from him and he staggered. He looked up to see each of the Dragoons gathering themselves, blinking and regaining their military bearing, just as he saw the woman shake her head. She looked at him with pity, but did not alter her guarded expression. She repeated her gesture for Chang to join her.

"It would be best, Cardinal Chang," she said, "that we move out of *range*."

They had walked in silence, Dragoons in line ahead of them and behind, Chang's pounding heart yet to shake free of the bitter impact of Angelique's vision, his sweetest memories now stained with regret, until he saw the woman glance down at the book in his hand. He said nothing. Chang was caught between fury and despair, physically ruined, his mind drifting deeper into acrid fatalism with each step. He could not look at a soldier, the woman—or at any of the curious well-fed faces from the household that peered at him past the Dragoons as they walked by—without rehearsing in his thoughts the swiftest and most savage angle of attack with his razor.

"May I ask where you acquired that?" the woman asked, still looking at the book.

"In a room," snapped Chang. "It had transfixed the lady it had been given to. When I came upon her she was quite unaware of the soldier in the process of her rape."

He spoke in as sharp a tone as he could. The woman in the black feather mask did not flinch.

"May I ask what you did?"

"Apart from taking the book?" Chang asked. "It's so long ago I can barely recall—you don't mean to say you *care*?"

"Is that so strange?"

Chang stopped, his voice rising to an unaccustomed harshness. "From what I have seen, Madame, it is *impossible*!"

At his tone the Dragoons stopped, their boots stamping in unison on the marble floor, blades ready. The woman raised her hand to them, indicating patience.

"Of course, it must be very upsetting. I understand the Comte's work is difficult—both to imagine and to bear. I have undergone the Process, of course, but that is nothing compared to what . . . what you must have seen . . . in the tower."

Her face was entirely reasonable, even sympathetic—Chang could not bear it. He gestured angrily behind them to the blood-stained floor.

"And what happened there? What *difficult* piece of work? Another execution?"

"Your own hands, Cardinal, are quite covered with blood—are you in any place to speak?"

Chang looked down despite himself—from Mr. Gray to the troopers down below, he was fairly spattered with gore—but met her gaze with harsh defiance. None of them mattered. They were dupes, fools, animals in harness . . . perhaps exactly like himself.

"I cannot tell you what happened here," she went on. "I was elsewhere in the house. But surely it can only reinforce, for us both, how *serious* these matters are."

His lips curled into a sneer.

"If you will continue," she said, "for we are quite delayed . . ."

"Continue where?" asked Chang.

"To where you shall answer your *questions,* of course."

Chang did not move, as if staying would somehow put off the confirmation of the deaths of Miss Temple and the Doctor. The soldiers were staring at him. The woman looked directly into his dark lenses and leaned forward, her nostrils flaring at the indigo stench but her expression unwavering. He saw the clarity in her eyes that spoke to the Process, but none of the pride or the arrogance. As he was closer to the heart of the Cabal, had he here met a more advanced and trusted minion?

"We must go," she whispered. "You are not the center of this business."

Before Chang could respond they were interrupted by a loud shout from the corridor ahead of them, a harsh voice he knew at once.

"Mrs. Stearne! Mrs. Stearne!" shouted Colonel Aspiche. "Where is Mr. Blenheim—he is wanted this instant!"

The woman turned to the voice as the line of Dragoons broke apart to make way for their officer, approaching with another squad of his men behind him. Chang saw that Aspiche was limping. When Aspiche saw him, the Colonel's eyes narrowed and his lips tightened—and he then pointedly fixed his gaze on the woman.

"My dear Colonel—" she began, but he bluntly overrode her.

"Where is Mr. Blenheim? He is wanted some time ago—the delay cannot be borne!"

"I do not know. I was sent to collect—"

"I am well aware of it," snarled Aspiche, cutting her off, as if to expunge his previous employment of Chang he would not even allow the speaking of his name. "But you have taken so long I am asked to collect *you* as well." He turned to the men who had come with him, pointing to side rooms, barking orders. "Three to each wing—quickly as you can—send back at once with any word. He must be found—go!"

The men dashed off. Aspiche avoided looking at Chang and stepped to the woman's other side, offering her his arm—though Chang half-thought this was to help his limp, rather than the lady. He wondered what had happened to the Colonel's leg and felt a little better for doing so.

"Is there a reason he is not in chains, or dead?" asked the Colonel, as politely as he could through his anger at having to ask at all.

"I was not so instructed," answered Mrs. Stearne—who, Chang realized as he studied her, could not be older than thirty.

"He is uniquely dangerous and unscrupulous."

"So I have been assured. And yet"—and here she turned to Chang with a curiously blank face—"he truly has no choice. The only help for Cardinal Chang—whether it merely be to soothe his soul—is information. We are taking him to it. Besides, I have no wish to lose a book in an unnecessary struggle—and the Cardinal holds one."

"Information, eh?" sneered Aspiche, looking around the woman at Chang. "About what? His whore? About that idiot Svenson? About—"

"Do be *quiet,* Colonel," she hissed, fully out of patience.

Chang was gratified, and not a little surprised, to see Aspiche pull his head back and snort with peevishness. And stop talking.

The ballroom was near. It only made sense to use it for another such gathering—perhaps already the crowds from the great chamber were convening too, along with those from the theatre at the end of the spiral staircase. Chang suddenly wondered with a sinking heart, not having found her in the great chamber, if this theatre was where Miss Temple had been taken. Had he walked right past her, just close enough and in time to hear the applause at her destruction?

With Aspiche in tow, their pace had slowed. The stamping bootsteps of the Dragoons made it difficult to hear any other movement in the house, and he wondered if his own execution or forced conversion was to be the main source of entertainment. He would smash the book over his own head before he allowed that to happen. To all appearances it seemed a quick enough end, and one equally horrible to watch as to experience. It would be something to at least, in his last moments, unsettle his executioners' stomachs.

He realized that Mrs. Stearne was looking at him. He cocked his head in a mocking invitation for her to speak... but she was, for the first time, hesitant to do so.

"I would... if I may, I would be grateful—for as I say, I was elsewhere occupied—if, with the Comte... if you could tell me what you saw... down below."

It was all Chang could do not to slap the woman's face.

"What I *saw*?"

"I ask because I do not know. Mrs. Marchmoor and Miss Poole—I knew them—I know that they have undergone—that the Comte's great work—"

"Did they go to him *willingly*?" demanded Chang.

"Oh yes," Mrs. Stearne replied.

"Why not you?"

She hesitated just a moment, looking into his veiled eyes.

"I... I must... my own responsibilities for the evening—"

She was interrupted by a peremptory snort from Aspiche, a clear admonishment at this topic of conversation—or indeed, conversation with Chang at all.

"Instead of you, it was Angelique."

"Yes."

"Because *she* was willing?"

Mrs. Stearne turned to Aspiche before he could snort again and snapped, "Colonel, do be quiet!" She looked back at Chang. "I *will* go in my turn. But you must know from Doctor Svenson—yes, I know who he is, as I know Celeste Temple—what happened to that woman at the Institute. Indeed, I am led to understand that you yourself were there, even perhaps responsible—I do not mean *intentionally*," she said quickly as Chang opened his mouth to speak, "but only that you well know that her state was grave. In the Comte's mind this was her only chance."

"Chance for *what*? You have not seen what—what—the *thing* she has become!"

"Truly, I have not—"

"Then you should not speak of it," cried Chang.

Aspiche chuckled.

"Does something amuse you, Colonel?" snarled Chang.

"*You* amuse me, Cardinal. A moment."

Aspiche stopped walking and pulled his arm from Mrs. Stearne. He reached into his scarlet coat and removed one of his thin black cheroots and a box of matches. He bit off the tip of the cheroot and spat. He looked up to Chang with a vicious grin and stuck the cheroot into his mouth, fiddling with the matches for a light.

"You see, I was introduced to you as a man of unfettered depravity—a figure without scruple or conscience, ready to hunt and kill for a fee. And yet, what do I find—in your final hours, with your life boiled down to its essence? A man in shackles to a whore who thinks as little of him as she does yesterday's breakfast, and working in league—the lone wolf of the riverside!—with an idiot surgeon and an even more idiotic girl—or should I say spinster? She is what—twenty and five?—and the only man who'd have her has come to his senses and thrown her aside like a spent nag!"

"They're alive then?" Chang asked.

"Oh . . . I did not say *that*." Aspiche chuckled, shaking out the match.

The Colonel inhaled through the cheroot's glowing tip and sent a thin stream of smoke out of the side of his mouth. He offered his arm again to Mrs. Stearne, but Chang made no move to continue.

"You will know, Colonel, that I have just come from killing Major Blach and three of his men—or perhaps five, there was no time to be sure. It would give me as much pleasure to do the same to you."

Aspiche scoffed and blew more smoke.

"Do you know, Mrs. Stearne," Chang pitched his voice loud enough that every Dragoon would hear him clearly, "how I was first introduced to the Colonel? I will tell you—"

Aspiche growled and reached for his saber. Chang raised the book high over his head. The two lines of Dragoons all raised their blades in readiness to attack. Mrs. Stearne, her eyes at once quite wide, stepped between them all.

"Colonel—Cardinal—this must not happen—"

Chang ignored her, glaring into Aspiche's hate-filled eyes, hissing with relish. "I met the Colonel-*Adjutant* when he *hired* me—to execute—to *assassinate*—his commanding officer, Colonel Arthur Trapping of the 4th Dragoons."

The words were met with silence, but their impact on the surrounding soldiers was palpable as a slap. Mrs. Stearne's eyes were wide—she had known Trapping as well. She turned to Aspiche, speaking hesitantly.

"Colonel Trapping . . ."

"Preposterous! What else will you say to divide me from my men?" cried Aspiche, in what, Chang had to admit, was a very credible impression of impugned honor—though Aspiche, being such a blind egotist, had probably already convinced himself that the contract for murder had never occurred. "You are a well-known lying, murdering rogue—"

"Who *did* kill him, Colonel?" taunted Chang. "Have you found that out? How long will you survive before they do it to you? How much time will the sale of your honor purchase? Did they ask you to attend when they sunk his body in the river?"

With a cry, Aspiche drew his saber in a wide scything arc but then, partially unsteadied by his rage, put his weight on his weak leg and just for a moment tottered. Chang shoved Mrs. Stearne to the side and snapped his right fist into Aspiche's throat. The Colonel staggered back, hand at his collar, choking, his face red. Chang immediately stepped away, close to Mrs. Stearne, raising his arms in peace. Mrs. Stearne at once shouted to the Dragoons, who were clearly an instant away from running Chang through.

"Stop! Stop it—*stop it*—all of you!"

The Dragoons hesitated, still poised to attack. She wheeled to Chang and Aspiche.

"Cardinal—you will be silent! Colonel Aspiche—you will behave like a proper escort! We will continue at once. If there is any more nonsense, I will not be responsible for what happens to *any* of you!"

Chang nodded to her and took another careful step away from the Colonel. He had grown so accustomed to Mrs. Stearne's calm manner that her genuine authority had surprised him. It was as if she had somehow *invoked* it from within, like something learned, like a soldier's automatic response from training—only this was emotion, a force of character that allowed a woman who knew nothing of command to assert control over twenty hardened soldiers—and in the direct place of their officer. Once more, the true impact of the Process left Chang amazed and unsettled.

They continued in silence, turning into another back corridor, skirting the kitchens. Chang looked through every open door or archway they passed, searching for any sign of Svenson or Miss Temple, or any hope of escape. The momentary pleasure at baiting Aspiche had gone, and his mind was once more plagued with doubt. If he could smash the book in the direction of one line of soldiers and then dash through the gap it created, he knew he had a chance—but it was useless if he didn't know where he was going. A blind rush was likely to lead straight into another band of soldiers or a malevolent crowd of adherents. He'd be cut to pieces without a qualm.

Chang turned at the sound of running steps behind them. It was one of the Dragoons Aspiche had sent to find Blenheim. The trooper made his way through the rear line of soldiers and saluted the Colonel, reporting that Blenheim was still missing, and that the other groups were fanning out through the interior rooms. Aspiche nodded curtly.

"Where is Captain Smythe?"

The trooper had no answer.

"Find him!" snapped Aspiche, as if he had asked for Smythe in the first place, and the trooper was impossibly stupid. "He should be outside—arranging the sentries—bring him to me at once!"

The Dragoon saluted again and dashed off. Aspiche said nothing more and they continued on.

More than once they were forced to wait while a group of guests crossed their corridor, moving on a different path toward—he assumed—the ballroom. The guests were formally dressed and masked, usually all smiles and eagerness—much like the two men he'd overheard in the drawing room earlier, and they tended to stare at the soldiers and the three in their midst—Chang, Aspiche, and Mrs. Stearne—as if they made some strange allegorical puzzle to be read: the soldier, the lady, the demon. He made a point of leering wickedly at anyone who looked for too long, but with each such meeting Chang felt more his isolation, and saw the extreme degree of his presumption to come to Harschmort at all . . . and the imminence of his doom.

They walked for perhaps another forty yards before they approached a short figure in a heavy cloak and dark spectacles, with an odd sort of bandolier slung across his chest from which hung perhaps two dozen metal flasks. He held up his hand for them to stop. Aspiche shook himself free of Mrs. Stearne and limped forward, speaking low, but not low enough that Chang could not hear.

"Doctor Lorenz!" the Colonel whispered. "Is something amiss?"

Doctor Lorenz did not share the Colonel's need for discretion. He spoke in a needle-sharp tone directed equally to Aspiche and the woman.

"I require some number of your men. Six will do, I am sure. There is not a minute to spare."

"Require?" snapped Aspiche. "Why should you *require* my men?"

"Because something has *happened* to the fellows detailed to help me," barked Lorenz. "Surely that is not too much to grasp!"

Lorenz gestured behind him to an open doorway. Chang noticed for the first time a bloody handprint on the wooden frame, and a split in the wood clearly ripped by a bullet.

Aspiche turned and with a finger snap detailed six men from the first line, limping with them through the doorway. Lorenz looked after them but did not follow, one hand idly tapping one of the dangling flasks. His attention wandered to Chang and Mrs. Stearne, and then pointedly settled on the book under Chang's arm. Doctor Lorenz licked his lips.

"Do you know which one that *is*?" The question was put to Mrs. Stearne but his gaze did not shift from the glass book.

"I do not. The Cardinal tells me he took it from a lady."

"Ah," replied Lorenz. He thought for a moment. "Beaded mask?"

Chang did not answer. Lorenz licked his lips again, nodded to himself.

"Must have had. Lady Mélantes. And Lord Acton. And Captain Hazelhorst. And I believe, actually, originally Mrs. Marchmoor herself. If I recall correctly. Rather an important volume."

Mrs. Stearne did not reply, which was, Chang knew, her way of saying she was well aware of its importance and not in need of Doctor Lorenz to apprise her.

A moment later Aspiche appeared at the head of his men, all six of them carrying an apparently very heavy stretcher, covered by a sheet of canvas that had been sewn to the frame, sealing in whoever was beneath it.

"Excellent," announced Lorenz. "My thanks to you. This way . . ." He indicated a door on the opposite side of the hall to the stretcher-bearers.

"You're not joining us?" asked Aspiche.

"There is no time," replied Lorenz. "I've lost precious minutes as it is—if the thing's to be done at all it must be done at once—our supply of ice has been exhausted! Please do offer my respects to all. Madame." He nodded to Mrs. Stearne and followed the soldiers out.

They walked on to the end of the corridor and stopped again, Aspiche sending a man forward to confirm they were clear to continue. As they waited, Chang shifted his grip on the book. The line of Dragoons in front had diminished now from ten to four. An accurate throw of the book could incapacitate them all and open the way . . . but the way to where? He studied the backs of the soldiers walking in front of him and pictured how the book might shatter . . . and then could not but think of Reeves, and of his delicate alliance with Captain Smythe. What had the Dragoons done to him? How could he face Smythe after slaughtering any of his men in such a foul manner? If there was no other way, he would not hesitate . . . but if there was truly no way out, why should he bother with the Dragoons at all? He would keep the book—either as a way to kill what main figures in the Cabal that he could—Rosamonde or the Comte—or use it to bargain, if not for his own life then Svenson's or Celeste's. He had to hope they were alive.

He swallowed with a grimace and saw Mrs. Stearne's eyes on him. Whether it had been intentional or not, their deliberate passage from the turret had taken long enough that the fire of his rage had faded, leaving his body to bear the full weight of exhaustion and sorrow. He felt something on his lip and wiped it with his glove—a smear of bright blood. He looked back at Mrs. Stearne, but her expression betrayed no feeling at all.

"You see I have very little left to lose," he said.

"Everyone always thinks that," commented Colonel Aspiche, "until that little bit is taken away—and feels like the whole of the world."

Chang said nothing, resenting bitterly the slightest glimmer of actual insight coming from the Colonel.

The Dragoon reappeared in the doorway, clicking his heels and saluting Aspiche.

"Begging your pardon, Sir, but they're ready."

Aspiche dropped the cheroot to the floor and ground it with his heel. He limped forward to enter the ballroom at the head of his men. Mrs. Stearne watched Chang very closely as they followed, and had quite subtly drifted beyond the immediate reach of his arms.

When they entered the ballroom, there were so many people gathered that Chang could not see through the throng as their path was opened by the wedge of Dragoons, spectators retreating like a whispering tide of elegance. They made their way to the center, when at a crisp bark from Aspiche, the Colonel and his Dragoons expanded the open area, marching some six paces in each direction, driving the crowd farther back, before wheeling to face Cardinal Chang and Mrs. Stearne, alone in the open circle.

Mrs. Stearne took a deliberate step forward and curtseyed deeply, dropping her head as if she faced royalty. Before them all, standing like a row of monarchs on a raised dais, were the uncrowned heads of the Cabal: the Contessa di Lacquer-Sforza, Deputy Minister Harald Crabbé, and, his arm satisfyingly swathed with bandages, Francis Xonck. To their side was the Prince, with Herr Flaüss, masked and apparently having regained the power to stand, to his left and to his right, clinging smilingly to his arm, a slim blonde woman in white robes and a white feather mask.

"Very well managed, Caroline," said the Contessa, returning the curtsey with a nod. "You may go on with your duties."

Mrs. Stearne stood again and looked once more at Cardinal Chang before walking quickly away through the crowd. He stood alone before his judges.

"Cardinal Chang—" began the Contessa.

Cardinal Chang cleared his throat and spat, the scarlet mass flying perhaps half the distance to the dais. An outraged whisper ran throughout the crowd. Chang saw the Dragoons nervously glancing at one another as the guests behind them inched forward.

"Contessa," said Chang, returning her greeting, his voice now unpleasantly hoarse. His gaze fell across the rest of the dais. "Minister... Mr. Xonck... Highness..."

"We require that book," stated Crabbé. "Place it on the floor and walk away from it."

"And then what?" sneered Chang.

"Then you will be killed," answered Xonck. "But killed *kindly.*"

"And if I do not?"

"Then what you have already seen," said the Contessa, "will be a trivial prologue to your pain."

Chang looked at the crowd around him, and the Dragoons—still no sign of Smythe, Svenson, or Celeste. He was acutely aware of the luxurious fittings of the ballroom—the crystal fixtures, the gleaming floor, the walls of mirror and glass—and the finery of the masked spectators, all in contrast to his own filthy appearance. He knew that for these people the state of his garments and his body were definitive indicators of his inferior caste. It was also what pained him about Angelique—in this place as much a piece of chattel as he, as much a specimen of livestock. Why else had she been first to undergo the hideous transformation—why had she been taken to the Institute to begin with? Because it did not matter if she died. And yet she could not see their contempt—just as she could not see him (but this was wrong, for of course she did—she merely rejected what she saw), nor beyond her own desperate ambition to the truth of how she had been used. But then Chang recalled the great figures of the city he'd found, one after another, slumped over the glass books in the string of private rooms, and Robert Vandaariff, now a parchment-scratching automaton. The contempt of the Cabal was not limited to those of lower birth or insufficient station.

He had to admit a certain equity of abuse.

Yet Chang sneered at the expressions of disdain and fury that pressed at him through the ring of uncertain Dragoons. Each guest had been offered the chance to lick the Cabal's boots, and now they clamored for the privilege. Who *were* these people to so easily blind so many?

He thought bitterly that half of the Cabal's work was done for it already—the fevered ambition that ran through their adherents had always lurked in the shadows of those lives, hungrily awaiting the chance to come forward. That the chance was only as honest as a baited hook never occurred to anyone—they were too busy congratulating themselves on swallowing it.

He held the gleaming glass book in front of him for all to see. For some reason the act of raising his arm exerted pressure on his seething lungs and Cardinal Chang erupted into a fit of agonized coughing. He spat again and wiped his bloody mouth.

"You *will* make us clean the floor," observed the Contessa.

"I suppose it's inconvenient of me not to have died at the Ministry," Chang hoarsely replied.

"Terribly so, but you've established yourself as quite a worthy opponent, Cardinal." She smiled at Chang. "Would you not agree, Mr. Xonck?" she called, and at least Chang knew she was mocking Xonck's injury.

"Indeed! The Cardinal illustrates the difficult task that is before us all—the determined struggle we must prepare ourselves to undergo," answered Francis Xonck, his voice pitched to reach the far corners of the room. "The vision we embrace will be resisted with all the tenacity of the man you see before you. Do not underestimate him—nor underestimate your own unique qualities of wisdom and courage."

Chang scoffed at this blatant flattery of the crowd, and wondered why it was Crabbé in politics making speeches and not the unctuously eloquent Xonck. He recalled the prostrate form of Henry Xonck—it might not be long before Francis Xonck was more powerful than five Harald Crabbés put together. Crabbé must have sensed this, for he stepped forward, also addressing the whole of the audience.

"Such a man has even this night committed murders—too many to name!—in his quest to destroy our mission. He has killed our soldiers, he has defiled our women—like a savage he has broken into our Ministry and this very house! And why?"

"Because you're a lying, syphilitic—"

"*Because*," Crabbé shouted down Chang's hoarse voice easily, "we offer a vision that will break the stranglehold this man—*and his hidden masters*—have over you all, to keep you at bay, offering scraps while they profit from your labor and your worth! We say all this must end—and their bloody man has come to kill us! You see it for yourselves!"

The crowd erupted into a chorus of angry cries, and once more Chang felt he had no real understanding of human beings at all. To him, Crabbé's words were every bit as idiotic and servile as Xonck's, every bit as fawning and conjured, patently so. And yet his listeners bayed like hounds for Chang's blood. The Dragoons were losing ground as the crowd pressed nearer. He saw Aspiche, shoved from behind, looking nervously up to the dais—and then to Chang, self-righteously glaring as if this was all *his* fault.

"Dear friends . . . please! Please—a moment!" Xonck was smiling, raising his good hand, calling over the noise. The cries fell away at once. The control was astonishing. Chang doubted that these people had even undergone the Process—how could there have been time? But he could scarce understand such a uniform response from an untrained (or un-German) collection of individuals.

"Dear friends," Xonck said again, "do not worry—this man shall pay . . . and pay directly." He looked at Chang with an eager smile. "We must merely determine the means."

"Put down the book, Cardinal," repeated the Contessa.

"If anyone moves toward me I will smash it across your beautiful face."

"Will you indeed?"

"It would give me *pleasure*."

"So petty, Cardinal—it makes me think less of you."

"Well then, I do apologize. If it helps at all, I would choose to kill you not because you have surely killed me already with the glass in my lungs, but because you are truly my most deadly foe. The Prince is an idiot, Xonck I've already beaten, and Deputy Minister Crabbé is a coward."

"How very bold you are," she replied, unable to prevent the slightest smile. "What of the Comte d'Orkancz?"

"He works his art, but you determine that art's path—he is finally your creature. You even weave your plots against your fellows—do any of them know the work assigned to Mr. Gray?"

"Mr. . . . who?" The Contessa's smile was suddenly fixed.

"Oh, come now—why be shy? Mr. *Gray*. From the Institute—he was with you in the Ministry—when Herr Flaüss was given the gift of the Process." He nodded to the portly Macklenburger who, despite the doubting look on his face, nodded back. Before the Contessa could reply Chang called out again. "Mr. Gray's work was assigned by you, I assume. Why else would I have found him in the depths of the prison tunnels, tampering with the Comte's furnaces? I have no idea whether he did what you wanted him to do or not. I killed him before we had a chance to exchange our news."

He had to give her credit. The words were not two seconds from his mouth before she turned to Crabbé and Xonck with a deadly serious hiss, barely audible beyond the dais.

"Did you know about this? Did *you* send Gray on some errand?"

"Of course not," whispered Crabbé, "Gray answered to *you*—"

"Was it the Comte?" she hissed again, even more angrily.

"Gray answered to *you*," repeated Xonck, his mind clearly working behind his measured tone.

"Then why was he in the *tunnels*?" asked the Contessa.

"I'm sure he was not," said Xonck. "I'm sure the Cardinal is *lying*."

They turned to him. Before she could open her mouth Chang pulled his hand from his coat pocket.

"I believe this is his key," Chang called out, and he tossed the heavy metal key to clatter on the floor in front of the dais.

Of course, the key could have been anyone's—and he doubted any of them knew Gray's enough to recognize it—but the palpable artifact had the desired effect of seeming to prove his words. He smiled with a grim pleasure, finally feeling a welcoming coldness enter his heart with this final charade of baiting conversation—for Chang knew there was little more dangerous than a man beyond care, and welcomed the chance to sow what dissension he could in these final, doomed moments. The figures on the dais were silent, as was the crowd—though he was sure the crowd lacked the barest idea of what this might mean, seeing only that its leaders were unpleasantly at a loss.

"What *was* he doing there—" began Crabbé.

"Open the doors!" shouted the Contessa, glaring at Chang but raising her voice so it cut like a razor to the rear of the room. Behind him Chang heard the sound of bolts being drawn. At once the crowd began to whisper, looking back and then shifting away. Someone else was entering the ballroom. Chang glanced at the dais—they all seemed as fixed on the new entry as the crowd—and then back, as the whispering became punctuated by gasps and even cries of alarm.

The crowd made way at last, clearing the floor between Cardinal Chang and, walking slowly toward him, the Comte d'Orkancz. In his left hand was a black leather leash, attached by a metal clasp to the leather collar around the neck of the woman who walked behind him. Despite everything, the breath clutched in Chang's throat.

She was naked, her hair still hanging black in lustrous curls, walking pace by deliberate pace behind d'Orkancz, her eyes roving across the room without seeming to fix on any one thing in particular, as if she were seeing it all for the very first time. She moved slowly, but without modesty, as natural as an animal, each footfall carefully placed, feeling the floor deliberately as she looked at their faces. Her body was gleaming blue, shimmering from its indigo depths, its surface slick as water, pliant but still somehow stiff as she walked, giving Chang the impression that each movement required her conscious thought and preparation. She was beautiful and unearthly—Chang could not look away—the weight of her breasts, the perfect proportion of her ribs and her hips, the luscious sweep of her legs. He saw that, apart from her head, there was now no hair on Angelique's face or body—the lack of eyebrows somehow opening the expression on her face like a blankly beatific medieval Madonna's, at the same time her bare sex was both impossibly innocent and lewd.

Only the whites of her eyes were bright. Her eyes settled on Chang.

The Comte flicked her leash and Angelique drifted forward. The ballroom was silent. Chang could hear the click of each footfall on the polished wood. He wrenched his eyes to d'Orkancz and saw cold hatred. He looked to the dais: shock on the faces of Crabbé and Xonck, but the Contessa, however troubled, looking at her companions, as if to gauge the success of this distraction. Chang looked back at Angelique. He could not stop himself. She stepped closer . . . and he heard her speak.

"Car-din-al *Chang,*" she said, enunciating each syllable as carefully as ever . . . but her voice was different, smaller, more intense—as if half of what had made it had been boiled away.

Her lips were not moving—*could* they move?—and he realized with a shock that her words were in his head alone.

"Angelique . . ." His voice was a whisper.

"It is finished, Cardinal, . . . you know it is . . . look at me."

He tried to do anything else. He could not. She came nearer and nearer.

"Poor Cardinal . . . you desired me so very much . . . I desired so very much also . . . do you remember?"

The words in his mind expanded, like Chinese paper balls in water, blooming out into bright flowers, until he felt her presence overwhelm him and her projected thoughts take the place of his own senses.

He was no longer in the room.

They stood together at the river bank, gazing into the grey water at twilight. Had they ever done such a thing? They had, he knew, once—once they had by chance met in the street and she allowed him to walk her back to the brothel. He remembered the day vividly even as he experienced it again through her own projected memory. He was speaking to her—the words meaningless—he had wanted to say anything to reach her, relating the history of the houses they passed, of his daring experiences, of the true life of the river bank. She'd barely said a word. At the time he had wondered if it was a matter of language—her accent was still strong—but now, crushingly, with her thoughts in his mind, he knew that she had merely chosen not to speak, and that the entire episode had nothing to do with him at all. She had only agreed to walk with him—had deliberately gone to him in the street—so as to avoid another jealous client who had followed her all the way from Circus Garden. She had barely heard Chang's words, smiling politely and nodding at his foolish stories and wanting solely to be done with it . . . until they had paused for a moment at the quayside, looking down at the water. Chang had fallen silent, and then spoken quietly of the river's passage to an endless sea—observing that even they in their squalid lives, by being in that place, for that time, could truly situate themselves at the border of mystery.

For that image of possible escape, that unintended echo of her own vast imagined life, so far removed . . . she had been surprised. She had remembered that moment, and offered him, here at the end, that much thanks.

Cardinal Chang blinked. He looked at the floor. He was on his hands and knees, bloody saliva hanging from his mouth. Colonel Aspiche loomed above him, the glass book cradled in his hands. Angelique stood with the Comte d'Orkancz, her gaze wandering with neither curiosity nor interest. The Comte nodded to the dais and Chang forced himself to turn. Near the dais the crowd parted again . . . for Mrs. Stearne. She entered leading by the hand a small woman in a white silk robe. Chang shook his head—he could not think—the woman in white . . . he knew her . . . he blinked again and wiped his mouth, swallowing painfully. The robe was sheer, clinging tightly to her body . . . her feet were bare . . . a mask of white feathers . . . hair the color of chestnuts, in sausage curls to either side of her head. With an effort Chang rose up on his knees.

He opened his mouth to speak as Mrs. Stearne reached behind her and pulled the feathered mask from Miss Temple's face. The scars of the Process were vivid around each grey eye, and burned in a line across the bridge of her nose.

Chang tried to say her name. His mouth would not work.

Colonel Aspiche moved behind him. The force of the blow so spun the room that Chang wondered, in his last moment before darkness, whether his head had been cut off.

NINE

Provocateur

As a surgeon, Doctor Svenson knew that the body did not remember pain, only that an experience had been painful. Extreme fear however was seared into the memory like nothing else in life, and as he pulled himself, hand over agonizing hand, toward the metal gondola, the dark countryside spinning dizzily below him, the freezing winds numbing his face and fingers, the Doctor's grasp on his own sanity was tenuous at best. He tried to think of anything but the sickening drop below his kicking boots, but he could not. The effort denied him the breath to scream or even cry out, but with each wrenching movement he whimpered with open terror. All his life he had shrunk away from heights of any kind—even climbing ladders aboard ship he willed his eyes to look straight ahead and his limbs to move, lest his mind or stomach give way to even that meager height. Despite himself he scoffed—a staccato bark of saliva—at the very notion of *ladders.* His only consolation, feeble in the extreme, was that the noise of the wind and the darkness of the sky had so far hidden him from anyone looking out of a window. Not that he knew for certain he had not been seen. The Doctor's own eyes were tightly shut.

He had climbed perhaps half-way up the rope and his arms felt like burning lead. Already it seemed all he could do to hold on. He opened his eyes for the briefest glimpse, shutting them at once with a yelp at the vertigo caused by the swinging gondola. Where before he'd seen a face at the circular window there was only black glass. Had it truly been Elöise? He had been sure on the ground, but now—now he barely knew his own name. He forced himself upwards—each moment of letting one hand go to stab above him for the rope was a spike of fear in his heart, and yet he made himself do it again and again, feeling his way, his face locked in a shocking rictus of effort.

Another two feet. His mind assailed him—why not stop? Why not let go? Wasn't this the underlying dread behind his fear of heights to begin with—the actual impulse to jump? Why else did he shrink away from balconies and windows, but for the sudden urge to hurl himself into the air? Now it would be so simple. The grassy pastures below would be as good a grave as any sea—and how many times had he contemplated that, since Corinna's death? How many times had he grown cold looking over the iron rail of a Baltic ship, worrying—like a depressive terrier with a well-gnawed stick—the urge to throw himself over the side?

Another two feet, gritting his teeth and kicking his legs, driving himself by pure will and anger. That was a reason to live—his hatred for these people, their condescension, their assumption of privilege, their unconscionable *appetite.* He thought of them in the gondola, away from the freezing cold, no doubt wrapped in furs, soothed by the whispering wind and the whistling buzz of the rotors. Another foot, his arms slack as rope. He opened his hand and snatched for a new grip . . . kicked his boots . . . again . . . again. He forced his mind to think of anything but the drop—the dirigible—he'd never seen anything like it! Obviously full of some gas—hydrogen, he assumed—but was that all? And how was it powered? He didn't know how it could bear the weight of the gondola much less a steam engine . . . could there be some other source? Something with Lorenz and the indigo clay? In the abstract Svenson might have found these questions fascinating, but now he threw himself into them with the mindless fervor of a man reciting multiplication tables to stave off an impending *crise.*

He opened his eyes again and looked up. He was closer than he thought, hanging some ten yards below the long iron cabin. The upper end of the rope was secured to the steel frame of the gasbag itself, just behind the cabin. The rear of the cabin had no window that he could see . . . but did it have a door? He closed his eyes and climbed, three agonizing feet, and looked up again. Doctor Svenson was suddenly appalled . . . climbing with his eyes closed he hadn't realized . . . and for a moment he simply clung where he was. Below and to each side of the cabin were the rear rotors—each perhaps eight feet across—and his path on the rope led right between them. Between the wind and his own exertions, the rope swung back and forth—the blades themselves were turning so fast he couldn't tell how wide the gap really was. The higher he got, the more any exertion might send him too far in either direction—and straight into the blades.

There was nothing he could do except drop, and the longer he delayed out of fear, the less strength was in his arms. He pulled himself up, clamping shut his eyes, and gripped the cable more firmly between his knees to steady the swinging. As he inched higher he could hear the rotors' menacing revolutions more clearly, a relentless chopping of air. He was just beneath them. He could smell the exhaust—the same sharp tang of ozone, sulphur, and scorched rubber that had nearly made him sick in the attic of Tarr Manor—the flying vehicle *was* another emanation of the Cabal's insidious science. He could sense the rotors near to him, invisibly slicing past. He extended a hand up the rope, then another, and then hauled his entire body into range, braced for the savage impact that would shear off a limb. The blades roared around him but he remained somehow unscathed. Svenson inched higher, his entire body shaking with the effort. The gondola was right in front of him—some three feet out of reach. Any attempt to nudge the rope toward it—if he didn't catch hold—would send him straight into the rotors on the backswing. Even worse, there was nothing on the rear of the gondola to grab on to even if he risked the attempt. He looked up. The cable was attached to the metal frame by an iron bolt . . . it was his only option. Another two yards. His head was above the rotors. He could almost touch the bolt. He inched up another foot, gasping, his body expending itself in a way he could not comprehend. Another six inches. He reached up in agony, felt the bolt, and then above it the riveted steel strut. A spasm of fear shot through him—he was only holding to the rope with one hand and his knees. He swallowed, and fixed his grip on the strut. He was going to have to let go and pull himself up. It should be possible to wrap his legs around the strut and creep over the rotors to the top of the gondola. But he would have to let go of the rope. Suddenly—it was perhaps inevitable—his nerves got the best of him and his rope hand slipped. At once Doctor Svenson thrust both arms toward the metal strut and caught hold, his legs flailing wildly. He looked down to see the rope disappear into the right side rotor, flayed to pieces. He pulled his knees to his chest with a whimpering cry—before the rotors hacked off his feet—and kicked them over the metal bar. He looked up at the canvas gasbag just above his head. Directly below him was death—by dismemberment if not by impact. He slowly slid along the strut, painfully shifting his grip on the freezing metal around the intervening cross-pieces. His hands felt numb—he was gripping as tightly with his forearms as his fingers.

It took him ten minutes to crawl ten feet. The gondola was directly beneath him. As gently as he could he let down his legs and felt the solid metal beneath his feet. His eyes were streaming—whether with tears or the wind, Doctor Svenson hadn't a clue.

The gondola was a smooth metal box of blackened steel, suspended some three feet below the massive gasbag by metal struts bolted to its frame at each corner. The surface of the roof was slick from the cold and the moisture in the foggy coastal air, and Doctor Svenson was both too paralyzed with fear and too numbed by exertion to allow himself so near the edge to cling to one of these corner struts. Instead, he crouched in the center of the roof with his arms wrapped around the same metal brace he'd used to climb forward. His teeth chattered as he forced his staggered mind to examine his circumstances. The gondola was perhaps twelve feet across and forty feet in length. He could see a round hatch set into the rooftop, but going to it would require him to release his hold on the metal brace. He shut his eyes and focused on breathing, shivering despite his greatcoat and his recent exertion—or even because of it, the sweat over his body and in his clothing now viciously chilling his flesh in the bitter wind. He opened his eyes at a sudden lurch, holding on to the metal brace for his life. The dirigible was turning and Svenson felt his grip inexorably weakening as the force of the turn pulled him away. With an insane bark of laughter he saw himself—in a desperate attempt to manage his grip on a swiftly turning airship—in comparison to his lifelong anxiety at climbing *ladders*. He remembered just the day before—was it so recently?—emerging on his hands and knees onto the rooftop of the Macklenburg compound! If he'd only known! Svenson tightened his grip and cackled again—the rooftop! He was clinging to the very answer to the mystery of the Prince's escape—they'd come for him with the dirigible! The rotors would be silent at a lower speed—they could have easily drifted into position and lowered men to liberate the Prince with no one being the wiser. Even the crimped cigarette butt made sense—discarded by the Contessa di Lacquer-Sforza as she watched from a gondola window. What still made no sense however, was *why* the Prince had been stolen without the other Cabal members—Xonck and Crabbé at the least—being aware of it. Like the death of Arthur Trapping, it lay between his enemies without explanation . . . if he could just unravel either mystery . . . he might understand it all.

The dirigible straightened out of the turn. The fog thickened around Svenson, and he moved forward on the strut, careful not to step too heavily—the last thing he wanted was for anyone below to know he was there. He shut his eyes once more and tried to ease his heaving breath to mere gasps and chattering teeth. He would not move until his arms fell off or until the dirigible found its destination, whichever happened first.

When he opened his eyes the dirigible was making another turn, less precipitous than before and—he hadn't realized, but now saw through ragged gaps in the fog—at a lower altitude, some two hundred feet above what looked like a low fennish grassland, with scarcely a single tree in sight. Were they possibly crossing the sea? He saw lights through the gloom, first dim and winking, but as they went on emerging with a growing clarity that allowed him to sketch out the entirety of their destination—for indeed, as he studied it the dirigible continued to descend.

It was an enormous structure, but relatively low to the ground—Svenson's guess was two or three stories—giving out an impression of massive strength. The place as a whole was shaped something like a disconnected jawbone, with the center space taken up by some sort of ornamental garden. As they soared closer he could hear a variation in the sound of the rotors—they were slowing down—as he saw more detail: the large open plaza in front, thronged with coaches and dotted with the ant-like (or as they neared, mouse-like) figures of drivers and grooms. Svenson looked to the other side and saw a pair of waving lanterns on the rooftop and behind the lanterns a group of men—no doubt waiting to wrangle the mooring ropes. They drifted closer . . . a hundred feet, seventy feet . . . Svenson was suddenly concerned about being seen, and against all his better wishes dropped down to hang on to the hatch handle, flattening his body over the roof of the gondola. The steel plate was freezing. He had one hand on the handle and the other spread out across the roof for balance, with each boot splayed toward a different corner. They sank lower. He could hear shouts from below, and then the pop of a window being opened and an answering shout from the gondola.

They were landing at Harschmort House.

Doctor Svenson shut his eyes again, now more out of dread at being discovered than at his still-precarious altitude, as all around him he heard the calls and whistles of the craft coming in to land. No one came up through the hatch—apparently the mooring cables were lowered from the front of the gondola. Perhaps once the rotors stopped the cables were re-attached to the bolt where he'd climbed. He had no idea—but it was only a matter of time before he was discovered. He forced his mind to think about his situation, and his immediate odds.

He was unarmed. He was physically spent—as well as his ankle twisted, head battered, and hands raw from the climb. There was on the rooftop a gang of assuredly burly men more than willing to take him in hand, if not fling him to the plaza below. Within the gondola lurked another handful of enemies—Crabbé, Aspiche, Lorenz, Miss Poole . . . and in their power, in who knew what state—or, if he was perfectly honest, with what loyalties—Elöise Dujong. Below him he heard another popping sound and then a loud metallic rattle that ended in a heavy ring of steel striking stone. He suppressed the urge to raise his head and peek. The gondola began to rock slightly as he heard voices—Crabbé calling out and then after him Miss Poole. Someone answered them from below and then the conversation grew to too many voices for him to follow—they were descending from the gondola via some lowered ladder or staircase.

"At long last," this was Crabbé, calling to someone across the rooftop, "is everything ready?"

"A most delightful time," Miss Poole was saying to someone else, "though not without *adventure*—"

"Damnable thing," Crabbé continued. "I've no idea—Lorenz says he can, but that is news to me—yes, twice—the second straight through the heart—"

"Gently! Gently now!" This was Lorenz calling out. "And ice—we're going to need a washtub full at once—yes, all of you—take hold! Quickly now, there is no time!"

Crabbé was listening as someone speaking too low for Svenson to hear briefed him on events elsewhere—could this be Bascombe?

"Yes . . . yes . . . I see . . ." He could picture the Deputy Minister nodding along as he muttered. "And Carfax? Baax-Saornes? Baroness Roote? Mrs. Kraft? Henry Xonck? Excellent—and what of our illustrious host?"

"The Colonel has injured his ankle, yes," Miss Poole chuckled—was there ever a thing that woman did not find amusing?—"in *battle* against the dread Doctor Svenson. I am afraid the poor Doctor's death was hard—my complexion is quite *ashen* at the prospect!"

Miss Poole—and joining her with a bellowing "haw haw haw" was Colonel Aspiche—erupted in laughter at her pun. In Svenson's spent emotional state, it was something of an abstraction to realize that the object of their sport was his being burnt in an oven.

"This way—this way—yes! I do declare, Miss Poole, the ride does not seem to have suited her!"

"And yet she seemed so recently *tractable,* Colonel—perhaps the lady merely requires more of your kind *attention.*"

They were taking Elöise away—she was alive. What had they done to her? Worse, what did Miss Poole mean by "tractable"? He tormented himself with the image of Elöise on the wooden staircase, the confusion in her eyes . . . she had come to Tarr Manor for a reason, no matter that it was gone from her memory. Who was Svenson to say who she truly was? Then he remembered the warm press of her lips against his and had no idea what to think at all. Still Svenson's fear at being discovered would not let him look up. The seconds crawled by and he muttered to himself, fervently wishing the pack of them off the rooftop as quickly as possible.

Finally the voices were gone. But what of the men mooring the craft, or guarding it? Doctor Svenson heard a muffled clicking from the hatch beneath him, then felt the handle turning in his hand. He scuttled back as the handle caught the bolt. The hatch rose, and directly after it appeared the grease-smeared face of a man in coveralls. He saw Svenson and opened his mouth in surprise. Svenson drove the heel of his boot into the man's face with all his strength, grimacing at the crunch of impact. The fellow abruptly dropped back through the open hatch,

Svenson scrabbling after him. He thrust both legs through the round hole, ignoring the line of iron rungs bolted to the wall, and launched himself down onto the groaning, stunned body sitting at its feet. Svenson landed squarely on the man's shoulders, flattening him hard against the floor with a meaty thud. He stumbled from his unmoving victim and grabbed on to the rungs for balance. Sticking out from a pocket of the man's coveralls was an enormous, greasy wrench. Weighing it in his hand, Svenson recalled both the wrench with which he had doomed Mr. Coates at Tarr Village, and the candlestick with which he had murdered the unfortunate Starck. Had such mayhem become so necessary, so natural a tactic? Was it only the night before when the Comte had brought to mind Svenson's guilt upon poisoning the fellow—the villain, did it matter—in Bremen? Where were those tender scruples now?

He stepped carefully through the gondola, which was divided up into smaller cabins like the cramped yet well-appointed interior of a yacht. Against the wall were leather upholstered benches and small inset tables and what seemed to be a drinks cabinet—the lashed-down bottles visible through the secured glass front. Svenson's numbed fingers fumbled with the leather straps across the cabinet door. His hands were still half-frozen and raw and he could not get them to perform such fine work as unbuckling a simple clasp. He whimpered with impatience and snatched up the wrench. He swung it once against the glass panel and then jammed it through the shattered hole to clear away the jagged fragments from the edge. He carefully extricated a bottle of cognac and pried out the cork with stiff, claw-like fingers. He took a deep swig, coughing once and happy for the warmth, and then took another. He exhaled fiercely, tears at the corner of each eye, and then took another swig. Svenson put the bottle down—he wanted to be warm and revived, not insensible.

On the opposite wall was another, taller wooden cabinet. He stepped to this and tried to pull it open. It was locked. Svenson raised the wrench and with one solid blow smashed in the wood around the lock. He pulled apart cabinet doors to reveal a well-oiled row of five gleaming carbines, five polished cutlasses, and hanging from hooks behind them, three service revolvers. Svenson tossed the wrench onto a leather seat and quickly availed himself of a revolver and a box of cartridges, snapping open the cylinder to load. He looked up, listening as his fingers went about sliding shell after shell into the gun and, after six, snapping the cylinder home. Was someone else outside? He reached for one of the cutlasses. It was a ridiculously vicious weapon, rather like thirty inches of razor-sharp butcher's cleaver, with a shining brass bell hilt that covered his entire hand. He had no idea how to use it, but the thing was so fearsome he was nearly convinced it would kill by itself.

The man in coveralls was not moving. Svenson took a step toward the front, paused, sighed, and then quickly knelt by the man, stuffing the revolver in his pocket. He felt for a pulse at the carotid artery... it was there. He sighed again at the man's clearly broken nose, and shifted his position so the blood would drain without choking him. He wiped his hands and stood up, pulling out the revolver. Now that he was sure he retained his humanity, he set forth for revenge.

Doctor Svenson advanced through the next smaller cabin to the doorway—another hatch with a collapsible metal staircase opened out to the surface of the roof some ten feet below. Another staircase led up to the cockpit of the dirigible. He made sure no one at the base of the stairs could see him and listened once more. This center cabin seemed much like the other—benches and tables—when his eye caught an innocuous litter of rope on the floor beneath a metal wall brace. Svenson knelt with dismay. The fragments were cut on one end and bloody... Elöise's bonds, her hands, her feet, her mouth. Whoever had confined her had done so without scruple—tight enough to draw blood. Svenson felt a chill at what she had endured, and an answering glimmer of rage in his veins. Did this not demonstrate her virtue? He sighed, for of course it showed nothing other than the Cabal's cruelty and thoroughness. Just as they sacrificed potential adherents at Tarr Manor, so they would hardly scruple to make sure of a new adherent's loyalty—and, of course, any true adherent would undergo every trial without protest. If only he knew what they had said to her, what urgings and temptations, what questions... if only he knew how she had replied.

He pulled the revolver from his pocket. With a deep breath—he was not so transformed that he could descend such a thing, trusting to balance with a weapon in each hand, without some tangle of anxiety—he stepped through the hatch and as swiftly as possible climbed (or careened) down the gangway. He whipped his gaze across the rooftop, looking for any other guard. But as far as he could see he was alone. The craft was moored to the roof by two cables attached to the underside of the gondola, but otherwise unattended. He decided he should not tempt his fate further and strode toward the only way his quarry could have gone—a small stone shed some twenty yards off, its door propped open by a brick.

As Doctor Svenson walked he looked down at his hands—the cutlass in the left, the revolver in the right. Was this the proper arrangement? He was no particular shot at anything but short range, nor had he any experience with the cutlass. For each, using his right hand would make for a more effective weapon—but which would be least hampered in his left? He thought who he might be struggling against—his own Ragnarok troopers or Colonel Aspiche's Dragoons—all of whom would be carrying sabers and savagely trained in their use. With the cutlass in his left hand he hadn't a prayer to parry a single blow. And yet, if the thing was in his right—did he still have any chance—or, more importantly, did he have a better chance than shooting at them? He did not. He kept each weapon where it was.

He opened the door and looked to an empty staircase with smooth white plaster walls and flagstone steps. He heard nothing. Svenson eased the door to its brick stop and stepped back, crossing quickly, swallowing the rising fear in his throat, to the far edge of the rooftop overlooking the garden. This edge was lined, like an ornamental castle, with a low wall of defensive crenellations from which he could both hang on and peer out simultaneously. The fog was still thick, but below him he could see the massive garden as through a veil, with conical tops of formally trimmed fir trees, tips of statuary and decorative urns, and then moving torches all piercing the lurking gloom. The torches seemed to be carried by Dragoons, and he heard cries, but it was difficult to place where they'd come from, as clearly not all the men in the garden had torches. Then the shouts were louder—somewhere near the center? This was followed by a shot and then a strangled cry. Two more shots rang out in direct succession and Svenson could see the torches converging and he scanned ahead of them to find their quarry. The fog was still too thick—yet the fact that they were in motion told him that whoever had been shot was not sufficiently wounded—or not alone.

Suddenly Doctor Svenson saw a movement, nearly below him, as a figure crept from the line of hedges to the grass border of the garden, preparing to dash across the strip of gravel to the house itself. The fog clung to the moist vegetation and dissipated at its border . . . it was Cardinal Chang. The Dragoons were hunting Chang! Svenson waved his arms like a lunatic, but Chang was looking instead at some window—the fool! Svenson wanted to scream, but what good would that do—aside from getting a squadron of Dragoons running directly to the roof?

Then Chang was gone, darting back into the shadow of the garden—creeping who knew where—a pair of Dragoons arriving at the spot only moments later. Svenson realized with a shudder that if he *had* succeeded in catching Chang's attention, the man would most likely be dead. The Dragoons looked around them with suspicion—and then glanced up, forcing Svenson to duck behind the wall.

What was Chang doing here? And how could none of these running men have noticed the arrival of the airship? Svenson supposed it was the fog and dirigible's dark color and counted himself lucky to have arrived so secretly . . . if only he could turn it to his advantage.

At the sharp crack of breaking wood in the garden Svenson looked back down and to his surprise found Chang at once, visible from the waist up through the fog—which meant he stood well off the ground—kicking at something inside a massive stone urn. The torches converged around him—there were shouts. With a sudden impulse Svenson leaned over the edge of the roof and flung the cutlass with all his might toward a ground-floor window beneath him. He ducked into cover just as the sound of breaking glass cut through the cries of pursuit. At once there was a confused crossing of shouts and then charging footsteps on the gravel below. At least some men had been diverted to the window, giving Chang that much more time to do whatever it was he was doing . . . hiding in an urn? Svenson risked one more glimpse but could no longer see him. There was nothing else to do—and the more he stayed in one place, the more vulnerable he was to capture. He dashed back to the staircase door and began his descent into the house. He might attribute some of this energy to the cognac, but the knowledge that—somehow, somewhere—he was not alone, gave his mission a new hope.

The staircase led him ten steps down to the third-floor landing and went no farther, being for roof access alone. Svenson listened at the door and gingerly turned the knob, releasing a breath he had not realized he had been holding when it was not locked. He wondered idly at these people's confidence—but with the exception of three ragged random individuals, who had they not been able to sway? He thought again of Chang—what had brought him? With a jolt—and another snarl of recrimination—he knew it must be Miss Temple. Chang had found her—had traced her to Harschmort. And now Chang was doing his best to survive capture. But Svenson's presence was unknown to them. While they occupied themselves with hunting Cardinal Chang—Svenson could only trust in his comrade's ability to evade them—he himself must supply Miss Temple's rescue.

And what of Elöise? Doctor Svenson sighed in spite of himself. He did not know. Yet, if she was who he hoped—the smell of her hair still sang in his memory—how could he leave her? The house was very large—how could he hope to accomplish both of these goals? Svenson paused and placed a hand over his eyes, balancing in his exhaustion the pull of his heart against that of his mind—for what were these rescues next to his unquestioned larger aim—to reclaim the Prince and the honor of Macklenburg itself? He did not know. He was one man, and for the moment at least, quite alone.

Svenson slipped silently from the staircase onto an open landing. To either side extended corridors to each wing, and before him was the highest point of the splendid main staircase of the house, and a marble balcony that, should he care to look over its edge (which he did not), would allow him to see down to the main entrance two floors below. Both side corridors were empty. If Miss Temple or Elöise had been stashed into a room for safe-keeping, he was certain there would be a guard at the door. He would need to go down another floor.

But what was he looking for? He tried to focus on what he knew—what plans were in motion that might guide his steps? As far as he could tell, the Cabal had used Tarr Manor to gather and refine a massive quantity of the indigo clay—either to make more of the malevolent glass, or to build and house the dirigible, or for something still more sinister... the alchemical genius of Oskar Veilandt as exploited by the Comte d'Orkancz. A second purpose had been to gather—to capture in glass—personal information from the discontented intimates of the highly placed and powerful. So armed, there would be small limit to the Cabal's powers of compulsion and subversion. Who did not have such secret shames? Who would not do what they could to preserve them? This specter of raw power brought to Svenson's mind the fallen Duke of Stäelmaere. The third purpose had been his introduction—in relative isolation—to the Cabal, an attempt to gain his favor and participation. With the Duke dead, at least Crabbé's Palace intrigues had been thrown into disarray.

And what did it mean for Elöise, the author of his death? Perhaps, he thought with a chill, her loyalties did not matter at all—having demonstrated such boldness the Cabal would give her over to the Process and make her theirs forever. As soon as the thought formed he knew it was true. And if his logic was right—and Svenson was dreadfully certain it was—the exact same fate awaited Miss Temple.

The Doctor slipped down the wide oaken staircase, his back against the wall, head craned for the first glimpse of any guard below. He reached the inter-floor landing and looked down. No one. He slid to the far wall and crept on to the second floor proper. He heard voices rising up from the main foyer below, but a quick glance back and forth showed the second-floor corridors empty of guards. Where was everyone from the dirigible? Had they just gone straight to the main floor? How could he follow into the thick of the household?

He had no idea, but crossed the landing to the final staircase leading down—this flight being even wider and more ostentatious than the others, as it was part of a visitor's first impression of the house from the main entrance. Svenson swallowed. Even from his partial perspective he could see a knot of black-coated footmen and a steady passage of elegantly dressed guests coming in from the front. A moment later he heard a clatter of boots and saw a furious-faced balding man with heavy whiskers march through his frame of vision at the head of a line of Dragoons. The footmen snapped to attention at his appearance and saluted like soldiers, calling out his name—Plengham?—all of which the man ignored. Then he was gone and Svenson sighed bitterly—looking down at a mere five or six men he'd have to overcome in the presence of a hundred onlookers.

He whipped his head around at a noise behind him and startled a squeak from each of a pair of girls dressed in black with white aprons and white caps—housemaids. Svenson took in the ingrained deference on their fearful faces and wasted no time in exploiting it—the more time they had to think, the more likely it was they'd scream.

"There you are!" he snarled. "I've just arrived with Minister Crabbé—they directed me here to clean up—I'll need a basin and my coat brushed—just do what you can—quickly now, quickly!"

Their eyes were wide on the revolver in his hand as he thrust it back into his coat pocket and then pulled the coat from his shoulders as he walked, driving the two girls back down the hall where they'd come. He tossed the filthy coat over the arms of one and nodded curtly at the other.

"I'll be speaking with Lord Vandaariff—vital information—extraordinary activity. You've seen the Prince, of course—Prince Karl-Horst? Speak when you're spoken to!"

Both girls bobbed on their knees. "Yes, Sir," they said nearly in unison, one of them—without the coat, dirty brown hair escaping from her cap near her ear, perhaps a bit stouter than her companion—adding, "Miss Lydia's just gone to meet the Prince, I'm sure."

"Excellent," snapped Svenson. "You can tell by my accent, yes—I'm the Prince's man—vital information for your master, but I can hardly meet him like this, can I?"

The girl with the coat darted forward to open a door. The other hissed at her with dismay, and the first hissed back, as if to ask where else they were to take him. The second gave in—all of this happening too rapidly for Svenson to complain at the delay—and they ushered him into a washroom whose trappings dripped with white lace and whose air was a near-suffocating *mélange* of scented candles and dried flowers doused with perfume.

All business, the girls directed Doctor Svenson to the mirror, where it was all he could do not to flinch bodily at what greeted him. As one maid brushed ineffectually at his coat, the other soaked a cloth and began to dab at his face—but he could see the arrant futility of either task. His face was a mask of dirt, sweat, and dried blood—from his own lacerations or his victims', he could not say until the rough surface of the cloth either cleaned it away or caused him to wince. His ice blond hair, normally plastered back in a respectable manner, had broken forward, matted with blood and grime. His intention had been to merely use the maids to get out of sight and find information, but he could not help but take some action at his wretched state. He brushed the fussing hands aside and slapped at his dusty jacket and trousers.

"Attend to my uniform—I'll manage this."

He stepped to the basin and plunged his head directly in it, gasping despite himself at the cold water. He brought up his dripping head, groped for a towel which the girl thrust into his hand, and then stood, vigorously rubbing his hair and face, pressing repeatedly at his re-opened cuts, dappling the towel with tiny red spots. He threw the towel aside, exhaled with some pleasure and smeared his hair back as best he could with his fingers. He caught the maid with his coat watching his face in the mirror.

"Your Miss Lydia," he called to her. "Where is she now—she and the Prince?"

"She went with Mrs. Stearne, Sir."

"Captain," the other corrected her. "He's a Captain, aren't you, Sir?"

"Very observant," answered Svenson, forcing an avuncular smile. He looked again at the basin and licked his lips. "Excuse me . . ."

Svenson leaned over to the copper pitcher and held it up to his mouth, awkwardly drinking, splashing water on his collar and jacket. He didn't care, any more than he cared what the maids might think—he was suddenly parched. When had he last had a drink—at the little inn at Tarr Village? It seemed half a lifetime past. He set down the pitcher and picked up another towel to wipe his face. He dropped the towel and dug his monocle from his pocket, screwing it into place.

"How is the coat?" he asked.

"Begging your pardon, Captain, but your coat is very unkempt," replied the maid meekly. He snatched it from her hands.

"Unkempt?" he said. "It is *filthy*. You have at least made it recognizable *as* a coat, if not a presentable one—and that is quite an achievement. And you"—he turned to the other—"have turned me into a recognizable *officer,* if not an entirely respectable one—but that fault lies entirely with me. I thank you both." Svenson dug into his trouser pocket and came up with two silver coins, giving one to each girl. Their eyes were wide... even suspiciously so. It was too much money—did they think he required some additional unsavory service? Doctor Svenson cleared his throat, his face reddening, for now they were smiling at him coyly. He adjusted his monocle and thrashed his way awkwardly into the greatcoat, his haughty tone giving way to an uncomfortable stammer.

"If you would be kind enough to point me in the direction taken by this M-Mrs. Stearne?"

Doctor Svenson was happily directed by the maids' pointing fingers to a side staircase he never would have seen, reached through a bland-looking door next to a mirror. Still Svenson was unsure as to his responsibility, his best intention. He followed the path of Karl-Horst and his fiancée—yet might it not just as well lead to that of Miss Temple or Elöise? The Cabal would strive to keep the likes of Miss Temple from the sight of its guests—or "adherents" as Miss Poole might arrogantly term them—for as long as possible, as she was sure to give the impression of a prisoner under guard. As they were not on this floor or the one above, this was at least a way for him to descend unseen. But what if he found the Prince before either woman—would that end his search entirely? For an instant he imagined a successful return to Macklenburg, to that life of arid duty, idiot successfully in tow, his heart as ever in its fog of despair. Yet what of the compact he had made on the rooftop of the Boniface, with Chang and Miss Temple? How could he choose between these paths? Svenson left the maids looking after him in the hallway, their heads a-tilt like a pair of curious cats. He fought the urge to wave good-bye and strode on to the staircase.

It was smaller than the main stairs, but only as if to say the Sphinx is smaller than the Pyramids, for it was still magnificent. Every step was intricately inlaid wood of many colors, and the walls were painted with an extremely credible copy, in miniature, of the Byzantine mosaics of Justinian and Theodora at Ravenna. Svenson suppressed an appreciative whistle at the amount Robert Vandaariff must have spent to refinish this one side staircase, and then attempted without success to extrapolate from that imagined sum the cost of fitting out Harschmort Prison into Harschmort House. It was a fortune whose vastness stretched beyond the Doctor's ability with numbers.

At the foot of the steps he had expected to see a door to the first-floor hallway, but there was none. Instead, he found an unlocked door, like a kitchen door on a spring. *Was* he near the kitchens? He frowned for a moment, placing himself in the house. On his previous visit, he had come in the front entrance with the Prince and spent his entire time in the left wing—around the ballroom—and then in the garden, where he'd seen Trapping's body. He was now in unknown territory. He pushed the swinging door gently until there was enough of a gap to peek through.

It was a room of bare wooden tables and a plain stone floor. Around one table were two men and three women—two sitting, and a younger woman pouring beer from a jug into wooden cups—all five in plain, dark woolen work clothes. Between them on the table was an empty platter and a stack of wooden bowls—servants taking a late repast. Svenson threw his shoulders back and marched forward in his best impression of Major Blach, deepening his accent and worsening his diction for maximum haughtiness.

"Excuse me! I am requiring after the Prince Karl-Horst von Maasmärck—he has come this way? Or—excuse me—*this* way he shall be found?"

They stared at him as if he were speaking Chinese. Again Doctor Svenson assumed the natural actions of Major Blach, which was to say he screamed at them.

"The Prince! With your Miss Vandaariff—this way? One of you tells me at once!"

The poor servants shrank back in their chairs, the pleasant end of their evening meal ruined by his insistent, threatening bellow. Three of them pointed with an abject eagerness at the opposite door and one of the women actually stood, nodding with cringing deference, indicating the same door.

"That way, Sir—not these ten minutes—begging your pardon—"

"*Ach,* it is very kind of you I am sure—please and be back to your business!" snapped Svenson, stepping to the door before anyone thought to question who in the world he was and why a man in such a filthy, unkempt state was following the Prince in such a hurry. He could only hope that the demands of the Cabal were as oblique, and the figures just as imperious.

It was not difficult to believe.

Once through the swinging door, Svenson stopped again, reaching behind him to still its movement. He stood at one end of a wider, open drawing room—a sort of servants' corridor with a low overhanging ceiling, designed to allow passage without it being intrusive to the room at large. Above him was a musicians' balcony from which Svenson could hear the delicate plucking of a harp. Directly across the corridor was another swinging door, perhaps ten yards away, but the way across was fully open to the larger room. He threw himself against the small abutment of wall that hid the swinging door and listened to the raised voices of those people directly beyond it.

"They must *choose,* Mr. Bascombe! I cannot suspend the natural order indefinitely! As you know, beyond this immediate matter looms the Comte's transformations, the initiations in the theatre, the many, many important guests identified for collection—to all of which my personal attention is crucial—"

"And as I have told *you,* Doctor Lorenz, I do not know their wishes!"

"One way or the other—it is very simple! He is made use of at once or he is given over to putrefaction and waste!"

"Yes, you have made those choices clear—"

"Not clear enough that they will act!" Lorenz began to sputter with the condescending pedantry of a seasoned academic. "You will see—at the temples, at the nails, at the lips, the discoloration—the seepage—you will no doubt, even *you,* discern the *smell*—"

"Berate me as you please, Doctor, we will wait for the Minister's word."

"I *will* berate you—"

"And I remind you that the fate of the Queen's own brother is not for *you* to decide!"

"I say . . . what was that noise?"

This was another voice. One that Svenson felt he knew but could not place.

More importantly, it referred to the sound of his own entry through the swinging door. The others stopped their argument.

"What noise?" snapped Lorenz.

"I don't know. But I thought I heard something."

"Aside from the harp?" asked Bascombe.

"Yes, that lovely harp," muttered Lorenz waspishly. "Exactly what every slaughtered Royal needs when lying in state in a leaking tub of ice—"

"No, no . . . from over *there* . . ." said the voice, quite clearly turning to the side of the room where Svenson stood, quite minimally concealed.

The voice of Flaüss.

The Envoy was with them. He would name Svenson and that would be the end of it. Could he run back through the servants? But where after that—up the stairs?

His thoughts were broken by the sound of a large party entering from the far doors, near the others—many footsteps . . . or more accurately bootsteps. Lorenz called out a greeting in his flat, mocking voice.

"Excellent, how kind of you to finally arrive. You see our burden—I will require two of your fellows to collect a supply of ice, I am told there is an ice *house* somewhere on the premises—"

"Captain," this was Bascombe cutting smoothly through the Doctor's words, "could you make sure we are not troubled by any unwanted visitors from the servants' passage?"

"As soon as you send two men for more ice," insisted Lorenz.

"Indeed," said Bascombe, "two men for ice, four men for the tub, one man to respectfully ask the Minister if there is further word, and one to check the passage. Does that satisfy us all?"

Svenson slipped back to the door and pushed gently against it, straining for silence. It held fast. The door had been bolted from the inner side—the servants making sure he'd not again trespass upon their meal. He shoved again, harder, to no avail. He quickly fished out the pistol—for within the noises of scraping metal and scuffling feet from his enemies across the room came the rapping of deliberate bootsteps advancing directly toward him.

Before he was prepared the man was looking right at him, not two yards away: a tall fellow with hanging lank brown hair, Captain of Dragoons, red coat immaculate, brass helmet under one arm, drawn saber in the other. Svenson met his sharp gaze and tightened his grip on the revolver, but did not fire. The idea of killing a soldier went against the grain—who knew what these fellows had been told, or what they'd been ordered to do, especially by a government figure like Crabbé or even Bascombe? Svenson imagined Chang's lack of hesitation and raised the revolver to fire.

The man's eyes flicked up and down, taking in Svenson's uniform, his rank, his unkempt person. Without any comment he turned to look in the other direction and then casually took a step toward Svenson, ostensibly—for the purpose of anyone watching from the room—to examine the door behind him. Svenson flinched—but still could not pull the trigger. Instead, the Captain leaned near to Svenson, reaching past him to the door and confirming it was locked. Svenson's revolver was nearly pressed against the Captain's chest, but the Captain's saber had been deliberately dropped to his side.

"Doctor Svenson?" he whispered.

Svenson nodded, unprepared to form actual words.

"I have seen Chang. I will take these people to the center of the house—please go in the opposite direction."

Svenson nodded again.

"Captain Smythe?" called Bascombe.

Smythe stepped back. "Nothing unusual, Sir."

"Were you *speaking* to someone?"

Smythe gestured vaguely toward the door as he walked back, out of Svenson's sight.

"There are servants in the next room. They've seen no one—perhaps their movement was what the Envoy heard. The door is now locked."

"Undoubtedly," agreed Lorenz, impatiently. "May we?"

"If you will follow me, gentlemen?" called Smythe. Svenson heard the doors opening, the scuffle and creak of the men lifting the fallen Duke, the *thwop* of water slopping out of the tub, the scuffle of footsteps and finally the closing of the door. He waited. There was no sound. He sighed and stepped around the corner, shoving the revolver back into his coat pocket.

Herr Flaüss stood just inside the far doorway, grinning smugly. Svenson dragged out the revolver. Flaüss snorted.

"What will you do, Doctor, shoot me and announce yourself to every soldier in the house?"

Svenson began to walk deliberately across the wide room toward the Envoy, his aim never wavering from the man's chest. After all the torments he had passed through, it was bitter to imagine his downfall at the hands of *this* petty and puling creature.

"I knew what I had heard," smiled Flaüss, "just as I knew Captain Smythe was not telling the truth. I've no idea why—and I am indeed curious what power you might have over an officer of Dragoons, especially in your present wholly decrepit state."

"You're a traitor, Flaüss," answered Svenson. "You always have been."

He was within two yards of the Envoy, the main door perhaps a yard beyond that. Flaüss snorted again.

"How can I be a traitor when I do my own Prince's bidding? It is true I did not always understand that—it is true that I have been assisted to my present level of *clarity*—but you are as wrong about me, and the Prince, as you have always been—"

"He's an idiot and a traitor himself," spat Svenson hotly, "betraying his own father, his own nation—"

"My poor Doctor, you are quite behind the times. Much has changed in Macklenburg." Flaüss licked his lips and his eyes gleamed. "Your Baron is dead. Yes, Baron von Hoern—his feeble network of operatives was well known—why else should I attend the every move of an obscure naval *physician*? And of course the Duke himself is also very unwell—your brand of patriotism is *passé*—very soon Prince Karl-Horst will *be* the nation, and perfectly placed to welcome the cooperative financial ventures of Lord Vandaariff and his associates."

Flaüss wore a plain black half-mask across his eyes. With grim recognition Svenson could see the lurid scarring peeking out from the edges.

"Where is Major Blach?" he asked.

"Somewhere about, I am sure—as I am sure he will be most happy at your capture. He and I finally see eye to eye, of course—another blessing! It really is a matter of looking beyond to deeper *truths*. If, as you say, the Prince is not especially gifted in matters of policy, it is all the more important that those who support him are able to make up that lack."

It was Svenson's turn to scoff. He looked behind him. Adding another bizarre touch to his confrontation with the mentally altered Envoy, the concealed harpist continued to play. He turned back to Flaüss.

"If you knew I was there, why didn't you say anything to your *masters,* to Lorenz or Bascombe?" He gestured with the revolver. "Why give me the upper hand?"

"I've done nothing of the kind—as I say, you can't shoot me without dooming yourself. You're no more a fool than you are a brawler—if you want to stay alive, you'll give me your weapon and we shall walk together to the Prince—and I will establish myself as trustworthy in my new role. Especially so, I should say—for to get this far, I imagine you must have avoided a great number of ostensible foes."

The Envoy's smug expression demonstrated for Dr. Svenson the extent and the limit of the Process's transformation. Never before would the man have been so bold as to risk an open confrontation—much less so brazen an admission of his secret plans. Flaüss had always been one for honeyed agreement followed by backhanded plotting, for layered schemes and overlapping patronage. He had despised the blunt arguments of Major Blach and Svenson's own diffident independence as quite equal levels of defiance—and, indeed, personal offense. There was no doubt that the man's *loyalty* had—as he put it—been "clarified" by his alchemical ordeal and his hesitancies weakened, but Svenson saw that his conniving, narcissistic nature remained quite whole.

"Your weapon, Doctor Svenson," repeated Flaüss, his voice pointedly yet somehow comically stern. "I have you boxed with logic. I *do* insist."

Svenson flipped his grip on the revolver, holding on to its barrel and cylinder. Flaüss smiled, as this seemed the first step to politely handing him the butt of the gun. Instead, feeling another uncharacteristic surge of animal capacity, Svenson raised his arm and cracked the pistol butt across the Envoy's head. Flaüss staggered back with a squawk. He looked up at Svenson with an outraged glare of betrayal—as if in flouting the man's "logic" Svenson had broken all natural law—and opened his mouth to scream. Svenson stepped forward, arm raised for another swing. Flaüss darted away, quicker than his portly frame would seem to allow, and Svenson's blow went wide. Flaüss opened his mouth again. Svenson abruptly switched his grip on the revolver and aimed it directly at the Envoy's face.

"If you scream, I *will* shoot you! I'll have no more reason for silence!" he hissed.

Flaüss did not scream. He glared at Svenson with hatred and rubbed the welt above his eye. "You are a *brute*," he insisted. "An outright *savage*!"

Svenson padded quietly down the hallway—now sporting the Envoy's black silk mask, the better to blend in with the locals—following Smythe's directions away from the center of the house, with no idea if this path brought him anywhere near his ostensible targets of rescue. Most likely he was squandering what time he had to save them—he scoffed aloud—like so much else in his life had been squandered. His mind bristled with questions about the Dragoon Captain—he "had seen" Chang (though hadn't Chang been fleeing Dragoons in the garden?), but how had he known *him*? If only there had been time to actually *speak*—it was more than likely the man knew the location of Elöise or Miss Temple. For a moment he'd entertained the idea of interrogating Flaüss, but his skin crawled at the man's physical presence. Leaving him gagged and trussed behind a divan was more than enough time spent with such a toad. Yet he knew Flaüss would be missed—it was frankly odd he'd not been looked for already—and that his period of anonymity inside Harschmort was severely limited. But at the same time, the house was massive, and blundering senselessly through its hallways would only waste his temporary advantage.

The hallway ended at a T junction, with a path to either side. Svenson stood, undecided, like a figure in the forest of a fairy tale, knowing that the wrong choice would lead to the equivalent of a malevolent ogre. One way led to a succession of small parlors, following one to the next like links in a chain. The other opened onto a narrow corridor whose walls were plain, but whose floor was strikingly laid with black marble. Then as he stood, Doctor Svenson quite clearly recognized a woman's scream... dimly, as if the cry passed through a substantial intervening wall.

Where had it come from? He listened. It was not repeated. He strode into the black corridor—less comfortable, less wholesome, and altogether more dangerous—for if he chose wrong, the sooner he knew it the better.

The corridor was pocked with small niches for statuary—mostly simple white marble busts on stone pillars with the occasional limb-free torso. The heads were copies (though, given Vandaariff's wealth, who knew?) from antiquity, and the Doctor recognized the varyingly vacant, cruel, or thoughtful heads of Caesars high and low—Augustus, Vespasian, Gaius, Nero, Domitian, Tiberius. As he passed this last, Svenson stopped. Dimly—though louder than the scream—he heard... *applause.* He spun to place the source of the noise, and saw, cut into the white wall behind the bust of that pensive, bitter emperor, regular grooves running up to the ceiling... *rungs.* Svenson edged behind the pillar and looked up. He looked around him and—taking a breath and shutting his eyes—began to climb.

There was no hatch. The ladder continued into darkness before his hands found a new surface to grasp. The Doctor opened his eyes and blinked, allowing his eyes to adjust to the dark. He was gripping a piece of wooden scaffolding, the end of a low catwalk. He heard distant voices... and then again the whisper, like a sudden rustle of leaves, of an audience's applause. Was he backstage at some sort of theatre? The Doctor swallowed, for the dizzying heights from which stagehands operated the lifts and curtains always made him queasy (and his compulsion was to look up again and again, just to torment himself with vertigo). He recalled a performance of Bonrichardt's *Castor und Pollux* where the triumphant finale, the titular pair ascending to heaven—an excruciatingly extended duet as they were raised (the twins operatically portly, the ropes audibly protesting) some hundred feet from view—had him near to heaving with dread into the lap of the unfortunate dowager seated next to him.

Doctor Svenson clambered onto the catwalk and crept along it quietly. Ahead he saw a thin glimmer of light, perhaps a distant door set ajar, allowing a single beam to fall into the darkness. What performance might be hosted in Harschmort on a night like this? The engagement party had been a dual event—a public celebration of the engagement of Karl-Horst and Lydia and a private occasion for the Cabal to transact its private business. Was tonight a similarly double-edged event—and could this performance be the respectable side of whatever other malevolence was at work elsewhere in the house?

Svenson continued forward, wincing at a tightness in his legs and a renewed pain from his twisted ankle. He thought of Flaüss's boasting words—the Baron was dead, the Duke to follow. The Prince was a fool and a rake, eminently subject to manipulation and control. Yet if the Doctor could prise the Prince from the clutches of the Cabal—Process or no—might there not be yet some hope, providing the ministers around him were responsible and sane?

But then with a grim snort he recalled his own brief conversation with Robert Vandaariff over Trapping's corpse. Such was the great man's irresistible influence that any unfortunate or scandalous occurrence—like the Colonel's death—was made to disappear. The grandson of Robert Vandaariff—especially if inheriting as a child and requiring a regent—would be the best return the financier could realize on the investment of his daughter. After the child's birth Karl-Horst would be unnecessary—and, given everything, wholly unregretted at his death.

But what were Svenson's choices? If Karl-Horst were to die *without* issue, the Macklenburg throne would pass to the children of his cousin Hortenze-Caterina, the oldest of whom was but five. Wasn't this a better fate for the Duchy than being swallowed by Vandaariff's empire? Svenson had to face the deeper truth of his mission from the Baron. Knowing what he did of the forces in play, if he could not prevent the marriage, which seemed impossible, he would have to shoot Prince Karl-Horst down—to be a traitor in service to a larger patriotism.

The reasoning left the taste of ash in his mouth, but he could see no other way.

Svenson sighed, but then, like the shift of a mountebank's con-trick, the line of light in front of him—which he had, in the darkness, taken to be a distant door—was revealed for what it was: the thin gap between two curtains, not two feet in front of his face. He gently pushed it aside, both light and sound flooding through the gap, for the fabric was actually quite heavy, as if it had been woven with lead to prevent fire. But now Doctor Svenson could see and hear everything... and he was appalled.

It was an *operating* theatre. His catwalk door was perched just to the right of the audience and led across the stage itself at the height of the ceiling—some twenty feet above the raised table and the white-robed, white-masked woman bound to its surface with leather straps. The gallery was steeply raked and full of well-dressed, masked spectators, all gazing with rapt attention at the masked woman who spoke from the stage. Doctor Svenson recognized Miss Poole at once, if only by the woman's irrepressible glow of self-satisfaction.

Behind them all, on a large blackboard, were inscribed the words "AND SO THEY SHALL BE REBORN".

Standing unsteadily next to Miss Poole was another masked woman in white, her blonde hair somewhat disturbed, as if from physical exertion. As she stood Svenson noticed, distracted and disapproving, the very thin and clinging nature of the nearly transparent silk, making plain every contour of her body. To her other side stood a man in a leather apron, ready to support her if she fell. Behind, next to the woman on the table, stood another such man, wearing leather gauntlets and holding under his arm what looked like a brass and leather helmet—just what the Comte d'Orkancz had worn when Svenson had taken the Prince at pistol-point from the Institute. The man by the table set down his helmet and began to remove pieces of machinery from a nest of wooden boxes—the same boxes they'd seen taken from the Institute by Aspiche's Dragoons. The man attached several lengths of twisted copper wire to mechanical elements within the boxes—from his vantage Svenson could only see that they were bright steel with glass dials and brass buttons and knobs—and then to either side of a pair of black rubber goggles, taking a moment to get the wire properly attached. Svenson realized—the electrified rubber mask, the facial scars—that they were about to perform the Process on the woman on the table, as they had no doubt just done to the woman standing with Miss Poole (the cause of the screams!).

The man finished with the wires and raised the hideous mask to the woman's face, pausing quickly to remove one of the white feathers that she presently wore. She shook her head from side to side, a futile bid to avoid his hands—her eyes wide and her mouth—which he saw was blocked with a gag—working. Her eyes were riveting, a cold, glittering grey... Svenson gasped. The man strapped and then brutally tightened the device across her face, his body blocking the Doctor's view. Svenson could not determine her state—was she drugged? Had she been beaten? He knew he had only until Miss Poole was finished with the blonde woman—who was *she,* he wondered?—until their vicious intent was worked irrevocably upon Miss Temple.

Miss Poole stepped to a small rolling side table—intended, Svenson knew, to hold a tray of medical implements—and took up a glass-stoppered flask. With a knowing smile she uncorked the flask and took a step to the front row of the gallery, holding the open flask up for her spectators to sniff. One after another—and always to Miss Poole's delight—the elegant masked figures recoiled with immediate disgust. After the sixth person, Miss Poole stepped back to the brighter light and her blonde charge.

"A challenge to the most sturdy of sensibilities—as I believe all of you that have smelled this mixture will attest—yet such is the nature of our science and our need that this lovely subject, a veritable arrow in flight toward a target of *destiny,* has been made to consume it not once, but daily, for twenty-eight consecutive days, until her *cycle* is completely prepared. Before this day, such a task could not have been accomplished save by forcibly holding her down, or—as it has actually been managed—hiding tiny amounts of the substance in chocolate or an aperitif. Now, witness the strength of her new-minted will."

Miss Poole turned to the woman and held out the flask.

"My dear," she said, "you understand that you must drink this, as you have in these past weeks."

The blonde woman nodded, and reached out to take the flask from Miss Poole.

"Please smell it," asked Miss Poole.

The woman did. She wrinkled her nose, but showed no other response.

"Please drink it."

The woman put the flask to her lips and tossed off the contents like a sailor quaffing rum. She primly wiped her mouth, held her body still for a moment, as if to better keep the substance down, and then returned the flask.

"Thank you, my dear." Miss Poole smiled. "You've done very well."

The audience erupted into fervent applause, and the young blonde woman shyly beamed.

The Doctor looked ahead of him on the catwalk. Bolted to an iron frame suspended from the ceiling—and in reach, for he realized that the catwalk's sole purpose was to tend them—hung a row of metal-boxed paraffin lamps, as in a theatre. The front of each box was open, to aim the light in one direction, and fixed with a ground-glass lens to focus the light onto a more precise area. For a moment he considered—if he were able to climb out unseen—the possibility of blowing out each lamp and throwing the theatre into darkness . . . but there were at least five lamps over a fifteen-foot length of the iron grid. He could not reach them all before he was seen and most likely shot. But what else could he do? Moving as delicately and as quickly as he could, Doctor Svenson crawled through the curtain and into view of anyone who happened to look up.

Miss Poole whispered in her blonde charge's ear and then led her closer to the audience. The young woman sank into a curtsey, and the audience politely applauded once more. Svenson could swear she was blushing with pleasure. The woman rose again and Miss Poole handed her to one of the Macklenburg soldiers, who offered an arm with a click of his heels. The blonde woman draped her arm in his and with a distinct brightening of her step they disappeared down one of the rampways.

From the same rampway emerged two more Macklenburg soldiers propelling between them a third masked woman in white. Her feet dragged in awkward steps and her head dipped—she was either drugged or injured. Her brown hair unspooled behind her back and around her shoulders, obscuring her features. Again, despite his best intentions, Doctor Svenson found his gaze falling to the lady's body, the white silk clinging across the curve of her hips, her pale arms sticking from the balled-up sleeves.

At their entrance, Miss Poole whipped around in annoyance. Svenson could not hear what she hissed to the soldiers, nor what they deferentially whispered in return. In the moment of disturbance he looked to Miss Temple, the hideous mask in place across her face, twisting ineffectually against her bonds.

Miss Poole gestured to the new arrival.

"It is a different sort of case I present to you here—perhaps one emblematic of the *dangers* attending our great enterprise, and of the *correc-*

tive power of this work. The woman here before you—you see her ragged appearance and lowly condition—is one who had been invited to participate, and who then took it upon herself, in league with our enemies, to *reject* this invitation. More than this, her rejection took the form . . . of *murder*. The woman before you has killed one of our blameless number!"

The audience whispered and hissed. Svenson swallowed. It was Elöise Dujong. He hadn't recognized her—her hair had been back in a braid and now it wasn't—such a foolish detail, but it nearly caused his heart to crack. All his doubts as to her loyalty fell away before this sudden pang of emotion. Seeing her hair down should have been an intimacy given to him from her, and now she was insensible, vulnerable, the intimacy blithely trammeled. He crawled quickly to the next lamp and dug in his pocket for the revolver.

"And yet," continued Miss Poole, "she has been brought before you to demonstrate the greater wisdom—and the greater *economy*—of our purpose. For despite everything this woman's actions carry with them undenied qualities of resilience and courage. Should these be destroyed simply because she lacks the will or the vision to see her true avenue of advantage? We say it shall not be—and so we will *welcome* this woman into our very bosom!"

She gestured to her attendant. He bent over Miss Temple once more to make sure of his electrical connections and then knelt at the boxes. Svenson looked wildly about him. In a moment it would be too late.

"Both these women—I promise you, more determined villains you could not find outside the *Thuggee* cult!—will join us, one after the next, by way of the clarifying Process. You have seen its effect with a willing subject. Now see it transform a defiant enemy to the fiercest adherent!"

The first shot crashed out from the darkness above the theatre. The man near Miss Temple abruptly stumbled back, and then dropped beneath the blackboard, the blood from his wound pooling in the leather apron. Screams erupted from the gallery. The figures on the stage looked up, but straight into the lamps and could not—at least for another precious moment—see past the glare. The second shot tore through the shoulder of the other aproned man, spinning him away from Elöise and to his knees.

"He is there!" shrieked Miss Poole. "Kill him! *Kill him!*"

She pointed up at Svenson, her face an emblem of fury. The Macklenburg trooper had been pulled off balance by the second man's fall, suddenly taking up the whole of Elöise's weight. He released her—she dropped at once to her hands and knees—and swept out his saber. Svenson ignored him. He was well out of reach of the blade, and knew the Ragnarok troopers did not carry firearms. He aimed the revolver at Miss Poole, but then—what was he thinking! How could he forget her cruelty at the quarry?—hesitated to pull the trigger.

The catwalk behind him lurched. Svenson turned to see two hands grabbing hold of the edge. He shifted on his knees and rapped the gun butt down on each hand one after the other, dropping the man back into the seats. The catwalk lurched again. Now three sets of hands pulled on the edge, tipping the Doctor into the wooden rail. For a moment he looked helplessly down into the outraged crowd—men on each other's shoulders, women shrieking at him as if he were a witch. He shot a foot forward and smashed it down on the nearest hand—but now there were men on either side of him, hefting themselves above the edge. To his left was an athletic young man in a tailcoat, no doubt an ambitious second son of a Lord determined to take an inheritance away from an older brother. Svenson shot him through the upper leg and didn't wait to watch him fall before turning to the second man—a wiry fellow in his shirtsleeves (thoughtful enough to doff an encumbering coat before climbing)—who leapt the rail and crouched like a cat not three feet away. Svenson fired again, but more hands jostled the catwalk. The bullet flew wide and directly into one of the paraffin lanterns, shattering it completely. A shower of hot metal, broken glass, and burning paraffin spattered onto the stage.

The shirtsleeved man launched himself at Svenson, knocking him flat. A woman screamed from the stage—there was smoke—the paraffin—did he smell burning hair? The man was younger, stronger, fresher—an elbow across Svenson's jaw stunned him. He thrust a hand ineffectually at the fellow's eyes, and the catwalk careened as more hands pulled at them and more men climbed aboard—a creak, a popping snap of wood—it could not hold. The woman still screamed. The shirtsleeved man took hold of Svenson's coat with both hands and raised him up—face-to-face with a triumphant leer—as a prelude to flattening the Doctor's nose with his fist.

The catwalk gave way, tipping toward the stage and dumping them both over the rail and into the row of lamps—Svenson hissing with pain at the hot metal against his skin—and then (in one ghastly moment of weightless terror that convulsed Svenson from the top of his spine to his genitals) to the theatre floor.

The impact jarred the Doctor to his teeth and for a moment he merely lay where he was, dimly aware of a great deal of activity around him. He blinked. He was alive. There were screams and shouts from every direction . . . smoke . . . a great deal of smoke . . . and heat—in fact, everything pointed to the theatre being on fire. He tried to move. To his surprise he was not on the floor—he was not on anything *smooth*. He rolled on one shoulder and saw the waxen face of the shirtsleeved man, neck folded unnaturally to the side, tongue blue. Svenson heaved himself to his hands and knees—realizing as it hit the floor with a *clunk* that he still held the revolver.

The fallen lamps had set a line of flame between the stage and the gallery, effectively blocking one from the other. Through the rising wall of smoke he could see figures and hear their screams and shouts, but he quickly turned away at another scream, much nearer. It was Elöise, terrified but still dulled by the drug, kicking weakly at the flames that licked her smoking silken robe. Svenson stuffed the revolver into his belt and tore off his greatcoat. He lurched forward on his knees and threw it over her legs, patting out any flames, and then quickly pulled her clear of the fire. He turned to the table and felt his way to Miss Temple's hand. Her fingers took hold of his arm—a desperate silent plea—but he was forced to wrench himself away in order to reach the buckle for her leather straps. He fumbled to free her arms and that done was gratified to see her own hands shoot up to the infernal mask around her face. He released her feet and then helped her from the table, once more—for Svenson was never one to become used to the matter—surprised at the meager weight of such an enterprising person. As she tore the wadded gag from her mouth he bent to her ear and shouted above the roar of flame and popping wood.

"This way! Can you walk?"

He pulled her down below the line of smoke and saw her eyes widen at the identity of her rescuer.

"Can you walk?" he repeated.

Miss Temple nodded. He pointed to Elöise, just visible, hunched against the curved wall of the theatre.

"She cannot! We must help her!"

Miss Temple nodded again, and he took her arm—wondering idly if he might not be in the more shattered physical condition. Svenson looked up at a rush of footsteps within the gallery, and then a crashing hiss and a cloud of steam. Men had arrived with buckets. They raised Elöise between them—Miss Temple a good six inches shorter than the woman she supported. Svenson called to her.

"I have seen Chang! There is a flying machine on the roof! The Dragoon officer is a friend! Do not look into the glass books!"

He was babbling—but there seemed so much to say. More water was flung from above—the steam clouds now rivaled the smoke—and more bootsteps. Svenson turned to face them. He raised the revolver and shoved behind him at the ladies, pushing them on.

"Go! Go at once!"

The Macklenburg trooper had returned with a host of others. Svenson aimed the revolver just as more water flew down from the gallery and a plume of ash and steam rose in front of the other rampway. He felt suddenly nauseous at the mix of exhaustion and light-headed recklessness—he'd just shot three men and wrestled a fourth to his death in what seemed like as many seconds. Was this how men like Chang spent their lives? Svenson gagged. He took a step backwards and tripped over the carcass of a shattered lamp, sprawling headlong onto his back with a grunt, smacking the back of his head into the floorboards. Pain exploded across Doctor Svenson's body—all of his injuries from the quarry and Tarr Manor brought back to vivid life. He opened his mouth but could not speak. He would be taken. He moved feebly on his back like a tortoise. The room was nearly dark—only one of the lights remained, its cover dislodged and blocking the beam, sending an eerie orange glow through the murk.

He expected to be swarmed by his enemies, slit like a pig by five sabers at once. Around him were the sounds of flame and water, the shouts of men and, more distant, the cries of women. Had they not seen him? Were they only fighting the fire? Had the flames so cut them off from pursuit? With an effort Svenson rolled over and began to crawl through the glass and metal after the women. He was coughing—how much smoke had he inhaled? He kept going, his right hand still holding the revolver. With a dull apprehension he remembered that the box of cartridges was in the pocket of his greatcoat, which he had given to Elöise. If he did not catch up to her, he was left with just two shells remaining in the gun—against all of the forces of Harschmort.

Svenson reached the ramp and crawled down. The path turned and he felt something in the way—a boot... and then a leg. It was the man he'd shot in the shoulder. In this light there was no telling if the man was dead, dying, or merely overcome by smoke. Svenson had no time. He stumbled to his feet and past the fellow and found a door. He pushed his way through and took a heaving lungful of clean air.

The room was empty. Thickly carpeted and lined with wooden cabinets and mirrors, it reminded him of a dressing room for the opera—or, as if there was any real difference, of Karl-Horst's own attiring room at the Macklenburg Palace. The idea that it was connected to a theatre for demonstrations of surgery was perhaps all the more sickening for what it said about Robert Vandaariff. The cabinets were open and in disarray, various garments spilling onto the floor. He took several steps, brushing glass and ash from his uniform, his feet sinking deeply into the luxurious carpet, and stopped. On the floor near the cabinets, in ruins and quite clearly cut from her body, was the dress Elöise had been wearing at Tarr Manor. He looked behind him. Still no sounds of pursuit. Where were the women? His throat was aching. He pushed himself across the room to another door and turned the handle carefully, peering out with one eye through the gap.

He closed it at once. The corridor was full of activity—servants, soldiers, cries for buckets, cries for help. There was no possible way he would not be taken. But could the women have had any better hope? He turned again to the rampway door. His enemies would be coming through it any moment—someone—he had caused too much damage to ignore. Svenson was wracked with regret for the men he had shot, for the injury—flame? falling debris?—that had stricken Miss Poole, despite his hatred for her. But what else could he have done? What else would he yet be forced to do?

There was no time for any of this. Could the women be hiding in the room? Feeling a fool, he whispered aloud.

"Miss Temple? Miss Temple! Elöise?"

There was no reply.

He crossed to the wall of opened cabinets to quickly sort through them, but got no farther than Elöise's dress on the floor. Svenson picked it up, fingering with a distressed intimacy the ripped edges of her bodice and the sliced, dangling bits of lacing. He pressed it to his face and breathed in, and sighed at his own hopeless gesture—the dress smelled of indigo clay—acrid, biting, offensive—and dried sweat. With another sigh he let the dress fall to the floor. He was bound to find the women—of course he must—but—he wanted to cry aloud with distress—what of the Prince? Where was he? What could Svenson possibly do aside from killing him before the wedding? This thought brought the words of Miss Poole back to his mind, in the theatre with the blonde woman and the loathsome potions. She had mentioned the girl's monthly cycle... "until the cycle is prepared"... obviously this was more of the Comte's (or Veilandt's) alchemical evil. Svenson was chilled—Miss Poole had also mentioned the woman's "destiny"—for he was suddenly sure the pliant blonde woman, proven to be the passive instrument of the Cabal, was Lydia Vandaariff. Could Vandaariff be so heartless as to sacrifice his own daughter? Svenson scoffed at the obviousness of the answer. And if the Lord's own flesh meant so little, what would he possibly care for the Prince—or the succession?

He shook his head. His thoughts were too slow. He was wasting time.

Svenson stepped toward the cupboard and felt his boot crunch on broken glass. He looked down—this was not where he'd brushed it from himself—and saw the carpet littered with bright shards... glittering... reflective... he looked up... a mirror? The doors of two nearby cupboards were opened toward each other... the open panels blocking whatever might be behind. He pulled them apart to reveal a large jagged hole in the wall, punched through what had been a full-length mirror with an ornate gold-leaf frame. He stepped carefully over the shards. The glass was slightly odd... discolored? He picked up one of the larger pieces and turned it side to side in his hand, then held it up to the light. One side was a standard mirror—but the other side was somehow, granting a slightly darker cast to the image, transparent. It was a spy mirror—and one of the women (it could only be Miss Temple) had known of it and smashed it through. Svenson dropped the shard and stepped through the gap—taking care to pull the cupboards to behind him, to slow any pursuit—and then over a wooden stool that she had evidently used to break the glass, for he could see tiny glittering needles embedded in the wooden seat.

The room on the other side of the mirror confirmed all that Doctor Svenson feared about life in Harschmort House. The walls were painted a bordello red, with a neat square of Turkish carpet that held a chair, a small writing table, and a plush divan. To the side was a cabinet that held both notebooks and inks, but also bottles of whisky, gin, and port. The lamps were painted red as well, so no light would give the game away through the mirror. The experience of standing in the room struck the Doctor as both tawdry and infernal. On one hand, he recognized that there were few things more ridiculous than the trappings of another person's pleasure. On the other, he knew that such an arrangement only served to take cruel advantage of the innocent and unsuspecting.

He knelt quickly on the carpet, feeling for any bloodstains, in case either woman had cut a foot making her way through the glass. There were none. He stood and continued after them—a poor shambling trot. The way was lined with the same red-painted lamps, and twisted and turned without any reason he could see. How long would it take to truly understand the ways of this house? Svenson wondered how often the servants got lost, or for how long—and further what the punishment might be for the wrong servant mistakenly stumbling into an extremely sensitive room, such as this. He half-expected to find a caged skeleton, set up as a sign to warn off all curious maids and footmen.

He stopped—this tunnel just went on—and risked another whisper.

"Miss Temple!" He waited for a reply. Nothing. "*Celeste! Elöise!* Elöise Dujong!"

The corridor was quiet. Svenson turned behind him and listened. He could scarce credit their pursuit had not reached him already. He tried to flex his ankle and winced with pain. It had been twisted again in his fall from the catwalk and soon it would be all he could do to drag it, or lapse again into his absurd hopping. He steadied himself with a hand on the wall. Why hadn't he had more to drink in the airship? Why had he walked right past the bottles in the first red room? By God, he wanted another swallow of brandy. Or a cigarette! The urge fell onto him like a wave of agitated need. How long had it been without a smoke? His case was in the inner pocket of his greatcoat. He wanted to swear out loud. Just a bit of tobacco—hadn't he earned that much? He stuffed a knuckle into his mouth to stifle the urge to scream and bit down, hard as he could bear. It didn't help in the least.

He limped ahead to a crossroads. To his left the corridor went on. Ahead it dead-ended at a ladder going up. To the right was a red cloth curtain. Svenson did not hesitate—he'd had his fill of ladders and his fill of walking. He whipped aside the curtain and extended the revolver. It was a second observation chamber, its far wall another transparent mirror. The red chamber was empty, but the room beyond the mirror was not.

The spectacle before him was like a medieval pageant, a *Danse Macabre* of linked figures from all walks of life being led away by Death and his minions. The line of figures—a red-coated churchman, an admiral, men in the finest topcoats, ladies dripping with jewelry and lace—shambled into the room one after another, assisted by a crew of black-masked functionaries, guiding each to a chaise or chair where they slumped unceremoniously, obviously insensible. If he were a native of the city Svenson was sure he would have known them all—as it was he could pick out Henry Xonck, the Baroness Roote (a *salon* hostess who had invited Karl-Horst once and then never again after he'd spent the entire time drinking—and then sleeping—in his corner chair), and Lord Axewithe, chairman of the Imperial Bank. Such a gathering was simply unheard-of—and a gathering where they had all been so overborne was unthinkable.

In the center of the room was a table, upon which one of each pair of functionaries would—while the other settled their personage—deposit a large brilliant rectangle of blue glass . . . another glass book . . . but how many were there? Svenson watched them pile up. Fifteen? Twenty? Standing at the table and watching it all with a smile was Harald Crabbé, hands tucked behind his back, eyes darting with satisfaction between the growing stack of books and the procession of vacant luminaries arranged around the steadily more crowded room. Next to Crabbé, as expected, stood Bascombe, making notes in a ledger. Svenson studied the young man's expression as he worked, sharp nose and thin earnest lips, hair plastered into position, broad shoulders, perfectly schooled posture, and nimble fingers that flipped the ledger pages back and forth and stabbed his pencil in and out of them like an embroidery needle.

Doctor Svenson had seen Bascombe before of course, at Crabbé's side, and had overheard his conversation with Francis Xonck in the Minister's kitchen, yet this was the first time he'd observed the man knowing he had been Celeste Temple's fiancé. It was always curious what particular qualities might bring two people together—a shared taste for gardening, a love of breakfast, snobbery, raw sensual appetite—and Svenson could not help but ask the question about these two, if only for what it revealed about his diminutive ally, to whom he felt a duty to protect (a duty naggingly compromised by the memory of the thin silk robes hanging closely around her body... the suddenly soft weight of her limbs in his arms as he helped her from the table... even the animal spate of effort as she pulled the gag from her stretched lips). Svenson swallowed and frowned anew at Bascombe, deciding then that he very much disliked the man's proud manner—one could just tell by the way he ticked his notebook. He'd seen enough naked ambition in the Macklenburg Palace to make the man's hunger as plain to his trained eyes as the symptoms of syphilis. More, he could imagine how Bascombe had been served by the Process. What before must have been tempered with doubt or deference had been in that alchemical crucible hardened to steel. Svenson wondered how long it would be before Crabbé felt the knife in his back.

The last functionaries laid the final victim on a divan, next to the uncaring elderly churchman—a handsome woman with vaguely eastern features in a blue silk dress and a fat white pearl dangling from each ear. The last book was set down—the whole pile had to number near thirty!—and Bascombe made his final jabs with the pencil... and then frowned. He flipped back through the notebook and repeated his calculations, by his darkening frown coming up with the same unsatisfactory answer. He spoke to the men quickly, sorting through their responses, winnowing their words until he was looking at the somnolent figure of a particularly lovely woman in green, with a mask woven of glass beads that Svenson guessed would be Venetian and extremely expensive. Bascombe called again, as clearly as if Svenson could hear the words, "Where is the book to go with this woman?" There was no answer. He turned to Crabbé and the two of them whispered together. Crabbé shrugged. He pointed to one of the men who then dashed from the room, obviously sending him back to search. The rest of the books were loaded carefully into an iron-bound chest. Svenson noted how all of them wore leather gloves to touch the glass and treated them with deliberate and tender care—their efforts reminding him keenly of sailors nervously stacking rounds of ammunition in an armory.

The clear association of particular books with specific individuals—individuals of obvious rank and stature—had to relate to the Cabal's earlier collection of scandal from the minions of the powerful, at Tarr Manor. Was it merely another level of acquisition? In the country, they had gathered—had stored within those books—the means to manipulate the powerful... could the aim have merely been to blackmail those powerful figures into journeying to Harschmort, and then forcing this next step upon them? He shook his head at the boldness of it, for the next step was to seize hold of the knowledge, the memories, the plans, the very dreams of the most mighty in the land. He wondered if the victims retained their memories. Or were they amnesiac husks? What happened when—or was it if?—they awoke to full awareness... would they know where they were... or who?

Yet there was more to it, if only in simple mechanics. The men wore gloves to touch the glass—indeed to even look within it was perilous, as those who had died at Tarr Manor made clear. But how then did this precious information serve the Cabal—how was it *read*? If a person could not touch a book without risking their life or sanity, what was the point? There must be a way... a key...

Svenson glanced behind him. Had there been a noise? He listened... nothing... merely nerves. The men finished loading the chest. Bascombe tucked the notebook under his arm and snapped his fingers, issuing orders: these men to take the chest, these to go with the Minister, these to stay. He walked with Crabbé to the doors—and had the Minister handed something to his assistant? He had . . . but Svenson could not see what it was. And then they were gone.

The two remaining men stood for the barest moment and then, with a palpable relaxation of their manner, stepped one to the sideboard and the other to a wooden cigar box on a side table. They spoke smilingly to one another, nodding at their charges. The one at the sideboard poured two tumblers of whisky and crossed to the other, who was even then spitting out a bitten tip of tobacco. They swapped gifts—tumbler for cigar—and lit up, one after another. Their masters not gone for ninety seconds, they were smacking their lips and puffing away like princes.

Svenson looked around him for ideas. This observation room was less fully appointed than the other—there was no drink and no divan. The two men walked around the room, making a circuit of the furniture and commenting on their charges, and it was only another minute before they were fumbling through the pockets of a tailcoat or a lady's handbag. Svenson narrowed his eyes at the actions of these scavengers, and waited for them to come nearer. Right before him was the divan holding the churchman and the Arabic woman—with her head lolling back (eyes dreamily half-open to the ceiling) the pearl earrings shone brightly against her dark skin . . . they would have to notice them.

As if they had heard his thought, one man looked up, saw the pearls and ignored the five victims in between to hurry directly to them. The other followed, sticking the cigar in his mouth, and soon they were both leaning over the passive woman, their black backs facing Svenson, not two feet away from the glassy barrier.

He placed the barrel flat against the mirror and pulled the trigger. The bullet slammed into the back of the nearest man and then, with an unexpected flourish, out his chest to shatter the tumbler in his hand, sprawling him across the unfortunate cleric. His companion wheeled at the shot and stared without comprehension at the round hole in the mirror. Svenson fired again. The glass starred at this second puncture, a sudden spider's web clouding his vision. He quickly stuffed the revolver into his belt and reached for a small side table of inks and paper, tipping them brusquely to the floor. Three strokes with the table, swinging it like an axe, and the mirror fell away.

He dropped the table and looked behind him. The sound of the shots would have traveled for the most part back through the tunnels, not forward into the house, and he had to trust that they'd been well-insulated for secrecy's sake. *Why* was no one following? On the carpet at his feet the second man was breathing heavily, shot through the chest. Svenson sank to his knees to find the entry-point and quickly concluded the wound was mortal—it would be a matter of a minute. He stood, unable to bear the gaze of the gasping man, and stepped to his fellow, quite dead, rolling him off of the elderly churchman. Svenson shifted the body to the floor, already assailed by feelings of guilt and recrimination. Could he not have wounded them? Shot once and bluffed them into submission, tied with curtain cords like Flaüss? Perhaps . . . but such niceties—had human life become a *nicety*?—left no time to find the women, to secure his Prince, to stop these fellows' masters. Svenson saw that the dead man still held a burning cigar between his fingers. Without a thought he reached down and took it, inhaling deeply and closing his eyes with long-missed pleasure.

The men were unarmed, and with no weapons to pillage Svenson resigned himself to more stealth and theatre, holding the empty revolver as he walked. He'd left the room's other occupants as they were and picked his way through an empty string of parlors, watching for any trace of Bascombe or Crabbé, but hoping it was Bascombe that he found. If what he had guessed of the books from Tarr Manor was true, that they were capable of absorbing—of *recording*—memories, then the chest of books rivaled an unexplored continent for value. He also realized the particular worth of Bascombe's notebook, where the contents of each book—of each mind!—were cataloged and detailed. With those notes as a guide, what question could not be answered from that unnatural library? What advantage not be found?

Doctor Svenson looked around him with annoyance. He'd walked through another sitting room to an airy foyer with a bubbling fountain whose sound obscured any distant footfalls that might point him in the right direction. The Doctor wondered idly if the labyrinth of Harschmort had a Minotaur. He crossed heavily to the fountain and looked into the water—could one ever *not* look into the water?—and laughed aloud, for the Minotaur was before him: his own haggard, soot-smudged, battered visage, cigar in his face, weapon in hand. To the guests of this gala evening, was *he* not their determined, monstrous nemesis? Svenson outright cackled at the idea—and cackled again at the antic hoarseness of his voice, a raven trying to sing after too many cups of gin. He set down his smoke and stuffed the pistol into his belt, and reached into the fountain's pool, scooping water first to drink and then to splash across his face, and to once again smooth back his hair. He shook his hands, the droplets breaking his reflection to rippling pieces, and looked up. Someone was coming. He threw the cigar into the water and pulled out the gun.

It was Crabbé and Bascombe, with two of their functionaries walking behind, and between them, unmistakably, his posture characteristically sharp as a knife-point, Lord Robert Vandaariff. Svenson scrambled to the other side of the fountain and dropped to the floor, for all his fear and fatigue feeling caught out like a character in a comic operetta.

"It is astonishing—first the theatre, and now this!" The Minister was speaking, and with anger. "But the men are now in place?"

"They are," answered Bascombe, "a squad of Macklenburgers."

Crabbé snorted. "That lot has been more trouble than they are worth," he said. "The Prince is an idiot, the Envoy's a grub, the Major's a Teuton boor—and the *Doctor*! Did you hear? He is alive! He is at Harschmort! He must have come with us—but honestly, I cannot imagine how it was accomplished. He can only have been stowed away—hidden by a confederate!"

"But who could that be?" hissed Bascombe. When Crabbé did not reply, Bascombe ventured a hesitant guess. "Aspiche?"

Crabbé's answer was lost, for they had moved through the foyer to the edge of his hearing. Svenson rose to his knees, relieved they had not seen him, and carefully followed. He did not understand it . . . though Vandaariff walked between the two Ministry conspirators, they paid him no attention at all, speaking across his body . . . nor did the Lord take part in the plotting. What was more, what had happened to Bascombe's treasure chest of blue glass books?

"Yes, yes—and it's for the better," Crabbé was saying, "both of them are to take part. Poor Elspeth has lost a quantity of hair, and Margaret—

well, she was keen to press ahead. She is *ever* keen, but . . . apparently she had a *confrontation* with this Cardinal at the Royale—she—well, I cannot say—she seems in a *mood* about it—"

"And this is along with the . . . ah . . . other?" Bascombe politely cut in, bringing the conversation back to its subject.

"Yes, yes—*she* is the *test case,* of course. In my own opinion, it all goes too fast—too much effort in too many places—"

"The Contessa *is* concerned about our time-table—"

"As am *I,* Mr. Bascombe," Crabbé replied sharply, "but you will notice for yourself—the confusion, the risk—when we have tried to simultaneously manage *initiations* in the theatre, the Comte's *transformations* in the cathedral, the *collections* in the inner parlors, the *harvest* from Lord Robert"—he gestured casually to the most powerful man in five nations—"and *now* because of that blasted woman, the Duke—"

"Apparently Doctor Lorenz is confident—"

"He is *always* confident! And yet, Bascombe, science is pleased if one experiment out of twenty actually succeeds—the mere *confidence* of Doctor Lorenz is not enough when so much hangs at risk—we need certainty!"

"Of course, Sir."

"Just a moment."

Crabbé stopped, and turned to the two retainers walking behind—prompting Svenson to abruptly crouch behind a molting philodendron.

"Dash ahead to the top of the tower—I don't want any surprises. Make sure it's clear, then one of you return. We will wait."

The men ran off. Svenson peeked through the dusty leaves to see Bascombe in the midst of a deferent protest.

"Sir, do you really think—"

"What I think is that I *prefer* not to be overheard by *anyone.*"

He paused to allow the two men to fully vanish from sight before going on.

"Before anything," began the Deputy Minister, glancing once at the figure of Robert Vandaariff, "what book do we have for Lord Vandaariff, here? We need something as a place-holder, yes?"

"Yes, Sir—though for now it can be the one missing, from Lady Mélantes—"

"Which *must* be recovered—"

"Of course, Sir—but for the moment it may also stand in as the keeper of Lord Vandaariff's secrets—until such time as we have occasion to irreparably *damage* another."

"Excellent," muttered Crabbé. His eyes darted around them and the small man licked his lips, leaning closer to Bascombe. "From the beginning, Roger, I have offered you this opportunity, have I not? Inheritance and title, new prospects for marriage, advancement in government?"

"Yes, Sir, I am well in your debt—and I assure you—"

Crabbé waved away Bascombe's obsequiousness as if he were brushing off flies. "What I have said—about there being too many elements in motion at once—is for your ears alone."

Again, Svenson was astonished to find neither man referring in the slightest to Lord Vandaariff, who stood not two feet away.

"You are intelligent, Roger, and you are cunning as any person in this business—as you have well proven. Keep your eyes open, for both our sakes, for any out of place comment or action . . . from *anyone.* Do you understand? Now is the sticking point, and I find myself brimming with suspicion."

"Do you suggest one of the others—the Contessa, or Mr. Xonck—"

"I suggest nothing. Yet, we have suffered these . . . *disruptions*—"

"But these *provocateurs*—Chang, Svenson—"

"And your Miss Temple," added Crabbé, a tinge of acid in his tone.

"Including her only strengthens the truth, Sir—which they each have sworn—that they have no master, nor any plan beyond plain antagonism."

Crabbé leaned closer to Bascombe, his voice dropping to an anxious hiss. "Yes, yes—and *yet*! The Doctor arrives by way of the airship! Miss Temple penetrates our plans for Lydia Vandaariff and somehow resists—without assistance, which one can scarcely credit—submersion in a glass book! And Chang—how many has he killed? What havoc has he not set off? Do you flatter these so much that they have done all this without aid? And where else, I ask you, Roger, could that aid have come from, save within our number?"

Crabbé's face was white and his lip shaking with rage—or fear, or both, as if the very idea of being vulnerable set off the Minister's fury. Bascombe did not answer.

"You know Miss Temple, Roger—possibly better than anyone in this world. Do *you* think she could have killed those men? Shrugged off that book? Located Lydia Vandaariff and quite nearly spirited her from our grasp? If it was not for Mrs. Marchmoor's arrival—"

Bascombe shook his head.

"No, Sir . . . the Celeste Temple I know is capable of none of those things. And yet—there *must* be some other explanation."

"Yet do we have it? Is there an explanation for Colonel Trapping's death? All three of our *provocateurs* were in this house that night, yet it is impossible that they would know to kill him without some betrayal from within our ranks!"

They fell silent. Svenson watched them, and with patient slowness reached up to scratch his nose.

"Francis Xonck *was* burned by Cardinal Chang." Bascombe began to speak quickly, sorting out their options. "It is unlikely he would undergo such an injury on purpose."

"Perhaps . . . yet he is extremely cunning, and personally reckless."

"Agreed. The Comte—"

"The Comte d'Orkancz cares for his glass and his transformations—his *vision.* I swear that in his heart he considers all of this but one more canvas—a masterwork, perhaps—but still, his thought is to my taste a bit too . . ." Crabbé swallowed with some discomfort and brushed his moustache with a finger. "Perhaps it is simply his horrid plans for the girl—not that I even trust those plans have been fully *revealed* . . ."

Crabbé looked up at the young man, as if he had said too much, but Bascombe's expression had not changed.

"And the Contessa?" Bascombe asked.

"The Contessa," echoed Crabbé. "The Contessa *indeed* . . ."

They looked up, for one of their men was returning at a jog. They let him arrive without any further conversation. Once he reported the way ahead was clear, Bascombe nodded that the man should rejoin his companion ahead of them. The man crisply turned and the Ministry men again waited for him to disappear before they followed in silence—evidently not finished with their brooding. Svenson crept after them. The possibility of mistrust and dissension within the Cabal was an answer to a prayer he had not dared to utter.

Without the trailing men to block his view, he could see the Minister more clearly—a short determined figure who carried a leather satchel, the sort one might use for official papers. Svenson was sure it was not present when they had collected the books, which meant Crabbé had acquired it since—along with his acquisition of Lord Vandaariff? Did that mean the satchel carried papers *from* Lord Vandaariff? He could still make no sense of the Lord's apparent participation—his unforced accompaniment—at the same time they utterly ignored him. Svenson had assumed Vandaariff to be the plot's prime mover—for not two days before the man had quite deliberately manipulated him away from Trapping's body. However long the Cabal might have planned to spring their trap, whatever control they had established, whatever somnambulism . . . it had been recently done—for surely they had drawn on the full resources of the Lord's house and name to achieve their ends, which only could have been begun with his full participation and approval. And now he followed along—in his own house—as if he were an affable pet goat. Yet Svenson's first glimpse of the man, as he crouched behind the fountain, had shown his face free of the scars of the Process. How else was he compelled? By way of a glass book? If it were only possible to get Vandaariff to himself for five minutes! Even that much time would afford a quick examination, would give the Doctor some insight into the corporeal effects of this *mind control,* and who could say . . . some insight into its reversal.

For now however, unarmed and outnumbered, he could only follow them deeper into the house. He could hear from the rooms around them a growing buzz of human activity—footsteps, voices, cutlery, wheeled carts. So far their path had skirted any open place or crossroads—undoubtedly to keep Vandaariff from public view. Svenson wondered if the servants of the house knew of their master's mental servitude, and how they might react to the knowledge. He did not imagine Robert Vandaariff to be a kindly employer—perhaps the household *did* know, and happily celebrated his downfall—perhaps the Cabal had dipped into Vandaariff's own riches to purchase his people's loyalty. Either possibility kept Svenson from trusting the servants . . . but he knew his opportunity was quickly slipping away. With each step they traveled closer to the other members of the Cabal.

* * *

Svenson took a deep breath. The three men were perhaps ten yards ahead of him, just turning the corner from one long corridor into—he presumed—another. As soon as they disappeared he dashed ahead to make up ground, reached the corner and peeked—five yards away, and onto a thin runner of carpeting! Svenson stepped out, revolver extended, and rapidly advanced, his padded footfalls mixing with theirs—ten feet away, then five, and then he was right behind them. Somehow they sensed his presence, turning just as Svenson reached out and took rough hold of Vandaariff's collar with his left hand, and pressed the revolver barrel against the side of the Lord's temple with his right.

"Do not move!" he hissed. "Do not cry out—or this man will die, and then each of you in turn. I am a crack shot with a pistol, and few things would give me more pleasure!"

They did not cry out, and once again Svenson felt the disquieting capacity for savagery creeping up his spine—though he was no particular shot at all even when his gun was loaded. What he didn't know was the value they placed on Vandaariff. With a sudden chill he wondered if they might actually *want* him killed—something they desired but shrank from doing themselves—especially now that Crabbé had the satchel of vital information.

The satchel. He must have it.

"That satchel!" he barked at the Deputy Minister. "Drop it at once, and step away!"

"I will not!" snapped Crabbé shrilly, his face gone pale.

"You *will*!" snarled Svenson, pulling back the hammer and pressing the barrel hard into Vandaariff's skull.

Crabbé's fingers fidgeted over the leather handle. But he did not throw it down. Svenson whipped the gun away from Vandaariff and extended his arm directly at Crabbé's chest.

"Doctor Svenson!"

This was Bascombe, raising his own hands in a desperate conciliatory gesture that was still for Svenson too much like an attempt to grab his weapon. He turned the barrel toward the younger man, who flinched visibly, then back toward Crabbé who now hugged the satchel to his body, then again to Bascombe, pulling Vandaariff a step away to give himself more room. Why did he not get *better* at this sort of confrontation?

Bascombe swallowed and took a step forward. "Doctor Svenson," he began in a hesitant voice, "this cannot stand—you are inside the hornets' nest, you will be taken—"

"I require my Prince," said Svenson, "and I require that satchel."

"Impossible," piped Crabbé, and to the Doctor's great exasperation the Deputy Minister turned and spun the satchel like a discus down the length of the corridor. It bounced to a stop against the wall some twenty feet beyond them. Svenson's heart sank—God damn the man! If he'd possessed a single bullet he would have put it straight between Harald Crabbé's ears.

"So much for *that,*" Crabbé bleated, babbling fearfully. "How did you survive the quarry? Who helped you? Where were you hidden on the airship? How are you still tormenting my *every plan*?"

The Minister's voice rose to a high-pitched shout. Svenson took another step back, dragging Vandaariff with him. Bascombe—though frightened the man had courage—again stepped forward in response. Svenson put the gun back against Vandaariff's ear.

"Stay where you are! You will answer me—the whereabouts of Karl-Horst—the Prince—I insist..."

His words faltered. From somewhere below them in the house Svenson heard a screaming high-pitched whine, like the brakes of a train slamming down at high speed... and within it, like the silver thread run through a damask coat made for a king, a desperate woman's shriek. What had Crabbé said about the Comte's activity... "the cathedral"? All three stood fixed as the noise rose to an unbearable peak and then just as suddenly cut away. He dragged Vandaariff back another step.

"Release him!" hissed Crabbé. "You only make it worse for yourself!"

"Worse?" Svenson sputtered at the man's arrogance—O for one bullet! He gestured at the floor, at the hideous noise. "What horrors are these? What horrors have I already seen?" He tugged Vandaariff. "You will not have this man!"

"We have him already," sneered Crabbé.

"I know how he is afflicted," stammered Svenson. "I can restore him! His word will be believed and damn you all!"

"You know nothing." Despite his fear, Crabbé was tenacious—no doubt a valuable quality in negotiating treaties, but to Svenson galling as all hell.

"Your infernal Process may be irreversible," announced Svenson, "I have had no leisure to study it—but I know Lord Vandaariff has not undergone that ritual. He bears no scars—he was perfectly lucid and in his own mind but two evenings ago, well before such scars would fade—and what is more, I know from what I have just observed in your theatre that if he *had* been so transformed he would be fighting my grip quite violently. No, gentlemen, I am confident he is under the temporary control of a drug, for which I will locate an antidote—"

"You'll do nothing of the kind," cried Crabbé, and he turned his words to Vandaariff, speaking in a sharp, wheedling tone that one would use to order a dog. "*Robert!* Take his gun—at once!"

To Svenson's dismay, Lord Vandaariff spun and dove for the pistol with both arms. The Doctor stepped away but the Lord's insistent grasping hands would not let go and it was instantly apparent that the automaton Lord was more vigorous than the utterly spent surgeon. The Doctor looked up to see Crabbé's face split with a wicked smile.

It was the last stroke of arrogance that Doctor Svenson could bear. Even as Vandaariff grappled him—a hand across his throat, another stabbing at the weapon—Svenson wrenched the pistol away and thrust it at the Minister's face, drawing back the hammer.

"Call him off or you die!" he shouted.

Instead, Bascombe leapt for Svenson's arm. He slashed the gun at Bascombe as he came, the jagged sight at the end of the barrel digging a raw line across the younger man's cheekbone, knocking him off his feet. At that moment Vandaariff's hand clamped over Svenson's, squeezing. The hammer clicked forward. Svenson desperately looked up and met Bascombe's gaze. They both knew the gun had not fired.

"He has no bullets!" cried Bascombe and he pitched his voice to the far end of the corridor. "Help! Evans! Jones! Help!"

Svenson turned. The satchel! He threw himself away from Vandaariff and ran for it, though it carried him straight toward the returning escorts. His boots clattered against the slippery polished wood, his ankle spasmed in protest, but he reached the satchel, scooped it up, and began his hobbling run back toward Bascombe and Crabbé. Crabbé screamed to the men who—he had no doubt—were all too close behind him.

"The satchel! Get the satchel! He must not have it!"

Bascombe had regained his feet and came forward, hands out, as if to bar Svenson's way—or at least tackle him until the rest could dash his brains out. There were no side doors, no alcoves, no alternatives but to charge the man. Svenson recalled his days at university, the drunken games played inside the dormitories—sometimes they would even manage horses—but Bascombe was younger and angry, with his own foolish game-playing to draw upon.

"*Stop* him, Roger—*kill* him!" Even enraged, Crabbé managed to sound imperious.

Before Bascombe could tackle him Svenson swung the satchel at his face, an impact more ignominious than painful, but it caused Bascombe to turn his head at the moment of collision. Svenson dropped his shoulder and knocked Bascombe backwards. The man's hands grabbed at his shoulders, but he bulled himself free and Bascombe's grip slipped down his body. Svenson was nearly past, stumbling, when Bascombe caught both hands on his left boot and held fast, pulling him off balance and sending him to the floor. He rolled on his back to see Bascombe sitting in a heap, his face red and blood-smeared. Svenson raised his right boot and kicked it at Bascombe's face. The blow landed on Bascombe's arm—both men crying out at the impact, for this was the Doctor's twisted ankle. Two more hideous kicks and he was free.

But the men in black were there—he had no chance. He scrabbled to his feet—and then in a sudden moment of joy saw that the two men had by instinct and deference stopped to aid both Crabbé and Bascombe. On a sudden urge, Doctor Svenson ran right at them, the satchel in one hand and the revolver in the other. He could hear Crabbé's protests—"No, no! Him! Stop *him*!" and Bascombe's cries of "Satchel! Satchel!"—but he was on them and swinging just as the men looked up. Neither blow—pistol or satchel—landed, but both caused their targets to flinch, and he gained yards of valuable space as he dashed past them down the hall. They were following, but despite his fear and his ankle Doctor Svenson's game-playing spirits were high.

He raced down the corridor, boots slipping, wincing at the impact of each step. Where had Crabbé sent the two men to wait—the "top of the tower"? He frowned—his view from the airship had shown him quite clearly that there was no tower to speak of at Harschmort. What was more, the men had come quite quickly at Bascombe's call for help—that is, they could not have scaled any height. Unless . . . he rounded a corner into a wide marble foyer, the floor a black and white checkerboard, the far wall marked by a strange iron door, wide open onto a dark spiral staircase . . . this place marked the top of a tower leading *down.* Before he could even fully process the thought, Doctor Svenson lost his footing completely and crashed to the floor, sliding all the way across the marble to the far wall. He shook his head and tried to stand. He was dripping with . . . blood! He'd stepped into a wide scarlet pool and with his fall smeared it across the width of the marble, soaking the right side of his body in gore.

He looked up. His two pursuers appeared in the far doorway. Before anyone could move, another piercing mechanical shrieking rose from beyond the open tower door, rising to a head-splitting level of loathsome discomfort. His ears did not deceive him, there was definitely the voice of a woman within the shriek.

Svenson threw the pistol with all his strength at the men, catching one dead on the knee. The man groaned and slumped back against the doorframe, the pistol spinning away across the floor. The second man dove after the gun and snatched it up as Svenson broke for the only other door—a wide hallway leading away from the tower (the last thing he wanted was to go nearer to the screaming). He could hear the clicking of the hammer on empty chambers behind him and then a snarl of anger from the man—as Svenson again stretched his lead.

He rounded a corner into another small foyer, with doors to each side. Quickly and quietly, Doctor Svenson stepped through a swinging door, easing it shut behind him so the door was still, careful not to leave any smear of blood. He had entered some part of the kitchens. The Doctor stepped past barrels and lockers toward an inner door. He had just reached it when the door swung open. He ducked swiftly behind it as it did, hiding him from the rest of the room. A moment later, the far door opened—where he'd come in—and he heard the voice of his pursuer.

"Did anyone come in here?"

"When?" asked a gruff voice not ten inches from where the Doctor presently skulked.

"Just now. Bony fellow, foreigner, covered in blood."

"Not in here. Do you see any blood?"

There was a scuffling pause as both men looked around them. The man nearest him leaned against the door as he looked, causing Svenson to shrink further into the wall.

"Don't know where else he could've run," muttered the man from the hallway.

"Across the way—that goes to the trophy room. Full of guns."

"I'll be damned," hissed his pursuer, and Svenson heard the blessed sound of the door swinging shut. A moment later he heard a locker being opened, the man rooting around in it, and what seemed like the spilling sound of gravel. This done, as quickly as that the man walked back out of the room, pulling the door closed behind him. Svenson breathed a sigh of relief.

He looked at the wall—quite covered in blood from his pressing against it. He sighed—nothing to be done—and wondered if there was anything to drink in one of the lockers. He was hardly safe—enemies but yards away in either direction—but that was becoming a common condition. What was more . . . gravel? Curiosity got the better of him, and Svenson crept to the largest of the lockers—fully large enough to stand in—where he was sure the man had gone. He pulled it open and winced as the frigid air inside flowed over his face. It had not been gravel at all, but ice. A bag of chipped ice poured over the body of the Duke of Stäelmaere, skin blue, reptilian eyes half-open, lying in grisly state in an iron tub.

Why were they keeping him? What did Lorenz think he could do—bring him back to life? That was absurd. Two bullets—the second of which had blown out his heart—had inflicted grievous damage, and now for so many hours, the blood would be cooled and pooling, the limbs stiffened . . . what did they possibly intend? Svenson had a sudden urge to dig out a penknife and do more mischief to the body—open the jugular, perhaps?—to further frustrate Lorenz's unnatural plans, but such actions seemed too unsavory. Without concrete reason, he was not going to stoop to desecrating even this disreputable corpse.

But as he looked down at that corpse, Doctor Svenson felt the nearness of his own despair. He hefted the satchel in his hands—did it bring him any nearer the Prince, any closer to saving the lives of his friends? The corners of his mouth flicked with a wan smile at the word. He did not really remember the last time he'd made what he could call a friend. The Baron was—had been—an employer and gouty mentor to his life in the Palace, but they shared no confidences. Officers he'd served with, in port or shipboard, became companions for that tour of duty, but rarely came to mind once subsequent postings had split them apart. His friends from university were few and mostly dead. His family relations were cast under the shadow of Corinna and quite out of mind. The idea that in these few days he had thrown his lot—not just his life, but whatever that life stood for—with an unlikely pair (or was it now three?) that had he passed them on the street would not have turned his head... well, that was not completely true. He would have smiled knowingly at Miss Temple's contained willfulness, shaken his head at Chang's garish advertisement of mystery... and contented himself with a tactful appraisal of Elöise Dujong in her no doubt demure dress. And he would have perilously undersold them all—as their own first impressions of him might not have allowed for his present achievements. Svenson winced at this, glancing down at the sticky blood congealing down the side of his uniform. What had he achieved, at the end? What had he ever achieved at all? His life was a fog since Corinna's death... must he fail these others as he had failed her?

He was tired, dangerously so, standing without the first idea of his next step, in the doorway of a meat locker, enemies waiting on the other side of a door whichever way he went. Hanging from a metal pole that went across above his head were a number of wicked metal hooks, set at the end with a small wooden cross-piece for a handle. Intended for handling large cuts of meat, one in each hand would suit him very well indeed. Svenson reached up and selected a pair and smiled. He felt like a pirate.

He looked down at the Duke, for something had caught his eye... it did not seem as if anything had changed—the corpse was no more animated and no less blue. He realized that was it... the blue was not the normal color of icy dead flesh, of which he had seen more than his share in his Baltic service. No, this was somehow brighter... *bluer.* The ice shifted, slipping down as it melted, and Svenson's eye was drawn to the water in the tub... the ice and the water... the ice was piled at the edge of the tub and over the Duke's lower body, while the water, which must be the center of melting, was pooled over his chest, over his wound. With a sudden curiosity, Svenson stepped behind the Duke and placing his hooks under each of the man's arms lifted him some inches out of the tub, until he could see the actual wound. As the torn flesh broke the surface, he was astonished to see it had been patched—and the wound cavity filled—with indigo clay.

The door in the room opened and with a start Svenson let go of the body, which slid back into the tub, ice and water spilling loudly onto the floor. He looked up—whoever had entered would have heard the sound as they saw the locker door was open—and quickly freed his two hooks. The satchel! Where was the satchel? He'd put it down when he'd reached up for the hooks. He cursed himself for a fool, dropped one hook into the tub and snatched up the satchel just as the locker door began to move. Svenson threw himself forward, driving his shoulder into the door and, with a satisfying *thud,* the door into whoever stood behind it. Another of the black-coated functionaries tottered backwards, his hands laden with another burlap sack of broken ice, and fell. The sack split and ice slid across the floor in a gleaming sheet. Svenson charged over the man, stepping on him rather than risking a slip on the ice, and burst through the swinging door, leaving a wide red smear on its butter-cream paint as he passed.

This was a kitchen room proper—a wide long table for preparation, an enormous stone hearth, stoves, racks of pots and pans and metal. On the other side of the table stood Doctor Lorenz, black cloak thrown back over his shoulders, thick glasses on the end of his nose, peering at a page of densely written parchment. To the savant's right was spread a cloth roll of metal tools, picks and knives and tiny sharp shears, and to his left was a row of glass vials connected to one another by distilling coils. Svenson saw the bandolier of metal flasks slung over a chair—the Doctor's store of refined indigo clay from the quarry.

On the side of the table nearer to Svenson sat another functionary smoking a cigar. Two others stood by the hearth, tending several metal vessels hanging over the fire, unsettling combinations of a tea kettle and a medieval helmet, vaguely round, banded and bolted with steel, with shiny metal spouts that spat steam. These men wore heavy leather gauntlets. All four men looked up at Svenson in surprise.

As if he was born to it, fear and fatigue curling in an instant into brutal expedience, Svenson took two steps to the table, swinging with all his strength before the man in the chair could move. The hook landed with a *thwock,* pinning his right hand to the table top. The man screamed. Svenson released the hook and kicked the chair out from under the man, who cried out again as he fell to the floor and drove more weight against his pinioned hand. Svenson dropped the satchel and swung the chair as hard as he could at the nearest man from the fire, already charging at him. The chair struck the man's outstretched arms cruelly and broke his momentum. Stepping aside like a bullfighter—or how he *imagined* a bullfighter might step—Svenson swung again, this time across the fellow's head and shoulders. The chair snapped to pieces and the man went down. The first man was still shrieking. Lorenz was bawling for help. The second man from the fire had charged. Svenson dashed away toward the rack of pans—beyond the rack was a heavy butcher block. Svenson dove to it as he felt the man's hands take hold of his jacket. There was a row of knives but his grasping hand could not reach them. The man pulled him away and spun him around, driving an elbow across his jaw. Svenson was knocked into the butcher block with a grunt, the edge slamming across his arching back with a vicious impact. His hand groped behind him and caught some handle, some tool, and he whipped it forward at the man, just as a fist slammed into his stomach. Svenson doubled over, but his own blow struck hard enough to cause his opponent to stumble back. The Doctor looked up, gasping for breath. He was holding a heavy wooden mallet for tenderizing meat, the flat hammer head cut into sharp wooden spikes for quicker, deeper work. Blood trickled down the staggered fellow's head. Svenson swung again, landing square on the ear, and the man went down.

He looked to Lorenz. The man at the table was still pinned, his face white and drawn. Doctor Lorenz dug furiously at his cloak, glaring at Svenson with hatred. If he could get that bandolier! Svenson heaved himself back toward the table, raising the mallet. The pinned man saw him coming and dropped to his knees with another scream. Lorenz's face contorted with effort and he finally freed his prize—a small black pistol! The Doctors stared at each other for a brief suspended moment.

"You're as persistent as bed lice!" hissed Lorenz.

"You're all doomed," whispered Svenson. "Every one of you."

"Ridiculous! *Ridiculous!*"

Lorenz extended his arm, taking aim. Svenson threw the hammer into the line of glass vials, smashing them utterly, and flung himself to the floor. Lorenz cried out with dismay—both at the ruined experiment and the broken glass flying up at his face—and the bullet sailed across the room to splinter the far door. Svenson felt the satchel under his hand and once more snatched it up. Lorenz fired again but Svenson had the luck to trip on a pan (screaming himself at yet another searing jolt to his ankle) and so was no longer where Lorenz had aimed. He reached the door and burst through—a third shot splitting the wood near his head—stumbled into the hall, slipped, and sat down hard in a heap. Behind him Lorenz bellowed like a bullock. Svenson lurched across the main hall to another passage, in hopes that he might find Lord Vandaariff's trophy room . . . before his stuffed head took up a place of honor in it.

He limped blindly down the corridor, seeing no doors, his anxiety rising toward paralysis as he realized what he had just done—the compressed savagery, the calculated mayhem. What had happened to him—potting men from the catwalk as if they were unfeeling targets, murdering the helpless fellows through the mirror, and now this awful slaughter in the kitchens—and he had done it all so easily, so *capably,* as if he were a seasoned killer—as if he were Cardinal Chang. But he was not Chang—he was not a killer—already his hands were shaking and face slick with cold sweat. He stopped, leaning heavily against the wall, his mind suddenly assailed by the image of the poor man's hand, pinned like a pale flipping fish. Doctor Svenson's throat rose and he looked about him for an urn, a pot, a plant, found nothing, and forced his gorge down by strength of will, the taste of bile sharp in his mouth. He could not go on, careening from collision to collision, with no longer the slightest idea of what he sought. He needed to sit, to rest, to weep—any respite, however brief. All around him were the sounds of guests and preparations, music, footsteps—he must be very near the ballroom. With a grateful groan he spied a door, small, plain, unlocked, prayed with all his bankrupt faith that the room was empty, and slipped inside.

He stepped into darkness, closed the door and immediately barked his shin, tripped, and set off an echoing clatter that seemed to take minutes to die. He froze, waiting... breathed in the silent dark... there were no other noises from within the room... and nothing from the hallway. He exhaled slowly. The clatter was wooden, wooden poles... mops, brooms... he was in a maids' closet.

Doctor Svenson carefully set down the satchel and groped around him to either side. He felt shelves—one of which he'd kicked—and his hands moved cautiously, not wanting to knock anything else to the floor. His fingers sought quickly, moving from shelf to shelf until his right hand slipped over and then into a wooden box, full of slick, tubular objects... candles. He plucked one from the box and then continued his search for a box of matches—surely they would be in the same place. In fact, the box was on the next shelf down, and crouching, Svenson carefully struck a match by feel—how often had he done the same in the darkness of a ship at night?—in a stroke transforming his little chamber of mystery into a mundane catalog of house management: soap, towels, brass polish, buckets, mops, brushes, brooms, dusters, pans, smocks, vinegar, wax, candles... and, he blessed the thoughtful maid who put it there, a tiny stool. He shifted his body and turned, sitting so he faced the door. A *very* thoughtful maid... for stuck into the wall near the door was a small loop of chain on a nail, made to slip around the knob and serve as a lock—but only usable from *within* the closet. Svenson made the chain fast and saw, near the box of matches, a cleared foot of shelf marked with melted wax—the place for occupants to place their candles. He'd ducked into someone's sanctuary, and made it his own. Doctor Svenson shut his eyes and allowed his fatigue to slump his shoulders. If only the maid had left a stash of tobacco.

* * *

It would be terribly simple to fall asleep, and he knew it was a real possibility. With a grimace he forced himself to sit up straight, and then—why did it keep slipping his mind?—he remembered the satchel, fetching it onto his lap. He untied the clasp and fished out the contents, a thick sheaf of parchment, densely covered with finely written notes. He leafed through the stack... angling the pages so they caught more candlelight.

He read, quickly, his eyes skimming from line to line, and then from that page to the next, and to the next again. It was a massive narrative of acquisition and subterfuge, and clearly from the pen of Robert Vandaariff. At first Svenson recognized just enough of the names and places to follow the geographical path of finance—money houses in Florence and Venice, goods brokers in Vienna, in Berlin, fur merchants in Stockholm, then diamond traders in Antwerp. But the closer he read—and the more he flipped back and forward between the pages to re-sort out the facts (and which initials stood for institutions—"RLS" being Rosamonde Lacquer-Sforza not, as he'd first suspected, Rotterdam Liability Services, a major insurer of overseas shipping)—the more he understood it was a narrative with two conjoined threads: a steady campaign of leverage and acquisition, and a trail of unlikely individuals, like islands in a stream, determining each in their way how the money flowed. But more than anything what cried out to the Doctor were the many references to his country of Macklenburg.

It was quite clear that Vandaariff had undergone protracted negotiations, both openly and through a host of intermediaries, to purchase an enormous amount of land in the Duchy's mountain district, with an ever-present emphasis on mining rights. This confirmed what Svenson had guessed from the reddish earth at the Tarr Manor quarry, that the Macklenburg hills were even richer in deposits of indigo clay. It also confirmed Vandaariff's knowledge of this mineral as a commodity—its special properties and the insidious uses to which they might be put. Finally, it convinced him again, as he had thought two days ago, that Robert Vandaariff had been very much personally involved in this business.

Bit by bit Doctor Svenson identified the other major figures in the Cabal, noting how each one entered Vandaariff's tale of conquest. The Contessa appeared by way of the Venetian speculation market, and it was through her that Lord Robert became acquainted in Paris with the Comte d'Orkancz as someone who could initially—and discreetly—

advise him on the purchase of certain antiquities from a recently discovered underground Byzantine monastery in Thessalonika. But this was a ruse, for the Comte was truly enlisted to study and verify the characteristics of certain mineral samples that Lord Vandaariff had apparently acquired in secret from the same Venetian speculators. Yet he was surprised to see no mention, as far as he could tell, of Oskar Veilandt, from whose alchemical studies so much of the conspiracy's work seemed to spring. Could Vandaariff have known Veilandt (or suborned him) for so long that he saw no need to mention the man? It made no sense, and Svenson flipped ahead to see if the painter was mentioned later, but the narrative quickly branched out to tales of exploration and diplomacy, from scientists and discoverers at the Royal Institute who were also invited to study these samples, the resources of industry given over to certain experiments in fabrication (here Doctor Lorenz and Francis Xonck first appeared), and then to Macklenburg proper, with the subtle interactions between Lord Vandaariff, Harald Crabbé, and their Macklenburg contact—of *course,* Svenson rolled his eyes—the Duke's dyspeptic younger brother, Konrad, Bishop of Warnemünde.

With these agents in motion and his money behind them, Vandaariff's plans moved ahead seamlessly, using the Institute to locate the deposits, Crabbé to negotiate for the land with Konrad, who acted as an agent for the cash-poor aristocratic property holders. But in a twist he saw there was more to it, for instead of gold, Konrad was selling the land in exchange for contraband munitions supplied by Francis Xonck. The Duke's brother was amassing an arsenal—to assert control of Karl-Horst upon his inheritance. Svenson smiled at the irony. Unbeknownst to Konrad the Cabal had used him, enabling him to essentially import a secret army that, once *they* ruled by proxy through the Prince's soon-to-arrive infant son (and necessarily managed Konrad's death), they could use themselves to defend their investment—whereas bringing in foreign troops would have provoked an uprising. It was exactly the sort of stratagem that made Vandaariff's reputation. And moving between them all were the Comte and the Contessa. For Svenson could see what Vandaariff had not, that as much as the financier imagined himself the architect of this scheme, in fact he was merely its engine. The Doctor had no doubt the Contessa and the Comte had set it all in motion from the start, manipulating the great man. The exact point where they joined forces with the others—

whether they had been in league before or after Vandaariff had recruited them—was unclear, but he sensed immediately why they had all agreed to turn on their benefactor. Vandaariff uncontrolled could dictate the profit to them all... with him in thrall, the whole of his wealth lay at their disposal.

There was much Svenson didn't understand—still no mention of Veilandt, for one, and how exactly had the Cabal managed to overcome Vandaariff, who was fully his powerful self the night of the engagement party? Could that have been why Trapping had been killed—that he had threatened to tell Vandaariff what was in store for him? But then why did at least some of the Cabal seem ignorant of Trapping's killer? Or did Trapping threaten to tell Vandaariff about the Comte's plans for Lydia, if Lord Robert had not known already? But no, what did Vandaariff's feelings matter if the man was going to be made their slave in any case? Or had Trapping discovered something else—something that implicated one member of the Cabal against the others? But which one—and what was their secret?

Svenson's head was already swimming with too many names and dates and places and figures. He returned to the pages of tightly scrawled text. So much had happened within Macklenburg itself that he'd never even glimpsed. The roots of the conspiracy had worked their way deeper and deeper, amassing property and influence and, he shook his head to read it, doing whatever they needed to acquire more. There were fires, blackmail, threats, even murder... even... how long had this been going on? It seemed like *years*... he read of experiments—"usefully serving both scientific and practical purposes"—where disease had been introduced into districts where the tenants would not sell.

Doctor Svenson's blood went cold. Before him were the words "blood fever." Corinna... could it be that these people had killed her... killed *hundreds*... infected his cousin... in order to drive down the price of *land*?

He heard steps outside his door. Quickly and quietly he stuffed the pages back into the satchel and blew out the light. He listened... more steps... was that speaking? Music? If only he knew where exactly he was in the house! He scoffed—if only he had a loaded weapon, if only his body was not a painful wreck—he might as well wish for wings! Doctor Svenson covered his eyes with his palm. His hand trembled... his own immediate danger... the need to find the others... the Prince—but it was all thrown to pieces with the idea—no, the *truth,* he had no doubt at all—that this same business, these same people, had—casually, offhandedly, uncaringly—murdered his Corinna. It was as if he could no longer feel his own body, but was somehow suspended above it, commanding his limbs but not inhabiting them. All this time spent wrestling and railing against cruel destiny and a heartless world—and now to find these forces embodied not in the dispassionate course of a disease but in the deliberate handiwork of men. Doctor Svenson put his hand over his mouth to stifle a sob. It had been preventable. It needn't have happened at all.

He wiped his eyes and exhaled with a shuddering whisper. It was too much to bear. Certainly it was too much to bear in a closet. He unlooped the chain from the knob and opened the door, stepping out into the corridor before his nerves got the better of him. All around—visible to either side through open archways—were guests, masked, cloaked. He met the eyes of a cloaked man and woman and smiled, bowing his head. They returned the bow, their expressions a mix of politeness and horror at his appearance. Taking advantage of the moment, the Doctor quickly beckoned them to him with a finger. They paused, the traffic continuing to flow about them, all in the direction of the ballroom. He motioned again, a bit more conspiratorial, with an inviting smile. The man took a step closer, the woman holding his hand. Svenson gestured once more, and the man finally left the woman's grasp and came near.

"I beg your pardon," whispered Svenson. "I am in the service of the Prince of Macklenburg, who you must know is engaged to Miss Vandaariff"—he indicated his uniform—"and there has been an intrigue—indeed, violence—you will see it on my face—"

The man nodded, but it was clear this seemed as much a reason to run from Svenson as to trust him.

"I need to reach the Prince—he will be with Miss Vandaariff and her father—but as you can see, there is no way for me to do this in such a crowd without causing distress and uproar, which I assure you would be dangerous for everyone concerned." He looked either way and dropped his voice even lower. "There may still be confidential agents at large—"

"Indeed!" replied the man, visibly relieved to have something to say. "I am told they have captured one!"

Svenson nodded knowingly. "But there may be others—I must deliver my news. Is there any way—I am dreadfully hesitant to ask—but is there any way you could see fit to lend me your cloak? I will certainly mention your name to the Prince—and his partners, of course, the Deputy Minister, the Comte, the Contessa—"

"You know the Contessa?" the man hissed, risking a guilty glance back to the woman waiting in the archway.

"O yes." Svenson smiled, leaning closer to the man's ear. "Would you care for an introduction? She is *incomparable.*"

With the black cloak covering his uniform and its stains of blood, smoke, and orange dust, and the black mask he'd taken from Flaüss, the Doctor plunged into the crowd moving toward the ballroom, shouldering through as brusquely as he dared, responding to any complaint in muttered German. He looked up and saw the ballroom ceiling through the next archway, but before he could reach it heard raised voices—and then above them all a sharp, commanding cry.

"Open the doors!"

The Contessa's voice. The bolts were pulled and then a sharp hiss of alarm came from those up front who could see . . . and then an unsettled, *daunted* silence. But who had arrived? What had happened?

He shoved forward with even less care for decorum until he passed the final archway and entered the ballroom. It was thronged with guests who pushed back at him as he came, as if they made room for someone in the center of the chamber. A woman screamed, and then another—each cry quickly smothered. He threaded his way through the palpably disturbed crowd to reach a ring of Dragoons, and then through a gap between red-coated troopers saw the grim face of Colonel Aspiche. Doctor Svenson immediately turned away and found, in the circle itself, the Comte d'Orkancz. He twisted past one more ring of spectators and stopped dead.

* * *

Cardinal Chang crouched on his hands and knees, insensible, drooling. Above him stood a naked woman, for all the world like an animated sculpture of blue glass. The Comte led her by a leather leash linked to a leather collar. Svenson blinked, swallowing. It was the woman from the greenhouse—Angelique!—at any rate it was her body, it was her hair... His mind reeled at the mere implications of what d'Orkancz had done—much less *how* he had done it. His eyes went back to Chang with dismay. Was it possible he'd seen greater distress than Svenson himself? The man was a ruin, his flesh slick and pale, spattered with blood, his garish coat slashed and stained and burned. Svenson's gaze darted past Chang to a raised dais... all of his enemies in a row: the Contessa, Crabbé (but no Bascombe, that was odd), Xonck, and then his own Karl-Horst, arm in arm with the blonde woman from the theatre—as he had feared, Lydia Vandaariff was as much a tool for the Cabal's cruel usage as her father.

Another rolling whisper, like the hiss of incoming surf, and the crowd parted to allow two more women to enter the circle behind Chang. The first was simply clad in a dark dress, with a black mask and black ribbon in her hair. Behind her was a woman with chestnut hair wearing the white silk robes. It was Miss Temple. Chang saw her and pushed himself up on his knees. The woman in black pulled away Miss Temple's mask. Svenson gasped. She bore the scars of the Process vividly imprinted on her face. She said nothing. Out of the corner of his eye Svenson saw Aspiche, a truncheon in his hand. His arm flashed down and Chang fell flat to the floor. Aspiche motioned to two of the Dragoons and pointed them toward where the women had entered.

Chang was dragged away. Miss Temple did not pay him a single glance.

His allies were shattered. One overborne physically, the other mentally, and—he had to face it—both beyond hope of rescue or recovery. And if Miss Temple had been taken, what but death or the same servitude could have been dealt to Elöise? If only he hadn't abandoned them—he had failed again—all one disaster after another! The satchel... if he could get the satchel into the hands of some other government—at the least someone else would *know*... but standing in the thick of the crowded ballroom, Doctor Svenson knew this was just one more vain hope. There was scant chance of escaping the house much less of reaching the frontier or a ship... he had no idea what to do. He looked up at the dais, narrowing his eyes at the simpering Prince. If he'd a pistol he would have stepped forth to blaze away—if he could kill the Prince and another one or two of them, it would have been enough... but even that sacrificial gesture was denied.

The voice of the Contessa broke into his thoughts.

"My dear Celeste," she called, "how fine it is that you have... *joined* us. Mrs. Stearne, I am obliged for your timely entrance."

The woman in black sank into a respectful curtsey.

"Mrs. Stearne!" called the rasping voice of the Comte d'Orkancz. "Do you not wish to see your transformed companions?"

The great man gestured behind him and Svenson was jostled as his fellow guests twisted and craned to see two more gleaming blue women, also naked, also wearing collars, step slowly and deliberately into view, their feet clicking against the parquet floor. Each woman's flesh was shining and bright, transparent enough to show darker streaks of murky indigo within its depths. Both women held in their hands a folded-up leash, and as they neared the Comte each extended her hand for him to take... and, once he did, stood gazing over the crowd with clinical dispassion. The woman nearest him... he swallowed... the hair on her head—in fact, as he looked, he realized with an uncomfortable frisson up the back of his neck that this was the only hair on her body—had been burned above her left temple... the operating theatre... the paraffin... he was looking at Miss Poole. Her body was both beautiful and inhuman—the splendid *tension* of its surface, glassy yet somehow soft—Svenson's skin crawled to look at it, yet he could not turn away, and, appalled, felt his lust begin to stir. And the third woman—it was hard to read their features, but it could only be Mrs. Marchmoor.

The Comte tugged lightly on Miss Poole's leash, and she advanced toward the woman in black. Suddenly that woman's head lolled to the side and she staggered, her eyes dulled. What had happened? Miss Poole turned toward Svenson's side of the crowd. He inched away from her strange eyes, for it was as if they could see to his bones. At once his knees trembled and for a terrible moment the entire room fell away. Svenson was on a settee in a darkened parlor... his hand—a delicate woman's hand—was stroking Mrs. Stearne's unbound hair as, on that lady's other side, a masked man in a cloak leaned over to kiss her mouth. The gaze of Miss Poole (the vision was from her experience, like the blue glass cards, or like the books... she was a *living* book!) turned slightly as, with her other hand, she reached for a glass of wine—her arm in a white robe like Miss Temple's, in fact, *both* women wore the same silk robes of initiation!—but then the parlor snapped away and Svenson was back in the ballroom, fighting the first stirrings of nausea in his throat. All around him, the other guests were shaking their heads, dazed. What violation was this—the effect of the glass cards projected across the audience at large—into every mind!

Doctor Svenson desperately groped to make sense of it—the cards, the Process, the books, and now these women, like three demonic Graces—there was no time! He thought he understood the rest, the Process and the books, for blackmail and influence were standard things, even on such an evil scale, but this—this was alchemy, and he could not comprehend it any more than he could imagine *why* anyone would give themselves over to such—such—abomination!

The Comte was saying something else to Mrs. Stearne—and to the Contessa, and the Contessa was replying—but he could not follow their words, the insistent vision still muddied his brain. Svenson stumbled into the equally disoriented people behind him, then turned to force his way through the crowd, away from his enemies, away from Miss Temple. He did not get seven steps before his mind reeled with another vision... a vision of himself!

He was back at Tarr Manor, facing Miss Poole on the quarry steps, Crabbé scuttling free, the men racing at him, beating aside his feeble blows and snatching him bodily up—and then hurling him over the rail. Again, he was plunged into Miss Poole's experience—of watching his own defeat!—and so immediate that he felt in his nerves the ethereal glide of Miss Poole's amusement at his pathetic efforts.

Svenson gasped aloud, coming back to his senses, on his hands and knees on the parquet floor. People were backing away from him, making room. This is what had happened to Chang. She had sensed him somehow in the crowd. He scrambled wildly to rise, but was rebuffed by the hands around him and propelled against his will toward the center of the room.

He slipped again and fell, flailing with the satchel. It was over. Yet—something... he fought to think—ignoring everything—there were shouts, steps... but Doctor Svenson shook his head, holding on—to—to what he had just seen! In Miss Poole's first vision—of Mrs. Stearne—the man on the settee had been Arthur Trapping, his face marked with the fresh scars of the Process. The memory was of the evening he had died—the very half hour before his murder... and as Miss Poole turned her head to collect her wine, Svenson had seen on the far wall a mirror... and in that mirror, watching from the shadow of a half-open doorway... the unmistakable figure of Roger Bascombe.

He could not help it. He turned his desperate face to Miss Temple, his heart breaking anew to meet her flat indifferent gaze. Aspiche ripped the satchel from his hand and Dragoons took fierce hold of his arms. The Colonel's truncheon swept savagely down and Doctor Svenson was dragged without ceremony to his doom.

TEN

Inheritrix

The Comte d'Orkancz had led them all—Miss Temple, Miss Vandaariff, Mrs. Stearne, and the two soldiers—up the darkened rampway into the theatre. It was as desolate of good feeling as Miss Temple had remembered and her gaze fell upon the empty table with its dangling straps and the stack of wooden boxes beneath it, some pried open, spilling sheets of orange felt, with a dread that nearly buckled her knees. The Comte's iron hand had kept hold of Miss Temple's shoulder and he looked behind to confirm they had all arrived before he passed her off with a nod to Mrs. Stearne, who stepped forward between the two white-robed women, taking a hand from each and squeezing. Despite her deeply rooted anger, Miss Temple found herself squeezing back, for she was finally very frightened, though she prevented herself from actually glancing at the woman. The Comte set his monstrous brass helmet onto one of the table's rust-stained cotton pads (or was that dried blood?) and crossed to the giant blackboard. With swift broad strokes he inscribed the words in bold capital letters: "AND SO SHALL BE REBORN". The writing struck Miss Temple as strangely familiar, as if she recognized it from some place other than this same blackboard on her previous visit. She bit her lip, for the matter seemed somehow important, but she could not call up the memory. The Comte dropped the chalk into the tray and turned to face them.

"Miss Vandaariff shall be first," he announced, his voice again sounding crafted of rough minerals, "for she must take her place in the celebration, and to do so must be sufficiently recovered from her *initiation.* I promise you, my dear, it is but the first of many pleasures on your card for this gala evening."

Miss Vandaariff swallowed and did her best to smile. Where a few moments ago her spirits had been gay, the combination of the room and the Comte's dark manner had obviously rekindled her worry. Miss Temple thought they would have kindled worry in the iron statue of a saint.

"I did not know this room was here," Lydia Vandaariff said, her voice quite small. "Of course there are so many rooms, and my father . . . my father . . . is most occupied—"

"I'm sure he did not think you'd an interest in science, Lydia." Mrs. Stearne smiled. "Surely there are storerooms and workrooms you've never seen as well!"

"I suppose there must be." Miss Vandaariff nodded. She looked out beyond the lights to the empty gallery, hiccuped unpleasantly and covered her mouth with one hand. "But will there be people watching?"

"Of course," said the Comte. "You are an example. You have been such all your life, my dear, in the service of your father. Tonight you serve as one for our work and for your future husband, but most importantly, Miss Vandaariff, for your *self*. Do you understand me?"

She shook her head meekly that she did not.

"Then this is still more advantageous," he rasped, "for I do assure you . . . you *will*."

The Comte reached under his leather apron and removed a silver pocket watch on a chain. He narrowed his eyes and tucked the timepiece away.

"Mrs. Stearne, will you stand away with Miss Vandaariff?"

Miss Temple took a breath for courage as Caroline released her hand and ushered Lydia to the table. The Comte looked past them to nod at the two Macklenburg soldiers.

Before Miss Temple could move the men shot forward and held her fast, raising her up so she stood on the very tips of her toes. The Comte removed his leather gauntlets, tossing them one after the other into the upturned brass helmet. His voice was as deliberate and menacing as the steady strop of a barber's razor.

"As for you, Miss Temple, you will wait until Miss Vandaariff has undergone her trial. You will watch her, and this sight will increase your fear, for you have utterly, utterly lost your very self in this business. Your self will belong to me. And worse than this, and I tell you now so you may contemplate it fully, this *gift,* of your autonomy to my keeping, will be made willingly, happily... *gratefully*... by you. You will look back with whatever memories you keep at the willful gestures of these last days and they will seem the poor antics of a child—or not even, the actions of a disobedient lap-dog. You will be *ashamed.* Trust this, Miss Temple, you will be reborn in this room, contrite and wise... or not at all."

He stared at her. Miss Temple did not—could not—reply.

The Comte snorted, then reached for the pocket watch again and frowned, stuffing it back behind the apron.

"There *was* a disturbance in the outer hallway—" Mrs. Stearne began.

"I am aware of it," rumbled the Comte. "Nevertheless, this... *lateness*—the prospective adherents are sure to be waiting already. I begin to think it was a mistake not to send *you*—"

He turned at the sound of an opening door from the opposite rampway and strode to it.

"Have you an *inkling* of the time, Madame?" he roared into the darkness, and marched back to the table, crouching amidst the boxes beneath it. Behind him, stepping up from the darkened rampway, was the figure of a short curvaceous young woman with curling dark brown hair, a round face, and an eager smile. She wore a mask of peacock feathers and a shimmering pale dress the color of thin honey, sporting a silver fringe around her bosom and her sleeves. Her arms were bare, and in her hands she carried several dull, capped metal flasks. Miss Temple was sure she had seen her before—it was an evening for nagging suspicions—and then it came to her: this was Miss Poole, the third woman in the coach to Harschmort, initiated to the Process that night.

"My goodness, Monsieur le Comte," Miss Poole said brightly. "I am perfectly aware of it, and yet I assure you there was no helping the delay. Our business became dangerously protracted—"

She stopped speaking as she saw Miss Temple.

"Who is this?" she asked.

"Celeste Temple—I believe you *have* met," snapped the Comte. "Protracted how?"

"I shall tell you later." Miss Poole let her gaze drift to Miss Temple, indicating none too subtly the reason she preferred not to speak openly of her delay, then turned to wave girlishly at Mrs. Stearne. "Suffice it to say that I simply *had* to change my dress—that orange dust, don't you know—though before you rail at me, it took no more time than Doctor Lorenz took to prepare your precious clay."

Here she handed the flasks to the Comte and once again danced away from the man toward Miss Vandaariff, lighting up with another beaming smile.

"Lydia!" she squeaked, and took the heiress by the hands as Mrs. Stearne looked on with what to Miss Temple seemed a watchful, veiling smile.

"O Elspeth!" cried Miss Vandaariff. "I came to see you at the hotel—"

"I know you did, my dear, and I *am* sorry, but I was called away to the country—"

"But I felt so *ill*—"

"Poor darling! Margaret was there, was she not?"

Miss Vandaariff nodded silently and then sniffed, as if to say that she did not *prefer* to be soothed by Margaret, as Miss Poole was well aware.

"Actually, Miss Temple was there first," observed Mrs. Stearne rather coolly. "She and Lydia had quite some time to converse before Mrs. Marchmoor was able to intervene."

Miss Poole did not reply, but looked over to Miss Temple, weighing her as an adversary. Returning this condescending gaze, Miss Temple remembered the petty struggle in the coach—for it was Miss Poole's eyes she had poked—and knew that humiliation would remain, despite the Process, in the woman's mind like a whip mark turned to scar. For the rest of it, Miss Poole had just that sort of willfully merry temperament Miss Temple found plain galling to be around, as if one were to consume a full pound of sweet butter at a sitting. Both Mrs. Marchmoor (haughty and dramatic) and Mrs. Stearne (thoughtful and reserved) appeared to be informed by injuries in their lives, where Miss Poole's insistence on gaiety seemed rather a shrill denial. And to Miss Temple's mind all the more repellent, for if she posed as Lydia's true friend, it was only to better ply their awful *philtre*.

"Yes, Lydia and I got on quite well," Miss Temple said. "I have taught her how to poke the eyes of foolish ladies attempting to rise beyond themselves."

Miss Poole's smile became fixed on her face. She glanced back at the Comte—still occupied with the boxes and flasks and lengths of copper wire—and then called to Mrs. Stearne, loud enough for all to hear.

"You did miss so much of interest at Mr. Bascombe's estate—or should I say Lord Tarr? Part of our delay involved the capture and execution of the Prince's physician, Doctor—O what is his name?—a strange fellow, now quite dead, I'm afraid. The other part was one of our subjects; her reaction to the *collection* was averse but not fatal, and she ended up causing, as I say, rather an important problem—though Doctor Lorenz is confident it may be remedied..."

She glanced back to the Comte. He had stopped his work and listened, his face impassive. Miss Poole pretended not to notice and spoke again to Mrs. Stearne, a sly smile gracing the corners of her plump mouth.

"The funny thing, Caroline—and I thought you would be *particularly* interested—is that this Elöise Dujong—is tutor to the children of Arthur and Charlotte *Trapping*."

"I see," said Caroline, carefully, as if she did not know what Miss Poole intended with this comment. "And what happened to this woman?"

Miss Poole gestured to the darkened rampway behind her. "Why, she is just in the outer room. It was Mr. Crabbé's suggestion that such spirited defiance be put to use, and so I have brought her here to be initiated."

Miss Temple saw she was now looking at the Comte, pleased to be giving him information he did not have.

"The woman was intimate with the Trappings?" he asked.

"And thus of course the Xoncks," Miss Poole said. "It was through Francis that she was *seduced* to Tarr Manor."

"Did she reveal anything? About the Colonel's death, or—or about—" With an uncharacteristic reticence, the Comte nodded toward Lydia.

"Not that I am aware—though of course it was the Deputy Minister who interrogated her last."

"Where is Mr. Crabbé?" he asked.

"Actually, it is Doctor Lorenz you should be seeking first, Monsieur le

Comte, for the *damage* the woman has done—if you will remember who else was attending our business at Tarr Manor—is such that the Doctor would very much appreciate your consultation."

"Would he?" snarled the Comte.

"Most urgently." She smiled. "If only there were two of you, Monsieur, for your expertise is required on so many fronts! I do promise that I will do my best to ferret out any clues from this lady—for indeed it seems that a good many people might have wished the Colonel dead."

"Why do you say that, Elspeth?" asked Caroline.

Miss Poole kept her gaze on the Comte as she replied. "I only echo the Deputy Minister. As someone in *between* so many parties, the Colonel was well-placed to divine . . . secrets."

"But all here are in allegiance," said Caroline.

"And yet the Colonel is dead." Miss Poole turned to Lydia, who listened to their talk with a confused half-smile. "And when it is a matter of *secrets* . . . who can say what we don't know?"

The Comte abruptly snatched up his helmet and gloves. This caused him to step closer to Miss Poole—who quite despite herself took a small step backwards.

"You will initiate Miss Vandaariff first," he growled, "and then Miss Temple. Then, if there is time—and *only* if there is time—you will initiate this third woman. Your higher purpose here is to inform those in attendance of our work, not to initiate *per se*."

"But the Deputy Minister—" began Miss Poole.

"His wishes are not your concern. Mrs. Stearne, you will come with me."

"Monsieur?"

It was quite clear that Mrs. Stearne had thought to remain in the theatre.

"There are more *important* tasks," he hissed, and turned as two men in leather aprons and helmets came in dragging a slumped woman between them.

"Miss Poole, you will address our spectators, but do not presume to operate the machinery." He called up to the dark upper reaches of the gallery. "Open the doors!"

He wheeled and was at the rampway in two strides and was gone.

Mrs. Stearne looked once at Miss Temple and then to Lydia, her expression tinged with concern, and then met the smiling face of Miss Poole whose dashing figure had just—in her own opinion at least—somehow turned Mrs. Stearne, in her plain severe dark dress, from her place.

"I'm sure we shall speak later," said Miss Poole.

"Indeed," replied Mrs. Stearne, and she swept after the Comte.

When she was gone Miss Poole flicked her hand at the Comte's two men. Above them all the door had opened and people were flowing into the gallery, whispering at the sight below them on the stage.

"Let us get dear Lydia on the table. Gentlemen?"

Throughout Miss Vandaariff's savage ordeal the two soldiers from Macklenburg held Miss Temple quite firmly between them. Miss Poole had stuffed a plug of cotton wadding into Miss Temple's mouth, preventing her from making a sound. Try as she might to shift the foul mass with her tongue, her efforts only served to dislodge moistened clots at the back of her mouth that she then worried she might swallow and choke upon. She wondered if this Dujong woman had been with Doctor Svenson at the end. At the thought of the poor kind man Miss Temple blinked away a tear, doing her best not to weep, for with a sniffling nose she'd have no way to breathe. The Doctor... dying at Tarr Manor. She did not understand it—Roger had been on the train to Harschmort, he was not *at* Tarr Manor. What was the point of anyone going there? She thought back to the blue glass card, where Roger and the Deputy Minister had been speaking in the carriage... she had assumed Tarr Manor was merely the prize with which Roger had been seduced. Was it possible it was the other way around—that the need for Tarr Manor necessitated their possession of Roger?

But then another nagging thought came to Miss Temple—the last seconds of that card's experience—metal-banded door and the high chamber... the broad-shouldered man leaning over the table, on the table a woman... that very card had come from Colonel Trapping. The man at the table was the Comte. And the woman... Miss Temple could not say.

These thoughts were driven from her head by Lydia's muffled screams, the shrieking machinery, and the truly unbearable smell. Miss Poole stood below the table, describing each step of the Process to her audience as if it were a sumptuous meal—every moment of her smiling enthusiasm belied by the girl's arching back and clutching fingers, her red face and grunts of animal pain. To Miss Temple's lasting disgust, the spectators whispered and applauded at every key moment, treating the entire affair like a circus exhibition. Did they have any idea who lay in sweating torment before them—a beauty to rival any Royal, the darling of the social press, heiress to an empire? All they saw was a woman writhing, and another woman telling them how fine a thing it was. It seemed to her that this was Lydia Vandaariff's whole existence in a nutshell.

Once it was over however, Miss Temple chided herself bitterly. She did not think she actually could have broken from the two soldiers, but she was certain that this period of sparking, ghastly chaos was the only time she might have had a chance. Instead, as soon as the Comte's men unstrapped Lydia and eased her limp form from the table—the unctuous Miss Poole whispering eagerly into the shattered girl's ear—the soldiers stepped forward and hefted Miss Temple into her place. She kicked her legs but these were immediately caught and held firmly down. In a matter of helpless seconds she was on her back, the cotton pads beneath her hot and damp from Lydia's sweat, the belts cinched close across her waist, neck, and bosom and each limb tightly bound. The table was angled so those in the gallery could see the whole of her body, but Miss Temple could only see the glare of the hot paraffin lamps and an indistinct mass of shadowed faces—as uncaring to her condition as those waiting with empty plates are to the frightened beast beneath the knife.

She stared at Lydia as the tottering young woman—sweat-sheened face, hair damp against the back of her neck, eyes dull and mouth slack—was briskly examined by Miss Poole. With a tremor Miss Temple thought of the defiant course of her short life—itself a litany of governesses and aunts, rivals and suitors, Bascombes and Pooles and Marchmoors . . . she would now join them, edges stripped away, her velocity set to their destinations, her determination yoked like an ox to work in someone else's field.

And what had she wanted instead? Miss Temple was not without insight and she saw how genuinely free the Process had made both

Marchmoor and Poole, and—she did not frankly doubt it—how Lydia Vandaariff would now find her will of steel. Even Roger—her breath huffed around the gag with a plangent whine as his visage crossed her inner eye—she knew had been formerly restrained by a decency rooted in fear and timid desire. It did not make them *wise*—she had only to recall the way Roger could not reconcile her present deeds with the fiancée he had known—but it made them fierce. Miss Temple choked again as the cotton wadding nudged the slick softness at the back of her throat. She was *already* fierce. She required none of this nonsense, and if she'd carried a man's strength and her father's horsewhip these villains would as one be on their knees.

But in addition Miss Temple realized—barely listening to Miss Poole's disquisition—that so much of this struggle came down to dreams. Mrs. Marchmoor had been released from the brothel, Mrs. Stearne from fallow widowhood, and Miss Poole from a girlish hope to marry the best man within reach... which was all to say that of course she understood. What *they* did not understand—what no one understood, from her raging father to her aunt to Roger to the Comte and the Contessa with their wicked violations—was the particular character of her own desires, her own sunbaked, moist-aired, salt-tinged dreams. In her mind she saw the sinister *Annunciation* fragments of Oskar Veilandt, the expression of astonished sensation on Mary's face and the gleaming blue hands with their cobalt nails pressing into her giving flesh... and yet she knew her own desire, however inflamed at the rawness of that physical transaction, was in truth elsewhere configured... her colors—the pigments of her need—existed before an artist's interposition—crumbled, primal minerals and untreated salts, feathers and bones, shells oozing purple ink, damp on a table top and still reeking of the sea.

Such was Miss Temple's heart, and with it beating strong within her now she felt no longer fear, but near to spitting rage. She knew she would not die, for their aim was corruption—as if to skip the act of death completely and leap ahead to the slow decomposition of her soul, through worms that they would here place in her mind. She would not have it. She would fight them. She would stay who she was no matter what—no matter what—and she would kill them all! She snapped her head to the side as one of the Comte's attendants loomed over her and replaced her white mask with the glass and metal goggles, pushing them tight so the black rubber seal sucked fast against her skin. She whined against the gag, for the metal edges pressed sharply and were bitter cold. Any moment the copper wires would surge with current. Knowing that agony was but seconds away, Miss Temple could only toss her head again and decide with all the force of her will that Lydia Vandaariff was a weakling, that it would not be difficult at all, that she should thrash and scream only to convince them of their success, not because they made her.

Into the theatre two soldiers brought this Miss Dujong, slumped and unresponsive, and deposited her onto the floor. The unfortunate woman had been bundled into the white robes, but her hair hung over her face and Miss Temple had no clear picture of her age or beauty. She gagged again on the wadding in her mouth and pulled at the restraints.

They did not pull the switch. She cursed them bitterly for toying so. They would *die*. Every one of them would be punished. They had killed Chang. They had killed Svenson. But this would not be the end . . . Miss Temple was not *prepared* to allow—

The straps around her head were fast, but not so tight that she did not hear the gunshots . . . then angry shouts from Miss Poole—and then more shots and Miss Poole's voice leapt from outrage to a fearful shriek. But this was shattered by a crash that shook the table itself, another even louder chorus of screams . . . and then she smelled the smoke and felt the heat of flame—flame!—on her bare feet! She could not speak or move, and the thick goggles afforded only the most opaque view of the darkening ceiling. What had happened to the lights? Had the roof fallen in? Had her "gunshots" actually been exploding joists from an unsound ceiling? The heat was sharper on her feet. Would they abandon her to burn alive? If they did not, if she pretended to be injured they would not hold her tightly—a stout push and she could run the other way . . . but what if her captors had already fled and left her behind to burn?

A hand groped at her arm and she twisted to take hold of whoever it was—she could not turn her head, she could not see through the thickening smoke—and squeeze—they must free her, they must! She curled her toes away from the rising flames, biting back a cry. The hand pulled away and her heart fell—but a moment later hands fumbled at the belt. She was a fool—how could the fellow free her if she held his arm? After another desperately distended moment the strap gave way and her hands were free. Her rescuer's attention dropped to her feet and without a thought Miss Temple's hands flew to her face, ripping at the mask. She found the release screw—for she had felt the point from which the thing was tightened—and scraped her finger tearing it loose. The goggles fell away and Miss Temple caught a handful of copper wire and sat up, dangling the contraption behind her like a medieval morning star, ready to bring it down on the head of whatever conscience-stricken functionary had thought to save her.

He'd managed the other straps and she felt the man's arms snake under her legs and behind her back to scoop her from the table and set her feet down on the floor. Miss Temple snorted at the presumption—the silk robes might as well have been her shift, a shocking intimacy no matter the circumstance—and raised her hand to swing the heavy goggles (which bore all sorts of jagged metal bolts that might find vicious purchase), while with her other hand she pried the sopping gag from her mouth. The smoke was thick—across the table the flames flickered into view, an orange line dividing gallery from stage and blocking off the far rampway, where she could hear shouts and see figures looming in the murk. She took a lungful of foul air and coughed. Her rescuer had his hand around her waist, his shoulder leaning close. She took aim at the back of his head.

"This way! Can you walk?"

Miss Temple stopped her swing—the voice—she hesitated—and then he pulled her down below the line of smoke. Her eyes snapped open, both in unlooked-for delight at the man she found before her, and at the desperately stricken image that man presented, as if he had indeed crawled up through hell to find her.

"Can you walk?" Doctor Svenson shouted again.

Miss Temple nodded, her fingers releasing the goggles. She wanted to throw her arms around his shoulders and would have done that very thing had he not then pulled her arm and pointed to the other woman—

Dujong?—who had come from Tarr Manor and was now hunched against the curved wall of the theatre with the Doctor's coat thrown across her legs.

"She cannot!" he shouted above the roaring flames. "We must help her!"

The woman looked up to them as the Doctor took her arm and duty-bound Miss Temple took her other side. They lifted her with an awkward stumble—in the back of her mind Miss Temple was entirely unsure—in fact, annoyed—about the choice to adopt this new companion, though at least now the woman was able to move and mutter whatever she was muttering to Doctor Svenson. Hadn't Miss Poole described her as "seduced by Francis Xonck"? Wasn't she some sort of adherent possessing privileged information? The last thing Miss Temple desired was the company of such a person, any more than she appreciated the Doctor's earnest frown of concern as he brushed the hair from the woman's sweat-smeared face. Behind them she heard steps and a piercing wave of sharp hissing—buckets emptied into the fire—and then coughed at the roiling smoky steam that billowed into their faces. The Doctor leaned across the Dujong woman to call to her.

"—Chang! There is a—machine—the Dragoon—do not—glass books!"

Miss Temple nodded but even apart from the noise the information was too thick to make sensible in her mind—too many other sensations crowded for her attention—hot metal and broken wood beneath her bare feet, with one hand under the woman's arm and the other out before her, feeling in the gloom. What had happened to the lights? From the once-blazing array she saw but one distracted orange glow, like a weak winter sun unable to reach through fog—what *had* happened to Miss Poole? Doctor Svenson turned—there was motion behind them—and thrust his half of the woman wholly onto Miss Temple, who stumbled forward. His hand was shoving at her, driving her on. In the shadows she saw Doctor Svenson extend a revolver toward their pursuers and heard him shout.

"Go! Go at once!"

Never one to misunderstand her own immediate needs, Miss Temple dipped her knees, threw the burdensome woman's arm over her shoulder and then stood straight with a grunt, Miss Temple's other hand around her waist, doing her best to carry what weight she could, rolling on her tiptoes away from the wall to stumble down the rampway, hoping the slope would create enough momentum to keep Miss Dujong propelled. They slammed into the far wall at the curve, both of them crying out (the bulk of the impact absorbed by the taller woman's shoulder), careened backwards and wavered, nearly toppling, until Miss Temple managed to angle them along the next part of the pitch-black passage. Her feet caught on something soft and both women went down in a heap, their fall broken by the inert body that had tripped them. Miss Temple's groping hand fell onto leather—the apron—this was one of the Comte's attendants—and then into a sticky trail on the floor that must be his blood. She wiped her hand on the apron and got her feet beneath her and her hands under the arms of Miss Dujong, heaving her over the body. She heaved her again—Miss Temple huffed with the knowledge that she simply was not meant for this sort of work—and felt in front of her for the door. It was not locked, nor did the fallen man block its opening. With another gasp she pulled Miss Dujong through its bright archway, into light and cool sweet air.

She dragged the woman as far as she could onto the carpet with one sustained burst of effort, until her legs caught beneath her and she tripped, sitting down. On her hands and knees Miss Temple crawled back to the open door and looked for any sign of Doctor Svenson. Smoke seeped into the room. She did not see him, and slammed the door, leaning against it to catch her breath.

The attiring room was empty. She could hear the commotion in the theatre behind her, and racing footsteps in the mirrored hall on the other side. She looked down to her charge, presently attempting to rise to her hands and knees, and saw the blacked soles of the woman's bare feet and the singed, discolored silk at the hem of her robes.

"Can you understand me?" Miss Temple hissed impatiently. "Miss Dujong? *Miss Dujong.*"

The woman turned to her voice, hair across her face, doing her best to move in the awkward robe that, with Doctor Svenson's greatcoat, was tangling her legs. Miss Temple sighed and crouched in front of the woman, doing her best to give an impression of kindness and care, knowing well there was precious little time—or, to be honest, feeling—for either.

"My name is Celeste Temple. I am a friend of Doctor Svenson. He is behind us—he will catch up, I am sure—but if we do not escape his efforts will be wasted. Do you understand me? We are at Harschmort House. They are keen to murder us both."

The woman blinked like a rock lizard. Miss Temple took hold of her jaw.

"Do you *understand*?"

The woman nodded. "I'm sorry... they..." Her hand fluttered in a vague and indefinite gesture. "I cannot think..."

Miss Temple snorted and then, still gripping her jaw, sorted the woman's hair from her face with brisk darts of her fingers, tucking away the wisps like a bird stabbing together its nest. She was older than Miss Temple—in her presently haggard condition it was unfair to guess by how many years—and as she allowed herself to be held and groomed, there emerged in her features a delicate *wholeness* with which Miss Temple grudgingly found a certain reluctant sympathy.

"Not thinking is perfectly all right." Miss Temple smiled, only a little tightly. "I can think for the pair of us—in point of fact I should prefer it. I cannot however *walk* for the pair of us. If we are to live—to *live,* Miss Dujong—you must be able to move."

"Elöise," she whispered.

"I beg your pardon?"

"My name is Elöise."

"Excellent. That will make everything much easier."

Miss Temple did not even risk opening the far door, for she knew the corridor beyond would be full of servants and soldiers—though why they did not come at the fire through this room she had no idea. Could the prohibition against entering such a secret room—one that so obviously loomed in the Cabal's deepest designs—carry over in the staff to even this time of crisis? She turned back to Elöise, who was still on her knees, holding in her arms a savaged garment—no doubt the dress she had arrived in.

"They have destroyed it," Miss Temple told her, crossing past to the open cabinets. "It is their way. I suggest you turn your head..."

"Are you changing clothes?" asked Elöise, doing her best to stand.

Miss Temple pushed aside the open cabinet doors and saw the wicked mirror behind. She looked about her and found a wooden stool.

"O no," she replied, "I am breaking glass."

Miss Temple shut her eyes at the impact and flinched away, but all the same the destruction was enormously satisfying. With each blow she thought of another enemy—Spragg, Farquhar, the Contessa, Miss Poole—and at every jolting of her arms her face glowed the more with healthy pleasure. Once the hole was made, but not yet wide enough to pass through, she looked back at Miss Dujong with a conspiratorial grin.

"There is a secret room," she whispered, and at Miss Dujong's hesitant nod wheeled round to swing again. It was the sort of activity that could easily have occupied another thirty minutes of her time, chipping away at this part and at that, knocking free each hanging shard. As it was, Miss Temple called herself to business, dropped the stool, and carefully stepped back to Elöise's tattered dress. Between them they spread it across their path to absorb at least what fallen glass it could, and made their way through the mirror. Once in, Miss Temple gathered the dress and, balling it in her hands, threw it back across the room. She looked a last time at the inner door, her worry grown at the Doctor's non-arrival, and reached for the cabinet doors on either side, pulling them to conceal the open mirror. She turned to Elöise, who clutched the poor man's coat close to her body.

"He will find us," Miss Temple told her. "Why don't you take my arm?"

They did not speak as they padded along the dim carpeted passageway, their pale, smoke-smeared faces and their silken robes made red in the lurid gaslight. Miss Temple wanted to put as much distance as she could between themselves and the fire, and only then address escape and disguise... and yet at each turn she looked back and listened, hoping for some sign of the Doctor. Could he have effected their rescue only to sacrifice himself—and what was more, maroon her with a companion she neither knew nor had reason to trust? She felt the weight of Elöise on her arm and heard again his urgent words to go, go at once... and hurried forward.

Their narrow path came to a crossroads. To the left it went on, the dead-end wall ahead of them was fitted with a ladder rising into a darkened shaft, while to the right was a heavy red curtain. Miss Temple cautiously reached out with one finger and edged the curtain aside. It was another observation chamber, looking into a rather large, empty parlor. If she truly wanted to evade pursuit, the last thing she needed to do was leave a second broken mirror in her trail. She stepped back from the curtain. Elöise could not climb the ladder. They kept walking to the left.

"How do you feel?" Miss Temple asked, putting as much hearty confidence as she could into a stealthy whisper.

"Palpably better," answered Elöise. "Thank you for helping me."

"Not at all," said Miss Temple. "You know the Doctor. We are old comrades."

"Comrades?" Miss Dujong looked at her, and Miss Temple saw disbelief in the woman's eyes—her size, her strength, the foolish robes—and felt a fresh spike of annoyance.

"Indeed." She nodded. "It would perhaps be better if you understood that the Doctor, myself, and a man named Cardinal Chang have joined forces against a Cabal of sinister figures with sinister intent. I do not know which of these you know—the Comte d'Orkancz, the Contessa di Lacquer-Sforza, Francis *Xonck*"—this name offered rather pointedly with a rise of Miss Temple's eyebrows—"Harald Crabbé, the Deputy Foreign Minister, and Lord Robert Vandaariff. There are many lesser villains in their party—Mrs. Marchmoor, Miss Poole—whom I believe you know—Caroline Stearne, Roger Bascombe, far too many Germans—it's all quite difficult to summarize, of course, but there is apparently something about the Prince of Macklenburg and there is a *great* deal to do with a queer blue glass that can be made into books, books that hold—or consume—actual memories, actual experiences—it's really quite extraordinary—"

"Yes, I have seen them," whispered Elöise.

"You have?" Miss Temple's voice was tinged with disappointment, for she found herself suddenly eager to describe her own astonishing experience to someone else.

"They exposed each of us to such a book—"

"Who 'they'?" asked Miss Temple.

"Miss Poole, and Doctor... Doctor Lorenz." Elöise swallowed. "Some of the women could not bear it... they were killed."

"Because they would not look?"

"No, no—because they did look. Killed by the book itself."

"*Killed?* By looking in the books?"

"I do believe it."

"I was not killed."

"Perhaps you are very strong," answered Elöise.

Miss Temple sniffed. She rarely discredited flattery, even when she knew the point of the moment lay elsewhere (as when Roger had praised her delicacy and humor at the same time that his hand around her waist sought to wander exploratively southward), but Miss Temple *had* pulled herself from the book, by her own power—an achievement even the forever condescending Contessa had remarked upon. The idea that the opposite was possible—that she could have been swallowed utterly, that she could have *perished*—sent a brittle shiver down her back. It would have been absolutely effortless, true—the contents of the book had been so seductive. But she had not perished—and what was more, Miss Temple felt fully confident that should she look into another of these books its hold would be even weaker, for as she had pulled free once, she would know she could do so again. She turned back to Elöise, still unconvinced of the woman's true character.

"But you must be strong as well, of course, as a person our enemies sought to add to their ranks—just as you were brought to Tarr Manor to begin with. For this is why we wear these robes, you know—to initiate our minds into their insidious mysteries, a Process to bend our wills to their own."

She stopped and looked down at herself, plucking at the robes with both hands.

"At the same time, though I would not call it *practical,* the feel of silk against one's body is nevertheless . . . *well* . . . so . . ."

Elöise smiled, or at least made the attempt, but Miss Temple saw the woman's lower lip hesitantly quiver.

"It is just . . . you see, I do not *remember* . . . I know I went to Tarr Manor for a reason, but for my life I cannot call it to mind!"

"It is best we keep on our way," Miss Temple said, glancing to see if the quivering lip had been followed by tears, and breathing with relief that it had not. "And you can tell me what you do remember of Tarr

Manor. Miss Poole mentioned Francis Xonck, and of course Colonel Trapping—"

"I am tutor to the Colonel's children," said Elöise, "and known to Mr. Xonck—indeed, he has been most attentive ever since the Colonel disappeared." She sighed. "You see, I am a confidante of Mr. Xonck's sister, the Colonel's wife—I was even present here, at Harschmort House, the night the Colonel disappeared—"

"You were?" asked Miss Temple, a bit abruptly.

"I have asked myself if I inadvertently witnessed some clue, or overheard some secret—anything to entice Mr. Xonck to curiosity, or that he might use against his siblings, or even to conceal his own part in the Colonel's death—"

"Is it possible you knew who had killed him or why?" asked Miss Temple.

"I have no idea!" cried Elöise.

"But if those memories are gone, then it follows they must have been worth taking," observed Miss Temple.

"Yes, but because I learned something I should not have? Or because I was—there is no other word—seduced to even take part?"

Elöise stopped, her hand over her mouth, tears gleaming in each eye. The woman's despair struck Miss Temple as real, and she knew as well as anyone—after her experience of the book—how temptation might sway the sternest soul. If she could not remember what she'd done, if she was here stricken with regret, did the truth of it really matter? Miss Temple had no idea—no more than she might parse the relative state of her own bodily innocence. For the first time she allowed a gentle nudge of pity to enter her voice.

"But they did not enlist you," she said. "Miss Poole told the Comte and Caroline that you were quite a nuisance."

Elöise exhaled heavily and shrugged Miss Temple's words away. "The Doctor rescued me from an attic, and then was taken. I followed, with his gun, and tried to rescue him in turn. In the process—I'm sorry, it is difficult to speak of it—I shot a man. I shot him dead."

"But that is excellent, I'm sure," replied Miss Temple. "I have not shot anyone, but I have killed one man outright and another by way of a co-operative coach wheel." Elöise did not reply, so Miss Temple helpfully went on. "I actually spoke of it—well, as much as one speaks of anything—with Cardinal Chang, who you must understand is a man of few words—indeed, a man of *mystery*—the very first time I laid eyes upon him I knew it was so—granted, this was because he was wearing all red in a train car in the very early morning holding a razor and reading poetry—and wearing dark spectacles, for he has suffered injury to his eyes—and though I did not know him I did remark him, in my mind, and when I saw him again—when we became comrades with the Doctor—I knew who he was at once. The Doctor said something about him—about Chang—just now, I mean to say, in the theatre—I didn't make sense of any of it for that abominable shouting and the smoke and the fire—and do you know, it is a queer thing, but I have noticed it, how at times the extremity of, well, *information,* assaulting one of our senses overwhelms another. For example, the *smell* and the *sight* of the smoke and flames absolutely inhibited my ability to *hear*. It is exactly the sort of thing I find fascinating to think on."

They walked for a moment before Miss Temple recalled the original drift of her thought.

"But—*yes*—the reason I spoke to Cardinal Chang—well, you see, I must explain that Cardinal Chang is a *dangerous* man, a very deadly fellow—who has probably killed a man more often than I have purchased shoes—and I spoke to him about the men I had killed, and—well, honestly it was very difficult to talk about, and what he ended up telling me was exactly how someone like myself ought to use a pistol—which was to grind the barrel as tightly into the body of your target as you can. Do you see my point? He was telling me what to *do* as a way of helping me sort out how to *feel*. Because at the time, I had no idea how to talk of anything. Yet these things that have happened—they tell us what kind of world we are in, and what sort of actions we must be prepared to take. If you had not shot this fellow, would either yourself or the Doctor be still alive? And without the Doctor to take me off that table, would I?"

* * *

Elöise did not answer. Miss Temple saw her wrestling with her doubts and knew from experience that to overcome those doubts and accept what had occurred was to become a significantly less innocent person.

"But this was the Duke of Stäelmaere," Elöise whispered. "It is assassination. You do not understand—I will assuredly hang!"

Miss Temple shook her head.

"The men *I* killed were villains," she said. "And I am sure this Duke was the same—most Dukes are simply *horrid*—"

"Yes, but no one will care—"

"Nonsense, for I care, as you care, as I am sure Doctor Svenson cared—it is the exact heart of the matter. What I do *not* give a brass farthing for is the opinion of our enemies."

"But—the *law*—their word will be believed—"

Miss Temple gave her opinion of the law with a dismissive shrug.

"You may well have to leave—perhaps the Doctor can take you back to Macklenburg, or you can escort my aunt on a tour of Alsatian restaurants—but there is always a remedy. For example—look how foolish we are, waltzing along who knows where without a second's thought!"

Elöise looked behind them, gesturing vaguely. "But—I thought—"

"Yes, of course." Miss Temple nodded. "We will surely be pursued, but have either of us had the presence of mind to look through the Doctor's pockets? He is a resourceful man—one never knows—my father's overseer would not step foot from his door, as a rule, without a knife, a bottle, dried meat, and a twist of tobacco that could fill his pipe for a week." She smiled slyly. "And who can say—in the process it may afford a glimpse into the secret life of Doctor Svenson . . ."

Elöise spoke quickly. "But—but I am sure there is no such thing—"

"O come, every person has some secrets."

"I do not, I assure you—or at least nothing indecent—"

Miss Temple scoffed. "*Decent?* What are you wearing? Look at you—I can see your legs—your bare legs! What use is decency when we have been thrust into this peril—treading about without even a corset! Are we to be judged? Do not be silly—here."

She reached out and took the Doctor's coat, but then wrinkled her nose at its condition. The ruddy light might hide its stains but she could smell earth and oil and sweat, as well as the strongly unpleasant odor of indigo clay. She batted at it ineffectually, launching little puffs of dust, and gave up. Miss Temple dug into the Doctor's side pocket and removed a cardboard box of cartridges for his revolver. She handed it to Elöise.

"There—we now know he is a man to carry bullets."

Elöise nodded impatiently, as if this were against her wishes. Miss Temple met her gaze and narrowed her eyes.

"Miss Dujong—"

"Mrs."

"Beg pardon?"

"Mrs. Mrs. Dujong. I am a widow."

"My condolences."

Elöise shrugged. "I am well accustomed to it."

"Excellent. The thing is, Mrs. Dujong," Miss Temple's tone was still crisp and determined, "in case you had not noticed, Harschmort is a house of masks and mirrors and lies, of unscrupulous, brutal advantage. We cannot afford illusion—about ourselves least of all, for this is what our enemies exploit *most* of all. I have seen notorious things, I promise you, and notorious things have been done to me. I too have undergone—" She lost her way and could not speak, taken unawares by her own emotion, gesturing instead with the coat, shaking it. "*This* is nothing. Searching someone's *coat*? Doctor Svenson may have given his *life* to save us—do you think he would scruple the contents of his pockets if they might help us further—or help us to save him? It is no time to be a foolish woman."

Mrs. Dujong did not answer, avoiding Miss Temple's gaze, but then nodded and held out her hands, cupping them to take whatever else might come from the coat pockets. Working quickly—despite the pleasure it gave her, Miss Temple was not one to continue with criticism once her point was made—she located the Doctor's cigarette case, matches, the other blue card, an extremely filthy handkerchief, and a mixed handful of coins. They gazed at the collection and with a sigh Miss Temple began to restore them to their places in the coat—for that seemed the simplest way to carry them.

"After all of that, it appears you are right—I do not think we have learned a thing." She looked up to see Elöise studying the silver cigarette case. It was simple and unadorned save for, engraved in a simple, elegant script, the words "*Zum Kapitänchirurgen Abelard Svenson, vom C. S.*"

"Perhaps it commemorates his promotion to Captain-Surgeon," whispered Elöise.

Miss Temple nodded. She put the case back in its pocket, knowing they were both wondering at who had given it to him—a fellow officer, a secret love? Miss Temple draped the coat over her arm and shrugged—if the last initial was "S" it needn't be interesting at all, most likely a dutiful token from some dull sibling or cousin.

They continued down the narrow red-lit passage, Miss Temple dispirited that the Doctor had not caught up, and a bit curious that no one else had pursued them either. She did her best not to sigh with impatience when she felt the other woman's hand on her arm, and upon turning tried to present a tolerant visage.

"I am sorry," Elöise began.

Miss Temple opened her mouth—the last thing she appreciated after berating a person was that they should *then* waste her time with apology. But Elöise touched her arm again and kept on speaking.

"I have not been thinking... and there are things that I must say—"

"Must you?"

"I was taken aboard the airship. They asked me questions. I do not know what I could have told them—in truth I know nothing that they cannot already know from Francis Xonck—but I do remember what they asked."

"Who was it asking?"

"Doctor Lorenz gave me the drug, and bound my arms, and then he and Miss Poole made certain I was under their influence by the most impertinent demands... I was powerless to refuse... though I am ashamed to think of it..."

The woman's voice dipped deeper in her throat. Miss Temple thought of her own experience at the mercy of the Comte and Contessa, and her heart went out—yet she could not help speculating on the exact details of what had happened. She patted the woman's silk-covered arm. Elöise sniffed.

"And then Minister Crabbé interrogated me. About the Doctor. And about you. And about this Chang. And then about my killing the Duke—he would not believe I had not been put up to it by another party."

Miss Temple audibly scoffed.

"But *then* he asked me—and in a voice that I do not think was heard by the others—about Francis Xonck. At first I thought he meant my employment by Mr. Xonck's sister, but he wanted to know about Mr. Xonck's plans *now*. Was I in service to him *now*. When I replied that I was not—or at least did not *know*—he asked about the Comte and the Contessa—especially about the Contessa—"

"It seems a long list," replied Miss Temple, who was already impatient. "What about them *exactly*?"

"If they had killed Colonel Trapping. He was particularly suspicious of the Contessa, for I gather she does not always tell the others what she plans to do, or does things without caring how it may ruin their plans."

"And what did you tell Deputy Minister Crabbé?" Miss Temple asked.

"Why, nothing at all—I *knew* nothing."

"And his response?"

"Well, I do not know the man, of course—"

"If you were to hazard a *guess*?"

"That is just it . . . I should say he was frightened."

Miss Temple frowned. "I do not mean to insult your former employer," she said, "but from all accounts . . . well, it seems the Colonel is not exactly *missed* for his good qualities. Yet as you describe Deputy Minister Crabbé's curiosity, so I heard the Comte d'Orkancz pressing Miss Poole for the same information—and indeed the Contessa and Xonck asking as well, in a coach from the station. Why should all of them care so much for such a, well . . . such a *wastrel*?"

"I cannot think they would," said Elöise.

Whoever killed the Colonel defied the rest of the Cabal in doing so . . . or was it that they had *already* defied the Cabal—already planned to betray them? Somehow Trapping knew and was killed before he told the others! The Colonel still breathed when Miss Temple had left him: either he had just been poisoned or was poisoned directly afterwards. She had been on her way to the theatre . . . by the time she got there, the Comte was *in* the theatre . . . as was Roger—she'd watched Roger climb the spiral staircase before her. She had not seen Crabbé or Xonck—she'd no idea then who Xonck *was*—nor any of the Macklenburgers. But behind her—behind everyone and alone in the corridor . . . had been the Contessa.

Their passage came to an end. To one side was a third curtained alcove, and to the other was a door. They peeked around the curtain. This viewing chamber was dominated by a larger chaise draped with silken quilts and furs. In addition to the drinks cabinet and writing desk they had seen before, this room was fitted with a brass speaking tube and a metal grille that must allow for instructions to be relayed between each side of the mirror. It was not a room for observation alone, but for interrogation . . . or a more closely directed private performance.

The room that lay beyond the wall of glass was like no other Miss Temple had seen at Harschmort, but it might have disturbed her even more than the operating theatre. It was a pale room with a simple floor of unvarnished planking, lit by a plain hanging lamp that threw a circle of yellow light onto the single piece of furniture, a chaise identical to the one before them, distinguished by both an absence of silks and furs and the metal shackles bolted to its wooden frame.

But it was not for the chaise that upon looking through the mirror Miss Temple's breath stopped fast, for in the open doorway of the room, looking down at its single piece of furniture, stood the Contessa di Lacquer-Sforza, red jewel-teared mask over her face and a smoking cigarette holder at her lips. She exhaled, tapped her ash to the floor and snapped her fingers at the open door behind her, stepping aside to allow two men in brown cloaks to carry in between them one of the long wooden boxes. She waited for them to pry open the box top with a metal tool and leave the room, before snapping her fingers again. The man who entered, his manner an awkward mix of deference and amused condescension, wore a dark uniform and a gold-painted mask over the upper half of his face. His pale hair was thin and his chin was weak, and when he smiled she saw his teeth were bad as well. On his finger however was a large gold ring . . . Miss Temple looked again at the uniform . . . the ring was a signet . . . this was Doctor Svenson's Prince! She had seen him in the suite at the Royale—and had not recognized him at once in a more formal uniform and different mask. He sat on the chaise and called back to the Contessa.

They could not hear. Moving quietly to the brass grille, Miss Temple saw a small brass knob fitted to it. The knob did not pull, so she tried to turn it, moving ever so slowly if it should squeak. Its movement was silent, but suddenly they could hear the Prince.

"—gratified of course, most enthusiastically, though not surprised, you must know, for as the mighty among animals will recognize one another across an expanse of forest, so those in society matched by a natural superiority will similarly gravitate, it being only fitting that spirits united in an *essential* sympathy be followed by a sympathy of a more *corporeal* nature—"

The Prince was in the midst of unbuttoning the collar of his tunic. The Contessa had not moved. Miss Temple could not readily credit that such a man could be so shamelessly describing to such a woman the destined aspect of their imminent assignation—though she knew one could scarcely underestimate the arrogance of princes. Still, she pursed her lips with dismay at his droning prattle, as he all the while dug at the double row of silver buttons with a pale hooked finger. Miss Temple looked to Mrs. Dujong, whose expression was equally unsteady, and leaned her lips quite close against her ear.

"That is the Doctor's Prince," she whispered, "and the Contessa—"

Before she could say more the Contessa took another step into the room and closed the door behind her. At the sound the Prince paused, interrupting his words with an unhealthily gratified leer that revealed a bicuspid gone grey. He dropped a hand to his belt buckle.

"Truly, Madame, I have longed for this since the moment I first kissed your hand—"

The Contessa's voice was loud and sharp, her words spoken clearly and without regard for sense.

"Blue Joseph blue Palace ice consumption."

The Prince went silent, his jaw hanging open, his fingers still. The Contessa stepped closer to him, inhaled thoughtfully from her lacquered holder and let the smoke pour from her mouth as she spoke, as if upon exercising her hidden power she had become that much more demonic.

"Your Highness, you will believe you have had your way with me in this room. Though it would very much give you pleasure, you will be unable to convey this information to anyone else under any circumstances. Do you understand?"

The Prince nodded.

"Our *engagement* will have occupied your time for the next thirty minutes, so it will be impossible that I have in this time seen either Lydia Vandaariff or her father. During our encounter I have also confessed to you that the Comte d'Orkancz prefers the erotic companionship of boys. You will be unable to convey this information to anyone else either, though because of it you will not begrudge any request the Comte might have for unaccompanied visits to your bride. Do you understand?"

The Prince nodded.

"Finally, despite our encounter this evening, you will believe that upon this night you have taken the virginity of Miss Vandaariff, before you are married, so rapacious is your sexual appetite, and so little can she resist you. In the event she conceives, it is therefore entirely as a result of your own impulsive efforts. Do you understand?"

The Prince nodded. The Contessa turned, for at the door behind her came a gentle knock. She opened it a crack, and then, seeing who it was, wide enough for that person to enter.

Miss Temple put her hand over her mouth. It was Roger Bascombe.

"Yes?" asked the Contessa, speaking quietly.

"You wanted to know—I am off to collect the books from this night's *harvest,* and meet the Deputy Minister—"

"And deliver the books to the Comte?"

"Of course."

"You know which one I need."

"Lord Vandaariff's, yes."

"Make sure it is in place. And watch Mr. Xonck."

"For what?"

"I'm sure I do not know, Mr. Bascombe—thus the need to watch him closely."

Roger nodded. His eyes glanced past the Contessa to the man on the chaise, who followed their words with an ignorant curiosity, like a cat captivated by a beam of light thrown from a prism. The Contessa followed Roger's gaze and smirked.

"Tell the Comte this much is done. The Prince and I are in the midst of a torrid assignation, do you see?"

She permitted herself a throaty chuckle at the ridiculousness of that prospect and then sighed with contemplative pleasure, as if she were in the midst of a thought.

"It is a terrible thing when one is unable to resist one's impulses..." She smiled to Bascombe and then called to the Prince. "My dear Karl-Horst, you are having your way with my body even now—your mind is writhing with sensation—you have never felt such ecstasy and you never will again. Instead you will always measure your future pleasure against this moment... and find it lacking."

She laughed again. The Prince's face was pink, his hips twitching awkwardly on the chaise, his nails scratching feebly at the upholstery. The Contessa glanced at Roger with a wry smile that to Miss Temple was confirmation that her ex-fiancé was just as much subject to this woman's power as the Prince. The Contessa turned back to the man on the chaise.

"You... may... *finish,*" she said, teasing him as if he were a dog awaiting a treat.

At her words the Prince went still, breathing air in gulps, whimpering, both hands clutching the chaise. After what seemed to Miss Temple a very brief time, he exhaled deeply, his shoulders sagged from his effort, and the unpleasant smile returned to his face. He absently plucked at his darkening trousers and licked his lips. Miss Temple scoffed with abhorrence at the entire spectacle.

Her eyes snapped to the Contessa and her hand flew up to cover her mouth. The Contessa glared directly into the mirror. The speaking tube—the knob had been turned. Miss Temple's scoff had been heard.

The Contessa barked harshly at Roger. "Someone is there! Get Blenheim! Around the other side—*immediately*!"

Miss Temple and Elöise stumbled back to their curtain as Roger dashed from sight and the Contessa strode toward them, her expression dark with rage. As she passed, the Prince attempted to stand and take her into his arms.

"My darling—"

Without a pause she struck him across the face, knocking him straight to his knees. She reached the mirror and screamed as if she could see their startled faces.

"Whoever you are—whatever you are doing—you will die!"

Miss Temple dragged Elöise by the hand through the curtain and to the nearby door. It did not matter where it went, they had to get out of the passage at once. Even wearing a half-mask the fury on the Contessa's face had been that of a Gorgon, and as her hand tore at the doorknob Miss Temple felt her entire body trembling with fear. They barreled through the door and slammed it behind—and then both squealed with alarm at the brooding figure that loomed suddenly over them. It was only the back side of the door, covered by a striking, somber portrait in oils of a man in black with searching eyes and a cold thin mouth—Lord Vandaariff, for behind the figure rose the specter of Harschmort House. And yet, even as she continued to run, her heart in her mouth, Miss Temple recognized the painting as the work of Oskar Veilandt. But—was he not dead? And Vandaariff only in residence at Harschmort for two years? She groaned at the annoyance of not being able to pause and think!

As one she and Elöise cut through a strange ante-room of paintings and sculpture, its floor inlaid with mosaic. They could already hear approaching footsteps and dashed heedlessly in the other direction, careening around one corner and then another, until they reached a foyer whose flooring was slick black and white marble. Miss Temple heard a cry. They had been seen. Elöise ran to the left, but Miss Temple caught her arm and pulled her to the right, to a formidable dark metal door she thought they might close behind them to seal themselves off from pursuit. They rushed through, bare feet pattering across the marble and onto a landing of cold iron. Miss Temple thrust the coat at Elöise and shoved the woman toward a descending spiral staircase of welded steel while she tried to close the door. It did not move. She heaved again without success. She dropped to her knees, pried out the wooden wedge that had held it and then thrust the heavy door shut just as she heard footsteps echoing off the marble. The latch caught and she quickly dropped to her knees again and with both hands drove the wedge back under the door. She leapt after Mrs. Dujong, her pale feet soft and moist against the metal steps.

Being a spiral staircase, as the steps reached the iron column in the center they became quite narrow, and so because she was smaller Miss Temple felt it only fair she take the inside going down, half a step behind Elöise but holding on to her arm—as Elöise with her other hand held on to the rail. The metal staircase was very cold, especially so on their feet. Miss Temple felt as if she were scampering around the scaffolds and catwalks of an abandoned factory in her nightdress—which was to say it felt very like one of those strange dreams that always seemed to end up in unsettling situations involving people she but barely knew. Racing down the stairs, still genuinely amazed at this dark metal tower's very existence—*under* the *ground*—Miss Temple wondered what new peril she had launched them into, for the pitiless tower struck her as the most unlikely wrinkle yet.

Was there someone behind—a noise? She pulled Elöise to a stop, patting her arm to indicate urgency and silence, and looked back up the stairs. What they heard was not footsteps from within the tower, but what seemed very much like footsteps—and scuffles and snippets of talk—*outside* of it. For the first time Miss Temple looked at the tower walls—also welded steel—and saw the queer little sliding slats, like the ones sometimes seen between a coach and driver. Elöise slid the nearest open. Instead of an open window, it revealed an inset rectangle of smoked glass through which they could see... and what they saw quite took their breath away.

They looked out and down from the top of an enormous open chamber, like an infernal beehive, walls ringed with tier upon tier of walled prison cells, into which they could gaze unimpeded.

"Smoked glass!" she whispered to Elöise. "The prisoners cannot see when they are spied upon!"

"And look," her companion answered, "are these the new prisoners?"

Before their eyes, the upper tier of cells were filling up like theatre boxes with the elegantly dressed and masked guests of the Harschmort gala, climbing down through hatches in the cell roofs, setting out folding chairs, opening bottles, waving handkerchiefs to one another across the open expanse through fearsome metal bars—the whole as unlikely, and to Miss Temple's mind inappropriate, as spectators perched in the vault of a cathedral.

So high were they that even pressing their faces angled down against the glass did not allow them to see the floor below. How many cells were there? Miss Temple could not begin to count how many prisoners the place might hold. As for the spectators, there seemed to be at least a hundred—or who knew, numbers not being her strongest suit, perhaps it was three—their mass emitting a growing buzz of anticipation like an engine accelerating to speed. The only clue to the purpose of the gathering, or indeed the cathedral itself, was the bright metal tubing that ran the height of the chamber, lashed together in bunches, emerging from the walls like creeping vines the width of a tree trunk. While Miss Temple was sure that the layers of cells covered the whole of the chamber, she could not see the lower tiers for all the metal pipes—which told her sensible mind that the pipes, not the cells, had become the main concern. But where were the pipes going and whatever substance did they hold?

Miss Temple's head spun back, where a grating shove echoed down to them like a whip crack—someone was opening the wedged door. At once Miss Temple took Elöise's arm and leapt ahead.

"But where are we going?" hissed Elöise.

"I do not know," whispered Miss Temple, "take care we do not get tangled in that coat!"

"But"—Elöise, annoyed but obliging, shifted the coat higher in her arms—"the Doctor cannot find us—we are cut off! There will be people below—we are marching directly to them!"

Miss Temple simply snorted in reply, for about no part of this could anything be done.

"Mind your feet," she muttered. "It is slippery."

As they continued their descent, the noise above them grew, both from the spectators in their cells and then, with another sharp scraping exclamation of the door being forced, from their pursuers at the top of the tower. Soon there were hobnails clattering against the steel steps. Without a word to each other the women increased their speed, racing around several more turns of the tower—how far down could it extend?—until Miss Temple abruptly stopped, turning to Elöise, both of them out of breath.

"The coat," she panted, "give it to me."

"I am doing my best to carry it safely—"

"No no, the bullets, the Doctor's bullets—quickly!"

Elöise shifted the coat in her arms, trying to find the right pocket, Miss Temple feeling with both hands for the bulky box, and then desperately digging it out and prying up the cardboard lid.

"Get behind me," hissed Miss Temple, "keep going down!"

"But we have no weapon," whispered Elöise.

"Exactly so! It is dark—and perhaps we can use the coat as a distraction—quickly, remove whatever else—the cigarette case and the glass card!"

She pushed past Elöise, and working as quickly as she could began to scatter the bullets across the metal steps, emptying the box and covering perhaps four steps with the metal cartridges. The bootsteps above them were audibly nearer. She turned to Elöise, impatiently motioning her to *go on—quickly!*—and snatched away the coat, spreading it out some three steps lower than her bullets, plumping and plucking at the sleeves to make as intriguing a shape as possible. She looked up—they could only be a turn above—and leapt down, lifting up her robes, legs flashing pale, darting away from view.

She had just caught up to Elöise when they heard a shout—someone had seen the coat—and then the first crash, and then another, the cries, and the echoing clamor of scattered bullets, flailing blades, and screaming men. They stopped to look above them, and Miss Temple had just an instant to apprehend a swift metallic slithering and see the merest flash of reflected light. With a squeak she flung herself at Elöise with all her strength, lifting their bodies just enough that they each sat on the handrail, buttocks poorly balanced but feet clear of the disembodied saber that scythed at them, as if the steps were made of ice, then bounced past to ring and spark its way to the bottom of the steps. The women tumbled off the rail, amazed at their own sudden escape, and continued down, the rage of confusion and gruesome injury clamorous above them.

The saber was a problem, Miss Temple thought with a groan, for its arrival below would surely alert whoever was there that something was wrong. Or perhaps not—perhaps it would run them through! She snorted at her own unquenchable optimism. She had no more clever ideas. They came round the final turn of the spiral and faced a landing as cluttered with boxes as a holiday foyer. To the right, leading out to the base of the great chamber, was an open door. To the left, another man with a brass helmet and leather apron crouched near an open hatchway, perhaps the size of a large coal furnace, set directly into the steel column that rose through the center of the staircase. The man carefully examined a wooden tray of bottles and lead-capped flasks that he had obviously pulled from the hatch and set down on the floor. Next to the hatch, affixed into the column, was a brass plate of buttons and knobs. The column was a dumbwaiter.

In the middle of the floor, its blade imbedded—presumably in silence, given the man's inattention—in a discarded heap of packing straw, was the saber.

From the doorway marched a second helmeted man, walking directly past the pile of straw, to gather two wax-capped bottles, one bright blue, the other vibrant orange, and rush back through the door without another word. The women stood still, unconvinced they had yet to be seen—could the helmets so impede the men's peripheral vision and muffle their hearing? Through the open door Miss Temple heard urgent commands, the sounds of work, and—she was quite certain—the voices of more than one woman.

From above them came the deliberate pinging of a kicked bouncing bullet, striking the steps and the wall in turn. The men above had resumed their descent. The bullet flew past them and bounced off of the stack of crates on the far wall, coming to rest on the floor near the man's feet. He cocked his head and registered its unlikely presence. They were ruined.

Outside the door a man's voice erupted into speech at such a volume that Miss Temple was bodily startled. She had never before heard such a human noise, not even from the roaring sailors when she'd crossed the sea, but this voice was not loud because of any extremity of effort—its normal tone was mysteriously, astonishingly, and disturbingly exaggerated. The voice belonged to the Comte d'Orkancz.

"Welcome to you *all,*" the Comte intoned.

The man in the helmet looked up. He saw Miss Temple. Miss Temple leapt down the final steps, dodging past.

"It is time to begin," cried the Comte, "as you have been instructed!"

From the cells above them—incongruously, fully the last thing Miss Temple would have ever expected—the gathered crowd began to sing.

She could not help it, but looked through the open door.

The tableau, for it was framed as such by the door in front and the silver curtain of bright shining pipes behind, was the operating theatre writ large, the demonic interests of the Comte d'Orkancz given full free rein—*three* examination tables. At the foot of each rose a gearbox of brass and wood, into which, as if one might slide a bullet into the chamber of a gun, one of the helmeted men inserted a gleaming blue glass book. The man with the two bottles stood at the head of the first table, pouring the blue liquid into the funneled valve of a black rubber hose. Black hoses coiled around the table like a colony of snakes, slick and loathsome, yet more loathsome still was the shape that lurked beneath, like a pallid larva in an unnatural cocoon. Miss Temple looked past to the second table and saw Miss Poole's face disappear as an attendant strapped a ghoulish black rubber mask in place... and then to the final table, where a third man attached hoses to the naked flesh of Mrs. Marchmoor. Looking up at the cells was a final figure, mighty and tall, the mouth of his great mask dangling a thick, slick black tube, like some demonic tongue—the Comte himself. Perhaps one second had passed. Miss Temple reached out and slammed the door between them.

And just as suddenly she knew, this echoing vision provoking her memory of the final instant of Arthur Trapping's blue glass card... the woman on its table had been Lydia Vandaariff.

Behind her Elöise screamed. The helmeted man's arms took crushing hold around Miss Temple's shoulders and slammed her into the newly shut door, then threw her to the ground.

She looked up to see the man holding the saber. Elöise seized one of the bottles of orange liquid from the tray and hefted her arm back, ready to hurl it at him. To the immediate shock of each woman, instead of running her through, the man stumbled back and then sprinted up the stairs as fast as the awkward helmet and apron would allow. All he needed was a set of bat's wings, Miss Temple thought, to make a perfect shambling imp of hell.

The women looked at each other, baffled at their near escape. The platform door was shaken again from the outside, and the stairwell above them echoed with shouts from the running man—shouts that were answered as he met their initial pursuers. There was no time. Miss Temple took Elöise brusquely by the arm and shoved her toward the open hatch.

"You must get in!" she hissed. *"Get in!"*

She did not know if it had room for two, or even if the lift would carry their weight if there was, but nevertheless leapt to the brass plate of controls, forcing her tired mind—for her day had been more than full, and she had not eaten or drunk tea in the longest time—to make sense of its buttons . . . one green, one red, one blue, and a solid brass knob. Elöise folded her legs into the hatch, her mouth a drawn grim line, one hand a tight fist and the other still holding the orange bottle. The shouting above had turned and someone pounded on the outside door. At the green button the dumbwaiter lurched up. At the red, it went down. The blue did not seem to do a thing. She tried the green again. Nothing happened. She tried red, and it went down—perhaps a single inch, but all the way to the end.

The door to the platform shook on its hinges.

She had it. The blue button meant the dumbwaiter must continue its course—it was used to prevent needless wear on the engines caused by changing directions mid-passage. Miss Temple stabbed the blue button, then the green, and dove for the hatch, Elöise's arms around her waist, gathering her quickly in, Miss Temple's wriggling feet just barely slipping through the narrowing hatchway before they rose into the pitch-black shaft, their last view the black boots of Macklenburg soldiers limping down the final steps.

The fit was incredibly awkward and, after the initial relief that first they were indeed climbing and second the men had not stopped their way and third that she had not been sheared of any limbs, Miss Temple attempted to shift herself to a more comfortable position only to find that the effort ground her knees into her companion's side, and Elöise's elbow sharp against her ear. She turned her face the other way and found her ear pressed flat on the other woman's chest, Elöise's body warm and damp with perspiration, her flesh soft and the cushioned thrum of her heartbeat reaching Miss Temple despite the dumbwaiter's clanking chains, like a precious secret risked by whisper in a crowded parlor. Miss Temple realized that her torso was curled between the other woman's legs, legs drawn tightly up to Elöise's chin, while her own legs were cruelly bent beneath them both. There had not been time to shut the hatch, and Miss Temple held her feet tucked with one arm—the other close around Elöise—so they did not, with the jarring of the dumbwaiter, accidentally pop out into the shaft. They did not speak, but after a moment she felt the other woman tug free an arm and then Miss Temple, already grateful despite herself for the comfort afforded by the unintended and therefore unacknowledged close contact with her companion's body, felt the other woman's hand smoothing her hair with soft and gentle strokes.

"At the top, they will try to reverse it before we can get out," she whispered.

"They will," agreed Elöise quietly. "You must get out first. I will push you."

"And then I shall pull your feet."

"That will be fine, I am sure."

"What if there are more men?"

"It's very possible."

"We will surprise them," observed Miss Temple quietly.

Elöise did not answer, but held the younger woman's head to her bosom with an exhalation of breath that to Miss Temple was equal parts sweetness and sorrow, a mixture she did not completely understand. Such physical intimacy with another woman was unusual for Miss Temple, much less any emotional intimacy—but she knew that their adventures had already hastened a connection to each other, as a telescope eliminated the distance between a ship and the shore. It was the same with Chang and Svenson, men who she in truth knew not at all yet felt were the only souls in the world she could rely on or even—and this surprised her, for to form the thought was to place the events of the recent days within the context of her whole life—care about. She had never known her mother. Miss Temple wondered—self-conscious and rapidly becoming less sure of herself, as this was no time to drift into reckless contemplation or indulgent feeling—if her present sensations of warm flesh, of life, of contact, and, for the space of their isolated climb at least, unquestioned care resembled what having a mother might be like. Her cheeks flushing at the exposure of her frailty and her desire, Miss Temple burrowed her face into the crook between the woman's arm and bosom and let out a sigh that by its end left her entire body shuddering.

They rose in the darkness until the car lurched to a stop without warning. The door slid open and Miss Temple saw the astonished faces of two men in the black servants' livery of Harschmort, one having slid open the door and the other holding another wooden tray of flasks and bottles. Before they could close the door and before the men below could call the car back down, she kicked both feet—the soles of which she knew were filthy as any urchin's—vigorously in their faces, driving them back out of disgust if not fear. With Elöise shoving her from behind, Miss Temple shot out the door, screaming at the men like a mad thing, hair wild, face smeared with soot and sweat and then, her eyes desperately looking for it, lunged to the brass control panel, stabbing the green button that kept the car in place.

The men looked at her with their mouths open and expressions darkening, but their response was cut short as their gaze was pulled to Elöise clambering out, feet first, silk robes rising up to the very tops of her pale thighs as she scooted forward and revealing her own pair of small silk pants, the split seam gaping for one dark, flashing instant that rooted both men to the spot before she slid her upper body free and landed awkwardly on her knees. In her hand was the bottle of bright orange fluid. At the sight of it the men took another step back, their expressions shifting in a trice from curious lust to supplication.

The moment Elöise was clear Miss Temple released the button and stepped directly to the man without the tray and shoved him with both of her hands and all of her strength back into the man who held it. Both servants retreated tottering through the metal door and onto the slick black and white marble, their attention focused solely on not dropping any of their precious breakables. Miss Temple helped Elöise to her feet and took the orange bottle from her. Behind them the dumbwaiter clanked into life, disappearing downward. They dashed into the foyer, but the servants, recovered somewhat, would not let them past.

"What do you think you're *doing*?" shouted the one with the tray, nodding urgently at the bottle in Miss Temple's hand. "How did you get that? We—we could—we *all* could have—"

The other simply hissed at her. *"Put that down!"*

"*You* put it down," Miss Temple snapped. "Put down the tray and leave! Both of you!"

"We will do no such thing!" snapped the man with the tray, narrowing his eyes viciously. "Who are you to give orders? If you think—just because you're one of the master's *whores*—"

"Get out of the way!" the other man hissed again. "We have work to do! We will be whipped! And you've made us wait *again* for the dumbwaiter!"

He tried to edge around them toward the tower door, but the man with the tray did not move, glaring with a rage that Miss Temple knew arose from injured pride and petty stakes.

"They will not! They're not going anywhere! They need to explain themselves—and they'll do it to me or to Mr. Blenheim!"

"We don't need Blenheim!" his partner hissed. "The *last* thing—for God's sake—"

"*Look* at them," said the man with the tray, his expression growing by the moment more ugly. "They're not *at* any of the ceremonies—they're running *away*—why else was she screaming?"

This thought penetrated the other man, and in a pause both studied the two less-than-demurely-clad women.

"If we stop them I wager we'll be rewarded."

"If we don't get this work done we'll be sacked."

"We have to wait for it to come back up anyway."

"We do . . . do you reckon they've stolen those robes?"

Throughout this fatiguing dialog, Miss Temple debated her course, edging farther from the door, half-step by half-step, as the two men hesitated and bickered—but she could see that they were about to be ridiculous and manly, and so she must act. In her hand was the orange bottle, which evidently held some appallingly violent chemical. If she broke it over one of their heads, it was probable that both men would be incapacitated and they could run. At the same time, the way everyone flinched from it, like schoolgirls from a spider, she could not depend that once shattered it might not—by fumes, perhaps—afflict herself and Elöise. Further, the bottle was an excellent weapon to keep for a future crisis or negotiation, and anything of value Miss Temple much preferred to possess rather than spend. But whatever she did must be decisive enough to forestall these fellows' pursuit, for she was deeply annoyed at all this seemingly endless *running*.

With a dramatic gesture Miss Temple drew back the bottle and with a cry brought her arm forward, as if to break it over the head of the man who held the tray and who—because of the tray—could not raise his own hands to ward off the blow. But such was the threat of the bottle that he could not stop his hands from trying and as Miss Temple's arm swept down he lost his grip on the tray, which dropped to the marble floor with a crash, its contents of bottles and flasks smashing and bursting against each other with an especially satisfying clamor.

The men looked up at her, both hunched at the shoulders against the impact of her blow, their faces gaping at the fact that Miss Temple had never released—had never intended to release—the orange bottle. At once the gazes of all four dropped to the tray, whose surface erupted with hissing and steaming and a telltale odor that made Miss Temple gag. This odor was not, as she would have anticipated, the noxious indigo clay, but one that brought her back to the coach at night as she struggled free of Spragg's heavy spurting body—the concentrated smell of human blood. Three of the broken flasks had pooled together and in their mixture transformed—there was no other way to say it—into a shining bright arterial pool that spilled from the tray onto the floor in a quantity larger than the original fluids—as if the combination of chemicals not only made blood, but made *more* of it, gushing like an invisible wound across the marble tile.

"What is this *nonsense*?"

All four looked up at the flatly disapproving voice that came from the doorway behind the two men, where a tall fellow with grizzled whiskers and wire spectacles stood holding in his arms an army carbine. He wore a long dark coat, whose elegance served to make his balding head appear more round and his thin-lipped mouth more cruel. The servants immediately bowed their heads and babbled explanations.

"Mr. Blenheim, Sir—these women—"

"We were—the dumbwaiter—"

"They attacked us—"

"Fugitives—"

Mr. Blenheim cut them off with the finality of a butcher's cleaver. "Return this tray, replace its contents, and deliver them at once. Send a maid to clean this floor. Report to my quarters when you are finished. You were told of the importance of your task. I cannot answer for your continued employment."

Without another word the men snatched up the dripping tray and trotted past their master, hanging their heads obsequiously. Blenheim sniffed once at the smell, his eyes flitting over the bloody pool and then back to the women. His gaze paused once at the orange bottle in Miss Temple's hand, but betrayed no feeling about it either way. He gestured with the carbine.

"You two will come with me."

They walked in front of him, directed at each turn by blunt monosyllabic commands, until they stood at an aggressively carved wooden door. Their captor looked about him quickly and unlocked it, ushering them through. He followed them in, showing a surprising swiftness for a man of his size, and once more locked the door, tucking the key—one of many on a silver chain, Miss Temple saw—back into a waistcoat pocket.

"It will be better to speak in isolation," he announced, looking at them with a cold gaze that in its flat and bland nature belied a capacity for pragmatic cruelty. He shifted the carbine in his hand with dangerous ease.

"You will put that bottle on the table next to you."

"Would you like that?" asked Miss Temple, her face all blank politeness.

"You will do it at once," he answered.

Miss Temple looked about the room. Its ceilings were high and painted with scenes of nature—jungles and waterfalls and expansively dramatic skies—that she assumed must represent someone's idea of Africa or India or America. On each wall were display cases of weapons and artifacts and animal trophies—stuffed heads, skins, teeth, and claws. The floors were thickly carpeted and the furniture heavily upholstered in comfortable leather. The room smelled of cigars and dust, and Miss Temple saw behind Mr. Blenheim an enormous sideboard bearing more bottles than she thought were made in the civilized world, and reasoned that, given the exploratory nature of the decor, there must among them be many liquors and potions from the dark depths of primitive cultures. Mr. Blenheim cleared his throat pointedly, and with a deferent nod she placed her bottle where he had indicated. She glanced to Elöise and met the woman's questioning expression. Miss Temple merely reached out and took hold of Elöise's hand—the hand that held the blue glass card—effectively covering it with her own.

"So, you're Mr. Blenheim?" she asked, not having the slightest idea what this sentence might imply.

"I am," the man answered gravely, an unpleasant tang of self-importance clinging to his tone.

"I had wondered"—nodded Miss Temple—"having heard your name so many times."

He did not reply, looking at her closely.

"*So* many times," added Elöise, striving to push her voice above a whisper.

"I am the manager of this household. You are causing trouble in it. You were in the master's passage just now, spying on what you shouldn't have been like the sneaks you are—do not bother to deny it. And now I'll wager you've disrupted things in the tower—as well as having made a mess of my floor!"

Unfortunately for Mr. Blenheim, his litanies—for he was clearly a man whose authority depended on the ability to catalog transgression—were only damning to those who felt any of this was a source of guilt. Miss Temple nodded to at least acknowledge the man's concerns.

"In terms of management, I should expect a house this size is rather an involving job. Do you have a large staff? I myself have at various times given much thought to the proper size of a staff in relation to the size of a house—or the ambition of the house, as often a person's social aim outstrips their physical resources—"

"You were *spying*. You broke into the master's inner passage!"

"And a wicked inner passage it is," she replied. "If you ask me, it is your *master* you should call a sneak—"

"What were you doing there? What did you hear? What have you stolen? Who has paid you to do this?"

Each of Mr. Blenheim's questions was more vehement than the one before, and by the last his face was red, quite accentuating the amount of white hair in his grizzled whiskers, making him appear to Miss Temple even more worth mocking.

"My goodness, Sir—your complexion! Perhaps if you drank less gin?"

"We were merely lost," Elöise intervened smoothly. "There was a fire—"

"I am aware of it!"

"You can see our faces—my dress—" and here Elöise helpfully drew his eyes to the blackened silk that fell about her shapely calves.

Blenheim licked his lips. "That means nothing," he muttered.

But to Miss Temple it meant a great deal, for the fact that the man had not by this time delivered them to his master told her that Mr. Blenheim had ideas of his own. She indicated the animal heads and the display cases of weapons with a vague wave and a conspiratorial smile.

"What a curious room this is," she said.

"It is not curious at all. It is the trophy room."

"I'm sure it must be, but that is to say it is a room of men."

"And what of that?"

"We are women."

"Is that of consequence?"

"*That,* Mr. Blenheim"—here she batted her eyes without shame—"is surely our question to you."

"What are your names?" he asked, his mouth a tightly drawn line, his eyes flicking quickly as he stared. "What do you know?"

"That depends on who you serve."

"You will answer me directly!"

Miss Temple nodded sympathetically at his outburst, as if his anger were at the uncooperative weather rather than herself. "We do not want to be difficult," she explained. "But neither do we want to offend. If you are, for example, deeply attached to Miss Lydia Vandaariff—"

Blenheim waved her past the topic with a violently brusque stab of his hand. Miss Temple nodded.

"Or you had particular allegiances with Lord Vandaariff, or the Contessa, or the Comte d'Orkancz, or Mr. Francis Xonck, or Deputy Minister Crabbé, or—"

"You will tell me what you know no matter what my allegiance."

"Of course. But first, you must be aware that the house has been penetrated by *agents.*"

"The man in red—" Blenheim nodded with impatience.

"And the other," added Elöise, "from the quarry, with the airship—"

Again Blenheim waved them to another topic. "These are in hand," he hissed. "But why are two adherents in white gowns running through the house and defying their masters?"

"Once more, Sir, which masters do you mean?" asked Miss Temple.

"But..." he stopped, and nodded vigorously, as if his own thoughts were confirmed. "Already, then... they plot against each other..."

"We knew you were not a fool." Elöise sighed, hopelessly.

Mr. Blenheim did not at once reply, and Miss Temple, though she did not risk a glance at Elöise, took the moment to squeeze her hand.

"While the Comte is down in the prison chamber," she said, speaking with bland speculation, "and the Contessa is in a private room with the Prince... where is Mr. Xonck? Or Deputy Minister Crabbé?"

"Or where are they *thought* to be?" asked Elöise.

"Where is your own Lord Vandaariff?"

"He is—" Blenheim stopped himself.

"Do you know where to find your own master?" asked Elöise.

Blenheim shook his head. "You still have not—"

"What do you *think* we were doing?" Miss Temple allowed her exasperation to show. "We escaped from the theatre—escaped from Miss Poole—"

"Who came with Minister Crabbé in the airship," added Elöise.

"And then made our way to overhear the actions of the Contessa in your secret room," resumed Miss Temple, "and from there have done our best to intrude upon the Comte in his laboratory."

Blenheim frowned at her.

"Who have we *not* troubled?" Miss Temple asked him patiently.

"Francis Xonck," whispered Mr. Blenheim.

"You have said it, Sir, not I."

He chewed his lip. Miss Temple went on. "Do you see . . . *we* have not divulged a thing . . . you have seen these things for yourself and merely deduced the facts. Though . . . if we were to help you . . . Sir . . . might it go easier with us?"

"Perhaps it would. It is impossible to say, unless I know what sort of *help* you mean."

Miss Temple glanced to Elöise, and then leaned toward Blenheim, as if to share a secret.

"Do you know where Mr. Xonck is . . . at this very moment?"

"Everyone is to gather in the ballroom . . . ," Blenheim muttered, ". . . but I have not seen him."

"Is that *so*?" replied Miss Temple, as if this were extremely significant. "And if I can show you what he is doing?"

"Where?"

"Not where, Mr. Blenheim—indeed, not *where* . . . but *how*?"

Miss Temple smiled and, slipping it from Elöise's grasp, held up the blue glass card.

Mr. Blenheim snatched at it hungrily, but Miss Temple pulled it from his reach.

"Do you know what this—" she began, but before another word could be uttered Blenheim surged forward and took hard hold of her arm with one hand and wrenched the card free from her grip with the other. He stepped back, and licked his lips again, glancing back and forth between the card and the women.

"You must be careful," said Miss Temple. "The blue glass is very dangerous. It is disorienting—if you have not looked into it before—"

"I know what it is!" snarled Blenheim, and he took two steps away from them, toward the door, blocking it with his body. He looked up at the women a last time, then down into the glass.

Blenheim's eyes dulled as he entered the world of the glass card. Miss Temple knew this card showed the Prince and Mrs. Marchmoor, no doubt more entrancing to Mr. Blenheim than Roger ogling her own limbs on the sofa, and she reached out slowly, not making a sound, to the nearest display case to take up a sharp short dagger with a blade that curved narrowly back and forth like a silver snake. Mr. Blenheim's breath caught in his throat and his body seemed to waver—the cycle of the card had finished—but a moment later he had not moved, giving himself over to its seductive repetition. Taking care to position her feet as firmly as she could and recalling Chang's advice for practical action, Miss Temple stepped to the side of Mr. Blenheim and drove the dagger into the side of his body to the hilt.

He gasped, eyes popping wide and up from the card. Miss Temple pulled the dagger free with both hands, the force of which caused him to stagger in her direction. He looked down at the bloody blade, and then up to her face. She stabbed again, this time into the center of his body, shoving the blade up under his ribs. Mr. Blenheim dropped the card onto the carpet and wrestled the dagger from Miss Temple's grasp, tottering backwards. With a grunt he dropped to his knees, blood pouring from his abdomen. He could not draw breath nor—happily for the women—make noise. He toppled onto his side and lay still. Miss Temple, gratified to see that the carpet bore a reddish pattern, knelt quickly to wipe her hands.

She looked up to Elöise, who had not moved, fixed on the fading breaths of the fallen overseer.

"Elöise?" she whispered.

Elöise turned to her quickly, the spell broken, eyes wide.

"Are you all right, Elöise?"

"O yes. I am sorry—I—I don't know—I suppose I thought we would creep past—"

"He would have followed."

"Of course. Of course! No—yes, my goodness—"

"He was our deadly enemy!" Miss Temple's poise was suddenly quite fragile.

"Of course—it is merely—perhaps the quantity of blood—"

Despite herself, the prick of criticism had punctured Miss Temple's grim resolve, for after all it was not as if murder came to her naturally or blithely, and though she knew she *had* been clever, she also knew what she had done—that it *was* murder—not even strictly a *fight*—and once more she felt it all had moved so quickly, too fast for her to keep her hold on what she believed and what her actions made of her. Tears burned the corners of each eye. Elöise suddenly leaned close to her and squeezed her shoulders.

"Do not listen to me, Celeste—I am a fool—truly! Well done!"

Miss Temple sniffed. "It would be best if we dragged him from the door."

"Absolutely."

They had each taken an arm, but the effort of transporting the substantial corpse—for he had finally expired—behind a short bookcase left them both gasping for breath, Elöise propped against a leather armchair, Miss Temple holding the dagger, wiping its blood on Mr. Blenheim's sleeve. With another sigh at the burdens one accepted along with a pragmatic mind, she set the dagger down and began to search his pockets, piling all of what she found in a heap: banknotes, coins, handkerchiefs, matches, two whole cigars and the stub of another, pencils, scraps of blank paper, bullets for the carbine, and a ring of so many keys she was sure they would answer for every door in the whole of Harschmort. In his breast pocket however was another key . . . fashioned entirely of blue glass. Miss Temple's eyes went wide and she looked up to her companion.

Elöise was not looking at her. She sat slumped in the chair, one leg drawn up, her face open, eyes dull, both hands holding the blue card in front of her face. Miss Temple stood with the glass key in her hand, wondering how long her work had taken . . . and how many times her companion had traveled through the sensations of Mrs. Marchmoor on the sofa. A little gasp escaped Elöise's parted lips, and Miss Temple began to feel awkward. The more she considered what she had experienced by way of the blue glass—the hunger, the knowledge, the delicious submersion, and of course her rudely skewed sense of self—the less she knew how she ought to feel. The attacks upon her person (that seemed to occur whenever she set foot in a coach) she *had* sorted out—they filled her with rage. But these *mental* incursions had transfigured her notions of propriety, of desire, and of experience itself, and left her usual certainty of mind utterly tumbled.

Elöise was a widow, who with her marriage must have found a balance with these physical matters, yet instead of reason and perspective Miss Temple was troubled to see a faint pearling of perspiration on the woman's upper lip, and felt a certain restless shifting at her thighs at being in the presence of someone else's unmediated desire (a thing she had never before faced, unless one could count her kisses with Roger and Roger's own attempts to grope her body, which now—by force of absolute will—she refused to do). Miss Temple could not, for she was both curious and proud, but wonder if this was how she had looked as well.

The widow's cheeks were flushed, her lower lip absently plucked between her teeth, her fingers white with pressure as they squeezed the glass, her breath shot through with sighs, the silk robe sliding as she moved, soft and thin enough to show the stiffened tips of each breast, the barely perceptible rocking of her hips, one long leg stretched out to the carpet, its toes flexing against some hidden force, and on top of all of this, to Miss Temple's discomforting attraction, was the fact that Elöise still wore her feathered mask—that, to some degree, Miss Temple felt she was not gazing at Elöise at all, but simply a Woman of Mystery, as she had made of herself in the Contessa's Dutch mirror. She continued to stare as Elöise repeated the cycle of the card, Miss Temple now able to locate, at the same slight inhalation of breath, the moment of Mrs. Marchmoor pulling the Prince's body into hers, hooking her legs around his hips and pressing him tight . . . and she wondered that she herself had been able to remove her attention from the card without difficulty—or without difficulty beyond her own embarrassment—where Elöise seemed quite trapped within its charms. What had she said about the book—about people being killed, about her own swooning? With a resolve that, as perhaps too often in her life, cut short her fascination, Miss Temple reached out and snatched the card from her companion's hands.

Elöise looked up, quite unaware of what had happened and where she was, mouth open and her eyes unclear.

"Are you all right?" Miss Temple asked. "You had quite lost yourself within this card." She held it up for Elöise to see. The widow licked her lips and blinked.

"My heavens . . . I do apologize . . ."

"You are quite flushed," observed Miss Temple.

"I'm sure I am," muttered Elöise. "I was not prepared—"

"It is the same experience as the book—quite as *involving,* if not as *deep*—for as there is not as much glass, there is not as much *incident.* You did say the book did not agree with you."

"No, it did not."

"The card seems to have agreed with you perhaps too well."

"Perhaps... and yet, I believe I have discovered something of use—"

"I blush at what it must be."

Elöise frowned, for despite her weakness she was not ready to accept the mockery of a younger woman so easily, but then Miss Temple smiled shyly and patted the woman's knee.

"I thought you looked very pretty," Miss Temple said, and then adopted a wicked grin. "Do you think Doctor Svenson would have found you even prettier?"

"I'm sure I don't know what you mean," muttered Elöise, blushing again.

"I'm sure he doesn't either," answered Miss Temple. "But what have you discovered?"

Elöise took a breath. "Is that door locked?"

"It is."

"Then you had best sit down, for we must *reason.*"

"As you know," Elöise began, "my position is—or at least was—tutor to the children of Arthur and Charlotte Trapping, Mrs. Trapping being the sister of Henry and Francis Xonck. It is generally held that Colonel Trapping's rapid advancement was due to the machinations of Mr. Henry Xonck, though I see now that in fact Mr. Francis Xonck manipulated it all to engineer—by way of his new allies—a way to wrest the family business from his brother, and all of it arranged—because the Colonel became privy to all sorts of useful government secrets—with that same brother's blessing. The unwitting key to this had been Colonel Trapping, who would report faithfully back to Henry—passing on both the information and *mis*-information that Francis could supply. Further, it was Francis who persuaded *me* to visit Tarr Manor with whatever secrets I might supply—again, designed to give him the leverage of blackmail over his siblings. But *this* was made suddenly necessary exactly because the Colonel had been killed—do you see? He was killed despite the fact that, either willingly or in ignorance, he was *serving* the Cabal."

Miss Temple nodded vaguely, perched on the arm of the chair, feet dangling, hoping that a larger point would soon emerge.

Elöise went on. "One wonders why precisely because the Colonel was so very unremarkable."

"The Doctor did find the second blue card on the Colonel's person," replied Miss Temple, "the one drawn from the experience of Roger Bascombe. It was evidently sewn into the lining of his uniform. But you said you discovered—"

But Elöise was still thinking. "Was there anything within it that seemed particularly... secret? That would justify concealing it—protecting it—so?"

"I should say not, save for the part containing *me*—except—well, except the very final moment, where I am sure one can glimpse Lydia Vandaariff on an examination table with the Comte d'Orkancz—well, you know, *examining* her."

"What?"

"Yes," said Miss Temple. "I only realized it now—when I saw the tables, and then of course I remembered seeing Lydia—and at the time I saw the card I did not know who Lydia was—"

"But, Celeste"—Miss Temple frowned, as she was not entirely sure of her companion even now, and certainly not comfortable with being so familiar—"that the card remained sewn into the Colonel's coat meant that no one had found it! It means that what he knew—what the card proved—died with him!"

"But it did not die at all. The Doctor has the card, and we the secret."

"Exactly!"

"Exactly what?"

Elöise nodded seriously. "So what I've found may be even more important—"

Miss Temple could only bear this for so long, for she was not one who stinted from absolutely shredding the wrapping paper around a present.

"Yes, but you have not said what it *is*."

Elöise pointed to the blue card on Miss Temple's lap. "At the end of the cycle," she said, "you will recall that the woman—"

"Mrs. Marchmoor."

"Her head turns, and one sees *spectators.* Among them I have recognized Francis Xonck, Miss Poole, Doctor Lorenz—others I do not know, though I'm sure you might. Yet beyond these people . . . is a *window*—"

"But it is *not* a window," said Miss Temple, eagerly, inching forward. "It is a *mirror*! The St. Royale's private rooms are fitted with Dutch glass mirrors that serve as windows on the lobby. Indeed, it was recognizing the outer doors of the hotel through this mirror that sent the Doctor to the St. Royale in the first place—"

Elöise nodded impatiently, for she had finally reached her news.

"But did he note who was *in* the lobby? Someone who had quite obviously stepped out of the private room for a chance to speak apart from those remaining in it, distracted by the, ah, *spectacle*?"

Miss Temple shook her head.

"Colonel Arthur Trapping," whispered Elöise, "speaking most earnestly . . . with Lord Robert Vandaariff!"

Miss Temple placed a hand over her mouth.

"It *is* the Comte!" she exclaimed. "The Comte plans to use Lydia—use the marriage, I can't say exactly how—in another part of Oskar Veilandt's alchemical scheme—"

Elöise frowned. "Who is—"

"A painter—a mystic—the discoverer of the blue glass! We were told he was dead—killed for his secrets—but now I wonder if he lives, if he might even be a prisoner—"

"Or his memories drained into a book!"

"O yes! But the point is—do the *others* know what the Comte truly intends for Lydia? More importantly, did her *father* know? What if Trapping found Roger's card and recognized Lydia and the Comte? Is it possible that the Colonel did not understand the truth of his associates' villainy and threatened them with exposure?"

"I am afraid you never met Colonel Trapping," said Elöise.

"Not to actually exchange words, no."

"It is more likely he understood exactly what the card meant and went to the one person with even deeper pockets than his brother-in-law."

"And we have not *seen* Lord Vandaariff—perhaps even now he weaves his own revenge against the Comte? Or does he even know—if Trapping promised him information but was killed before he could reveal it?"

"Blenheim had not seen Lord Robert," said Elöise.

"And the Comte's plan for Lydia remains in motion," said Miss Temple. "I have seen her drinking his poisons. If Trapping was killed to keep her father in ignorance—"

"He must have been killed by the Comte!" said Elöise.

Miss Temple frowned. "And yet... I am certain the Comte was as curious as anyone as to the Colonel's fate."

"Lord Robert must at least be warned by his secret agent's demise," reasoned Elöise. "No wonder he is in hiding. Perhaps it is he who now holds this missing painter—seeking some sort of exchange? Perhaps he now weaves his own plot against them all!"

"Speaking of *that,*" said Miss Temple, casting her eyes down to the heavy shoes of Mr. Blenheim, just visible behind a red leather ottoman, "what do we make of Mr. Blenheim's possession... of *this*?"

She held the key of blue glass to the light and studied its gleam.

"It is the same glass as the books," said Elöise.

"What do you think it opens?"

"It would have to be extremely delicate... something *else* made of the glass?"

"My exact conclusion." Miss Temple smiled. "Which leads me to a second point—that Mr. Blenheim had no business carrying this key at all. Can you imagine any of the Cabal trusting such a thing—which must be priceless—to someone not of their direct number? He is the overseer of the house, he can only figure in *their* plots as much as these Dragoons or Macklenburg stooges. Who would trust him?"

"Only one person," said Elöise.

Miss Temple nodded. "Lord Robert Vandaariff."

"I believe *I* have an idea," Miss Temple announced, and hopped off the armchair. Taking care to step over the darkened smear on the carpet—it had been difficult enough to shift the body, they agreed not to concern themselves with stains—she made her way to the cluttered sideboard. Working with a certain pleasurable industry, she found an unopened bottle of a decent age and a small sharp knife to dig past the wax seal and into the crumbling cork beneath, at least enough to pour through—for she did not mind if the cork dust crept into the liquid, for it was not the liquid that she cared for. Selecting a largely empty decanter, Miss Temple began, tongue poking from her mouth in concentration, to pour out the deep ruby port, doing her best to empty the bottle. When at last she saw the first bits of muddy sediment, she left off the decanter and reached for a wineglass, emptying the rest of the port bottle, sediment and all, into this. She then took another wineglass and, using the little knife as a dam, poured off the liquid until all that remained in her first glass were the ruddy, softened dregs. She looked up with a smile at Elöise, whose expression was tolerant but baffled.

"We cannot proceed with our investigations trapped within this room, nor can we rejoin the Doctor, nor can we escape, nor can we gain revenge—for even carrying sacrificial daggers we must be taken captive or killed once we attempt to leave."

Elöise nodded, and Miss Temple smiled at her own cunning.

"Unless, of course, we are clever in our disguise. The fire in the operating theatre was a site of great confusion and, I am willing to wager, one that prevented any clear account of exactly what occurred—too much smoke, too many shots and screams, too little light. My point being"—and here she waved her hand across the maroon dregs in the wineglass—"no one quite knows whether we underwent the Process or not."

They walked down the corridor in their bare feet, backs straight, unhurried, doing their level best to appear placid of character while paying attention to the growing turmoil around them. Miss Temple held the serpentine dagger in her hand. Elöise held the bottle of orange fluid and had tucked the cigarette case, the blue glass card and the glass key into her shift, as it had thoughtfully been made with pockets. They had pulled their masks around their necks to give everything a bit more time to dry, for meticulously applied and patted and smeared and dabbed around their eyes and across their noses, in as exact an imitation of the looping scars of the Process as they could manage, were the reddish-ruddy dregs of port. Miss Temple had been quite satisfied looking into the sideboard mirror, and only hoped that no one leaned so near as to smell the vintage.

During their time in the trophy room the traffic of guests and servants had increased dramatically. At once they found themselves amongst men and women in cloaks and topcoats and formal gowns, masked and gloved, all nodding to the white-robed pair with the calculated deference one might show to a tomahawk-bearing red Indian. They answered these greetings not at all, imitating the post-Process stupor that Miss Temple had seen in the theatre. The fact that they were armed only served to make room around them, and she realized the guests accorded them a higher status—acolytes of the inner circle, so to speak. It was all she could do not to shake the dagger in each obsequious set of faces and growl.

The traffic drove them toward the ballroom, but Miss Temple was not convinced it was where they ought to go. It seemed more likely that what they really needed—clothing, shoes, their comrades—would be found elsewhere, in some back room like the one where she'd met Farquhar and Spragg, the furniture covered with white sheets, the table littered with bottles and food. She reached for Elöise's hand and had just found it when a noise behind caused them both to turn and break the grip. Marching toward them, driving the hurrying guests to either side of the corridor, an action marooning Miss Temple even more obviously in its middle, was a double line of red-jacketed Dragoons in tall black boots, a scowling officer at their head. She nodded Elöise urgently into the crowd but was herself jostled back into the soldiers' path, ridiculously in their way. The officer did his best to stare her down, and she looked again to Elöise—vanished behind a pair of waspish gentlemen in oyster grey riding cloaks. The guests around them stopped to watch the impending collision. The officer snapped his hand up and his men immediately stamped themselves to a concise, orderly halt. The corridor was suddenly silent . . . a silence that allowed Miss Temple to hear what would have been a previously inaudible chuckle, somewhere behind her. She slowly turned to see Francis Xonck, smoking a cheroot, head cocked in an utterly contemptuous bow.

"What pearls are found," he drawled, "unexpected and unlooked-for, in the wilds of Harschmort House . . ."

He stopped speaking as he took in the markings on her face. Miss

Temple did not reply, merely inclining her head to acknowledge his authority.

"Miss Temple?" he asked, curious and warily skeptical. She dropped into a simple, bobbing curtsey, and rose again.

He glanced once at the officer, and reached out to take hold of her jaw. She passively allowed him to move her head around however he liked, never making a sound. He stepped away, staring at her evenly.

"Where have you come from?" he said. "You will answer me."

"The theatre," she said, as thickly as she could. "There was a fire—"

He did not let her finish, sticking the cheroot into his mouth and reaching forward with his one unbandaged hand to fondle her breast. The crowd around them gasped at the cold determination of his face as much as his brazen action. With the sternest resolve Miss Temple's voice did not shift in the slightest, nor did she pause as he continued to forcefully grope across her body.

"—from the lamps, there was smoke, and shooting... it was Doctor Svenson. I did not see him... I was on the table. Miss Poole—"

Francis Xonck slapped Miss Temple hard across the face.

"—disappeared. The soldiers took me off the table."

As she spoke, just as she had seen in the theatre, and with pleasure, her hand shot out toward Francis Xonck, doing her level best to stab him in the face with the serpentine dagger. Unfortunately, he had seen the blow coming. He parried the blow with his arm against her wrist, then took hold of her wrist and squeezed. As it would give her away to struggle, Miss Temple released the dagger, which hit the floor with a clang. Francis Xonck lowered her hand to her side, and stepped away. She did not move. He looked past her at the officer, flared his nostrils in a sneer—which she was sure meant the officer had shown his disapproval of what he'd just witnessed—and picked up the dagger. He stuck it in his belt and turned on his heels, calling airily over his shoulder.

"Bring the lady with you, Captain Smythe—and quickly. You're *late.*"

Miss Temple could only risk the barest glance for Elöise as she walked away, but Elöise was gone. Captain Smythe had taken her by the arm, not roughly but with insistence, enforcing her compliance with their speed. She allowed herself a look at the officer, masking herself with an expression of bovine disinterest, and saw a face that reminded her of Cardinal Chang, or of the Cardinal beset with the burdens of command, hated superiors, fatigue, self-disgust, and of course without the disfigurement of his eyes. The Captain's eyes were dark and warmer than the bitter lines around them seemed to merit. He glanced down at her with brisk suspicion and she returned her attention to the receding, well-tailored back of Francis Xonck, parting the crowds ahead of them with the imperious ease of a surgeon's scalpel.

He led them through the thickest knots of the gathering crowd, their passage a spectacle for whispers and gawking—Xonck reaching to either side for handshakes and hearty back-slaps to particular men and brief kisses to similarly high-placed or beautiful women—and then beyond them, skirting the ballroom proper to an open space at the meeting of several corridors. Xonck gave Miss Temple one more searching stare, crossed to a pair of wooden doors, opened them, and leaned his head from view, whispering. In a moment he had pulled his head back and shut the door, ambling again to Miss Temple. He pulled the cheroot from his mouth and looked at it with distaste, for he was nearing the stub. He dropped it to the marble floor and ground it beneath his shoe.

"Captain, you will position your men along this corridor in either direction, specifically guarding access to these"—he pointed to two doors farther down the hall away from the ballroom—"inner rooms. Colonel Aspiche will provide further instructions upon his arrival. For now, your task is one of waiting, and making sure of this woman's continued presence."

The Captain nodded crisply and turned to his men, detailing them along the length of the corridor and at each inner door. The Captain himself remained within saber's reach of Miss Temple, and, for that matter, Francis Xonck. Once he had spoken however, Xonck paid the officer no further mind, his voice dropping to a whisper as coiled with menace as the hiss of a snake preparing to strike.

"You will answer me quickly, Celeste Temple, and I will know if you lie—and if you *do* lie, *do* know it means your head."

Miss Temple nodded blankly, as if this meant nothing to her either way.

"What did Bascombe tell you on the train?"

This was not what she'd expected. "That we should be allies," she replied. "That the Contessa desired it."

"And what did the Contessa say?"

"I did not speak to her aboard the train—"

"Before that—*before*! At the hotel—in the *coach*!"

"She said I must pay for the deaths of her men. And she put her hands upon me, quite indecently—"

"Yes, yes," snapped Xonck, impatiently waving her on, "about *Bascombe*—what did she say about *him*?"

"That he would be Lord Tarr."

Xonck was muttering to himself, glancing over his shoulder at the wooden doors. "Too many others must have been there . . . what else, what else—"

Miss Temple tried to recall what the Contessa *had* said to her, or anything provocative that might inflame Xonck's obvious suspicions . . .

"The Comte was there too—"

"I am aware of that—"

"Because she did ask *him* a question."

"What question?"

"I do not think I was supposed to hear it—for I'm sure it made no sense to me—"

"Tell me what she said!"

"The Contessa asked the Comte d'Orkancz how he thought Lord Robert Vandaariff had discovered their plan to alchemically impregnate his daughter—that is, who did he think had betrayed them?"

Francis Xonck did not reply, his eyes boring into hers with a palpably dangerous intent, doing his best to measure the true degree of her compliance. Miss Temple somehow kept the fear from her face, concentrating upon the patterns of shadow on the ceiling beyond his shoulder, but she could tell that Xonck was so provoked by these last words that he was about to slap her again, or launch into an even more debasing physical assault—when behind them, topping his rising agitation as an erupting whistle announces the boiling of a kettle, the wooden doors opened and the Macklenburg Envoy's freshly scarred and deferential face poked through.

"They are ready, Mr. Xonck," the man whispered.

Xonck snarled and stepped away from Miss Temple, his fingers tapping the handle of the dagger in his belt. With one more searching stare at her face he spun on his heels to follow the Envoy into the ballroom.

It was perhaps the length of two minutes before Miss Temple concluded, with the rise of different voices piercing murkily through the doors, that the members of the Cabal were holding forth to their assembled guests. She was aware of the silent Captain Smythe behind her and the general presence of his soldiers, within direct call however distant their posts might be. She took a deep breath and let it out slowly. She could only hope that eagerness for information had blinded Xonck to her disguise—which was more designed to fool ignorant guests in the hall than seasoned members of the Cabal. With a sudden urge toward self-preservation, Miss Temple restored her feathered mask into position. She sighed again. She could not go anywhere... but perhaps she could measure the strength of her cage. She turned to Captain Smythe and smiled.

"Captain,... as you have seen *me* interrogated... may I ask *you* a question?"

"Miss?"

"You seem unhappy."

"Miss?"

"Everyone *else* at Harschmort House seems... well, eminently *pleased* with themselves."

Captain Smythe did not answer, his eyes flicking back and forth between his nearest men. Accordingly, Miss Temple dropped her voice to a demure whisper.

"One merely wonders *why*."

The Captain studied her closely. When he spoke it was near to a whisper.

"Did I hear Mr. Xonck correctly... that your name is... *Temple*?"

"That is so."

He licked his lips and nodded to her robes, the slight gaping around her bosom that allowed a glimpse of her own silk bodice showing through the layers of translucent white.

"I was informed . . . you did favor the color green . . ."

Before Miss Temple could respond to this truly astonishing comment, the doors behind her opened again. She turned, composing her face to a suitable blandness, and met the equally distracted Caroline Stearne, so preoccupied and so surprised to see Miss Temple in the first place as to pay no attention whatsoever to the officer behind her.

"Celeste," she whispered quickly, "you must come with me at once."

Miss Temple was led by the hand through a silent crowd that parted for them impatiently, each person begrudging the distraction from what held their attention in the center of the room. She steeled herself to be calm, expecting that at the words of Francis Xonck she must now submit to public examination by the entire Cabal in front of hundreds of masked strangers, and it was only this preparation that forestalled her gasp of shock at the sight, as she was pulled so briskly onto the open floor by Caroline Stearne, of Cardinal Chang, on his knees, spitting blood, his every inch the image of a man who had passed through the pits of hell. He looked up at her, and with his gaze, his face pale and bloodied, his movements slow, his eyes blessedly veiled behind smoked glass, came the gazes of those other figures before her—Caroline, Colonel Aspiche, and the Comte d'Orkancz, who stood in his great fur holding a leash that went to the neck of a small figure—a lady of perhaps Miss Temple's own height and shape—distinguished first by her nakedness and secondly, and more singularly, by the fact that she seemed to be completely fabricated of blue glass. It was when this statue turned *its* head to look at Miss Temple, its expression unreadable and its eyes as depthless as a Roman statue's, slick, gleaming, and swirled indigo marbles, that Miss Temple understood the woman—or creature—was *alive.* She was fully rooted to the ground with amazement, and could not have cried out to Chang if she had wanted.

Caroline Stearne pulled Miss Temple's white mask down around her neck. She waited through agonizing seconds of silence, sure that someone would denounce her . . . but no one spoke.

Chang's mouth opened haltingly, as if he could not form words or gather breath to speak.

Then, as if everything was happening too quickly to see, Colonel Aspiche was swinging his arm and whatever he held in it smashed down onto Cardinal Chang's head, knocking him flat in a stroke. With a brusque nod from their Colonel, two Dragoons detached themselves from the ring of men keeping back the crowd and took hold of Chang's arms. They dragged him past her, his body utterly lifeless. She did not turn to follow his passage, but made herself look up, despite her racing heart and the pressing nearness of her tears, into the intelligent, searching face of Caroline Stearne.

Behind, the voice of the Contessa snapped through the air like the crack of a particularly exultant whip.

"My dear Celeste," she called, "how fine it is that you have . . . *joined* us. Mrs. Stearne, I am obliged for your timely entrance."

Caroline, who was already facing the Contessa, sank into a respectful curtsey.

"Mrs. Stearne!" called the rasping voice of the Comte d'Orkancz. "Do you not wish to see your transformed companions?"

Caroline turned along with everyone else in the ballroom, for the Comte's gesture was one of grand showmanship, to see two more glass women stalking into the open circle with their deliberate, clicking gait, arms strangely floating, their uncovered bodies an arrogant assertion of ripe, ghastly, unsettling allure. It took Miss Temple a moment—what had the Comte said to Caroline, "companions"?—to recognize with shock Mrs. Marchmoor and, some new disfiguring scorch across her head, Miss Poole. What did it mean that her enemies had—*willingly?*—been transformed, *transfigured,* into such . . . such *things*?

The Comte gathered up Miss Poole's leash and flicked her toward Mrs. Stearne. Miss Poole's lips parted ever so slightly with a chilling smile and then Caroline staggered where she stood, her head lolling to the side. An instant later, as the effect spread to the first rank of the crowd like a rippling pool, Miss Temple felt herself swallowed up and thrust into a scene so enticingly real that she could scarcely remember the ballroom at all.

She was on a plush settee in a dark, candlelit parlor and her hand was occupied with stroking Caroline Stearne's lovely, soft unbound hair. Mrs. Stearne wore—as Miss Temple saw that she (that is, Miss Poole) wore as well—the white robes of initiation. On the other side of Mrs. Stearne sat a man in a black cloak and a tight mask of red leather, leaning over to kiss her mouth, a kiss to which Mrs. Stearne responded with a passionate moan. It was like Mrs. Marchmoor's story of the two men in the coach, only here it was a man and two women. Mrs. Stearne's hunger caused Miss Poole to condescendingly chuckle as she turned to reach for a glass of wine... and with this action her shifting gaze took in an open door and a lurking figure half-visible in the light beyond... a figure whose shape Miss Temple knew at once as that of Roger Bascombe.

The vision was withdrawn from Miss Temple's mind, like a blindfold whipped from her eyes, and she was back in the ballroom, where every person she could see was blinking with confusion, save for the Comte d'Orkancz, who smiled with a smug superior pleasure. He called again to Caroline—some vulgar jest about sisterhood and opportunities for taking the veil—but Miss Temple did not mark their conversation, so provoked were her thoughts by what she'd just beheld....

Miss Poole and Caroline Stearne had been wearing their white robes, and the man with them on the settee—she had seen him, she had taken that very cloak for her own!—was none other than Colonel Trapping. Miss Temple groped to make sense of it, as if she were in a hurry to open a door and could not get the right key in the hole... it had been that same night at Harschmort... and just before the Colonel's murder, for the women had changed into their white robes but not yet undergone the Process. This meant it had been while she was creeping through the hall of mirrors and past the queer man with the boxes—only minutes before she herself had entered Trapping's room. She had already worked out that Roger and the Contessa were the Cabal members nearest to the Colonel at his death... could these women have killed him instead—on instructions of the Comte? If the Colonel had been in secret agreement with Lord Vandaariff... but why, she suddenly wondered, had Miss Poole chosen to share *this* memory—one that must obviously stir up questions about the murdered Colonel—with Caroline Stearne? There had been a rivalry between them in the theatre—was it merely to mock Caroline's affections for a dead man, and what was more a dead traitor to the Cabal? In front of *everyone*?

She was startled—was she an idiot? She must pay attention—by a hoarse cry and then the total immersion without warning into another vision: a tall wooden staircase, lit by orange torchlight under a blackened sky, a sudden rush of men, a scuttling figure in a black topcoat—Minister Crabbé!—and then the mob converging upon and raising up a kicking figure in a steel-blue greatcoat, a flash of his drawn face and ice-pale hair confirming him as Doctor Svenson an instant before, with a heaving surge, the crowd of men launched him without ceremony over the rail.

Miss Temple looked up—just piecing together that this must be an image from the quarry at Tarr Manor—back in the ballroom again, to see a disturbance in the crowd, an undulating progress toward the center that with a lurch deposited the haggard figure of Doctor Svenson, breathless and battered, onto his hands and knees—exactly where Chang had been. Svenson looked up, his wild eyes searching for some escape but instead finding her face, the sight of which stopped him cold. Colonel Aspiche stepped forward, ripping a leather satchel from the Doctor's grasp with one hand, and then bringing his truncheon down pitilessly with the other. It was a matter of seconds. Like Chang before him, Doctor Svenson was dragged past Miss Temple from the room.

Unable to watch him go without giving herself away, Miss Temple instead found her gaze rooted to the gleaming glass women. As disturbing as they were—and the sight of Miss Poole, if this unconscionably animated statue could still so be named, licking her lips with the slick, livid tip of a cerulean tongue caused Miss Temple to shiver with an unnameable dismay—it nevertheless put off the moment when she must face the Contessa's piercing violet eyes. But then Caroline took her hand, spinning her to the raised dais where the members of the Cabal stood—the Contessa, Xonck, Crabbé, and then the Prince and Lydia Vandaariff, still in her mask and white robes, and behind this pair, like a furtive eavesdropping child, lurked the Envoy, Herr Flaüss. Against all reason Miss Temple's eyes went straight to the Contessa, who met her glance with an implacably cold stare. It was to her great relief when it was Harald Crabbé, and not the Contessa, who stepped forward to speak.

"Assembled *guests*... devoted *friends*... faithful *adherents*... now is the time when all our plans are ripe... hanging like fruit to be plucked. It is our present labor to *harvest* that fruit, and prevent it from falling fallow and uncared-for to the insensate *ground*. You all understand the gravity of this night—that we in truth usher in a new epoch—who could doubt it, when we see the evidence before us like angels from another age? Yet tonight all rests in the balance—the Prince and Miss Vandaariff will depart for their Macklenburg wedding... the Duke of Stäelmaere is appointed head of the Queen's Privy Council... the most mighty figures of this land have in this house given over their power... and all of *you*—perhaps most importantly of all!—all of *you* will execute your own assignments—achieve your own destinies! Thus shall we here construct our common dream."

Crabbé paused and met the eyes of first Colonel Aspiche—who rapped out a sharp command that cut through the buttery flattering tone of the Deputy Minister's speech, at which point every door to the ballroom was slammed shut with a crash—and next of the Comte d'Orkancz, who flicked his leashes like an infernal circus master, sending each glass creature stalking toward a different portion of the crowd. The impression was very much of lions in an arena sizing up an impressive number of martyrs, and Miss Temple was no less unsettled to find it was the third woman—the one of her own size and shape—the Comte had sent toward her. The creature advanced to the end of its leash and having pulled it taut stood flexing its fingers with impatience, the people nearest inching away with discomfort. Miss Temple felt a pressing on her *thoughts*—thoughts clouded now with sensations of ice-blue cold...

"You will all accept," continued Crabbé, "that there is no room for risk, no place for second thoughts. We must have *certainty*—every bit as much as all of you, having pledged yourselves, must have it of each man and woman in this ballroom! No one in this room has not undergone the Process, or submitted their interests to one of our *volumes,* or otherwise demonstrated total allegiance . . . or such is our assumption. As I say . . . you will understand if we make *sure.*"

The Comte tugged the leash of Mrs. Marchmoor, who arched her back and swept her gaze across the crowd. The men and women before her were staggered and stunned, they went silent, they whimpered or cried, they lost their balance and fell—all as their minds were scoured for any deception. Miss Temple saw that the Comte had his eyes shut as well in concentration . . . could Mrs. Marchmoor be sharing with him what she saw? Then the Comte abruptly opened his eyes. One of the two men in the oyster grey riding cloaks had dropped to his knees. The Comte d'Orkancz gestured to Colonel Aspiche and two Dragoons dragged the fallen man, now sobbing with fear, without mercy from the room. The Comte shut his eyes again and Mrs. Marchmoor continued her silent inquisition.

After Mrs. Marchmoor came Miss Poole, moving just as remorselessly through her portion of the crowd, isolating two more men and a woman who were given swift cause to regret their decision to attend. For a moment Miss Temple wondered if these could be people like herself—desperate enemies of the Cabal's villainy—but as soon as they were pulled from their places by the soldiers it was clear the exact opposite was the case. These were social climbers who had managed to forge an invitation or bluff their way into what they hoped was an especially exclusive *soirée* for the bright lights of society. As much as she was rattled by their pleas, she did not spare their fates another thought . . . for Miss Poole had finished, and the Comte had snapped the third woman's leash.

The invisible wave of the woman's scrutiny inched toward her like a fire, or like a burning fuse whose end must mean her death. Closer and closer; Miss Temple did not know what to do. She must be found out completely. Should she run? Should she try to push the woman over in hopes that she might shatter? Miss Temple's exposure was but seconds away. She took a breath for courage and tensed herself as if for a blow. Caroline stood straight, also waiting, and glanced once quickly at Miss Temple, her face more pale—Miss Temple realized suddenly that Caroline was terrified. But then the woman's gaze went past Miss Temple's shoulder.

There was a noise—the door?—and then the sudden sharp voice of Deputy Minister Crabbé.

"If you please, Monsieur le Comte, that is enough!"

Quite directly behind Miss Temple an astonishing party had entered the room. All around, people in the crowd lowered their heads with respect for the tall man, deathly pale with long iron-grey hair, with medals on his coat and a bright blue sash across his chest. He walked with great stiffness—he walked rather like the glass women, actually—with one hand clutching a black stick and the other the arm of a small, sharp-faced man with greasy hair and glasses who did not strike her as any kind of normal companion for a royal personage. Given the Deputy Minister's speech she knew it must be the Duke of Stäelmaere, a man who, if the rumors were true, only employed impoverished aristocrats as his servants, so much did he abhor the presence of common folk. What was such a man doing at so large—and so common—a gathering? Yet this was but the half of it, for walking directly next to the Duke—almost as if they were a bride and groom—was Lord Robert Vandaariff. Behind him, and supporting Lord Robert's near arm, walked Roger Bascombe.

"I do not believe we had quite finished with the examinations," said Francis Xonck, "which as you have said, Minister, are most *crucial.*"

"Indeed, Mr. Xonck." Harald Crabbé nodded, and spoke loud enough for the crowd to hear him. "But this business cannot stay! We have before us the two most eminent figures in the land—perhaps the continent!—one of them our very host. It strikes me as prudent, as well as polite, to allow their urgent needs to trump our own."

Miss Temple saw Francis Xonck glance once her way, and knew that he had been watching very closely for the results of her inquisition. She turned toward the new arrivals—as much as she did not want to see Roger she wanted to see Xonck and the Contessa even less—and realized, with the dull deliberate *clonk* of a brick hitting the floor, that Crabbé's halt of the examinations had nothing to do with her at all, but *these* figures, for the glass woman's scrutiny must have swept them up as well, revealing their inner minds to the waiting Comte d'Orkancz. But who was Harald Crabbé protecting? The Duke? Vandaariff? Or his own aide Bascombe—and the secret plans they'd hatched between them? And why had Caroline been so frightened? She wanted to stamp her foot with frustration at all she did not know—was Vandaariff the leader of the Cabal or not? Was he locked in a struggle with the Comte to save his daughter? Did Crabbé's action—and Roger's presence—indicate an allegiance with Vandaariff? But then what did she make of Roger being in the doorway just before Trapping must have been killed? Suddenly Miss Temple remembered her fiancé's appearance in the secret room, where the Contessa had tormented the Prince—could Roger have a secret allegiance of his own? If Roger *had* killed Trapping (her mind could scarcely accept it—*Roger*?) was it to serve the Contessa?

The Duke of Stäelmaere began to speak, his voice halting and dry as a mouthful of cold cinders.

"Tomorrow I become head of the Queen's Privy Council . . . the nation is in crisis . . . the Queen is unwell . . . the Crown Prince is without heir and without merit . . . and so he has this night been given the gift of his dreams, a gift which must ensnare his weakened soul . . . a *glass book of wonders* in which he will drown."

Miss Temple frowned. This did not sound like any Duke she'd ever heard. She glanced carefully behind her and saw the glass woman's attention fully fixed on the Duke, and behind her, his bearded lips moving ever so slightly with each word that issued from the Duke of Stäelmaere's mouth, the Comte d'Orkancz.

"The Privy Council will govern . . . our *vision,* my allies, . . . will find expression . . . will be written on the world. Such is my promise . . . before you all."

The Duke then turned to the man next to him with a glacial nod.

"My Lord . . ."

While Robert Vandaariff's voice was not so openly sepulchral as the Duke's, it nevertheless served to further chill Miss Temple's blood, for before he spoke a single word he turned to Roger and accepted a folded piece of paper, passed with all the deference of a clerk . . . yet the Lord had only turned at a squeeze from Roger on his arm. Vandaariff unfolded the paper and at another squeeze—she was watching for it—began to read, in a hearty voice that rang as hollow to her ear as footfalls in an empty room.

"It is not my way to make speeches and so I ask forgiveness that I rely upon this paper—yet tonight I send my only child, my Princess, Lydia, to be married to a man I have taken to my heart like a son."

At a third subtle squeeze from Roger—whose face, she saw, was directed at the floor—Lord Robert nodded to the Prince and his daughter on the dais. Miss Temple wondered what emotions about her father remained beneath the girl's mask . . . how the Process had rarefied her depthless need and her rage at being abandoned, and what effect these vacant formal words could have. Lydia bobbed in a curtsey and then curled her lips in a grin. Did she know her father was Roger Bascombe's puppet? Could that be why she smiled?

Lord Robert turned back to the assembled guests, and located his place on the page. "Tomorrow it must be as if this night had never been. None of you will return to Harschmort House. None of you will acknowledge you have been here, any more than you will acknowledge each other, or news from the Duchy of Macklenburg as anything other than unimportant gossip. But the efforts here of my colleague the Duke will be mirrored in that land, and from that nation to nations beyond. Some of you will be placed among my agents, traveling where necessary, but before you leave tonight, all will be given instructions, in the form of a printed cipher book, from my chamberlain, . . . Mr. *Blenheim.*"

Vandaariff looked up, instructed here to point out Blenheim from the crowd . . . but Blenheim was not there. The pause drifted toward confusion as faces glanced back and forth, and there were frowns on the dais and sharp glances in the direction of Colonel Aspiche, who answered them with haughty shrugs of his own. With a deft—and therefore to Miss Temple equally galling and impressive—display of initiative, Roger Bascombe cleared his throat and stepped forward.

"In Mr. Blenheim's absence, your instructive volumes can be collected from *me* in the chamberlain's offices, directly after this gathering adjourns."

He glanced quickly to the dais, and then whispered into Lord Robert's ear. Roger returned to his place. Lord Robert resumed his speech.

"I am *gratified* to be able to aid this enterprise, as I am *thankful* to those who have most imagined its success. I beg you all to enjoy the hospitality of my home."

Roger gently took the paper from his hands. The crowd erupted into applause for the two great men, who stood without any particular expression whatsoever, as if it were the rain and they insensible statues.

Miss Temple was astonished. There was no struggle between Vandaariff and the Comte at all—Lord Robert had been utterly overcome. Trapping's news had never reached him, and Lydia's fate—whatever hideous design had been in motion—was sealed. It did not matter if Oskar Veilandt was prisoner in the house, just as it no longer mattered who had killed Trapping—but then Miss Temple frowned. If Vandaariff was their creature, then why had Crabbé stopped the examinations? If the members of the Cabal themselves did not know Trapping's killer, could things be so settled? Could the struggle for Lydia's fate be just one fissure between her enemies? Could there be others?

At the same time, Miss Temple wondered who this performance by the Duke and Lord Robert was expected to fool—she had heard more elevating and persuasive words from half-drunken fishwives on the pier. Taking her cue from Caroline Stearne, she lowered her head as the two luminaries and their assistants—or should she say puppet-masters?—advanced across the ballroom. As they passed she looked up and met the eyes of Roger Bascombe, who frowned with a typically veiled curiosity at the scars across her face. As they reached the far side she was surprised to see the Comte hand Mrs. Marchmoor's leash to Roger and that of Miss Poole to the shorter sharp-faced man. As the doors were opened by the Dragoons—for she could only with difficulty shift her eyes from Roger for any length of time—she saw her fiancé step close to Colonel Aspiche and snatch—there was no gentler word for it—a leather satchel from the Colonel's grasp. A satchel, she realized, that had arrived in the possession of Doctor Svenson . . .

Behind her, the Contessa called out to the crowd, just before either Xonck or Crabbé could do the same, for each man's mouth was poised for speech, their expressions giving out just a flicker of frustration before they were agreeably nodding along with her words.

"Ladies and gentlemen, you have heard the words of our host. You know the preparations you must make. Once these duties are satisfied you are released. The pleasures of Harschmort House this night are yours, and after this . . . for every night . . . the pleasures of the world. I give you all good night . . . I give you all our victory."

The Contessa stepped forward and, beaming at her listeners, began to applaud them all. She was joined by every person on the dais, and then by the entirety of the crowd, each person eager to register delight at the Contessa's favor and to bestow—from that enhanced position—their own approval upon each other. Miss Temple clapped along, feeling like a trained monkey, watching the Contessa speak quietly to Xonck and Crabbé. At some silent agreement, the members of the Cabal swept off the dais and toward the doors. Before Miss Temple could react Caroline Stearne's voice was in her ear.

"We are to follow," she whispered. "Something is wrong."

As they walked toward the open doors, attracting inquisitive glances from the guests who were all gaily exiting in the opposite direction in the wake of Vandaariff and the Duke, Miss Temple felt someone behind her aside from Caroline. Though she dared not look—curiosity of that sort did not become the staid confidence born of the Process—the sound of clicking steps told her it was the Comte and the last remaining of the three glass Graces, the woman she did not know. This was some blessing at least—a fresh slate was better than the knowing sneers and penetrating disbelief she could expect from Marchmoor and Poole—but in her heart she knew it did not matter which of them ransacked her mind, her pose would be revealed. Her only hope was that the same instinct that had led Crabbé to prevent the examination of the Duke or Lord Vandaariff would prevent them from risking the woman's talents in such close quarters—for surely the rest of the Cabal would not choose to deliver their open minds to the Comte... at least not if they were betraying one another...

She entered the open foyer where she had waited with Captain Smythe, who had withdrawn some yards away so as not to intrude on the deliberations of his betters, betters who in turn waited in impatient silence for the last of their number to arrive, at which point the doors in every direction were closed, shielding their words from the tender ears of any passing *adherent.* As the latches caught and bolts were shot, Miss Temple wondered wistfully what had happened to Elöise, and whether Chang or Svenson might be alive, thoughts brusquely smothered by the figure of the Contessa di Lacquer-Sforza lighting a cigarette in her shining black holder, puffing on the thing three times in succession before she spoke, as if each ascending inhalation stoked the fires of her rage. Perhaps even more disturbingly, not one of the powerful men around her presumed to interrupt this openly menacing ritual.

"What was that?" she finally snarled, fixing her gaze on Harald Crabbé.

"I do beg your pardon, Contessa—"

"Why did you interfere with the examinations? You saw yourself how at least five interlopers were revealed—any one of whom might have undone our plans while we are in Macklenburg. You know this—you know this work is not *finished*."

"My dear, if you felt so strongly—"

"I did not say anything because Mr. Xonck *did* say something, only to be overruled—in front of *everyone*—by you. For any of us to disagree further would have presented the exact lack of unity we have—with some *great effort,* Deputy Minister—managed to avoid."

"I see."

"I don't believe you *do*."

She spat out another mouthful of smoke, her eyes burning into the man like a basilisk. Crabbé did his best to clear his throat and start fresh, but before he spoke a single word she'd cut him off.

"We are not fools, Harald. You stopped the examinations so certain people would not be revealed to the Comte."

Crabbé made a feeble gesture toward Miss Temple, but again whatever words he might have said were halted by the Contessa's condescending scoff.

"Do not insult me—we'll get to Miss Temple in time—I am speaking of the Duke and Lord Vandaariff. Both of whom should have presented no difficulty at all, unless of course, we are misled as to their true status. Enough of us have seen the Duke's corpse that I am willing to say that Doctor Lorenz has done his work fairly—work that perforce was done in cooperation with the Comte. This leaves us with Lord Robert, whose transformation I believe was your *own* responsibility."

"He is absolutely under our control," protested Crabbé, "you saw yourself—"

"I saw no proof at all! It would have been simple to counterfeit!"

"Ask Bascombe—"

"Excellent—of course, we shall rely on the word of your own trusted assistant—now I shall sleep soundly!"

"Do not take anyone's word," snapped Crabbé, growing angry in his turn. "Call Lord Robert back—go see him yourself, do whatever you like, you'll see he is our slave! Exactly as planned!"

"Then *why,*" said Francis Xonck in a calm dangerous tone, "did you interrupt the examination?"

Crabbé stammered, gesturing vaguely with his hands. "Not for the precise reason I stated at the time—I admit that—but so as not to compromise the apparent authority of the Duke and Lord Robert by publicly degrading them with scrutiny! Much rests on our remaining invisible behind these figureheads—including them in the examinations would have revealed them for what they are, our servants! So much is in turmoil already—Blenheim was to escort his master to begin with, to maintain appearances—if it were not for Roger's quick thinking to step forward—"

"Where *is* Blenheim?" snapped the Contessa.

"He seems to have vanished, Madame," answered Caroline. "I have questioned the guests as you asked, but no one has seen him."

The Contessa snorted and looked past Miss Temple to the door, where Colonel Aspiche stood, having entered last of all.

"I do not know," he protested. "My men searched the house—"

"Interesting, as Blenheim would be loyal to Lord Robert," observed Xonck.

"Lord Robert is under our control!" insisted Crabbé.

"The control of your man Bascombe, at least," said Xonck. "And what were those papers?"

This was to Aspiche, who did not understand the question.

"A satchel of papers!" cried Xonck. "You took them from Doctor Svenson! Bascombe took them from you!"

"I have no idea," said the Colonel.

"You're as bad as Blach!" scoffed Xonck. "Where is he anyway?"

The Comte d'Orkancz sighed heavily. "Major Blach is dead. Cardinal Chang."

Xonck took this in, rolled his eyes, then shrugged. He turned back to Colonel Aspiche.

"Where is Bascombe now?"

"With Lord Robert," said Caroline. "After Mr. Blenheim—"

"Where else *ought* he to be?" cried Crabbé, growing exasperated, "Where else? Distributing the message books—someone had to do it in Blenheim's absence!"

"How fortunate he thought to step in," said the Contessa icily.

"Mrs. Marchmoor is with him—surely you trust her as much as I trust Bascombe!" sputtered Crabbé. "Surely they have *both* proven their loyalty to us *all*!"

The Contessa turned to Smythe. "Captain, send two of your men to collect Mr. Bascombe as soon as he is finished. Bring him here, along with Lord Robert, if necessary."

Smythe gestured immediately to his men, and the Dragoons clattered off.

"Where is Lydia?" asked Xonck.

"With the Prince," answered Caroline, "saying good-bye to the guests."

"Thank you, Caroline," said the Contessa, "at least *someone* is paying attention." She called to Smythe. "Have your men collect them as well."

"Bring them to me," rasped the Comte d'Orkancz. "Their part of our business is not finished."

The Comte's words hung balefully in the air, but the others remained silent, as if to speak at all would restart a now-settled disagreement. The Captain detailed two more Dragoons and returned to his place on the far wall, looking at his boots as if he could not hear a word.

"All this can be settled with ease," announced the Deputy Minister, turning to the Comte d'Orkancz, "if we consult the book wherein Lord Robert's thoughts have been stored. That book will make it perfectly clear that I have done what we agreed. It should contain a detailed account of the Lord's participation in this entire affair—facts that only he could know."

"At least one book was destroyed," rasped the Comte.

"Destroyed *how*?" asked the Contessa.

"Chang."

"Damn his bloody soul!" she snarled. "That really is the *limit.* Do you know which book it was?"

"I cannot know until I compare those remaining against the ledger," said the Comte.

"Then let us do so," said Crabbé waspishly. "I would be *exonerated* as soon as possible."

"The books are in transit to the rooftop," said the Comte. "As for the ledger, as you well know it remains in the possession of your assistant."

"My goodness!" cried Xonck. "It seems Bascombe's become a powerfully valuable fellow!"

"He will bring it with him!" protested Crabbé. "It will be settled. All of this is a ridiculous waste of our time—it has divided our efforts and created dangerous delays—and the most likely explanation for all these questions stands before us." He thrust his chin toward Miss Temple. "She and her comrades have caused no end of trouble! Who is to say it was not *they* who have killed Blenheim!"

"Just as Cardinal Chang slew Mr. Gray . . . ," observed Xonck quietly, turning his gaze to the Contessa. Crabbé took in his words, blinked and then, heartened by the shift of inquiry, nodded with agreement.

"Ah! Yes! Yes! I had forgotten it—it had been quite blown from my mind! Contessa?"

"What? As Chang is a murderer and Mr. Gray gone missing, I have no doubt the man was killed. I know not where—my instructions for Mr. Gray were to assist Doctor Lorenz with the Duke."

"Yet Chang says they met underground—near the pipes!" cried Crabbé.

"I had not heard this . . . ," rasped the Comte d'Orkancz.

The Contessa looked up at him and pulled her spent cigarette from the holder, dropping it to the floor and stepping on the smoking butt while she screwed a new one in its place.

"You were occupied with your *ladies,*" she replied. Miss Temple perceived just a whisper of discomfort cross the Contessa's face as she took in the small glass woman, standing placidly as a tamed leopard, careless of their bickering, her brilliant indigo color more striking for her proximity to the Comte's dark fur. "Chang claimed Mr. Gray had been tampering with your works—at my instruction. The clearest evidence of this, of course, would be if something had gone wrong with your efforts—however, as far as I can tell, you have produced three successful transformations. As this is a process I quite freely admit I do not understand *in the slightest,* I offer your results as evidence that Cardinal Chang is a liar."

"Unless he killed Gray *before* he could do his damage," said Crabbé.

"Which is idle, baseless speculation," growled the Contessa.

"Which does not mean it is not true—"

The Contessa swept to the Deputy Minister and her hand—apparently occupied with replacing her cigarette case in her bag—was now wrapped with the bright band. Its glittering spike was hard against Crabbé's throat, digging at a visibly throbbing vein.

Crabbé swallowed.

"Rosamonde . . . ," began the Comte.

"Say it again, you bothersome little man," hissed the Contessa, "and I will rip you open like a poorly sewn sleeve."

Crabbé did not move.

"Rosamonde . . . ," said the Comte again. Her attention did not shift from Crabbé.

"Yes?"

"Might I suggest . . . the young lady?"

The Contessa moved two quick steps away from Crabbé—clear of any counter-stroke from a weapon of his own—and wheeled to Miss Temple. The woman's face was flushed—with open pleasure, it seemed—and her eyes flared with excitement. Miss Temple doubted she had ever been in such peril.

"You underwent the Process in the theatre?" The Contessa smiled. "Is that it? Yes, directly after Lydia Vandaariff?"

Miss Temple nodded quickly.

"What a shame Miss Poole cannot confirm it. But *here* we are not helpless . . . let me see . . . orange for Harschmort . . . attendant whore . . . hotel, I suppose . . . and of course, doomed . . ."

The Contessa leaned forward and hissed into Miss Temple's ear.

"Orange Magdalene orange Royale ice consumption!"

Miss Temple was taken by surprise, stammering for a response, then recalling—too late—the Prince in the secret room—

The Contessa took hold of Miss Temple's jaw, wrenching her head so the women stared at each other. With a cold deliberate sneer the Contessa's tongue snaked from her mouth and smeared its way across each of Miss Temple's eyes. Miss Temple whimpered as the Contessa licked again, pressing her tongue flat over her nose and cheek, digging its narrow tip along her lashes. With a triumphant scoff the Contessa shoved Miss Temple stumbling into the waiting arms of Colonel Aspiche.

Miss Temple looked up to see the elegant lady wiping her mouth with her hand and mockingly smacking her lips.

" 'Thirty-seven Harker-Bornarth, I should say . . . excellent vintage . . . shame to waste it on a savage. Get her out of here."

She was dragged without ceremony down a nearby hallway and thrown, there was no other word for it, like a sack of goods into a dimly lit room guarded by two black-coated soldiers of Macklenburg. She sprawled to her knees and wheeled back to the open door, hair hanging in her eyes, in time to see Aspiche abruptly slam it shut. A moment later it was locked, and his bootsteps retreated into silence. Miss Temple sank back on her haunches and sighed. She dabbed at her face, still sticky with saliva and port, with the sleeve of her robe, and looked around her.

It was, as she had speculated earlier, the exact sort of dusty, disused parlor where she had met Spragg and Farquhar, but with a cry Miss Temple saw that she was not alone. She leapt to her feet and lunged at the two figures sprawled facedown on the floor. They were warm—both warm and—she whimpered with joy—they breathed! She had been reunited at last with her comrades! With all her available strength, she did her best to turn them over.

Miss Temple's face was wet with tears, but she smiled as Doctor Svenson erupted into a fearsome spate of coughing, and she did her best to wedge her knees under his shoulders and help him to sit up. In the dim light she could not see if there was blood, but she could smell the pungent odors of the indigo clay infused throughout his clothing and his hair. She shoved again and swiveled his body so he could lean back against a nearby settee. He coughed again and recovered so far as to cover his mouth with a hand. Miss Temple brushed the hair from his eyes, beaming.

"Doctor Svenson—" she whispered.

"My dear Celeste—are we dead?"

"We are not, Doctor—"

"Excellent—is Chang?"

"No, Doctor—he is right here—"

"Are we still at Harschmort?"

"Yes, locked in a room."

"And your mind remains your own?"

"Oh yes."

"Capital . . . I am with you in a moment . . . beg pardon."

He turned away from her and spat, took a deep breath, groaned, and heaved himself to a full sitting position, his eyes screwed tightly shut.

"My suffering Christ . . . ," he muttered.

"I have just been with our enemies!" she said. "Absolutely everything is going on."

"Imagine it must be . . . pray forgive my momentary lapse . . ."

Miss Temple had scuttled to the other side of Cardinal Chang, doing her best not to cry at the spectacle he presented. If anything, the noxious smell was even more intense, and the dried crusts of blood around his nose and mouth and his collar, and the deathly paleness of his face, made clear the extremity of his health. She began to wipe his face with her robe, her other hand holding his head, when she realized that his dark glasses had come off as she'd rolled him over. She stared at the truly vicious scars across each eye and bit her lip at the poor man's torment. Chang's breath rattled in his chest like a shaken box of jumbled nails. Was he dying? Miss Temple pulled his head to her bosom and cradled it, whispering gently.

"Cardinal Chang, . . . you must come back to us . . . it is Celeste . . . I am with the Doctor . . . we cannot survive without you . . ."

Svenson heaved himself from his place and took hold of Chang's wrist, placing his other hand upon the man's forehead. A moment later his fingers were probing Chang's throat and then Svenson had placed his ear against Chang's chest, to gauge his ragged breath. He raised himself, sighed, and gently disengaged Miss Temple and searched with deliberate fingers along the back of Chang's skull, where he'd been struck by the Colonel's truncheon.

She stared helplessly at his probing fingers, stalking pale through Chang's black hair.

"I thought you'd undergone their Process," he observed mildly.

"No. I was able to counterfeit the scars," she said. "I'm sorry if—well, I did not mean to disappoint you—"

"Hush, it sounds an excellent plan."

"The Contessa found me out nevertheless."

"That is no shame, I'm sure . . . I am happy to find you whole. May I ask—I am almost afraid to say it—"

"Elöise and I became separated. She bore the same false scars—I do not think she has been taken, but do not know where she is. Of course I am not entirely sure I know *who* she is."

The Doctor smiled at her, rather lost and wan, his eyes achingly clear. "Nor am I . . . that is the strangest part of it." He looked pointedly at Miss Temple with the same troubling open gaze. "Of course, when does one ever know?"

He pulled his eyes from hers and cleared his throat.

"Indeed," sniffed Miss Temple, moved by this unexpected glimpse into the Doctor's heart, "still, I am terribly sorry to have lost her."

"We have each done our best . . . that we are alive is a marvel . . . these things are equal between us."

She nodded, wanting to say more but having no idea what those words might be. The Doctor sighed, thinking, and then with an impulsive gesture reached out to pinch tight Chang's nose with one hand and cover his mouth with the other. Miss Temple gasped.

"But what—"

"A moment . . ."

A moment was all it took. Like a man brought back to life Chang's eyes snapped open and his shoulders tensed, his arms groped at Svenson and the rattle in his lungs redoubled in strength. The Doctor removed his hands with a flourish and the Cardinal erupted with his own fit of coughing, dauntingly moist and accompanied by sprays of bloody saliva. Svenson and Miss Temple each took one of the Cardinal's arms and raised him to his knees where he could more easily vent his body's distress and its attendant discharge.

Chang wiped his mouth with his fingers and smeared them on the floor—there was no point in wiping them on his coat or trousers, Miss

Temple saw. He turned to them, blinked, and then groped quickly at his face. Miss Temple held out his glasses with a smile.

"It is so very good to see you both," she whispered.

They sat for a moment, giving each other time to gather their strength and wits, and in Miss Temple's case to wipe away her tears and regain control over her tremulous voice. There was so much to say and so many things to do, she scoffed at her own indulgence, even if the scoff was half-heartedly blown through a sniffling nose.

"You have the advantage, Celeste," muttered Chang hoarsely. "From the blood in the Doctor's hair, I assume we both lack any knowledge of where we are, who guards us . . . even the damned time of day."

"How long since we were taken?" asked Svenson.

Miss Temple sniffed again.

"Not long at all. But so much has happened since we spoke, since I left you—I am so sorry—I was childish and a fool—"

Svenson waved away her concerns.

"Celeste, I doubt there is time—nor does it matter—"

"It matters to me."

"Celeste—" This was Chang, struggling to rise.

"Be quiet, the both of you," she said, and stood up so she was taller than either of them. "I will be brief, but I must first apologize for leaving you at Plum Court. It *was* a foolish thing to do and one that nearly ended my life—and nearly finished both of yours as well." She held up a hand to stop Doctor Svenson from speaking. "There are two Macklenburg soldiers outside the door, and down the corridor at least ten Dragoons with their officer and their Colonel. The door is locked, and—as you both can see—our room is without windows. I assume we have no weapons."

Chang and Svenson patted their pockets somewhat absently, not finding a thing.

"We will acquire them, it does not signify," she said quickly, not wanting to lose her place.

"If we get out the door," said Svenson.

"Yes, of course—the important thing is stopping our enemies' plan."

"And what exact plan is that?" asked Chang.

"That is the issue—I only know a portion of it. But I trust you've each seen a portion of your own."

Keeping her promise to be brief, Miss Temple breathlessly launched into her tale: the St. Royale, Miss Vandaariff's potion, the painting in the Contessa's room, her battle with the book, her battle—in a strictly abbreviated version—with the Comte and Contessa in the coach, her train ride to Harschmort, and her journey to the theatre. Both Chang and Svenson opened their mouths to add details but she hushed them and went on—the secret room, the Contessa and the Prince, the killing of Blenheim, Elöise's discovery in the blue card, Trapping, Vandaariff, Lydia, Veilandt, the ballroom, and, finally, the vicious argument between the Contessa and her allies not ten minutes before. The entire narrative took perhaps two hurriedly whispered minutes.

When she was finished, Miss Temple took a deep breath, hoping she hadn't forgotten anything vital, though of course she had—simply too much had *happened.*

"So . . ." The Doctor pushed himself up from the floor onto the settee. "They have taken control of this government with the Duke—who I promise you was *killed*—and are on their way to taking over that of Macklenburg—"

"If it is not offensive to you, Doctor," said Miss Temple, "I do not understand the *to-do* about one amongst so many German kingdoms."

"Duchy, but yes—it is because our mountains hold more of this indigo clay than a hundred Tarr Manors put together. They have been acquiring the land for years . . ." His voice caught and again he shook his head. "In any case—if they journey tonight to Macklenburg—"

"We will need to travel—" muttered Chang. His words were followed by another wracking cough he did his best to ignore, digging into each side pocket of his coat. "I have carried these quite a way, for this exact moment . . ."

Miss Temple squeaked with happy surprise, blinking again at a new tickling of tears in each eye. Her green boots! She sat down on the floor without the slightest hesitation or thought of modesty and snatched them up, working her lost treasures joyfully onto each foot. She looked up at Chang, who was smiling—though still coughing—and set to tightening the laces.

"I cannot tell you what this means," she said, "you will laugh at me—you're laughing now—I know they are only shoes, and I have many shoes, and to be honest I should not have given a pin for these four days before, but now I would not lose them for the world."

"Of course not," said Svenson quietly.

"O!" Miss Temple said. "But there are things of yours—from your greatcoat, which we lost, but as I said, we took the card, and there was also a silver case, for your cigarettes! Well, now that I say it, I do not have it—Elöise does, but once we find her, you shall have it back."

"Indeed . . . I . . . that is excellent—"

"It seemed as if it might be precious to you."

The Doctor nodded, but then looked away, frowning, as if he did not want to say more. Chang coughed again, congestion echoing wetly in his chest.

"We must do something for you," said Svenson, but Chang shook his head.

"It is my lungs—"

"Powdered glass," said Miss Temple. "The Contessa explained how she'd killed you."

"I am sorry to disappoint the Lady . . ." He smiled.

Svenson looked at Chang quite soberly. "The glass alone would be harmful to your lungs—that it bears such toxic properties as well, it is a marvel you have not succumbed to hypnotic visions."

"I should prefer them to this coughing, I assure you."

"Is there any way to get it out?" asked Miss Temple.

The Doctor frowned in thought. The Cardinal spat again, and began to speak.

"My story is simple. When we did not know where you went, we split up, the Doctor to Tarr Manor and I to the Ministry, neither of us guessing correctly. I met Bascombe and the Contessa, witnessed the Process in action, fought Xonck, nearly died, then tracked you—too late—to the St. Royale—thus the boots—and made the train for Harschmort. Once here I have seen the most powerful figures overborne, their minds drained into these books, and Robert Vandaariff, mindless as an ape, filling page after page with a narrative of his secrets. I was unable to prevent the transformation of the three women . . ." Chang paused for a moment—Miss Temple was becoming steadily aware of the degree to which each man had pressed the limit of not only his strength but also his heart, and her own went out to them utterly—and then cleared his throat. "Though I did kill your Major Blach. But the rest was capture and failure—except I also managed to kill the Contessa's man, Mr. Gray—"

"O! They were arguing about it fiercely!" exclaimed Miss Temple.

"He was on some errand—secret from the others, I am sure. I do not know what it was." He looked up at Miss Temple. "Did you say our guards were Dragoons?"

"Not directly outside the door, no—but in the corridor, yes—perhaps a dozen men with their officer, Captain Smythe, and their Colonel—"

"Smythe, you say!" Chang's face visibly brightened.

"I met him," said Svenson. "He saved my life!"

"He knows me too, somehow," said Miss Temple. "It was actually rather unsettling..."

"If we can get rid of Aspiche then Smythe will come to our cause, I am sure of it," said Chang.

Miss Temple glanced back at the door. "Well, if *that* is all we require, then we will soon be on our way. Doctor?"

"I can speak as we go—save to say that there is an airship on the roof—it is how we came from Tarr Manor. They may use it to reach a ship at the canal, or farther up the coast—"

"Or go all the way to Macklenburg," said Chang. "These machines I have seen are prodigiously powerful."

Svenson nodded. "You are right—it is ridiculous to undervalue their capacity in any way—but this too can wait. We must stop the marriage. We must stop the Duke."

"And we must find Elöise," exclaimed Miss Temple, "especially as she has the glass key!"

"What glass key?" rasped Chang.

"Did I not mention it? I believe it is the way to safely read the books. We got it from Blenheim's pocket."

"How did *he* have it?" asked Chang.

"Exactly!" Miss Temple beamed. "Now, both of you—back on the

floor—or, all right, I'm sure it is fine if you are on a settee—but you must shut your eyes and remain inert."

"Celeste, what are you doing?" asked Svenson.

"Managing our escape, naturally."

She knocked on the door and called out as sweetly as she could to the guards on the other side. They did not answer, but Miss Temple kept knocking and although she was forced to switch several times from one hand to the other as her knuckles became tender, at last the lock was turned and the door cracked open a single suspicious inch, through which Miss Temple glimpsed the pale, cautious face of a young soldier from Macklenburg—younger than herself, she saw, which only increased the sweetness of her smile.

"I do beg your pardon, but it's very important that I see the Colonel. I have information for the Contessa—the *Contessa,* you understand—that she will be most anxious to have."

The trooper did not move. Did he even *understand* her? Miss Temple's smile hardened as she leaned forward and spoke more loudly, with a sharp, unmistakable intent.

"I must see the Colonel! At once! Or *you* will be *punished*!"

The trooper looked to his comrade, out of view, clearly unsure of what he should do. Miss Temple barked past him at the top of her lungs.

"*Colonel Aspiche!* I have vital news for you! If the Contessa does not get it, *she will cut off your ears*!"

At her scream the guard slammed the door and fumbled for the lock, but Miss Temple could already hear the angry stride of heavy boots. In a moment the door was flung wide by Aspiche, face crimson with rage, cheroot in one hand and the other on the hilt of his saber, glaring down at her like a red-coated schoolmaster ready to deal out a whipping.

"Thank you so much," said Miss Temple.

"What information are you screeching about?" he snarled. "Your manners are quite unbecoming—even more so if I find this is a *lie.*"

"Nonsense," said Miss Temple, shivering for the Colonel's benefit and slipping a theatrical quaver into her voice. "And you do not need to *scare* me so—the state of my allies and the Contessa's power have left me helpless. I am only trying to save my own life." She wiped her nose on her sleeve.

"What information?" repeated Aspiche.

Miss Temple glanced behind him at the guards, who were staring with undisguised curiosity, and then leaned forward with a whisper.

"It is actually rather *sensitive* . . ."

Aspiche leaned forward in turn with a tight, put-upon expression. Miss Temple brushed his ear with her lips.

"Blue . . . Caesar . . . blue . . . Regiment . . . ice . . . consumption . . ."

She looked up and saw the Colonel's eyes did not move, gazing at a point just beyond her shoulder.

"Perhaps we ought to be alone," she whispered.

Aspiche wheeled on the guards with fury.

"Leave me with the prisoners!" he barked. The guards stumbled back, as Aspiche reached out with both hands and slammed the door. He turned back to Miss Temple, his face without any expression at all.

"Cardinal, . . . Doctor, . . . you may rise . . ."

She kept to her whisper, not wanting the guards to hear. Chang and Svenson stood slowly, staring at the Colonel with morbid curiosity.

"Everyone who undergoes the Process is instilled with some sort of control phrase," Miss Temple explained. "I overheard the Contessa use one on the Prince, and again when she attempted to use one on me—to prove I had *not* been converted. I wasn't able to work it all out—it was a guess—"

"You risked this on a guess?" asked Svenson.

"As it was a *good* guess, yes. The phrase has several parts—the first is a color, and I deduced that the color was about where the Process was administered. You remember that the different boxes had different colors of felt packing—"

"Orange at Harschmort," said Chang. "Blue at the Institute."

"And seeing as he was converted *before* they moved the boxes from the Institute, the color for the Colonel was blue."

"What was the rest of the phrase?" asked Svenson.

"The second word is about their *role,* using a Biblical metaphor—I'm sure it is all part of the Comte's ostentation. For the Prince it was

Joseph—for he will be the father to someone else's child, as poor Lydia must be Mary—for me it would have been Magdalene, as for all of the white-robed initiates—and for the Colonel, as the representative of the state, I guessed correctly it would be 'Caesar' . . . the rest follows the same way—'Regiment' instead of 'Palace' or 'Royale'—"

"Is he understanding this?" asked Svenson.

"I think so, but he is also waiting for instructions."

"Suppose he should cut his own throat?" suggested Chang, with a moist chuckle.

"Suppose he tells us if they've captured Elöise," said Svenson, and he spoke slowly and clearly to Colonel Aspiche. "Do you know the whereabouts of Mrs. Dujong?"

"Shut your filthy hole before I shut it for you!" Aspiche roared.

Svenson darted back a step, his eyes wide with surprise.

"Ah," Miss Temple said, "perhaps only the person who speaks the phrase can command." She cleared her throat. "Colonel, do you know where we can find Mrs. Dujong?"

"Of course I don't," snapped Aspiche, sullenly.

"All right . . . when did you last see her?"

The Colonel's lips curled into an unabashed and wicked smile. "Aboard the airship. Doctor Lorenz asked her questions, and when she did not answer Miss Poole and I took turns—"

Doctor Svenson's fist landed like a hammer on the Colonel's jaw, knocking him back into the door. Miss Temple turned to Svenson—hissing with pain and flexing his hand—and then to Aspiche, sputtering with rage and struggling to rise. Before he could, Chang's arm shot forth and snatched the Colonel's saber from its sheath, a wheeling bright scythe that had Miss Temple scampering clear with a squeak. When she looked back, the Cardinal had the blade hovering dangerously in front of the man's chest. Aspiche did not move.

"Doctor?" she asked quietly.

"My apologies—"

"Not at all, the Colonel is a horrid beast. Your hand?"

"It will do fine."

She stepped closer to Aspiche, her face harder than before. She had known Elöise endured her own set of trials, but Miss Temple thought back to her own irritation at how the woman, drugged and stumbling, had slowed their progress in escaping the theatre. She was more than happy to expend the sting of her guilt and regret on the villain before her.

"Colonel, you will open this door and take us into the hall. You will order both of these guards into this room and then lock the door behind them. If they protest, you will do your level best to kill them. Do you understand?"

Aspiche nodded, his eyes wavering between her own and the floating tip of the saber.

"Then do it. We are wasting time."

The Germans gave them no trouble, so inured were they to following orders. It was only a matter of moments before they stood again in the open foyer where the members of the Cabal had argued with one another. The Dragoons lining the corridor were gone, along with their officer.

"Where's Captain Smythe?" she asked Aspiche.

"Assisting Mr. Xonck and the Deputy Minister."

Miss Temple frowned. "Then what were *you* doing here? Did you not have orders?"

"Of course—to execute the three of you."

"But why were you waiting in the corridor?"

"I was finishing my cigar!" snapped Colonel Aspiche.

Chang scoffed behind her.

"Every man reveals his soul eventually," he muttered.

Miss Temple crept to the ballroom doors. The enormous space was empty. She called back to her prisoner.

"Where is everyone?" He opened his mouth to answer but she cut him off. "Where are each of our enemies—the Contessa, the Comte, Deputy Minister Crabbé, Francis Xonck, the Prince and his bride, Lord Vandaariff, the Duke of Stäelmaere, Mrs. Stearne—"

"And Roger Bascombe," said Doctor Svenson. She turned to him, and to Chang, and nodded sadly.

"And Roger Bascombe." She sighed. "In an orderly manner, if you please."

The Colonel had informed them—sullen twitches around his mouth evidence of a useless struggle against Miss Temple's control—that their enemies had split into two groups. The first occupied themselves with a sweeping progress through the great house, gathering up their guests and collecting the stupefied luminaries whose minds had been drained into the glass books on the way, to send off the Duke of Stäelmaere with ceremony suitable to his imminent *coup d'état.* Accompanying the Duke's progress would be the Contessa, the Deputy Minister, and Francis Xonck, as well as Lord Vandaariff, Bascombe, Mrs. Stearne, and the two glass women, Marchmoor and Poole. The second group, about which Aspiche could provide no information as to their errand, consisted of the Comte d'Orkancz, Prince Karl-Horst von Maasmärck, Lydia Vandaariff, Herr Flaüss, and the third glass woman.

"I did not recognize her," said Miss Temple. "By all rights the third subject ought to have been Caroline."

"It is *Angelique,* the Cardinal's acquaintance," replied Doctor Svenson, speaking delicately. "The woman we searched for in the greenhouse. You were right—she did not perish there."

"Instead, the Comte kept her alive to use as a test subject," rasped Chang. "If his transformation failed, then he need not sacrifice the others—if it worked and made moot the issue of her damaged body, then all the better. All in all you see, it is an admirable expression of *economy.*"

Neither Miss Temple nor the Doctor spoke, letting Chang's bitterness and anger have their sway. Chang rubbed his eyes beneath his glasses and sighed.

"The question is what they are doing, and which group we ought to follow. If we agree that stopping the Duke and the Prince's marriage are both vital, it is of course possible that we split up—"

"I should prefer not to," said Miss Temple quickly. "In either place we shall find enemies *en masse*—it seems there is strength in numbers."

"I agree," said the Doctor, "and my vote is to go after the Duke. The rest of the Cabal journeys to Macklenburg—the Duke and Lord Vandaariff are their keys to maintaining power here. If we can disrupt that, it may upset the balance of their entire plot."

"You mean to kill them?" asked Chang.

"Kill them *again,* in the case of the Duke," muttered the Doctor, "but yes, I am for assassinations all round." He sighed bitterly. "It is exactly my plan for Karl-Horst, should his neck ever come within reach of my two hands."

"But he is your charge," said Miss Temple, a little shocked by Svenson's tone.

"My charge has become their creature," he answered. "He is no more than a rabid dog or a horse with a broken fetlock—he must be put down, preferably *before* he has a chance to sire an heir."

Miss Temple put her hand over her mouth. "Of course! The Comte is using his alchemy to impregnate Lydia—it is the height of *his* part of this plan—it is Oskar Veilandt's alchemical *Annunciation* made flesh! And they are doing it tonight—even now!"

Doctor Svenson sucked on his teeth, wincing, looking back and forth between Miss Temple and Chang.

"I still say we stop the Duke. If we do not—"

"If we do not, mine and Miss Temple's lives in this city are ruined," said Chang.

"And after that," asked Miss Temple, "the Prince and Lydia?"

Svenson nodded, and then sighed. "I'm afraid they are already doomed..."

Chang abruptly cackled, a sound as pleasant as a gargling crow. "Are we so different, Doctor? Save some of your pity for us!"

At Miss Temple's command Aspiche led them toward the main entrance of the house, but it became quickly clear they could not go far that way, so thronged had it become with the many, many guests gathered for the Duke's departure. With a sudden inspiration, Miss Temple recalled her own path with Spragg and Farquhar through the gardener's passage between the wings of the house and around to the carriages. Within two minutes—Aspiche huffing as sullenly as his conditioning allowed—they had arrived, their breath clouding in the chilly air, just in time to watch a procession flow down the main stairs toward the Duke's imperious, massive black coach.

The Duke himself moved slowly and with care, like a particularly delicate, funereal stick insect, guided on one side by the small greasy-haired man—"Doctor Lorenz," whispered Svenson—and on the other by Mrs. Marchmoor, no longer with a leash around her neck, her gleaming body now covered in a thick black cloak. Behind in a line came the Contessa, Xonck, and Deputy Minister Crabbé, and behind them, stopping at the steps and waving the Duke on his way, stood the similarly aligned knot of Robert Vandaariff, Roger Bascombe, and Mrs. Poole, also leashless and cloaked.

The Duke was installed in his coach and joined a moment later by Mrs. Marchmoor. Miss Temple looked to her companions—now was clearly the time to dash for the coach if they were going to do so—but before she could speak she saw with dismay, boisterously shouting to the Duke and to each other as they sought their own amongst the many coaches, the rest of the guests all preparing to leave. Any attack on the Duke's coach was all but impossible.

"What can we do?" she whispered. "We are too late!"

Chang hefted the saber in his hand. "I can go—one of us alone, I can move more quickly—I can track them to the Palace—"

"Not in your condition," observed Svenson. "You would be caught and killed—and you know it. Look at the soldiers! They have a full escort!"

As he pointed Miss Temple now saw that it was true—a double rank of mounted Dragoons, perhaps forty men, moving their horses into position ahead and behind the coach. The Duke was completely beyond their reach.

"He will convene the Privy Council," rasped Chang hollowly. "He will make whatever they want into law."

"With the Duke's power, and Vandaariff's money, the Macklenburg throne, and an inexhaustible supply of indigo clay . . . they'll be unstoppable . . ." whispered Svenson.

Miss Temple frowned. Perhaps it was a futile gesture, but she would make it.

"On the contrary. Cardinal Chang, if you would please return the Colonel's saber—I do insist."

Chang looked at her quizzically, but carefully passed the weapon to Aspiche. Before the man could do a thing with it, Miss Temple spoke to him quite firmly.

"Colonel Aspiche, listen to me. Your men protect the Duke—this is excellent. No one else—no one, mind—is to come within reach of the Duke during his journey back to the Palace. You will go now, collect a horse, and join his train—immediately, do not speak to anyone, do not return to the house, take the mount of one of your men if you must.

Once you reach the Palace, being very particular to avoid the scrutiny of Mrs. Marchmoor, you will find time—the appropriate time, for you must *succeed*—but nevertheless *before* the Privy Council can meet—to hack the Duke of Stäelmaere's head clean from his body. Do you understand me?"

Colonel Aspiche nodded.

"Excellent. Do not breathe a word of this to anyone. Off you go!"

She smiled, watching the man stride into the crowded plaza, possessed by his mission, toward the nearest stand of horses, pretending not to see the astonished expressions of Svenson and Chang to her either side.

"Let's see them stick it back on with library paste," she said. "Shall we find the Prince?"

The Colonel had not known exactly where the Comte and his party had gone, merely that it was somewhere below the ballroom. From his own journeys through Harschmort House, Cardinal Chang was convinced he could find the way, and so Miss Temple and Doctor Svenson followed him back through the gardener's passage and then indoors. As they walked, Miss Temple looked up at Chang, daunting despite his injuries, and wished for just a moment that she might see inside his thoughts like one of the glass women. They were on their way to rescue—or destroy, but the goal was the same—the Prince and Lydia, but the Cardinal's lost woman, Angelique, would be there as well. Did he hope to reclaim her? To force the Comte to reverse her transformation? Or to put her out of her misery? She felt the weight of her own sadness, the regret and pain of Roger's rejection, of her own habitual isolation—were these feelings, feelings that because they were hers felt somehow small, however keenly they plagued her, anything like the burdens haunting a man like Chang? How could they be? How could there not be an impassable wall between them?

"The two wings mirror each other," he said hoarsely, "and I have been up and down the lower floors on the opposite side. If I am right, the stairway down should be right . . . about . . . *here* . . ."

He smiled—and Miss Temple was struck anew, perhaps by his especially battered condition, of what a provocative mix of the bodily compelling and morally fearsome Cardinal Chang's smile actually was—and indicated a bland-looking alcove covered with a velvet curtain. He whisked it aside and revealed a metal door that had boldly been left ajar.

"Such *confidence*"—he chuckled, pulling it open—"to leave an open door . . . you'd think they might have learned."

He spun to look behind them, his face abruptly stern, at the sound of approaching footsteps.

"Or *we* would have . . . ," muttered Doctor Svenson, and Chang hurriedly motioned them through the door. He closed it behind them, letting the lock catch. "It will delay them," he whispered. "Quickly!"

They heard the door being pulled repeatedly above them as they followed the spiral staircase for two turns, reaching another door, also ajar, where Chang eased past Miss Temple and Svenson to peek through first.

"Might I suggest we acquire *weapons*?" whispered the Doctor.

Miss Temple nodded her agreement, but instead of answering Chang had slipped through the door, his footfalls silent as a cat's, leaving them to follow as best they could. They entered a strange curving corridor, like an opera house or a Roman theatre, with a row of doors on the inner side, as if they led to box seats, or toward the arena.

"It is like the Institute," Svenson whispered to Chang, who nodded, still focused on the corridor ahead. They had advanced, walking close to the inner wall, just so the staircase door was no longer visible behind them, when a scuffling noise beyond the next curve caused Chang to freeze. He held his open palm to indicate that they should stay, then carefully moved forward alone, pressed flat against the wall.

Chang stopped. He glanced back at them and smiled, then darted forward in a sudden rush. Miss Temple heard one brief squawk of surprise and then three meaty thuds in rapid succession. Chang reappeared and motioned them on with a quick toss of his head.

On the ground by another open door, his breathing labored, blood flowing freely from his nose, lay the Macklenburg Envoy, Herr Flaüss. Near his feebly twitching hand lay a revolver, which Chang snatched up, breaking it open to check the cylinder and then slamming it home. While Doctor Svenson knelt by the gasping man, Chang extended the weapon for Miss Temple to take. She shook her head.

"Surely you or the Doctor," she whispered.

"The Doctor, then," replied Chang. "I am more useful with a blade or my fists." He looked down to watch Svenson briskly ransack the Envoy's pockets, each search answered by an ineffectual gesture of protest from the injured man's hands. Svenson looked up, behind them toward the staircase—footsteps. He stood, abandoning the Envoy. Chang pressed the pistol into Svenson's hands and took hold of the Doctor's sleeve and Miss Temple's arm, pulling them both farther down the corridor until they could no longer see the Envoy. Svenson whispered his protest.

"But, Cardinal, they are surely *inside*—"

Chang tugged them both into an alcove and pressed a hand over his mouth to stifle a cough. Down the corridor Miss Temple heard rushing steps . . . that suddenly fell silent. She felt Chang's body tense, and saw the Doctor's thumb moving slowly to the hammer of the pistol. Someone was walking toward them, slowly . . . the footsteps stopped . . . and then retreated. She strained her ears . . . and heard a woman's haughty, angry hiss.

"*Leave* the idiot . . ."

Chang waited . . . and then leaned close to them both.

"Without getting rid of the body, we could not enter in secret—at this moment they are searching the room, assuming we have entered. This alone will halt whatever is happening inside. If we enter *now,* there is a chance to take their rearmost by surprise."

Miss Temple took a deep breath, feeling as if she had somehow in the last five minutes become a soldier. Before she could make sense of—or more importantly, protest against—this wrong-headed state of affairs Chang was gone and Doctor Svenson, taking her hand in his, was pulling her in tow.

The Envoy remained in the doorway, raised to a sitting position but still incapacitated and insensible. They stepped past with no reaction from Herr Flaüss save a snuffle of his bleeding nose, into a dim stone entryway with narrow staircases to either side to balconies that wrapped around the room. Chang swiftly ducked to the left, with Svenson and Miss Temple directly behind him, crowding as quietly as possible out of sight. Miss Temple wrinkled her nose with distaste at the harsh reek of indigo clay. Ahead of them, through the foyer, they heard the Contessa.

"He has been attacked—you heard nothing?"

"I did not," answered the dry, rumbling voice of the Comte. "I am *busy,* and my business makes noise. Attacked by *whom*?"

"I'm sure I do not know," replied the Contessa. "Colonel Aspiche has cut the throats of each *likely* candidate . . . thus my *curiosity.*"

"The Duke is away?"

"Exactly as planned, followed by those selected for book-harvest. As agreed, their distraction and loss of memory have been blamed on a virulent outbreak of blood fever—stories of which will be spread by our own adherents—a tale with the added benefit of justifying a quarantine of Harschmort, sequestering Lord Robert for as long as necessary. But that is not our present difficulty."

"I see," grunted the Comte. "As I am in the midst of a very delicate procedure, I would appreciate it if you explained what in the depths of hell you are all doing here."

Miss Temple did her best to follow the others up the narrow stairs in silence. As her head cleared the balcony floor, she saw a domed stone ceiling above, lit by several wicked-looking iron chandeliers that bristled with spikes. Miss Temple could never see a chandelier under the best of circumstances without imagining the destructive impact of its sudden drop to the floor (especially if she was passing beneath), and these instinctive thoughts, and these fixtures, just made the Comte's laboratory that much more a chamber of dread. The balcony was stacked with books and papers and boxes, all covered by a heavy layer of dust. Svenson indicated with a jab of his finger that she could inch forward to peek through the bars of the railing.

Miss Temple had not been to the Institute, but she had managed a powerful glimpse of the hellish platform at the base of the iron tower. This room (as the walls were lined with bookshelves it seemed to have once been some sort of library) was a strange mix of that same industry (for there were tables cluttered with steaming pots and boiling vials and parchment and wickedly shaped metal tools) and a sleeping chamber, for in the center of the room, cleared by pushing aside and stacking any number of tables and chairs, was a very large bed. Miss Temple nearly gagged, covering her mouth with her hand, but she could not look away.

On the bed, her bare legs dangling over the side, lay Lydia Vandaariff, her white robes around her thighs, each arm outstretched and restrained by a white silk cord. Her face shone with exertion, and each of her hands tightly gripped its cord, as if the restraint were more a source of comfort than punishment. The bedding between Lydia's legs was wet, as was the stone floor beneath her feet, a pooling of watered blue fluid streaked with curling crimson lines. The embroidered hem of Lydia's robe had been flipped down in a meager gesture toward modesty, but there was no ignoring the flecks of blue and red on her white thighs. She looked up at the ceiling, blinking.

Slumped in a nearby chair, a half-full glass in his hand and an open bottle of brandy on the floor between his legs, sat Karl-Horst von Maasmärck. The Comte wore his leather apron, his black fur slung over a pile of chairs behind him, and cradled a bizarre metal object, a metal tube with handles and valves and a pointed snout that he wiped clean with a rag.

On the walls behind them, hung on nails hammered carelessly into the bookcases, were thirteen distinct squares of canvas. Miss Temple turned to Chang and pointed. He had seen them as well, and made a deliberate gesture to flatten his hand and then turn it over, as to turn a page. At the St. Royale, Lydia had muttered something about the *rest* of the *Annunciation* fragments—indicating that she had seen them collected. Miss Temple knew the squares of canvas represented the entire reconstituted work, but she had not expected the Comte to hang each painting face to the wall, for what she saw was not the complete blasphemous image (which she was frankly by now more than a little curious to see), but its canvas backing—Oskar Veilandt's alchemical formulae as they traveled across every piece, for which the painting was but a decorative veil, a detailed recipe for his own Annunciation, the unspeakable impregnation of Lydia Vandaariff by way of his twisted science. Around each canvas were pasted scores of additional notes and diagrams—no doubt the Comte's own attempts to understand Veilandt's blasphemous instructions. Miss Temple looked down at the girl on the bed and bit her knuckle to keep silent...

She heard an impatient sigh below her and the flicking catch of a match. Miss Temple scooted forward on her belly and gained a wider view of the room. With a tremor of fear she saw, almost directly beneath, the Contessa's large party. How had they not heard them in the corridor? Next to the Contessa—smoking a fresh cigarette in her holder—stood Francis Xonck and Crabbé, and behind them at least six figures in black coats, carrying cudgels. She glanced again to Chang and Svenson and saw Chang's attention focused elsewhere, underneath the opposite balcony. Glittering in the shadows, as the orange flames from the Comte's crucibles reflected off her skin, stood the third glass woman, Angelique, silently waiting. Miss Temple stared at her, and was just beginning to examine the woman's body with the new understanding that it was the object of Chang's ardent affection—and in fact, its consummation, for the woman *was* a whore—which meant . . . Miss Temple's face became flushed, suddenly jumbling her memories from the book with thoughts of Chang and Angelique—when she shook her head and forced her attention to the rather agitated conversation below.

"We would not have bothered you," began Xonck, his eyes drawn with some distaste to the spectacle before them, "save we are unaccountably unable to locate a workable *key*."

"Where is Lorenz?" asked the Comte.

"Readying the airship," replied Crabbé, "and surrounded by a host of soldiers. I would prefer to leave him be."

"What of Bascombe?"

"He accompanies Lord Robert," snorted the Contessa. "We will meet him with the trunk of books and his ledger—but he does not have a key either, and for any number of reasons I would prefer not to involve him."

Crabbé rolled his eyes. "Mr. Bascombe is absolutely loyal to us all—"

"Where is *your* key?" the Comte asked, glaring pointedly at the Deputy Minister.

"It is not *my* key at all," replied Crabbé somewhat hotly. "I do not believe I am even the last to have it—as the Contessa says, we were collecting the books, not *exploring* them—"

"Who *was* the last to have it?" cried the Comte, openly impatient. He shifted his grip on the repulsive metal device in his hand.

"We do not *know*," snapped the Contessa. "I believe it was Mr. Crabbé. He believes it was Mr. Xonck. *He* believes it was Blenheim—"

"Blenheim?" scoffed the Comte.

"Not Blenheim directly," said Xonck. "*Trapping.* I believe Trapping took it to look at one of the books—perhaps idly, perhaps not—"

"*Which* book?"

"We do not *know,*" said the Contessa. "We were *indulging* him—I am still not satisfied as to his death. Blenheim either took it from Trapping's pocket when the body was moved, or he was given it by Lord Robert."

"I take it Blenheim is still missing?"

The Contessa nodded.

"The question is whether he is dead," said Crabbé, "or *independent*?"

"Perhaps we can *query* Lord Robert," said the Comte.

"We could if he retained his memory," observed Xonck. "But as you know it has been put into a book—a book we cannot find. If we did find it, we could not safely read it without a key! It is ridiculous!"

"I see . . ." said the Comte, his brooding face dark with thought. "And *what* has happened to Herr Flaüss?"

"We do not *know*!" cried Crabbé.

"But don't you think we should?" asked the Comte, reasonably. He turned to Angelique and clapped his hands. At once she stepped into the light like a tamed tiger, drawing the wary attention of every other person in the room.

"If there is someone hiding here," the Comte said to her, looking up to the balconies, "*find* them."

Miss Temple spun to Chang and Svenson, her eyes wide. What could they do? She searched around them—there was no other place to hide, to shield themselves! Doctor Svenson silently rolled back on his heels and pulled out the gun, his eyes measuring the distance to Angelique. Chang put a hand on the Doctor's arm. The Doctor shrugged it off and eased back the hammer. Miss Temple felt the strange blue coldness approaching her mind. Any moment they would be found.

Instead, the pregnant silence in the room was broken by a crash from the opposite balcony, directly above Angelique. In an instant Xonck had the serpentine dagger in his hand and was sprinting to the narrow stairs. Miss Temple heard a scuffle and then a woman's gasping protests as Xonck dragged her twisting body brusquely down the staircase and thrust her to her knees before the others. It was Elöise.

Miss Temple looked to Svenson and saw his frozen expression. Before he could do a thing she reached for his hand that held the pistol, gripping it tightly. This was no time for reckless impulse.

Xonck backed away from Elöise, indeed as did they all, for at a nod from the Comte Angelique stepped forward, her feet clicking against the stone floor like a new-shod pony's. Elöise shook her head and looked up, utterly bewildered by the splendid, naked creature, and screamed. She screamed again—Miss Temple squeezing the Doctor's arm as tightly as she could—but it died in her throat, as the expression of terror on her face faded to a quivering passivity. The glass woman had savagely penetrated her mind and was rummaging through its contents with pitiless efficiency. Again, Miss Temple saw the Comte d'Orkancz had closed his eyes, his face a mask of concentration. Elöise did not speak, her mouth open, rocking back and forth on her knees, staring helplessly into the cold blue eyes of her inquisitor.

Then it was done. Elöise dropped in a heap. The Comte came forward to stand over her, looking down.

"It is Mrs. Dujong," whispered Crabbé. "From the quarry. She shot the Duke."

"Indeed. She escaped from the theatre with Miss Temple," said the Comte. "Miss Temple killed Blenheim—his body is in the trophy room. Blenheim *did* have the key—she herself wondered why. It is tucked in Mrs. Dujong's shift, along with a silver cigarette case and a blue glass demonstration card. Both were acquired by way of Doctor Svenson."

"A glass card?" asked the Contessa. Her gaze darted judiciously across the room. "What does it happen to *show*?"

Elöise was panting with exertion, groping to rise to her hands and knees. The Comte shoved his hand roughly into her shift, feeling for the objects he'd described. He stood again, peering at the cigarette case, all the time not answering the Contessa's question. Xonck cleared his throat. The Comte looked up and tossed the silver case to him, which Xonck awkwardly managed to catch.

"Also Svenson's," he said, and glanced over at the Prince, who was still in his chair, watching it all through a veil of drunken bemusement. "The card is imprinted with an experience of Mrs. Marchmoor, within a room at the St. Royale... an *encounter* with the Prince. Apparently it made quite an *impression* on Mrs. Dujong."

"Is that... all?" asked the Contessa, again rather carefully.

"No." The Comte sighed heavily. "It is not."

He nodded again to Angelique.

To the immediate dismay of the other members of the Cabal, the glass woman turned toward them. They shrank back, as Angelique began to walk forward.

"W-what are you *doing?*" sputtered Crabbé.

"I am getting to the bottom of this *mystery,*" rasped the Comte.

"You cannot finish this without our help," hissed Xonck. He waved a hand at the girl on the bed. "Haven't we done enough for you—haven't we all accommodated your *visions*?"

"Visions at the core of your *profit,* Francis."

"I have never denied it! But if you think to turn me into a husk like Vandaariff—"

"I think nothing of the kind," answered the Comte. "What I am doing is in our larger interest."

"Before you treat us like animals, Oskar,... and make me your *enemy,*" said the Contessa, raising her voice and speaking quite fiercely, "perhaps you could explain what you intend."

Miss Temple clapped a hand over her mouth, feeling like a fool. Oskar! Was it so stupidly obvious? The Comte had not stolen the works of Oskar Veilandt, the painter was no prisoner or mindless drone... the two men were one and the same! What had Aunt Agathe told her—that the Comte was born in the Balkans, raised in Paris, an unlikely inheritance? How was that incompatible with what Mr. Shanck had said of Veilandt—school in Vienna, studio in Montmartre, mysteriously disappeared—into respectability and wealth, she now knew! She looked over to Chang and Svenson, and saw Chang shaking his head bitterly. Svenson had eyes for nothing but Elöise's slumped figure, glaring down at the poor woman with helpless agitation.

The Comte cleared his throat and held up the glass card.

"The *encounter* is attended by spectators—including you, Rosamonde, and you, Francis. But the clever Mrs. Dujong has perceived, through the viewing mirror, a *second* encounter, in the lobby... that of Colonel Trapping speaking most earnestly with Robert Vandaariff."

This revelation was met with silence.

"What does that *mean*?" asked Crabbé.

"That is not *all*," intoned the Comte.

"If you would simply tell us, Monsieur!" protested Crabbé. "There is no great amount of time—"

"Mrs. Dujong's memory tells of a *second* card—one the Doctor cut from the lining of Arthur Trapping's uniform. Evidently his body was not fully *searched*. Among other things this card conveys an image of myself performing a preparatory examination on Lydia."

"Arthur intended to give it to Vandaariff," said Xonck. "The greedy fool would not have been able to resist..."

Crabbé stepped forward, narrowing his eyes.

"Is this your way of informing us that *you* killed him?" he hissed at the Comte. "Without telling anyone? Risking everything? Pushing forward our entire time-table? No wonder Lord Robert was so agitated—no wonder we were forced to—"

"But that is the point, Harald," rumbled the Comte. "I am telling you *all* this exactly because *I* did not harm a hair on Arthur Trapping's head."

"But—but why else—" began Crabbé, but he then fell silent... as every member of the Cabal studied one another.

"You said she had this from Svenson?" the Contessa asked. "Where did *he* get it?"

"She does not know."

"From me, of course," drawled a sluggish voice from the other side of the room. Karl-Horst was attempting to pour himself more brandy. "He must have found it in my room. I never even noticed Trapping, I must say—more interested in *Margaret*! It was the first bit of glass I'd ever seen—a present to entice my participation."

"A present from whom?" asked Francis Xonck.

"Lord knows—is that important?"

"It is perhaps crucial, Your Highness," said the Contessa.

The Prince frowned. "Well... in *that* case..."

It seemed to Miss Temple that each member of the Cabal watched the Prince with the barest restraint, every one of them wishing they could slap his face until he spat out what he knew, but none daring to show the slightest impatience or worry in front of the others . . . and so they waited as he pursed his lips and scratched his ear and sucked on his teeth, all the time enjoying their undivided attention. She was beginning to get worried herself. What if Angelique were to continue her search? Who was to say the glass woman could not somehow smell the presence of their minds? Miss Temple's leg tingled from being crouched so long, and the dusty air was tickling her nose. She glanced at Chang, his lips pressed shut, and realized he had controlled his cough this entire time. She'd not given it a second thought, but suddenly the possibility—the inevitability!—of him exposing their presence terrified her. They must take some action—but what? What possibly?

"I suppose it must have been Doctor Lorenz, or—what was his name?—Mr. Crooner, from the Institute, the one who died so badly. They were the ones working the machines. Gave it to me as a sort of *keepsake*—don't know how that villain Svenson found it unless he had help—I stashed it most brilliantly—"

The Contessa cut him off. "Excellent, Your Highness, that's very helpful."

She crossed to the Comte and relieved him of the items he'd taken from Elöise, speaking with a barely veiled anger.

"This gets us nowhere. We have what we came for—the key. Let us at once return to the books, to find what we can from Lord Robert's *testimony*. Perhaps we will finally learn why the Colonel was killed."

"You don't believe it was Chang?" asked Crabbé.

"Do you?" scoffed the Contessa. "I would be happy to hear it—my life would be simpler. But no—we all remember the delicacy and risk involved in our final *swaying* of Robert Vandaariff, who up to that point quite believed the entire campaign was his own conception. We know the Colonel was brokering secrets—who can say how many secrets he knew?" She shrugged. "Chang's a killer—this is *politics*. We will leave you, Monsieur, to your work."

The Comte nodded to Lydia. "It is done . . . save for the settling."

"Already?" The Contessa looked down at Miss Vandaariff's spent body. "Well, I don't suppose she would have taken pleasure in drawing things out."

"The pleasure is in the final outcome, Rosamonde," the Comte rasped.

"Of course it is," she replied, her gaze drifting to the spattered bedding. "We have intruded enough. We will see you at the airship."

She turned to leave but stopped as Xonck stepped forward and nodded at Elöise.

"What will you do with *her*?"

"Is it up to me?" asked the Comte.

"Not if you'd prefer it otherwise." Xonck smiled. "I was being polite..."

"I would prefer to get on with my work," snarled the Comte d'Orkancz.

"I am happy to oblige you," said Xonck. He pulled Elöise to her feet with his good hand, and dragged her from the room. A moment later the Contessa, Crabbé, and their retinue followed.

Miss Temple looked to her companions and saw that Chang's hand was clapped across Svenson's mouth. The Doctor was in torment—yet if they made any noise at all, Angelique would sense their presence and overcome them as easily as she had Elöise. Miss Temple leaned forward again, peeking down into the laboratory. The Comte had watched the others depart, and then returned to his table. He glanced over to Lydia and to Angelique, ignored the Prince, and unscrewed a small valve that stuck out from the metal implement's side. With more delicacy than she would have credited a man of his size, Miss Temple watched the Comte pour steaming liquid from one of the heated flasks into the valve, never spilling a drop, and then screw the valve closed. He lifted the metal implement and walked back to the bed, setting it down next to Lydia's leg.

"Are you awake, Lydia?"

Lydia nodded. It was the first time Miss Temple had seen the girl move.

"Are you in pain?"

Lydia grimaced, but shook her head. She turned, distracted by movement. It was the Prince, pouring more brandy.

"Your fiancé will not remember any of this, Lydia," said the Comte. "Neither will you. Lie back... what cannot be reversed must be embraced."

The Comte picked up the implement and glanced up to their balcony. He raised his voice, speaking generally to the room.

"It would be better if you descended willingly. If the *lady* brings you down, it will be by dragging you over the edge."

Miss Temple turned to Chang and Svenson, aghast.

"I *know* you are there," called the Comte. "I have obviously *waited* to speak to you for a reason . . . but I will not ask a second time."

Chang took his hand away from Svenson's mouth and looked behind for some other way out. Before either could stop him, the Doctor shot to his feet and called out over the balcony to the Comte.

"I am coming . . . damn you to hell, I am coming down . . ."

He turned to them, his eyes a fierce glare, his hand held out for their continued silence. He made a loud stomping as he reached the staircase, but as he passed thrust the pistol into Miss Temple's hands and leaned close to her ear.

"If they never marry," he whispered, "the spawn is not *legitimate*!"

Miss Temple bobbled the gun and looked up at him. Svenson was already gone. She turned to Chang, but he was stifling a vicious cough—a thin stream of blood dripping down his chin. She turned back to the balcony rail. The Doctor stepped into view, his hands away from his body and open, to show he was unarmed. He winced with disgust at this new closer view of Lydia Vandaariff, then pointed to the glass woman.

"I suppose your *creature* sniffed me out?"

The Comte laughed—a particularly objectionable sound—and shook his head. "On the contrary, Doctor—and appropriately, as we are both men of science and inquiry. My glimpse through Mrs. Dujong's mind showed no memory of an attack on Herr Flaüss. It was mere deduction to assume the true culprit was still in hiding."

"I see," said Svenson. "Yet I do not see why you waited to expose me."

"Do you not?" the Comte said, with a smug condescension. "First . . . where are your companions?"

The Doctor groped for words, his fingers flexing, then let them burst forth with scorn and rage.

"Damn you, Sir! Damn you to hell—you heard for yourself! Their throats have been cut by Colonel Aspiche!"

"But not yours?"

Svenson scoffed. "There is no virtue in it. Chang was half-dead already—his dispatch was a matter of seconds. Miss Temple"—here Svenson passed a hand across his brow—"you will not doubt how she fought him. Her struggles woke me, and I was able to break the Colonel's skull with a chair... but not, to my undying shame, in time to save the girl."

The Comte considered the Doctor's words.

"A moving tale."

"You're a bastard," spat Svenson. He waved a hand at Lydia without taking his eyes from the Comte. "You're the worst of the lot—for you've wasted gifts the others never had. I would put a bullet through your brain, Monsieur—send you to hell right after Aspiche—with less remorse than I would squash a flea."

His words were met with laughter, but it was not from the Comte. To Miss Temple's surprise, the Prince had roused himself from his chair and taken a step toward his one-time retainer, the snifter still cradled in his hand.

"What shall we do with him, Monsieur? I suppose the task is mine—he is my traitor, after all. What would you suggest?"

"You're an ignorant fool," hissed Svenson. "You've never seen it—even now! For God's sake, Karl, look at her—your fiancée! She is given someone else's child!"

The Prince turned to Lydia, his face as blandly bemused as ever.

"Do you know what he means, darling?"

"I do not, dearest Karl."

"Do you, Monsieur?"

"We are merely ensuring her health," said the Comte.

"The woman is half-*dead*!" roared Svenson. "Wake up, you idiot! Lydia—for heaven's sake, girl—run for your life! *It is not too late to be saved!*"

Svenson was raving, shouting, flailing his arms. Miss Temple felt Chang take hold of her arm and then—chiding herself again for being one step behind the game—she realized that the Doctor was making noise enough to cover their way down the stairs. They descended quickly to the lowest steps, just out of sight of the room. She looked down at the pistol—why in the world had the Doctor given it to *her*? Why did he not try to shoot the Prince himself? Why not give it to Chang? She saw Chang look down at the weapon as well, then up to meet her eyes.

She understood in an instant, and despite everything, despite the fact she could not even see his eyes, felt the sting of tears in her own.

"Doctor, you will calm *down*!" cried the Comte, snapping his fingers at Angelique. In an instant Svenson cried out and staggered, dropping to his knees. The Comte held up his hand again and waited just long enough for the Doctor to regain his wits before speaking.

"And I will hear no more *disparagement* of this work—"

"Work?" barked Svenson, waving his arms at the glass beakers, at Lydia. "Medieval foolery that will cost this girl's life!"

"Enough!" shouted the Comte, stepping forward ominously. "Is it foolery that has created the books? Foolery that has eternally captured the very essence of how many lives? Because the science is ancient, you—a *doctor,* with no subtlety, no sense of energy's nuance, of elemental concepts—reject it out of hand, in ignorance. You who have never sought the chemical substance of desire, of devotion, of fear, of *dreams*—never located the formulaic roots of art and religion, the power to remake in flesh myths most sacred and profane!"

The Comte stood over Svenson, his mouth a grimace, as if he were angry for having spoken so intimately to such a person. He cleared his throat and went on, his words returned to their customary coldness.

"You asked why I waited to expose you. You will have overheard certain disagreements amongst my allies—questions for which I would have answers . . . without necessarily sharing them. You may speak willingly, or with the aid of Angelique—but speak to me you will."

"I don't know anything," spat Svenson. "I was at Tarr Manor—I am outside your Harschmort intrigues—"

The Comte ignored him, idly fingering the knobs on his metal implement as it lay next to Lydia's pale leg.

"When we spoke in my greenhouse, your Prince had been taken from you. At that time neither you nor I knew how or by whom."

"It was the Contessa," said Svenson, "in the airship—"

"Yes, I *know*. I want to know *why*."

"Surely she gave you an explanation!"

"Perhaps she did . . . perhaps not . . ."

"The falling-out of thieves," sneered the Doctor. "And the two of you seemed such *particular* friends—"

The Prince stepped forward and boxed Svenson's ear.

"You will not speak so to your betters!" he announced, as if he were making polite conversation, then snorted with satisfaction. Svenson looked up at the Prince, his face hot with scorn, but his words were still for the Comte.

"I cannot know, of course—I merely, as you say, *deduce*. The Prince was taken mere hours after I had rescued him from the Institute. You—and others—were not told. Obviously she wanted the Prince for her own ends. What is the Prince to your plans? A dupe, a pawn, a void in the seat of power—"

"Why, you damned ungrateful rogue!" cried the Prince. "The *audacity*!"

"To some this might seem obvious," said the Comte, impatiently.

"Then I should think the answer obvious as well," scoffed Svenson. "Everyone undergoing the Process is instilled with a control-phrase, are they not? Quite by accident the Prince was taken by me before any particular commands could be given to him—the Contessa, knowing that, and knowing the Prince's character would predispose everyone to think of him as an imbecile, seized the opportunity to instill within his mind commands of her own, to be invoked at the proper time against her putative allies—something unexpected, such as, let us say, pushing you out of an airship. Of course, when asked, the Prince will remember none of it."

The Comte was silent. Miss Temple was amazed at the Doctor's presence of mind.

"As I say . . . fairly obvious," sniffed Svenson.

"Perhaps . . . it is your own fabrication . . . yet credible enough that I must waste time scouring the memory of the Prince. But before that, Doctor—for I think you are lying—I will first scour *you*. Angelique?"

Svenson leapt to his feet with a cry, but the cry was cut to a savage choking bark as Angelique's mind penetrated his. Chang burst forth from the stairwell, running forward, Miss Temple right behind him. Svenson was on his knees holding his face, the Prince above him, raising a boot to kick the Doctor's head. To the side stood Angelique. The Prince looked up at them with a confused resentment at being interrupted. The Comte wrenched his attention from Svenson's mind with a roar. Angelique turned, a little too slowly, and Miss Temple raised the revolver. She was perhaps ten feet distant when she pulled the trigger.

The shot smashed into the glass woman's outstretched arm at the elbow, shearing through with a spray of bright shards and dropping the forearm and hand to the floor, where they shattered in a plume of indigo smoke. Miss Temple saw Angelique's mouth open wide but heard the scream within her mind, indiscriminately flaying the thoughts of every person in the room. Miss Temple fell to her knees, tears in her eyes, and fired again. The bullet pierced the cuirass of Angelique's torso, starring the surface. Miss Temple kept squeezing the trigger, each hole driving the cracks deeper, lancing into each other to form fissures—the scream redoubled and Miss Temple could not move, could barely see, flooded with random memories stabbing her mind like daggers—Angelique as a child at sea, the rank perfume of the brothel, silks and champagne, tears, beatings, bruises, distant embraces, and a piercingly tender hope, more than anything, that her desperate dreams had come true. Before Miss Temple's eyes the torso split wide below the ribs and gave, the upper body breaking against the lower in a cloud of indigo smoke and glimmering deadly dust, the pieces smashing apart as they struck the stone.

Miss Temple could not tell whether the silence was due to a shared inability to speak, or if the scream had made her deaf. Her head swam with the fumes in the air and she put a hand before her mouth, wondering if she'd already inhaled blue glass dust. The steaming ruins of Angelique lay scattered across the floor, blue shards in an indigo pool. She looked up and blinked. Chang lay with his back against the wall, staring. Svenson was on his hands and knees, groping to crawl free. Lydia was on the bed, whimpering and pulling at her ropes. The Prince lay on the ground near Svenson, hissing with pain and swatting feebly at his hand, where a splinter of glass cut open a patch of skin that had since turned blue. The Comte alone still stood, his face pale as ash.

Miss Temple turned the pistol toward him and pulled the trigger. The bullet shattered the chemical works on his table, spraying more glass and spattering his apron with steaming liquid. The sound woke the room. The Comte surged forward and swept up his metal implement from the bed, raising it up like a mace. Miss Temple aimed another shot at his head, but before she could fire felt Chang seize her arm. She grunted with surprise—his grip was painful—and saw that with his other hand he held Svenson's collar, pulling them both to the door with all his fading strength. She looked back at the Comte, who despite his rage took care to step around the sea of broken glass, and did her best to aim. Svenson got his feet beneath them as they reached the door but Chang did not let him go. Miss Temple extended her arm to fire, but Chang yanked her back and into the corridor.

"I must kill him!" she cried.

"You are out of bullets!" Chang hissed. "If you pull the trigger he will know!"

They'd not gone two more steps before the Doctor turned, struggling against Chang's grip.

"The Prince—he must die—"

"We've done enough—" Chang pulled them both forward, his voice thick, coughing with the effort.

"They will be married—"

"The Comte is formidable—we are unarmed and weak. If we fight him one of us—at least—will die." Chang could barely talk. "We have more to accomplish—and if we stop the others, we stop your idiot Prince. Remember Mrs. Dujong."

"But the Comte—" said Miss Temple, looking behind her for pursuit.

"Cannot chase us alone—he must secure the Prince and Lydia." Chang cleared his throat with a groan and spat past Svenson. "Besides . . . the Comte's vanity has been . . . *wounded* . . ."

His voice was raw. Miss Temple risked a glance, now finally running with the others on her own two feet, and saw with a piercing dismay the line of tears beneath Chang's glasses, and heard the terrible sobs within his heaving breath. She wiped at her own face and did her best to keep up.

They reached the stairwell and closed the door behind them. Chang leaned against it, his hands on his knees, and surrendered to another bout of coughing. Svenson looked at him with concern, his hand on Chang's shoulder for comfort. He looked up at Miss Temple.

"You did very well, Celeste."

"No more than anyone," she answered, a bit pointedly. She did not want to speak of herself in the presence of Chang's distress.

"That is true."

Miss Temple shivered.

"Her thoughts . . . at the end, in my mind . . ."

"She was cruelly used," said Svenson, "by the Comte . . . and by the world. No one should undergo such horror."

But Miss Temple knew the true horror for Angelique had not been transformation, but her untimely death, and her terrible silent scream was a protest as primal and as futile as the last cry of a sparrow taken by the hawk. Miss Temple had never been in the presence, been *possessed* by such fear—held tight to the very brink of death—and she wondered if she would die the same horrible way when it came to it—which it might this very night. She sniffed—or day, she had no idea what time it was. When they'd been outside watching the coaches it had still been dark, and now they were underground. Was it only a day since she'd first met Svenson in the Boniface lobby?

She swallowed and shook the dread from her mind. With a perhaps characteristic keenness Miss Temple's thoughts shifted from death to breakfast.

"After this is settled," she said, "I should quite enjoy something to eat."

Chang looked up at her. She smiled down at him, doing her level best to withstand the hardness of his face and the black vacuum of his glasses.

"Well . . . it *has* been some time . . . ," said Svenson politely, as if he were speaking of the weather.

"It will be some while more," managed Chang, hoarsely.

"I'm sure it will," said Miss Temple. "But being as I am *not* made of glass, it seemed like a reasonable topic of conversation."

"Indeed," said Svenson, awkwardly.

"Once this business is settled of course," added Miss Temple.

Chang straightened himself, his face somewhat composed. "We should go," he muttered.

* * *

Miss Temple smiled to herself as they climbed, hoping her words had served to distract Chang at least into annoyance, away from his grief. She was well aware that she did not understand what he felt, despite her loss of Roger, for she did not understand the connection between Chang and the woman. What sort of attachment could such *transacted* dealings instill? She was smart enough to see that bargains of some sort ran through most marriages—her own parents were a joining of land and the cash to work it—but for Miss Temple the objects of barter—titles, estates, money, inheritance—were always apart from the bodies involved. The idea of transacting one's own body—that this was the *extent*—involved a bluntness she could not quite comprehend. She wondered what her mother had felt when she herself had been conceived, in that physical union—was it a matter of two bodies (Miss Temple preferred not to speculate about "love" when it came to her savage father), or was each limb bound—as much as Lydia's had been in the laboratory—by a brokered arrangement between families? She looked up at Chang, climbing ahead of her. What did it feel like to be free of such burdens? The freedom of a wild animal?

"We did not see Herr Flaüss on our way out," observed Doctor Svenson. "Perhaps he went with the others."

"And where are they?" asked Miss Temple. "At the airship?"

"I think not," said Svenson. "They will be settling their own disagreements before they can go on—they will be interrogating Lord Vandaariff."

"And perhaps Roger," said Miss Temple, just to show she could say his name without difficulty.

"Which leaves us the choice of finding them or reaching the airship ourselves." Svenson called ahead to Chang. "What say you?"

Chang looked back, wiping his red-flecked mouth, out of breath. "The airship. The Dragoons."

Doctor Svenson nodded. "Smythe."

The house was disturbingly quiet when they reached the main floor.

"Can everyone be gone?" asked Svenson.

"Which way?" rasped Chang.

"It is up—the main stairs are simplest if they are free. I must also suggest, again, that we acquire weapons."

Chang sighed, then nodded with impatience.

"Where?"

"Well—" Svenson clearly had no immediate idea.

"Come with me," said Miss Temple.

Mr. Blenheim had been moved, though the stain on the carpet remained. They took a very brief time, but even then she smiled to see the curiosity and greed on the faces of her two companions as they plundered Robert Vandaariff's trophy chests. For herself, Miss Temple selected another serpentine dagger—the first had served her well—while Chang selected a matching pair of curved, wide-bladed knives with hilts nearly as long as the blade.

"A sort of *macheté*," he explained, and she nodded agreeably, having no idea what he meant but happy to see him satisfied. To her amusement, Doctor Svenson pulled an African spear from the wall, and then stuck a jeweled dagger in his belt.

"I am no swordsman," he said, catching her curious expression and Chang's dry smirk. "The farther I keep them from me, the safer I'll remain. None of which makes me feel any less ridiculous—yet if it helps us survive, I will wear a cap and bells." He looked over at Chang. "To the rooftops?"

As they walked to the front stairs, the dagger's unfamiliar weight in her hand, Miss Temple felt a troubling lightness in her breath and a prickling of sweat across her back. What if Captain Smythe did not reject his orders? What if Captain Smythe was not there at all? What if instead of soldiers they were met by the Contessa and Xonck and Crabbé? What must she do? A failure of nerve while she was alone was one thing, but in the company of Chang or Svenson? With every step her breathing quickened and her heart became less sure.

They reached the main foyer, an enormous expanse of black and white marble where Miss Temple had first met the Contessa di Lacquer-Sforza so long ago, now empty and silent save for their own echoing steps. The great doors were closed. Svenson craned his neck to look up the stairs and Miss Temple followed his gaze. From what she could tell, there was not a soul between the ground floor and the top.

Behind them in the house the dead air was split by a gunshot. Miss Temple gasped with surprise. Chang pointed to the far wing.

"Vandaariff's office," he whispered. Svenson opened his mouth but Chang stopped his words with an open hand. Could they have shot Elöise? Another few seconds . . . a door slam from the same direction . . . then distant footsteps.

"They are coming," snapped Chang. "Hurry!"

They were to the third floor when their enemies reached the foyer below. Chang motioned Miss Temple closer to the wall and lowered himself into a crouch. She could hear the Contessa, but not her words. Above, the Doctor groped his way to an unobtrusive door. Miss Temple dashed to meet him, bobbing past him in the doorway and trotting up the narrower steps to where Chang waited. Chang caught her arm and leaned his face close to hers, waiting until the Doctor had caught up to whisper.

"There will be a guard on the other side of the door. It is vital we not harm any Dragoon until we reach Smythe. His men ought to outnumber our other enemies—if we can but get his attention, we have a chance to sway him."

"Then I should be the one who goes," said Miss Temple.

Chang shook his head. "I know him best—"

"Yes, but any Dragoon will take one look at either of you and start swinging. He will not do so to me—giving *me* the time to call for the Captain."

Chang sighed, but Svenson nodded immediately.

"Celeste is right."

"I know she is—but I do not like it." Chang stifled another cough. *"Go!"*

Miss Temple opened the door and stepped through, the dagger tucked into her bodice, and winced at the bitter wind blowing across the rooftop, carrying the sharp salt tang of the sea. A red-jacketed Dragoon stood to either side of the door. Some twenty yards away was the dirigible, hovering ominously, like an unearthly predatory creature, an enormous gasbag dangling a long bright metal cabin, near the size of a sea-ship but all gleaming black metal like a train car. Dragoons were loading boxes into the cabin, handing them up to several black-uniformed Macklenburgers posted at the top of the gangway. Inside the cabin, through a gas-lit window, she saw the sharp-faced Doctor Lorenz, goggles around his neck, busy flipping switches. The rooftop was a hive of activity, but nowhere could she locate Smythe.

It took perhaps another second for the two Dragoons to cry out at her presence and take insistent hold of her arms. She did her best to explain herself above the whipping wind.

"Yes—yes, excuse me—my name is Temple, I am looking—I beg your pardon—I am looking for Captain—"

Before she could finish the one to her right was bawling toward the airship.

"Sir! We've got someone, Sir!"

Miss Temple saw Doctor Lorenz look up through the window, and the shock upon his face. At once he darted from view—no doubt coming down—and she took up the trooper's cry.

"Captain Smythe! I am looking for Captain Smythe!"

Her handlers exchanged a look of confusion. She did her best to exploit it and charge from their grasp but they kept hold, despite her kicking feet. Then, at the top of the gangplank, standing next to each other, appeared the figures of Captain Smythe and Doctor Lorenz. Miss Temple's heart sank. The pair began to walk down—Smythe's face too far away in the dim light to read his expression—when the door behind her slid open and Cardinal Chang laid a blade to the throat of each Dragoon. Miss Temple turned her head—surely this was an unwanted complication—to see Doctor Svenson, spear tucked under his arm, holding the doorknob fast by force.

"They are below us," he whispered.

"Who have we here?" called Doctor Lorenz, in a mocking tone. "Such a persistent strain of vermin. Captain—if you wouldn't mind?"

"Captain Smythe!" shouted Miss Temple. "You know who we are! You know what's been done tonight—you heard them speaking! Your city—your Queen!"

Smythe had not moved, still next to Lorenz on the gangway.

"What are you waiting for?" snapped Lorenz, and he turned to the Dragoons on the rooftop—a band of perhaps a dozen men. "Kill these criminals at once!"

"Captain Smythe," cried Miss Temple, "you have helped us before!"

"What?" Lorenz rounded on Smythe and the Captain, without hesitation, shot out his arm and shoved Doctor Lorenz cleanly off the gangplank to fall with a grinding thud on the graveled rooftop, some ten feet below.

At once Chang whipped back the blades and pulled Miss Temple free. The Dragoons leapt the other way and drew their sabers, facing Chang but glancing at their officer, unsure of what to do. Smythe descended the rest of the way, one hand on his saber hilt.

"I suppose this had to happen," he said.

Doctor Svenson grunted aloud as the door was pulled, testing his grip. He held it closed, but looked anxiously at Chang, who turned to Smythe. Smythe glanced at the top of the ramp, where two confused Macklenburg troopers stood watching. Satisfied they were not going to attack, Smythe called sharply to his men.

"Arms!"

As one the rest of the 4th Dragoons drew their sabers, Svenson let go of the door and leapt to join Miss Temple and Chang.

The door shot open to reveal Francis Xonck, a dagger in his hand. He stepped onto the rooftop, took in the drawn blades and the unguarded status of his enemies.

"Why, Captain Smythe," he drawled, "is something the matter?"

Smythe stepped forward, still not drawing his own blade.

"Who else is with you?" he called. "Bring them out now."

"I would be delighted." Xonck smiled.

He stepped aside to usher through the other members of the Cabal—the Contessa, the Comte, and Crabbé—and after them the Prince, Roger

Bascombe (notebooks tucked under his arm), and then, helping the unsteady Lydia Vandaariff, Caroline Stearne. After Caroline came the six functionaries in black, the first four manhandling a heavy trunk, the last two dragging Elöise Dujong between them. Miss Temple breathed a sigh of relief—for she was sure the shot they heard had meant the woman's death. As this crowd spread from the door the Dragoons withdrew, maintaining a strict cushion of space between the two groups. Xonck glanced toward Miss Temple and then stepped out into this borderland to address Smythe.

"Not to repeat myself... but is something *wrong*?"

"This can't go on," said Smythe. He nodded to Elöise and Lydia Vandaariff. "Release those women."

"I beg your pardon?" said Xonck, grinning as if he could not quite believe what he heard, yet found the possibility deeply amusing.

"Release those *women.*"

"Well," Xonck said, smiling at Lydia, "*that* woman does not wish to be released—for she would fall down. She's feeling poorly, you see. Excuse me—have you spoken to your Colonel?"

"Colonel Aspiche is a traitor," announced Smythe.

"To my eyes, the traitor here is *you.*"

"Your eyes are flawed. You are a villain."

"A villain who knows all about your family's debts, Captain," sneered Xonck, "all secured against a salary you may not live to collect—the price of disloyalty, you know, or is it idiocy?"

"If you want to die, Mr. Xonck, say one more word."

Smythe drew his saber and stepped toward Xonck, who retreated, his fixed smile now radiating malice.

Miss Temple groped for her dagger but did not pull it out—the air felt heavy and thick. Surely the Cabal would retreat in the face of Smythe and his men—how could they hope to withstand professional troops? It was clear that Captain Smythe was of the same opinion, for rather than pursuing Xonck, he pointed generally at the crowd around the doorway with his saber.

"Throw down your weapons and return to the house. We will settle this inside."

"That will not happen," answered Xonck.

"I am not looking for bloodshed, but I am not afraid of it," called

Smythe, pitching his voice to the others around Xonck—the women particularly. "Throw down your weapons and—"

"It really is not possible, Captain." This was Harald Crabbé. "If we are not in Macklenburg in two days, our entire effort is undone. I do not know what this rabble has told you"—he gestured vaguely to Miss Temple, Svenson, and Chang—"but *I* can tell you they are unscrupulous killers—"

"Where is Mr. Blenheim?" Smythe interrupted Crabbé without care.

"Ah! An excellent question!" cried Crabbé. "Mr. Blenheim has been murdered—and by *that* young woman!"

He pointed an accusing finger at Miss Temple, and she turned her eyes to Smythe, wanting to explain, but before she could get the words from her mouth the Captain tipped his brass helmet toward her in salute. He looked back to the Deputy Minister, whose condemnation clearly had not had the expected result.

"Then she has saved me the trouble—for Mr. Blenheim murdered one of my men," answered Smythe, and then he bawled at them with a harshness of command that made Miss Temple jump. "Put *down* your weapons! Get *back* in the house! Your effort is *undone* as of this minute!"

The crack of the pistol echoed flatly from the roof into the open air, the sound somehow less intrusive than the impact of its bullet, which spun Captain Smythe and knocked him forward to his knees, his helmet bouncing from his head. Miss Temple spun to see Doctor Lorenz, a smoking revolver in his hand, standing underneath the gangway. Without an instant's hesitation Xonck strode forward and landed a sweeping kick on the Captain's jaw, knocking him sprawling on his back. He turned back to the men behind and screamed aloud, his eyes disturbingly bright.

"Kill them!"

The rooftop exploded into mayhem. Lorenz fired again, bringing down the nearest Dragoon. The two Macklenburg troopers clattered down the gangplank, sabers drawn, with a clotted German war cry. The men in black dashed forward after Xonck, cudgels raised, some with pistols, snapping off shots where they could. The Dragoons, stunned by the attack on their officer and taken wholly wrong-footed, finally leapt to their own ragged defense. Blades swung wickedly through the air and errant bullets whipped past Miss Temple's ears. She fumbled for the dagger at the same time Chang seized her shoulder and thrust her toward the airship. She caught her footing and turned to see Chang parry a cudgel with one of his blades and bring the other down deep into the shoulder joint of one of the black-coated men.

He turned to her and shouted, *"Cut the ropes!"*

Of course! If she could shear through the cables, the craft would rise by itself, drifting derelict across the sea—there was no way they could reach Macklenburg inside two *weeks*! She dashed to the nearest mooring and dropped to her knees, sawing away with the dagger. The cable was thick hemp, black and clotted with tar, but the blade was sharp and soon clumps were twisting away, the gap she opened straining wider as the weight of the airship exerted its pull. She looked up, tossing the curls from her eyes, and gasped aloud at the hellish bloody confusion.

Chang fought one of the Macklenburgers, trying without success to work his shorter blades past the much longer saber. Xonck's face was spattered in blood as—now with a saber—he traded vicious blows with a Dragoon. Doctor Svenson waved his spear like a madman, keeping his assailant at bay. Then Miss Temple's eye was drawn to the Comte . . . and the flickering flash of blue beneath his arm. The Dragoon facing Xonck stumbled and his blade arm sagged, as if it had suddenly become too heavy. In an instant Xonck's blade flashed forward. A second Dragoon abruptly dropped to his knees—only to take a bullet from Doctor Lorenz. Miss Poole stood in the door, shrouded in her cloak, overwhelming the Dragoons one at a time on the Comte's instruction. Miss Temple screamed for help and desperately sawed at the cable.

"Cardinal Chang! Cardinal Chang!"

Chang did not hear, still dueling with the German soldier and fighting for his life—his cough piercing through the din. Another man went down, dispatched by Xonck. The remaining Dragoons saw what was happening and charged the knot of figures at the door, cutting down two more of the black-coated men in their way. At once the Cabal scattered—Crabbé and Roger stumbling into Caroline and Elöise, the Contessa screaming at Xonck, the Prince and Lydia dropping to their knees, hands over their heads, and the Comte thrusting Miss Poole forward to stop the attack. The Dragoons—perhaps six men—tottered in place, like saplings in the wind. Xonck stepped forward and hacked the nearest man across the neck. There was no stopping him—she had never seen such dispassionate savagery in her life.

Miss Temple's attention caught a swirl of movement at the corner of her eye. An instant later she was facedown on the gravel, shaking her head, blinking her eyes, and feeling for the dagger. She pushed herself up to her elbows, completely dazed, realizing that the concussive impact had burst within her mind. Like an answered prayer she saw Doctor Svenson's ridiculous spear sticking out from Miss Poole's back, pinning her to the wooden door. The stricken woman—creature—struggled like a fish in the air, but each twisting movement only worsened the damage. With a snapping lurch she stumbled and the pole ripped up several inches to her shoulder. Her breaking body was still hidden beneath the cloak and Miss Temple could only see her arching neck and snapping mouth—the Comte helplessly trying to still her movement to preserve her, but she would not or could not heed him. With a final crack she fell again. The spear tore from her body altogether, splitting her collapsing torso as she fell, jumbled on the ground like a broken toy.

Across the rooftop stunned faces groped for comprehension, for Miss Poole's silent screaming had battered them all, but the lull did not last, with Xonck and one of the Macklenburg men hurling themselves at the remaining Dragoons, Chang slashing away at his own opponent, and, most strangely, Roger Bascombe running to tackle Doctor Svenson. Miss Temple leapt back to her task, gripping the dagger with both hands.

The cable gave without warning, knocking her back on her seat. She scrambled up and ran at the other cable—but the suddenly tilting airship and careening gangway had alerted the others to her effort. She saw Lorenz take aim and, before she could do a thing, fire—but his gun was empty! He swore and broke it open, knocking out the empty shells and digging for fresh bullets in his coat. A Dragoon loomed up at Lorenz from behind, but Lorenz noticed her look and spun, firing the two shots he'd loaded straight into the soldier's chest. He snarled with satisfaction and wheeled back to Miss Temple, rushing again to reload. She did not know what to do. She sawed at the cable.

Lorenz watched her as he deliberately slotted in new shells. He glanced over his shoulder. Xonck had killed another Dragoon—there were only three left on their feet—one running for Xonck, the others charging the Cabal. Svenson and Roger were a kicking knot of bodies on the ground. The cable was coming apart. She looked up at Lorenz. He inserted the final bullet and slapped the pistol closed. He pulled back the hammer and aimed, striding toward her.

She threw the dagger, end over end—she had seen this done at carnivals—directly at his face. Lorenz flinched and fired the gun harmlessly, squawking as the dagger hilt caught his ear. Miss Temple ran the other way as she threw, back to the others. Another shot cracked out behind her, but she was small and dodging to each side, fervently hoping Lorenz was less interested in shooting a woman than protecting the cable.

Chang wheezed on one knee over the fallen Macklenburg trooper, Svenson held off Roger with his jeweled dagger, Xonck stood, his boot on the neck of a struggling Dragoon, and near the door were the two Dragoons who had charged the Cabal—one with his arm around the Contessa's neck holding off the Comte and the Prince. The other stood between Elöise and Caroline Stearne, both on their knees. Neither Macklenburger nor any man in black was visible. Everyone was out of breath, panting clouds in the cold air, and all around the fallen groaned. She tried to locate Smythe in the carnage but could not—either he had moved or was covered with another body. Miss Temple felt herself near tears, for she had not accomplished her task, but then saw the relief on Chang's face—and then as he too turned, on Svenson's—simply to see her still alive.

"What do you say, Sir?" called out Doctor Lorenz. "Should I shoot the girl or the men?"

"Or should I step on this man's neck," responded Xonck, as if the Dragoons by the door did not exist. "Issues of etiquette are always so *difficult*... my dear Contessa, what would *you* suggest?"

The Contessa answered with a shrug toward the Dragoon who seemed to hold her fast. "Well, Francis,... I agree it *is* difficult..."

"Damned shame about Elspeth."

"My thoughts exactly—I must admit to underestimating Doctor Svenson once again."

"It cannot work," called out Chang, his voice hoarse with exertion. "If you kill that man—or if Lorenz shoots us—these Dragoons will not scruple to kill the Contessa and the Comte. You must retreat."

"Retreat?" scoffed Xonck. "From you, Cardinal, this comes as a shock—or perhaps it is merely the perspective of a ruffian. I've always doubted your courage, man to man."

Chang spat painfully. "You can doubt what you like, you insufferable, worm-rotted—"

Doctor Svenson cut him off, stepping forward. "A great number of these men will die if they are not helped—your men as well as ours—"

Xonck ignored them both, calling out to the two Dragoons. "Release her, and you'll live. It is your only chance."

They did not answer, so Xonck bore down his foot on the fallen man's throat, driving out a protesting rattle like air from a balloon.

"It is your choice . . . ," he taunted them. Still they did not move. At once he wheeled and called to Lorenz. "Shoot someone—whoever you please."

"You're being stupid!" shouted Svenson. "No one need die!"

"Reason not the *need,* Doctor." Xonck chuckled, and he very deliberately crushed the man's windpipe beneath his boot.

In a blur of movement the Contessa's hand flew across the face of the Dragoon who held her, its pathway marked by a spurting line of blood—once more she wore her metal spike. Xonck hacked at the final stunned trooper, who could only parry the blow and then disappear beneath a crush of bodies as Caroline Stearne kicked his knee from behind, and the Comte himself grappled his sword arm. At once Miss Temple felt strong arms take hold of her waist and lift her off the ground. Chang flung her in the air toward the gangway, high enough to land on top of it. Lorenz's pistol cracked once, the bullet whistling past.

"Go on—go on!" shouted Chang, and Miss Temple did, realizing the airship held their only possible refuge. Again she was bundled up by stronger arms, this time it was Svenson, as she plunged into the cabin. He thrust her forward and wheeled to pull up Chang—bullets sending splinters of woodwork through the air. She raced ahead through one doorway and another, and then a third which was a dead end. She turned with a cry, the others colliding into her, and was knocked off her feet into a cabinet. With a desperate coordination Chang slammed the door and Svenson shot the bolt.

Somehow they had survived the battle, only to be imprisoned.

Miss Temple, on the floor, out of breath, face streaked with sweat and tears, gazed up at Svenson and Chang. It was hard to say which of them looked worse, for though his exertions had brought fresh blood to Chang's mouth and nose, the Doctor's glistening pallor was abetted by the utterly stricken cast of his eyes.

"We have left Elöise," he whispered. "She will be killed—"

"Is anyone injured?" asked Chang, cutting the Doctor off. "Celeste?"

Miss Temple shook her head, unable to speak, her thoughts seared by the savage acts she'd just witnessed. Could war possibly be worse? She squeezed shut her eyes as, unbidden, her mind recalled the grinding gasping crush of Francis Xonck bringing down his boot. She sobbed aloud and, ashamed, stuffed a fist in her mouth and turned away, her tears flowing openly.

"Get away from the door," muttered Chang hoarsely, shifting Svenson to the side. "They may shoot out the lock."

"We are trapped like rats," said Svenson. He looked at the dagger in his hand, useless and small. "Captain Smythe—all his men—*all* of them—"

"And Elspeth Poole," replied Chang, doing his best to speak clearly. "And their lackeys, and the two Germans—our position could be worse—"

"Worse?" barked Svenson.

"We are not yet dead, Doctor," said Chang, though his drawn, bloody face would not have seemed out of place in a graveyard.

"Neither is the Prince! Nor the Comte, nor the Contessa, nor that animal Xonck—"

"I did not cut the ropes," sniffed Miss Temple.

"Be *quiet*—the pair of you!" hissed Chang.

Miss Temple's eyes flashed—for even in these straits she did not appreciate his tone—but the Cardinal was not angry. Instead, his mouth was grim.

"You did not cut the ropes, Celeste. But you did your best. Did I kill Xonck? No—as pathetic as it sounds, it was all I could do to bring down one Macklenburg farmboy swinging an oversized cabbage-cutter. Did the Doctor save Elöise? No—but he preserved all of our lives—and hers—by destroying Miss Poole. Our enemies on the other side of this door—and we must assume they all are here—are less in number than they would have been, less confident, and just as unhappy—for *we* are not dead either."

That he followed this speech with a wrenching, racking cough, bent with his head between his knees, did not prevent Miss Temple from wiping her nose on her sleeve and brushing the loosened curls from her eyes. She sniffed and whispered to Doctor Svenson.

"We will save her—we have done it before."

He had no answer, but wiped his own eyes with his thumb and forefinger—any lack of outright scoffing she read as agreement. She pushed herself to her feet and sighed briskly.

"Well, then—"

Miss Temple grabbed at the cabinet to avoid falling back to the floor, squeaking with surprise as the entire cabin swung to the left and then back again with a dizzying swiftness.

"We are going up . . . ," said Svenson.

Miss Temple pushed herself to the one window, round like the porthole of a ship, and peered down, but already the roof of Harschmort House receded below her. Within seconds they were in dark fog, the rooftop and the brightly lit house swallowed up in the gloom below. With a brusque sputtering series of bangs the propellers sparked into life and the craft's motion changed again, pushing forward and steadying the side to side rocking, the low hum of the motors creating a vibration Miss Temple could feel through her hands on the cabinet and the soles of her boots on the floor.

"Well," she said, "it looks as if we shall visit Macklenburg after all."

"Unless they throw us into the sea on the way," observed the Doctor.

"Ah," said Miss Temple.

"Still wanting your breakfast?" muttered Chang.

She turned to glare at him—it not being a fair thing to say at all—when they were interrupted by a gentle knock at the door. She looked at both men, but neither spoke. She sighed, and called out as casually as she could.

"Yes?"

"Miss Temple? It is Minister Crabbé. I am wondering if you might open this door and join our conversation."

"What conversation is that?" she answered.

"Why, it is the one where we decide your lives, my dear. It would be better had not through a door."

"I am afraid we find the door *convenient,*" replied Miss Temple.

"Perhaps . . . yet I am forced to point out that Mrs. Dujong does not share your *partition.* Further, while I would prefer to avoid unpleasantness, the door *is* made of wood, and its lock must be subject to the force of bullets—it is in fact an *illusory* convenience. Surely there is much to discuss between us all—need this excellent oak panel be ruined for a conclusion you cannot dispute?"

Miss Temple turned to her companions. Svenson looked past her to the cabinet she leaned against. He stepped across and forced it open with a quick prying thrust of his dagger under its lock, but inside was merely a collection of blankets, ropes, candles, woolen coats, and a box of hats and gloves. He turned back to Chang, who leaned against the doorframe and shrugged.

"We cannot go out the window," Svenson said.

"You have the only weapon," said Chang, nodding to the Doctor's dagger, for he had dropped his own to throw Miss Temple on the gangway, "perhaps it were best stowed away."

"I agree, but surely by you."

Svenson passed the blade to Chang, who stuffed it in his coat. The Doctor reached for Miss Temple's hand, squeezed it once, and nodded to Chang, who unlocked the door.

The next room was the largest of the three in the dirigible's cabin, and was ringed with cabinets and inset settees, now occupied by the various members of the Cabal, all watching their entrance quite closely. On one side sat the Prince, Harald Crabbé, and Roger Bascombe, on the other the Comte, the Contessa, and in the far doorway, a saber in his hand, blood spoiling his once-white shirt, stood Francis Xonck. Beyond him lurked other figures and movement, and Miss Temple tried to deduce who was missing. Had more of them been brought down in the final struggle? Her questions were answered a moment later by the appearance of Lydia Vandaariff, changed from her robes to a brilliant blue silk dress, bobbing under Xonck's arm and stepping—still unsteadily—toward the Prince, prompting Roger to leave his place to make room. Emerging directly after Lydia—no doubt helping with her stays—was the ever-attentive Caroline Stearne, who slipped to an empty seat next to the Comte.

"I assume Doctor Lorenz pilots our craft?" asked Chang.

"He does," answered Harald Crabbé.

"Where is Mrs. Dujong?" asked Doctor Svenson.

Xonck nodded vaguely to the room behind him. "She is quite secure . . . something of a return to form, I'm told."

Svenson did not reply. Aside from Xonck, no one brandished any weapon—though, given Xonck's prowess and the small size of the room, Miss Temple doubted whether anyone else *needed* one. Yet if their immediate dispatch was not their enemies' intent, Miss Temple was mystified as to what their plan then was.

At the same time, simply where they sat revealed divisions among them: on one side Crabbé and Roger, and under their arm the Prince (though the Prince would go with whoever was ascendant), and on the other the Comte and Contessa, with Caroline under their sway (though how much she counted, Miss Temple had no clue—did she, Lorenz, and Roger make up a second tier of the Cabal, or were they simply three more drones of the Process?)—and then in the middle and unallied to either, Francis Xonck, his capacity for slaughter quite balancing, especially in these close quarters, the cunning of Crabbé, the knowledge of the Comte, and the provocative charm of the Contessa.

Crabbé looked across to the Contessa and raised his eyebrows in question. She nodded in agreement—or did she grant permission?—and Crabbé cleared his throat. He indicated a cabinet next to Mrs. Stearne.

"Before we start, would any of you care for some refreshment? You must be tired—I know *I* am tired, and the mere sight of you three—well, it amazes that you can *stand.* Caroline can get it—there is whisky, brandy, water—"

"If *you* are drinking," said Chang, "by all means."

"Excellent—of course, drinks all round—and my apologies, Caroline, for turning you into a barmaid—Roger, perhaps you will assist. Perhaps for simplicity it can be brandy for everyone."

There followed an awkward near silence where by tacit agreement all conversation paused until the business of pouring and handing out glasses was accomplished. Miss Temple watched Roger step to Chang and Svenson with a glass in each hand, his face a mask of professional diffidence that never once glanced her way. Her study was broken by Caroline's touch on her arm, as she was offered her own glass. Miss Temple shook her head, but Caroline pressed the glass hard into her hand, leaving Miss Temple the choice to hold on or let it drop. She looked down at the amber liquid and sniffed, detecting the familiar biting scent she associated with so much that was tiresome and foul.

The entire scene was strange—especially following the rooftop carnage, for she had braced herself for a second deadly struggle, yet here they stood, as sociably arrayed as any dinner party—save the men and women were drinking together—and all of it so patently false that Miss Temple narrowed her eyes. With an audible snort she set her glass on a nearby shelf and wiped her hands.

"Miss Temple?" asked Crabbé. "Would you prefer something else?"

"I would prefer you state your business. If Mr. Xonck will kill us, then let him try."

"Such *impatience.*" Crabbé smiled, unctuous and knowing. "We will do our best to satisfy. But first, I give you all the Prince of Macklenburg and his bride!"

He raised his glass and tossed off the contents, as the others followed suit amidst mutters of "the Prince!" and "Lydia!" The Prince smiled heartily and Lydia grinned, her small white teeth showing over her glass as she too drank, but then erupted into a fit of coughing to rival Cardinal Chang. The Prince patted her shoulder as she strove to breathe, her stomach now heaving unpleasantly with the stress. Roger stepped forward and offered a handkerchief which the young lady hurriedly snatched and held before her mouth, spitting into it wetly. The fit finally subsided and, face pale and out of breath, Lydia returned the cloth to Roger with an attempt at a smile. Roger deftly refolded the handkerchief before returning it to his pocket... but not before Miss Temple noticed the fresh, brilliant blue stain.

"Are you quite well, my dear?" asked the Prince.

Before Lydia could speak, Chang threw back his glass and gargled loudly before swallowing the brandy. Doctor Svenson poured his glass on the floor. Crabbé took all this in and exhaled sadly.

"Ah well... one cannot always please. Caroline?" Mrs. Stearne collected their glasses. Crabbé cleared his throat and gestured vaguely at the room around them.

"So we begin."

"Through your determined efforts at *destruction,* we are no longer able to easily determine what you know of our plans, or in whom you might have confided. Mrs. Marchmoor is well on her way to the city, Angelique and poor Elspeth are no more." He held up his hand. "Please know that *I* am speaking to you as the one most able to control my rage—if it were any of my associates, a recitation of even these facts would result in your immediate deaths. While it is true we could subject you to the Process, or distill your memories within a book, both of these endeavors demand time we do not have, and facilities beyond this craft. It is also true we could do both these things upon arrival in Macklenburg, yet our need for your knowledge cannot wait. Upon arrival we must know where we stand, and if... within our ranks... there is a Judas."

He held out his glass to Roger for more brandy, and continued speaking as it was poured.

"This latest confrontation on the rooftop—wasteful and distressing, I trust, to *all*—only reinforces our earlier decision that we would have been best served with your talents incorporated to our cause—via the Process. Thank you, Roger." Crabbé drank. "Do not bother to protest—we no longer expect any such conversions, nor—given the grief you have inflicted—would they now be accepted. The situation could not be clearer. We hold Mrs. Dujong. You will answer our questions or she will die—and I'm sure you can imagine the sort of death I mean, the time it will take, and how distressing such prolonged screams will be in such an enclosed place as this. And if she does manage to expire, then we shall merely move on to one of you—Miss Temple, perhaps—and on and on. It is inevitable as the dawn. As you have opened that door to avoid its being needlessly broken, I offer you the chance to avoid that same breaking of your comrades' bodies—and, indeed, their souls."

Miss Temple looked at the faces opposite her—Crabbé's smug smirk, the Prince's bemused disdain, Lydia's fox-faced hunger, Roger's earnest frown, Xonck's leer, the Comte's iron glare, the Contessa's glacial smile, and Caroline's sad patience—and found nowhere a suggestion that the Minister's words were anything but true. Yet she still saw the factions between them and knew their deeper interest lay no longer in what she and the others had discovered, but only in how those discoveries spelled out betrayals within the Cabal's circle.

"It would be easier to believe you, Sir," she said, "if you did not so blatantly *lie.* You ask us to talk to prevent our torture, yet what happens when we reveal some morsel of deduction that points to one among you—do you expect that person to accept our open word? Of course not—whoever is denounced will demand that your cruelties be brought to bear in *any* case, to confirm or disprove our accusations!"

The Deputy Minister's eyes twinkled as he shook his head, chuckling, and took another sip of brandy.

"My goodness—Roger, I do believe she *is* more than you'd perceived—Miss Temple, you have caught me out. Indeed, it is the case—so much for my attempts to save the woodwork! All right then—you will, all four, be killed at length, quite badly. If any of you have something to say, all the better—if not, well, we're rid of your damned stinking disruptions at last."

Xonck stepped forward, the saber dancing menacingly in the air before him. Miss Temple retreated, but a single step brought her flat against the wall. Once more the Doctor squeezed her hand, and then cried out in as hearty a voice as he could.

"Excellent, Minister—and perhaps Mr. Xonck will kill us *before* we talk—would that suit you even better?"

Crabbé stood up, impatient and angry. "Ah—here it comes! The vain attempt to turn us against one another—Francis—"

"By all means, *Francis*—kill us quickly! Serve the Minister as you always have! Just as when you sank Trapping in the river!"

Xonck paused, the tip of his blade within lunging range of Svenson's chest. "I serve *myself.*"

Svenson looked down at the saber tip and snorted—even as Miss Temple could feel the trembling of his hand. "Of course you do—just pardon my asking—what has happened to Herr Flaüss?"

For a moment, no one answered, and Crabbé was glaring at Xonck to *keep going* when the Contessa spoke aloud, picking her words carefully.

"Herr Flaüss was found to be . . . disloyal."

"The gunshot!" exclaimed Miss Temple. "You shot *him*!"

"It proved necessary," said Crabbé.

"How could he be disloyal?" croaked Chang. "He was your creature!"

"Why do you *ask*?" the Contessa pointedly demanded of the Doctor.

"Why do you *care*?" hissed Crabbé to her, behind Xonck's back. "Francis, *please*—"

"I just wonder if it had to do with Lord Vandaariff's missing *book,*" said Svenson. "You know—the one where his memory was—what is the word?—*distilled*?"

There was a pause. Miss Temple's heart was in her mouth—and then she knew the momentum toward their destruction had been stalled.

"That book was broken," rasped the Comte. "By Cardinal Chang in the tower—it killed Major Blach—"

"Is that what his *ledger* says?" Svenson nodded contemptuously to Roger. "Then I think you will find *two* books missing—one with the Lady Mélantes, Mrs. Marchmoor, among others—and another—"

"What are you waiting for?" cried Crabbé. "Francis! Kill him!"

"Or you *would,*" crowed Svenson, "if there was a second book at all! For to distill Robert Vandaariff's mind into a book—a mind holding the keys to a continent—to the future itself!—would have opened those riches to any one of you who owned it, who possessed a *key*! Instead, the man given the task to do just that did *not* create a book—so yes, there is one book broken, and another never made *at all*!"

The Contessa called out firmly to Xonck—"Francis, keep watching them!"—before turning to Crabbé. "Harald, can you answer this?"

"*Answer?* Answer *what?* Answer the—the desperate—the—"

Before the Minister could stop sputtering Chang called out again, a challenge to Roger. "I saw it myself, in Vandaariff's study—he wrote it all down on parchment! If I hadn't smashed a book they would have had to do it themselves—convincing you all that Vandaariff's memories were gone, when *they* held the only copy!"

"A copy I took from the Minister himself," cried Svenson, "in a leather satchel—and which Bascombe took from me in the ballroom. I'm sure he still has it with him—or is that what Flaüss noticed when he joined you at Lord Vandaariff's study . . . and why he had to die?"

In the silence Miss Temple realized she had been holding her breath. The words had flown so quickly back and forth, while in between stood Francis Xonck, eyes shifting warily, his blade an easy thrust from them all. She could feel the fearful state of Svenson's nerves, and knew Chang was tensed to futilely spring at Xonck—but she could also sense the changing tension in the room, as the Minister and Roger groped to refute their own prisoners.

"Aspiche took the satchel from Svenson in the ballroom," announced Xonck, not turning to the others. "And Bascombe took it from him . . . but I did not see it when we met up in the study."

"It was packed away," said Caroline Stearne, speaking quietly from her place. "When all was being readied for the journey—"

"Is the satchel here or isn't it?" snapped Xonck.

"I have its contents with me," said Roger smoothly. "As Caroline says, safely stowed. Doctor Svenson is wrong. They are Lord Vandaariff's planning papers—notes to himself for each stage of this enterprise. I do not know where this idea of Lady Mélantes's book comes from—*two* books—*no* books—"

"Doctor Lorenz identified the missing book as Lady Mélantes's," spat Svenson.

"Doctor Lorenz is *wrong*. Lady Mélantes's book—also containing Mrs. Marchmoor and Lord Acton—is safely stowed. The only book missing—the one broken in the tower—is that of Lord Vandaariff. You can check my ledger, but anyone is more than welcome to look in the books themselves."

It was an effective speech, with just the right amount of protest at being accused and an equally moving touch of professional supercilious-ness—a Bascombe specialty. And it seemed as if his upset superiors, perhaps persuaded by his own subservience via the Process, were convinced. But Miss Temple knew, from the way Roger's thumb restlessly rubbed against his leg, that it was a lie.

She laughed at him.

He glared at her, furiously willing her to silence.

"O *Roger*..." She chuckled and shook her head.

"Be quiet, Celeste!" he hissed. "You have no place here!"

"And you have surely convinced everyone," she said. "But you forget how well I know your ways. Even then you might have convinced me—for it *was* a fine speech—if it wasn't you who actually shot Herr Flaüss, after *convincing* everyone of his disloyalty, I am sure... or was it to keep him quiet? But it *was* you who shot him, Roger,... wasn't it?"

At her words the cabin went silent, save for the low buzz of the rotors outside. Xonck's saber did not waver, but his mouth tightened and his eyes flicked more quickly back and forth between them. The Contessa stood.

"Rosamonde," began Crabbé, "this is ridiculous—they are coming between us—it is their only hope—"

But the Contessa ignored him and crossed the cabin slowly toward Roger. He shrank away from her, first striking the wall and then seeming to retreat within his own body, meeting her gaze but flinching, for her eyes were empty of affection.

"Rosamonde," rasped the Comte. "If we question him together—"

But then the Contessa darted forward, sharp as a striking cobra, to whisper in Roger's ear. Miss Temple could only catch the odd word, but when she heard the first—"blue"—she knew the Contessa was whispering Roger's own control phrase, and that by speaking it before any of the others, the woman had made sure Roger must answer her questions alone. The Contessa stepped away and Roger sank down to sit on the floor, his expression empty and his eyes dulled.

"Rosamonde—" Crabbé tried again, but again the Contessa ignored him, speaking crisply down to Roger, his head at the level of her thighs.

"Roger... is what Doctor Svenson tells us true?"

"Yes."

Before Crabbé could speak the Contessa pressed Roger again.

"Were Lord Robert's memories distilled into a book?"

"No."

"They were written down."

"Yes."

"And those papers are on board?"

"Yes. I transferred them to the Prince's bag to hide them. Flaüss insisted on managing the Prince's bag and realized what they were."

"So you shot him."

"Yes."

"And in all of this, Roger, . . . who did you serve? Who gave the orders?"

"Deputy Minister Crabbé."

Crabbé said nothing, his mouth open in shock, his face drained of any color. He looked helplessly to the Comte, to Xonck, but could not speak. Still facing Roger, the Contessa called behind her.

"Caroline, would you be kind enough to ask Doctor Lorenz exactly where we are on our route?"

Caroline, whose gaze had been fixed on Roger Bascombe's slumped form, looked up with surprise, stood at once, and left the cabin.

"I say," muttered the Prince, aggrieved. "He put those papers in *my* bag? And shot my man because of it? Damn you, Crabbé! Damn your damned insolence!" Lydia Vandaariff patted her fiancé's knee.

"Your Highness," hissed Crabbé urgently, "Bascombe is not telling the truth—I do not know how—it could be any of you! Anyone with his control phrase! Anyone could order him to answer these questions—to implicate me—"

"And how would that person know what these questions were to be?" snarled the Contessa, and then pointed toward the captives. "At least one of them has been provided by Doctor Svenson!"

"For all any of us know, whoever has tampered with Bascombe's mind could be in league with these three!" cried Crabbé. "It would certainly explain their persistent survival!"

The Contessa's eyes went wide at the Deputy Minister's words.

"Bascombe's mind! Of course—of course, you sneaking little man! You did not halt the examinations in the ballroom for Lord Robert or the Duke—you did it because Roger was suddenly forced to accompany Vandaariff! Because otherwise the Comte would have seen inside his mind—and seen all of your plotting against us plain as day!" She wheeled to the Comte, and gestured to Bascombe on the floor. "Do not believe *me,* Oskar—ask your own questions, by all means—some questions I will not have *anticipated*! Or you, Francis—help yourself! For myself I am satisfied, but do go on! Roger—you will answer all questions put to you!"

The Comte's face betrayed no particular expression, but Miss Temple knew he was already suspicious of the Contessa and so perhaps was genuinely curious, unsure which—or was it both? Or all?—of his confederates had betrayed him.

"Francis?" he rasped.

"Be my guest." Xonck smiled, not even moving his eyes as he spoke.

The Comte d'Orkancz leaned forward. "Mr. Bascombe,... to your knowledge, did Deputy Minister Crabbé have anything to do with the murder of Colonel Arthur Trapping?"

The Contessa spun to the Comte, her expression wary and her violet eyes dauntingly sharp.

"Oskar, why—"

"No," said Roger.

The Comte's next question was interrupted by Caroline Stearne, whose return had brought Doctor Lorenz into the doorway.

"Contessa," she whispered.

"Thank you, Caroline—would you be so good as to fetch the Prince's bag?" Caroline took in the tension of the room, her face pale, bobbed her head once and darted from the cabin. The Contessa turned to Lorenz. "Doctor, how good of you to come—though I do trust *someone* remains at the wheel?"

"Do not trouble yourself, Madame—I have two good men *aloft,*" he answered, smiling at his nautical reference. The Doctor's smile faded as he took in that it was Bascombe on the floor being questioned, and not the prisoners.

"Our position?" the Contessa asked him crisply.

"We are just over the sea," Lorenz replied. "From here, as you know, there are different routes available—remaining over water, where there is less chance of being seen, or crossing straight to shadow the coast. In this fog it may not matter—"

"And how long until we reach Macklenburg proper?" asked the Comte.

"With either route it will be ten hours at the least. More if the wind is against us . . . as it presently is . . ." Lorenz licked his thin lips. "May I ask what is going on?"

"Merely a disagreement between partners," called Xonck, over his shoulder.

"Ah. And may I ask why *they* are still alive?"

The Contessa turned to look at them, her eyes settling at last upon Miss Temple. Her expression was not kind.

"We were waiting for *you,* Doctor. I would not have any bodies found on land. The sea will take them—and if one does happen to wash up on a beach, it will only be after days in the water. By that time even the lovely Miss Temple will be as grey and shapeless as a spoiled milk pudding."

Caroline appeared again, the bag in one hand and a sheaf of papers in the other.

"Madame—"

"Excellent as always, Caroline," said the Contessa. "I am so glad you retain your flesh. Can you read them?"

"Yes, Madame. They are Lord Vandaariff's writings. I recognize his hand."

"And what does he write *about*?"

"I cannot begin—the account is *exhaustive*—"

"I suppose it would be."

"Madame—would it not be better—"

"Thank you, Caroline."

Caroline bobbed her head and remained in the doorway with Lorenz, both of them watching the room with nervous fascination. The Comte frowned darkly, beads of sweat had broken out on Xonck's forehead, and Crabbé's face had gone so pale as to seem bloodless. Only the Contessa smiled, but it was a smile that frightened Miss Temple more than all the others rolled to one, for above her scarlet lips and sharp white teeth the woman's eyes glittered like violet knife-points. She realized that the Contessa was *pleased,* that she looked forward to what would come with the bodily hunger of a mother embracing her child.

The Contessa drifted to Xonck, placing her face next to his.

"What do you think, Francis?" she whispered.

"I think I should like to put down this sword." He laughed. "Or put it *in* someone." His eyes settled on Chang. The Contessa leaned her head against Xonck's, somewhat girlishly.

"That's a very good idea. But I wonder if you have ample room to swing."

"I might like more, it's true."

"Let me see what I can do, Francis."

In a turn as elegant as if she were dancing, the Contessa spun toward Deputy Minister Crabbé, the razor-sharp spike in place across her hand, and drove it like a hammer into the side of his skull, just in front of his ear. Crabbé's eyes popped open and his body jerked at the impact... then went still for the four long seconds it took for his life to fade. He collapsed onto Prince Karl-Horst's lap. The Prince hopped up with a cry and the Deputy Minister bounced forward and onto the cabin floor with a thud.

"And no blood to mop." The Contessa smiled. "Doctor Lorenz, if you would open the forward hatchway? Your Highness? If you might assist Caroline with the Minister's remains?"

She stood, beaming down as they bent over the fallen diplomat, his eyes wide with the shock of his dispatch, doing their awkward best to drag him to where Lorenz knelt in the cabin beyond. On the sofa, Lydia watched the corpse's progress with a groan, her stomach once more heaving. She erupted wetly into her hands and with a disgusted sigh the Contessa shoved a small silk handkerchief at the girl. Lydia snatched it gratefully, a smeared pearl of blue at each corner of her mouth.

"Contessa—" she began, her voice a fearful quaver.

But the Contessa's attention turned at the clicking of a bolt, as Lorenz raised an iron hatchway from the floor. A burst of freezing air shot through the cabin, the grasping paw of winter. Miss Temple looked through at the open hatch and realized that something seemed wrong...

the clouds outside . . . their pallid veneer of light. The round windows in the cabin were covered by green curtains . . . she had not noticed the dawn.

"It seems we divide the future in ever expanding portions," observed the Contessa. "Equal thirds, gentlemen?"

"Equal thirds," whispered the Comte.

"I am agreeable," said Xonck, a bit tightly.

"Then it's settled," she announced. The Contessa reached out to Xonck's shoulder and gave it a gentle squeeze.

"Finish them."

The dagger was in Chang's hand and he slashed toward Xonck, catching the saber on the dagger hilt and pushing Xonck's weapon aside as he rushed forward. But Xonck spun on his heels and chopped his bandaged arm across Chang's throat, knocking him backwards to the ground, both men crying with pain at the impact. Doctor Svenson darted for Xonck, a half-step too late, and Xonck whipped the saber hilt up and into Svenson's stomach, dropping the Doctor choking to his knees. Xonck retreated a step and wheeled to Miss Temple, his blade once more extended toward her face. Miss Temple could not move. She looked at Xonck, his chest heaving, wincing at the pain in his arm . . . hesitating.

"Francis?" said the Contessa, her voice glazed with amusement.

"What?" he hissed.

"Are you *waiting* for something?"

Xonck swallowed. "I was wondering if you'd prefer to do *this* one yourself."

"That's very sweet of you . . . but I am quite content to watch."

"I was merely asking."

"And I assure you, I appreciate the thought, as I appreciate that you might also wish to retain Miss Temple for intimate scrutiny . . . but I would appreciate it even more if you would get *on* with it and *stick* her like the vicious little pig she is."

Xonck's fingers flexed around the saber hilt, shifting his grip. Miss Temple saw its merciless tip not two feet from her chest, light rippling along the silver blade as it rose and fell with Xonck's breathing. Then Xonck leered at her. She was going to die.

"First it was the Minister wanting people to get on with it . . . now it's the Contessa," she said. "Of course, *he* had his reasons—"

"Must I do this myself?" asked the Contessa.

"Do not *hound* me, Rosamonde," snapped Xonck.

"But the Comte never finished his questions!" cried Miss Temple.

Xonck did not lunge. She shouted again, her voice rising up to a shriek.

"He asked if the Minister killed Colonel Trapping! He did not ask who *else* might have killed him! If *Roger* killed him! Or if he was killed by the *Contessa*!"

"What?" asked Xonck.

"Francis!" cried the Contessa. She snorted with rage and strode past Xonck to silence Miss Temple herself, the spike raised high. Miss Temple flinched, trembling at whether her throat would be cut or her skull perforated, unable to otherwise move.

Before any of these could occur, Xonck wheeled and hooked the Contessa about the waist with his bandaged arm and swept the woman off her feet and with a shriek of protest onto the nearest settee—exactly the spot where Harald Crabbé had just died.

The Contessa glared with an outrage Miss Temple had never seen in life—a ferocity to peel paint or buckle steel.

"Rosamonde—" began Xonck, and—too late again—Miss Temple darted for Chang's fallen dagger. Xonck slapped the flat of the saber blade hard across her head, sprawling her atop Doctor Svenson, who groaned.

She shook her head, the whole right side stinging. The Contessa still sat on the settee, next to the Prince and Lydia, miserable as children marooned in the midst of their parents' row.

"Rosamonde," said Xonck again, "what does she mean?"

"She means nothing!" the Contessa spat. "Colonel Trapping is no longer important—the Judas was Crabbé!"

"The Comte knows all about it," managed Miss Temple, her voice thick.

"All about what?" asked Xonck, for the first time allowing the saber to drift toward the Comte d'Orkancz, who sat opposite the Contessa.

"He won't say," whispered Miss Temple, "because he no longer knows who to trust. You have to ask *Roger*."

The Comte stood up.

"Sit down, Oskar," said Xonck.

"This has gone far enough," the Comte replied.

"Sit down or I will have your God damned head!" shouted Xonck. The Comte deigned to show actual surprise, and sat, his face now quite as grave as the Contessa's was livid.

"I will not be made a fool," hissed Xonck. "Trapping was my man—mine to discard! Whoever killed him—even if I would prefer not to believe—it follows they are my enemy—"

"Roger Bascombe!" shouted Miss Temple. "Do you know who killed Colonel Trapping?"

With a snarl and three iron-hard fingers of his sword hand Xonck took hold of Miss Temple's robes behind her neck, yanked her to her knees and then, with a roar of frustration, tossed her down the length of the cabin through the doorway to land with a cry at the feet of Caroline Stearne. The breath was driven from her body and she lay there blinking with pain, dimly aware that she was somehow even colder. She looked back to see her shredded robes hanging from Xonck's hand. He met her gaze, still furious, and Miss Temple whimpered aloud, convinced he was about to march over and step on her throat just like he'd done to the Dragoon . . . but then in the panting silence, Roger Bascombe answered her question.

"Yes," he said simply. "I know."

Xonck stopped where he stood, staring at Roger. "Was it the Contessa?"

"No."

"Wait—before that," broke in the Comte, "*why* was he killed?"

"He was serving Vandaariff instead of us?" asked Xonck.

"He was," said Roger. "But that is not why he was killed. The Contessa already knew Colonel Trapping's true allegiance."

Xonck and the Comte turned to her. The Contessa scoffed at their naïve credulity.

"Of course I knew," she sneered, looking up at Xonck. "You are arrogant, Francis, so you assume that everyone wants what you do—your brother's power—and Trapping especially. You hide your cunning behind the mask of a libertine, but Trapping had no such depth—he was happy to deliver every secret of your brother's—and yours—to whoever best indulged his appetite!"

"Then why?" asked Xonck. "To preserve the Comte's *Annunciation* project?"

"No," said Roger. "Trapping hadn't yet agreed on a price to save Lydia—he'd only given Vandaariff hints."

"Then it *was* Crabbé—Trapping must have learned his plans for distilling Vandaariff—"

"No," repeated Roger. "The Deputy Minister would have killed him, to be sure . . . just as the Comte would have . . . given time and opportunity."

Xonck turned to the Contessa. "So you *did* kill him!"

The Contessa huffed again with impatience.

"Have you paid any attention at all, Francis? Do you not remember what Elspeth Poole—stupid, insolent, and barely regretted—displayed for us all in the ballroom? Her *vision*?"

"It was Elspeth and Mrs. Stearne," said Xonck, looking through the doorway to Caroline.

"With Trapping," said the Comte. "The night of the engagement."

"We were sent to him," protested Caroline. "The Contessa ordered us—to—to—"

"Exactly," said the Contessa. "I was doing my best to *indulge* him where the other guests would not intrude!"

"Because you knew he could not be trusted," said the Comte.

"Though he could be *distracted*—until we had time to deal with Vandaariff ourselves," observed the Contessa, "which we then did!"

"If Colonel Trapping alerted Vandaariff then our entire enterprise could have been compromised!" cried Caroline.

"We are all aware of it!" snapped the Contessa.

"Then I don't understand," said Xonck. "Who killed Trapping? Vandaariff?"

"Vandaariff would not kill his own agent," said a hoarse voice behind Xonck, which Miss Temple recognized as Doctor Svenson's, pushing himself up to his knees.

"But Blenheim had Trapping's key!"

"Blenheim moved the body," said Svenson, "on Vandaariff's orders. At the time he still controlled his own house."

"Then who?" growled the Comte. "And why? And if it was not for Lydia's fate, or Vandaariff's legacy, or even control of the Xonck fortunes, how has the murder of this insignificant fool torn our entire alliance asunder?"

The Contessa shifted herself on the settee, and looked fiercely at Roger, whose lip betrayed the slightest quiver at his fruitless attempts to remain silent.

"Tell us, Roger," said the Contessa. "Tell us *now.*"

As Miss Temple watched the face of her former love, it seemed she looked at a puppet—remarkably life-like to be sure, but the falseness was readily, achingly, apparent. It was not his passive state, nor the even tone of his voice, nor the dullness of his eye, for these were explained by their strange circumstances—just as if he had screamed or gnashed his teeth. Instead, it was simply the content of his words, all the more strange, for Miss Temple had always attended instead to the way he said them—the way he took her arm or leaned across a table as he spoke, or even the stirring those words (whatever they might be) might spark in her own body. But now, *what* he said made clear the extent to which Roger's life had become separate from hers. She had assumed through their engagement—no matter where their own discrete days took them—they remained symbolically twinned, but now, spreading through her heart like the rising dawn outside the hatch, she saw that their wholeness—an idea beyond facts, however vain and foolish and doomed—lived only in her memory. She truly did not know who he was anymore, and never would again. And had she ever? It was a question she could not answer. The sadness she felt was no longer for him—for he was a fool, nor for herself—for she was rid of one. But somehow, listening to Roger speak in the freezing air, in Miss Temple's closely bound heart she mourned for the world, or as much of it as her sturdy chest could hold. She saw for the first time that it was truly made of dust . . . of invisible palaces that without her care—care that could never last—would disappear.

* * *

"The night before I underwent the Process," Roger began, "I met a woman at the St. Royale Hotel whose passion met my own in an exquisite union. In truth I had not decided to undergo the Process at all, and even then contemplated exposing everything to the highest authorities. But then I met this woman . . . we were both masked, I did not know her name, but she hovered hesitant on the same cusp of destiny, just as I did. As I strove to choose between the certain advancement brought by betraying the Deputy Minister and the utter risk of following him, I saw how she had given over the whole of her life to this new chance—that all before had been released, all attachment and all hope. And even though I knew that in giving myself to the Process I would give up my former aspirations to romance and marriage, this woman somehow in one night stirred me to my soul—a sadness matched with such tender care for our one lost instant together. But the next day I was changed and any thoughts I ever had of love were changed as well, directed and more reasoned, in service to . . . larger goals that could not contain her . . . and yet three days after that I met her again, once more masked, in the robes of an initiate to the Process . . . I knew her by her scent . . . by her hair—I had even been sent to collect her for the theatre, where she would undergo her own irrevocable change. I found her with another woman, and with a man I knew to be a traitor. Instead of collecting them I sent her friend ahead and the man away, and revealed myself . . . for I believed our temperaments were such that an understanding might survive, undetected by all . . . that we might ally . . . to share information about you, Contessa, about Minister Crabbé, Mr. Xonck, the Comte, Lord Robert—to serve both the goals we had sworn to and our own mutual ambition. And make an alliance we did, rooted no longer in anything called love . . . but in sensible expedience. And together we have served you all, our masters, and watched patiently as one after another those above us have been enslaved or slain, rising ourselves to the very edge of power until we are positioned to inherit everything, as each one of you turns on the other—as you are doing even in this instant. For we are without your greed, your lusts, your appetites, but have stood silently to the side of every plan, every secret, for the Process has made us stronger than you can know. All this we saw together, a dream when we both thought we would never dream again. It was later I found the man had not gone away as I'd thought. He'd seen us together . . .

overheard everything...and wanted payment—of many kinds. That was impossible."

"*You* killed him?" whispered Xonck. *"You?"*

"Not me," said Roger. "Her. Caroline."

Every eye in the room turned to Caroline Stearne.

"Hold her!" shouted Xonck, and Doctor Lorenz reached past Miss Temple to seize Caroline around the waist. Caroline lashed out with her elbow, driving it into the Doctor's throat. In an instant she turned on the choking man and pushed him with both hands. Doctor Lorenz vanished through the open hatch, his fading howl swallowed by the wind.

No one moved, and then Caroline herself broke the spell, kicking the Prince's leg and swinging a fist at Lydia's face, clearing a path to the iron staircase that rose to the wheelhouse. A moment later the cabin echoed with an ear-splitting scream and down the stairs bounced the body of one of Doctor Lorenz's sailors, blood pouring from a pulsing puncture on his back.

Miss Temple kicked herself away both from the bloody man and the open hatch, as chaos erupted around her. The Contessa was on her feet and after Caroline, lifting her dress with one hand to step over the sailor, the other hand holding her spike. The Comte and Xonck were close behind, but Xonck had not taken a step before he was tackled by Svenson and Chang. The Comte turned, looking back and then forward, hesitated, and then ripped open a cabinet near his head, revealing a rack of bright cutlasses. As Chang wrestled with Xonck for the saber, Svenson took a handful of Xonck's red curls and pulled his head away from the floor—Xonck snarling his protest—and then slammed it down as hard as he could. Xonck's grip on the saber wavered and Svenson smacked his head again on the planking, opening a seam of blood above his eye. The Comte ripped free a cutlass, the massive weapon looking in his hand like a particularly long kitchen cleaver. Miss Temple screamed.

"Doctor—look out!"

Svenson scuttled back as Chang finally scooped up the saber, forcing the Comte to pause. Miss Temple could not see the Comte's face, but she doubted his alchemical knowledge included swordplay—not when he faced a bitter opponent like Chang, even if Chang was weaving on his feet.

But her scream had another effect, which was to remind the Prince and Lydia of her presence. Karl-Horst dropped into a cunning crouch and leered at her, yet to her greater distress she saw Lydia weave the other way, behind the open hatch, where Elöise hung gagged and bound to the wall. Lydia clawed at the ropes with a determined grimace, watching Miss Temple across the whistling open hatchway.

Too much was happening at once. Chang was coughing horribly, Miss Temple could not see Svenson or Chang for the Comte's broad back and his enormous fur. Lydia pulled apart one knot, attacked another. Coming at her, his hands clutching wickedly, was the Prince, pausing to stare at Miss Temple's body. Miss Temple realized how exposed she was without her robes, but that the Prince could find the time—at this pitch of a crisis, to *ogle* a woman he was hoping to *kill*—was but another spur to her courage, for she had already seen what she must do.

She feinted to the stairs and then dashed the other way, leaping the hatch straight at Lydia, forcing the girl to drop the ropes. But Miss Temple dodged again, over Elöise's legs, just avoided the Prince's flailing arms, and then hurled herself at the Comte, digging at his fur with both hands, finding the pocket even as he turned and swatted her into the far settee with his mighty arm. Miss Temple landed in a sprawl, mid-way between the Comte and Chang, but in her hands, plucked from the pocket where the Comte himself had stowed it so many hours ago at the St. Royale, was her green clutch bag. She thrust her hand inside and did not bother to pull her revolver out, but fired through the fabric, the bullet shattering the cabinet near the Comte's head. He turned with a roar of alarm, and Miss Temple fired again, the bullet swallowed by his coat. She fired a third time. The Comte coughed sharply once, as if a bit of dinner had stuck in his throat, lost his balance and cracked his forehead hard against the corner of the cabinet. He straightened himself and stared at her, blood beading down above his eye. He turned to leave, almost casually, and caught his feet together. His knees locked, and the great man fell face down like a tree.

* * *

Xonck grunted, trying to crawl away. Chang sank to his knees and drove a brutal punch with the saber hilt across Xonck's jaw, stilling him like a pole-axed steer. Through the open doorway Miss Temple saw the Prince and Lydia watching in terror, but it was a terror mixed with defiance, for between them they had untied Elöise and held her precariously over the hatch, where with the gentlest push she would plummet to her death.

Miss Temple extracted the revolver from her bag and stood, taking a moment to yank what was left of her petticoats into position over her revealing silk pants, relieved that no one was looking at whatever parts she had exposed sprawling on the settee. Chang and Svenson advanced past her to the far doorway, Chang with Xonck's saber and Svenson availing himself of a cutlass from the cabinet. She stepped up between them, giving her petticoats just one more tug. The Prince and Lydia had not moved, rendered mute and still by the sudden fates of the Comte and Xonck, and by the truly vicious screaming that now reached them all from the wheelhouse.

The heated words passing back and forth between Caroline and the Contessa could not be made out over the roar of the open hatchway, but they were punctuated by the Contessa's snarls of rage and Caroline's shouts—tenacious, but terrified—the mix further complicated by the cries of the remaining crewman, who seemed by his pleading oaths to be German.

"Do not worry, Elöise," Miss Temple called out. "We shall collect you directly."

Still gagged, Elöise did not answer, for her gaze was fixed—indeed, it was held—on the freezing abyss beneath her, suspended by Lydia's tight handful of her hair, while, a step behind, the Prince had wrapped his arms around Elöise's legs. Wrists and ankles tied, Elöise could do nothing to prevent them dropping her through.

"Let her go!" cried Chang. "Your masters are down! You are alone!"

"Drop your weapons or the woman dies!" replied the Prince, shrilly.

"If you kill that woman," said Chang, "I will kill *you*. I will kill you *both*. If you release her, I will not. That is the extent of our negotiation."

The Prince and Lydia exchanged a nervous glance.

"Lydia," called Doctor Svenson. "It is not too late—we can reverse what has been done! Karl—listen to me!"

"If we *do* release her—" began the Prince, but Lydia had begun speaking at the same time and overrode his words.

"Do not treat us like children! You have no idea what we know or what we are worth! You do not know—*do* you?—that all the land in Macklenburg purchased by my father was settled in *my* name!"

"Lydia—" attempted the Prince, but she swatted at him angrily and kept on.

"I am the next Princess of Macklenburg whether I marry or no—whether my father is alive or no—no matter if I am the only person alive on this craft! I insist you drop your weapons! I have done nothing to any of you—to anyone!"

She stared at them wildly, panting.

"Lydia—" The Prince had finally noticed the smear of blue across her lips, and glanced to Svenson, suddenly confused.

"Be quiet! Do not talk to them! Hold her legs!" Lydia's stomach heaved again and she groaned painfully, spitting onto the front of her dress. "You should be fighting them yourself!" she complained. "You should have killed all three of them! Why is everyone so useless!"

The crewman above them screamed, and at once the entire airship careened to the left. Chang went into the wall, Miss Temple into Chang, and Doctor Svenson to his knees, the cutlass sliding from his hand. The Prince fell toward the open hatch, keeping his hold on Elöise so he drove her like a ram into Lydia, knocking both women into the opening. Lydia screamed and hit the lip of the hatch with her thighs and began to slide through. Elöise disappeared up to her waist—only the Prince's grip on her legs preventing her fall, a grip that was visibly slipping as he tried to decide whether to drop Elöise in order to save his bride.

"Hold her!" shouted Svenson, throwing himself forward to catch Lydia's feverishly clawing hands.

The airship careened again in the other direction, just as suddenly. Miss Temple lost her balance as she tried to reach Svenson. Chang leapt past them both toward the Prince. The Prince retreated in terror, releasing his hold on Elöise, but Chang caught her legs, digging his fingers in her ropes, and braced his foot on the hatch plate. He shouted to Miss Temple and gestured to the wheelhouse.

"Stop them—they'll kill us all!"

Miss Temple opened her mouth to protest, but as she watched—the Prince hunched in the corner beyond them—she saw Chang pull Elöise out to her hips, and Svenson do the same to Lydia.

She tightened her grip on the revolver and rushed to the stairs.

The second crewman lay draped over the topmost steps, blood bubbling on his lips. Lining either side of the wheelhouse were metal panels of levers and knobs, and at the far end, in front of the windows—where Miss Temple had first seen Doctor Lorenz from the roof—stood the wheel itself, made of brass and polished steel. Several levers had been broken off, with others jammed into positions that set the metal gears to grinding horribly. From the tilting floor it seemed certain the craft had swooned into a curve, spinning gently downwards.

In front of her lay Caroline Stearne, on her back, arms outstretched, an empty hand some inches from a bloody stiletto. Crouched on top of Caroline, her hair disheveled and her spike-hand smeared with blood like a glove, perched the Contessa di Lacquer-Sforza. A crimson pool drained to the side with the angle of the floor. The Contessa looked up at Miss Temple and sneered.

"Why, look who it is, Caroline—your little charge."

Her fist flashed forward, driving the spike into Caroline's throat with a meaty smack, causing Miss Temple to flinch and Mrs. Stearne's still body to react not at all.

"Where is everyone else?" she asked with a smirk. "Do not tell me you alone are left? Or if you're here, I suppose it is more accurate to say *I* am the only one left. How *typical.*"

She rose to her feet, her dress dripping blood, and gestured with her free hand to the whining machinery.

"Not that it mattered—I could have cared less who killed Trapping—if this romantic idiot hadn't killed Lorenz and our crewmen—much less set off my own *anger*—we could be sharing *tea.* All of this for nothing! *Nothing!* I merely want people I can control! But *now*—just listen!" She gestured at the grinding machinery and scoffed. "We're all finished! It makes me so very . . . *savage* . . ."

She stepped closer, and Miss Temple raised her pistol—she was still looking into the wheelhouse from the stairs. The Contessa saw the revolver and laughed. Her hand shot out to a lever and wrenched it down. With a shudder that shook the airship to its very frame—and threw Miss Temple all the way to the bottom of the staircase, her stinging fall broken only by the distressing cushion of the first crewman's body—the spinning momentum reversed direction. A broken chopping sound erupted from one of the propellers. The grinding from the wheelhouse rose nastily in pitch and volume, and as she shook her head Miss Temple heard the Contessa's footsteps coming down the iron steps.

She clawed her way free of the body—she was moving too slowly, she had dropped her revolver—and looked ahead of her, hair hanging in her eyes. The hatch was closed, but the sudden jolt had knocked everyone off their feet. Chang sat on the floor with Eloïse, cutting her bonds. Svenson was on his knees, facing Lydia and the Prince, skulking in a corner just beyond his reach. Miss Temple pulled herself toward them, feeling stiff as a tortoise.

"Cardinal!" Miss Temple gasped. "Doctor!"

Ignoring Miss Temple utterly, the Contessa's voice shot out from above.

"Roger Bascombe! Wake *up*!"

Chang and Svenson turned as Roger did just that, returning to awareness in an instant. Roger leapt to his feet, took in Xonck and the Comte on the floor, and threw himself at the open cabinet of weapons. Chang raised the saber—Miss Temple was dismayed to see still more blood around Chang's mouth—and struggled to stand. Doctor Svenson collected his own cutlass and reached his feet with the help of a brass wall bracket. He shouted to the Contessa.

"It is finished, Madame! The airship is falling!"

Miss Temple looked back, relieved she was not dead, but having no idea why it was so. The Contessa had paused on the little landing mid-way down the stairs, where in a small alcove—emblematic of the cunning use of space so necessary aboard vessels of all kinds—her minions had lashed into place an enormous steamer trunk.

Miss Temple heaved herself to her knees. She saw her revolver, slid half-way across the floor, and screamed at the Doctor as she flung herself toward it.

"She has the books! She has the books!"

The Contessa had both hands in the trunk and when she pulled them out each held a book—in her bare fingers! Miss Temple did not know how the woman did it—indeed the Contessa's expression was ecstatic—how was she not swallowed up?

"Roger!" called the Contessa. "Are you alive?"

"I am, Madame," he replied, having retreated at Chang's approach to the other side of the unmoving Francis Xonck.

"Contessa," began Svenson, "Rosamonde—"

"If I throw this book," the Contessa called, "it will surely shatter on that floor, and some of you—particularly those under-dressed and sitting—will be killed. I have many of them. I can throw one after another—and since the alternative means the end of *every* book, I will sacrifice as many as I need. Miss Temple, *do not touch that gun*!"

Miss Temple stopped her hand, hovering above her revolver.

"Every one of you," cried the Contessa. "Drop your weapons! Doctor! Cardinal! Do it now or this book goes *right... at... her*!"

She glared at Miss Temple with a wicked smile. Svenson dropped his cutlass with a clang, and it slid with the tipping of the craft toward the Prince, who snatched it up. Chang did not move.

"Cardinal?"

Chang wiped his mouth and spat, his blood-smeared jaw like the painted half-mask of a red Indian or a Borneo pirate, and his bone-weary voice from another world altogether.

"We are finished anyway, Rosamonde. I'll be dead by the end of the day no matter what, but we're all doomed. Look out the windows... we're going down. The sea will smother your dreams along with mine."

The Contessa weighed a book in her hand. "You've no care for your Miss Temple's painful death?"

"It would be quicker than drowning," answered Chang.

"I do not believe you. Drop your weapon, Cardinal!"

"If you answer a question."

"Don't be ridiculous—"

Chang shifted his grip on the saber and pulled back his arm, as if to throw it like a spear.

"Do you think your book will kill me before I put this through your heart? Do you want to take that chance?"

The Contessa narrowed her eyes and weighed her options.

"What question then? Quickly!"

"To be honest, it is *two* questions." Cardinal Chang smiled. "*First,* what was Mr. Gray doing when I killed him? And *second,* why did you take the Prince from his compound?"

"Cardinal Chang—*why*?" asked the Contessa, with a sigh of unfeigned frustration. "Why *possibly* do you want to know this *now*?"

Chang smiled, his sharp teeth pink with blood.

"Because one way or another, I shan't be able to ask you tomorrow."

The Contessa laughed outright and took two steps down the stairs, nodding Svenson and Miss Temple toward Chang, her expression darkening at Miss Temple's quite brazen snatch of her pistol before she went.

"Join your comrade," the Contessa hissed at them, then looked at Elöise with disdain. "*And* you, Mrs. Dujong—one wonders if you are professionally helpless for a living—*hurry*!" She turned to the Prince, her tone sweetening. "Highness . . . if you would climb to the wheelhouse and do what you can to slow our descent—I believe most of the panels have helpful *words* on them . . . Lydia, stay where you are."

Karl-Horst darted up the stairs as the Contessa continued down, stepping over the crewman, to face all four of them in the doorway. The Doctor had pulled Elöise to him and held her hand, while Miss Temple stood—feeling rather alone, actually—between the Doctor and Chang. She glanced once over her shoulder at Roger in the far doorway, his face pale and determined, another expression she had never seen.

"What a gang of unlikely rebels," said the Contessa. "As I am a rational woman I must recognize your success—however inadvertent—just as I can find myself truthfully wishing that our circumstances were other than they are. But the Cardinal is right. We will most likely perish—all of *you* will, certainly—just as I have lost my partners. Very well, Mr. *Gray*... it is no secret now—not even to the Comte, were he still alive. The mixture of indigo clay was altered to decrease the *pliability* of the new flesh of his *creations.* As a defense, you see, if they became too strong—they would be more brittle. As it happened, perhaps *too* brittle... ah, well... it seems I was rash." She laughed again—even at this extremity a lovely sound—and sighed, going on in a whisper. "As for the *Prince*—well, I do not like him to overhear. In addition to taking the opportunity of implementing my own control phrase for His Highness, he has also been introduced with a poison for which I alone have the antidote. It is a simple precaution. I have secretly made an adherent of his young cousin's mother—the cousin who must inherit if the Prince dies without issue. With Karl-Horst so dead, Lydia's child—and the Comte's dire plan for their offspring—is swallowed in a battle for the succession that I shall control. Or perhaps the Prince shall live, continuing to consume the antidote in ignorance—it is all preparation."

"And all of it rendered academic," muttered Svenson.

Above them the Prince had found a helpful switch, for one chopping propeller switched off, followed a moment later by the other. Miss Temple looked to the windows, but they were still covered with curtains—were they still losing altitude? The cabin righted itself, and grew silent save for the whistling outside wind. They were adrift.

"We shall see," said the Contessa. "Roger?"

Miss Temple turned at a noise behind her, but it did not come from Roger Bascombe. Francis Xonck had somehow regained his feet, steadying himself with his injured hand on a settee, the other holding his jaw, his lips pulled back in a wince of pain that revealed two broken teeth. He looked at Miss Temple with cold eyes and reached his good hand toward Roger, who immediately passed Xonck his cutlass.

"Why, hello, Francis," called the Contessa.

"We'll talk later," said Xonck. "Get up, Oskar. This isn't finished."

Before Miss Temple's eyes the enormous man on the floor, like a bear rousing itself from hibernation, began to stir, rearing up to his knees—the fur coat flashing briefly open to reveal a shirtfront drenched in blood, but she could see it had all seeped from one superficial line scored across his ribs—the crack on the head had brought him down, not her shooting. The Comte heaved himself onto a settee and glared at her with open hatred. They were trapped again, caught between the books and Xonck's cutlass. Miss Temple could not bear it an instant longer. She spun back to the Contessa and stamped her foot, extending the gun. The Contessa gasped with pleasure at the notion of being *challenged.*

"What is this, Celeste?"

"It is the finish," said Miss Temple. "You will throw the book if you are able. But I will do my best to put a bullet through the book in your other hand. It will shatter and you will lose your arm—and who knows, perhaps your face, perhaps your leg—perhaps it is you who will prove most *brittle* of all."

The Contessa laughed, but Miss Temple knew she laughed precisely because what Miss Temple said was true, and this was just the sort of thing the Contessa *enjoyed.*

"That was an interesting plan you described, Rosamonde," called Xonck. "The Prince, and Mr. Gray."

"Wasn't it?" she answered gaily. "And you would have been so surprised to see it unveiled in Macklenburg! It is such a pity I never got to see the finish of *your* secret plans—with Trapping or your brother's munitions—or *yours,* Oskar, the hidden instructions to your glass ladies, the triumphant birth of your creation within Lydia! Who can say what monstrosity you have truly implanted within her? How I should have been amazed and outflanked!" The Contessa laughed again and shook her head girlishly.

"You destroyed Elspeth and Angelique," rumbled the Comte.

"Oh, I did no such thing! Do not be temperamental—it is not becoming. Besides, who were they? Creatures of need—there are thousands more to take their place! There are more right before your eyes! Celeste Temple and Elöise Dujong and Lydia Vandaariff—another triumvirate for your great unholy sacrament!"

She sneered a bit too openly with this last word, caught herself, and then snickered. A certain lightness of mind was one thing, but to Miss Temple's wary eye the Contessa was becoming positively giddy.

"Karl-Horst von Maasmärck!" she bellowed. "Come down here and bring me two more books! I am told we must finish this—so finish it we shall!"

"There is no need," said Xonck. "We have them trapped."

"Quite right," laughed the Contessa. "If I did throw this book the glass might spray past them and hit you! That would be *tragic*!"

The Prince clomped down the stairs into view, with two books bundled in his coat under one arm, in the other carrying a bottle of orange liquid identical to the one Elöise had taken from the Comte's stores in the tower. Xonck turned to the Comte, who muttered, just loud enough for Miss Temple to hear.

"She does not wear gloves . . ."

"Rosamonde—" began Xonck. "No matter what has been done—our plans remain in place—"

"I can make him do anything, you know," laughed the Contessa. She turned to the Prince and shouted out, "A nice waltz, I think!"

As under her command as he'd been in the secret room, the Prince, his face betraying no understanding of what his body was doing, undertook a stumbling dance step on the slippery metal landing, all the time juggling his fragile burdens. The Comte and Xonck both took an urgent step forward.

"The books, Rosamonde—he will drop them!" cried Xonck.

"Perhaps I should just start throwing them anyway, and Celeste can try to shoot me if she can . . ."

"Rosamonde!" cried Xonck again, his face pale.

"Are you *afraid*?" she laughed. She motioned to the Prince to stop—which he did, panting, confused—and then raised her arm as if to make him continue.

"Rosamonde," called the Comte. "You are not yourself—the glass against your skin—it is affecting your mind! Put down the books—their contents are irreplaceable! We are still in alliance—Francis has them in hand with his blade—"

"But Francis does not trust me," she replied. "Nor I Francis. Nor I *you,* Oskar. How are you not dead when you've been shot? More of your *alchemy*? And here I had grown quite used to the idea—"

"Contessa, you must stop—you are frightening us all!"

This was from Lydia Vandaariff, who had taken several steps toward the Contessa, and reached out one hand, the other still clutching her belly.

She tottered, and her chin was streaked with blue-tinged drool—yet however hesitant her carriage, as always for Lydia, her tone was both restive and demanding.

"You are ruining everything! I want to be Princess of Macklenburg as you promised!"

"Lydia," rasped the Comte, "you must rest—take care—"

The girl ignored him, raising her voice, piercingly plaintive and peevish, to the Contessa. "I do not want to be one of the glass women! I do not want to have the Comte's child! I want to be a Princess! You must put down the book and tell us what to do!"

Lydia gasped at another spasm.

"Miss Vandaariff," whispered Svenson. "Step away—"

Another gout of blue, much thicker than before, heaved into Lydia's mouth. She gagged and swallowed, groaned and whined again at the Contessa, now in a tearful fury. "We can kill *these* others any time, but the books are precious! Give them to me! You promised me *everything*—my dreams! I insist you give them to me at once!"

The Contessa stared at her with wild eyes, but to Miss Temple it did seem the woman was genuinely attempting to consider Lydia's request—even as if the words came from a great distance and were only partly heard—when Lydia huffed with impatience and made the mistake of trying to snatch the nearest book. Showing the same speed she had used to overcome Crabbé, the Contessa, all sympathy vanished, whipped the one book from Lydia's reach and slashed the other book forward, chopping it with a cracking snap some two inches into Miss Vandaariff's throat.

The Contessa let go of the book and Lydia fell backwards, the flesh of her neck already turning blue, the blood in the back of her mouth and in her lungs hardening to crystal, popping like gravel beneath a wheel. The girl was dead before she hit the floor, her solidified throat breaking open and separating her head from her shoulders as neatly as an executioner's axe.

From the stairway the Prince let out a bellow of shock, roaring at the spectacle of Lydia dead, jaw quivering, mere words beyond him. Whether it was grief for the woman or outrage at an attack on one of his own, for the first time Miss Temple saw within the Prince a capacity for regret, for sentiment beyond mere appetite. But what to Miss Temple might have rendered the Prince infinitesimally admirable, for the Contessa changed him to a danger, and before he could take another step she hurled her second book into his knees. The glass shattered above his boots and with a piercing scream the Prince toppled back, legs buckling, juggling the books, landing heavily on the stairs, his boots still upright where he'd left them. His upper body slid down to rest against the fallen crewman and did not move.

The Contessa stood alone, flexing her fingers. The delirious gleam in her eyes grew dim and she looked around her, realizing what she'd done.

"Rosamonde . . ." whispered Xonck.

"Be quiet," she hissed, the back of her hand before her mouth. "I beg you—"

"You have destroyed my *Annunciation*!" The Comte's rasping voice betrayed an unbecoming whine, and he stood up, weaving, groping another cutlass from the cabinet.

"Oskar—stop!" This was Xonck, his face pale and drawn. "Wait!"

"You have ruined the work of my *life*!" the Comte shouted again, pulling free the cutlass and surging toward Miss Temple.

"Oskar!" the Contessa shouted. "Oskar—wait—"

Elöise took hold of Miss Temple's shoulders and yanked her from the Comte's path as the large man shouldered through, eyes fixed on the Contessa, who dug hurriedly to restore her metal spike. Miss Temple held her pistol, but it did not seem possible that she should shoot—for all this was the final confrontation with their enemies, she felt more a witness to their self-destruction than a combatant.

Cardinal Chang felt no such distance. As the Comte d'Orkancz passed by, Chang took hold of his massive shoulder and spun the man with all his strength. The Comte turned at this distraction, eyes wild, and raised the cutlass in an awkward, nearly petulant manner.

"You *dare*!" he cried at Chang.

"Angelique," spat Cardinal Chang in return. He drove the saber into the Comte's belly and up under his ribs, cutting deep into the great man's vitals. The Comte gasped and went rigid, and after one hanging moment

Chang gave the blade another push, grinding it in half-way to the hilt. The Comte's legs gave way and he took the blade from Chang with his fall, his dark blood pooling into the fur.

His cough trailing into a thick rattle, Chang dropped to his knees and then slumped back against the doorframe. Miss Temple cried out and sank to his side, feeling the Doctor's nimble fingers snatch the revolver from her hand as she did. She looked up from Chang's haggard face to see Svenson extend the gun at Francis Xonck—caught flat-footed by the Comte's death. Xonck stared into Svenson's hard eyes, his broken mouth desperately working for words.

"Doctor—too much hangs unfinished—your own nation—"

Svenson pulled the trigger. Xonck flew back as if he'd been kicked by a horse. The Doctor now stood face-to-face with Roger Bascombe.

He extended his arm, and then thought better of it and wheeled to the Contessa at the far end of the airship's cabin. He fired, but not before Roger had leapt forward and shoved the Doctor's arm. The bullet went wide and the Contessa ran for the stairs with a cry.

Svenson grappled with Roger for the gun, but Roger—younger, stronger—wrenched it away as the Doctor tripped over Xonck's leg. With an ugly grimace he aimed the gun at Svenson. Miss Temple cried out.

"Roger—do not!"

He looked up at her, his face disfigured by hatred and bitter rage.

"It is over, Roger. It has failed."

She knew there was one bullet left in the gun, and that Roger was too close to miss.

"It is *not,*" snarled Roger Bascombe.

"Roger, your masters are dead. Where is the Contessa? She has abandoned you. We are adrift. Both the Prince and the Duke of Stäelmaere are dead."

"The Duke?"

"He will be killed by Colonel Aspiche."

Roger stared at her. "Why would the Colonel do that?"

"Because I ordered him to. You see, I learned the Colonel's control phrase."

"His what?"

"Just as I know yours, Roger."

"I have no control phrase—"

"O Roger, . . . you really do not know after all, do you?"

Roger narrowed his eyes and raised the revolver to Doctor Svenson. Miss Temple spoke quickly and clearly, looking him straight in the eye.

"Blue Apostle blue Ministry ice consumption."

Roger's face went slack.

"Sit down," Miss Temple told him. "We will talk when there's time."

"Where is the Contessa?" asked Elöise.

"I do not know," said Miss Temple, "how is Chang?"

Doctor Svenson crawled to the Cardinal. "Elöise, help me move him. Celeste—" He pointed to the iron steps, to the Prince. "The orange bottle, if it is not broken, fetch it at once!"

She ran to it, stepping carefully around the glass—grateful for her boots—doing her best to avoid eye contact with the disfigured corpses.

"What is in it?" she called.

"I do not know—it is a chance for the Cardinal. I believe it is what saved Angelique—in the greenhouse, the mattress was stained orange—"

"But everyone we met was terrified of it," said Elöise. "If I made to break it they ran the other way!"

"I am sure they did—it must be deadly indeed, and yet—fire to fight fire, or in this case, ice."

Miss Temple found the bottle, nestled in the crook of the Prince's arm. She pulled it free, glancing just once at his horrible face, the open mouth with its stained teeth and blood-red gums, the lips and tongue now tinged with blue, and then looked up the stairs. The trunk of books was where it had been, and she heard no sound from the wheelhouse save the wind. She ran back to Chang. Elöise knelt behind him, propping up his head and wiping blood from his face. Svenson doused a handkerchief in the orange fluid and then, with a determined sigh, clamped it over Chang's nose and mouth. Chang did not react.

"Is it working?" asked Miss Temple.

"I do not *know,*" replied the Doctor. "I know he is dead without it."

"It does not *appear* to be working," said Miss Temple.

"Where is the Contessa?" asked Elöise.

Miss Temple looked down at Cardinal Chang. The Doctor's cloth had partially dislodged his spectacles, and she could see his scars, wounds of a piece with the blood that dripped down his face and neck. And yet beneath this history of violence—though she did not doubt it was integral to his soul—Miss Temple also saw a softness, an impression of what his eyes had been like before, of that underpinning and those margins where Chang located care and comfort and peace—if he ever did at all, of course. Miss Temple was no expert on the peace of others. What would it mean if Chang was to die? What would it have meant to him if their positions were reversed? She imagined he would disappear into an opium den. What would she do, lacking even that avenue into depravity? She looked down at Elöise and the Doctor working together, and walked back to Roger. She took the pistol from his hand and made her way to the iron steps.

"Celeste?" asked Svenson.

"Francis Xonck has your silver cigarette case—do not forget to collect it."

"What are you doing?" asked Elöise.

"Collecting the Contessa," said Miss Temple.

The wheelhouse was silent, and Miss Temple climbed past the dead crewman and onto the bloody deck, looking down at Caroline's body. The woman's eyes were open in dismay, her beautiful pale throat torn open as if a wolf had been at it. The Contessa was nowhere to be seen, but in the ceiling above another metal hatch had been pushed open. Before she climbed up, Miss Temple stepped to the windows. The cloud and fog had finally broken apart. Whatever its course had once been, the dirigible's path had become hopelessly skewed. She could see only grey cold water below them—not far below either, they were perhaps at the height of Harschmort's roof—and the pale flickers of white on top of the dark waves. Would they drown in the icy sea after all? After all of this? Chang was perhaps already dead. She'd left the room in part so as not to watch, preferring even at this extremity to avoid what she knew she would find painful. She sighed. Like a persistent little ape, Miss Temple clambered onto the shelf of levers and reached up to the hatch, pulling herself into the cold.

The Contessa stood on the roof of the cabin, holding on to a metal strut beneath the gasbag, wind whipping at her dress and her hair, which had become undone and flowed behind her head like the black pennant of a pirate. Miss Temple looked around her at the clouds, head and shoulders out of the hatch, her elbows splayed on the freezing metal roof. She wondered if she could just shoot the Contessa from here. Or should she simply take hold of the hatch and close it, marooning the woman outside? But this was the end, and Miss Temple found she could do neither of these things. She was transfixed, as perhaps she'd always been.

"Contessa!" she called above the wind, and then, the word feeling strangely intimate in her mouth, "Rosamonde!"

The Contessa turned, and upon seeing Miss Temple smiled with a grace and weariness that took Miss Temple by surprise.

"Go back inside, Celeste."

Miss Temple did not move. She gripped the gun tightly. The Contessa saw the gun and waited.

"You are an evil woman," shouted Miss Temple. "You have done wicked things!"

The Contessa merely nodded, her hair blowing for a moment across her face until with a toss of her head it flowed once more behind her. Miss Temple did not know what to do. More than anything she realized that her inability to speak and her inability to act were exactly how she felt when faced with her father—but also that this woman—this terrible, *terrible* woman—had been the birth of her new life, and somehow had *known* it, or at least appreciated the possibility, that finally she alone had been able to look into Miss Temple's eyes and see the desire, the pain, the determination, and see it—see her—for what she was. There was too much to say—she wanted an answer to the woman's brutality but would not get it, she wanted to prove her independence but knew the Contessa would not care, she wanted revenge but knew the Contessa would never admit her defeat. Nor could Miss Temple prove herself—overcome the one enemy who had always bested her effortlessly—by shooting her in the back, any more than she could have made her father care for her by burning his fields.

"Mr. Xonck and the Comte are dead," she shouted. "I have sent Colonel Aspiche to kill the Duke. Your plan has been ruined."

"I can see that. You've done very well."

"You have done things to me—changed me—"

"Why regret pleasure, Celeste?" said the Contessa. "There's little enough of it in life. And was it not exquisite? I enjoyed myself immensely."

"But I did not!"

The Contessa reached above her, the spike on her hand, and slashed a two-foot hole across the canvas gasbag. Immediately the blue-colored gas inside began to spew out.

"Go back inside, Celeste," called the Contessa. She reached in the other direction and opened another seam, out of which gushed air as blue as the summer sky. The Contessa held on to the strut within this cerulean cloud, in her windblown hair and bloody dress a perilous dark angel.

"I am not like your adherents!" Miss Temple shouted. "I have learned for myself! I have seen you!"

The Contessa ripped a third hole in the slackening gasbag, the plume of smoke roiling directly at Miss Temple. She choked and shook her head, eyes stinging, and groped for the hatch. With one last look at the glacial face of the Contessa di Lacquer-Sforza, Miss Temple pulled the hatch shut and dropped with a cry to the slippery wheelhouse floor.

"We are sinking to the sea!" she shouted, and with an aplomb she scarcely noticed stepped past and over mangled bodies all the way down to the others, never once slipping on blood or nicking herself on the scattered broken glass. To her utter delight, Chang was on his hands and knees, coughing onto the floor. The spray around his lips was no longer red but blue.

"It is working . . . ," said Svenson.

Miss Temple could not speak, just glimpsing in the prospect of Chang alive the true depths of her grief at Chang being dead. She looked up to see the Doctor watching her face, his expression both marking her pleasure and vaguely wan.

"The Contessa?" he asked.

"She is bringing us down. We will hit the water at any moment!"

"We shall help Chang—Elöise, if you could take the bottle—while you attend to *him.*" Svenson looked over his shoulder at Roger Bascombe, sitting patiently on a settee.

"Attend to him how?" asked Miss Temple.

"However you like," replied the Doctor. "Wake him or put a bullet through his brain. No one will protest. Or leave him—but I suggest *choosing,* my dear. I have learned it is best to be haunted by one's actions rather than one's lack of them." He re-opened the hatch in the floor and sucked his teeth with concern. Miss Temple could smell the sea. Svenson slammed the hatch shut. "There is no time—we must get to the roof at once—Elöise!"

Between them they caught Chang's arms and helped him up the stairs. Miss Temple turned to Roger. The dirigible shuddered, a gentle kick as the cabin struck a wave.

"Celeste—forget him!" shouted Elöise. "Come *now*!"

The airship shuddered again, settling fully onto the water.

"Wake up, Roger," Miss Temple called, her voice hoarse.

He blinked and his expression sharpened, looking around him, taking in the empty room without comprehension.

"We are sinking in the sea," she said.

"Celeste!" Svenson's shout echoed down the stairs.

Roger's eyes went to the pistol in her hand. She stood between him and the only exit. He licked his lips. The airship was rocking with the motion of the water.

"Celeste—" he whispered.

"So much has happened, Roger," Miss Temple began. "I find . . . I cannot contain it . . ." She sniffed, and looked into his eyes—fearful, wary, pleading—and felt the tears begin in her own. "The Contessa advised me, just now, against regret—"

"Please—Celeste, the water—"

"—but I am not like her. I am not even like myself, perhaps my character has changed . . . for I am awash in regret for everything, it seems—for what has stained my heart, for how I am no longer a child . . ." She gestured helplessly at the carnage around them. "For so many dead . . . for Lydia . . . even poor Caroline—"

"Caroline?" asked Roger, a bit too suddenly, the words followed by an immediate awareness that perhaps this wasn't the proper subject, given the circumstances, and the pistol. Miss Temple read the hesitation on his face, still grappling in her heart with the fact she had been found wanting twice in Roger's rejection—first as a matter of course to his ambition, and then as a companion—and a lover!—to Caroline Stearne. This was not what she intended to talk about. She met his eyes with hesitations of her own.

"She is dead, Roger. She is as dead as you and I."

Miss Temple watched Roger Bascombe take in this news, and understood that his next words were spoken not out of cruelty or revenge, but merely because she now stood for everything in his life that had thwarted him.

"She is the only one I ever loved," said Roger.

"Then it is good that you found her," said Miss Temple, biting her lip.

"You have no idea. You cannot *understand,*" he said, his voice bitter and hollow with grief.

"But I believe I do—" she began softly.

"How could you?" he shouted. "You never could understand—not me, nor any other, not in your pride—your very insufferable pride—"

She desperately wished Roger would stop speaking, but he went on, his emotions surging like the waves that slapped against the cabin walls.

"The wonders I have seen—the heights of sensation—of *possibility*!" He scoffed at her savagely, even as she saw tears in his eyes, tears rolling down his cheeks. "She *pledged* herself to me, Celeste—without even knowing who I was—without a care that we must die! That all is dust! That our love would lead to *this*! She knew even then!"

His hands shot out and shoved her hard, knocking her back into the cabinet. He stepped after her, arms flailing as he continued to yell.

"Roger, please—"

"And who are *you,* Celeste? How are you alive—so cold, so small of heart, so absent of feeling, without *surrender*!"

He caught her hard by the arm and shook her.

"Roger—"

"Caroline gave herself—gave everything! You have murdered her—murdered me—murdered the entire world—"

His groping hand found her hair and yanked her close—she felt his breath—and then his other hand was on her throat. He was sobbing. They stared into each other's eyes. She could not breathe.

Miss Temple pulled the trigger and Roger Bascombe reared back. His face was confused, and instead of snapping forward again he merely faded, like a dissipating curl of smoke, a shapeless figure in a black coat, falling onto the settee and then slipping with an easy movement to the floor. Miss Temple dropped the gun and sobbed aloud, no longer knowing who she was.

"Celeste!"

This was Chang, roaring out from the rooftop despite his pain. She looked up. Miss Temple felt an icy stab at her feet and saw that water was seeping through the floor. She stumbled to the iron staircase, blind with tears, and groped her way, gasping with unspent grief. Doctor Svenson crouched in the wheelhouse and hauled her up. She wanted to curl into a corner and drown. He lifted her high and more hands—Elöise and Chang—helped her onto the roof. What did it matter? They would die in the cabin or die above—either way they would sink. Why had she done it? What did it change? The Doctor followed her out, pushing her legs from below.

"Take her," Svenson said, and she felt Chang's arm around her shaking shoulders. The gasbag above was slackening, carried to the side with the wind, still enormous but sagging into the water—as opposed to collapsing on top of them—and tipping the roof at an angle. The spray slopped over the cabin, spattering Miss Temple's face, as waves rocked their precarious platform. Chang's other hand held on to a metal strut, as did the Doctor and Elöise. Miss Temple looked around her.

"Where is the Contessa?" She sniffed.

"She was not here," called Svenson.

"Perhaps she jumped," said Elöise.

"Then she is dead," said Svenson. "The water is too cold—her dress too heavy, it would pull her down—even if she survived the fall..."

Chang coughed, his lungs audibly clearer.

"I am in debt to you, Doctor, and your orange *elixir*. I feel quite well enough to drown."

"I am honored to have been useful," answered Svenson, smiling tightly.

Miss Temple shivered. What clothes she wore did nothing to cut the wind or the chilling water that splashed onto her trembling body. She could not bear it, no matter how the others tried to joke, she did not want to die, not after all this, and more than anything she did not care to drown. She knew it for an awful death—slow and mournful. She was mournful enough. She looked at her green boots and bare legs, wondering how long it would take. She had traveled so far in such a small amount of time. It was as if her rooms at the Boniface were as far away, and as much a part of the past, as her island home. She sniffed. At least she was back to the sea.

Miss Temple felt her flesh going numb, and yet when she looked down again the water had not climbed. She craned her head toward the open hatch to find the wheelhouse awash with rising water, with the sodden dress of Caroline Stearne swirling just under the surface. Yet why were they not sinking? She turned to the others.

"Is it possible we are *aground*?" she asked, through chattering teeth.

As one the other three echoed her look into the wheelhouse, and then all four searched around them for some clue. The water was too dark to reveal its depth. Ahead and to either side they could only find the open sea, while the view behind was blocked by the dirigible's billowing, sagging gasbag. With a sudden burst of energy Cardinal Chang hoisted himself over the metal strut and clambered onto the canvas bag itself, each step across it pushing out gouts of trapped blue smoke. He dropped from Miss Temple's view at the trough of each wave that passed beneath, and then she lost him altogether.

"We could be *anywhere*," said Doctor Svenson, adding after a silence where neither woman spoke, "speaking cartographically..."

A moment later they heard Chang's whooping cry. He was bounding back toward them, soaked to his waist, the canvas significantly flattened by his efforts.

"There is land!" he shouted. "God help us, it's land!"

Doctor Svenson averted his eyes as he lifted Miss Temple over the metal struts, and then did the same for Elöise, Miss Temple taking the other woman's hands. They helped each other over the dying gasbag, not halfway across before they were wet to their knees, but by then they could see it—a scumbled line of white breaking waves and a darker stripe of trees beyond.

Chang was waiting for her in the water and Miss Temple jumped into his arms. The sea was freezing, but she laughed aloud as it splashed against her face. She could not touch the sand with her toes and so she pushed herself away from Chang, took one look at the shore for a target, and then ducked herself under, the cold tingling the roots of her hair. Miss Temple swam, kicking her legs, unable to see in the dark water, the tears and sweat on her body dissolving in the sea, knowing she must hurry, that the cold would take her otherwise, that she would be even colder once outside the water, soaked and in the wind, and that from all of these things she still might perish.

She did not care about any of it. She smiled again, certain for the first time in so long exactly where she was, and where she was going to be. She felt like she was swimming home.